J. R. Ward lives in the South with her incredibly supportive husband and her beloved golden retriever. After graduating from law school, she began working in health care in Boston and spent many years as chief of staff for one of the premier academic medical centres in the nation.

Visit her and the Black Dagger Brotherhood at www.jrward.com

Also by J. R. Ward

The Black Dagger Brotherhood Series:

Dark Lover
Lover Eternal
Lover Awakened
Lover Revealed
Lover Unbound
Lover Enshrined
Lover Avenged

The Black Dagger Brotherhood: An Insider's Guide

Fallen Angels Series:

Covet

LOVER
MINE

J. R. WARD

piatkus

PIATKUS

First published in the United States in 2010 by New American Library,
A Division of Penguin group (USA) Inc, New York
First published in Great Britain as a paperback original in 2010 by Piatkus

A CIP catalogue record for this book
is available from the British Library.

ISBN 978-0-7499-4178-9

Typeset in Garamond 3 by
Palimpsest Book Production Limited, Grangemouth, Stirlingshire

Printed in the UK by CPI Mackays, Chatham ME5 8TD

Papers used by Piatkus are natural, renewable and recyclable
products sourced from well-managed forests and certified
in accordance with the rules of the Forest Stewardship Council.

Mixed Sources
Product group from well-managed
forests and other controlled sources
www.fsc.org Cert no. SGS-COC-004081
© 1996 Forest Stewardship Council

Piatkus
An imprint of
Little, Brown Book Group
100 Victoria Embankment
London EC4Y 0DY

An Hachette UK Company
www.hachette.co.uk

www.piatkus.co.uk

DEDICATED TO *YOU*:

I cannot believe you and I have come so far.
Your book is not a goodbye, however—
just another beginning.
But you're used to that . . .

ACKNOWLEDGMENTS

With immense gratitude to the readers of the Black Dagger Brotherhood and a shout-out to the Cellies!

Thank you so very much for all the support and guidance: Steven Axelrod, Kara Welsh, Claire Zion, and Leslie Gelbman.

Thank you also to everyone at NAL—these books are truly a team effort.

Thank you, Lu and Opal and all our Mods, for everything you do out of the goodness of your hearts!

As always with many thanks to my Executive Committee: Sue Grafton, Dr. Jessica Andersen, and Betsey Vaughan.

And with much respect to the incomparable Suzanne Brockmann and the ever-fabulous Christine Feehan (and family) and all the authors in my life who are such a source of comfort and advice (Christina and Linda and Lisa!).

Thank you also to Kara Cesare, who remains so close to my heart.

To D. L. B.—I am one of your biggest fans, please keep writing! Love u xxx mummy

To N. T. M.—thank you for sticking with me every step of the way, good and bad.

To Jac (and his Gabe!)—with thanks for Plastic Fantastic and the redefinition of romance.

To LeElla Scott—whom I love so much and not just because she takes such good care of my beloved nephuppy.

To Katie and our Kaylie-girl and their mama—who I'm so putting on speed dial.

To Lee for paving the way and Margaret and Walker for being such a source of joy.

None of this would be possible without: my loving husband, who is my adviser and caretaker and visionary; my wonderful mother, who has given me so much love I couldn't possibly ever repay her; my family (both those of blood and those by adoption); and my dearest friends.

Oh, and with love to the better half of WriterDog, as always.

GLOSSARY OF TERMS
AND PROPER NOUNS

abstrux nohtrum (n.) Private guard with license to kill
who is granted his or her position by the king.

ahvenge (v.) To commit an act of mortal retribution,
carried out typically by a male loved one.

Black Dagger Brotherhood (pr. n.) Highly trained
vampire warriors who protect their species against the
Lessening Society. As a result of selective breeding
within the race, Brothers possess immense physical
and mental strength, as well as rapid healing capa-
bilities. They are not siblings for the most part, and
are inducted into the Brotherhood upon nomination
by the Brothers. Aggressive, self-reliant, and secre-
tive by nature, they exist apart from civilians, having
little contact with members of the other classes except
when they need to feed. They are the subjects of legend
and the objects of reverence within the vampire world.
They may be killed only by the most serious of
wounds, e.g., a gunshot or stab to the heart, etc.

blood slave (n.) Male or female vampire who has been
subjugated to serve the blood needs of another. The
practice of keeping blood slaves has recently been
outlawed.

the Chosen (pr. n.) Female vampires who have been
bred to serve the Scribe Virgin. They are considered
members of the aristocracy, though they are spiritu-
ally rather than temporally focused. They have little
or no interaction with males, but can be mated to

Brothers at the Scribe Virgin's direction to propagate their class. Some have the ability to prognosticate. In the past, they were used to meet the blood needs of unmated members of the Brotherhood, and that practice has been reinstated by the Brothers.

chrih (n.) Symbol of honorable death in the Old Language.

cohntehst (n.) Conflict between two males competing for the right to be a female's mate.

Dhunhd (pr. n.) Hell.

doggen (n.) Member of the servant class within the vampire world. *Doggen* have old, conservative traditions about service to their superiors, following a formal code of dress and behavior. They are able to go out during the day, but they age relatively quickly. Life expectancy is approximately five hundred years.

ehros (pr. n.) A Chosen trained in the matter of sexual arts.

exhile dhoble (pr. n.) The evil or cursed twin, the one born second.

the Fade (n.) Nontemporal realm where the dead reunite with their loved ones and pass eternity.

First Family (n.) The king and queen of the vampires, and any children they may have.

ghardian (n.) Custodian of an individual. There are varying degrees of *ghardians*, with the most powerful being that of a *sehcluded* female.

glymera (n.) The social core of the aristocracy, roughly equivalent to Regency England's *ton*.

hellren (n.) Male vampire who has been mated to a female. Males may take more than one female as mate.

leahdyre (n.) A person of power and influence.

leelan (n.) A term of endearment loosely translated as "dearest one."

Lessening Society (pr. n.) Order of slayers convened by the Omega for the purpose of eradicating the vampire species.

lesser (n.) De-souled human who targets vampires for extermination as a member of the Lessening Society. *Lessers* must be stabbed through the chest in order to be killed; otherwise they are ageless. They do not eat or drink and are impotent. Over time, their hair, skin, and irises lose pigmentation until they are blond, blushless, and pale-eyed. They smell like baby powder. Inducted into the society by the Omega, they retain a ceramic jar thereafter into which their heart was placed after it was removed.

lewlhen (n.) Gift.

lheage (n.) A term of respect used by a sexual submissive to refer to her dominant.

lys (n.) Torture tool used to remove the eyes.

mahmen (n.) Mother. Used both as an identifier and a term of affection.

mhis (n.) The masking of a given physical environment; the creation of a field of illusion.

nalla (n., f.) or *nallum* (n., m.) Beloved.

needing period (n.) Female vampire's time of fertility, generally lasting for two days and accompanied by intense sexual cravings. Occurs approximately five years after a female's transition and then once a decade thereafter. All males respond to some degree if they are around a female in her need. It can be a dangerous time, with conflicts and fights breaking out between competing males, particularly if the female is not mated.

newling (n.) A virgin.

the Omega (pr. n.) Malevolent, mystical figure who has targeted the vampires for extinction out of resentment directed toward the Scribe Virgin. Exists in a nontemporal realm and has extensive powers, though not the power of creation.

phearsom (adj.) Term referring to the potency of a male's sexual organs. Literal translation something close to "worthy of entering a female."

princeps (n.) Highest level of the vampire aristocracy, second only to members of the First Family or the Scribe Virgin's Chosen. Must be born to the title; it may not be conferred.

pyrocant (n.) Refers to a critical weakness in an individual. The weakness can be internal, such as an addiction, or external, such as a lover.

rahlman (n.) Savior.

rythe (n.) Ritual manner of assuaging honor granted by one who has offended another. If accepted, the offended chooses a weapon and strikes the offender, who presents him- or herself without defenses.

the Scribe Virgin (pr. n.) Mystical force who is counselor to the king as well as the keeper of vampire archives and the dispenser of privileges. Exists in a nontemporal realm and has extensive powers. Capable of a single act of creation, which she expended to bring the vampires into existence.

sehclusion (n.) Status conferred by the king upon a female of the aristocracy as a result of a petition by the female's family. Places the female under the sole direction of her *ghardian*, typically the eldest male in her household. Her *ghardian* then has the legal right to determine all manner of her life, restricting at will any and all interactions she has with the world.

shellan (n.) Female vampire who has been mated to a male. Females generally do not take more than one mate due to the highly territorial nature of bonded males.

symphath (n.) Subspecies within the vampire race characterized by the ability and desire to manipulate emotions in others (for the purposes of an energy exchange), among other traits. Historically, they have been discriminated against and, during certain eras, hunted by vampires. They are near extinction.

the Tomb (pr. n.) Sacred vault of the Black Dagger Brotherhood. Used as a ceremonial site as well as a storage facility for the jars of *lessers*. Ceremonies performed there include inductions, funerals, and disciplinary actions against Brothers. No one may enter except for members of the Brotherhood, the Scribe Virgin, or candidates for induction.

trahyner (n.) Word used between males of mutual respect and affection. Translated loosely as "beloved friend."

transition (n.) Critical moment in a vampire's life when he or she transforms into an adult. Thereafter, he or she must drink the blood of the opposite sex to survive and is unable to withstand sunlight. Occurs generally in the mid-twenties. Some vampires do not survive their transitions, males in particular. Prior to their transitions, vampires are physically weak, sexually unaware and unresponsive, and unable to dematerialize.

vampire (n.) Member of a species separate from that of Homo sapiens. Vampires must drink the blood of the opposite sex to survive. Human blood will keep them alive, though the strength does not last long. Following their transitions, which occur in their mid-twenties, they are unable to go out into sunlight and must feed from the vein regularly. Vampires cannot "convert" humans through a bite or transfer of blood, though they are in rare cases able to breed with the other species. Vampires can dematerialize at will, though they must be able to calm themselves and concentrate to do so and may not carry anything heavy with them. They are able to strip the memories of humans, provided such memories are short-term. Some vampires are able to read minds. Life expectancy is upward of a thousand years, or in some cases even longer.

wahlker (n.) An individual who has died and returned to the living from the Fade. They are accorded great respect and are revered for their travails.

whard (n.) Equivalent of a godfather or godmother to an individual.

*Some things are destined to be—
it just takes us a couple of tries
to get there.*

LOVER MINE

PROLOGUE

He wished he had more time.

Although for truth, what would that change? Time mattered only if one did something with it, and he had already done what he could herein.

Darius, begotten son of Tehrror, forsaken son of Marklon sat on a dirt floor with his diary open on his knee and a beeswax candle in front of him. His illumination was naught but the small flame that swayed in a draft, and his room was the far corner of a cave. His clothing was made from rough, battle-ready leather, and his boots were of the same construction.

In his nose, the stench of male sweat and pungent earth mingled with the sweet death-decay of lessers' *blood.*

Each breath he took seemed to magnify the stink.

Flipping through the parchment pages, he went back in time, reversing the days one by one until he was no longer here at the war camp.

He longed for "home" with a physical ache, his sojourn in this camp an amputation, rather than a relocation.

He had been raised in a castle where elegance and grace had been the very fabric of life. Within the stout walls that had protected his family from humans and lessers *alike, every night had been as warm and rose-scented as those of July, the months and years passing with ease and leisure. The fifty rooms through which he had oft wandered had been appointed with satins and silks, and furniture made of precious woods, and woven rugs, not rushes. With oil paintings that glowed in their*

1

gilt frames, and marble statuary affecting dignified poses, it was a platinum setting to anchor a diamond existence.

And so it would have been unfathomable then that he would ever find himself where he was now. There had been, however, a vital weakness in the foundation of that life of his.

The beating heart of his mother had given him his right to be under that roof and held within that cosseted hearth. And when that loving, vital organ had stopped within her breast, Darius had lost not only his birthed mahmen, but the only home he had ever known.

His stepfather had cast him out and relegated him herein, an enmity long hidden thus exposed and acted upon.

There had been no time to mourn his mother. No time to puzzle over the abrupt hatred of the male who had all but sired him. No time to pine for the identity he'd had as a male of good breeding within the glymera.

He had been dropped at the entrance of this cave like a human who had succumbed to the plague. And the battles had begun afore he ever saw a lesser or began training to fight the slayers. In his first night and day within the belly of this camp, he had been attacked by fellow trainees who viewed his fine clothing, the only set he'd been permitted to take with him, as evidence he was weak of arm.

He had surprised not only them, but himself during those dark hours.

It was then that he had learned, as did they, that although he had been reared by an aristocratic male, in Darius's blood were the components of a warrior. Indeed, not just a soldier. Nay, a Brother. Without being taught, his body had known what to do and had responded to physical aggression with chilling action. Even as his mind struggled with the brutality of his deeds, his hands and feet and fangs had known precisely what exertion was necessary.

There had been another side of him, unknown, unrecognized . . . that somehow seemed more "him" than the reflection he had so long regarded within leaded glass.

Over time, his fighting had grown even more proficient . . . and his horror at himself had lessened. For truth, there was no other path upon which to tread: The seed of his true father and his father's father and his grandfather's sire had determined his skin and bone and muscles, the pure warrior bloodline transforming him into a powerful force.

And a vicious, deadly opponent.

Indeed, he found it highly disturbing to have this other identity. It was as if he cast two shadows upon the ground o'er which he tread, as if wherever he stood there were two separate light sources that illuminated his body. And yet, although conducting oneself in such a loathsome, violent manner offended the sensibilities he'd been taught, he knew it was part of the higher purpose he was destined to serve. And it had saved him time and time again . . . from those who sought to harm him inside the camp, and from the one who seemed to wish them all dead. Indeed, the Bloodletter was supposedly their whard, but he acted more like an enemy, even as he instructed them in the ways of war.

Or perhaps that was the point. War was ugly no matter the facet shown, whether it was preparation or participation.

The Bloodletter's teaching was brutal and his sadistic dictates demanded actions of which Darius would have no part. Verily, Darius was always the winner in conflict contests between trainees . . . but he did not partake of the raping that was punishment inflicted upon those bested. He was the only one whose refusal was honored. His denial had been challenged once by the Bloodletter, and when Darius had nearly beaten him, the male had never approached again.

Darius's losers, among which all in the camp were numbered, were punished by others, and it was during these times, when the rest of the camp was occupied by spectacle, that he most frequently took solace in his diary. Verily, at the now, he could not countenance even a glance in the direction of the main fire pit, for one of the sessions was taking place.

He hated that he had caused the events to transpire yet

3

again . . . but he had no choice. He had to train, he had to fight, and he had to win. And the sum resulting from that equation was determined by the Bloodletter's law.

From over at the fire pit, grunting and cheers of lusty derision rose.

His heart ached so at the sounds and he closed his eyes. The one currently exacting the punishment in Darius's place was a vicious male, out of the mold of the Bloodletter. He frequently stepped up to fill the void as he enjoyed the dispensation of pain and humiliation as much as he did his mead.

But mayhap it would be no longer thus. At least for Darius.

This night would be his test in the field. After having been trained for a year, he was going out not just with warriors, but Brothers. It was a rare honor—and a sign that the war with the Lessening Society was, as always, dire. Darius's innate expertise had gained notice, and Wrath, the Fair King, had decreed that he was to be taken out of the camp and developed further by the best fighters the vampire race had.

The Black Dagger Brotherhood.

All could be for naught, however. If this night he proved to be capable solely of training and the sparring with others of his ilk, then he would be cast back unto this cave for more of the Bloodletter's brand of "teaching."

Never to be tried by the Brothers again, relegated to serve as a soldier.

One had a single chance with the Brotherhood, and the test this moonlit eve was not about fighting styles or weaponry. It was a test of heart. Could he look into the pale eyes of the enemy and smell their sweet odor and keep his head calm whilst his body did act upon those slayers—

Darius's eyes lifted up from the words he had put upon parchment a lifetime ago. In the cave's innermost entryway, a band of four stood tall and thick shouldered and heavily weaponed.

Members of the Brotherhood.

He knew this quartet by name: Ahgony, Throe, Murhder, Tohrture.

Darius closed his diary, slid it into a fissure of rock, and licked the slice in his wrist that he had made to create "ink." His quill made from a pheasant's tail feather was failing fast, and he wasn't sure whether he would ever be back here again to use it; but he tucked it away.

As he picked up the candle and lifted it to his mouth, he was struck by the buttery quality of the light. He'd spent so many hours writing by such kind, soft illumination . . . in fact, that seemed the only tie he had between his life of the past and his current existence.

He blew out the small flame with a single breath.

Getting to his feet, he gathered his weapons: a steel dagger that he had been given off the cooling body of a dead trainee, and a sword that was from the communal training weapons stall. Neither hilt had been fitted for his palm, but his wielding hand cared not.

As the Brothers looked his way and offered neither greeting nor dismissal, he wished that among them was his real father. How different this would all feel if he had at his side one who cared what his outcome would be: He looked not for quarter given, and sought no special dispensation, but he was ever alone now, set apart from those around him, separated by a divide he could see across but never cover.

To be without family was a strange, unseeable prison, the bars of loneliness and rootlessness enclosing ever more tightly as years and experience accumulated, isolating a male such that he touched naught and naught touched him.

Darius did not look back at the camp as he walked toward the four who had come for him. The Bloodletter knew that he was going out into the field and didn't care whether or not he returned herein. And the other trainees were likewise.

On the approach, he wished he had more time to ready himself for this test of will and strength and courage. But it was now and here.

Verily, time moved forward even if you wanted it to slow to a crawl.

Stopping afore the Brothers, he yearned for a bracing word or a well wish or a pledge of faith from someone. As there was none coming, he offered up a brief prayer to the sacred mother of the race:

Dearest Virgin Scribe, please let me not fail in this.

ONE

Another fucking butterfly.

As R.I.P. looked at what was coming through the door of his tat shop, he knew he was going to end up doing another fucking butterfly. Or two.

Yup. Given the pair of long, blond, and bubbly that was jiggling their giggly way up to his receptionist, he was so not going to be rocking any skull-and-bones shit into their skin.

These Paris Hiltons and their we're-so-bad excitement had him looking at the clock . . . and wishing he closed now, instead of one a.m.

Man . . . the shit he did for money. Most of the time he could be all *yeah, whatever* about the lightweights who came in to get marked up, but tonight the bright ideas of cutie-pies annoyed him. Hard to get enthused about the Hello Kitty set when he'd just spent three hours doing a memorial portrait for a biker who'd lost his best friend on the road. One was real life, the other a cartoon.

Mar, his receptionist, came over to him. "You got time to do a quickie?" Her pierced eyebrows went up as her eyes rolled. "Shouldn't take long."

"Yeah." He nodded to his padded chair. "Get the first one over here."

"They want to be done together."

Of course they did. "Fine. Grab the stool from the back."

As Mar disappeared behind a curtain and he got set up, the two by the cash register held each other's hands and twittered over the consent forms they had to sign. From time to time, both of them shot him wide looks, like with

7

all his tats and his metal, he was an exotic tiger they'd come to admire at a zoo . . . and totally approved of.

Uh-huh. Right. He would cut his own balls off before he threw them as much as a pity fuck.

After Mar took their money, she brought them over and introduced them as Keri and Sarah. Which was more than he'd expected. He'd been bracing himself for Tiffany and Brittney.

"I want a rainbow carp," Keri said as she got into his chair with what she clearly intended to be an enticing arch. "Right here."

She pulled up her tight little shirt, undid the zipper on her jeans, and pushed down the top of her pink thong. Her belly button had a hoop with a pink rhinestone heart dangling off of it and it was clear she was into electrolysis.

"Fine," R.I.P. said. "How big."

Keri the Seductress seemed to deflate a little—as if her no doubt one hundred percent success rate with college football players had led her to assume he would pant all over the real estate she was showing him.

"Um . . . not too big. My parents would kill me if they knew I was doing this . . . so it can't show over a bikini bottom."

Of course not. "Two inches?" He held up his tatted hand and gave her a sense of dimension.

"Maybe . . . a little smaller."

With a black pen, he made a sketch on her, and after she asked him to stay on the inside of the lines, he snapped on his black gloves, got out a fresh needle, and tuned up his gun.

It took Keri about a second and a half to sport tears and hang onto Sarah's hand as if she were giving birth without an epidural. And that was the difference, wasn't it. There was a huge divide between the hard-core and the wannabe. Butterflies and carps and pretty little hearts were not—

The shop's door opened wide . . . and R.I.P. sat up a little straighter on his rolling stool.

The three men who walked in were not in military uniforms, but they were definitely not civilians. Dressed in black leather from their jackets to their pants to their shitkickers, they were huge men who sucked the walls of the shop in closer and shrank the ceiling down tight. Lot of bulges hidden underneath those coats. The kinds made by guns and maybe knives.

With a subtle shift, R.I.P. moved in the direction of his counter, where the emergency alarm button was.

The one on the left had mismatched eyes and gunmetal piercings and a killer's cool stare. The one on the right seemed a little closer to mainstream, with his pretty-boy puss and the red hair—except for the fact that he carried himself like someone who'd been to war and back.

The one in the middle, however, was trouble. Slightly larger than his buddies, he had dark brown hair that was cut short and a classically handsome face—but his blue eyes were lifeless, with about as much reflection as old asphalt.

A dead man walking. With nothing to lose.

"Hey," R.I.P. called out to greet them. "You guys need some ink?"

"He does." The one with the piercings nodded at his blue-eyed buddy. "And he's got the design. It's a shoulder piece."

R.I.P. gave his instincts a chance to weigh in on the project. The men didn't eye Mar inappropriately. There was no casing of the cash register and no one went for their metal. They waited politely—but with expectation. Like either he did what they wanted, or they'd find someone else who would.

He eased back into position, thinking they were his peeps. "Cool. I'll be finished in no time here."

Mar spoke up from behind the counter. "We were supposed to be closing in less than an hour—"

9

"But I'll do you," R.I.P. told the one in the center. "You don't worry about the time."

"And I think I'll stay," Mar said, eyeing the one with the piercings.

The blue-eyed guy's hands came up and moved with distinct gestures. After he was finished, the pierced one translated, "He says thanks. And he's brought his own ink, if that's okay."

Not exactly the norm, and against the health code, but R.I.P. had no trouble being flexible for the right customer. "No prob, my man."

He got back to work with the carp and Keri resumed her bitten lip and little-girl moaning routine. When he was finished, he was not at all surprised that Sarah, after having watched her friend go through "agony," decided that she wanted a refund instead of some pretty, rainbow-colored ink of her own.

Which was good news. It meant that he could get to work on the guy with the dead eyes right away.

As he snapped off his black gloves and cleaned up, he wondered what in the hell the design was going to look like. And exactly how long it was going to take Mar to get inside the pierced guy's pants.

Former was likely to be fairly good.

And the latter . . . he'd give that about ten minutes, because she'd caught his mismatched stare and Mar was a fast worker—not just behind the counter.

Across town, away from the bars and tat shops on Trade Street, in an enclave of brownstones and cobbled lanes, Xhex stood in a bay window and stared out of wavy antique glass.

She was naked and cold and bruised.

But she was not weak.

Down below, on the sidewalk, a human female strolled along with a little yappy dog on a string and a cell phone up to her ear. Across the way, people in other elegant walk-ups were drinking and eating and reading. Cars went by slowly out of both respect for the neighbors and fear for their suspension systems on the uneven street.

The Homo sapiens peanut gallery couldn't see or hear her. And not just because the capacities of that other race were so diminished in comparison to those of vampires.

Or in her case, half-*symphath* vampires.

Even if she turned the ceiling light on and screamed until her voice box gave out, even if she waved her arms until they fell out of their sockets, the men and women who were all around would just keep up whatever they were doing, unaware that she was trapped in this bedroom, thick in their midst. And it wasn't as if she could pick up the bureau or the bedside table and break the glass. Same with kicking down the door or crawling through the bathroom vent.

She'd tried all that.

The assassin in her had to be impressed by the pervasive nature of her invisible cell: There was, quite literally, no way to get around, through, or out of it.

Turning away from the window, she paced around the king-size bed with its silk sheets and horrible memories . . . and went by the marble bathroom . . . and kept going by the door that led out into the hall. Given the way things went with her captor, it wasn't as if she needed more exercise, but she couldn't keep still, her body twitchy and humming.

She'd done this against-her-will thing once before. Knew how the mind, like a starved body, could cannibalize itself after too long if you didn't feed it something to churn over.

Her favorite distraction? Mixed drinks. After having worked in clubs for years, she knew legions of cocktails and concoctions and she ran through them, picturing the bottles and the glasses and the pouring and the ice and the spice.

That Bartender-pedia routine had kept her sane.

Up until now, she had banked on a mistake, a slipup, an opportunity for escape. None had come and that hope was starting to fade, exposing a huge black hole that was ready to eat her. So she just kept making drinks in her head and searching for her opening.

And her past experience helped in a strange way. Whatever happened here, however bad it got, however much it hurt physically, it was nothing compared to what she'd been through before.

This was the minor leagues.

Or . . . at least she told herself that. Sometimes it felt worse.

More with the pacing, past the two bay windows in front, by the bureau, and then around the bed again. This time she went into the bathroom. There were no razors or brushes or combs, just some towels that were slightly damp and a bar of soap or two.

When Lash had abducted her, using the same kind of magic that was keeping her in this suite of rooms, he had brought her to this elegant crib of his and their first night and day together had been indicative of how it was going to be.

In the mirror over the double sinks, she saw herself and performed a dispassionate review of her body. There were bruises all over her . . . cuts and scrapes, too. He was brutal in what he did, and she fought back because she'd be damned if she let him kill her—so it was hard to tell what marks had been made by him and what had been incidental to what she'd done to the bastard.

Get his ass naked in front of some glass, and she'd bet her last breath he didn't look any better than she did.

Eye for an eye.

The unfortunate corollary was that he liked that she met fire with fire. The more they battled it out, the more he got turned on, and she sensed he was surprised at his own emotions. For the first couple of days, he'd been in punishment mode, trying to pay her back for what she'd done to his last girlfriend—evidently, those bullets she'd put in that bitch's chest had really ticked his shit off. But then things had changed. He'd started to talk less about his ex and more about body parts and fantasies involving a future that included her bearing his spawn.

Pillow talk for the sociopath.

Now his eyes glowed for another reason when he came to her, and if he knocked her out, she usually regained consciouness with him wrapped around her body.

Xhex turned away from her reflection, and froze before taking another step.

Someone was downstairs.

Leaving the bathroom, she went to the door that led out into the hall and inhaled slow and deep. As the scent of sweaty roadkill wafted into her sinuses, it was clear whatever was hoofing around down below was a *lesser*— but it wasn't Lash.

Nope, this was his minion, the one who came every night before her captor arrived to make him something to eat. Which meant Lash was on the way to the brownstone.

Man, wasn't it just her luck: She got snatched by the only member of the Lessening Society who ate and fucked. The rest of them were impotent as a ninety-year-old and existed on an air diet, but Lash? Fucker was fully functional.

Going back over to the window, she put her hand out toward the glass. The boundary that marked her prison was an energy field that felt like a prickling heat as she came into contact with it. The damn thing was like an invisi-fence for things bigger than dogs—with the added bene of no collar being required.

There was a little give in it . . . as she pressed forward, there was a hint of flexibility, but only up to a point. Then the molecules that were agitated pulled together

13

and the burning sensation got so acute she had to shake her hand out and walk off the pain.

As she waited for Lash to come back to her, her mind drifted to the male she tried never to think of.

Especially if Lash was around. It was unclear how much her captor could get into her head, but she didn't want to take chances. If the bastard got an itch that that mute soldier was her well-of-soul, as her people called it, he would use that against her . . . and John Matthew.

An image of the male came to her mind, his blue eyes resonating in her recollection so clearly, she could see the flecks of navy in them. God, those beautiful blue eyes.

She could remember when she first met him, back when he was a pretrans. He had looked at her with such awe and wonder, as if she were larger than life, a revelation. Of course, at that point, all she knew was that he was packing heat in ZeroSum, and as head of security for the club, she'd been hell-bent on disarming him and throwing him out into the street. But then she'd learned the Blind King was his *whard* and that had changed everything.

Following the happy little news flash about who was all up in his biz, John was not just welcome to be armed; he was a special guest, along with his two boys. After that, he'd come in regularly and had always watched her, those blue eyes on her wherever she was. And then he'd transitioned. Holy hell, had he turned into a big one, and abruptly that stare had something hot added to the gentle shyness.

It had taken a lot to kill that kindness. But true to her assassin's nature, she'd managed to strangle the warmth out of—the way he looked at her.

Focusing on the street below, she thought of that time they had been together at her basement place. After the sex, when he'd tried to kiss her, when his blue eyes had

14

glowed with the trademark vulnerability and compassion she'd come to associate with him, she'd pulled away and shut him down.

It was a case of lost nerve. She just couldn't handle the pressure of all that hearts-and-flowers stuff . . . or the responsibility that came with being around someone who felt like that about her . . . or the reality that she had the capacity to love him back.

The payback had been the death of that special look.

The solace she took was that among the males who were likely to try to come after her—Rehvenge, iAm, and Trez . . . the Brotherhood—John was not on a crusade. If he was searching for her, it was because he had to as a soldier, not because he was compelled to as part of a personal suicide mission.

No, John Matthew wouldn't be on the warpath because of how he felt about her.

And having already watched a male of worth destroy himself trying to rescue her, at least she didn't have to do that again.

As the smell of fresh grilling steak permeated the brownstone, she shut off her thoughts and gathered her will around her like a suit of armor.

Her "lover" would be here any minute, so she needed to batten down her mental hatches and get ready for tonight's battle. Pervasive exhaustion dragged at her, but her will ushered that deadweight out on its ass. She needed to feed, even more than she needed proper sleep, but neither of those was happening anytime soon.

It was a question of putting one foot in front of the other until something broke.

That and taking out the male who dared to hold her against her will.

TWO

Chronologically speaking, Blaylock son of Rocke had known John Matthew for just over a year.

But that was not a true reflection of the bromance. There were two timelines to people's lives: the absolute and the perceived. The absolute was the universal day-and-night cycle that for them added up to something like three hundred and sixty-five. Then there was the way that time period had gone, the events, the deaths, the destruction, the training, the fighting.

He figured all told . . . that pegged the two of them at about four hundred thousand years.

And counting, he thought, looking over at his buddy.

John Matthew was staring at the ink designs on the walls of the tat place, his eyes going over the skulls and daggers and American flags and Chinese symbols. With his size, he absolutely dwarfed the three-room shop—to the point where it was like he came from another planet. In contrast to his pretrans state, the guy now had the muscle mass of a pro wrestler, although because his skeleton was so big, the weight was stretched out on long bones, giving him a more elegant look than those swoll'd up humans in tights. He'd taken to buzz-cutting his dark hair and this made the lines of his face seem harsh rather than handsome—with the dark circles under his eyes giving the hard-ass look some serious backup.

Life had beaten the shit out of him, but instead of folding, each strike and blow had forged him harder and stronger and tougher. He was straight steel now, nothing lingering of the boy he'd once been.

But that was growing up for you. Not only your body changed; your head did, too.

Staring at his friend, the loss of innocence seemed a crime.

And on that note, the receptionist behind the counter caught Blay's attention. She was leaning on the glass display of piercing supplies, her breasts swelling against the black bra and black muscle shirt she was wearing. She had two sleeves, one in black and white and one in black and red, and she had gunmetal gray hoops in her nose, her eyebrows, and both ears. Amid all the tat drawings on the walls, she was a living example of the work you could get if you wanted. A very sexy, hard-core example . . . who had lips the color of red wine and hair the color of night.

Everything about her matched Qhuinn. She was like a female him.

And what do you know. Qhuinn's mixed eyes had already locked on her and he was smiling tightly in his trademark *gotcha* way.

Blay slipped a hand into his leather jacket and felt around for his pack of Dunhill reds. Man, nothing made him jones for a smoke more than Qhuinn's love life.

And clearly he'd be lighting up another couple coffin nails tonight: Qhuinn sauntered over to the receptionist and drank her in like she was a long, tall beer fresh from the tap and he'd been working in the heat for hours. His eyes locked on her breasts as he traded names with her, and she helped him get a clearer picture of her assets by easing forward onto her forearms.

Good thing vampires didn't get cancer.

Blay turned his back on the Spice Channel by the cash register and went over to stand next to John Matthew.

"That's cool." Blay pointed at a dagger sketch.

You going to get ink ever? John signed.

17

"I don't know."

God knew he liked it on skin . . .

His stare shifted back over to Qhuinn. The guy's huge body was arching into the human woman, his broad shoulders and his tight hips and his long, powerful legs guaranteeing her one hell of a ride.

He was amazing at sex.

Not that Blay would know firsthand. He'd seen it and he'd heard it . . . and he'd imagined what it would be like. But when the opportunity had arisen, he'd been relegated to a small, special class: denied.

Actually, it was more of a category than a class . . . because he was the only one who Qhuinn would not have sex with.

"Um . . . is it going to sting like this forever?" a female voice asked.

As a deep male rumble replied, Blay glanced over to the tat chair. The blond who'd just been worked on was gingerly tucking her shirt in over her cellophane bandage and staring at the guy who'd inked her like he was a doctor telling her the odds of surviving rabies.

The pair of girls then went over to the receptionist, where the uninked one who'd changed her mind got a refund and both of them checked out Qhuinn.

It was like that wherever the guy went and it used to be the kind of thing that made Blay worship his best friend. Now, it was a never-ending rejection: every time Qhuinn said yes, it made that one single no louder.

"I'm ready if you guys are," the tattoo artist called out.

John and Blay headed to the rear of the shop and Qhuinn dropped the receptionist like a bad habit and followed. One good thing about him was the seriousness with which he took his role as John's *ahstrux nohtrum*: he was supposed to be around the guy twenty-four/seven, and that was a responsibility he took more seriously even than sex.

18

As John sat in the padded chair in the center of the workspace, he took out a piece of paper and unfolded it on the artist's counter.

The man frowned and looked over what John had sketched out. "So it's these four symbols across your upper shoulders?"

John nodded and signed, *You can embellish them any way you want, but they have to be clear.*

After Qhuinn translated, the artist nodded. "Cool." He grabbed a black pen and started making a picture box of elegant swirls around the simple design. "What are these things, by the way?"

"Just symbols," Qhuinn answered.

The artist nodded again and kept sketching. "How's this?"

All three of them leaned in.

"Man," Qhuinn said softly. "That's vicious."

It was. It was absolutely perfect, the kind of thing John would wear on his skin with pride—not that anyone would see the Old Language characters or all that spectacular swirl work. What was spelled out was not something he wanted widely known, but that was the thing with tats: they didn't have to be public, and God knew the guy had plenty of T-shirts to cover up with.

When John nodded, the artist stood up. "Let me get the transfer paper. Copying it onto you won't take long and then we'll get to work."

As John put a crystal jar of ink on the counter and started to take off his jacket, Blay sat on a stool and held out his arms. Given the number of weapons John was packing in his pockets, it wouldn't do anyone any good for him to just hang his shit up on a hook.

When he was shirtless, John settled into a forward lean position, his heavy arms resting on a padded bar stand. After the tattoo artist got the image on the transfer paper, the guy smoothed the sheet over John's upper back, then peeled it off.

The design formed a perfect arch across the span of muscles, taking up all of John's considerable acreage.

The Old Language really was beautiful, Blay thought.

Staring at the symbols, for one brief, ridiculous moment he imagined his own name across Qhuinn's shoulders, carved into that smooth skin in the manner of the mating ritual.

Never going to happen. They were destined to be best friends . . . which, compared to strangers, was something huge. Compared to lovers? It was the cold side of a locked door.

He glanced over at Qhuinn. The guy had one eye on John and one eye on the receptionist—who had locked the front door and come to stand by his side.

Behind the fly of his leathers, the bulge he was sporting was obvious.

Blay looked down at the mess of clothes in his lap. One by one, he carefully folded the undershirt, the long-sleeve, and then John's jacket. When he glanced up, Qhuinn was running his forefinger slowly down the woman's arm.

They were going to end up ducking behind that curtain over to the left. The front door to the shop was secured, the curtain was fairly thin, and Qhuinn would do the woman with his weapons on. So John would be safe at all times . . . and that itch would get scratched.

Which meant Blay would only have to suffer hearing them.

Better than the full bifta. Especially because Qhuinn was beautiful to watch when he had sex. Just . . . beautiful.

Back when Blay had tried to do the hetero thing, the two had tag-teamed a number of human females—not that he could have recalled any of the women's faces, bodies, or names.

It had always been about Qhuinn for him. Always.

The nibbling pain of the tattoo needle was a pleasure.

As John shut his eyes and breathed deep and slow, he thought about the intersection of metal and skin, how the sharp entered the soft, how the blood flowed . . . how you knew exactly where the penetration was.

Like right now, the tattoo artist was directly over the top of his spine.

John had a lot of experience with the whole slice-and-dice shit—only on a much larger scale, and more as a giver rather than a receiver. Sure, he'd been cut up out in the field a couple of times, but he'd left more than his fair share of holes behind, and like the tattoo artist, he always took his equipment to work with him: His jacket carried all kinds of daggers and switches, even a length of chain. Also a matched set of just-in-case guns.

Well . . . all that and a pair of barbed cilices.

Not that he ever used those on the enemy.

No, those weren't weapons. And although they hadn't been cinched on anyone's thigh for almost four weeks now, they weren't useless. Currently, they functioned as a kind of fucked-up security blanket. Without them, he felt naked.

Thing was, those brutal ties were the only tie he had to the one he loved. Which, considering the way things had been left between them, made cosmic sense.

They didn't go far enough for him, however. What Xhex had worn around her legs to tame her *symphath* side didn't offer the kind of permanence he was looking for, and that was what had led to his own metal-on-skin convention. When he was through here, she would always be with him. In his skin as well as under it. On his shoulders as well as his mind.

Hopefully this human was doing a good job with the design.

When the Brothers needed tattoos for whatever reason, Vishous worked the needle and the guy was a pro at it—hell, the red tear on Qhuinn's face and the black scrolling date around the back of his neck were spank. Trouble was, you went to V with a job like this one and suddenly there were going to be questions—not just from him, but from everyone else.

Not many secrets in the Brotherhood, and John would just as soon keep his feelings for Xhex to himself.

The truth was . . . he was in love with her. Totally over-the-line, no-going-back, not-even-dead-would-he-part kind of shit. And although his hearts and flowers hadn't been unrequited, that didn't matter. He'd come to peace with the fact that the one he wanted didn't want him.

What he could not live with was her being tortured or dying a slow, excruciating death.

Or him not being able to give her a proper burial.

He was obsessed with her disappearance. Single-minded to the point of self-destruction. Brutal and unforgiving toward the one who'd taken her. But that was nobody else's biz.

The only good thing in the sitch was that the Brotherhood was likewise committed to figuring out what the hell had happened to her. The Brothers didn't leave anyone behind on a mission, and when they'd gone up to get Rehvenge out of that *symphath* colony, Xhex had been very much a member of the team. When the dust had cleared, and she'd disappeared entirely, the assumption was that she'd been abducted, and there were two possible ways to go: *symphaths* or *lessers*.

Which was kind of like saying, Do you want her to come down with polio or Ebola?

Everyone, including John, Qhuinn, and Blay, was on

the case. As a result? It just looked as though finding her was part of John's job as a soldier in war.

The humming of the needle stopped and the artist wiped at his back.

"It's looking good," the guy said, resuming his work. "You want to do it in two sessions or just this one."

John glanced at Blay and signed.

"He says he wants it done tonight if you have the time," Blay translated.

"Yeah, I can do that. Mar? Call Rick and tell him I'm going to be late."

"Dialing as we speak," the receptionist said.

Nope, John wasn't going to let the Brothers see this ink—no matter how great it looked.

The way he saw it, he'd been born in a bus station and left for dead. Thrown into the human child welfare system. Picked up by Tohr and his mate, only to have her killed and the guy disappear. And now Z, who'd been the one assigned to reach out to him, was understandably busy with his *shellan* and their new young.

Even Xhex had shut him out before the tragedy.

So, whatever, he could take a hint. Besides, it was curiously liberating not to give a shit about anyone else's opinion. Freed him up to nurture his violent obsession with tracking down her abductor and ripping the fucker limb from limb.

"You mind telling me what this is?" the tattoo guy asked.

John lifted his eyes and figured there was no reason to lie to the human. Besides, Blay and Qhuinn knew the truth.

Blay looked a little surprised, but then translated. "He says it's his girl's name."

"Ah. Yeah, I figured. You two getting married?"

After John signed, Blay said, "It's a memorial."

There was a pause and then the tattoo guy put his

gun down on the rolling table where the ink was. After yanking up the sleeve of his black shirt, he put his forearm in front of John. On it was the picture of a gorgeous woman, her hair breezing out over her shoulder, her eyes focused so that she looked out of his skin.

"That was my girl. She's not here anymore either." With a sharp tug, the guy covered up the picture. "So I get it."

As the needle got back to work, John found it difficult to breathe. The idea that Xhex was probably dead by now ate him alive . . . and what was worse was imagining the way she might have died.

John knew who'd taken her. There was only one logical explanation: While she had gone into the labyrinth and helped to free Rehvenge, Lash had shown up, and when he'd disappeared so had she. Not a coincidence. And though no one had seen anything, there had been about a hundred *symphaths* in the cave where Rehv had been and a lot going on . . . and Lash was not your garden-variety *lesser*.

Oh, no . . . he was apparently the son of the Omega. The very spawn of evil. And that meant the cocksucker had tricks.

John had seen a few of his fancy dancies up close and personal during the fight at the colony: If the guy could palm up energy bombs and go nose-to-nose with Rhage's beast, then why couldn't he snatch someone right from under everyone's noses. The thing was, if Xhex had been killed that night, they would have found a body. If she was breathing, but had an injury, she would have tele-pathically reached out *symphath*-to-*symphath* to Rehvenge. And if she was alive, but needed a little vacation, she would have left only after she was sure everyone else was home safe.

The Brothers were working off the same logical assumptions, so they were all out looking for *lessers*. And although most of the vampires had left Caldwell for out of state safe houses after the raids, the Lessening Society, under Lash's rule, had turned to drug dealing to make ends meet, and that went down mainly around the clubs here in town on Trade Street. Trolling seedy alleys was the name of the game, with everyone looking for things that were undead and smelled like a cross between a bled-out skunk and a Glade PlugIn.

Four weeks and they'd found nothing other than signs that *lessers* were moving product on the street to humans.

John was going insane, mostly from all the not-knowing and the fear, but partially from having to hold his violence inside. Although it was amazing what you could do when you had no choice—he had to appear normal and levelheaded if he wanted to be a part of this, so that was what he presented himself to be.

And this tattoo? It was a stake shoved into the territory he was in. His declaration that even if Xhex hadn't wanted him, she was his mate and he would honor her, alive or dead. Here was the thing: People felt the way they did and it wasn't their fault or yours if the connection was one-sided. It just . . . was.

God, he wished he hadn't been so cold when they'd had sex the second time.

That final time.

Abruptly, he cut off his emotions, putting that genie of sadness and regret and rejection back into its bottle. He couldn't allow himself to break down. He had to keep going, keep searching, keep putting one foot in front of the other. Time was moving forward even though he wanted to slow it down so that they had a better chance of finding her alive.

The clock was not interested in his opinions, however.

Dear God, he thought. Please let me not fail in this.

THREE

"Induction? What, like it's a fucking club?"

As the words bounced around the inside of the Mercedes, Lash tightened his hands on the steering wheel and stared out the windshield. He had a switchblade in the inside pocket of his Canali suit and the urge to out the blade and slice this human's throat open was goddamned tempting.

Of course, then he'd have a dead body to deal with and blood all over the leather.

Both of which were bores.

He looked across the seats. The one he had picked out of a cast of hundreds was your typical bottom-feeding, drug-dealing, shifty-eyed motherfucker. The kid's history of child abuse was written in the old circular scar on his face—perfectly round and the size of the burning end of a cigarette—and his hard life on the street was in his smart, twitchy eyes. His greed was in the way he looked around the inside of the car, like he was trying to figure out how to make it his own, and his resourcefulness was obvious by how quickly he'd made a name for himself as a go-to dealer.

"More than a club," Lash said in a low voice. "Much more. You've got a future in this business and I'm offering it to you on a silver platter. I'll have my men pick you up here tomorrow night."

"What if I don't show?"

"Your choice." Of course, then the fucker was going to wake up dead in the morning, but details, details . . .

The kid met Lash's eyes. The human wasn't built like

a fighter; he was more the size of someone who'd gotten his ass cheeks duct-taped together in the school locker room. But it had become amply clear that the Lessening Society needed two kinds of members now: moneymakers and soldiers. After having had Mr. D scope the Xtreme Park and watch who was moving the most product, this wiry little shit with the reptilian stare was at the top of the heap.

"Are you queer?" the kid said.

Lash allowed one of his hands to leave the steering wheel and duck into his jacket. "Why do you ask that?"

"You smell like one. Dress like one, too."

Lash moved so fast, his target didn't have a chance to even lean back in the seat. With a quick lunge, he rocked out the switch and laid that sharp blade right against the vital, beating pulse at the side of the white neck.

"The only thing I do to males is kill them," Lash said. "You want to get fucked like that? Because I'm ready if you are."

The kid's eyes went cartoon wide and his body trembled beneath his dirty clothes. "No . . . I don't got a problem with the queers."

Fidiot was missing the point, but whatever. "Do we have a deal?" Lash said, pressing the point of his knife in. As the penetration was achieved, blood welled up in a bubble and stayed put for a split second, like it was trying to decide whether to flow down the shiny metal or the smooth column of skin.

It picked the blade, meandering forth in a ruby red stream.

"Please . . . don't kill me."

"What's your answer."

"Yeah. I'll do it."

Lash pressed in harder, watching the blood run. He was momentarily captivated by the reality that if he took the weapon and pushed it farther through the flesh, this

27

human would cease to exist, like a breath of air disappearing into a chilly night.

He enjoyed feeling like a god.

As whimpering breached the kid's chapped lips, Lash relented, easing back. With a quick lick, he cleaned off the blade and flicked the weapon shut. "You're going to like where you end up. I promise you."

He gave the guy a chance to recover and knew it wasn't going to take long for the kid to get his groove back. Asswipes like this one had egos like balloons. Pressure, particularly the kind that came with a knife at the throat, caused them to collapse in on themselves. But the instant the stress was relieved, they rebounded, puffing back up into place.

The kid snapped his crappy leather jacket down. "I like where I is just fine."

Bingo. "Then why are you looking at my car like you want it in your garage?"

"I got a better ride than this."

"Oh. Really." Lash eyeballed the bitch from head to foot. "You come here every night on a BMX. Your jeans are torn and not because they're designer. How many jackets you got in your closet? Oh, wait, you keep your shit in a cardboard box under the bridge." Lash rolled his eyes as all kinds of surprise bubbled up from the passenger seat. "You think we didn't check you out? You think we're that stupid?"

Lash jabbed a finger toward the Xtreme Park, where skateboarders were making like metronomes on the ramps, up and down, up and down. "You are the shit in this playground over here. Fine. Congratulations. But we want you to go farther. You join with us, you've got muscle behind you . . . money, product, protection. You hit it with us, you're going to be something more than a two-bit punk swinging your cock around a concrete lot. We've got your future."

The kid's calculating stare shifted toward his little slice of territory in Caldwell and then floated over to the horizon where the skyscrapers loomed. The ambition was there, and that was why he'd been chosen. What this little bastard needed was a way up and a way out.

The fact that he'd have to sell his soul to do it was going to dawn on him only when it was too late, but that was the way of the Society. From what Lash had been told by the *lessers* he now commanded, there was never a full-disclosure thing before they got inducted— and this was understandable. Like any of them would have believed that evil was waiting on the other side of the door they were knocking on? Like any one of them would have volunteered for what they were getting into?

Surprise, motherfucker. This ain't no Disney World, and once you get on the ride, you are never, ever getting off.

Lash was totally fine with deception, however.

"I'm ready for bigger shit," the kid murmured.

"Good. Now get the fuck out of my car. My associate will pick you up tomorrow night at seven."

"Cool."

With business concluded, Lash was impatient to move the little bastard along. The kid smelled like a sewer and was screaming for more than a shower—he needed to be hosed down like a dirty stretch of sidewalk.

As soon as the door was shut, Lash backed out of the parking lot and hooked up with the road that ran parallel to the Hudson River. He headed for home, his hands gripping the steering wheel for another reason than the urge to kill.

The urge to fuck was just as strong a motivator for him.

The street he lived on in Old Caldwell had Victorian-era brownstones running down it and sidewalks planted with trees and property values no lower than a million dollars. The neighbors picked up after their dogs, never made any noise, and put their trash out only in the back alleys, and only on the right days. As he drove past his town house and cut around the block to the garage, he was tickled fucking pink to think all these tight-ass WASPs had a neighbor like him: He might have looked and dressed like them, but his blood ran black and he was as soulless as a wax statue.

As he hit the garage door opener, he smiled and his fangs, a gift from his mother's side, elongated as he got ready for his Hello, Lucy-I'm-home shit.

Never got old. Coming back to Xhex never got old.

After he'd parked the AMG, he got out and had to stretch his body. She put him through the wringer, she abso did, and he loved how she left him stiff . . . and not just in the cock.

Nothing like a good opponent to cheer his shit up.

Cutting through the back garden and entering the house through the kitchen, he smelled grilled sirloin and fresh bread.

He wasn't into food at the moment, though. Thanks to that convo at the park, that little shit skater was going to be his first induction, the first offering he brought to his father, the Omega. And didn't that make him jones for some sex.

"Y'all ready to eat?" Mr. D asked from the stove as he flipped the piece of meat over. The little Texan had proved useful not only as an initial tour guide through the Lessening Society, but also as a killer and a halfway decent cook.

"Nah, I'm going up now." He tossed his keys and his cell phone on the granite countertop. "Leave the food in the fridge and lock the door behind you."

"Yessuh."

"We're on for tomorrow night. You pick the target up at seven. You know where to take him."

30

"Yessuh."

That two-syllable word was the SOB's favorite response—which was another reason he remained upright and the second in command.

Lash passed through the butler's pantry and the dining room and hung a right to the carved staircase. When he'd first seen the place, it had been emptied out, with nothing but the remnants of graceful living left behind: silk wallpaper, damask drapes, and one wing chair. Now, the brownstone was filling up with antiques and statuary and proper rugs. It was going to take longer than he'd thought to get it where it needed to be, but you couldn't pull a household of shit out of your ass overnight.

Mounting the stairs, his feet were light and his body humming as he unbuttoned his coat and then his jacket.

As he closed in on Xhex, he was well aware that what had started out for him as payback had turned into an addiction: What was waiting for him on the other side of his bedroom door was much more than he'd bargained for.

It had been so simple at first: He'd taken her because she'd taken from him. When she'd been up at the colony in that cave, she'd pointed her gun and pulled the trigger and pumped a shitload of lead into his bitch's chest. Not acceptable. She'd robbed him of his favorite toy and he was exactly that flavor of dickhead where an eye for an eye was his theme song.

When he'd brought her here and locked her into his room, his goal had been to take pieces out of her, to trim off bits from her mind and her emotions and her body, putting her through shit that was going to bend her until she snapped.

And then, like any broken thing, he was going to throw her away.

At least, that had been the plan. It was becoming amply clear, however, that her edges didn't dull.

Oh, no. She was titanium, this one. Her reserves of strength were proving inexhaustible and he had the bruises to prove it.

As he came up to the door, he paused to take all his clothing off. Generally speaking, if he liked the threads he had on, they needed to hit the floor before he went inside, because he got trashed pretty quick the moment he got near her.

Unplugging his button-down from his slacks, he released his cuff links, left them on the hall table and took his silk shirt off.

He had marks on him. From her fists. Her nails. Her fangs.

The tip of his cock tingled as he looked at his various wounds and bruises. He healed quickly, thanks to his father's blood running thick in his veins, but sometimes the damage she did lasted and that thrilled him to the core.

When you were the son of evil, there was little you couldn't do, own, or kill, and yet her mortal self was an elusive trophy he could touch, but not put on his shelf.

This made her rare. This made her precious.

This made him . . . love her.

Fingering a blue-black contusion on the inside of his forearm, he smiled. He had to go to his father's tonight to confirm the induction, but first he would spend some QT with his female and add to his collection of scrapes. And before he took off, he would leave some food for her.

Like all prized animals, she needed to be provided for.

Reaching out to the doorknob, he frowned as he thought about the larger feeding issue. She was only half *symphath* and that vampire side of her worried him. Sooner or later, she was going to require something that couldn't be bought at the local Hannaford . . . and wasn't something he could give her.

Vampires needed to take the vein of the opposite sex.

It was immutable. If you had that biology in you, you died unless you put the hardware in your mouth to use and swallowed fresh blood. And she couldn't have what was in his body—everything in him ran black now. As a result, his men, what few he had left, were searching for a male of good age, but they'd been coming up with nothing. Caldwell was close to empty when it came to civilian vampires.

Although . . . he did have that one in deep freeze.

Trouble was, he'd known that motherfucker in his old life, and the idea of her taking the vein of someone he'd been friends with just cranked his shit right out.

Plus the bastard was Qhuinn's brother—so yeah, not a bloodline he wanted her to have anything to do with.

Whatever. Sooner or later, his men were going to come up with something—they just had to. Because his new favorite toy was the kind of thing he wanted to have around for a very long time.

As he opened the door, he started to smile. "Hi, honey, I'm home."

Across town, in the tat shop, Blay stayed mostly focused on what was doing on John's back. There was just something hypnotic about watching that needle trace over the blue transfer lines. Then from time to time, the artist paused to swipe the skin with a white paper towel before resuming his work, the whirring sound of the gun filling the silence once again.

Unfortunately, as captivating as it all was, he still had enough attention span left over to be very aware of when Qhuinn decided to fuck that human woman: After the pair chatted softly and swapped a lot of casual stroking down arms and shoulders, those astounding, mismatched eyes drifted over to the front door.

And a moment later, Qhuinn strolled across and checked to make sure it was locked.

That green-and-blue stare didn't meet Blay's as he came back to the tat station.

"You doing good?" he asked John.

When John glanced up and nodded, Qhuinn quickly signed, *You mind if I get a little exercise behind that curtain?*

Please say yes, you do mind, Blay thought. Please tell him he has to stay here.

Not at all, John signed. *You take care of yourself.*

I'll be on it if you need me. Even if I have to come out with my cock out.

Yeah, if we could avoid that, I'd appreciate it.

Qhuinn laughed a little. "Fair enough." There was a heartbeat of a pause; then he turned away without looking at Blay.

The woman went into the other room first, and given the way she was working her hips, she was as ready for what was going to happen as Qhuinn was. Then Qhuinn's big shoulders shifted as he ducked out of sight and the veil fell back into place.

The overhead light in the room and the curtain's anorexic fibers provided plenty of get-a-load-of-this, so Blay got a distilled picture of Qhuinn reaching out and pulling her by the neck against him.

Blay redirected his eyes to John's tattoo, but the refocusing didn't last. Two seconds later he was locked on that peep show, not so much watching it happen as absorbing the details. In typical Qhuinn fashion, the woman was now on her knees and the guy had his hands bunched into her hair. He was working her head, his hips flexing and releasing as he drilled her mouth.

The muted sounds were as incredible as the visual and Blay had to shift in his seat, his body hardening. He wanted to be in there, on his knees, led by Qhuinn's hands. He wanted to be the one whose mouth was full. He wanted to be responsible for making Qhuinn pant and strain.

Not going to be in the cards.

Man, what the hell? The guy had fucked people in clubs and bathrooms and cars and alleys and occasionally in beds. He'd done ten thousand strangers, men and women and males and females alike . . . he was Wilt Chamberlain with fangs. To be denied was like getting shut out of a public park.

Blay took another shot at looking away, but the ripple of a deep moan once again brought his eyes to the—

Qhuinn's head had turned so that he was staring out of the curtain. And as their eyes met, his mismatched stare flashed . . . almost like he was turned on more by who was watching him, than who he was hooking up with.

Blay's heart stopped. Especially as Qhuinn dragged the woman up, spun her around, and bent her over the desk. One yank and her jeans were to her knees. And then it was . . .

Jesus Christ. Was it possible his best friend was thinking like he was?

Except then Qhuinn pulled the woman's upper body against his chest. After he whispered something in her ear, she laughed and turned her head to the side so he could kiss her. Which he did.

You stupid fuck, Blay thought to himself. You stupid motherfucker.

The guy knows precisely who he's doing . . . and who he's not.

Shaking his head, he muttered, "John, you mind if I go have a cigarette outside?"

When John shook his head, Blay got to his feet and put the clothes on the seat. To the tattoo guy he said, "I just flip the lock?"

"Yup, and you can leave it open if you're just outside the door."

"Thanks, man."

"No prob."

Blay walked away from the buzz of the tattoo gun and the symphony of groans behind that curtain, slipping out of the shop and leaning against the building right next to the entrance. Palming up a flat pack of Dunhill reds, he withdrew a cigarette, put it between his lips, and lit the thing with his black lighter.

The first drag was heaven. Always the best out of all that followed.

As he exhaled, he hated that he read into things, saw connections that weren't there, misinterpreted actions and stares and casual touches.

Pathetic, really.

Qhuinn hadn't been looking up as he'd been getting blown to meet Blay's eyes. He'd been checking on John Matthew. And he'd spun that woman around and taken her from behind because that was how he liked it.

Fuckin' A . . . hope didn't so much spring eternal as it drowned out common sense and self-preservation.

Inhaling hard, he was so tangled in his own thoughts that he failed to notice the shadow at the head of the alley across the street. Unaware he was being watched, he smoked along, the chilly spring night eating up the puffs that rose from his lips.

The realization that he couldn't keep going like this anymore was a deep freeze that went right into his bones.

FOUR

"Okay, I think we're done."

John felt a last dragging pull across his shoulder and then the tattoo gun went silent. Sitting up from the rest he'd been curled against for the last two hours, he stretched his arms over his head and pulled his torso back into shape.

"Gimme a sec and I'll clean you up."

As the human male sprayed some paper towels with antibacterial wash, John settled his weight on his spine once again, and let the tingling hum from the needle's work reverberate through his whole body.

In the lull, an odd memory came to him, one he hadn't thought of for years. It was from his days of living at Our Lady's orphanage, back when he hadn't known what he truly was.

One of the church's benefactors had been a rich man who owned a big house on the shores of Saranac Lake. Every summer, the orphans had been invited to go up for a day and play on his football-field-size lawn and go for rides on his beautiful wooden boat and eat sandwiches and watermelon.

John had always gotten a sunburn. No matter how much goo they slathered on him, his skin had always burned to a crisp—until they finally relegated him to staying in the shade on the porch. Forced to wait things out on the sidelines, he'd watched the other boys and girls do their thing, listening to the laughter roll across the bright green grass, having his food brought to him and eating alone, playing witness instead of being a part of it.

Funny, his back felt now as his skin had then: tight and prickly, especially as the tattoo artist hit the raw spots with the wet cloth and made circles over the fresh ink.

Man, John could remember dreading that annual ordeal at the lake. He'd wanted so badly to be with the others . . . although if he was honest, that had been less about what they were doing, and more because he was desperate simply to fit in. For fuck's sake, they could have been chewing on glass shards and bleeding down the front of their shirts and he still would have been all sign-me-up.

Those six hours on that porch with nothing but a comic book or maybe a fallen bird's nest to inspect and reinspect had seemed as long as months. Too much time to think and yearn. He'd always hoped to be adopted and in lonely moments like that the drive had consumed him: Even more than being among the other little boys, he'd wanted a family, a real mother and a father, not just guardians who were paid to raise him.

He'd wanted to be owned. He'd wanted someone to say, *You're mine.*

Of course, now that he knew what he was . . . now that he lived as a vampire among vampires, he understood that "owning" thing much more clearly. Sure, humans had a concept of family units and marriage and all that shit, but his true kind were more like pack animals. Blood ties and matings were far more visceral and all-consuming.

As he thought about his younger, sadder self, his chest ached—although not because he wished he could reach back in time and tell that little kid that his parents were coming for him. Nope, he ached because the very thing he'd wanted had nearly destroyed him. His adoption had indeed come, but the "owning" hadn't stuck. Wellsie and Tohr had waltzed into his life, told him what he was, and shown him a brief glimpse of home . . . and then disappeared.

So he could say categorically that it was far worse to have had and lost parents, than not to have had them at all.

Yeah, sure, Tohr was technically back in the Brotherhood's mansion, but to John he was ever away: Even though he was now saying the right things, too many takeoffs had occurred such that now that a landing might actually have happened, it was too late.

John was through with that whole Tohr thing.

"Here's a mirror. Check 'er out, my man."

John nodded a thank-you and went over to a full-lengther in the corner. As Blay returned from his extended cigarette break and Qhuinn emerged from behind the side room's curtain, John turned around and got a look-see at what was on his back.

Oh, God. It was exactly what he wanted. And the scrollwork was boss.

He nodded as he moved the hand mirror around, checking out every angle. Man, it was kind of a shame that no one other than his boys were ever going to see this. The tat was spectacular.

And more to the point, no matter what happened next, whether he found Xhex dead or alive, she would always be with him.

Damn him to hell, these last four weeks since her abduction had been the longest of his life. And he'd had some pretty fucking long days before this shit. To not know where she was. To not know what had happened to her. To have lost her . . . He felt as if he'd been mortally injured, though his skin was intact and his arms and legs unbroken and his chest unpenetrated by bullet or blade.

But then again, in his heart, she was his. And even if he got her back just so she could live a life that didn't include him, that was okay. He only wanted her safe and alive.

John looked at the artist, put his hand over his heart, and bowed deeply. As he rose from his position of gratitude, the guy stuck his palm out.

"You're welcome, man. Means a lot that you approve. Let me cover it up now with some cream and a wrap."

After they shook, John signed and Blay translated, "Not necessary. He heals lightning-quick."

"But it's going to need time to—" The tattoo artist leaned in and then frowned as he inspected where he'd worked.

Before the guy started asking questions, John stepped back and grabbed his shirt from Blay. The fact was, the ink they'd brought with them had been lifted from V's stash—which meant part of its composition included salt. That name and those fabulous swirls were permanent—and his skin had already healed.

Which was one advantage of being a nearly purebred vampire.

"The tat rocks," Qhuinn said. "It's pure sex."

As if on cue, the woman who he'd just balled came out from behind the side room's curtain, and it was hard not to notice Blay's pained expression. Especially as she slipped a piece of paper into Qhuinn's back pocket. Undoubtedly her number was on the thing, but she really didn't need to get her hopes up. Once the guy had someone, that was it—kind of like his sex partners were a meal that couldn't be re-eaten and never had any leftovers. Unfortunately said Kat von D look-alike had stars in her eyes.

"Call me," she murmured to him with a confidence that would fade as the days passed.

Qhuinn smiled a little. "Take care."

At the sound of the two words, Blay relaxed, his big shoulders easing up. In Qhuinn-landia, *take care* was

40

synonymous with *I'm never going to see, call, or fuck you again.*

John took out his wallet, which was stuffed with tons of bills and absolutely no identification, and peeled off four hundreds. Which was twice what the tat cost. As the artist started shaking his head and saying it was too much, John nodded at Qhuinn.

The two of them lifted their right palms at the humans, and then reached into those minds and covered up the memories of the last couple hours. Neither the artist nor the receptionist would have any concrete recollection of what had happened. At the most, they might have hazy dreams. At the least, they'd have a headache.

As the pair slipped into trances, John, Blay, and Qhuinn walked out of the shop's door and into the shadows. They waited until the artist shook himself back into focus, went over, and flipped the lock . . . and then it was time to get down to business.

"Sal's?" Qhuinn asked, his voice lower than usual thanks to postcoital satisfaction.

Blay fired up another Dunhill as John nodded and signed, *They're expecting us.*

One after another, his boys disappeared into the night. But before John ghosted out, he paused for a moment, his instincts ringing.

Looking left and right, his laser-sharp eyes penetrated the darkness. Trade Street had a lot of neon lights and there were cars going by because it was only two a.m., but he wasn't interested in the lit parts.

The dark alleys were the thing.

Somebody was watching them.

He put his hand inside his leather jacket and closed his palm around his dagger's hilt. He had no problem killing the enemy, especially now, when he knew damn well who had his female . . . and he hoped something that smelled like a week-old dead deer stepped up to him.

41

No such luck. Instead, his cell phone went off with a whistle. No doubt Qhuinn and/or Blay were wondering where the fuck he was.

He waited a minute more and decided the information he hoped to get from Trez and iAm was more important than knuckle busting whatever slayer was hanging back in the shadows.

With vengeance flowing thick in his veins, John dematerialized into thin air and took form again in the parking lot of Sal's restaurant. There were no cars around and the lights that usually shone up on the outside of the brick building were off.

The double doors under the porte cochere opened right away and Qhuinn stuck his head out. "What the hell took you so long?"

Paranoia, John thought.

Double-checked my weapons, he signed as he walked over. "You could have asked me to wait. Or done it here."

Yes, Mother.

The inside of the place was done in old-school Rat Pack with red flocked wallpaper and plush carpeting as far as the eye could see. Everything from the club chairs to the linen-covered tables to the plates and silverware was a reproduction of what had been around in the sixties and the vibe was Dean Martin redux: smooth, rich, and Sands Casino classy.

Ol' Blue Eyes was even singing "Fly Me to the Moon."

The overhead speakers would probably refuse anything else.

The three of them walked past the hostess stand and into the bar room, where the pungent aroma of cigars lingered in spite of New York's anti-smoking laws. Blay went back behind the teak counter to fix himself a Coke, and John walked around, hands on hips, eyes on the marble floor, path delineated by the leather booths that were arranged around the space.

Qhuinn took a seat in one of them. "They told us to hang and make a drink. They're coming out in a sec—"

At that moment, from the staff-only room in back, a *thump-thump* and a groan cut into Sinatra's scooby-doo's. With a curse, John followed Qhuinn's lead and parked it across from the guy. If the Shadows were working some POS out, they were likely to be longer than a second.

As Qhuinn stretched his legs under the black table and cracked his back, he was still glowing, his cheeks flushed from exertion, his lips swollen from kissing. For a moment, John was tempted to ask why the guy insisted on fucking people in front of Blay, but he canned the Q as he stared at the red tear that was tatted on the guy's cheek.

How else was the bastard going to get laid? He was literally joined at the hip with John and all they did was go out and fight . . . with Blay a member of their team.

Blay came over with his Coke, sat next to John, and stayed quiet.

Awkward much, John thought as none of them said a thing.

Ten minutes later, the door marked STAFF ONLY swung wide and Trez came in from the back. "Sorry about the wait." He grabbed a hand towel from behind the bar and wiped the blood from his knuckles. "iAm's just dumping some trash in the alley. He'll be right in."

John signed, *Do we know anything?*

After Qhuinn translated, Trez's brows dropped and the Shadow's eyes grew calculating. "About what."

"Xhex," Qhuinn said.

Trez made elaborate work out of refolding the now red-stained towel. "Last thing I knew, Rehv was living at the compound with you."

"He is."

The Shadow planted his palms on the teak and leaned in, his shoulder muscles bunching up thick. "So why do you have to ask me about her search and rescue."

You know her very well, John signed.

After the translation, Trez's dark eyes flashed bright green. "I do. She is a sister, though not of mine blood."

So what's the problem? John signed.

As Qhuinn hesitated, like he wanted to be sure John really needed to say that to a Shadow, John motioned for the guy to get talking.

Qhuinn shook his head a little. "He said he understands that. He just wants to make sure all avenues are covered."

"Word up, I don't think that's what he signed." Trez's smile was cold. "And here's my problem. You coming here and being all what's-up suggests you and your king don't trust Rehv to tell you where it's at—or you don't think he's busting his balls to find her. And you know . . . that shit don't fly with me."

iAm came in through the staff door and just nodded as he stepped up to his brother—which was about as much welcome as you ever got from him. He didn't spare words. Or punches, going by how much blood had stained his gray T-shirt. And the guy didn't ask for a recap of the convo thus far. He seemed to be fully up to speed, which meant either he'd seen something on a security camera in the back, or he was accurately reading the tension in his brother's powerful body.

We didn't come here to fight or offend, John signed. *We just want to find her.*

There was a pause after Qhuinn did his bit. And then Trez asked the sixty-four-thousand-dollar question. "Your king know you're here?"

When John shook his head, Trez narrowed his eyes even further. "And what precisely do you expect to get from us?"

Anything you know or believe to be true about where Xhex is. And any information on the drug trade here in Caldwell. He waited for Qhuinn to catch up, then continued. *Assuming Rehv is right and Lash was the one knocking off those dealers in town, then it's damn obvious that he and the Lessening Society will fill the void they created.* Another pause for Qhuinn. *So where do people go for buys, apart from the clubs down on Trade? Is there a crack row? And who are the big suppliers Rehv worked with? If Lash is trying to deal, he's got to be getting the shit from someone.* One last breather for Qhuinn. *We've been down in the alleys, but up until now, it's getting us nowhere. Just humans dealing with humans.*

Trez eased back off his palms and you could practically smell the wood burning as his brain worked. "Lemme ask you something."

Sure, John signed.

Trez looked around and then met John's eyes again. "Privately."

FIVE

As the Shadow threw out the demand, John saw Qhuinn and Blay both stiffen and knew where his boys were coming from. Trez was an ally, but he was also dangerous by definition. Shadows ran by their own code and no one else's and they were capable of things that would make *symphaths* gag.

But when it came to Xhex, he was willing to walk into any ring of fire.

Long as I have a pad and pen, we're good to go, John signed. When neither Blay nor Qhuinn translated, he frowned and elbowed them both.

Qhuinn cleared his throat and stared across the bar at Trez. "As his *ahstrux nohtrum*, I go anywhere he does."

"Not in my house, you don't. Or in my brother's."

Qhuinn rose to his feet, like he would throw down with the Shadow if he had to. "That's the way it works."

John slid out of the booth and planted his body in Qhuinn's path before the motherfucker got all linebacker. With a nod toward the back, where he was assuming he and Trez would go, he waited for the Shadow to lead the way.

Naturally, Qhuinn just had to open his pie hole. "Fuck that, John."

John wheeled around and signed, *Do I have to give you a goddamned order? I'm going with him and you're staying out here. Period. End of.*

You suck, Qhuinn's hands spelled out. *I'm not just jacking you for kicks and giggles—*

The sound of a doorbell going off broke the argument up as they both looked to the Shadows. After iAm glanced at the security monitor under the bar, he said, "Our two-thirty meeting is here."

As he strode around the counter and headed out for the front door, Trez focused on Qhuinn for a long moment, then said to John, "Tell your boy it's hard to protect someone when you're dead."

Qhuinn's voice grew hard as a punch. "I'd go to the death for him."

"You keep up the attitude and that will not be a hypothetical."

Qhuinn bared his fangs and hissed down low in his throat, becoming the deadly animal that humans made up all kinds of horror mythology around. As he glared at Trez, it was pretty clear that in his mind, he was already mounting the bar and going for the Shadow's throat.

Trez smiled coldly and didn't budge an inch. "Tough guy, huh. Or are you all show."

Hard to know which fighter to back. The Shadow had tricks up his sleeve, and yet Qhuinn was looking like a bulldozer prepared to take down a building. But whatever, this was Caldwell, not Las Vegas, and John wasn't a bookie to take odds.

The right answer was to not let the unstoppable force meet the immovable object.

John balled up his fist and slammed it on the table. The crack was so loud, it brought everyone's head around, and Blay had to catch his Coke on the upswing as it bounced into the air.

After John grabbed the undivided attention of the combatants, he fingered up two birds and flashed one in each of their directions: Being mute, it was the closest he was going to get to telling them to chill the fuck out.

Qhuinn's mismatched stare swung back to the Shadow.

"It's just like you would do for Rehv. Can't blame me for that."

There was a pause . . . and then the Shadow eased up a little. "True enough." As the testosterone surge faded to a dull roar, Trez nodded. "Yeah . . . true enough. And I'm not going to hurt him. If he's a gentleman, I'll be a gentleman. I give you my word."

Stay with Blay, John signed, before turning around and heading for the Shadow.

Trez led the way into a hall that was wide and stacked with cases of beer and liquor. The kitchen was at the far end, separated by a pair of flap-doors that made no sound when you went through them.

Brightly lit and with a red tile floor, the heart of the restaurant was neat as a pin and the size of a house, with a bank of stoves, a meat locker, and yards and yards of stainless-steel countertops. Pans hung up above and down below and something gorgeous was stewing on a front burner.

Trez went over and lifted the lid. After a deep inhale, he glanced over with a smile. "My brother is a helluva cook."

Sure was, John thought. Although with Shadows you always had to wonder what the protein was. Rumor had it they liked to eat their enemies.

The guy replaced the top and reached up to a stack of pads. Taking one of them off the pile, he slid the thing across the counter and snagged a pen from a cup.

"That's for you." Trez crossed his arms over his huge chest and leaned back against the stove. "When you called and asked to see us, I was surprised. Like I said, Rehv lives under the same roof you do, so it's not as if you aren't aware of what he's doing up north in the colony. Therefore you must know, as your bosses do, that he's searching the northern-most corner of the labyrinth this week . . . and you must also be aware that he's found

48

absolutely, positively nothing that leads him to believe Xhex was captured by a *symphath*."

John didn't make a move, neither confirming nor denying.

"And I also find it curious that you want to ask me about drug deals, given that Rehv knows everything about the trade here in Caldwell."

At this point, iAm came into the kitchen. He went to the pot and gave it a stir as well, then braced himself next to his brother, assuming the same pose. John hadn't heard they were twins, but damn, you had to wonder.

"So what's doing, John," Trez murmured. "Why doesn't your king know what you're up to and why aren't you talking to my man Rehvenge?"

John faced off at the pair of them and then picked up the pen and wrote for a little bit. When he flashed the paper forward, the Shadows leaned in.

You are perfectly aware of what's going on here. Stop wasting our time.

Trez laughed and iAm even smiled. "Yeah, we can read your emotions. Just figured you might want to explain yourself." When John shook his head, Trez nodded. "Okay, fair enough. And I gotta respect your no-bullshit policy. Who else knows that this is personal to you?"

John went back to the pad-and-pen routine. *Rehv, most likely, given that he's a* symphath. *Qhuinn and Blay. But none of the Brothers.*

iAm spoke up. "So that tattoo you just got . . . it have to do with her?"

John was momentarily surprised, but then figured they could either smell the fresh ink or feel the reverberations of the faded pain.

With a quiet scribble, he wrote, *That is none of your business.*

"Cool, I can respect that," Trez said. "Listen . . . no

offense, but why can't you trust the Brothers with this shit? Is it because she's a *symphath* and you're worried about how they'll take it? Because they're down with Rehv."

Use your head. I go all guns-blazing about her with them and we find her? Everyone in that house is going to expect a mating ceremony at the homecoming. You think she'd appreciate that? And if she's dead? I don't want to stare across the dinner table every morning at a bunch of people waiting to see if I hang myself in the bathroom.

Trez barked out a laugh. "Well . . . there you go. And I can't fault logic like that."

So I need your help. Help me help her.

The two Shadows looked at each other and there was a long stretch of quiet. Which John took to mean they were having a conversation gray matter–to–gray matter.

After a moment, they glanced back to him, and as usual Trez did the talking. "Well, now . . . since you've done us the courtesy of cutting the shit, we'll do the same. Talking to you like this puts us in a difficult position. Our relationship with Rehv is tight, as you know, and he's as personally invested in this as you are." Just as John was trying to figure out a way around all that, Trez murmured, "But we will tell you . . . neither one of us is picking up on her. Anywhere."

John swallowed hard, thinking that was not good news.

"No, it isn't. She's either dead . . . or she's being held somewhere with a block." Trez cursed. "I think Lash has her, too. And I totally buy the idea that he's working the streets for cash, and that's the only way to find him. If I had to guess, he's trying out human dealers first before converting them to the Lessening Society—and mark my balls, he's going to start inducting them ASAP. He'll want to have total control over his retail team and the only way he's going to get that is by turning them. As for hotbeds of dealing, the malls are always jumping.

So is the high school, although that's going to be tough because of daylight problems for you. Municipal construction zones, too—the vendors in those catering trucks always used to buy from us. Also, that Xtreme skating park. Lotta shit goes down there. And under the bridges—although that's mostly homeless, bottom-feeder real estate, so the crank ratio for cash will probably be too low for Lash to get a hard-on over."

John nodded, thinking this was precisely the info he'd been hoping to get. *What about the suppliers*, he wrote. *If Lash stepped into Rehv's shoes, wouldn't he need relationships with them?*

"Yup. The big one in town, Ricardo Benloise, is pretty fucking insulated, though." Trez glanced at his brother and there was another silence. When iAm nodded, Trez turned back. "Okay. We'll see if we can get you some intel on Benloise—at least enough so you can trail his ass in the event he meets with Lash."

John signed without thinking, *Thank you so much.*

Both of them nodded, and then Trez said, "Two caveats."

With his hands, John urged the guy to continue.

"One, my brother and I don't keep anything from Rehv. So we're going to tell him you came to see us." As John frowned, Trez shook his head. "Sorry. That's the way it is."

iAm interjected, "It's cool with us that you're digging deep. Not that the Brothers aren't, it's just the more hands on deck, the better her chances are."

John could see that, but he still wanted to keep shit private. Before he could get scribbling, Trez kept going.

"And two, you must fully inform us of any information you get. Rehvenge, that fucking control-freak bastard, has commanded us to stay out of it. Your turning up here? Well, isn't that just a convenient way for us to get involved."

As John wondered why in the hell Rehv would tie the hands of the two warriors, iAm said, "He figures we'll get ourselves killed."

"And because of our . . ." Trez paused, as if looking for the right word. ". . . 'relationship' with him, we're locked in."

"He might as well have chained us to the cocksucking wall."

Trez shrugged. "Which was why we agreed to meet with you. The moment you texted, we knew—"

"—here was the opening we—"

"—were looking for."

As the Shadows completed each other's sentences, John took a deep breath. At least they understood where he was coming from.

"We totally do." Trez put his knuckles out and, as John gave them a pound, the guy nodded. "And let's just keep this little backroom convo to ourselves."

John leaned over the pad. *Wait, I thought you said you were going to tell Rehv I was here?*

Trez read over the handwriting and laughed again. "Oh, we're going to tell him you came to visit and have a meal."

iAm smiled darkly. "But he doesn't need to know the rest of it."

After Trez and John went into the back, Blay finished off his Coke and tracked Qhuinn with his peripheral vision. The guy was pacing around the bar area like he'd had his wings clipped and didn't appreciate the trim.

He just couldn't stand getting shut out of shit. Whether it was a dinner or a meeting or a fight, he preferred an all-access pass to life.

His kinetic silence was worse than cursing, frankly.

Blay got up and went behind the bar with his empty glass. As he refilled his Coke and watched the frothing dark rush hit the ice, he wondered why he was so attracted to the guy. He was a please-and-thank-you kind of male. Qhuinn was more of a fuck-off-and-die type.

Guess opposites attracted. At least on his side—

iAm came back in and had with him what could only be described as a male of worth: The guy was dressed impeccably, from the cut of his dark gray overcoat to the shine on his wingtips, and instead of a tie, he was wearing a cravat. Thick blond hair was cut short in the back and left long in the front and his eyes were the color of pearls.

"Jesus fucking Christ, what the hell are you doing here?" Qhuinn's voice boomed out as iAm disappeared into the back. "You slick bastard."

Blay's first response was to tighten up all over. Last thing he needed was another ride on the spectator merry-go-round, assuming Qhuinn was attracted to the guy.

Except then he frowned. Could it be . . . ?

The male who'd just arrived laughed as he embraced Qhuinn. "You have *such* a way with words, cousin. I would say . . . trucker meets sailor crossed with a twelve-year-old."

Saxton. It was Saxton, son of Tyhm. Blay could remember meeting him once or twice before.

Qhuinn pulled back. "*Fuck* is actually a comma. Or didn't they teach that shit to you at Harvard?"

"They were more concerned with contract law. Property. Torts—which covers actionable wrongs against others, by the way. I'm surprised you weren't on the final exam."

Qhuinn's fangs flashed bright and white as he truly smiled. "That's human law. They can't handle me."

"Who can."

"So what are you doing here?"

"Property transactions for the Shadow brothers. Lest you think I just learned all that human jurisprudence for my health." Saxton's eyes shifted over and met Blay's. Instantly, the guy's expression changed to something serious and speculative. "Well, hello."

Saxton turned his back on Qhuinn and came over with a focus that made Blay check behind himself.

"Blaylock, is it not?" The male extended his elegant arm across the bar. "I haven't seen you in years."

Blay had always felt a little tongue-tied in Saxton's presence because the "slick bastard" always had a comeback. And a vibe like he not only knew the right answers to everything but might not choose to let you in on the secrets if you weren't up to his standards.

"How do you do?" Blay said as their palms met.

Saxton smelled really good and had a handshake that was firm. "You've grown up a lot."

Blay found himself flushing as he took his hand back. "You're just the same."

"Am I?" Those pearl eyes flashed. "Is that good or bad?"

"Oh . . . good. I didn't mean—"

"So tell me how you've been. Are you mated to some nice female your parents set you up with?"

Blay's laugh was sharp and hard. "God, no. There's no one for me."

Qhuinn inserted himself in the conversation, all but putting his body between them. "So, how *you* been, Sax?"

"Rather well." Saxton didn't even glance over at Qhuinn as he answered, his attention staying on Blay. "Although my parents want me out of Caldwell. I am not inclined to leave, however."

Needing somewhere else to look, Blay got busy drinking his soda and counting the ice cubes that floated in it.

"And what are you doing here?" Saxton asked.

There was a long pause and eventually, Blay swung his eyes back up as he wondered why Qhuinn hadn't replied.

Oh. Right. Saxton wasn't addressing his cousin.

"You going to speak up there, Blay," Qhuinn prompted with a frown.

For the first time in . . . God, forever, it seemed . . . he went to fully meet his best friend's stare. Although it wasn't like he needed to brace himself. As always, those mismatched eyes were trained on someone else: Saxton was getting a once-over that would have rendered lesser males several inches shorter. But Qhuinn's cousin was either unaware of it or possibly didn't care.

"Do answer me, Blaylock," the male murmured.

Blay cleared his throat. "We're here to help a friend."

"Admirable." Saxton smiled, flashing a set of fangs that gleamed. "You know, I think we should go out sometime."

Qhuinn's voice was mostly edge. "Sure. Sounds great. Here's my number."

Just as he recited his digits, John, Trez, and iAm came back in. There were some introductions and conversating, but Blay stayed out of it, polishing off the Coke and putting his glass in the washer.

As he came around the bar and passed the guy, Saxton reached out. "Good to see you again."

On reflex, Blay clasped the palm that was offered . . . and after the shake, he realized there was a business card in his hand. As he covered his surprise, Saxton just smiled.

While Blay tucked the card into his pocket, Saxton turned his head and glanced at Qhuinn. "I'll be giving you a call, cousin."

"Yeah. Sure."

The good-bye-ing was considerably less friendly on Qhuinn's side, but again Saxton didn't seem to give a damn or didn't notice—the latter being hard to believe.

"Will you excuse me," Blay said, to no one in particular.

He left the restaurant by himself, and when he stepped out under the porte cochere, he lit up a cigarette and leaned back against the cool brick, bracing the sole of one boot on the building.

He took the card out as he smoked. Thick, creamy stock. Engraved, not embossed—naturally. Black, old-school font. As he lifted the thing to his nose, he could smell that cologne.

Nice. Very nice. Qhuinn didn't believe in the stuff . . . so he just smelled like leather and sex most of the time.

As he tucked the card inside his jacket, he took another drag and exhaled long and slow. He wasn't used to being looked at. Or approached. He was always the one doing the focusing and Qhuinn had been the target for as long as he could remember.

The doors burst open and his boys walked out.

"Man, I hate cigarette smoke," Qhuinn muttered, waving away the cloud that had just been exhaled.

Blay extinguished his Dunhill on his boot heel and tucked the half-finished length into his pocket. "Where we off to?"

The Xtreme Park, John signed. *The one close to the river. And they've given us another lead, which is going to take a couple of days to set up.*

"Isn't that park in gang territory?" Blay asked. "Aren't there a lot of police around?"

"Why worry about the cops?" Qhuinn laughed in a hard burst. "If we get into trouble with the CPD, Saxton can always come bail us out. Right?"

Blay glanced over, and this time, he should have braced himself. Qhuinn's blue-and-green stare was boring into him and, as it registered, that old, familiar thrill licked into his chest.

God . . . this was who he loved, he thought. And always would.

It was the thrust of that stubborn jaw, and the dark, slashing eyebrows, and those piercings up his ear and in his full lower lip. It was that thick, glossy black hair and the golden skin and that heavily muscled body. It was the way he laughed and the fact that he never, ever cried. It was the scars on his inside no one knew about and the conviction that he would always be the first to run into a burning building or a bloody fight or a car wreck.

It was all the things Qhuinn had been and was ever going to be.

But things were never going to change.

"What's not going to change?" Qhuinn said with a frown.

Oh, shit. He'd spoken aloud. "Nothing. Are we going, John?"

John glanced back and forth between them. Then nodded. *We've only got three hours before daylight. Let's hustle.*

SIX

"I love the way you look at me."

From over in the opposite corner of the bedroom, Xhex made no reply to the words Lash spoke. From the way he was collapsed in front of the bureau, with one of his shoulders higher than the other, she thought it was entirely possible she had dislocated his upper arm. And that wasn't his only injury. Black blood dripped off his chin from the split lip she'd given him and he was going to walk with a limp after she'd bitten him in the thigh.

His eyes roamed over her and she didn't bother to cover herself with her hands. If he was up for round two, she needed every ounce of strength she had left. And besides, modesty mattered only if you gave a shit about your body and she'd long ago lost that connection.

"Do you believe in love at first sight?" he asked. With a grunt, he pushed himself up off the floor, and he needed the edge of the dresser for support as he did some experimentation with that arm of his.

"Do you?" he prompted.

"No."

"Cynical." He gimped over to the archway that led into the bathroom. Standing in between the jambs, he braced one hand against the wall, faced off to the left, and took a deep breath.

With a slam, he put his upper arm back into its socket and the crack and curse were loud. As he sagged afterward, his breath coming in hard draws, the cuts on his face left black smudges of *lesser* blood on the white molding. Turning toward her, he smiled.

"Care for a shower with me?" When she stayed silent, he shook his head. "No? Pity."

He disappeared into the marble expanse and after a moment, water came on.

It was only after she could hear him washing himself and smelled the fragrance of that milled soap that she carefully rearranged her legs and arms.

No weakness. She showed him no weakness. And it wasn't just about wanting to appear strong so he would think twice about tangoing with her again. Her nature refused to relent to him or anyone else. She would die fighting.

It was just how she was hardwired: She was invincible—and that wasn't her ego talking. The sum of her experience was, no matter what was done to her, she could handle it.

But dear Lord, she hated fighting him. Hated this whole fucking thing.

When he came out a little later, he was clean and already healing up, the bruises fading, the scrapes disappearing, the bones reknitting like magic.

Just her luck. The goddamn Energizer Bunny.

"I'm off to see my father." As he came over to her, she bared her fangs and he seemed momentarily complimented. "I love your smile."

"Not a smile, asshole."

"Whatever you call it, I like it. And someday I'll introduce you to dear old Dad. I have plans for us."

Lash went to lean down, no doubt to try to kiss her, but as she hissed deep in her throat, he paused and reconsidered.

"I'll be back," he whispered. "My love."

He knew she hated the "love" crap, so she was careful to swallow her reaction. She also didn't taunt him as he turned and left.

The more she refused to play into the situation,

the more tangled he became and the clearer her head was.

Listening to him moving around in the room next door, she pictured him getting dressed. He kept his clothes in the other room, having moved them out after it became clear how things were going to roll between them: He hated messes and was fastidious about his threads.

When things quieted down and she heard him descend the stairs, she took a deep breath and dragged herself up off the floor. The bathroom was still steamy and tropical from his shower, and though she hated using the same soap he did, she disliked what was on her skin even more.

The moment she stepped under the hot spray, the marble at her feet turned both red and black as two kinds of blood washed off of her body and disappeared down the drain. She was quick with the suds and rinse, because Lash had left only moments before and you could never tell with him. Sometimes he came right back. Other times he didn't show again for a whole day.

The fragrance of the fancy-ass French shit Lash insisted on stocking his bathroom with made her gag, even though she supposed most females would have enjoyed the blend of lavender and jasmine. Man, she wished she had a dose of Rehv's good ol' Dial. Although no doubt that would sting like a bitch on the cuts, she was okay with agony, and the idea of scrubbing herself raw was appealing.

Each sweep up the arm or down the leg was marked with aches as she bent to the side or leaned forward, and for no reason at all, she thought of the cilices she'd always worn to control her *symphath* nature. With all the fighting out in that bedroom, she'd had enough pain in her body to dampen her evil inclinations—not that it mattered, really. She wasn't around "normals," and that dark part of her helped her deal with this situation.

Still, after two decades of wearing the barbs, it was odd not to have them with her. She'd left the pair of spiked chains behind at the Brotherhood mansion . . . on the bureau in the room she'd stayed in that day before they'd gone up to the colony. She'd had every intention of returning at the end of the night, showering, and putting them back on . . . but now they were no doubt gathering dust as they waited for her return.

She was losing faith that there was going to be a happy reunion with those fuckers.

Funny how your life could be interrupted: You left a house expecting to come back, but then the path you were on took you left instead of around again to the right.

How long would the Brothers let her personal items sit out? she wondered. How long before her few belongings, whether they were at the Brotherhood mansion or her hunting cabin or her basement place, got relegated to nothing but clutter? Two weeks was probably approaching the outside limit—although as no one except John knew about her underground crash pad, that stuff would linger far longer.

After a couple of weeks, her shit would no doubt be shoved into a closet. Then a small box in the attic.

Or maybe it would simply be pitched into the trash.

That was what happened when people died, though. What had been a possession became litter—unless the shit was adopted by someone else.

And it wasn't like there was a great demand for cilices.

Turning off the water, she got out, toweled off, and went back into the bedroom. Just as she sat down by the window, the door opened and the little *lesser* who ran the kitchen came in with a tray full of food.

He always seemed confused as he put what he'd prepared down on the bureau and looked around—like after all this time, he still had no clue why in the hell he was leaving hot meals in an empty room. He also inspected the walls, tracing the fresh dings and streaks of black blood. Given how tidy he seemed, no doubt he wanted to pull a DIY: When she'd first come here, the silk paper had been in perfect shape. Now, the stuff looked like it had been put through the wringer.

As he went over to the bed and straightened the scrambled duvet and scattered pillows, he left the door wide open and she stared out into the hall and down the stairs.

No reason to make a run for it. And tackling him hadn't worked, either. Nor had going the *symphath* route, because she was blocked mentally as well as physically.

All she could do was watch him and wish she could get at him somehow. God, this impotent drive to kill must be the same for zoo lions when their keepers entered their cage with the brooms and the eats: The other guy could come and go and change your environment, but you were stuck.

Kind of made you want to bite down on something.

After he left, she went over to the food. Getting angry at the steak wasn't going to help her and she needed the calories to fight back, so she ate everything there was. To her tongue, the shit all tasted like cardboard and she wondered whether she would ever again have something because she wanted to and liked the way it was seasoned.

The whole food-as-fuel thing was logical, but sure as hell didn't give you anything to look forward to during mealtime.

When she was finished, she went back to the window, settled in the wing chair, and brought her knees up against her breasts. Staring down into the street, she was not at rest, but merely motionless.

Even after all these weeks, she was looking for an escape . . . and she would be that way until she drew her last breath.

Again, like her urge to fight Lash, the drive was not just a function of her circumstance, but who she was as a female, and the realization made her think of John.

She had been so determined to get away from him.

She thought of when they'd been together—not the last time, when he'd paid her back for all the rejection, but the other one at her basement place. After the sex, he'd made a move to kiss her . . . clearly, he'd wanted more than just a quick, hard fuck. Her response? She'd pulled away and gone into the bathroom, where she'd washed herself off as if he'd dirtied her. Then she'd hit the door.

So she didn't blame him for the way their last good-bye had gone.

She glanced around her dark green prison. She was probably going to die here. Probably soon, too, as she hadn't taken a vein in a while and she was under a great deal of physical and emotional stress.

The reality of her own demise made her think of the many faces she'd stared down into as lives had leached out of bodies and souls went soaring free. As an assassin, death had been her job. As a *symphath*, it had been a kind of calling.

The process had always fascinated her. Every one of the people she'd killed had fought the tide, even though they knew, as she'd stood over them with whatever weapon she'd palmed up still in her hand, that if they managed to pull themselves out of the spiral she was just going to strike again. Hadn't seemed to matter, though. The horror and the pain had acted as an energy source, food for their fight, and she knew what that felt like. How you struggled to breathe even though you couldn't get air down your throat. How the cold sweat formed on top of your overheated skin. How your muscles became weak, but you still called on them to *move, move, move, damn it.*

Her previous captors had taken her to the brink of rigor mortis a number of times.

Although vampires believed in the Scribe Virgin, *symphaths* had no conception of an afterlife. To them, death was an exit ramp not to another highway, but to a brick wall that you slammed into. After which there was nothing.

Personally, she didn't buy the whole holy-deity bullshit, and whether that was breeding or intellect, the outcome was the same. Death was lights-out, end of story. For fuck's sake, she'd seen it up close so many times—after the great struggle came . . . nothing. Her victims had just stopped moving, frozen in whatever position they'd been in when their hearts had halted. And maybe some people died with a smile on their face, but in her experience, that was a grimace, not a grin.

You'd think if they were getting a boatload of bright white light and kingdom-of-heaven crap, they'd be beaming like they'd won the lottery.

Except maybe the reason they looked so bitched was less about where they were going and more about where they'd been.

The regrets . . . you did think about your regrets.

Aside from the fact that she wished she'd been born under different circumstances, there were two transgressions among her many that weighed more than all the others.

She wished she'd told Murhder, all those years ago, that she was half-*symphath*. That way, when she'd been taken up to the colony, he wouldn't have come to rescue her. He'd have known it was inevitable that the other side of her family would come claim her and he wouldn't then have ended up where he had.

She also wished she could go back and tell John Matthew she was sorry. She still would have pushed him away, because that was the only construct under which he wouldn't have repeated the mistakes of her other lover. But she would have let him know it wasn't him. It was her.

At least he was going to be okay in all of this. He had the Brothers and the king of the race to look after him, and, courtesy of her shutting him down, he wasn't going to do anything stupid.

She was on her own in this and it was going to play out as it would.

Having led a violent life, it was entirely unsurprising that she was going to meet a violent end . . . but true to form, she was sure as fuck going to take out a pound or two of flesh with her on the way to the exit.

SEVEN

Shit, they were losing the darkness.

As John glanced at his watch, the time check was a waste of effort. The sting in his eyes was telling him all he needed to know about how little night they had left.

Even the promise of daylight was enough to make him blink fast.

Then again, the activity at the Xtreme Park was winding down for the evening anyway, the drugged-out stragglers getting vertical on the benches or ducking into the public bathrooms for a last fix. Unlike Caldwell's other parks, this one was open twenty-four/seven, with fluorescent lights on tall poles illuminating the expanse of concrete. Hard to tell what the city planners had been thinking with the round-the-clock business—because that was what they had here. *Round-the-clock business.* With all the drugs changing hands, the place was like a bar away from the bars down on Trade.

No *lessers*, though. Just humans dealing to humans who used in the shadows.

Still, it was promising. If Lash hadn't infiltrated the zone yet, he was going to. Even with the cops doing their idle-bys in their marked cars, there was plenty of privacy and plenty of notice. The park was laid out like a huge terrace, with sinkholes in the ground alternating with ramps and jumps. Bottom line was, the people could see the CPD coming and duck behind or into all kinds of shelter.

And, man, they were trained well. From their vantage point behind the work shed, he and his boys had seen it happen over and over again. Kind of made you wonder why the CPD didn't send unmarkeds over or infiltrate in plain clothes.

Or maybe they were doing that already. Maybe there were others who, like John, were invisible to the crowd. Well, not exactly like him and Qhuinn and Blay. There was no way even a fully trained and decorated member of the CPD could present himself as nothing—which was what John and his buddies had been doing for the last three hours. Every time someone passed, they wiped out the memory.

It was kind of odd to be in a place, but not of it . . . sensed, but not seen.

"We gonna get ghost?" Qhuinn asked.

John glanced up at the brightening sky and told himself that in approximately thirteen hours that fucking heat lamp of a sun was going back under wraps and they could take up res in their little hidden corner and wait again.

Goddamn it.

"John? Let's go."

For a split second, he almost tore his buddy's head off, his hands coming up and getting ready to fly through all kinds of fuck-you, you're-not-my-babysitter shit.

What stopped him was the fact that just as no amount of waiting around here was going to produce Lash, yelling at Qhuinn wasn't going to get them closer to a sighting, either.

He nodded once and took a last look around. There was a single dealer type who seemed to run the show and the kid was hanging out to the very end. His main lean was against the center ramp, which was smart—it meant he could see everything in the park, from the far corners to the road where the cops came and went.

Kid looked to be about seventeen or eighteen and his clothes were loose on his frame, which was part of the skater style, and also probably a function of his using what he sold. He looked like he needed to be scrubbed with a car brush a couple of times, but he was alert and he was savvy. And he seemed to work alone. Which was interesting. To dominate a drug territory, usually the dealer in question had enforcers to back him up— otherwise he got jumped for either his product or his cash. But this young guy . . . he was by himself the whole time.

Either he had some serious meat in the shadows, or he was about to get taken down.

John stood up from where he'd braced himself against the side of the outbuilding and nodded at his boys. *Let's go.*

When he took form again, pea gravel crunched under his shitkickers as his weight became real and a brisk breeze hit him square in the face. The courtyard of the Brotherhood's mansion was demarcated by the front flank of the house and the tall shoulders of the twenty-foot-high retaining wall that ran all around the property. The white marble fountain in the middle had yet to be filled and jump-started for the warmer months and the half dozen cars that were parked in a row were waiting for action as well.

The whispered sound of well-oiled gears turning brought his head up. In a coordinated descent, the steel shutters were coming down over the windows, the panels unfurling and covering the leaded glass panes like the lids of many eyes closing for sleep.

He dreaded going inside. Even though there must be upward of fifty rooms to wander through, the fact that he was going to have to stay put until sundown made the mansion feel like a shoe box.

As Qhuinn and Blay materialized on either side of him, he walked up the steps to the huge double doors and pushed his way into the vestibule.

Inside, he presented his mug for viewing in the security camera. Instantly, the lock was popped and he walked into a foyer that was right out of czarist Russia. Malachite and claret marble columns supported a three-story-high painted ceiling. Gold-leafed sconces and mirrors generated and reflected buttery light that further enriched the colors. And that staircase . . . the thing was like a carpeted landing strip that stretched up to the heavens, its golden balustrade splitting at the top to form the anchors of the second floor's open balcony.

His father had spared no expense and obviously had a flair for the dramatic. All you needed was orchestral backup and you could imagine a king floating down in robes—

Wrath appeared at the top, his huge body clothed in black leather, his long black hair falling around his tremendous shoulders. His wraparound sunglasses were in place, and although he was at the head of a vast expanse of fall-on-your-ass, he didn't look down. No reason to. His eyes were now utterly blind.

But he was not sightless. At his side, George had things covered. The Seeing Eye dog was in control of the king, the two united through the harness that went around the golden retriever's chest and haunches. They were the ultimate Mutt and Jeff, a canine Good Samaritan with beauty-contestant looks and a brutal warrior who was obviously capable of tearing your throat open on a whim. But they worked well together and Wrath was pretty much in love with his animal: The dog was treated like the royal pet he was—to hell with even Iams; George ate whatever his master did, which meant prime cuts of beef and lamb. And word was that the retriever slept in bed with Beth and Wrath—although that had yet to be independently verified, as no one was allowed in the First Family's quarters.

As Wrath started down for the foyer, he walked with

a limp, the result of something he did over on the Far Side at the Scribe Virgin's. No one knew who he saw or why he sported a black eye or a split lip on a regular basis, but everyone, even John, was glad for the sessions. They kept Wrath on an even keel and away from the field.

With the king descending, and some of the other Brothers coming through the door John had just used, he had to make his escape. If those Shadows had sensed he had fresh ink, the people gathering for last meal would pick up on it in a heartbeat if they got close enough.

Fortunately, there was a wet bar in the library and John went there and helped himself to a shot of Jack Daniel's. The first of many.

While he started to make deposits into his buzz account, he braced himself against the marble slab and wished like hell he had a time machine—although it was hard to know whether he'd choose to go forward or backward with it.

"You want any food?" Qhuinn said from the doorway.

John didn't look in the guy's direction, just shook his head and poured some more liquid relief into his squat glass.

"Okay, I'll bring you a sandwich."

With a curse, John pivoted around and signed, *I said no*.

"Roast beef? Good. And I'll hitch you some carrot cake. Tray'll be left in your room." Qhuinn turned away. "If you wait about five more minutes in here, everyone will be seated at the table, so you'll have a clear shot up the stairs."

The guy took off, which meant short of braining him with the glass, there was no other way of expressing his I-am-an-island opinion.

Although really, that would just be a waste of good booze—Qhuinn was so hardheaded, you could have hit his frontal lobe with a crowbar and made no impression on him whatsoever.

Fortunately, the alcohol began to take effect, its numb blanket settling on John's shoulders first before sweeping up and down his body. The shit did nothing to quiet his mind, but his bones and muscles did ease out.

After waiting the suggested five minutes, John took his drink and his bottle and hit the stairs two at a time. As he ascended, the subdued voices from the dining room followed him, but that's all there was. Lately, there hadn't been much to laugh about over meals.

When he got to his room, he opened the door and walked into a jungle. There were clothes draped on every conceivable surface—the dresser, the wing chair, the bed, the plasma-screen TV. Kind of like his closet had thrown up all over everything. Empty bottles of Jack cluttered up the two side tables by the headboard, and the dead soldiers spread out from there, clustering on the floor and nesting in the twisted sheets and duvet.

Fritz and his cleaning crew hadn't been let in for two weeks, and at the rate things were going, they were going to need a backhoe when he finally threw the doors open to them.

Undressing, he let his leathers and shirt fall where they did, but his jacket he was careful with. At least until he took his weapons out—then he dumped the thing on the corner of the bed. In the bathroom, he double-checked his two blades and then he swiftly cleaned his guns with the kit that he just left out by the second sink.

Yeah, he'd let his standards slide lower than even frat-boy levels, but his weapons were different. Utility had to be maintained.

His shower was quick, and as he worked the soap over his chest and abs, he thought back to the time when even the brush of warm water over his cock was enough to make him hard. No more. He hadn't had an erection . . . since the last time he'd been with Xhex.

He just didn't have the interest—even in his dreams, which was a new one. Hell, before his transition, when he wasn't supposed to have any awareness of his sexuality, his subconscious had kicked up all sorts of hot and heavy. And those sex-fests had been so real, so detailed, it was as if they were memory and not REM-induced fabrications.

Now? All that played on his internal screen was *Blair Witch Project* chase scenes where he was running in a jerky panic but didn't know what was after him . . . or whether he would ever get to safety.

When he came out of the bathroom, he found a tray with a roast beef sandwich and a big-as-your-head wedge of carrot cake on it. Nothing to drink, but Qhuinn knew that he was taking his liquid refreshment from Mr. Daniel alone.

John ate standing up in front of the bureau, naked as the day he was born, and when the food hit his stomach, it sucked the energy from him, draining everything from his head. Wiping his mouth with the linen napkin, he put the tray out in the hall and then headed for the bathroom, where he brushed his teeth only from habit.

Lights off in the bath. Lights off in the room.

Him and the Jack sitting on the bed.

As exhausted as he was, he was not looking forward to lying down. There was an inverse relationship between his energy level and the distance between his ears and the floor: Even though he was cross-eyed, the second his head hit the pillow, his thoughts were going to start spinning and he was going to end up wide awake and staring at the ceiling, counting hours and aches.

He polished off what was in his glass and propped his elbows on his knees. Within moments, his head was bobbing, his lids slamming down. When he started to list to the side, he let himself go even though he was unsure which direction he was going in, toward the pillows or the wadded-up duvet.

Pillows.

Shifting his feet up on the bed, he dragged the covers over his hips and had a moment of blissful collapse. Maybe tonight the cycle would break. Maybe this glorious sinking relief would suck him down into the black hole he was hoping for. Maybe he'd . . .

His eyes popped open and he stared into the thick darkness.

Nope. He was exhausted to the point of being jittery, not just wide awake . . . but goosed-in-the-ass alert. As he rubbed his face, he figured this contradictory state of things was the cognitive equivalent to bumblebees being able to fly: Physicists maintained it wasn't possible, and yet it happened all the time.

Rolling over onto his back, he crossed his arms over his chest and yawned so hard his jaw cracked. Tough to know whether to turn on the light. The darkness amplified the whirling in his skull, but the lamp stung his eyes until he felt like he was crying sand. Usually, he alternated between clicking on the bulb and turning it off.

From out in the hall of statues, he heard Zsadist and Bella and Nalla walk down to their room. As the couple talked about the dinner, Nalla cooed and squeaked in the way babies did when their bellies were full and their parents were right with them.

Blay came down the way next. Aside from V, he was the only other person who smoked in the house, so that was how John knew it was him. And Qhuinn was with the guy. Had to be. Otherwise Blay wouldn't have lit up outside of his own room.

It was payback for that receptionist at the tat shop and who could blame him?

There was a long silence out there. And then a final pair of boots.

Tohr was heading to bed.

It was obvious who it was by the quiet more than the sound—the footfalls were slow and relatively light for a Brother: Tohr was working on getting his body back into shape, but he hadn't been cleared for fieldwork, which made sense. He needed to put on another fifty pounds of muscle before he had any business going toe-to-toe with the enemy.

There wouldn't be anyone else coming down. Lassiter, a.k.a. Tohr's golden shadow, didn't sleep, so the angel usually stayed down in the billiard room and watched highbrow television. Like paternity tests on *Maury* and *The People's Court* with Judge Milian and *Real Housewives* marathons.

Silence . . . silence . . . silence . . .

When the sound of his heartbeat started to annoy him, John cursed and stretched up, turning on the light. As he settled back against the pillows, he let his arms flop down. He didn't share Lassiter's fascination with the boob tube, but anything was better than the quiet. Fishing around the empty bottles, he found the remote, and when he hit the *on* button, there was a pause like the thing had forgotten what it was used for—but then the picture flared.

Linda Hamilton was running down a hallway, her body bouncing with power. Down at the far end, an elevator was opening . . . revealing a short dark-haired kid and Arnold Schwarzenegger.

John hit the power button and killed the image.

Last time he'd seen that movie had been when he and Tohr had watched it together . . . back when the Brother had taken him out of his sad pitiful exisitence and shown him who he really was . . . back before all the seams in both their lives had gotten yanked apart.

At the orphanage, in the human world, John had always been aware he was different . . . and the Brother had given him the "why" that evening. The flash of fangs had explained it all.

Now, naturally, there had been a shitload of anxiety that came with finding out you weren't who or what you'd always assumed you were. But Tohr had stuck by his side, just chilling and watching TV, even though he'd been on rotation to fight and also had a pregnant *shellan* to look after.

Kindest thing anyone had ever done for him.

Coming back to reality, John pitched the remote onto the side table and it bounced around, knocking over one of the empties. As the last half inch of bourbon splashed out, he reached across and picked up a shirt to mop up the mess. Which, considering what a shambles the rest of the room was in, was like backing up a Big Mac and fries with a Diet Coke.

But whatever.

He wiped off the tabletop, lifting the bottles one by one, and then opened the little drawer to swipe across the—

Tossing his T-shirt onto the floor, he reached in and picked up an ancient leather-bound book.

The diary had been in his possession for about six months now, but he hadn't read it.

It was the one thing he had of his father's.

With nothing else to do and nowhere to go, he opened the front cover. The pages were made of vellum and they smelled old, but the ink was still totally legible.

John thought of those notes he'd written to Trez and iAm back at Sal's and wondered if his and his father's handwriting were at all similar. As the entries in the diary were done in the Old Language, there was no way of knowing.

Focusing his tired eyes, he started out just examining

75

how the characters were formed, how the ink strokes whipped about to form the symbols, how there were no mistakes or cross-outs, how even though the pages were not lined, his father had nonetheless made neat, even rows. He imagined how Darius might have bent over the pages and written by candlelight, dipping a quill pen . . .

An odd shimmer went through John, the kind that made him wonder whether he was going to have to be sick . . . but the nausea passed as an image came to him.

A huge stone house not unlike the one they were living in now. A room kitted out with beautiful things. A hurried entry made on these pages at a desk before a grand ball.

The light of candle, warm and soft.

John shook himself and kept turning the pages. Sometime along the way he started not just measuring the lines of characters, but reading them . . .

The color of the ink changed from black to brown when his father wrote about his first night in the warrior camp. How cold it was. How scared he was. How much he missed home.

How alone he felt.

John empathized with the male to the point where it seemed as though there was no separation between the father and the son: In spite of the many, many years and an entire continent of distance, it was as though he were in his father's shoes.

Well, duh. He was in the exact same situation: a hostile reality with a lot of dark corners . . . and no parents to back him up now that Wellsie was dead and Tohr was a living, breathing ghost.

Hard to know when his eyelids went down and stayed there.

But at some point he fell asleep with what little he had of his father held reverently in his hands.

EIGHT

Darius materialized in a stretch of thick forest, taking form beside the entrance of a cave. As he scanned the night, he listened for any sounds worthy of notice . . . There were deer tiptoeing around down by the quietly running stream, and the breeze whistled through the pine needles, and he could hear his own breathing. But there were no humans or lessers *about.*

A moment longer . . . and then he slipped beneath the overhang of rock and walked into a natural room created aeons ago. Deeper and deeper he went, the air thickening with a smell he despised: The musty dirt and cold humidity reminded him of the war camp—and even though he'd been out of that hellish place for twenty-seven years, the memories of his time with the Bloodletter were enough to make him recoil even now.

At the far wall, he ran his hand over the wet, uneven rock until he found the iron pull that released the hidden door's locking mechanism. There was a muffled squeal as hinges turned and then a portion of the cave slid to the right. He didn't wait for the panel to fully retract, but stepped through as soon as he could wedge his thick chest in laterally. On the other side, he hit a second lever and waited until the section was secured back in place.

The long pathway to the Brotherhood's sanctum sanctorum was lit with torches that burned ferociously and cast hardlined shadows that jerked and spasmed on the rough floor and ceiling. He was about halfway down when the voices of his brothers reached his ears.

Clearly, there were a lot of them at the meeting, given the symphony of bass, male tones that overlapped and competed for airspace.

He was probably the last to arrive.

When he got to the iron-barred gate, he took a heavy key from his breast pocket and pushed it into the lock. Opening the way took strength, even for him, the huge gate swinging free of its anchor only if he who sought to enter could prove himself worthy of forcing it wide.

When he got down into the wide-open space deep in the earth, the Brotherhood was all there and, with his appearance, the meeting commenced.

As he took a stand next to Ahgony, the voices silenced and Wrath the Fair regarded the assembled. The Brothers respected the race's leader, even if he was not a warrior among them, for he was a regal male of worth whose sage council and prudent restraint were of great value in the war against the Lessening Society.

"My warriors," the king said. "I address you this eve with grave news and a request. A doggen emissary came unto my private home during the sunlight and sought a personal audience. After refusing to present his cause unto mine own attendant, he broke down and wept."

As the monarch's clear green eyes circled the faces, Darius wondered where this was leading. Nowhere good, he thought.

"It was then that I interceded." The king's lids lowered briefly. "The doggen's master had sent him forth unto me with the worst possible news. The unmated daughter of the family is missing. Having taken an early retire, all appeared well with her until her maid brought forth a midday repast in the event she was of a mind for sustenance. Her room was empty."

Ahgony, the lay leader of the Brotherhood, spoke up. "When was she last seen?"

"Prior to Last Meal. She came unto her parents and informed them she had no appetite and would be requiring a lie-down." The king's gaze continued around. "Her father is a righteous

male who has rendered unto me personal favors. Of greater weight, however, is the service he has offered unto the race as a whole as leahdyre *of the Council."*

As curses echoed around the cave, the king nodded. "Verily, it is the daughter of Sampsone."

Darius crossed his arms over his chest. This was very bad news. Daughters of the glymera *were like fine jewels to their fathers . . . until such time as they were passed unto the care of another male of substance, who would treat her thusly. These females were watched over and cloistered . . . They did not just disappear out of their families' houses.*

They could be taken, however.

Like all things of rarity, well-bred females were of very high value—and as always when it came to the glymera, *the individual was less important than the family: Ransoms were paid not to save her life, but her bloodline's reputation. Indeed, it was not unheard-of for such a virginal female to be abducted and held for money, the sole leverage being social terror.*

The Lessening Society was not the only source of evil in the world. Vampires had been known to prey upon their own.

The king's voice resonated around the cave, deep and demanding. "As my private guard, I look to you to provide redress of this situation." Those royal eyes locked on Darius. "And there is one among you whom I shall ask to go forth and right this wrong."

Darius bowed low before the request was put out. As always, he was fully prepared to discharge any duty for his king.

"Thank you, my warrior. Your statesmanship shall be of value under the roof of that now broken home, as shall your sense of protocol. And when you discover the malfeasor, I am confident of your ability to ensure an appropriate . . . outcome. Avail yourself of those who stand shoulder to your shoulder and, above all, find her. No father should have to bear this empty horror."

Darius couldn't agree more.

And it was a wise assignment made by a wise king. Darius

was a statesman, true. But he had a particular commitment to females after having lost his mother. Not that the other Brothers wouldn't have given themselves over with similar dedication—except for Hharm, perhaps, who had a rather dim view of female worth. But Darius was the one who would feel this responsibility most and the king was nothing if not calculating.

That being said, he was going to need help and he glanced around his brothers to determine who he would pick, sifting through the grim, now familiar faces. He stopped looking when he saw a stranger's visage among them.

Across the altar, the Brother Hharm was standing beside a younger, thinner version of himself. His boy was dark haired and blue eyed in the manner of the sire, and shared the potential of the broad shoulders and wide chest that was characteristic of Hharm. But there the similarity ended. Hharm was lounging with an insolent lean against the wall of the cave—which was not a surprise. The male preferred combat to conversation, having little time or attention span to spare for the latter. The boy, however, was engaged to the point of transfixion, his intelligent eyes locked on the king in awe.

His hands were behind his back.

In spite of his outward appearance of calm, he was twisting those hands where no one could see, the movement in the tops of his forearms belying his nervous churning.

Darius could understand how the boy felt. After this address, they were one and all going out into the field and Hharm's son would be tested for the first time against the enemy.

He was not properly armed.

Fresh from the war camp, his weapons were no better than Darius's had been . . . just more of the Bloodletter's castoffs. Which was deplorable. Darius had had no sire to provide for him, but Hharm should have taken care of his boy, giving him well-balanced, well-made instruments that were as good as his own.

The king raised his arms and looked up unto the ceiling. "May the Scribe Virgin look upon those herein assembled with all grace and blessing as these soldiers of worth go out unto the fields of conflict."

The war cry exploded from the Brothers, and Darius joined in with all his breath, the roar echoing and rebounding and continuing as a chant started up. As the thundering sound rose higher and higher, the king held his palm out to the side. From the shadows, the young heir to the throne came forward, his expression far older than his seven years. Wrath, son of Wrath, was, like Tohrment, the spitting image of his sire, but there the comparison between the two pairs ended. The regent king was sacred, not just to his parents, but to the race.

This small male was the future, the leader to come . . . evidence that in spite of the affronts committed by the Lessening Society, the vampires would survive.

And he was fearless. Whereas many a wee one had shrunk back behind a parent when facing a single Brother, the young Wrath stood his own, staring up at the males before him as if he knew, regardless of his tender age, that he would command the strong backs and fighting arms of those before him.

"Go forth, my warriors," the king said. "Go forth and wield thy daggers with lethal intent."

Bloodythirsty things to say in front of tender ears, but in the midst of the war, there was no advantage to shielding the next generation of royalty. Wrath, son of Wrath, would never be out in the field—he was too important to the race—but he would be trained so he could appreciate what the males under his authority were facing.

As the king stared down upon his begotten issue, the elder's eyes misted with pride and joy and hope and love.

How different Hharm and his son were. That young was beside his blooded sire, but for all the attention that was paid to him, he might have stood next to a stranger.

Ahgony leaned into Darius. "Someone needs to watch o'er that boy."

Darius nodded. "Aye."

"I fetched him from the war camp this night."

Darius glanced over at his brother. "Indeed? Where was his sire?"

"Betwixt the legs of a maiden."

Darius cursed under his breath. Verily, the Brother was of brutish constitution in spite of his breeding and courtesy of his base instincts, he had sons aplenty, which may have explained though certainly not excused his thoughtlessness. Of course, his other sons were not eligible for the Brotherhood because their mothers were not of Chosen blood.

However, Hharm appeared to be unconcerned.

As the poor boy stood so separate, Darius remembered well his own first night in the field: how he'd been tied to no one . . . how he'd feared facing the enemy with nothing but his wits and what little training he'd had to fortify his courage. It wasn't that the Brothers had cared naught how he fared. But they had had to watch after themselves and he'd had to prove he could hold his own.

This young male clearly was in the same predicament—it was just that he had a father who should have eased his way.

"Be well, Darius," Ahgony said as the royals went in among the Brothers, clasping palms and preparing to take their leave. "I am escorting the king and the prince."

"Be well, my brother." The two embraced quickly and then Ahgony joined the Wraths and went with them out of the cave.

As Tohrture stepped up and began apportioning territories for the night, pairs started to form and Darius looked through the heads at Hharm's son. The boy had faded back against the wall and was standing stiffly, still with those hands behind his back. Hharm seemed uninterested in anything other than trading hyperbole with the others.

Tohrture put two fingers up to his mouth and whistled. "My brothers! Attention!" The cave went stone silent. "Thank you. Are we clear on territories?"

There was a collective affirmation and the Brothers started to leave—and Hharm didn't even look back at his son. He just went for the exit.

In the wake, the boy brought his hands forward and rubbed them one into the other. Stepping forward, he said his father's name once . . . twice.

The Brother turned back, his expression like that of one confronted by an unwelcome obligation. "Well, come on, then—"

"If I may," Darius said, stepping between them. "It would be my pleasure to have him aid me in my duty. If it would not offend."

Truth was, he cared naught if it offended. The boy needed more than his father would give him and Darius was not the kind to sit aside while a wrong unfolded.

"You think I cannae take care of my blood?" Hharm snapped.

Darius turned to the male and went nose-to-nose with him. He preferred peaceful negotiation when it came to conflict, but with Hharm, there was no reasoning. And Darius was well endowed to meet force with force.

As the Brotherhood froze around them, Darius dropped his voice even though all assembled would hear every word. "Give me the boy and I will deliver him whole unto the dawn."

Hharm growled, the sound like that of a wolf amid fresh blood. "As shall I, brother."

Darius leaned in closer. "If you take him out to fight, and he dies, you shall carry that shame upon your lineage fore'er-more." Although for truth it was hard to know whether the male's conscience would be affected. "Give him to me and I will save you that burden."

"I never liked you, Darius."

"And yet back in camp you were more than willing to service those I bested." Darius flashed his fangs. "Given how much you enjoyed that, I should think you'd hold me in kinder regard. And know this—if you do not allow me to o'ersee the boy, I shall take you down to this floor at our feet and beat you until you relent unto me."

Hharm broke eye contact, lifting his gaze above Darius's shoulder as the past sucked the Brother down. Darius knew the moment that he had been drawn into. It was the night when Darius had won against him back at the camp—and as Darius had refused to redress the deficiency, the Bloodletter had. Brutal *was* a pale word to describe that session, and though Darius was loath to bring it up, the boy's safety was a worthy end for the unworthy means.

Hharm knew who would win in a contest of fists.

"Take him," the male said flatly. "And do what you will with him. I hereby renounce him as my son."

The Brother pivoted, strode out . . .

And took all the air from the cave with him.

The warriors watched him go, their silence louder than the war cry had been. To disavow offspring was antithetical to the race, as much as daylight would be to a family meal: it was ruination.

Darius went over to the young male. That face . . . Dearest Virgin Scribe. The boy's frozen gray face wasn't sad. Wasn't heartbroken. Wasn't even ashamed.

His features were a veritable death mask.

Putting out his palm, Darius said, "Greetings, son. I am Darius, and I shall function as your fighting *whard.*"

The young's eyes blinked once.

"Son? We shall go anon to the cliffs."

Abruptly, Darius was subjected to a sharp regard; the boy was clearly searching for signs of obligation and pity. He would find none, however. Darius knew with precision the dry, hard earth upon which the boy's boots stood, and therefore he was well aware that any kind of softness offered would only result in further disgrace.

"Why," came a hoarse question.

"We go anon to the cliffs to find that female," Darius said with calm. "That is why."

The boy's eyes bored into Darius's. Then the young placed his hand upon his breast. With a bow, he said, "I shall endeavor to be of service rather than weight."

It was so hard to be unwanted. Harder still to hold one's head up after such an affront.

"What is your name," Darius asked.

"Tohrment. I am Tohrment, son of . . ." The throat was cleared. "I am Tohrment."

Darius stepped in beside the young male and put his palm on a shoulder that had yet to fill out to its fullest potential.

"Come with me."

The boy followed with purpose . . . out of the audience of the Brotherhood . . . out of the sanctuary . . . out of the cave . . . into the night.

The shift within Darius's chest happened sometime between that initial footstep forward and the moment they dematerialized together.

Verily he felt for the first time as if he had a family of his own . . . because even though the boy wasn't his by blood, he had assumed care of him.

Accordingly, he would go before a blade intended for the younger if it came down to that, sacrificing himself. Such was the code of the Brotherhood—but only toward one's brothers. Tohrment was not yet among that number; he was but an initiate by virtue of his bloodline, which gained him access into the Tomb, and nothing further. If he failed to prove himself, he would be barred forever therein.

Indeed, for all the code required, the boy could well be slain on the field and left for dead.

But Darius would not permit that.

He'd always wanted a son of his own.

NINE

"Holy . . . shit. They got some kind of trees here."

Well, yeah, that summed it up. As the *Paranormal
Investigators* satellite-link van eased off Rural Route SC
124, Gregg Winn braked and leaned forward over the
steering wheel.

Fucking . . . *perfect*.

The plantation house's entrance was marked on both
sides by live oaks the size of RVs and Spanish moss hung
off all those massive branches, swaying in the soft breeze.
Down at the end of the framing alley, about half a mile
away, the columned mansion sat pretty as a lady in a chair,
the noontime sun painting her face in lemon yellow light.

From the back, *PI*'s "host," Holly Fleet, leaned in.
"Are you sure about this?"

"It's a B and B, right?" Gregg hit the gas. "Open to
the public."

"You called four times."

"They didn't say no."

"They didn't get back to you."

"Whatever." He needed to make this happen. *PI*'s
prime-time specials were on the verge of breaking
through to the next advertising-dollar level at the
network. They weren't in *American Idol* territory, true,
but they'd kicked the shit out of the most recent *Magic
Exposed* episode, and if that trend continued, the money
was going to get thicker than blood.

The long drive up to the house was like a trail that led not just deeper into the property, but backward in time. For God's sake, as he glanced around the grass-covered grounds, he expected to see Civil War soldiers and antebellum Vivien Leighs strolling beneath the scarved trees.

The gravel lane took visitors directly to the formal front enterance and Gregg parked off to the side in case any other cars needed to pass by.

"You two stay here. I'm going in."

As he stepped out from behind the wheel, he covered up his Ed Hardy shirt with a black windbreaker and pulled the cuff down over his gold Rolex. The van with its *PI* logo of a magnifying glass over a black, shadowy ghost was flashy enough, and no doubt the house was owned by a local. Thing was, Hollywood style wasn't necessarily a value-add outside of L.A.—and this gracious place was about as far from plastic surgery and spray tans as you could get.

His Prada loafers shifted through the stone confetti of the driveway as he walked over to the entry. The white house was a simple three-story box with porches on the first and second floors and a hip roof with dormers, but the elegance of the proportions and the sheer size of the damn thing were what put it so solidly in mansion terri-tory. And to top off the grande dame routine, all the windows were framed on the inside by jewel-toned drapes, and through the leaded glass, he could see the chandeliers hanging from high ceilings.

Hell of a bed-and-breakfast.

The front door was big enough to belong on a cathe-dral and the knocker was a brass lion's head that seemed nearly life-size. Lifting the weight, he let it fall back into place.

While he waited, he checked to make sure Holly and Stan were where he'd left them. Backup was the last thing he needed when he was on what amounted to a sales call—especially when the hello-my-name-is was an unwelcome one. And the truth was, if they hadn't just been on an assignment up in Charleston, he might not have tried a face-to-face, but for a half-hour drive that wasn't even out of their way, it was worth the effort. They weren't due to start setup for the special in Atlanta for a couple of days, so there was time for this. More to the point, he would kill to—

The door swung wide and he had to smile at what was on the other side. Man . . . it just kept getting better. The guy had *English butler* stamped all over him, from his shiny shoes to his black waistcoat and blazer.

"Good afternoon, sir." And he had an accent. Not quite British, not quite French—high-class European. "How may I help you?"

"Gregg Winn." He put out his hand. "I think I've called you a couple of times? Not sure you've gotten the messages."

The butler's shake was fast. "Indeed."

Gregg waited for the man to continue. When there was nothing coming, he cleared his throat. "Ah . . . I was hoping you'd allow us to do some investigating of your lovely house and grounds. The Eliahu Rathboone legend is pretty remarkable, I mean . . . the reports from your guests are amazing. My team and I—"

"Permit me to interrupt. There will be no filming or recording on the premises—"

"We would pay."

"—at all." The butler smiled tightly. "I'm sure you can understand that we prefer our privacy."

"Quite frankly, I don't. What's the harm in allowing us to poke around?" Gregg dropped his voice and leaned in. "Unless, of course . . . you're making those footsteps yourself in the middle of the night? Or suspending a candle in that upstairs bedroom by fishing wire?"

The butler's face didn't change, and yet he reeked of disdain. "I believe you were on your way."

Not a comment. Not a suggestion. A demand. But fuck that, Gregg had dealt with tougher stuff than some nancy in a penguin suit.

"You know, you must get a lot of traffic as a result of those haunting stories." Gregg lowered his voice even further. "Our TV audience is huge. If you think you're getting visitors now, imagine what it would do for your business if you went national. And even if you are cooking up the Rathboone stuff yourself, we can work with you, rather than against you. If you know what I mean."

The butler stepped back and began to close the door. "Good day, sir—"

Gregg put his body in the way. Even if he hadn't wanted to check out the stories badly, the whole *no* thing just wasn't his bag. And as usual, getting shut out sharpened his interest like nothing else.

"We'd like to stay the night, then. We're doing workups on some of the neighboring Civil War sites and need a place to crash."

"I'm afraid we're full."

At that moment, like a gift from God, a couple came down the gracious stairway, their suitcases in hand. Gregg smiled as he looked over the butler's shoulder.

"Not as full as you were." Shifting through his deck of personality cards, he put forth his best I'm-going-to-be-no-trouble expression. "No is no, I get that. So we won't record anything, audio or video. Swear on my grandmother's life." Lifting his hand in greeting, he said loudly, "Hey, you guys—enjoy your stay?"

"Oh, my God, it was incredible!" the girlfriend, wife, casual lay, whatever said. "Eliahu is real!"

The boyfriend, husband, wanted-to-score nodded. "I didn't believe her. I mean, ghosts—come on. But yeah . . . I heard the thing."

"We saw the light, too. Have you heard about the light?"

Gregg put his hand over his chest in shock. "No, what light? Tell me everything . . ."

As they launched into a detailed recitation of all the "incredibly amazing things" that were so "incredible and amazing to witness" during their "incredible . . . ," the butler's eyes narrowed into slits. Clearly, his manners overrode his urge to kill as he stepped aside to let Gregg meet up with the departing pair, but the temperature in the foyer had dropped into chilly land.

"Wait—is that . . ." The male guest frowned and leaned to the side. "Holy crap, are you with that show—"

"*Paranormal Investigators*," Gregg filled in. "I'm the producer."

"Is the host . . ." The guy glanced at his lady friend. "Is she here, too?"

"Sure is. You want to meet Holly?"

The guy put down the suitcase he was carrying to tuck in his polo shirt a little more tightly. "Yeah, could I?"

"We were just leaving," his other half interjected. "Weren't we. Dan."

"But if I—we—have the chance to—"

"Get on the road now, we'll be home by nightfall." She turned to the butler. "Thank you for everything, Mr. Griffin. We've had a lovely stay."

The butler bowed with grace. "Please do come again, madam."

"Oh, we will—this is going to be a perfect place for our wedding in September. It's incredible."

"Just amazing," her fiancé tacked on, like he wanted to be back on her good side.

Gregg didn't push the meet-and-greet with Holly as the pair went out the front door—even though the guy paused and looked over as if he were hoping Gregg would follow them.

"So I'll just go get our bags," Gregg said to the butler. "And you can get our room ready, Mr. Griffin."

The air around the man seemed to warp. "We have two rooms."

"That's fine. And because I can tell you're a man with standards, me and Stan will bunk together. For propriety's sake."

The butler's brows lifted. "Indeed. If you and your friends would be good enough to wait in the drawing room to your right, I shall have the housekeepers ready your accommodations."

"Fantastic." Gregg clapped the man on the shoulder. "You won't even know we're here."

The butler pointedly stepped back. "A word of caution, if I may."

"Hit me."

"Do not go up to the third floor."

Well, wasn't that an invitation . . . and a line right out of a *Scream* movie. "Absolutely not. I swear to it."

The butler went off down the hall and Gregg leaned out of the front door, motioning for his crew. As Holly got out, her double-Ds bounced under the black T-shirt she was wearing, and her Sevens were so low-cut her flat, tanned belly flashed. He'd hired her not for her brains, but for her Barbie dimensions, and yet she'd proven to be more than he'd expected. Like a lot of dummies, she wasn't completely stupid, just largely so, and she had an eerie ability to position herself where it would most suit her advancement.

Stan slid the van's side panel back and stepped out, blinking hard and shoving his long, straggly hair out of the way. Perpetually stoned, he was the perfect person for this kind of work: technically adept, but mellow to the point where he took orders well.

Last thing Gregg wanted was an artiste running the camera lenses.

"Get the luggage," Gregg called over to them. Which was code for, *Bring not only your overnight bags but the small-scale equipment.*

This wasn't the first site he'd had to talk his way into.

As he ducked back inside, the couple who had departed were driving past in their Sebring convertible, the guy watching Holly bend into the van instead of where he was going.

She tended to have that effect on men. Another reason to keep her around.

Well, that and she had no problem with casual sex.

Gregg walked into the drawing room and did a slow around-the-world. The oil paintings were museum quality, the rugs were Persian, the walls were hand-painted with a pastoral scene. Sterling-silver candlesticks were on every surface and not one piece of furniture had been made in the twenty-first or twentieth . . . or maybe even nineteenth century.

The journalist in him sat up and hollered. B and Bs, even first-rate ones, weren't kitted out like this. So there was something going on here.

Either that or the Eliahu legend was putting a helluva lot of heads on those pillows every night.

Gregg went over to one of the smaller portraits. It was of a young man in his mid-twenties, and painted in another time, another place. The subject was seated in a stiff-backed chair, his legs crossed at the knees, his elegant hands off to one side. Dark hair was pulled back and tied with a ribbon, revealing a face that was a stunner. The clothes were . . . Well, Gregg was no historian, so who the fuck knew, but they sure as hell looked like what George Washington and his ilk wore.

This was Eliahu Rathboone, Gregg thought. The secret abolitionist who had always left a light on to encourage those who needed to escape to come his way . . . the man who had died to protect a cause before it even took root up in the North . . . the hero who had saved so many, only to be cut down in the prime of his life.

This was their ghost.

Gregg made a frame with his hand and panned around the room before zeroing in on that face.

"Is that him?" Holly's voice came from behind. "Is that really him?"

Gregg beamed over his shoulder, his body positively tingling. "And I thought the pictures on the Internet were good."

"He's, like . . . gorgeous."

And so were his backstory and his house and all of those people who left here talking about hauntings.

Fuck the Atlanta trip to that asylum. This was their next live special.

"I want you to work on the butler," Gregg said softly. "You know what I mean. I want access to everything."

"I'm *not* sleeping with him. I draw the line at necrophilia and that one is older than God."

"Did I *ask* you to get on your back? There are other ways. And you have tonight and tomorrow. I want to do the special here."

"You mean . . ."

"We're broadcasting live from here in ten days." He walked over to the windows that faced out toward the alley of trees, and with every step he took, the floorboards creaked.

Daytime Emmys, here we come, Gregg thought.

Fucking perfect.

TEN

John Matthew woke up with his hand on his cock. Or rather, he semi woke up.

What he had his palm on was fully ready to go, however.

In his foggy mind, images of him and Xhex were lighting him up from the inside out . . . He saw them on her bed in that basement place of hers and there was a whole lot of naked going on, her straddling his hips, him reaching up to touch her breasts. She felt good and solid on top of him, her core hot and wet against his erection, her powerful body arching and releasing as she rubbed herself on what ached to penetrate her.

He needed to get in her. Needed to leave something of himself behind.

Needed to mark her.

The instinct was overwhelming to the point of compulsion . . . and yet his conscience prickled as he sat up and took one of her nipples into his mouth. As he drew her flesh between his lips, sucking on it, tonguing it, nipping it ever so gently, on some level, he knew this was not really happening—and that even in a fantasy, it was wrong. It wasn't fair to her memory, and yet the visions had too much momentum and his palm as he worked himself had too much grip . . . and the moment was too undeniable and electric to turn away from.

There was no going back.

John imagined that he rolled her over onto her back and loomed above her, looking down into her gunmetal gray eyes. Her thighs were split on either side of his hips, her lush sex ready for what he wanted to give her, her scent burrowing into his nose until all he knew was her. Running his palms over her breasts and down her stomach, he marveled at how similar their bodies were. She was smaller compared to him, but their muscles were all the same, hard and toned, ready for use, tight as bone when they were engaged. He loved how unyielding she was beneath her soft, smooth skin, loved how strong, how tough . . .

He wanted her like crazy.

Except suddenly he could go no further.

It was as if the fantasy jammed up, the tape breaking, the DVD scratched, the digital file corrupted. And all he had left was his attraction and this wrenching, on-the-brink ecstasy that was going to drive him insane—

Xhex reached up to his face and cupped it, and with the gentle contact, she abruptly commanded all of him, his head and his body and his soul: She owned him and everything he was from his eyes to his thighs. He was hers.

"Come to me," she said, tilting her head to the side.

Tears turned his vision wavy. Finally, they were going to kiss. Finally, what she had denied him was going to happen—

When he leaned down . . . she guided his mouth back to her nipple.

He felt a momentary sting of rejection, but then this weird elation hit him. The deflection was so true to her, he figured that maybe it wasn't a dream. Maybe this was actually happening. Pushing aside his sadness, he concentrated on what she was willing to give him.

"Mark me," she said in a deep voice.

Baring his fangs, he ran one sharp white tip around her areola, circling, stroking. He wanted to ask her if she was sure, but she answered that question herself. In a quick move, she jacked off the mattress and held his head down to her skin so that he struck her and a sliver of blood was drawn.

John jerked back, afraid he'd hurt her . . . but he hadn't, and as she arched in an erotic wave, the glistening wellspring of her life made him orgasm.

"Take from me," she commanded as his cock jerked and hot pulses poured out over her thighs. "Do it, John. *Now.*"

She didn't have to ask him twice. He was captivated by the bead of deep red that bloomed up, and with slow grace eased down the pale side of her breast. Leading with his tongue, he caught the trail and swept it back home with a flick that ended with her nipple—

His whole body shimmered at the taste of her, another release shuddering out of him and marking her skin as he fell into the throes of another release. Xhex's blood was bold and heady in his mouth, an addiction fully formed on the first try, a destination he didn't want to ever leave now that he was there. As he savored what he'd taken, he thought he heard her laugh in satisfaction, but then he was lost to what she gave him.

His tongue dragged over both her nipple and the cut and then his lips formed a seal and he suckled on her, taking her dark flavor down his throat and into his gut. The communion with her was all he'd ever wanted, and now that he was feeding from her, joy overtook him along with the nuclear energy that came to him from her blood.

Wanting to give her something back, he shifted his arm down so that his hand swept over her hip and between her thighs. Tracing the taut muscles he found her core . . . Oh, God, she was slippery smooth and hella hot, ready and aching to receive him. And although he didn't know a shitload about female anatomy, he let her moans and thrashes tell him where his fingers should go and what they should be doing.

It didn't take long before what he was touching her with was as wet as what he was stroking and it was then that he slid his middle finger in deep. Using his thumb, he massaged the top of her and found a rhythm to match the pulls he was making at her breast.

He was bringing her to the edge, taking her with him, giving back as much as he was getting, when he knew he needed more. He wanted to be in her when she came. Then he would be completed in some ethereal way, made whole inside his skin.

It was a bonded male's drive and necessity. What he had to have in order to feel at peace.

Lifting his lips from her breast, he dragged his hand from her sex and repositioned himself so that his glossy cock was poised over her open legs. Meeting her eyes in the incendiary moment, he brushed the short hair around her face. Slowly, he dropped his mouth downward—

"No," she said. "That's not what this is about."

John Matthew shot upright, the fantasy of the dream shattered, his chest banding in frigid cords of pain.

With disgust, he let go of his arousal—not that he was hard anymore. His cock had positively shriveled up, in spite of the orgasm that had been on its way out of the thing's head.

That's not what this is about.

Unlike the dream, which had been a total hypothetical, those words were ones she'd actually said to him— and in precisely that sexual context.

As he looked down at his naked body, the releases he'd had, the ones he'd imagined he'd had on her, were all over his belly and the sheets.

Why the hell did that spell out *alone* like nothing else could.

Glancing at the clock, he saw he'd slept through his alarm. Or more likely he hadn't bothered to set it. One bene to insomnia was that you didn't need to recharge your phone from all the snooze buttons you hit.

In the shower, he washed himself quickly and started

with his cock. He hated what he'd done in that odd half-asleep zone. It felt totally wrong to jerk off, considering the situation, and from now on, he was going to sleep in his jeans if he had to.

Although knowing his hand, the damn thing would have probably ended up behind the fly anyway.

Fuck it, he was gonna chain his wrists to the frickin' headboard.

After he shaved, which like tooth maintenance was out of habit rather than pride in his appearance, he braced his palms on the marble and leaned into the main spray nozzle, letting the water sweep over him.

Lessers were impotent. *Lessers* . . . were impotent.

Hanging his head, he felt the hot rush over the back of his skull.

Sex kicked up all kinds of bad shit for him, and as the image of a grungy stairwell bloomed like a stain on his brain, he popped his lids and dragged himself back to the present. Not that it was an improvement.

He'd have gone through what had happened to him a thousand times to save Xhex from being mistreated that way once.

Oh . . . God . . .

Lessers were impotent. Always had been.

Moving like a zombie, he stepped out, dried himself, and headed for the bedroom to get dressed. Just as he was pulling on his leathers, his phone went off and he reached over to his jacket to fish the thing out.

Flipping it open . . . he found a text from Trez.

All it said was: *189 st. francis ave 10 2nite.*

Clipping the phone closed, his heart beat with brutal intent. Any crack in the foundation . . . he was just looking for one little crack in Lash's world, a fissure, something he could wedge himself into and blow the whole fucking thing to pieces.

Xhex might well be dead, and this new reality without

her might be his forever more, but that didn't mean he couldn't avenge her.

In the bathroom, he strapped on his chest holster, weaponed up, and after grabbing his jacket, he went out into the hall. Pausing, he thought of all the people who would be gathering downstairs . . . as well as the time. Shutters were still down.

Instead of going left toward the grand staircase and the foyer, he went right . . . and walked silently in spite of his shitkickers.

Blaylock left his room a little before six because he wanted to check in on John. Usually the guy gave a knock around mealtime, but there had been none. Which meant he was either dead or dead drunk.

At his buddy's door, he paused and leaned in. Nothing doing on the other side that he could hear.

After a soft knock wasn't answered, he pulled a fuck-it and opened the thing in. Man, the place looked ransacked, with clothes everywhere and a bed that might possibly have been used as a demolition derby site.

"He in there?"

At the sound of Qhuinn's voice, he stiffened and had to stop himself from turning around. No reason to. He knew that the guy would be wearing some kind of Sid Vicious or Nine Inch Nails or Slipknot T-shirt tucked into black leathers. And that his hard face would be cleanly shaven and very smooth. And that his spiky black hair would be slightly wet from the shower.

Blay walked into John's space and headed for the bathroom, figuring his actions would answer the question well enough. "J? Where are you, J?"

When he pushed his way into all that marble, the air was thick with humidity and smelled like Ivory soap, which was what John used. Wet towel was on the counter.

As he turned around to go, he slammed right into Qhuinn's chest.

The impact was like getting hit with a car and his best friend reached out to steady him.

Oh, no. No touching.

Blay stepped back quickly and stared out into the bedroom. "Sorry." There was an odd pause. "He's not here."

Duh.

Qhuinn leaned to the side and put his face, that beautiful face, in the line of Blay's vision. When the guy straightened, Blay's eyes followed because they had to.

"You don't look at me anymore."

No, he didn't. "Yes, I do."

Desperate to get away from that blue-and-green stare, he cut himself some slack and went over to the towel. Wadding it up, he shoved the thing down the laundry chute, and damn if the cramming didn't help a little.

Especially as he imagined it was his own head he was forcing into the hole.

Blay was calmer when he turned around. Even met those eyes. "I'm going down to dinner."

He was feeling quite proud of himself as he walked by—

Qhuinn's hand snapped out and latched onto his forearm, stopping him dead. "We have a problem. You and me."

"Do we." Not a question. Because this was one convo he had no interest in encouraging.

"What the hell is the matter with you?"

Blay blinked. What was wrong with *him*? He wasn't the one fucking anything with a hole.

No, he was the pathetic fidiot who pined for his best friend. Which put him into wee-wee-wee-all-the-way-home territory. Any closer to chicking out and he'd have to carry Kleenex tucked into his sleeve to catch his tears.

Unfortunately, the flash of anger deflated fast and left him hollow. "Nothing. There's nothing wrong."

"Bullshit."

Right. Okay. This was unfair. They'd already been over this territory and Qhuinn might be a slut, but the guy's memory was perfectly functional.

"Qhuinn . . ." Blay shoved a hand into his hair.

On cue, that fucking Bonnie Raitt song shot into his brain, her rich voice singing . . . *I can't make you love me if you don't . . . You can't make your heart feel something it won't . . .*

Blay had to laugh.

"What's so funny?"

"Is it possible to be castrated without being aware of it?"

Now Qhuinn was doing the blink. "Not unless you're really fucking drunk."

"Well, I'm sober. Dead sober. As usual." And on that note, maybe he needed to take a page from John's book and start liquoring it up. "I think I might have to change that, however. Excuse me—"

"Blay—"

"No. You do not get to 'Blay' me like that." He stuck his finger in his best friend's face. "You just do your thing. It's what you're best at. Leave me alone."

He walked out, his head tangled but his feet mercifully on the ball.

Taking the hall of statues down to the grand staircase, he passed by the Greco-Roman masterpieces, and ran his eyes over those male bodies. Naturally, he Photoshop'd Qhuinn's head on top of each one—

"You don't have to change anything." Qhuinn was right on his tail, the words low.

Blay got to the head of the stairs and looked down. The yawning, resplendent foyer before him was like a gift you opened with your body as you entered it, each step forward bringing you into a visual embrace of color and gold.

Perfect place for a mating ceremony, he thought for no particular reason.

"Blay. Come on. Nothing has changed."

He glanced over his shoulder. Qhuinn's pierced brows were tight, his eyes fierce. But as much as it was clear the guy wanted to keep talking, Blay was so done.

He started down the steps, moving fast.

And was not at all surprised when Qhuinn stuck with him—and the conversation. "What the hell's that supposed to mean?"

Oh, right, like they needed to do this in front of the people in the dining room. Qhuinn was fine with audiences for all sorts of things, but Blay did not find peanut galleries helpful in the slightest.

He marched back up two steps, until they were face-to-face. "What was her name?"

Qhuinn recoiled. "Excuse me?"

"The receptionist's name."

"What receptionist?"

"From last night. At the tat shop."

Qhuinn rolled his eyes. "Oh, come on—"

"Her name."

"God, I have no fucking clue." Qhuinn went palms-up, the universal language for *whatever.* "Why does it matter?"

Blay opened his mouth, on the verge of spelling out that what had meant nothing to Qhuinn had been hell to watch. But then he knew it would sound possessive and stupid.

Instead of talking, he reached into his pocket, took out his Dunhills, and fingered one up. Popping it into his mouth, he lit the thing while staring into those mismatched eyes.

"I hate that you smoke," Qhuinn muttered.

"Get over it," Blay said, turning away and heading downward.

ELEVEN

"Where you going, John?"

Down in the mudroom at the back of the mansion, John froze with his hand on one of the doors that led into the garage. Goddamn it . . . a house this big, you'd think you could leave without an audience. But no . . . eyes everywhere. Opinions . . . everywhere.

It was like the orphanage in that respect.

He turned and faced Zsadist. The Brother had a napkin in one hand and a baby bottle in the other, having obviously just gotten up from the dining room table and come in through the kitchen. And gee, guess what . . . next person through the door was Qhuinn, and he had a half-eaten turkey leg with him as if it were his last hope of food for, like, the next ten hours.

Blay's arrival turned it into a fucking convention.

Z nodded at the grip John's hand had on the knob, somehow managing to look like a serial killer in spite of the baby paraphernalia. Probably the facial scar. More likely the eyes that were flashing black.

"I asked you a question, boy."

I'm taking the frickin' garbage out.

"So where's your Rubbermaid."

Qhuinn polished off his dinner and then deliberately walked over to the trash bins to toss the cleaned-off bone. "Yeah, John. You wanna answer that."

No, he fucking didn't.

I'm out of here, he signed.

Z leaned forward and planted a palm on the door panels, the napkin hanging loose like a flag. "You've been taking off a little earlier and a little earlier every night, but you've reached the cutoff. I'm not letting you go this early. You'll be burned to a crisp. And P.S., if you ever think of leaving without your private guard again, Wrath's going use your face as a hammer, feel me?"

"Jesus fucking Christ, John." Qhuinn's voice was a growl of disgust and he had an expression on his puss like someone had cleaned a bathroom with his bedsheets. "I've never stopped you. Ever. But you fuck me like this?"

John stared at a place somewhere over Z's left ear. There was a temptation to sign that he'd heard when the Brother had been looking for Bella, he'd gone shit wild and done all kinds of crazy things. Except bringing up that *shellan*'s abduction was a red cape in front of a bull and John was already doing the cloven-hoof thing about a female. Two would be overkill.

Z's voice dropped. "What's doing, John?"

He stayed quiet.

"John." Z leaned in further. "I will beat an answer out of you if I have to."

Just got the time wrong. The lie sucked ass, because if that were true, he'd have made a move to go out the front door and not covered his tracks with the trash story. But he honestly didn't care whether the bucket that carried his bullshit had a hole in the bottom.

"I'm not buying it." Z straightened and checked his watch. "And you're not leaving for another ten minutes."

John crossed his arms over his chest to keep from commenting on the lockdown, and as the *Jeopardy!* theme played in his head, he felt like he was going to explode.

Z's hard stare sure as hell didn't help.

Ten minutes later, the sound of those shutters lifting all around the mansion broke up the standoff and Z nodded at the door. "Okay, go now if you want. At least you won't fry out." John turned away. "I catch you without your *abstrux nohtrum* again, I'm turning you in."

Qhuinn cursed. "Yeah, and then I'll get fired. Which means V'll Donald Trump my ass with a dagger. You're welcome."

John gripped the knob and yanked his way out of the house, his skin feeling too tight. He didn't want trouble with Z because he respected the guy, but he was pretty damned volatile and the trend suggested that was only going to get more true.

In the garage, he hung a louie and headed for the outside door that was on the back wall. As he went along, he refused to look at the coffins that were stacked across the way. Nope. Didn't need the image of even one in his head right now. Sixteen? Whatever.

Opening the steel door, he stepped onto the long rolling lawn that stretched out around the drained swimming pool and eased down to the forest edge and the retaining wall. He knew that Qhuinn was right on his ass because the scent of disapproval contaminated the fresh air sure as mold in a basement. And Blay was with them as well, going by the cologne.

Just as he was about to dematerialize, his arm was grabbed hard. As he wheeled around to tell Qhuinn to fuck himself, he stopped.

Blay was the one doing the holding and the redhead's blue eyes were burning.

The guy signed as opposed to spoke, probably because it forced John to pay attention.

You want to get yourself killed, fine. At this point, I'm resigning myself to that possibility. But you don't endanger others. I won't stand for that. Don't leave without telling Qhuinn again.

John glanced over the guy's shoulder at Qhuinn, who was looking as if he wanted to hit something he was so frustrated. Ah, so that was why Blay was doing the signing thing. Didn't want the third wheel in this dysfunctional triumvirate to see what was being said.

We clear? Blay signed.

It was a rarity that Blay ever punched a hole in the wall of opinion. And that made John explain himself.

I can't promise I won't need to bolt, John signed. *Just can't do it. But I will swear that I will tell him. At least that way he can get out of the house.*

John—

He shook his head and squeezed Blay's arm. *I just can't promise anyone that. Not with where my head's at. But I won't leave without telling him where I'm going or when I'll be back.*

Blay's jaw worked, clenching and releasing. He wasn't stupid, however. He knew when there was a nonnegotiable on the table. *Okay. I can live with that.*

"You two want to share some love?" Qhuinn demanded.

John stepped back and signed, *We're going to the Xtreme Park until ten. Then we go to St. Francis Avenue. Trez texted me.*

He dematerialized, traveling south and west, taking form behind the shed they'd hung around the night before. As his crew appeared behind him, he ignored the tension that clouded and weighted down the air.

Staring across the concrete, he traced the various players. That young gun with the busy pockets was still smack in the center of it all, leaning against one of the ramps, flicking a lighter so that it sparked but didn't catch. There were about a half dozen skaters riding the hard stone and another dozen talking and spinning the wheels on their boards. Seven cars of various meh description were parked in the lot, and as the police rolled by slowly and kept going, John was feeling like this was a colossal waste of time.

Maybe if they headed deeper into downtown and trolled the alleys they'd have more—

106

The Lexus that wheeled up into the lot didn't park in one of the spaces. It stopped perpendicular to those seven rear bumpers . . . and what got out from behind the wheel looked like a high school kid, what with the baggy jeans and the cowboy hat.

But the breeze that floated over smelled like a morgue with no central AC.

And also of . . . Old Spice?

John straightened, his heart going all hi-how're-ya. His first thought was to lunge out and tackle the bastard, but Qhuinn caught him with an arm bar.

"Wait for it," the guy said. "Better to find out the whys."

John knew his buddy was right, so he pulled the parking brake on his body and got busy memorizing the license plate on the chromed-out LS 600h.

The sedan's other doors opened and three guys got out. They were not as pale as really old *lessers* got, but they were a fair shade of white boy, for sure, and they stank to high heaven.

Man, that baby-powder shit was straight-up nasty in the nose.

With one slayer staying behind to watch the ride, the other two fell into formation with the little cowboy in front. As they walked onto the concrete, all the eyes in the park went to them.

The kid by the middle ramp straightened and put his lighter in his pocket.

"Shit, I wish we had my fucking ride," Qhuinn whispered.

True enough. Unless there was a skyscraper nearby where they could get a roof's-eye view, there would be no way of tracking the Lexus.

The dealer didn't move as he was approached and didn't seem surprised by the visit, so chances were this was an arranged meeting. And what do you know, after some conversating, the slayers surrounded the guy and the bunch walked back over to the sedan.

All but one *lesser* got in the car.

Decision time. Did they bust into a vehicle, hot-wire it, and take off in pursuit? Did they materialize onto the hood of the fucking Lexus and throw down? Trouble was, both of those solutions ran the risk of a serious disturbance of the peace—and there was only so much mental cleanup they could do on a group of twenty humans.

"I think one's staying behind," Qhuinn murmured.

Yup. Flyboy was getting left in the lot as the Lexus K-turned and started to head out.

Letting the car go was the hardest thing John had ever done. But the reality was, that bunch of bastards had just picked up one of the prime dealers of the territory—so they were going to be back. And they'd left a *lesser* behind.

So there were things to keep him and his boys busy.

John watched the slayer walk into the park. Unlike the guy he was taking the place of, he was a roamer, pacing off the perimeter, meeting all of the eyes that were on him. He clearly made the skaters anxious and a couple of them who'd made buys the night before left. But not everyone was wary . . . or sober enough to be concerned.

As a soft ticking sound rose up, John looked down at himself. His foot was tapping in the dirt, going up and down as fast as a rabbit's.

But he wasn't going to blow it. He waited behind the shed . . . and waited . . . and waited.

It took the fucker nearly an hour to wander his nasty ass around, but when he was finally in range, all that foot tapping was so worth it.

With a quick shot of mental will, John canned the closest street lantern to give them a little privacy. And as the bastard looked up, John stepped out from behind the shed.

The *lesser*'s head snapped around and clearly he recognized that the war had just come and knocked on his door: The sonofabitch smiled and put his hand into his jacket.

John was not concerned that he was going to flash heat. The one rule of engagement was that there was no going at it in front of human bystand—

An autoloader appeared and went off in a quick one-two punch, the discharged shot sounding out with a pop that carried loud as a curse through the park.

John dived for cover, a whole lot of what-the-fuck giving him wings. And then more bullets went flying, the lead ricocheting off concrete as humans screamed and scrambled.

Behind the shed, he slammed his back against the wood and pulled his own piece. As Blay and Qhuinn slid into home, there was a split second of who's-bleeding? that coincided with a pause in the bullet shower.

What the fuck is he thinking? Qhuinn signed. *Public much?*

Heavy footsteps approached and there was the clicking sound of a sleeve of ammo being changed. John glanced at the shed door. The Master Lock on a chain was a godsend, and he reached up with his palm, mentally unlocking the thing and slipping it free of its links so that it hung loose.

Go around the next corner, John told his boys. *And make like you're wounded.*

Oh, hell, no—

John swung his gun muzzle into Qhuinn's face.

As the guy recoiled, John just stared right into his buddy's blue and green eyes. This was going down John's way: He was going to be the one to do business with the slayer. End of discussion.

Fuck. You, Qhuinn mouthed before he and Blay dematerialized.

With a loud groan, John let himself fall hard to the side, his body hitting the ground like a massive bag of concrete. Sprawling out on his stomach, he kept his SIG under his chest with the safety still off.

The footsteps grew closer. And so did a low laugh, like the *lesser* was having the time of his life.

When Lash returned from his father's, he took form in the bedroom next to the one he kept Xhex in. As much as he wanted to see her, he stayed away. Every time he came back from *Dhunhd*, he was a waste of space for a good half hour and he wasn't about to be stupid and give her a chance to kill him.

Because she would. And wasn't that sweet?

Lying down on the bed and closing his eyes, his body was slow and cold, and as he breathed deep, he felt as though he was thawing out like a slab of beef. Not that it was freezing on the other side. In fact, his father's digs were toasty and well-appointed—assuming you were into the Liberace shit.

Daddy-o had almost no furniture, but enough candelabra to sink a ship.

The oh-chillies seemed to have something to do with the leap back into this reality and every time he returned to this side, it was more of a struggle to rebound. The good news was that he didn't think he was going to have to go over there as much. Now that his bag of tricks had been fully explored and mastered, there was really no need, and truth was, the Omega wasn't exactly stimulating company.

It was a case of enough-about-me-what-do-you-think-about-me. And even if said demand for ego masturbation was being thrown out by an admittedly powerful, evil fucker who happened to be your pops, it got old fast.

Besides, his father's love life was disturbing as shit.

Lash didn't even know what those fucking things in that bed were. Black beasts, yeah, but the sex of them was as indiscernible as their species, and the way they oiled around was creepy. Plus they were always looking for a fuck even if there was company present.

And his father never said no.

As a beep sounded out, Lash reached into his suit jacket for his phone. It was a text from Mr. D: *On the way. Gots the guy.*

Lash looked at the clock and shot upright, thinking that the time couldn't be right. He'd come back two hours ago—how had he lost track so badly?

Going vertical threw his stomach in a roll and putting his hands up to rub his face took more effort than it should have. The deadweight of his body, coupled with the aches, made him remember back to a time when he'd gotten colds or flus. Same feeling. Was it possible he was getting sick?

Made him wonder if anyone had come up with a product like Dead-quil or some shit.

Probably not.

Letting his arms fall into his lap, he glanced over to the bathroom. The shower seemed miles away and not really worth the effort.

It took him another ten minutes before he could throw off the lethargy, and when he got to his feet, he stretched hard to get his black blood flowing. The bathroom turned out to be not miles away but a matter of yards, and with each step he felt stronger. Heading over to start the hot water, he admired himself in the mirror and checked out his collection of bruises. Most of them from the night before were gone, but he knew he was going to get more—

Lash frowned and lifted up his arm. The sore on the inside of his forearm was larger, not smaller.

When he prodded it with his finger, it didn't hurt, but the thing looked nasty as shit, a flat, open wound that was gray in the middle and bordered by a black line.

His first thought was that he needed to go see Havers . . . except that was ridiculous and nothing but a remnant from his old life. Like he was going to show up at the clinic and be all, Hey, could you fit my ass in?

Besides, he didn't know where they'd moved the damn thing to. Which was the problem with a successful raid. Your target took your threat seriously and went deep underground.

Getting under the warm spray, he was careful to scrub the spot with some soap, figuring if it was some kind of infection that had to help; and then he thought about other things.

He had a big-ass night. The induction at eight. Meeting with Benloise at ten.

Back here for some more lovin'.

When he got out, he dried himself and inspected the sore. The damn thing appeared to be pissed off at the attention he'd given it, a thin black ooze welling up over its surface.

Oh, that stuff was going to be great to get out of his fucking silk shirts.

He slapped a Band-Aid the size of an index card on the thing and thought that maybe tonight he and his GF would play nice.

He'd tie her up for a change.

It took him no time at all to put on a sweet Zegna suit and head out. As he passed by the master bedroom's door, he paused and made a fist. Banging on the wood loud enough to wake the dead, he smiled.

"Be back soon and I'm bringing chains."

He waited for a response. When there was none, he reached for the knob and put his ear to the door. The sound of her even breathing was soft as a gentle current of air, but it was there. She lived. And she would be alive still when he returned.

With deliberate self-control, he released the knob. If he opened the door, he'd lose another couple of hours and his father was not into waiting.

Down in the kitchen, he took a stab at some eats and came up with nothing. The coffee machine had been timed to start up two hours ago, so a quick lift of the pot showed something close to crankcase oil. And cracking the fridge, he didn't see anything that appealed even though he felt starved.

Lash ended up dematerializing from the kitchen empty-handed and with a bottomless gut. Not a great combo for his mood, but he wasn't going to miss the show—if for no other reason than he wanted to see what had been done to him during his induction.

The farmhouse was out north and east of the brownstone, and the instant he took form on the lawn, he knew his father was inside: An odd shiver in his blood bubbled up every time he was around the Omega, like an echo in an enclosed space . . . although he wasn't sure whether he was the sound and his father the cave, or if it was the other way around.

The front door was open, and as he mounted the porch steps and went into the shitty little hall, he thought about his induction.

"When you became truly mine."

Lash wheeled around. The Omega was in the living room, his white robes covering his face and hands, his black energy seeping out onto the floor, a dark shadow formed by no illumination.

"Are you excited, my son?"

"Yeah." Lash glanced over his shoulder at the dining room table. The bucket and the knives that had been used on him were right there. Ready and waiting.

The sound of gravel crunching under tires had him turning to the door. "They're here."

"My son, I should like you to bring me more. I find myself hungry for fresh ones."

Lash went to the doorway. "No problem."

In this at least, they were fully aligned. More inductees meant more money, more fighting.

The Omega came up behind Lash and there was a soft brushing movement as a black hand ran down his spine. "You are a good son."

For a split second, Lash's dark heart ached. The phrase was exactly the one the vampire who'd raised him had said from time to time. "Thanks."

Mr. D and the two others got out of the Lexus . . . and brought the human forward. It hadn't dawned on the little bastard yet that he was a pair of jeans and a T-shirt away from being a sacrificial lamb. But the instant he got a look-see at the Omega, shit was going to become clear as a bell.

TWELVE

As John lay facedown and the footsteps of his enemy got closer, he breathed through his nose and got a sinus-load of fresh dirt. Pulling a possum was not a bright idea generally speaking, but this motherfucker with the epileptic trigger finger didn't fit the profile of someone who was going to be too careful about whether he'd hit his mark or not.

Letting loose the lead in the middle of a public park?

Had the idiot never heard of the Caldwell Police Department? The *Caldwell Courier Journal*?

The boots stopped and that sweet, choking smell *lessers* carried on their skin nearly made him gag. But funny how life and death got the attention of your esophagus.

He felt something blunt push at his left arm, like the slayer was checking with his boot to see if they were in toe tag territory. And then on cue, Qhuinn let out a low, pathetic moan from around the far side of the shed.

Like his liver was leaking into his colon.

The boots moved down John's body as the bastard wandered forward to investigate and John cracked an eye. The slayer was pulling a Hollywood, his gun held straight out in a double-palm grip, the muzzle swinging from side to side with more affect than effect. Still, though he looked all Crockett-and-Tubbs ridiculous with that theatrical bust-a-move, bullets were bullets and it would take only a quick shift in direction and John was at point-blank range.

Good thing he didn't give a shit. As the fucker

wedding-marched it toward Qhuinn's moans, an image of Xhex's face sprang John up off the ground in a single lithe move. He landed on top of the *lesser's* thick back, latching on with his free arm and both of his legs as he put his gun to that pale temple.

The slayer froze for a split second, and John whistled between his teeth, the signal for Qhuinn and Blay to come up from behind.

"Time to drop the gun, asshole," Qhuinn said as he reappeared. Then, without giving the bastard time to comply, he reached out, locked his hands on the slayer's forearm, and made like he was snapping a stick.

The crack of bones was louder than John's whistle had been and the result was a limp wrist and a Glock no longer under the enemy's control.

As the *lesser* bucked in pain, sirens from far off sounded out . . . and closed in.

John dragged the bastard back to the double doors of the shed, and after Blay opened the way in, he pulled his prey out of sight.

With overexaggerated words, he mouthed to Qhuinn, *Go get your Hummer.*

"If those cops are coming for us, we've got to blow."

Not leaving. Get the Hummer.

Qhuinn took out his keys and tossed them to Blay. "You go. And lock us in, feel me?"

Blay didn't waste a second, backing out and closing the door. There was the subtle sound of metal clinking as he reset the chain and then a click as that Master Lock was popped into place.

The *lesser* was starting to struggle with greater strength, but this was not a bad thing—consciousness was what they were going for.

John flipped the fucker onto his stomach and pulled back on that neck until the thing's spine pretzeled.

Qhuinn knew exactly what to do. Kneeling down, he

put his face right into the slayer's. "We know you hold a female prisoner. Where is she?"

As the sirens intensified, the slayer managed only a series of grunts, so John relented a little and allowed some air down in those lungs.

Qhuinn drew back his palm and slapped the *lesser*. "I asked you a question, bitch. Where is she?"

John eased up a little further, but not so much as to offer an escape route. With the added leeway, the *lesser* shuddered in fear, proving that whereas the motherfucker had been all business with his showy shooting, here during crunch time, he was nothing but a young punk in over his head.

Qhuinn's second slap was harder. "Answer me."

"No . . . prisoner."

As Qhuinn threw back his arm again, the slayer recoiled—yup, although the fuckers were dead, their pain receptors worked just fine. "Female abductee held by your *Fore-lesser*. Where is she?"

John reached forward and gave his gun to Qhuinn and then, with his now-free hand, he went to the small of his back and withdrew his hunting knife. It went without saying that he was the only one who was going to do any real damage and he brought the blade around and put it right up to the *lesser's* eyes. Wild bucking ensued, but the struggle was quickly contained, John's huge body blanketing what was under him.

"You're going to want to talk," Qhuinn said dryly. "Trust me on this."

"I don't know no female." The words were nothing but a hiss, that windpipe constricted by John's forearm.

John gave a jerk backward and the slayer yelled, "I don't!"

Sirens were screaming now, and out in the parking lot there were multiple tire squeals.

Time to tread carefully. The *lesser* had already demonstrated a total disregard for the single rule in the war, so whereas with any other slayer you could be sure of silence, that was a not-so-much with Mr. Click-click Bang-bang.

John met Qhuinn's mismatched stare, but the guy was already on it. Reaching over to a pile of oily rags, Qhuinn snagged one and stuffed it into the *lesser's* mouth. Then it was freeze-frame time.

From outside, the voices of the cops were muffled: "Cover me."

"Roger that."

As John put away his knife so he could hold on with both hands, there was lots of foot shuffling, most of which was off in the distance. But would no doubt come near eventually.

While the uniforms scattered, the radios in the cop cars provided a chatty sound track to their initial search-and-secure. Which didn't take long. Within a couple of minutes, the policemen were pooling around the cars, right next to the shed.

"Unit Two-forty to base. Area is secure. No victims. No perp—"

With a quick kick, the *lesser* creamed a gas can with its boot. And you could practically hear all those CPD gun muzzles come back up and train on the shed.

"What the fuck?"

Lash smiled as the kid's eyes locked on the Omega. Although everything was covered with robing, you'd have to be a total moron not to realize there was something way off under there—and ding-ding-ding, they had a winner in the cognitive lottery.

As those feet started to paddle backward out of the farmhouse, Mr. D's backup slayers flanked the little bastard and caught him by the arms.

Lash nodded to the dining room table. "My father will do him in there."

"Do what!" Now there was full-on panic, with the kid thrashing like a gutted pig. Which was nothing but good practice for what was coming, really.

The slayers muscled him over and flipped him up on top of the pitted wood, holding him down at the feet and ankles as the Omega came forward amid all the squeaking and flapping.

As the evil lifted his hood, everything went quiet.

And then the scream that came out of the human's mouth ripped through the air, echoing up to the ceiling, filling the decrepit house with noise.

Lash hung back and let his father go to work, watching the human's clothes get shredded with a mere pass of that black, transparent palm. And then it was time for the knife, the blade catching the light of the cheapo chandelier that dangled from the grungy ceiling.

Mr. D was the one who helped with the technicalities—positioning the buckets under the arms and legs, scurrying around.

Lash had been dead when his veins got drained; he'd awoken only when a shock that had been generated from God only knew where had tunneled through his body. So it was interesting to see how it all worked: How the blood was emptied from the body. How the chest was split open and the Omega slit its own wrist to drip black oil into the cavity. How the evil called up a ball of energy out of thin air and sent into the corpse. How the reanimation carried what had been given to every vein and artery. The final step was removal of the heart, the organ shriveling up in the Omega's palm before being put into a ceramic container.

As Lash remembered his own coming-back-from-the-dead routine, he recalled his father dragging Mr. D over to serve as a feeding source for him. He'd needed the blood, but then again, he'd been dead for a while at that point—and was at least half vampire. This human, on the other hand, came awake with nothing more than a gaping, fish mouth and a whole lot of confusion.

Lash put his hand up to his own chest and felt the beat of his heart—

Something was leaking. In his sleeve.

While the Omega started to do depraved things to the initiate, Lash jogged upstairs to the bathroom. Taking off his suit jacket, he folded the thing in half . . . and realized there was nowhere to lay it down. Everything was covered with two decades' worth of grime.

Christ, why hadn't he sent someone over to clean the place?

He ended up hanging the jacket from a hook and— Oh, shit.

As he lifted his arm, there was a black stain right over where he'd put the bandage, and at the bottom of his elbow, there was a wet patch.

"God*damn* it."

Ripping free his cuff links, he unbuttoned his shirt and froze as he looked down at his chest.

Lifting his eyes to the cloudy mirror, as if that were going to change what he was seeing, he leaned in toward the glass. There was another sore on his left pectoral, of the same flat, dime-size shape as the first. And a third by his belly button.

Wings of panic fanned up a light-headed dizziness and he caught himself on the sink. His first thought was to run to the Omega and ask for help, but he held off—going by the screams and grunts downstairs, there was some serious action happening in the dining room, and only an idiot interrupted that.

The Omega was fickle by nature, but had OCD concentration about some things.

Bracing his hands on the basin, Lash dropped his head as his empty stomach pulled a churn and burn on him.

He had to wonder how many more of those spots he had—and didn't want to know the answer.

His induction, rebirth, whatever, was supposed to be permanent. That's what his father had told him. He was born from the evil, spawned from a dark well that was eternal.

Rotting in his own skin had not been part of the deal.

"Y'all okay there?"

Lash shut his eyes, the sound of the Texan's voice like claws raking down his back. Except he just didn't have the energy to fuck-off the guy.

"How are things going downstairs?" he asked instead.

Mr. D cleared his throat. And still the disapproval made him choke on his words. "I do believe it'll be 'while yet, suh."

Great.

Lash forced his sagging spine to straighten and turned to face his deputy—

In a sharp rush, his fangs punched into his mouth, and for a moment, he couldn't figure out why. Then he realized his eyes had locked on the guy's jugular.

Deep in Lash's belly, his hunger grew horns and went haywire, thrashing and gouging his gut.

It happened too fast to stop or question or think. One second he was rooted where he stood in front of the sink. The next he was all over Mr. D, shoving the *lesser* back against the door, and going hard into the guy's throat.

The black blood that hit his tongue was the tonic he needed and he drew with desperation, even as the Texan struggled and then fell still. But the fucker didn't have to worry. There was nothing sexual in the sucking. It was nutrition, plain and simple.

And the more he swallowed, the more he needed.

Jacking the slayer tight against his chest, he fed like a motherfucker.

THIRTEEN

As the sound of the slayer's boot against that gas can faded, Qhuinn moved down and sat on the SOB's legs. The bastard might have gotten one kick in, but he was not getting a second chance.

Outside, the human cops gathered around the shed.

"It's locked," one of them said as the chain rattled.

"I have shell casings over here."

"Wait, there's something inside . . . phew, man, what a stench."

"Whatever it is, it's been dead at least a week. That smell—I'd take even my mother-in-law's tuna casserole over that."

There was a ripple of agreement.

In the darkness, John and Qhuinn locked eyes and waited. The only solution if the door got popped was to dematerialize and leave the *lesser* behind; there was no way of moving the weight of the slayer through thin air. But none of these policemen could possibly have the key—so that left shooting their way in as their only option.

And chances were good they'd assume a quick pop just to get into the shed was not worth the paperwork.

"Only one shooter, according to the nine-one-one call. And he can't be in there."

There was a cough and a curse. "If he is, his nose is falling off from the stank."

"Call the groundskeeper," a deep voice said. "Someone's gotta get that dead animal out of there. Meantime, let's head into the neighborhood."

There was chatter and footsteps. A little later one of the cars drove off.

"We gotta off him," Qhuinn whispered over John's shoulder. "Take that knife and let's do him and get the fuck out of here."

John shook his head. There was no way he was losing this prize.

"John, we're not leaving with him. Kill him so we can bounce."

Even though Qhuinn couldn't see his lips, John mouthed, *Fuck that. He's mine.*

Letting this source of information slide was not going to happen. If anything, the human police could be dealt with mentally . . . or physically if it came down to it.

There was the smooth sound of a knife being unsheathed. "Sorry, John, we're outtie."

No! John yelled over his shoulder soundlessly.

Qhuinn's hand locked on the collar of John's jacket and dragged him off balance, so it was a case of either letting go of the slayer's neck or snapping the fucker's head off his spine. Since an incapacitated *lesser* couldn't talk, John released his hold—and caught himself by planting his palm on the cold cement.

No fucking way was he going to let his buddy cheat him out of this.

As he lunged at the male, all hell broke loose. He and Qhuinn wrestled for control over the dagger, knocking into a lot more than a gas can, and the *lesser* rolled free and sprang for the door. As the cops started hollering, the slayer pounded to get out—

The next sound that made any impression over the din was a gunshot. The chaser of which was a metallic ringing.

The police had blasted off the Master Lock.

From down on the floor, John whipped his arm around to the small of his back, and as he pivoted on his knees, he and Qhuinn threw their knives in sync, their blades traveling end over end across the shallow space.

The penetrations were of such force that even though they went into the slayer's torso between the shoulder blades, clearly one or both hit home: In a flash bright as lightning and with a sonic boom loud enough to make ears bleed, the *lesser* went back to his maker, leaving nothing but a smoky stink . . . and a hole the size of a refrigerator in the shed door.

With adrenaline running so high, neither he nor Qhuinn could dematerialize, so they leaped up and back-flatted it on either side of the gaper, staying put as first one gun muzzle then another eased inside.

Forearms were next.

Then profiles and shoulders. And flashlights.

Fortunately, the humans stepped fully inside.

"Psst. Your fly's down." As the cops turned on Qhuinn's smart ass, John unsheathed both his SIGs, and with a quick cross-strike on those heads, CPD's finest were seeing stars and sinking down onto the floor.

Which was precisely when Blay showed up with the Hummer.

John jumped over the policemen and hightailed it down to the SUV with Qhuinn right behind him, those New Rocks the fucker insisted on wearing positively pounding the earth. John gunned his way for the rear door, which Blay had popped, catching the handle and flipping himself inside as Qhuinn slid into the back-seat.

As Blay took off, flooring the engine and blasting out of there, John was glad they'd had to tango with only one set of cops—although sure as shit the other two badges would be back ASAP.

They were heading north toward the highway as John clawed his way into the backseat . . . and relocked his hands around Qhuinn's throat.

As they went back at it, Blay shouted from up front, "What the fuck is wrong with you two?"

No time to answer that. John was busy squeezing and Qhuinn was trying to give him a black eye—and succeeding.

Sixty-something miles an hour. In and around downtown. With a possible ID on the Hummer if either of those cops had come to enough to focus his peepers while Blay got them out of Dodge.

And a brawl going down.

Later, John would realize that of course there was only one place Blay could go.

By the time the guy pulled into Sal's parking lot—in the back of the restaurant, where there were no lights—John and Qhuinn had both drawn blood. And the fight ended only when John was yanked out of the door by Trez—which suggested the redhead had phoned ahead. Qhuinn was handled with similar muscle by iAm.

John spit to clear out his mouth and glared at all of them.

"I believe we'll call this a draw, boys," Trez said with a half smile. "What do ya think?"

As John was released, rage made him shake. That slayer could have been the one thing they needed to crack the locale . . . the story . . . the *anything*. And because Qhuinn had insisted on wasting the bastard, they were no closer to where they had to be. Plus there was the fact that the *lesser* had died so easily. Just a prick in the heart cavity and he was home free—or at least back to the Omega.

Qhuinn wiped his mouth on the back of his hand. "For fuck's sake, John! You think I don't want to find her? You think I don't give a shit? Christ, I've been out every night with you, looking, searching, praying for a break." He pointed his finger straight out. "So get this straight. The pair of us getting busted with a leaking *lesser* by a bunch of humans is *not* going to help us. You want to tell Wrath how you rolled with that one? I don't. And if you *ever* put a gun in my face again, I will fuck you up no matter what my job is."

John didn't trust himself to respond. One thing was clear, though—if he didn't have the hope of something turning up at Benloise's St. Francis place, he would have been tearing shit up no matter who tried to stop him, Shadow or otherwise.

"Are you hearing me?" Qhuinn demanded. "Am I clear to you?"

John paced around, hands on his hips, head down low. As his temper started to cool, the logical side of him knew his buddy was right. He was also very aware he'd temporarily lost his damn mind in that shed. Had he really put a forty in his friend's puss?

His sudden clarity made him sick to his stomach.

If he didn't stitch it up here, he was going to have more problems than a missing female. He was going to end up dead, either because he was sloppy in combat or because Wrath gave him a serious case of boot-up-the-ass-itis.

He looked over at Qhuinn. Man, the hard expression on that pierced face was right close to an edge a friendship couldn't go back from—the kind of thing that didn't have to do with Qhuinn being a tough guy, but rather John being the kind of asshole no one wanted to hang out with.

He walked up to the male and wasn't surprised when Qhuinn held his ground in spite of the throw-down in the car. When he stuck his hand out, there was a long pause.

"I'm not the enemy, John."

John nodded, focusing on that tattooed tear beneath the guy's eye. Retracting his palm, he signed, *I know that. I just . . . I need to find her. And what if that slayer was the way?*

"Maybe he was—but the sitch got critical and you're going to have to choose yourself over her sometimes. Because if you don't, there's no way you're ever going to find out what happened. You can't search for her from inside a coffin."

He couldn't find a way to argue with that.

"So listen up, you crazy fuck, we're in this together," Qhuinn said softly. "And I'm here to make sure you don't wake up dead. I get the drive, I do. But you've got to work with me."

I'm going to kill Lash, John signed in a rush. *I'm going to hold his throat in my hands and I'm going to stare into his eyes as he dies. I don't care how much it costs me . . . but his ashes will be sprinkled on her grave. I swear on . . .*

What did he have to swear on? Not his father. Not his mother.

. . . I swear on my own life.

Anyone else might have tried to placate him with a shitload of have-faith, you-gotta-believe crap. But Qhuinn clapped him on the shoulder. "Have I told you how much I love you lately?"

Every night you come out with me to help find her.

"It's not because of the fucking job."

This time when John put his palm out, his friend used it to pull them into a hard embrace. Then Qhuinn shoved him away and checked the watch on his wrist. "We should head over to St. Francis Avenue."

"You got ten minutes." Trez put his arm around the guy and started walking for the back door into the kitchen. "Let's get you two cleaned up. You can leave the Hummer in our receiving dock and I'll switch the plates for you while you're gone."

Qhuinn looked over at Trez. "That's really fucking nice of you."

"Yeah, I'm a prince, all right. And to prove it, I'll even tell you all I know about Benloise."

As John followed them inside, the fact that he hadn't gotten anything out of the slayer focused him, steeled him, resolved him further.

Lash wasn't going to leave Caldwell. He couldn't. As long as he was head of the Lessening Society, he was going to go toe-to-toe with the Brotherhood, and the Brothers weren't budging from the city—the Tomb was here. So although the civilian vampires had scattered, Caldie remained the focal point of the war because there would be no winning for the enemy if the Brothers still breathed.

Sooner or later, Lash was going to slip up and John was going to be there.

But goddamn the waiting could wear a guy out, it really could. Every dragging night with nothing new and nothing really to go on . . . was a forever in hell.

FOURTEEN

When Lash finally released Mr. D's vein, he pushed him away like a dirty plate after a meal. Sagging on the counter, he reveled in the fact that his hunger was sated and that his body seemed stronger already. But now he was logy as fuck, which was what always happened after he fed.

He'd been taking Xhex's throat periodically just for kicks and giggles, but that clearly wasn't what he needed to fill his gut.

Which left him living off of . . . *lessers?*

Nah, he didn't fly that way. Never had. No fucking way he was going to be latching onto the throats of guys with any regularity.

Lifting up his arm, he checked his watch. Ten minutes of ten. And he looked like a homeless guy. Felt like one, too.

"Clean yourself up," he told Mr. D. "I have shit you need to do."

As he started to give out the orders, his mouth tripped over the words he was speaking.

"You got that?" he said.

"Yes, suh." The Texan looked around the bathroom like he was searching for a towel.

"Downstairs," Lash snapped. "Kitchen. And you need to go get me a change of clothes and bring them here. Oh, and while you're at the brownstone, set some more food out in the bedroom."

Mr. D just nodded and headed out, walking on loose legs.

"Did you get the new recruit a cell phone? ID?" Lash called after him.

"They're down in the messenger bag. And I texted you the number."

Fucker really was an excellent PA.

As Lash leaned into the shower and cranked the knobs on the tile wall, he wouldn't have been surprised if either nothing came out or there was only a thin trail of brown muck. He lucked out, though. Fresh, clean rain fell from the showerhead and he quickly undressed.

It felt good to wash off, kind of like he was rebooting his body.

After he was finished, he used his shirt to dry himself and then stumbled into a bedroom. Lying down, he closed his eyes and put his hand on his stomach over where the sores were. Which was dumb. Not like he needed to protect them from anything.

As the sounds from downstairs seemed to indicate things were progressing, he was relieved . . . and a little surprised. The noises weren't all painful and frightened anymore; they were heading into porno territory, the groans and moans now rising up the result of orgasms.

Are you queer? he recalled the kid asking.

Maybe that had been more of an I-hope-so kind of thing.

Whatever. Lash didn't want to be all out-of-it around his father, so with any luck the new recruit would be used for a while.

Lash closed his eyes and tried to shut his head off. Plans for the Society, thoughts of Xhex, frustration at the whole feeding thing . . . His brain waves coalesced into a whirl, but his body was too exhausted to sustain consciousness.

Which was just as well—

It was as he sank down into sleep that he had the vision. Sharp and clear, it came into him, not to him, entering his mind from somewhere else and shoving all other preoccupations out of the way.

He saw himself walking the grounds of the estate he'd grown up on, going over the lawn toward the grand house. Inside, the lights were glowing and folks were moving around . . . exactly as they had the night he had gone in and murdered those two vampires who had raised him. These were not the profiles of people he knew, however. They were different. They were the humans who had bought the house.

To the right was the ivy bed that he'd buried his parents in.

He saw himself standing over the place where he'd dug the hole and dumped the bodies. It was still slightly uneven, although some gardener had planted it over with new ivy growth.

Kneeling down, he reached forward . . . only to see that his arm was not his own.

He was as his true father existed: a black, shimmering shadow.

For some reason, the revelation panicked him and he tried to rouse himself. In his motionless skin, he thrashed.

But he had sunk too low to get free of the pull.

Ricardo Benloise's art gallery was downtown, over near the St. Francis Hospital complex. The sleek, six-story building stood out amid its sister 1920s-era "skyscrapers" thanks to a face-lift that left it with a brushed-steel exterior and windows the size of barn doors.

Rather like a starlet seated next to a bunch of dowagers.

As John and the boys appeared on the sidewalk across from the facade, the place was hopping. Through those huge panels of glass, he could see men and women dressed in black carrying around champagne glasses as they inspected the art on the walls. Which at least from the street seemed to be a fusion between five-year-old finger painting and the work of a sadist with a rusty nail fetish.

John was not impressed with the cultivated avant-garde routine—and as always, he had no idea why he had an opinion about art. Like any of it mattered?

Trez had told them to head around back, so he and his boys walked down the block and cut into the alley that ran behind the gallery. Whereas the front of the place was all eye-catching and welcoming, the opposite was true for the business's ass. No windows. Everything painted matte black. Two flush doors and a loading dock that was locked up tighter than a chastity belt.

Based on the intel from Trez, piss-poor excuses for "art" like the ones being discussed by those self-important Warhol-wannabes weren't the only products going in and out of the place. Which was clearly why there was a fuckload of security cameras mounted over the rear exit.

Fortunately, there were plenty of shadows to take cover behind, and instead of walking by all those lenses, they dematerialized over to a stack of wooden pallets in a dark corner.

The city was still full of life at this hour, the muted honks of cars and the distant sirens of the police and the lumbering groans of the CTA buses marking the cool air with an urban symphony—

At the far end of the alley, a car turned in and shut off its lights as it came forward toward the gallery.

"Right on time," Qhuinn whispered. "And it's that Lexus."

John took a deep breath and prayed for a break before he lost his ever-loving mind.

The sedan rolled to a stop parallel to the loading dock and the door opened. As the interior light came on . . .

The little *lesser* from the park, the one who'd smelled like Old Spice, got out of an otherwise empty car. No Lash.

John's first instinct was to jump on the slayer . . . but according to Trez, Lash was supposed to be at the meeting. If they disturbed a prearranged flow of bodies, there was a chance he'd be tipped off.

And given his bag of tricks, surprise was mission critical.

For a moment, John wondered whether he should text the Brothers. Let them know. Get some serious backup . . . except the instant it occurred to him his vengeance sat up and roared.

Which was precisely what had him reaching into his pocket and taking out his phone. As the slayer headed inside, the text he sent to Rhage was short and factual: *189 St. Francis. Lash on way. 3 of us in the rear alley.*

When he put the phone back into his pocket, he could feel Blay and Qhuinn staring over his shoulder. One of them gave him a squeeze of approval.

The thing was, Qhuinn was right. If the goal truly was to take down Lash, there were better odds of nailing the guy if he got help. And he needed to be smart about this—because stupid clearly wasn't getting him where he needed to be.

A moment later, Rhage materialized at the head of the alley with Vishous and the pair strode down. Hollywood was the go-to guy when it came to Lash because the Brother was packing the one weapon that could go head-to-head with the bastard: That dragon of his went wherever he did.

The two of them flashed down right beside John and before either of them could ask, he started signing.

I need to be the one who kills Lash. Do you understand? It has to be me.

Vishous immediately nodded and signed, *I know your history with that piece of shit. But if it comes to a point where it's either you or the motherfucker, your honor's going to get benched and we're going to intercede. Clear?*

John took a deep breath, thinking that the extrapolation worked well enough for a why. *I'm gonna make it so you don't have to worry about that.*

Fair enough.

They all froze as the *lesser* who'd driven the Lexus came back out, got behind the wheel . . . and took off as if the meeting had been canceled.

"Roof it," Rhage said, disappearing.

With an inner curse, John took the cue and assumed form on the top of Benloise's place, looking over the lip and watching the sedan come to a stop on St. Francis Street. Fortunately, the slayer was a law-abider and hit its directional signal to the left, so John scattered his molecules and coalesced two buildings down. As the car progressed, he repeated and repeated until the *lesser* took a right into the even older section of Caldwell.

Where the flat roofs ended and all you had to land on was a bunch of pointed Victorian shit.

Good thing the soles of shitkickers had some grab in 'em.

Making like a gargoyle, John perched on turrets and dormers and sills, following his prey from the air . . . until the Lexus turned off on an alley and ducked behind a row of brownstones.

John knew the neighborhood only nominally—from his one trip to Xhex's basement place, which was close by—but it was not normal Lessening Society territory. Usually their cribs were in much lower-profile zip codes.

So there was only one explanation. This was where Lash stayed.

Guy like him, who'd been into the bling and the clothes and that shit when he was growing up, would need a personality transplant to be able to settle for anything less than good real estate. It was what he'd grown up around, and undoubtedly he would see it as his due.

John's heart started to beat hard and fast.

The Lexus stopped in front of a garage, and when the door was up, it went in. A moment later, the little slayer walked through a garden to the back of one of the nicer brownstones.

Rhage appeared right next to John and signed, *You go in the rear with me. Vishous and the boys are going to dematerialize in through the front door. V's already on the porch and says there's no steel.*

When John nodded, the two of them flashed down onto a slate terrace—just as the *lesser* popped the door into what looked like a gourmet kitchen. They waited a moment, frozen in time and space, as the slayer turned off the security system.

The fact that the thing needed to be disarmed didn't necessarily mean Lash wasn't inside. *Lessers* required time-outs to recharge on a regular basis and only an asshole left himself unsecured.

John just had to believe what he was looking for was in that house.

FIFTEEN

Xhex was sitting in the wing chair by the window when she heard the noise up above on the roof. The muffled *bump-bump* was loud enough to pull her free of the mental aerobics she did to keep herself sharp.

She looked to the ceiling . . .

Downstairs, the security system went off and her precision hearing picked up the *beep-beep-beep-beep-beep* of it being disarmed. And then there were the light footsteps of the *lesser* who brought her food—

Something was off. Something . . . just wasn't right.

Sitting forward in her chair, she tensed up from neck to foot and cast out mental feelers. Although she couldn't send *symphath* signals, her ability to sense emotional grids was compromised but workable . . . and that was how she knew there was somebody other than that slayer around the house.

A number of bodies. Two out the back. Three in the front. And the emotions of the individuals who had surrounded the brownstone were appropriate to those of soldiers: deadly calm, utterly focused.

But they were not *lessers*.

Xhex shot to her feet.

Jesus . . . Christ. They'd found her. The Brothers had fucking found her.

And the ambush was executed with perfect timing. Downstairs, she heard a shout of surprise, a scramble of bodies, and then the pounding of boots as hand-to-hand combat was thrown around and back-up came roaring in from another direction.

Even though no one but Lash could hear her, she started

to yell as loud as she could in the hopes that for once, she could reach out beyond the invisible walls of her cage.

John Matthew couldn't believe the *lesser* hadn't known they were there. Unless the fucker was compromised in some way, it should have tweaked to the fact that there were vampires all around the place. But oh, no—it just went about its biz, stepping inside while leaving the damn door open.

First order of infiltration was control, and as soon as John was over the brownstone's threshold, he subdued the *lesser* by cranking the bastard's arms behind its back, forcing it facedown on the tile, and sitting on its ass like a grand piano. Meanwhile, Rhage blasted past on surprisingly light feet just as V and the boys emerged into the kitchen from the dining room.

As the first level of the house was searched fast, John felt a tickling go down his back . . . as if a razor-sharp knife was tracing his spine. Looking around, he couldn't tease out the origin of the sensation, so he banked the instinct.

"Cellar," Rhage hissed.

Vishous headed down with the Brother.

With his boys left to guard his back, John was able to focus his attention on the *lesser* beneath him. Fucker was too quiet, too still. Breathing, but that was it.

Had it hit something on the way down to the floor? Was it leaking? Usually they fought back.

Kicked gas cans, for fucking instance.

As he searched for signs of bleeding or other injury, John shifted his head around without giving the slayer a chance to get free. Grabbing onto the fucker's hair, he pulled up—

He found something, all right . . . but it sure as shit wasn't caused by the tackle. On the left side of the slayer's neck, there were two puncture wounds and a circular bruise caused by sucking.

Qhuinn came over and kneeled down. "Who's been workin' your neck, big guy?"

The *lesser* didn't reply as V and Rhage dematerialized up from the basement and headed for the second floor.

As the Brothers moved silently through the house, Qhuinn took ahold of the slayer's jaw. "We're looking for a female. And you can make shit easier on yourself if you tell us where she is."

The *lesser* frowned . . . and slowly shifted its eyes above.

That was all John needed.

He lunged forward, grabbing Blay's palm and yanking it down to the slayer. As possession changed hands, John leaped off and ran through a dining room and a front hall. The stairwell was broad and carpeted, which meant he had excellent traction as he took the steps three at a time. The higher he went, the more his instincts screamed.

Xhex was in the house.

Just as he came to the top, Rhage and V appeared in front of him, blocking the way.

"House is empty—"

John cut Rhage off. *She's here. She's here somewhere. I know it.*

Rhage caught his arm. "Let's go down and question the slayer. We'll get more that way—"

No! She's here!

Vishous stepped up into John's grille, his diamond stare glowing. "Listen to me, son. You want to go back downstairs."

John narrowed his eyes. They didn't just want him down below. They didn't want him *up* here.

What did you find. Neither answered. *What did you find!*

Breaking away from them both, he heard Rhage curse as V leaped in front of a door.

Hollywood's voice was hollow. "Nah, V, let him go. Just let him go . . . he already hates Lash enough for a lifetime."

V's stare flashed as if he were going to argue, but then he took a hand-rolled out of his jacket and stepped aside with a curse.

With the back of his neck as tight as a fist, John burst through the door and skidded to a halt. The sadness in the room was a tangible threshold he had to breach, his body penetrating the cold wall of desolation only because he forced his feet forward.

She had been kept here.

Xhex had been kept here . . . and hurt here.

His lips parted and he breathed through his mouth as his eyes traced the scratches on the walls. There were legions of them, along with black stains . . . and other dried blood.

Which was a deep, purpley red.

John went over and ran his hands down one gouge that was so deep, the silk wallpaper had given way to the lath and plaster beneath.

His inhales grew sharper and his exhales shorter as he went around the room. The bed was an absolute mess, the pillows scattered to the floor, the duvet a tangle . . .

There was blood on it.

Reaching out, he picked up one of the pillows and held it gently. Bringing it to his nose, he inhaled . . . and caught a stronger version of what he dreamed of every night: Xhex's scent.

His knees weakened and he went down like a stone through still water, collapsing by the side of the mattress. Burying his face into the softness, he drew her into him, her fragrance lingering like a memory, at once tangible and elusive.

She had been here. Recently.

He glanced at the bloodied sheets. The bloodied walls. *He was too late.*

John's face grew wet and he felt something drip off his chin, but he didn't give a shit. He was consumed with the thought that he'd come so close to saving her . . . but just not arrived soon enough.

The sob that breached his throat actually made a sound.

For all of her life, Xhex's heart had not been prone to breaking. She'd long suspected that it was a result of her *symphath* side, a kind of congenital condition that hardened her about things that most females lost it over.

Turned out that was wrong, however.

As she stood beside John Matthew, and watched his huge body crumple down by the bed, the organ that beat behind her sternum shattered like a mirror.

Nothing but shards.

She was utterly and completely ruined as he cradled that pillow like it was a newborn, and in this moment of his utter despair, she would have done anything to ease his pain: Even though she had no idea why he felt the way he so clearly did, the reasons were unimportant.

His suffering was paramount.

Weakened herself, she knelt down next to him, her eyes sending the tragic image he cut straight into the core of her brain.

It felt like centuries since she had seen him, and God, he was still so beautiful—even more than she remembered in her quiet moments. With his strong, hard profile and his extraordinary blue eyes, his face was that of a warrior, and he had the huge body to match, his shoulders making three of hers. All his clothes were leather except for the T-shirt under his jacket and his hair was essentially shaved off, like he'd stopped giving a shit and was cutting it with a buzz razor.

There was *lesser* blood down the front of his jacket and on his shirt.

He had killed tonight. And maybe that was why he'd found her.

Well, almost found her.

"John?" a male voice said softly.

She looked over toward the doorway, even if he did not. Qhuinn was standing with the Brothers Rhage and Vishous, having just joined them.

In an absent way, she noted the shock on the Brothers' faces—and got the sense that they hadn't guessed there'd been any serious connection between her and John. They knew it now though. Loud and clear.

As Qhuinn stepped inside and approached the bed, his tone continued to be gentle. "John, we've been here for a half hour. If we're going to interrogate that *lesser* downstairs about her, we need to move him pretty damn quick. We don't want to do it here and I know you want to be in charge of things."

Oh, God . . . no . . .

"Take me with you," Xhex whispered desperately. "Please . . . don't leave me here."

Abruptly, John glanced up at her, as if he heard her plea.

Except no, he was just staring through her to his friend.

As he nodded, she memorized his face, knowing that it was the last time she'd see him. When Lash found out about the break-in, he'd either kill her outright or move her somewhere else—and chances were good she wouldn't survive long enough to be found again.

Lifting her hand, even though it would do no good, she laid it on the side of John's face and swept her thumb back and forth over the tracks of his tears. She imagined she could almost feel the warmth of his skin and the wetness on his cheeks.

She would have given anything to be able to take him into her arms and hold him close. More still to go with him.

"John . . ." she croaked. "Oh, God . . . why are you doing this to yourself."

He frowned, but no doubt it was because of something Qhuinn was saying. Except then his own palm lifted and he placed it where she was touching him.

It was just to sweep his tears away, though.

When he stood up, he took the pillow with him, and he stepped right through her.

Xhex watched his back retreat, her blood thundering in her ears. This was, in some ways, an echo of the process of death, she thought. Little by little, inch by inch, what tied her to life was leaving, heading off, departing. With each step John took toward that door, her breath was evaporating in her lungs. Her heart was stopping. Her skin was growing cold.

Her chance of rescue was walking away. Her chance at . . .

It was then that she knew what she had been fighting all along, and for once, she felt no inclination to hide her emotions. No need to. Though he was with her, she was totally alone and separate from him, but more to the point, her own mortality clarified her priorities.

"John," she said softly.

He paused and looked over his shoulder toward the bed.

"I love you."

His handsome face tightened in pain, and he rubbed the middle of his chest, as if someone had fisted up his heart and squeezed it dead.

And then he turned away.

Xhex's body overrode her mind. With a frantic leap, she ran for the open door, arms outstretched, mouth cranked wide.

As she hit the confines of her prison, she heard a loud noise, like a siren . . . or the shrill whistle of fireworks after they were lit . . . or maybe it was the security system's alarm going off.

But it was none of those.

She was screaming at the top of her lungs.

SIXTEEN

John had to tear himself away from that bedroom. If it hadn't been for the overriding logic and the need to crack open that lesser, he wouldn't have been able to budge his boots an inch.

He could have sworn he felt her presence . . . but he knew that was a mind trick born out of his quest. She wasn't in the room. She'd *been* in the room. Two totally different things . . . and his only chance at finding out what had happened to her was downstairs in the kitchen.

As he headed for the first floor, he rubbed his eyes and his face and found that one hand wanted to linger over his cheek. The skin there was tingling . . . kind of like it did when Xhex had touched him the few times she had.

God . . . the blood in that room. All that blood. She'd been fighting Lash off, and though it was a source of pride to think she'd shanked the fucker a good number of times, he couldn't stand the reality that had rolled out in that bedroom.

John hung a left and stalked through the dining room, trying to get his game head back while feeling as if he'd had his skin stripped off and been thrown raw into the ocean. Pushing through the butler's door into the kitchen—

The instant his eyes locked on the *lesser*, an earthquake ripped through him, his firmament breaking open all the way down to his hot core.

His mouth stretched wide and he let loose a mute bellow.

As he lunged forward, rage punched his fangs out into his mouth and his body went on autopilot, dematerializing through the space, taking form in front of the bastard. Shoving Blay off the slayer, John's bonded vampire attacked with a kind of ferocity he'd heard about . . . but never seen.

Certainly never experienced.

With his vision on whiteout and his muscles energized by mania, he was all action, no thought as he attacked, his hands cranking into claws, his fangs slicing like daggers, his inner wrath so great he was an animal.

He had no idea how long it took him . . . or even what he did. The only thing that registered was the dim awareness that a sweet stench was all he could smell.

Sometime later . . . much later . . . a lifetime later . . . he paused to catch his breath and found that he was down on all fours, his head dangling off the top of his spine, his lungs burning from exertion. His palms were planted on tile that was slick with black blood and something was dripping off his hair and out of his mouth.

He spit a couple of times to try to get rid of a foul taste, but whatever it was, the shit wasn't just around his tongue and teeth; it was down the back of his throat and into his gut. His eyes were also stinging and blurry.

Was he crying again? He didn't feel sad anymore . . . he felt empty.

"Jesus . . . Christ . . ." someone said softly.

Abruptly overcome with exhaustion, John allowed his elbow to go lax and let his weight shift to the side. Laying his head down in a cooling puddle, he closed his eyes. He had no strength. It was all he could do to breathe.

A while later, he heard Qhuinn talking to him. Innate politeness, rather than any clue what was going on, made him nod when there was a pause.

He was momentarily surprised when he felt hands on his shoulders and his legs and his lids managed to flicker open as he was lifted up.

Weird. The countertops and cabinets had been white when they'd first come in. Now . . . they'd been painted in a high-gloss black.

With delirium, he wondered why someone had done that.

Black was hardly a welcoming color.

Closing his eyes, he felt the bumps and shifts as he was carried out and then there was a final hefting followed by his body landing in a heap. Car engine turned over. Doors shut.

They were en route. No doubt back to the Brotherhood compound.

Before he passed out completely, he took his hand and raised it to his cheek. Which made him realize he'd forgotten the pillow.

Coming awake with a flash, he jacked himself up, all Lazarus back from the dead.

Blay was right there with what he'd taken, however. "Here. I made sure we didn't leave without it."

John took what still smelled like Xhex and curled his huge body around it. And that was the last thing he remembered of the trip back home.

When Lash woke up, he was in precisely the same position he'd been in when he'd fallen asleep: flat on his back, arms crossed over his chest . . . like a corpse laid out in a coffin. Back when he'd been a vampire, he'd moved around during the day, usually waking up on his side with his head under a pillow.

As he sat up, the first thing he did was look at the lesions on his chest and stomach. Unchanged. No worse, but unchanged. And his energy level hadn't improved significantly.

In spite of the fact that he'd slept . . . Jesus Christ, three hours? What the hell?

Thank fuck he'd had the sense to postpone that appointment with Benloise. You didn't meet a man like that when you looked and felt like you'd been on a bender for a week and a half.

Shifting his legs off the bed, he braced himself and then pushed his ass free of the mattress, going all the way vertical. As his body weaved, he heard nothing but silence from downstairs. Oh . . . wait. Someone was throwing up. Which meant the Omega had finished his biz with the new recruit and the kid was starting on a fun-filled six to ten hours of vomiting.

Lash picked up his stained shirt and his suit and wondered where in the hell his wardrobe change was. It didn't take three hours for Mr. D to get his ass over to Benloise's, reschedule things, and then head over to the brownstone to feed Xhex and pick out a new set of threads from the closet.

On his way down the stairs, Lash dialed the idiot, and as voice mail kicked in, he snapped, "Where the fuck are my clothes, asshole?"

He hung up and stared through the hall into the dining room. The new recruit was not on the table anymore; he was partially underneath, and huddled over a bucket, dry heaving like there was a rat in his gut that couldn't find either exit.

"I'm leaving you here," Lash said loudly. This caused a pause and the recruit looked over. His eyes were blood-shot and there was something like dirty dishwater running out of his open mouth.

"What's . . . happening to me?" Small voice. Small words.

Lash's hand went to the sore on his chest and he found it difficult to breathe as he thought once again that the recruits were never told the full story. They never knew what to expect or the full value of what they gave up and what they received.

He'd never thought of himself as a recruit before. He was the son, not another cog in the Omega's machine. But how much did he really know?

He forced his hand away from his lesion.

"You're going to be okay," he said roughly. "Everything's . . . going to be okay. You're going to pass out in a little bit and when you wake up . . . you're going to feel like yourself only better."

"That thing . . ."

"Is my father. You're still going to work for me, like I said. That hasn't changed." Lash headed for the door as the urge to run got too strong to fight. "I'll send someone for you."

"Please . . . don't leave me." Watery eyes implored and a stained hand reached out. "Please . . ."

Lash's ribs seized up hard, compressing his lungs to the point of malfunction, until he could draw no more air down his throat.

"Someone will come for you."

Out of the door, out of the house, out of the mess. He hustled for his Mercedes, got behind the wheel, and locked himself in the car. Tearing out of the farm-house's short driveway, it took him about three miles before he could breathe properly and it wasn't until he saw the skyscrapers of downtown that he felt more himself.

As he headed to the brownstone, he called Mr. D two more times and got voice mail, and then . . . voice mail.

Taking a right down the alley to the garage, he was ready to fire the phone out the window in frustration—

Easing off on the gas pedal, he let another car go past him . . . but he didn't slow down just to be courteous to his neighbor's Porsche.

The door to the brownstone's garage was wide open

and Mr. D's Lexus was parked right in there. Not protocol.

That and all the no-answering was a red flag the size of Texas and Lash's first thought was of Xhex. If those motherfucking Brothers had taken her, he was going to stake them out on the lawn and let the sun take them nice and slow.

Closing his eyes, he sent his instincts outward . . . and after a moment, he could sense Mr. D, but the signal was way dim. Nearly imperceptible.

The fucker had obviously been dusted, but not finished off yet.

When a car came up behind him and honked its horn, he realized he was stopped dead in the middle of the lane.

Ordinarily, his first move would have been to pull the Mercedes into the garage and flash into the brownstone with his fists up . . . but he was half-mast at best, all sluggish and woozy. And in the event the Brothers were still inside, now was not the time to engage his enemy.

Even *lessers* could wake up dead. Even the son of the evil could be sent home.

But what about his female?

Dogged by an odd, cold terror, Lash went farther down the alley, and took one right and then another. As he trolled by the front of his house, he prayed like a little bitch that she was still—

Looking up to the windows on the second floor, he saw her in the bedroom—and his relief was so powerful his breath left him on a wheeze. No matter what might have gone down in that house, no matter who had infiltrated, Xhex was still there where he had left her: Her face was plain for him, and only him, to see on the far side of that glass, her eyes lifted up to the sky, her hand raised to her throat.

What a lovely picture, he thought. Her hair was growing out and starting to curl and the moonlight on her high cheekbones and perfect lips was downright romantic.

She was still his.

Lash forced himself to keep driving. The thing was, she was safe where she was—his invisible prison was impenetrable by any vampire or human or *lesser*, whether it was a Brother or just any old schmo with a gun and an attitude.

If he went in there, and got into a skirmish with the Brothers? If he was injured? He was going to lose her, because that spell she was trapped in took energy for him to maintain. He was already having enough trouble summoning the strength to keep it going—and though he despised his weakness, he was a fucking realist.

It killed him to keep going. Absolutely killed him.

But it was the right decision. If he wanted to keep her, he had to leave her behind until dawn cleared that brownstone out.

It took him a while to realize he was driving around aimlessly, but the truth was, the idea of going back to crash at one of those shitty little ranches that the Lessening Society owned made him want to peel the skin off his face.

Man, was the dawn never going to come . . .

On some level, he couldn't believe he was so ball-less as to be pulling a drive-off. But on the other hand, he was having trouble keeping his head up and his eyes open behind the wheel. As he started over Caldwell's westbound bridge, he just didn't get the tired routine. The sores could well be from the battles with Xhex, but the exhaustion was—

The answer occurred to him as he glanced over at the eastbound lanes. It was so obvious and yet it struck him with such force that his foot eased off the accelerator.

East and west. Left and right. Night and day.

Of course feeding from Mr. D had only nominally helped him.

He needed a female. A female *lesser*.

Why hadn't it dawned on him sooner? Male vampires were strengthened only by the blood of the opposite sex. And although his father's side was very much dominant in him, clearly there was enough of the fang left over in there that he needed to feed.

Only after he'd taken Mr. D's vein had he felt even partially satisfied.

Well, didn't this change everything . . . and give Xhex a whole new future.

SEVENTEEN

The sounds of the bloody melee down below had carried up to Xhex's ears, and given the stench that now wafted through the bedroom's doorway, she could only guess what had been done to that little *lesser* who'd brought her food.

Apparently some portion of the first floor had just been redecorated in slayer paisley.

She was surprised that the Brothers had chosen to rip the bastard limb from limb in the house. From what she knew, Butch O'Neal usually inhaled the slayers to keep them from going back to the Omega. But downstairs? She'd be surprised if there was anything left you could pick up without a mop.

Unless it was a message to Lash.

Following the slaughter's loud chaos, there was an odd stretch of quiet and then lots of footfalls. They were leaving now that there was nothing left to kill.

Panic rose again in her chest and the effort of pulling herself back together was nearly physical . . . but goddamn it, she was not going to come undone. All she had in this situation was herself. She was her weapon; her mind and her body were the only things that Lash couldn't take away from her.

She lost them, she was as good as dead.

Fuck that, she lost them and she couldn't take Lash with her when she went.

The reality of the situation was where she found the strength to keep going, the weight on her grounding her emotions when they otherwise would have flown the coop and taken her logic with them. She locked away everything, shutting down anything she'd felt when she'd been beside John Matthew.

Nothing got through. Nothing bubbled up.

Snapping into war mode, she realized she hadn't heard a pop or seen the echo of a flash, so they hadn't stabbed the slayer. And the smell was so vivid, she was betting they were leaving the body behind.

Lash was going to fucking lose it. She'd heard him interacting with the little Texan and although he'd have denied it, he was attached to the bastard. What she needed to do was exploit this weakness in him. Tee him up even further when he got scrambled. Maybe he'd crack in some fundamental way . . .

Amid the silence and the sweet stench, she paced around and ended up at the window. Without thinking of the force field, she put both her hands up and leaned in against the jambs—

Xhex leaped back, expecting a wave of pain.

Instead . . . she just got a tingle.

There was something different about her prison.

Keeping a lid on her head, she came back at the barrier with her palms, pressing them against her containment. Complete and utter objectivity was what she needed to assess things—but it turned out, the change was so obvious that even distracted she would have registered it: There was weakness within the tensile weave of the spell. Unmistakable weakness.

The question was why. And whether it was going to get even looser or this blip was something she needed to take advantage of right now.

Her eyes rimmed the window. Visually, there was nothing out of the norm with her prison and she put her hand up to the glass, just to be sure—yup, she'd been right.

Had Lash died? Been wounded?

At that moment, a big black Mercedes eased by the front of the house, and she sensed the sonofabitch inside. And whether it was because he'd been taking her vein or because the barrier was weakening, his emotional grid was crystal clear to her symphath side: He was feeling isolated. Anxious. And . . . weak.

Well, well, well . . .

Didn't that give credibility to the loosening she'd sensed. And an idea why he wasn't all Johnny-on-the-spot to come get her. If she were Lash, and she were not feeling particularly strong, she would wait for the dawn to come before going inside.

Either that or she would head off and get some serious-ass reinforcements.

But then, that's what they made cell phones for, right?

When the Mercedes left the neighborhood and didn't show signs of returning, she took two steps back from the window. Tensing her thighs, she sank down into a fighter's stance, curling up her fists and angling her body slightly back on her hips. She breathed deep and focused and . . .

Snapping out her right fist with all the strength in her shoulder, she punched the barrier hard enough so that if it had been the jaw of a male, she'd have cracked the fucker into pieces.

The spell stung her back, but all around the room, ripples appeared, her prison cell shimmering as if recalibrating itself after an injury. Before there could be a complete regathering, she pitched another punch—

The glass on the far side of the barrier shattered on impact.

At first, she was struck stupid . . . even as she felt the breeze on her face, and looked down at her now-bleeding knuckles for confirmation there was no other reason why the window had broken.

Holy . . . shit.

Quickly considering her potential exit strategies, she looked over her shoulder at the door John and the Brothers had left open.

The last thing she wanted to do was go out through the house, because she didn't know the layout and had no clue what she was going to run into along the way. But instinct told her she was probably too weak to dematerialize—so if she tried to bust out through the window, she didn't know if she'd be able to pull off a midair disappearance.

In which case she'd yard-sale in the road down below.

The open doorway was her best shot. She could use her own body as a fist, and with a running start, she'd have even more power behind her.

Turning around, she put her shoulder blades against the wall, sucked in a deep breath . . . and sprinted across the room, the balls of her feet driving her weight over the floor, her arms pumping.

She hit the barrier and the pain was incandescent, firing through every single cell in her body, lighting her up from the inside out. The agony blinded her at the same moment that the spell held her in place, trapping her inside its confines and rendering her as good as dead—

Except then there was a tearing as her momentum won out over her prison's invisible bars . . . and goddamn it if she didn't end up on the far side of that bedroom.

As her body broke free, she slammed into the corridor's wall, to the point where she expected to take a layer of paint off with her face and chest as she slid down onto the floor.

With her head spinning and her eyes filled with flashing lights, she kicked her own ass into gear. She was out, but was not free.

Glancing back, she watched the rippling of the spell as it recast itself . . . and wondered if her breaching it didn't send some kind of signal out to Lash.

Go . . . now . . . get out . . . run!

Dragging herself off the floor and down the hall, she hit the stairs on unreliable legs, careening around, stumbling. In the foyer below, the stink of *lesser* blood choked her to the point of gagging, and she moved away from it, although not because of her nose. All of the egress and ingress at the house happened in the back. If she had nothing but a sliver of time on her side, she needed to focus on finding another way out.

Up ahead, the front door was a massive, ornately carved thing, with glass into which iron bars were set. But all they had for locks were simple dead bolts.

Candy-from-a-baby time.

She walked up, put her hand on the Schlage mechanism, and focused what she had left of her energy on shifting the pins. One . . . two . . . three . . . and the fourth.

Throwing the door wide, she had one foot outside when she heard the creak of someone coming into the kitchen.

Oh shit, Lash was back. He'd come back for her.

In a flash she was gone, panic giving her wings that her focused mind put to good use. Given the shape she was in, she knew she wasn't going to make it far and decided the best she could do was her basement place. At least there, she could be safe while she regrouped.

Xhex took form in the sheltered alcove that led down into her studio and sprang the copper locks with her mind. As she went through the door, the motion-sensing lights came on in the whitewashed corridor, and she lifted her arm to shield her eyes as she stumbled down the steps. Locking the door with her thoughts, she tripped forward, becoming dimly aware she had a limp.

The impact of the wall? The scramble down the stairs? Who the fuck knew or cared.

She made it into her bedroom and shut herself in. As

155

the automatic lights came on, she looked at the bed. Clean white sheets. Pillows all arranged. Duvet spread flat.

She didn't make it to the mattress. As her knees gave out, she let herself go, her skeleton collapsing in on itself until she was nothing but a pile of sticks covered by skin.

It was not sleep that claimed her as she hit the floor. But that was okay.

Unconsciousness worked better anyway.

Blaylock reentered the brownstone with Rhage and Vishous a mere twenty minutes after they'd left with John. As soon as they'd gotten him back to the compound safely, they'd returned to finish the sweep of the premises: this time, they were looking for the small stuff like ID, computers, cash, drugs, anything that gave them intel.

Having watched the carnage John Matthew had thrown around, the aftermath barely registered as Blay walked in the kitchen, and immediately started pulling open cupboards and drawers. Vishous headed up to the second floor while Rhage rooted around the front of the house.

He was just finding his groove when Rhage called out, "The front door's wide open."

So someone had been back here since they'd pulled out with John. *Lesser?* Not likely as they would never have left things unsecured. Maybe a human thief? The Brothers hadn't locked up the back when they'd taken off so perhaps someone had waltzed right in.

If it had been a human, what a sight they'd gotten. Might have explained a rushed exit out the other way.

Blay popped his heat just in case there was someone in the house, and with his free hand, he was quick as he rifled around. He found two cell phones in a drawer with the knives, neither of which had chargers—but V would solve that. There were also some business cards by the phone, but they were all for humans in the contracting trade—who had probably been used to work on the brownstone.

He was tackling the cupboards under the counter when he frowned and looked up. Right in front of him was a bowl of fresh apples.

Glancing down in the direction of the stove, he saw some tomatoes. And a loaf of French bread in a paper wrapper.

Straightening, he walked over to the Sub-Zero and cracked the thing open. Organic milk. Takeout from Whole Foods. A fresh turkey ready to be cooked. Smoked Canadian bacon.

Not exactly prisoner food.

Blay looked up at the ceiling, where heavy footsteps sounded out as V went from room to room. Then his eyes traced the kitchen as a whole, from the cashmere dress coat draped over a stool to the copper pans stacked in the open shelving to the coffeepot that had a brew in its belly.

Everything was name-brand and new and neater than a picture out of a catalog.

This was up to Lash's standards for real . . . but *lessers* weren't supposed to be able to eat. So unless he was treating Xhex like a queen, which was highly unlikely . . . someone was chowing down on a regular basis in this house.

The butler's pantry was right off the kitchen and Blay stepped through the wet remains of the slayer to give the shelved room a quick once-over: enough canned foods to keep a household going for a year.

He was on his way out when his eyes caught something on the floor: There was a subtle series of scratches across the otherwise mirror-perfect surface of the hardwood . . . and they were arranged in a half-moon shape.

Blay's knees cracked as he got down on his haunches and shoved aside a canister vacuum cleaner. The bead-board wall looked flush and uninterrupted by any seams that shouldn't have been there, but a quick rapping trip around with his knuckles and he found a hollow space. Taking out his knife, he used the hilt as a sonar device to determine the precise dimensions of the hidden tuck hole; then he flipped the weapon around and penetrated the tongue-and-groove pattern with the tip of the blade.

Forcing open the cover, he took a penlight and flashed it inside.

Trash bag. The Hefty kind that was the color of *lesser* blood.

Dragging it out, he pulled open the drawstring. "Holy . . . shit."

Rhage appeared behind him. "What you got?"

He shoved his hand in and pulled out a palmful of wrinkled bills. "Cash. Lotta cash."

"Grab it. V found a laptop and a broken window upstairs that was not there before. I closed the front door just so no humans get nosy." He checked his watch. "We need to blow before the sun gets rolling."

"Roger that."

Blay grabbed the sack and left the space all open and violated, figuring the more evidence of a break-in, the merrier. Although it wasn't like the bits and pieces of *lesser* could be ignored.

If only he could see Lash's face when the motherfucker came home.

The bunch of them headed out the back into the garden, and he and Rhage dematerialized while Vishous hot-wired the Lexus in the garage so they could confiscate it.

It went without saying that they'd rather stay and wait to see what showed up. But there was no negotiating with the dawn.

Back at the Brotherhood mansion, Blay walked into the foyer with Hollywood and there was a receiving line of people waiting for them. All of the booty got handed over to Butch for processing at the Pit, and as soon as Blay could break away, he went upstairs to John's bedroom.

His knock was answered by a grunt, and as he opened up and walked in, he saw Qhuinn seated in a wing chair by the bed. The lamp on the table next to him cast a yellow pool within the darkness, illuminating both him and the recumbent mountain underneath the duvet.

John was out cold.

Qhuinn, on the other hand, was laying into the Herradura, the bottle of Seleccion Suprema at his elbow, his crystal glass full of the outstanding tequila that had recently become his drink of choice.

Christ, with him sucking back that and John into Jack, Blay was thinking he needed to upgrade his own tipple. Beer abruptly seemed sophomoric.

"How's he doing?" Blay asked softly.

Qhuinn took a sip and swallowed. "Pretty rough. I called Layla. He needs to feed."

Blay approached the bed. John's eyes were not so much closed as on lockdown, his brows drawn so tightly it looked like he was trying to solve a law of physics in his sleep. His face was preternaturally pale, his hair appearing darker in contrast, and his breathing was too shallow. His clothes had been removed and most of the *lesser* blood had been washed off him.

"Tequila?" Qhuinn asked.

Blay held his hand out to the guy without looking, still focused on their buddy. What hit his palm was the glass instead of the bottle, but he didn't care and he drank hard.

Well, at least he knew why Qhuinn liked the stuff.

As he gave the glass back, he crossed his arms over

his chest and listened to the quiet, glugging refill. For some reason, the loose, charming sound of that expensive booze hitting cut crystal eased him.

"I can't believe he cried," Blay murmured. "I mean . . . I can, but it was a surprise."

"She'd obviously been held in that room." The Herradura was put back on the side table with a subtle thump. "And we'd just missed her."

"Did he talk at all?"

"Nope. Not even when I shoved him in the shower and got in with him."

Okay, that was a visual Blay could do without. Good thing John didn't flip that way—

There was a soft knock at the door and then a waft of cinnamon and spice. Blay walked over and let Layla in, bowing to her in deference.

"How may I be of . . ." The Chosen frowned and glanced toward the bed. "Oh, no . . . he is injured?"

As she went over to John Matthew, Blay thought, Yeah, but mostly on the inside.

"Thanks for coming," Qhuinn said as he got up out of his chair. Leaning down over John, he gently pushed on the guy's shoulder. "Hey, my man, can you wake up for a sec."

John roused like he was fighting against a tidal wave, his head lifting slowly, his eyelids flipping up and down like there was a rush of water on his puss.

"Time to feed." Without glancing over his shoulder, Qhuinn motioned for Layla by holding out his hand. "We need you to focus for just a little longer and then we'll leave you alone."

The Chosen paused . . . then stepped forward. She took the outstretched palm slowly, sliding her skin against Qhuinn's and stepping in with a kind of shy beauty that made Blay feel sorry for her.

Going by the blush that suddenly flared in her cheeks,

he had a feeling she, like everyone else, it seemed, had a spark for Qhuinn.

"John . . . my man? Come on, I need you to pay attention here." Qhuinn tugged at Layla so that the Chosen took a seat on the bed, and the instant she got a good look at John, she was all about him.

"Sire . . ." Her voice was quiet and impossibly kind as she pulled up the sleeve of her robe. "Sire, rouse thyself and take what I may give you. Verily, you are in need."

John started to shake his head, but Qhuinn was on it. "You want to go after Lash? Ain't going to be in this shape. You can't lift your fucking head—'scuse the language, Chosen. You need some strength . . . Come on, don't be an asshole, John."

Qhuinn's mismatched eyes shot to Layla as he mouthed, *Sorry*. And she must have smiled at him because for a moment, he tilted his head as if he were struck by her.

Or maybe she'd just mouthed something back.

Had to be it.

Really.

And then both their heads snapped downward and Layla let out a gasp as John's fangs struck deep and he started to take what she offered. Evidently satisfied, Qhuinn returned to where he'd been sitting and refilled his glass. After he'd drunk half, he held it out toward Blay.

Best idea anyone had had in ages. Blay positioned himself against the high back of the wing chair, running one arm along the top of the thing as he took a deep sip, and then another, before passing the tequila back.

They stayed like that, sharing the drink while John fed from Layla . . . and sometime into the process of both nourishments, Blay became aware that he was putting his lips on the very rim Qhuinn was taking from.

Maybe it was the alcohol. Maybe it was the glass. Maybe

it was the fact that from where he stood, with every breath Blay took he smelled Qhuinn's dark scent . . .

He knew he had to leave.

He wanted to support John, but with each passing minute, he was leaning closer and closer and . . . closer to Qhuinn. To the point that as his hand hung over the chair, he was nearly stroking that thick black hair.

"I have to go," he said roughly, returning the glass one last time and heading for the door.

"You okay?" Qhuinn called out.

"Yup. Sleep well and take care, Layla."

"Don't you need to feed?" Qhuinn demanded.

"Tomorrow."

The Chosen said something lovely and pleasant, but there was no turning around. Nope. Couldn't turn around.

And please God, let him not run into anyone out in the hall.

He hadn't checked to see how bad it was, but he knew when he was aroused . . . and that was one thing that, no matter how polite a male was, he couldn't hide in tight leather.

EIGHTEEN

Over on the Far Side, Payne paced around in her mother's fountain, her feet making circles in the pool that caught the falling water. As she splashed, she held her robing aloft and she listened to the colorful birds that sat in the white tree over in the corner. The little ones chirped and carried on, flitting from branch to branch, pecking at each other, fussing with their feathers.

How in the hell they found such limited activity worth waking up for she hadn't a clue.

In the sanctuary there was no conception of time, and yet she wished she had a pocket watch or a chiming clock to figure out how late the Blind King was. They had a standing sparring session every afternoon.

Well, afternoon for him. For her, stuck here on this side, everything was perpetually daytime.

She wondered exactly how long it had been since her mother had sprung her from that deep freeze and allowed her some freedom. No way to know. Wrath had started to show up regularly about . . . fifteen times ago and she'd been reanimated maybe . . . well, long before that. So maybe over six months?

The real question was how long she'd been kept under frosted lock and key—but it wasn't like she was going to ask her mother about that. They weren't talking at all. Until that "divine" female who'd birthed her was prepared to let her out of here, Payne didn't have anything to say.

For truth, the silent treatment didn't seem to be making a difference at all, but she hadn't expected it to.

When your mother-mare was the creator of the race and answerable to no one, even the king . . .

It was rather easy to become trapped in your own life.

As her pace through the fountain intensified and her robing started to get soaked, she leaped out of the pool and jogged around, her fists up in front of her, the punches she threw out pumping the air.

Being the good, dutiful Chosen was not in her hard-wiring, and that was the root of all of the problems between her and her mother. Oh, the waste. Oh, the disappointment.

Oh, do get over it, mother dear.

Those standards of behavior and belief were for someone else. And if the Scribe Virgin had been looking for another robed ghost to drift around like a silent draft through a temperate room, she should have picked another sire for her young.

The Bloodletter's vital makeup was in Payne, the traits of the father carrying through to the next generation—

Payne wheeled around and met Wrath's falling fist with a forearm block and a scissor kick to his liver. The king was quick to retaliate and the hammering elbow that returned at her was a concussion waiting to happen.

Fast duck had her barely out of the way. Another kick from her sent the king jumping back—though he was blind, he had an unerring ability to know precisely where she was in space.

Which meant he would guess she would come at his flank. Indeed, he was already spinning his weight around, ready to punch her with the sole of his boot around the back.

Payne changed her mind, hit the ground, and swept both of her legs out, catching him at the ankle and throwing him off balance. A quick jog to her right and she was out of the way of his huge, lurching body; another leap and she was latched onto his back as he landed hard, his neck caught in a choke hold within the crook of her elbow. To gain extra leverage, she grabbed onto her own wrist and used her other biceps as she pulled against his throat.

The king's way of dealing with it? He turtled on her.

His incredible brute strength gave him the power to get his feet under both their weight and rise up. Then it was a jump in the air that had them landing with her underneath, flattened on the marble.

Hell of a bedding platform—she could practically feel her bones bending.

The king was first and foremost a male of worth, however, and in deference to her inferior muscularity, he never kept her down for long. Which irked her. She'd have preferred a no-holds-barred contest of skill, but there were differences in the sexes that were not negotiable and males were simply bigger and therefore stronger.

As much as she resented the fact of biology, there was nothing to be done about it.

And anytime her superior speed got him a good one, it was extra sweet.

The king was nimble as he popped back to his feet and swung around, his long black hair fanning out in a circle before resetting on his white *judogi*. With the set of dark lenses over his eyes, and that tremendous spread of muscles, he was magnificent, the very best of the vampire bloodlines undiluted with anything human or otherwise.

Although that was part of his problem. She had heard that that blindness of his was the result of all that pure blood.

As Payne went to get up, her back let out a spasm, but she ignored the sharp shooting strike and faced off with her opponent once again. This time, she was the one who came out swinging and chopping, and for a blind male, Wrath's ability to parry her was downright amazing.

Maybe that was why he never complained about his impairment. Then again, they didn't talk much, which was fine with her.

Although she did wonder what his life was like on the Other Side.

How she envied him his freedom.

They continued to go at it, working their way around the fountain, then over to the columns and toward the door that led out into the sanctuary. And back again. And around again.

They were both bruised and bleeding by the finish of the session, but it was no bother. As soon as their hands dropped to their sides and no more hits were exchanged, the injuries would begin to heal up.

The last punch that was thrown was hers and it was a stunner of an uppercut, catching the king's chin like a ball and chain, throwing his head back, that hair once again flying.

They always seemed to agree without speaking when it was time to end.

They cooled down by walking side by side to the fountain, stretching out their muscles, cracking their necks back into place. Together, they washed their faces and fists in the clear, clean water and they dried themselves on soft cloths that Payne had asked to have at the ready.

In spite of the fact that they traded punches and not words, she had come to think of the king as a friend. And to trust him as one.

First time she'd ever had that.

And it was truly just friends. As much as she could admire from afar his considerable physical attributes, there was no spark of attraction between them—and that was part of the reason this worked. She wouldn't have been comfortable any other way.

No, she wasn't interested in something sexual from him or anyone else. Male vampires had a tendency to take over, especially highbred ones. They couldn't help it—it was, once again, a case of what was in the blood determining behavior. She'd had quite enough of someone with an opinion about her life. The last thing she needed was another one of those.

"You okay?" Wrath asked as they sat on the lip of the fountain.

"Yes. You?" She didn't mind that he always asked if she was all right. The first couple of times it had offended her—as if she couldn't handle the post-sparring aches? But then she realized it had nothing to do with her sex—he would have asked it of anyone he so exerted himself with.

"I feel great," he said, his smile revealing tremendous fangs. "That arm bar at the beginning was boss, by the way."

Payne grinned so broadly her cheeks hurt. Which was another reason she liked to be with him. As he couldn't see, there was no reason to hide her emotions—and nothing got her beaming more than him telling her she'd impressed him.

"Well, Your Highness, your turtles always kill me."

Now he was smiling even wider and she was momentarily touched to think her praise meant something to him. "Deadweight has its uses," he murmured.

Abruptly, he turned to her, the dark spectacles he always wore making her think, once again, that he looked cruel. And yet he'd proved that wasn't the case over and over again.

He cleared his throat. "Thanks for this. Things are bad back home."

"How so?"

Now he looked away, as if he were staring at the horizon. Which was likely a holdover from when he hid his emotions from people. "We've lost a female. The enemy has her." He shook his head. "And one of ours is suffering for it."

"Were they mated?"

"No . . . but he's behaving as though they were." The king shrugged. "I missed the connection between them. We all did. But . . . it's there and it came out tonight in a big way."

A hunger for the down-below, for the earthbound lives that were traumatic but vivid, had her leaning in. "What happened?"

The king pushed his hair back, his widow's peak showing starkly against his golden brown skin. "He slaughtered a *lesser* tonight. Just slaughtered the bastard."

"That's his duty, no?"

"It wasn't in the field. It was in the house where the slayers had imprisoned the female. The bastard should have been used for interrogation, but John just lit his ass up. John's a good kid . . . but that kind of bonded-male shit—stuff . . . can be deadly and not in a good way, feel me?"

Memories of being on the Other Side, of righting wrongs and fighting, of—

The Scribe Virgin appeared through the doorway of Her private quarters, Her black robes floating slightly above the marble floor.

The king rose to his feet and bowed . . . and yet somehow didn't appear subservient in the slightest. Another reason to like him. "Dearest Virgin Scribe."

"Wrath, son of Wrath."

And that was . . . it. As you weren't supposed to address any questions to the mother of the race, and as Payne's mother remained silent thereafter, there was a whole lot of nothing but air happening.

Yeah, because—fates preserve us—you wouldn't want to tax that female with any inquiries. And it was clear why the interruption had occurred: Her mother didn't want an intersection between Payne and the outside world.

"I'm going to retire now," Payne said to the king. Because she would not be responsible for what came out of her mouth if her mother dared to dismiss her.

The king put his fist out. "Farewell. Tomorrow?"

"With pleasure." Payne punched her knuckles against his, as he had taught her was customary, and headed for the door that led into the sanctuary.

On the other side of the white panels, the bright green grass was a shock to her eyes and she blinked as she went past the Primale Temple and down to the Chosen's quarters. Yellow, pink, and red flowers grew in random bunches now, cheerful tulips mixing with jonquil and iris.

All spring blooms, if she remembered from her brief time on the earth.

It was always spring here. Ever on the verge, never to reach the full magnificence and brash heat of summer. Or least . . . what she had read summer was like.

The columned building wherein the Chosen resided was cut into cubelike rooms that offered a modicum of privacy to their tenants. Most of the spaces were empty now, and not only because the Chosen were a dying breed. Ever since the Primale had "freed" them, the Scribe Virgin's private collection of ethereal do-nothings were thinning out thanks to trips to the Other Side.

Surprisingly, none of them had chosen to un-Chosen themselves—but unlike before, if they went over to the Primale's private compound, they were allowed back into the sanctuary.

Payne went directly to the baths and was relieved to find she was alone. She knew her "sisters" didn't understand what she did with the king and she'd just as soon enjoy the calming aftermath of the exercise without the eyes of others.

The communal washing suite was set up in a lofty marble space, the huge pool marked with a waterfall at the far end. As with all things in the sanctuary, the laws of rationality didn't apply: The warm, rushing stream pouring over the lip of white stone was ever clean, ever fresh, even though it had no source and no evident drainage.

Taking off her modified robe, which she'd tailored to match Wrath's *judogi*, as he called it, she waded into the pool with her undergarments still upon her. The temperature was always perfect . . . and made her long for a bath that was either too hot or too cold.

In the center of the great marble bowl, the water was deep enough to swim through, and her body relished the stretching motion of her weightless strokes.

Yes, indeed this was the best part of the sparring. Save for when she caught Wrath a good one.

When she got to the waterfall, she waded up toward it and unplaited her hair. It was longer than Wrath's was, and she'd learned to not just braid the stuff, but tuck it up at the base of her neck. Otherwise, it was like handing him a tether to yank her around with.

Under the falling spray, bars of sweet-smelling soap awaited her palm, and she used one all over herself. As she turned around to rinse, she found that she was no longer alone.

But at least the dark-robed figure who had limped in was not her mother.

"Greetings," Payne called out.

No'One bowed, but did not answer, as was her way, and Payne was abruptly sorry that she'd just left her robe on the flooring.

"I can get that," she said, her voice echoing around the cavern.

No'One just shook her head and gathered up the cloth. The maid was so lovely and quiet, doing her duties without complaint even though she had some kind of disability.

Although she never spoke, it wasn't hard to guess what her sad story was.

One more reason to despise She who had birthed the race, Payne thought.

The Chosen, like the Black Dagger Brotherhood, had been bred within certain parameters with a desired result intended. Whereas the males were to be thick of blood and stout of back, aggressive and worthy in battle, the females were calculated to be intelligent and resilient, capable of harnessing the males' baser tendencies and civilizing the race. Yin and yang. Two parts to a whole, with the requirement of blood feedings ensuring the sexes were tied together forever.

But all wasn't well within the divine scheme. The truth was, inbreeding had led to problems, and though in Wrath's case the laws provided that, as son of the king, he was to take the throne with or without impairments, the Chosen were not so lucky. Defects were shunned by the breeding laws. Always had been. And so someone like No'One, who was handicapped, was relegated to serving her sisters under a cloak . . . a hidden, unspoken-of embarrassment that was nonetheless regarded with "love."

Or "pity" was more like it.

Payne knew precisely how the female must feel. Not about a physical defect, but about being relegated to a slot of expectation that one couldn't possibly live up to.

And speaking of expectation . . .

Layla, another of the Chosen, entered the bath and removed her robing, handing it over to No'One with the gentle smile that was her trademark.

The expression was lost as she lowered her eyes and entered the water. Indeed, the female seemed to be tangled in thoughts that were not pleasing.

171

"Greetings, sister," Payne said.

Layla's head whipped up and her brows rose. "Oh . . . verily, I knew not you were herein. Greetings, sister."

After the Chosen bowed deeply, she sat on one of the submerged marble benches, and although Payne wasn't a conversationalist, something about the dense quiet around the other female drew her.

Finishing her rinse-off, she swam over and settled beside Layla, who was sluicing puncture wounds on her wrist.

"Whom did you feed?" Payne asked.

"John Matthew."

Ah, yes, the male to whom the king referred, perhaps. "Did it go as it should?"

"Indeed. It did indeed."

Payne leaned her head back against the edge of the pool and stared at the Chosen's blond beauty. After a moment, she murmured to the female, "May I inquire something of you?"

"But of course."

"Wherefore the sadness. Always with you . . . you return in sorrow." Even though she knew. For a female to be forced into sex and feeding just because it was tradition was an unconscionable violation.

Layla regarded the puncture marks on her vein with a kind of dispassionate absorption, as if she were puzzling over the wounds of another. And then she shook her head. "I shall not bemoan the glory I have been given."

"Glory? Verily, you appear to have been given something else entirely." A curse was more apt.

"Oh, no, 'tis a glory to be of service—"

"For truth, do not hide behind such words when your visage belies your heart. And as always, if you carry criticism of the Scribe Virgin upon your lips, come sit around my fire." As a pair of shocked pale green eyes flipped up, Payne shrugged. "I've made no secret of how I feel. Ever."

"No . . . indeed you have not. It just seems so . . ."

"Unladylike? Inappropriate?" Payne cracked her knuckles. "What a pity."

Layla exhaled long and slow. "I have been properly trained, you know. As an *ehros*."

"And that is what you don't like—"

"Not at all. That is what I don't know, but wish to."

Payne frowned hard. "You are not used?"

"Verily, I was denied by John Matthew on the evening of his transition after I saw him safely through the change. And when I go to feed the Brothers, I am ever untouched."

"I beg your . . ." Was she hearing that right? "You *want* to have sex. With one of them."

Layla's tone turned shrewd. "Surely you of all my sisters understand what it is like to be naught but a potential."

Well . . . hadn't she gotten the scenario all wrong. "With all due respect, I can't fathom why you would want . . . *that* . . . with one of those males."

"Why would I not? The Brothers and those three younger males are beautiful, *phearsome* creatures of strength. And with the Primale leaving us all unserved . . ." Layla shook her head. "To have been well taught and had it described and read about the act . . . I want to experience it for myself. Even if it is but once."

"For truth, I cannot summon even the slightest inclination. Never have, don't think I ever will. I'd rather fight."

"Then I envy you."

"Oh?"

Layla's eyes seemed ancient. "Far better to be uninterested than unfulfilled. One is a relief. The other an emptiness with heavy weight."

As No'One appeared with a tray of cut fruit and fresh juice, Payne said, "No'One, won't you join us?"

Layla smiled up at the maid. "Indeed. Please do."

With a shake of her head and a bow, No'One just left them the repast she had so thoughtfully prepared and went about her business, limping through the archway and out of the baths.

Payne's frown stayed in place as she and the Chosen Layla fell into silence. Mulling over what had been exchanged, it was hard to understand how they could have opinions of such total opposite regard—and both be in the right.

For Layla's sake, Payne wished she herself was wrong; what a disappointment it would be to pine for something that was far, far less than expectation bore it to be.

NINETEEN

"A female . . ." The Omega's soft, echoing voice carried farther than its volume would have suggested, the two words suffusing every corner of the smooth stone room that formed his private chamber.

Lash did his best to appear unconcerned as he lounged against one of the black walls. "I need her to service me for blood."

"Do you."

"It's biology."

In his white robing, the Omega cut a stunning figure as he circulated around the space. With his hood up in place, his arms crossed, and his hands tucked into his billowing sleeves, he resembled a bishop in the game of chess.

Except, of course, he was the king down here.

The evil's receiving area was about the size of a ballroom and decked out like one, with plenty of black chandeliers and stanchions that supported legions of black candles. It was far from stark, however. For one thing, those wicks were spouting red flames. And to top it off, the walls and floor and ceiling were made of the most extraordinary marble Lash had ever seen. From one angle it was black, from another it was metallic bloodred, and given that the source of illumination was constantly flickering, you got both colors at once all around you.

It wasn't hard to figure out the why of the decor. Given the Omega's wardrobe, which was limited to those driven-snow drapery things, he was the prime focal point, the only thing that stood out. The rest was window dressing.

He ran his world like that, too.

"And would this be a mate for you, my son?" the Omega asked from way across the room.

"No," Lash lied. "Just a blood source."

You did not give the Omega more information than you had to: Lash was well aware of how fickle his father could be and off-the-radar was key.

"Have I not given you enough strength?"

"My vampire nature is what it is."

The Omega turned and faced Lash. After a pause, that distorted voice whispered, "Indeed. I find that to be true."

"I'll bring her to you," Lash said, straightening from the wall. "To the farmhouse. Tonight. You turn her and I'll have what I need."

"And I cannot provide that to you?"

"You would be providing it to me. You induct her and I have the blood source required to give me power."

"So you say that you are weak?"

Damn him to hell, but it must be obvious that he was. The Omega could sense things and surely it had been apparent for some time now.

When Lash stayed quiet, the Omega drifted forward until they were eye to eye. "I have never inducted a female."

"She wouldn't have to be in the Lessening Society. She would just be for me."

"For you."

"No reason to have her out there fighting."

"And this female. You have chosen her already."

"I have." Lash laughed shortly, thinking of Xhex and the damage she was capable of. "I'm sure you'll approve of her."

"You are so certain."

"I have very good taste."

All around, the red flames trembled on their wicks as if a breeze had ruffled them.

Abruptly, the Omega's hood lifted, revealing the shadowy, translucent face that had angles just like Lash's flesh-and-blood version did.

"Return from whence you came," the Omega pronounced as his dark, smoky hand rose up. With a stroke down Lash's cheek, the evil turned away. "Return from whence you came."

"I'll meet you at nightfall," Lash said. "At the farmhouse."

"Night. Fall."

"You want it later? How about one. We'll see each other then."

"You shall see me, indeed."

"Thank you, Father."

As the Omega drifted across the floor, that hood settled back into place of its own volition, and a panel slid open across the way. A moment later, Lash was alone.

Taking a deep breath, he rubbed his face and looked around at all the red flames and the spectacular walls. The place was kind of like a womb.

With a flash of will, he shot himself out of *Dhunhd* and back to the nasty little ranch house he'd had to use as a launching pad. As he came awake in his corporeal form, he hated the fact that he was stretched out on a couch that had cheesy autumnal leaves on its slipcover. And God, the nap of the fabric was like a buzz cut on a dog . . . and smelled the same, really.

Assuming said four-legged fucker had rolled in a damp ashtray.

Lifting his head up, he pulled his shirt to his neck. Still there. The lesions were still there and getting larger. And he felt like ass.

His hands shook as he got himself vertical, and

when he checked his phone, he saw nothing from anybody. No voice mail back from Mr. D and no other slayers checking in. Both made sense. Everyone and everything was routed through his second in command so if the SOB had bit it, the Society couldn't find Lash.

Maybe the little Texan had been too good as a PA.

With hunger spurring him on, he shuffled into the kitchen and peeled open the refrigerator door. Empty. Except for a box of Arm & Hammer baking soda that should have been used on that couch.

Slamming the Frigidaire shut, he absolutely despised the world and everyone in it—although that was mostly a function of not having his eggs and bacon already waiting for him.

Plus crappy real estate did that to a guy. The ranch house was a new acquisition and one he'd been to only once before—hell, not even Mr. D knew the Society owned it. The thing was, Lash had bought it out of foreclosure because they were going to need places to make meth and the POS had a large basement. Stunning that whoever had owned it hadn't been able to cover the mortgage cost. The bitch was one step up from an outhouse.

Maybe half a step.

He headed out into the garage and it was a frickin' relief to be back in the Mercedes . . . although it galled him to have to hit a McDonald's drive-through for an Egg McMuffin and a coffee. He'd even had to wait in line along with a bunch of guys in trucks and moms in minivans.

As he went back to his brownstone, his attitude sank further into Manson territory—and then shot completely into the sewer as he pulled up to the garage. The door was still up, but the Lexus was gone.

Parking the Mercedes under cover, he shut the thing

in with the remote and got out. The garden in the back was relatively undisturbed, but he could smell the *lesser* the instant he—

Stopping on the terrace, his eyes shot to the second floor. Oh, God . . .

Energized by panic, Lash started to run full tilt and he took the back steps on a oner, bursting through the door—

His loafers skidded to a halt as he saw the carnage. Jesus . . . Christ . . . *his kitchen.*

The place looked like it had been hit with an oil shower. And duh, there wasn't much left of Mr. D. The slayer's torso was in the middle of the room, by the island, but his arms and legs were scattered all around . . . and his digestive tract was like macramé hanging from the pulls on the cupboards.

By some miracle, the guy's head was still attached and his eyes opened wide, his mouth starting to move as he saw he was no longer alone; a guttural plea came out of lips glossy with congealed black blood.

"You fucking pussy," Lash spat. "Look at you. For fuck's sake!"

And goddamn it, he had bigger problems than his second in command getting shredded. He leaped over the mess, tore through the dining room, and raced up the stairs.

Bursting into the bedroom he'd shared with Xhex, he found nothing but a whole lot of empty . . . and a window with a hole in it.

"Motherfucker!"

Wheeling around, he looked through the open door and saw the mark outside on the hall wall. Stalking over, he pressed his nose against the silk wallpaper and inhaled. Her scent was in the fibers of the weave.

She had broken out physically.

Yet she'd still been in the room after Mr. D had been

attacked. Had the Brothers come back and helped her get out?

A quick run through the house and Lash's mood went from nasty to toxic. Laptop gone. Cell phones missing.

Mother*fucker.*

Down in the kitchen, he headed into the pantry to get the—

"Oh, fuck me!" Kneeling down, he checked out the panel that had been torn open. His stash was gone, too? How the hell had they found it?

Then again, Mr. D looked like an anatomy class had had at him. Maybe he'd spilled. Which meant Lash couldn't be sure what other addresses had been compromised.

On a burst of rage, he threw his fist out, winging it hard and catching whatever he did.

A massive glass jar of olives.

The thing shattered, juice going everywhere, those little eyelike rollers hitting the floor and making bids for freedom in all directions.

Lash stomped back into the kitchen and went over to Mr. D. As that bloody mouth started working again, the pitiful struggle was positively nauseating.

Reaching over the counter, Lash extracted a Henckels, palmed the hilt, and sank down. "Did you tell them anything?"

As Mr. D shook his head, Lash stared down into the guy's eyes. The whites were darkening to a gray shade and the pupils had dilated to the point where there was almost no iris. However, although he appeared to be on the brink of demise, left on his own, Mr. D would languish and rot forever in this condition. There was only one way to "kill" him.

"Are you sure?" Lash murmured. "Even when they pulled your arms out of those sockets?"

Mr. D's mouth moved, the gurgling sounds like wet dog food falling out of a can.

With a revolted curse, Lash stabbed the empty chest of that *lesser*, getting rid of at least that part of the mess. The pop and flash both faded quickly and then Lash shut himself in, locking the back door before heading up for the second floor once again.

It took him a half hour to pack his clothes, and as he muscled six Prada duffels down the stairs, he couldn't remember when he'd ever had to carry his own luggage.

After lining up his load out on the back step, he set the security alarm, locked up, and shuffled his shit to the Mercedes.

As he drove away, he hated the idea of returning to that fucking ranch. But at the moment, he was out of options—and had other things to fucking worry about rather than where he stayed.

He needed to find Xhex. If she'd been on her own, there was no way she could have gone far. She'd been too weak. So the Brotherhood had to have her.

Jesus Christ . . . with his father showing up at one a.m. for the induction, he had to get her back fast. Either that or find someone he could make do with.

The knock that woke John up was a real knuckle-bouncer, loud as a gun.

The instant he heard it, he was totally upright. As he rubbed his eyes, he whistled a "come in" and prayed it was nothing but Qhuinn with a tray of First Meal.

The door wasn't opened.

John frowned and dropped his hands.

Shifting to his feet, he grabbed a pair of jeans and pulled them up to his hips, then went over and . . . Wrath was standing in the doorway with George by his side, and he was not alone. The boys and Rehvenge were with him, as were all of the other Brothers, including Tohr.

Oh . . . God . . . no.

His hands signed fast even as his heart stopped dead. *Where was the body found?*

"She's alive," Rehvenge answered as he held out a phone. "I just got the message. Hit four."

John took a second to internalize the information. Then he snapped the cell out of the male's hand and punched the key. There was a beep and then . . .

Holy shit . . . her voice. *Her voice.*

"Rehv . . . I'm out. I got out." There was a low, deep sigh. "I'm okay. I'm intact. I'm out." Long pause. To the point that John was about to check to see if the— "I need some time. I'm safe . . . but I'm not coming back for a little while. I need some time. Tell everyone . . . tell . . . everyone. I'll be in touch." Another pause and then her voice grew strong to the point of anger. "As soon as I can . . . Lash is mine. Do you understand me? No one takes him out but me."

The message ended.

John hit four again and listened.

After the second time, he handed the thing back to Rehv and met those amethyst eyes head-on. He was well aware Rehv had been around Xhex for years and years. Knew the guy shared not just experience with her but the *symphath* blood that in many ways changed everything. Knew that the male was older and wiser and all that shit.

But the bonded male in John put them on equal footing when it came to her.

And then some.

Where would she go? he signed.

After Qhuinn translated, Rehv nodded. "She's got a hunting cabin about fifteen miles north of here. On the Hudson River. I'm thinking that's where she is. She'd have access to a phone there and it's safe. I'm going up at nightfall alone. Unless you join me."

No one seemed surprised by the exchange . . . but then

John realized his secret had to be out. After the way he'd behaved up in that bedroom at the brownstone— to say nothing of how he'd torn into that *lesser*, they all knew how he felt about Xhex.

That was the reason the group had come. They were recognizing his status, paying it due. The rights and boundaries of bonded males were respected when it came to their females.

John glanced at Qhuinn and signed, *Tell him I'll go.*

After his boy translated, Rehv nodded and then turned to Wrath. "I go with him and him alone. He can't bring Qhuinn. We're going to have enough trouble with her if the pair of us show up unannounced."

Wrath frowned. "Damn it, Rehv—"

"She's a flight risk. I've been through this once before with her. Anyone else shows, she's going to bolt and she's not going to call again. Besides, John here . . . he'll follow me anyway, won't you, son. You'll ditch Qhuinn and follow me anyway."

John didn't hesitate to nod.

As Qhuinn cursed like a motherfucker, Wrath shook his head. "Why in the hell I gave you him as an *ahstrux . . .*"

There was a period of tense silence, during which the king measured both John and Rehv. Then he said, "Oh, for fuck's sake, fine—I'll let you go without your guard this one time, but you do not engage the enemy. You go to that cabin, and only there, and then you come back and get Qhuinn before you head out into the field. We clear?"

John nodded and turned away to hit the bathroom.

"Ten minutes," Rehv said. "You got ten minutes and we're driving out."

John was ready in four and downstairs pacing the foyer in six. He was fully weaponized, as was protocol, and covered in protective leather. More to the point, he was alive to the point of mania, his blood humming at a tornadic pitch.

As he paced, he felt eyes on him. From the billiard room. From the dining room. From up above on the second floor's balcony. Silent mouths, but eyes that missed nothing.

The Brotherhood and the other members of the house were clearly reeling from the Xhex connection and he supposed he could understand. Surprise! He'd bonded with a *symphath*.

But you couldn't help who you fell in love with—or change the feelings of someone who didn't love you back.

God, not that that part mattered. *She was alive!*

Rehvenge came down the grand stairs, his red cane hitting the carpeted steps every time his right foot came forward. He was dressed not for war, but for warmth, his floor-length mink skimming the tops of his wingtips and the cuffs of his elegant black suit.

As he came up to John, he just nodded and opened the way into the vestibule. Together, they stepped through and penetrated the cool night.

The air smelled like clean, unfrozen earth.

The perfume of spring. The very scent of hope and rebirth.

Walking over to the Bentley, John drew the fragrance into his lungs and held it there as he told himself that Xhex was doing the very same thing on this very same night.

And not because she was buried underground.

Tears pricked his eyes as gratitude washed through every vein he had, pumped around by a singing heart.

He couldn't believe he was going to get to see her . . . God, to see her once again. To look into her gunmetal eyes. To . . .

Shit, it was going to be hard not to throw his arms around her and hold her until tomorrow morning. Or maybe next week.

When they got into the car, Rehv started the engine, but didn't put it in drive. He just stared out through the windshield at the cobblestone drive ahead.

In a quiet voice, he said, "How long's this been going on for you? With her."

John took out a small pad he'd brought with him and wrote: *Since the moment I first met her.*

After Rehv read the scribble, he frowned. "She feel the same way?"

John did not drop his eyes as he shook his head. No sense hiding shit. Not with a *symphath*.

Rehv nodded once. "That's so like her. Goddamn it . . . okay, let's do this."

With a roar, they were off into the night.

TWENTY

Hope was a treacherous emotion.

It was two evenings hence when Darius finally walked into the home of the abducted female's family, and as the grand door opened to both himself and Tohrment, they were met by a doggen whose eyes were filled with the tragedy of hope. Verily, the butler's expression was of such high regard, it was clear he felt he was ushering into his master's house saviors, rather than mortals.

Only time and the vagaries of fortune would bear out whether his faith was well- or misplaced.

With alacrity, Darius and Tohrment were led into a formal study and the gentlemale who rose from a silk-covered sitting chair had to steady his weight.

"Welcome, sires, thank you for coming," Sampsone said as he reached out with both palms to shake Darius's hands. "I'm sorry that I have not been receiving these last two evenings. My beloved shellan . . . *"*

The male's voice cracked and in the silence, Darius stepped aside. "May I present my colleague, Tohrment, son of Hharm."

As Tohrment bowed low with his hand over his heart, it was clear that the son had all the manners his sire did not.

The master of the house returned the deference. "Would you care for libations or gastronomic provision?"

Darius shook his head and took a seat. As Tohrment came to stand behind him, he said, "Thank you. But mayhap we could speak of what has happened within this manse."

"Yes, yes, of course. What may I tell you?"

"All things. Tell us . . . all things."

"My daughter . . . my light in the darkness . . ." The male

took out a handkerchief. "*She was of worth and virtue. A more caring female you should never come across . . .*"

Darius, aware that they'd already lost two evenings, allowed the father a certain time of remembrance before refocusing him. "*And that night, sir, that terrible night,*" he cut in when there was a pause. "*What happened here within this house?*"

The male nodded and dabbed at his eyes. "*She awoke from her slumbers feeling a certain disquiet and was advised to attend to her private quarters for her health. She was brought a meal at midnight and then another well before the dawn's arrival. That was the last she was seen. Her evening quarters are upstairs, but she also has, along with the rest of the family, rooms underground. She often elected not to move down below with us for the day, however, and as we have access to her through inner hallways, we assumed she would be safe enough—*"

The male choked up at this point. "*How I wish I had insisted.*"

Darius could very much understand the regret. "*We shall find your daughter. One way or the other, we shall find her. Would you permit us to go now unto her bedroom?*"

"*Please do.*" As the male nodded at his *doggen*, the butler came forward. "*Silas will be pleased to escort you. I shall . . . prefer to wait here.*"

"*But of course.*"

When Darius stood up, the father reached forward and snagged his hand. "*A word, if I may? Between you and me.*"

Darius acquiesced, and after Tohrment and the *doggen* left, the master of the house collapsed back into his formal chair.

"*Verily . . . my daughter was of worth. Of virtue. Untouched by . . .*"

In the pause that stretched out, Darius knew what the male was concerned with: If they didn't get her back in that virginal condition, her honor, as well as the family's, was in jeopardy.

"*I cannot say this in front of my beloved* shellan," the male continued. "*But our daughter . . . If she has been defiled . . . perhaps it would be better to leave . . .*"

Darius's eyes narrowed. "You would prefer her not be found."

Tears sprang up in those pale eyes. "I . . ." Abruptly, the male shook his head. "No . . . no. I want her back. No matter the outcome, no matter her condition . . . of course I want my daughter."

Darius was not inclined to offer support—that such a denial of his blooded child had even crossed the male's mind was grotesque. "I should like to go to her room now."

The master of the house snapped his fingers and the doggen stepped back into the archway of the study.

"This way, sire," the butler said.

As he and his protégé were taken through the house, Darius scanned the reinforced windows and doors. There was steel everywhere, either separating the panes of glass or fortifying the stout oak panels. To get in without welcome would not be easy . . . and he was willing to bet that every room on the second and third floors was similarly well-appointed—as were the servants' quarters.

He also measured every painting and rug and precious object as they ascended. This family was high up within the glymera, with coffers choked with coin and an enviable blood-line. Thus, the fact of their unmated daughter going missing affected more than just their heartstrings: She was a marketable asset. With this sort of background, a female of mate-able age was a thing of beauty . . . and social and finan-cial implication.

And that was not the full extent of it. As with all such valuations, the converse was true as well: To have such a daughter ruined, either in fact or by rumor, was a taint that would take generations to even dim. The master of this mansion no doubt loved his daughter honestly, but the weight of all this distorted the relationship.

Darius quite believed that in the male's eyes it was better that she come home in a pine box as opposed to breathing, but defiled. The latter was a curse, the former a tragedy that would garner much sympathy.

Darius hated the glymera. *He truly did.*

"Here are her private quarters," the doggen *said, swinging open a door.*

As Tohrment stepped inside the candlelit room, Darius asked, "Have these been cleaned? Have they been tidied since she was herein?"

"Of course."

"Leave us, please?"

The doggen *bowed deeply and disappeared.*

Tohrment wandered around, looking at the silk draperies and the beautifully appointed sitting area. A lute was in one corner and a fine piece of needlework that was partially completed in another. Books by human authors were stacked neatly on shelves along with scrolls in the Old Language.

The first thing one noticed was that nothing was out of place. But whether that was a case of the staff or the circumstance of the disappearance, it was hard to know.

"Touch nothing, yes?" Darius said to the boy.

"But of course."

Darius went into the lush bedroom. The draperies were made of thick, heavy tapestry such that the sunlight couldn't hope to penetrate and the bed was ringed with more of the same, great panels of cloth hanging from the canopy.

Over at the wardrobe, he pulled open the carved doors. Gorgeous gowns in sapphire and ruby and citrine and emerald hung together, full of beautiful potential. And a single empty hanger rested on a hook on the inside of the panels, as if she had taken the night's choice from its padded shoulders.

The dressing table had a hairbrush on it and various pots of unguents and scented oils and tinting powders. All of which were arranged in neat rows.

Darius pulled open a drawer . . . and let out a soft curse. Jewelry cases. Flat leather jewelry cases. He picked one up, popped the golden clasp, and lifted the lid.

Diamonds gleamed in the candlelight.

As Darius returned the box to its comrades, Tohrment stopped in the doorway, his eyes focusing on the fine woven rug that was done in peaches, yellows, and reds.

The faint blush on the male's face made Darius sad for some reason. "You've never been in a female's boudoir then?"

Tohrment got even redder. "Ah . . . no, sire."

Darius motioned with his hand. "Well, this is business. Best to put aside any shyness."

Tohrment cleared his throat. "Yes. Of course."

Darius went over to the two sets of French doors. Both opened onto a terrace and he went out with Tohrment right on his heels.

"You can see through the distant trees," the boy murmured, walking to the balcony.

Indeed one could. Through the spindly arms of the leafless branches, the mansion on another property was visible. The great house was of comparable size and distinction, with fine metalwork on its turrets, and gracious grounds . . . but as far as Darius was aware, it was not inhabited by vampires.

He turned away and walked the length of the terrace, inspecting all the windows and all the doors and all of the handles, hinges, and locks.

There had been no kind of break-in, and given how cold it was, she wouldn't have tallied with anything wide open to the elements.

Which meant she had either left of her own volition . . . or let whoever had taken her in. Assuming the entrance had been gained up here.

He looked through the glass into her rooms, trying to imagine what had transpired.

To hell with the ingress, the exit was more the point, wasn't it. Highly unlikely the abductor would have dragged her out through the house: She must have been spirited away during darkness or else she would have been burned to ash and there were always people out and about during the night hours.

No, he thought. They had to have left from this suite of rooms.

Tohrment spoke up. "Nothing is disturbed, inside or out. No scratches on the floors or marks on the wall, which means . . ."

"She may well have let them in and not struggled o'er much."

Darius went back inside and picked up the hairbrush. Fine strands of pale hair were caught in the stiff bristles. Not a surprise, as both of the parents were fair.

The question was, what caused a female of worth to bolt out of her family's house right before dawn, leaving nothing in her wake . . . and taking nothing with her?

One answer came to mind: a male.

Fathers didn't necessarily know all of their daughters' lives, did they.

Darius stared out into the night, tracing the grounds and the trees . . . and the mansion next door. Threads . . . there were threads to the mystery herein.

The answer he was searching for was here somewhere. He just had to stitch it all together.

"Where to?" Tohrment asked.

"We shall confer with the servants. Privately."

For the most part, in houses such as this one, the doggen would never dream of speaking anything out of turn. But these were not normal circumstances and it was entirely possible that pity and compassion for the poor female would override the staff's reticence.

And sometimes the back of the house knew things the front did not.

Darius turned away and strode for the door. "We shall become lost now."

"Lost?"

They stepped out together and Darius looked up and down the hallway. "Indeed. Come this way."

He chose the left because, in the opposite direction, there was a set of double doors that led out onto another second-story terrace—so it was obvious the staff stairwell wasn't down there. As they walked along, passing many well-appointed rooms, his heart ached such that his breath became tight. After two decades, *his losses registered still, his fall from his station echoing as yet along the bones of his body. His mother he missed the most, 'twas true. And behind that pain was the demise of the civilized life he had once lived.*

He did what he was trained and born to do for the race, and he fed certain . . . indulgences, and he had earned a respect from his comrades at war. But there was no joy for him in this existence of his. No wonder. No captivation.

Had it all just been about pretty things to him? Was he that shallow? If he someday had a big, lovely house with countless rooms filled with fine things, would he be light of heart?

No, he thought. Not if there was no one under the lofty ceilings.

He missed people of like minds living together, a community held within stout walls, a group that was family both by blood and choice. Indeed, the Brotherhood did not live together, as it was viewed by Wrath the Fair as a risk to the race—if their position was compromised to the enemy in some way, all of them would be exposed.

Darius could understand the thinking, but he wasn't sure he agreed with it. If humans could live in fortified castles among their own battlefields, vampires could do the same.

Although the Lessening Society was a far more dangerous foe, to be accurate.

After going along the corridor for some time, they finally encountered what he had hoped to find: a flap panel to a back stairwell that was utterly unadorned.

Following the pine steps downward, they went into a small kitchen and their emergence stopped the meal that was in progress at the long oak table across the way. The assembled doggen *dropped their mugs of ale and chunks of bread and shot to their feet.*

"Verily, resume your imbibing," Darius said, urging them with his hands to sit back down. "We should wish to speak to the second-floor steward and the daughter's personal maid."

All resumed their places along the benches save for two, a female with white hair, and a young male with a kind face.

"If you could suggest a place of some privacy?" Darius said to the steward.

"We have a sitting room through there." He nodded toward a door by the hearth. "You shall have what you seek therein."

Darius nodded and addressed the maid, who was pale and shaky, as if she were in trouble. "You have done naught wrong, dear one. Come, this shall be quick and painless, I assure you."

Better to start with her. He wasn't sure whether she would make it through waiting for them to finish with the steward.

Tohrment opened the way and in the three of them went, to a parlor with as much character as a blank sheaf of parchment.

As was always true in big estates, the family's rooms were done up to luxurious effect. And the staff's were nothing but utility.

TWENTY-ONE

As Rehv's Bentley pulled off Route 149 North and eased onto a narrow dirt road, John leaned forward toward the windshield. The headlights hit bare tree trunks as the sedan snaked closer and closer to the river, the landscape overgrown and unwelcoming.

The small hunting cabin that was revealed was absolutely, positively nothing worth noticing. Small, dark, and unassuming, with a detached garage, it was rustic, but in perfect condition.

He had the car door open before the Bentley was in park and he was walking for the front entrance before Rehv was out from behind the wheel. The overriding sense of dread he got was actually a good sign. He'd felt the same thing up at the *symphath* camp and it made sense that she would protect her private quarters with a similar force field.

The sound of his boots was loud in his ears as he crossed the packed earth of the drive and then all went quiet as he hit the scruffy brown grass of the shallow lawn. He didn't knock, but reached for the knob and willed the lock free.

Except . . . it didn't budge.

"You're not going to be able to get in there with your head." Rehv came up with a copper key, put the thing to use, and opened the way.

As the stout, solid door was pushed aside, John frowned into the darkness and cocked his head, expecting an alarm to go off.

"She doesn't believe in them," Rehv said quietly—

before catching John as he went to rush in. On a louder note, the male called out, "Xhex? Xhex? Put the gun down—it's me and John."

His voice didn't sound right somehow, John thought.

And there was no reply.

Rehv hit the lights and released John's arm as they both went inside. The kitchen was nothing but a stretch of galley with the bare essentials: gas oven, older refrigerator, stainless-steel sink that was functional, not chic. But everything was spotless and there was no clutter at all. No mail, no magazines. No weapons left out.

Musty. The air was still and musty.

Across the way, there was a single large room with a bank of windows that faced the water. Furniture was minimal: nothing but two wicker chairs, a rattan couch, and a short table.

Rehv walked right through, heading for a single closed door to the right. "Xhex?"

Again with that voice. And then the male put his palm on the jamb and leaned in to the panels, closing his eyes.

On a shudder, Rehv's huge shoulders lowered.

She wasn't there.

John strode forward, and went for the handle, pushing his way into her bedroom. Empty. And so was the bathroom beyond.

"Goddamn it." Rehv turned on his heel and strode off. When a door slammed on the river side of the cabin, John figured the guy had gone out onto the porch and was staring at the water.

John cursed in his head as he looked around. Everything was neat and tidy. Nothing out of place. No windows cracked for fresh air or doors that had been recently opened.

The fine dust on the knobs and the fastenings told him that.

She might have been here, but she was gone now. And if she had come, she hadn't stayed long or done much, because he could detect nothing of her scent.

He felt like he'd lost her all over again.

Christ, he'd thought that her being alive would be enough to carry him through—but the idea she was somewhere on the planet and yet not with him was strangely crippling. Plus he felt blinded by the situation; he still didn't know the hows and whats and wheres of any of it.

Flat out sucked, to be honest.

Eventually, he went out to join Rehv on the little porch. Grabbing his pad, he scribbled quickly and prayed to hell the *symphath* could understand where he was coming from.

Rehv looked over his shoulder and read what John held up. After a moment, he said, "Yeah. Sure. I'll just tell them she wasn't here and you came with me to go eat at iAm's place. It'll buy you a good three, four hours of space minimum."

John put his palm over his pec and bowed deeply.

"Just don't go out fighting. I don't need to know where you're going, that's your biz. But if you get yourself killed, I got ninety-nine problems and you're the biggest one of them." Rehv looked back out to the river. "And don't worry about her. She's done this once before. This is the second time she's been . . . taken away like that."

John's hand snatched out and grabbed hard onto the male's forearm. Rehv didn't even flinch . . . then again, there were rumors he couldn't feel anything because of what he did to control his *symphath* side.

"Yup. This is number two. She and Murhder had been going together—" As John's fangs made an appearance, Rehv smiled a little. "That's long passed. No need to worry there. But she ended up heading to the colony for family reasons. They played her, though, and wouldn't let her out. When Murhder went up to get her, the *symphaths* snatched him as well, and shit got critical. I had to make a bargain to get them both out, but her family sold her at the last second, right out from under my nose."

John swallowed hard and signed without thinking. *To who?*

"Humans. She got herself free, though, just like she did this time. And then she went away for a while." Now Rehv's amethyst eyes flashed. "She'd always been tough, but after whatever those humans did to her, she got hard."

When, John mouthed.

"Some twenty years ago." Rehv resumed staring out at the water. "FYI, she wasn't kidding in that message. She's not going to appreciate anyone coming in and being her hero with Lash. She's going to have to do that herself. You want to help the situation? Let her come to you when she's ready—and stay out of her way."

Yeah, well, she probably wasn't going to be in a hurry to text his ass, John thought. And as for the Lash thing? He wasn't sure he could let that one go. Even for her.

To cut off his own thinking, John put out his palm. The two of them met chest-to-chest in a brief hug and then John dematerialized.

When he took form, he was back at the Xtreme Park, behind the shed, looking out over the empty ramps and bowls. The head drug pusher wasn't back. No skating, either. Both made sense. Raid the night before with a shitload of cops coming? To say nothing of the bullet shower?

Place was going to be a ghost town for a while.

John leaned against rough wood, his senses alert. He was aware of time passing, both because of the position of the moon pinwheeling in an arc overhead, and because his brain downshifted from manic spin to a more reasonable churn. Which still sucked but was easier to sit with.

She was out and he didn't even know what condition she was in. Was she hurt? Did she need to feed? Did—

Right. Time to stop playing that loop.

And he probably should take off. Wrath had been pretty damned clear about that no-fighting-without-Qhuinn business and this would still be considered a hot spot for the enemy.

Abruptly, he realized where he had to go.

Pushing himself out of his lean, he paused and looked around with a frown. The sensation of being watched, of being followed, cloaked him once again—just like it had back at that tat shop.

Tonight, however, he just didn't have the energy to support a good dose of paranoia, so he simply dematerialized, figuring whoever or whatever it was would either track him again or he'd lose them in the ether—and he didn't care which it would be.

He was pretty fucking worn-out.

When he took form again, he was a mere handful of blocks from where he'd done the number on that *lesser* the night before. From the inner pocket of his leather jacket, he took out a copper key that was just like the one Rehv had put to use on the hunting cabin.

He'd had the thing for about a month and a half. Xhex had given it to him the night he had told her she could trust him with her *symphath* secret, and like her cilices, he took it with him wherever he went.

Ducking under the stairs of a brownstone, he inserted the sliver of metal and opened the door. The lights in the basement hall were motion-activated and the stretch of whitewashed stone was instantly illuminated.

He was careful to lock up behind himself and then he went down to the only door.

She had given him sanctuary in this private place once

before. Had granted him access to her basement room when he had needed to be alone. And when he'd taken advantage of the hospitality, it had led to her taking his virginity.

She'd refused to kiss him, though.

The same key worked in the door to the bedroom, the locking mechanism shifting smoothly. As he swung the metal panels wide, the light came on and he stepped in—

John died a little at what he saw on the bed: His heart and breath stopped, his brain waves ceased, his blood froze in his veins.

Xhex's bare-naked body was curled up on the sheets.

As the room was flooded with illumination, her hand tightened on the gun that lay flat on the mattress and was pointed at the door.

She didn't have the strength to lift either her head or the weapon, but he was highly confident she could pull that trigger.

Raising up his arms and showing his palms, he stepped to the side and kicked the door shut to protect her.

Her voice was barely a whisper. "John . . ."

A single, bloodred tear pooled in the eye he could see and he watched it slowly ease over the bridge of her nose and drop onto the pillow.

Her hand retreated from the weapon and went to her face, moving inch by inch, as if it took all she had in her to draw it upward. She covered herself the only way she was able, her shield of palm and fingers hiding her tears from him.

She was marked all over with welts and bruises in various stages of healing and she'd lost so much weight, her bones seemed about to break through her flesh. Her skin was gray instead of a healthy pink and her natural scent was nearly nonexistent.

She was dying.

The horror of it all weakened his knees to the point that he listed and had to catch himself back against the door.

But even as he wobbled, his mind kicked into gear. Doc Jane needed to come look at her and Xhex needed to feed.

They didn't have a lot of time left.

If she was going to live, he was going to have to take charge here.

John ripped off his leather jacket and yanked up his sleeve as he headed to her. The first thing he did was gently cover her nakedness by folding the top sheet across her. The second was shoving his cocked wrist right up to her mouth . . . and waiting for her instincts to take over.

Her mind might not want him, but her body was not going to be able to resist what he had to offer.

Survival always won out over matters of the heart. He was living proof of it.

TWENTY-TWO

Xhex felt a soft brush across her shoulder and hip as John drew the sheet around her.

From behind the shelter of her hand, she inhaled and all she smelled was good, clean, healthy male . . . and the scent stirred hunger deep in her gut, her appetite and needs waking from their slumber with a roar.

And that was before John put his wrist up so close she could kiss it.

Her *symphath* instincts snaked out and read his emotions.

Calm and purposeful. Utterly tight in the head and the heart: John was going to save her ass if it was the last thing he did.

"John . . ." she whispered.

The problem with this situation . . . well, one of them . . . was that he wasn't alone in knowing how close to death she was.

Her anger at Lash had been a sustenance while she'd been jailed and abused, and she'd thought it would have kept her going outside as well. But the instant she'd made that call to Rehv, all her energy had drained out of her and left her nothing but a heartbeat. And not much of one at that.

John moved his wrist even closer . . . so that his skin brushed against her mouth.

Her fangs elongated in a sluggish push at the same time her heart hiccuped like it wasn't working right.

She had a choice in this quiet, charged moment: Take his vein and stick around. Deny him and die in front of him in the next hour or so. Because he was going nowhere.

Moving her hand from her face, she shifted her eyes to him. He was as beautiful as always, his face the kind of thing females dreamed of.

Lifting her palm, she reached up to him.

Surprise flared in his eyes and then he bent down so that her hand landed against his warm cheek. The effort of keeping her arm elevated proved to be too much, but as her fingers trembled, he put his own palm over hers, holding it in place.

His deep blue eyes were a kind of heaven, the color like that of a warm, darkening sky.

She had a decision to make here. Take his vein or . . .

As she couldn't find the energy to finish the thought, she felt as though she'd lost herself: going by the fact that she appeared to be conscious, she guessed she was alive—and yet she wasn't in her own skin. Her fight was long gone, the thing that had defined her most in the world having evaporated. Which made sense. She had no interest in living anymore and she couldn't fake that, not for him, not for herself.

Two trips around the prisoner park had taken her too far down.

So . . . what to do, what to do.

She licked her dry lips. She hadn't been born on any terms she would have chosen or volunteered for, and her time of breathing and eating and fighting and fucking hadn't improved where she'd started from. She could, however, leave on her terms—and do so after she had put things right.

Yeah, that was the answer. Thanks to the last three and a half weeks, she had one hell of a bucket list. Granted, there was only a single entry on it, but sometimes that was enough to motivate you.

In a rush of resolve, her hard outer skin re-formed,

the odd floaty feeling that had fogged her out dissipating and leaving a sharp awareness in its wake. Abruptly, she pulled her hand out from under John's, and the withdrawal spiked a flare of pure, silvery fear on his emotional grid. But then she drew his wrist to her and bared her fangs.

His triumph was a heat wave.

At least until it became apparent that she didn't have the strength to break his skin—her incisors did nothing but scratch his surface. John was on it, though. With a fast move, he punctured his own vein and brought the source of him to her lips.

The first taste was . . . a transformation. His blood was so pure it blazed in her mouth and down her throat . . . and the fire it ignited in her stomach tore throughout her body, thawing her, enlivening her. Saving her.

With greedy pulls, she took from him to revive herself, each swallow a life raft for her to crawl into, each draw a rope slung over the cliff of her demise, each pull on his vein the compass she needed to find the trail back home.

And he gave without expectation or hope or the stirrings of emotions.

Which even in her frenzy caused her pain. She had well and truly broken his heart: There was nothing left for him to anticipate with. But she had not broken him— and didn't that make her respect the guy like nothing else could.

As she fed, time flowed as his blood did, into the infinite and into her.

When she finally had taken her fill, she released her seal on his skin and licked the wound closed.

The shaking started soon thereafter. It began in her hands and feet and quickly centralized in her chest, the uncontrollable tremors rattling her teeth and her brain and her vision until she felt as though she was a limp sock thrown in a dryer.

Through the trembling, she caught sight of John taking his cell phone out of his jacket.

She tried to snag his shirt. "N-n-n-no. D-d-don't—"

He ignored her, cocking the damn thing and texting.

"F-f-f-fuck . . ." she groaned.

When he clipped the phone shut, she said, "Y-y-you try to t-t-take me to H-H-Havers right n-now—not gonna g-g-go well."

Her fear of clinics and medical procedures was going to throw her right over the edge, and thanks to him, she now had the energy to do something with her panic. And wasn't that going to be a joy for all of them to handle.

John took out a pad and scribbled something. He turned the thing around, and then left a moment later, and all she could do was close her eyes as the door shut.

Parting her lips, she breathed through her mouth and wondered if she had enough energy to get up, get dressed, and head out before John's bright idea showed up. Quick check told her that was a no-go. If she couldn't lift her head and hold it off the pillow for more than a second and a half, she was fucked for getting vertical.

It didn't take John long to come back in with Doc Jane, the Black Dagger Brotherhood's personal physician. The ghostly female had a black bag with her and exuded the kind of medical competence that Xhex valued—but would infinitely have preferred to be applied to others and not herself.

Doc Jane approached and put her stuff down on the floor. Her white jacket and her scrubs were solid to the eye, though her hands and face were translucent. That all changed, however, as she sat on the edge of the bed.

Everything about her took form and the hand she laid upon Xhex's arm was warm and weighted.

Even the compassionate doctor made Xhex's skin crawl, however. She really didn't want to be touched by anyone.

As the good doctor removed her hand, she had a feeling the female knew that. "Before you tell me to go, a few things you should know. First of all, I will not divulge your location to anyone and I will not share whatever you tell me or whatever I find with anybody. I will have to report that I've seen you to Wrath, but any clinical findings are yours and yours alone."

Sounded good. In theory. But she didn't want the female anywhere near her with what was in that black bag.

Doc Jane went on. "Second, I don't know a damn thing about *symphaths*. So if there's something anatomically distinct or significant to that half of you . . . I'm not going to necessarily know how to treat it. Do you still consent to be seen by me?"

Xhex cleared her throat and tried to lock her shoulders so she didn't shake so much. "I don't w-want to be seen."

"That's what John said. But you've been through a trauma—"

"It w-w-wasn't that bad." She sensed John's emotional response to that from the corner, but didn't have the energy to tease out the details of what he was feeling. "And I'm f-f-fine—"

"Then you should view this as simply a formality."

"Do I l-l-look like someone who's formal?"

Doc Jane's forest green stare narrowed. "You look like someone who's been beaten. Hasn't fed properly. And hasn't slept. Unless you want to tell me that purple bruise on your shoulder is makeup? And those bags under your eyes are a mirage?"

Xhex was well familiar with people who wouldn't accept no for an answer—for shit's sake, she'd worked with Rehv for years. And going by that hard, level tone, it was pretty damn clear that the doctor was going to have her way or she wasn't leaving. Ever.

"G-g-g-goddamn it."

"FYI, the sooner we start, the sooner it's over."

Xhex glanced at John, thinking that if she had to be seen, he was so not a value-add. He really didn't need to know anything more than what he'd probably guessed about the condition she was in.

The doctor looked over her shoulder. "John, will you please wait in the hall?"

John ducked his head and bowed out of the room, the tremendous spread of his back disappearing through the door. When the lock clicked into place, the good doctor opened that fucking bag of hers and the stethoscope and the blood-pressure cuff were the first to come out.

"I'm just going to listen to your heart," the female said, putting the wishbone up to her ears.

The sight of the medical instruments was gasoline to Xhex's shivers, and as out-of-it as she was, she cringed away.

Doc Jane paused. "I'm not going to hurt you. And I won't do anything you don't want me to do."

Xhex closed her eyes and rolled over onto her back. Every muscle in her body hurt all of a sudden. "Let's just get this over with."

As the sheet lifted, a draft of cold air breathed over her skin and the cool disk was placed against her sternum. Flashbacks threatened to send her on a screamer-coaster, and she stared up at the ceiling, just trying to keep herself from levitating off the frickin' mattress.

"B-be fast, D-D-Doc." She could hold the panic back for only so long.

"Could you take a deep breath for me?"

Xhex did the best she could and ended up wincing. Clearly, one or more of her ribs were broken, probably from her hitting the wall outside of that bedroom.

"Can you sit up?" Doc Jane asked.

Xhex groaned a curse as she tried to push her torso off the bed and failed. Doc Jane ended up having to help her, and when the doctor got a load of her back, she hissed a little.

"It doesn't hurt that bad," Xhex bit out.

"Somehow I doubt that." Again with the metal disk going around. "Breath as deep as you can without hurting yourself."

Xhex gave it a shot and was relieved when the doc's kind hand urged her back against the pillows and the sheet was floated into place once more.

"May I check your arms and legs for injury?" When Xhex shrugged, Doc Jane put her stethoscope aside and moved down the bed. There was another draft as the sheet was drawn back . . . and then the other female hesitated.

"Very deep ligation marks around your ankles," the doctor murmured, almost to herself.

Well, that was because Lash had tied her up with wire sometimes.

"Lot of bruising . . ."

Xhex stopped the inspection when the sheet was pushed up to her hips. "Let's just say they go all the way north, 'kay?"

Doc Jane resettled the sheet where it had been. "Can I palpate your belly?"

"Knock yourself out."

Xhex stiffened at the idea of being uncovered again, but Doc Jane just stretched the sheet flat and pushed and prodded. Unfortunately, there was no hiding the winces, especially as things headed to her lower stomach.

The doc settled back and stared straight into Xhex's eyes. "Any chance you'll let me do an internal exam on you?"

"Internal as in . . ." As she got the meaning, Xhex shook her head. "Nope. Not going to happen."

"Were you sexually assaulted?"

"No."

Doc Jane nodded once. "Is there anything I need to know that you haven't told me? Pain in any particular place?"

"I'm fine."

"You're bleeding. I'm not sure you're aware of it. But you're bleeding."

Xhex frowned and looked at her trembling arms.

"There's fresh blood on the insides of your thighs. Which is why I asked if I could do the internal exam."

Xhex felt a wash of dread come over her.

"I'll ask you one more time. Were you sexually assaulted." There was no emotion behind the clinical words, and the doctor had guessed right. Xhex wouldn't have been interested in any hysteria or drippy, over-the-top pity.

When she didn't reply, Doc Jane read into the silence correctly and said, "Any chance you could be pregnant."

Oh . . . God.

Symphath cycles were weird and unpredictable, and she'd been so caught up in the drama of the capture and captivity, she hadn't even thought about the repercussions.

At that moment, she despised being a female. She truly did.

"I don't know."

Doc Jane nodded once. "How can you tell if you are?"

Xhex just shook her head. "There's no way I am. My body's been through too much."

"Let me do the internal, okay? Just to be certain there's

nothing going on that I can feel inside. And then I'd like to take you to the Brotherhood compound and do an ultrasound on you. You were really uncomfortable when I went over your belly. I had V come with a car—he should almost be here by now."

Xhex was barely hearing a word that was being spoken to her. She was too busy tracing back over the last couple weeks. She'd been with John the day before the abduction. That last time. Maybe . . .

If she was pregnant, she flat-out refused to believe it had anything to do with Lash. That would just be too cruel. Too fucking cruel.

Besides, maybe there was another reason for the bleeding.

Like a miscarriage, part of her brain insisted on pointing out.

"Do it," Xhex said. "But make it quick. I don't deal well with this shit and I'm going to flip out on you if it takes longer than a few minutes."

"I'll be fast."

As she closed her eyes and braced herself, a quick slide show set up shop in her head. Flash: her body on a stainless-steel table in a tiled room. Flash: her ankles and wrists locked in place. Flash: human doctors with spastic, lookie-here eyes coming at her. Flash: a video camera in her face and panning down. Flash: a scalpel catching the light from above.

Snap. Snap.

Her lids flipped open at the sounds because she was unsure whether what she'd heard was in her head or in the room. It was the latter. Doc Jane had her latex gloves on.

"I'll be gentle," Jane said.

Which would be a relative term, of course.

Xhex fisted the sheets and felt the muscles that ran up her inner thighs spasm as she went rigid from head to toe. The good news with the frozen-stiff act was that it cured her of that stutter. "I'd rather you be fast."

"Xhex . . . I want you to look right at me. Right now."

Xhex's scattered stare swung around. "What."

"Hold my eyes. Right here." The doctor pointed to her peepers. "Hold 'em. You lock on my face and know that I've had this done to me, okay? I know exactly what I'm doing, and not just because I've been trained."

Xhex forced herself to focus and . . . Jesus, it did help. Meeting that evergreen stare did help. "You'll feel it."

"Excuse me?"

Xhex cleared her throat. "If I'm . . . pregnant, you'll feel it."

"How."

"When you . . . there'll be a pattern. Inside. It won't . . ." She took a shallow breath, drawing on the tales she'd heard from her father's people. "The walls won't be smooth."

Doc Jane didn't even blink. "Got it. You ready?"

No. "Yes."

Xhex was in a cold sweat by the time it was over and that rib she'd broken was screaming from her sawing gulps of air.

"Tell me," she said hoarsely.

TWENTY-THREE

"I'm telling you . . . Eliahu is alive. Eliahu Rathboone
. . . he's *alive*."

Standing in his room at the Rathboone mansion,
Gregg Winn stared out the window at some of South
Carolina's signature Spanish moss. In the moonlight, the
shit was creepy as a shadow thrown by no discernible
object . . . or body.

"Gregg, did you hear me?"

After rubbing the sleep out of his eyes, he looked over
his shoulder at his nubile young narrator. Holly Fleet was
just inside the door, her long blond hair pulled straight
back from her makeup-less face, her eyes not nearly as
wide or captivating without the false lashes or the sparkly-
sparkly stuff she wore on camera. But the pink silk robe
did nothing, absolutely nothing to hide her banging body.

And she was practically vibrating, her inner tuning
fork struck by one hell of a ringer.

"You are aware," Gregg drawled, "that the SOB died
over one hundred and fifty years ago."

"Then his ghost is really here."

"Ghosts don't exist." Gregg turned back to the view.
"You of all people should know that."

"This one does."

"And you woke me up at one a.m. to tell me this?"

Not a good move on her part. They'd all gotten next
to no sleep the night before, and he'd spent the day
pushing and shoving on the phone to L.A. He'd hit
the pillow an hour ago, not expecting to crash—but
fortunately his body had had different plans.

Either that or his brain was telling him to give it up because shit was not going well. That butler was refusing to budge on the permission thing; both of Gregg's reapproaches had been shut down, the one at breakfast politely declined, the one at dinner flat-out ignored.

Meanwhile they had some great footage that he'd already sent in. Thanks to the evocative shots captured on the sly, the brass had given him the go-ahead to switch the special's location—but they were pressuring him for a presell cut they could broadcast ASAP.

Which couldn't happen until the butler relented.

"Hello?" Holly snapped. "Are you listening to me?"

"What."

"I want to go."

He frowned, thinking she didn't have the brains to be frightened by anything short of an eighteen-wheeler with her name on the front grille. "Go where?"

"Back to L.A."

He nearly recoiled. "L.A.? Are you kidding—Okay, so not going to happen. Unless you want to get on Orbitz and ship yourself back like a piece of luggage. We have a job to do here."

Which given the hair across that butler's ass included a lot of doctoring and begging. The latter being Holly's milieu. And actually . . . if she was scared, that worked to an advantage. She could leverage fear with the guy. Men normally responded well to that kind of thing— especially proper gentleman types who surely channeled chivalry through every one of their dry, spindly bones.

"I really . . ." Holly pulled the silk lapels closer to her neck . . . so that the front of the robe stretched tight against her hard nipples. "I'm freaking out."

Hmm. If this was a ploy to get him into bed . . . he wasn't *that* tired. "Come here."

He held out his arms, and as she came forward and put her body against his, he smiled as he stared over her head. God, she smelled good. Not that flowery shit she usually wore, but something darker. Nice.

"Baby, you know you've got to stay with us. I need you to work your magic."

Outside, the Spanish moss swayed in the breeze, the moonlight catching it and creating the illusion of chiffon, so that the trees looked like they were be-gowned.

"Something's not right here," she said into his chest.

Down below, on the lawn, a lone figure ambled into view. Clearly, Stan going for a stoner stroll.

Gregg shook his head. "The only thing that's not right is that damn butler. Don't you want to be famous? A special here's going to open doors for you. You could be hosting *Dancing with the Stars* next. Or *Big Brother*."

He could tell he'd gotten her attention, because her body relaxed, and to help her along, he rubbed her back.

"That's my girl." He watched Stan wander along, hands in pockets, head looking away from the house, long hair moving in the wind. Another couple of yards and he was going to be bathed in moonlight as he stepped out from under the trees. "Now, I want you to stay here with me—like I said, you of all people should know these ghost stories are never anything more than creaking floorboards. We have a job just because people want to believe in creepy shit."

As if on cue, someone came up the stairs, the soft footfalls accompanied by some real Vincent Price specials, the whines and groans of the old wood penetrating the quiet.

"Is that what you're afraid of? Just some bumps in the night?" he said, pulling away and looking down at her. Her plump lips brought back some very fine memories and he brushed her mouth with his thumb, thinking that maybe she'd gotten more silicon pushed into them. They seemed extra puffy and pretty.

"No . . ." she whispered. "It's not that."

"So why do you think there's a ghost."

A knock on the door sounded out and Stan's voice was muffled. "Are you two fucking or can I go to bed now."

Gregg frowned and whipped his head toward the window. That lone figure stepped out into the wash of moonlight . . . and disappeared right into thin air.

"Because I just had sex with him," Holly said. "I had sex with Eliahu Rathboone."

TWENTY-FOUR

Outside in the basement hallway at Xhex's, John was wearing a path in the stone floor. Up and back. Up and back. While he heard absolutely nothing through the door to the bedroom.

Which he supposed was a good thing—no screaming or curses hopefully meant that Doc Jane's exam wasn't causing pain.

He'd texted Rehvenge and told the male that Xhex had been found and they were going to try to get her back to the compound. He didn't mention the basement place, however. Clearly she wanted to keep this private, because if Rehv had known about it, the guy would have insisted on coming here after she wasn't at the hunting cabin.

After checking his watch, John raked his hands through his hair again and wondered how bonded males like Wrath and Rhage and Z handled shit like this— Christ, Z had had to go through watching Bella give birth. How the hell did they—

The door opened and he wheeled around, his soles squeaking on the floor.

Doc Jane was grim. "She's agreed to go to the compound. V should be outside waiting in the Escalade— can you see if he's there?"

John signed, *Is she okay?*

"She's been through a lot. Go check if the car's there, will you? And you're going to have to carry her out, okay? I don't want her walking and I'm not using a stretcher because we don't need to cause a scene on the street."

John didn't fuck around and bolted out of the basement. Right on the curb, with lights off but the engine running, was the SUV. Behind the wheel, there was a flare of orange as V took an inhale from his hand-rolled.

The Brother put his window down. "We taking her in?"

John nodded once and rushed back inside.

When he came up to the door of Xhex's room, it was closed, so he knocked softly.

"One minute," Doc Jane called out, her voice muffled. "Okay."

He opened up and found Xhex still on her side. A towel had been wrapped around her and a fresh sheet draped her from head to foot. Christ . . . he wished her skin offered a little more contrast to all that white shit.

John approached and thought it was odd. He'd never seen himself as taller than her before. Now he towered and not just because she was prone.

I'm going to pick you up now, he signed while mouthing the words.

Her eyes locked on his and then she nodded and tried to sit up. As she struggled, he bent down and scooped her into his arms.

She didn't weigh enough.

When he straightened, Doc Jane quickly flipped the covers on the bed into a fold and motioned toward the door.

The stiffness in Xhex's body was costing her energy and he wanted to tell her to relax, but even if he'd had a voice, that would have been a waste. She wasn't the kind to be carried under any circumstances, by anyone.

At least . . . normally.

The corridor seemed twelve miles long, and outside, the three yards that it took for him to cross the sidewalk to the SUV was twice that far.

V hopped out from behind the wheel and opened the

rear door. "She can stretch out here. I put down blankets before I left."

John nodded and went to lay her on the soft nest that had been made.

Her hand reached up and locked onto his shoulder. "Stay with me. Please."

He froze for a split second . . . and then with brute strength, he stepped up and in while keeping his hold on her. Settling in was awkward . . . but eventually he got them situated against the wall of the car's interior with his legs bent at the knees and her in his lap, cradled against his chest.

The doors were shut and then there were two more *thunch*es and a roar of the engine.

Through the darkened windows, lights flared and receded as they sped out of town.

As Xhex started to shiver, he wrapped his arms more tightly around her, keeping her flush against his body and willing his warmth to go into her. And maybe it worked, because after a moment, she laid her head against his pec and the trembling eased off.

God . . . he had wanted her in his arms for so long. Had imagined it and envisioned scenarios where it happened.

This was so not it.

He inhaled deeply, intending to let out a sigh . . . and caught the scent he was throwing off. Dark spices. The kind he smelled on the Brothers when their *shellans* were around. The kind that meant his body was weighing in on his emotions and there was no going back.

Damn him to hell, there was no hiding the bonding and no stopping it. All along, since he'd first met her, he'd been inching closer and closer to that cliff, and clearly he'd pitched over the side of it when she'd fed from him.

"John?" she whispered.

He tapped lightly on her shoulder so she knew he'd heard her.

"Thank you."

He put his cheek down on her hair and nodded his head so she could feel it.

When she pulled herself out from under, he wasn't surprised—at least not until he realized that she wanted to look up at him.

Oh, Jesus, he hated the expression on her gaunt face. She was afraid to the point of terror, her deep gray eyes the color of flat asphalt.

You're okay, he mouthed. *You're going to be okay.*

"Am I." Her eyes squeezed shut. "Am I really."

If he had anything to do with it, shit, yeah.

Her lids popped open again. "I'm so sorry," she said hoarsely.

What for?

"Everything. Treating you like I did. Being who I am. You deserve so much better. I'm . . . really sorry."

Her voice cracked at the end and as she started to blink, she laid her head back down and put her palm right on his beating heart.

It was moments like this when he desperately wished he could speak. After all, it wasn't like he was going to shuffle her around so he could get to his frickin' pad of paper.

In the end, he just held her with care because that was all he had to offer.

And he wasn't mistaking this exchange for what it wasn't. An apology wasn't a declaration of love and it wasn't even necessary, because he'd all but forgiven her anyway. Yet it helped him, somehow. It was still a far distance from the way he'd hoped things would have gone between them, but it was a damn lot better than nothing.

John tugged the sheet up higher on her shoulder, then

let his head fall back. Staring out of the darkened window, his eyes searched the stars that dotted the dense, velvety black of the night sky.

Funny, felt like heaven was up against his chest instead of all above the whole world.

Xhex was alive. And in his arms. And he was taking her home.

Yup. All in all, things could have been a fuckload worse.

TWENTY-FIVE

Lash would later reflect that you never knew who you were going to cross tracks with. You just never knew how a simple decision to go left or right at a corner would change things. Sometimes the choices didn't matter. Others . . . took you into unexpected places.

At the current moment, however, he had yet to come to that realization. He was just out in farm country, driving along, thinking about the time.

Just a little past one.

"How much longer?"

Lash glanced across the interior of the Mercedes. The prostitute he'd picked up in an alley downtown was sufficiently good-looking and had enough silicon in her to do porn, but Plastic Fantastic's drug habit had left her bony and twitchy.

Desperate, too. So strung out it had taken only a hundred-dollar bill to get her into the AMG on the way to a "party."

"Not far," he replied, refocusing on the road ahead.

He was disappointed as shit. When he'd played this out in his head, Xhex was bound and gagged in the backseat—much more romantic. Instead, he was stuck with this nasty 'hood rat. But he couldn't fight the reality he was in: he needed to feed and his father was expecting some business to be done and finding Xhex was going to require more time than there was to spare.

Among the worst of the concessions was that this bitch riding shotgun was a human: Far less useful than a female vampire, but he was hoping her ovaries worked in his favor when it came to sucking her blood.

More to the point, he hadn't been able to find one of his kind in a skirt.

"You know," she said with a slur, "I used to model."

"Really."

"Down in Manhattan. But you know, those bastards . . . they don't really care about you. They just want to use you, you know."

Right. First, she needed to forget she'd ever heard the phrase *you know*. And second, like she was doing so much better on her own up in Caldwell?

"I like your car."

"Thanks," he muttered.

She leaned over, her breasts bunching up over the pink basque she had on. The thing had grease smudges from dirty hands on the sides, like she hadn't washed it for a couple of days, and she smelled like fake cherries, BO and crack smoke.

"You know, I like you . . ."

Her hand went to his thigh and then her head went down into his lap. When he felt her rooting around for his zipper, he grabbed a hunk of bleached-blond tangle and yanked her back up.

She didn't even notice the pain.

"Let's not start this now," he said. "We're almost there."

The woman licked her lips. "Sure. Okay."

The shorn fields on either side of the road were washed in moonlight and the clapboard houses that dotted the scruffy patches glowed white. Most places had a porch light on and that was it. Around here, anything after midnight was waaaaaaay past bedtime for these folks.

Which was part of the reason it made sense to have an outpost here in the land of hot apple pie and American flags.

Five minutes later, they pulled up to the farmhouse and parked close to the front door.

"No one else is here," she said. "We the first ones?"

"Yeah." He reached forward to turn off the engine. "Let's—"

The clicking sound next to his ear had him freezing.

The prostitute's voice was no longer fuzzy. "Get out of the car, motherfucker."

Lash swiveled his head around, and all but French-kissed the muzzle of a nine-millimeter. On the other end of the weapon, the whore's hands were stone steady and her eyes burned with the kind of canny smarts he had to respect.

Surprise, surprise, he thought.

"Get. Out," she snapped.

He smiled slowly. "You ever shot that thing before?"

"Loads." She didn't blink. "And I don't have a problem with blood."

"Ah. Well, good for you."

"Get out—"

"So what's the plan here. Order me from the car. Shoot me in the head and leave me for dead. Take the Mercedes, my watch, and my wallet?"

"And what's in your trunk."

"You need a spare tire? You know, you can buy one at any Firestone or Goodyear outlet. Just FYI."

"You think I don't know who you are?"

Oh, he was quite fucking sure she hadn't a clue. "Why don't you tell me."

"I've seen this car. I've seen you. I've bought your drugs."

"A customer. How sweet."

"Get. Out."

When he didn't move, she shifted the gun an inch to the side and pulled the trigger. As the bullet blew out the window behind him, he got pissed. It was one thing to play around. Another to cause property damage.

As she shifted the business end of the nine back between his eyes, he dematerialized.

Taking form around the other side of the car, he watched as she flipped out in her seat, looking all around, her frizzy hair flying this way and that.

Ready to teach her a thing or two about plans, he ripped open her door, and dragged her out by the arm. Getting control of the gun and her was the work of a moment, just a snatch and grab. And then he was tucking the nine into his belt at the small of his back and cranking her into a choke hold against his chest.

"What . . . what—"

"You told me to get out of the car," he said into her ear. "So I did."

Her slender body was all kinds of leaf-in-the-wind weak, nothing but a shimmer in her cheapo whore clothes. Compared to the physical battles with Xhex, this was a single breath versus a hurricane gale. What a bore.

"Let's go inside," he murmured, lowering his mouth to her throat and running a fang up her jugular. "The other partygoer should be waiting for us."

As she shrank away from him, her face turned around and he smiled, flashing his hardware. Her scream flushed an owl from its perch overhead, and to make sure she cut the Hitchcocking, he slapped his free palm over her piehole and forced her to the front door.

Inside, the place smelled like death, thanks to the induction the night before and all the blood in the buckets. There was an advantage to the residual, however. As he willed the lights on and the chick got a look-see at the dining room, she went rigid with terror and then passed the fuck out.

Damn good of her. Made getting her on the table and tied up splayed wide easy.

After catching his breath, he took the buckets into the kitchen, rinsed them out in the sink, cleaned up the knives, and wished like hell Mr. D was still around to take care of the shit work.

He was just putting the spray nozzle back where it belonged when it dawned on him the *lesser* they'd done the night before was nowhere to be seen.

Taking the buckets into the dining room, he set them out under the whore's wrists and ankles and then did a quick double-check of the downstairs. When all he got was a whole lot of not-there, he jogged up to the second floor.

The closet door in the bedroom was open and there was a hanger on the bed like a shirt had been macked. Shower in the bath had fresh water dripping down its side walls.

What the fuck?

How in the hell did that guy take off? There hadn't been a car, so the only other option was walking out the lane. And then hitching a ride. Or hot-wiring one of these farmers' trucks.

Lash went downstairs and found that the whore had come around and was fighting against the gag in her mouth, her eyes bugging as she writhed on the table.

"Won't be long," he told her, glancing down at her spindly legs. She had tattoos on both, but they were a hot mess with no theme at all, just random blotches— some of which you could maybe identify, others of which were ruined either by bad reinking or scars.

Lot of butterflies done in neon, he supposed. Maybe that had been the plan at first.

He paced around, going out to the kitchen and then coming back through the dining room and heading down the hall again. The sharp sound of stilettos knocking against the table and the squeak of bare skin faded into the distance as he wondered where the hell the new recruit was and why his father was late.

Half an hour later he still had a whole lot of nothing doing and he sent a mental ping to the other side.

His father did not answer.

Lash went upstairs and shut the door, thinking that maybe he wasn't concentrating properly because he was pissed off and frustrated. Sitting on the bed, he put his hands on his knees and calmed himself. When his heartbeat was slow and steady, he took a deep breath, pinged again . . . and got nothing.

Maybe something had happened to the Omega?

In a rush of emotion, he decided to go over to *Dhunhd* himself.

His molecules scrambled well enough, but when he tried to re-form on the other plane of existence, he was blocked. Shut out. Denied.

It was like hitting a solid wall, and as he bounced back to the crappy bedroom in the farmhouse, his body absorbed the shock on a wave of nausea.

What. The. Fuck—

As his cell phone went off, he snatched it out of his suit coat pocket and frowned when he saw the number.

"Hello?" he said.

The giggle that came through was boyish. "Hi ya, asswipe. It's your new boss. Guess who just got promoted? By the way, your daddy says not to bother him anymore. Bad move asking about the ladies—you should know your father better than that. Oh, and I'm supposed to kill you now. See you soon!"

The new recruit started laughing, that sound punching through the connection, drilling into Lash's head as the call was ended.

By the other party.

She was not pregnant. At least, not that Doc Jane knew.

But courtesy of that happy little pause in panic-ville, Xhex didn't remember anything of the trip to the compound. The idea that there was even a chance she could have been . . .

After all, she hadn't been wearing her cilices—and their purpose was to kill the *symphath* tendencies in her, including ovulation.

What would she have done?

Okay, moot point there, and she needed to cut that shit right out. God knew she had enough to worry about in the "actually happening" category.

Breathing deep, she inhaled John's scent and concentrated on the strong, steady beat of his heart under her ear. It wasn't long before sleep took her hard, the combination of exhaustion, postfeeding loginess, and the need to peace out of life for a while carrying her into a deep, dreamless state in the back of the SUV.

She woke up to the sensation of being lifted and her eyes opened.

John was carrying her through some kind of parking area that, given the cavelike walls and ceiling, had to be underground. A massive steel door was opened by Vishous, who seemed to be in a surprising mood to help, and on the far side . . . was a nightmare.

The long, anonymous hall had pale tile on the floor, concrete-block walls, and a low ceiling that had fluorescent box lights in it.

The past slid into place, the filter of prior experience replacing what was actually occurring with a remembered nightmare. In John's arms, her body went from weak to manic and she started to fight the hold on her, battling to get free. The commotion was instantaneous, people rushing toward her, a loud sound like a siren blaring—

As it dimly occurred to her that her jaw hurt, she realized she was yelling.

And then suddenly all she saw was John's face.

He'd somehow managed to turn her around in his

arms and they were nose-to-nose, eye-to-eye, his hands digging into her sides and her hips. With the sight of that institutional corridor replaced with his blue stare, the grab of the past was broken and she was caught by him.

He didn't say a thing. Just stayed still and let her look at him.

It was exactly what she needed. She locked onto his eyes and used them to turn her brain off.

When he nodded, she nodded back to him and he started moving forward again. From time to time, his stare flicked away from hers to check where they were going, but it always returned.

It always came back.

There were voices, a number of them, and a lot of doors opening and shutting, and then a whole lot of pale green tile: She was in an examination room, with a multi-light chandelier above her and all kinds of medical supplies in glass-front cabinets everywhere she looked.

As John put her on the table, she lost control of her reins again. Her lungs refused to do their job, as if the air were poisoned, and her eyes bounced around, hitting all kinds of panic triggers like equipment, and instruments, and the table . . . the table.

"Okay, we're losing her again." Doc Jane's tone was relentlessly level. "John, get in there."

John's face came back in close and Xhex held on to his eyes.

"Xhex?" Doc Jane's voice came from over on the left. "I'm going to give you a sedative—"

"No drugs!" The answer leaped out of her mouth. "I'd rather be terrified . . . than helpless . . ."

Her breath was painfully short, and each impotent draw of her rib cage convinced her as nothing else could that life was about suffering more than it was about joy. There had been too many of these moments, too many times the pain and fear took over, too many dark shadows that didn't just lurk, but sucked out all the illumination from the night in which she existed.

"Let me go . . . let me go away . . ." When John's eyes went wide, she realized that she'd found one of his knives, unsheathed it, and was trying to put it in his palm. "Please let me go . . . I don't want to be here anymore . . . put me out forever, *please* . . ."

Lot of frozen bodies around her and the lack of movement refocused her a little. Rhage and Mary were in the corner. Rehv was there. Vishous and Zsadist. No one was speaking or budging an inch.

John took the dagger from her hand and the removal was what made her cry. Because he wasn't going to use it. Not on her. Not now . . . not ever.

And she lacked the strength to do it herself.

All at once, a tremendous emotion boiled in her gut, and as it expanded and pressure grew inside her body, she looked around frantically as shelves started to rattle and the computer over in the corner began to bounce on the desk.

John was on it, though. And he was on it fast. He started to sign with the same kind of urgency she was feeling, and a moment later, everyone left.

Except for him.

Trying desperately not to explode, she looked down at her hands. They were shaking so badly, they were like the wings of a fly . . . and it was when she was staring at them that she hit bottom.

The scream pealed out of her and the sound was utterly foreign, all high-pitched and horrified.

John stood his ground. Even when she screamed again.

He wasn't going anywhere. He wasn't rattled. He was just . . . there.

Grabbing the sheet that circled her, she tightened it around her body, very aware she was breaking down, that the fissure had been tapped by that trip down the hall and now she had splintered. In fact, she felt as though there were two of her in the room, the mad one on the table screaming her head off and crying bloody tears . . . and a calm, sane one in the far corner, watching herself and John.

Would the two parts of her cleave together again? Or would she be ever thus, wrenched asunder?

Her mind chose the observer persona over the hysterical one and she retreated into that soundless place where she witnessed herself sob to the point of asphyxiation. The streaks of blood that ran down her paper white cheeks didn't disgust her and nor did the crazy, wide eyes or epileptic thrashing of her arms and legs.

She felt sorry for the female who had been driven to such straits. Who had kept herself apart from all emotions.

The female had been born under a curse. The female had done evil and had evil done unto her. The female had hardened herself, her mind and her emotions becoming steel.

The female had been wrong about that locking down, that self-containment.

It was not a case of strength, as she had always told herself.

It was strictly survival . . . and she simply couldn't keep it up any longer.

TWENTY-SIX

"You had . . . sex. With Eliahu Rathboone."

Gregg set Holly back from him and stared into her face, thinking she'd lost her damn mind—well, lost what little of a one she had. And that made two of them, because he had clearly imagined what he'd just "seen" outside.

Except her eyes were utterly clear and without guile. "He came to me. I'd fallen asleep—"

Another round of banging on the door cut her off, and then Stan's voice came through. "Hello? Which room am I—"

"Later, Stan," Gregg clipped out. As the grumbling faded, footsteps in the hall went down to Holly's room and a door was slammed.

"Come here." He tugged Holly over to the bed. "Sit down and tell me . . . what the hell you think happened."

He focused on her puffy lips as she spoke. "Well, I'd just gotten out of the shower. I was exhausted and I lay down on the bed to rest my eyes before I got into my nightgown. I must have fallen asleep . . . because the next thing I knew I had this dream—"

Oh, for God's sake. "Holly, just because you had a nightmare doesn't mean you—"

"I'm not finished," she snapped. "And it wasn't a nightmare."

"I thought you were freaking out."

"The scary stuff came afterward." She arched a brow. "Are you going to let me talk?"

"Fine." But only on the hope that he could get her

mouth to do something else later. Damn, her lips looked good . . . "Go 'head."

Head. Yup. That's what he was thinking.

"I started to have this dream that this man came into my room. He was very tall and muscular . . . one of the biggest men I've ever seen. He was dressed in black and he stood over my bed. He smelled amazing . . . and he just stared at me. I . . ." Her hand wrapped around her neck and slowly slid down between her breasts. "I took off my towel and pulled him on top of me. It was . . . indescribable . . ."

Which was good news. Because he suddenly didn't want to hear anything about what happened next.

"He took me." More with that hand-on-the-neck thing. "As I've never been had before. He was so—"

"—hung like a fire hose and did you twelve different ways to Sunday. Congratulations. Your subconscious should be directing porn. What does this have to do with Eliahu Rathboone."

Holly glared at him . . . and then yanked her lapel to the side. "Because when I woke up, I had this." She jabbed at what certainly appeared to be a hickey on her neck. "And I'd actually had sex."

Gregg frowned hard. "You . . . How do you know?"

"How do you think I know."

Gregg cleared his throat. "Are you okay?" He put his hand on her arm. "I mean . . . ah, do you want to call the police."

Holly's laugh was low and achingly sexy. "Oh, it was consensual. Whatever it was." Her expression lost its glow. "That's the point . . . I don't know what it was. I thought I'd dreamed it. I didn't think it was real until . . ."

Until there was some undeniable evidence to the contrary.

Gregg brushed her blond extensions over her shoulder. "You sure you're all right?"

231

"I guess so."

Man, it didn't take him even a moment to make up his mind. "Well, that's it. We're leaving tomorrow."

"What? Oh, my God, Gregg . . . I didn't mean to cause problems—" She frowned. "Maybe . . . maybe I dreamed the after part where I woke up, too. I took another shower . . . maybe none of it really happened."

"Fuck it, I'll call Atlanta in the a.m. and tell them it's back on. I'm not going to have you staying where you're not safe."

"Jesus, I mean, that's very chivalric of you, but . . . I don't know. Everything's so fuzzy, and now I wonder if I'll just feel better in the morning. I'm really confused . . . it was weird." Her fingertips went to her temples and started rubbing in circles, like her head was aching. "I will say that I wanted it to happen, every step of the way—"

"Was your door locked?" He wanted an answer to the question, but he also didn't need to hear about the Ghost with the Mostest, thank you very much.

"I always lock a hotel room door before I have a shower."

"Windows?"

"Closed. I guess they're locked. I don't know."

"Well, you stay with me tonight. You'll be safe here." And not just because he wasn't going to hit on her now. He had a gun with him. Always. And the thing was permitted and he knew how to use it: Back when people had been getting popped in L.A. traffic, he'd decided to get armed.

Together they stretched out on the bed. "I'll leave the light on."

"It's okay. Just lock the door."

He nodded and slipped off the bed, throwing the dead bolt as well as the chain; then he did a quick pass by the windows to inspect the latches. When he lay back down, she nestled into the crook of his arm and sighed.

With a lean, he pulled the duvet out from under their legs and over them, turned off the lamp and eased back into the pillows.

He thought of that man out walking the grounds and nearly growled. Fuck. This. Shit. Either it was a local with a passkey, or a staff member who could jimmy the lock.

Assuming anything had happened at all. Which she seemed less and less sure of—

Whatever. They were leaving in the morning and that was that.

He frowned in the darkness. "Holly?"

"Yes?"

"Why did you think it was Rathboone."

She yawned widely. "Because he looked exactly like the portrait in the living room."

TWENTY-SEVEN

Down in the exam room at the underground clinic, John stood before Xhex and felt utterly powerless to help her. As she sat screaming on the stainless-steel table, her arms strained against her hold on the sheet, and her face stretched long, her mouth tearing open, red tears spilling out of her eyes and falling down her white cheeks . . . And he could do nothing about any of it.

He knew the rough place she was in. Knew that he couldn't possibly reach the well that she was down at the bottom of: He'd been there himself. He knew exactly what it was like to trip and fall and be in agony from hard impact . . . even though your body technically hadn't gone anywhere.

The only difference was that she had a voice to give her pain wings.

As his ears rang and his heart broke for her, he stayed strong against the gale force she let loose. After all, there was a reason why *here* and *hear* were separated by so little and sounded one like the other. Bearing witness to her, he heard her and was there for her because that was all you could do during a fall apart.

But God, it pained him to see how she suffered. Pained him and focused him, Lash's face gathering like a ghost taking physical form in John's mental eye. As she screamed and screamed, he vowed vengeance until his heart beat not blood, but the need for revenge.

And then Xhex took a series of big breaths. And a couple more.

"I think I'm done with that," she said roughly.

He waited a moment to make sure. When she nodded, he took out his pad and wrote quickly.

As he flashed the page to her, her eyes went to the writing and it took her a couple of tries to get the gist.

"Can I wash my face first?"

He nodded and went over to the stainless-steel sink. Running a stream of cool water, he got a clean towel from a stack and wet it before returning to her. As she held out her hands, he put the damp cloth in her palms and watched as she slowly pressed it against her face. It was hard to see her so frail and he thought back to how he had always known her: strong, powerful, edged-out.

Her hair had grown longer and was starting to curl up at the ends, suggesting that if she didn't cut it, it would have a thick wave in the length. God, he wanted to touch the softness.

His eyes moved down to the table and abruptly popped wide. The sheet had twisted out from under her . . . and there was a dark spot on the towels that had been wrapped around her hips.

As he inhaled deeply, he caught the scent of fresh blood and was surprised he hadn't before. Then again, he'd been pretty fucking distracted.

Oh . . . Christ. She was bleeding . . .

He tapped her lightly on the arm and mouthed, *Doc Jane.*

Xhex nodded. "Yeah. Let's get this over with."

Frantic, John stalked over to the door of the exam room. Out in the hall, there was a legion of worried faces, with Doc Jane at the head of the group.

"She ready for me?" When John stepped to the side and motioned urgently with his arm, the doctor came forward.

He stopped her, though. With his back to Xhex, he signed, *She's injured somewhere. She's bleeding.*

Doc Jane put her hand on his shoulder and maneuvered him around in a circle so they traded places. "I know. Why don't you wait outside. I'll take good care of her. Ehlena? Would you mind coming in—I'm going to need a second set of hands."

Rehvenge's *shellan* went into the exam room and John watched over the doctor's head as the female started washing her hands.

Why isn't Vishous assisting? he signed.

"We're just doing an ultrasound to make sure she's all right. I'm not operating." Doc Jane smiled at him in a professional way—which was oddly frightening. And then the door was shut in his face.

He looked around at the others. All the males were locked out in the hall. Only females in there with her.

His mind started to churn and it didn't take him long to come to a conclusion that couldn't possibly be right.

A heavy hand landed on his shoulder and V's voice was low. "No, you need to stay out here, John. Let go."

That was when he realized his palm had locked on the door handle. Looking down, he told himself to release his hold . . . and had to send the command twice before his grip slid off the metal.

There was no more screaming. No sounds at all.

He waited. And waited. And paced and waited some more. Vishous lit another hand-rolled. Blay joined him, firing up a Dunhill. Qhuinn drummed a beat out on his thigh. Wrath petted George's head while the golden retriever watched John with kind brown eyes.

Eventually, Doc Jane poked her head around the door and looked at her mate. "I need you."

Vishous put out his cig on the sole of his boot and tucked the butt into his back pocket. "Scrubbing in?"

"Yup."

"Let me go change."

As the male jogged off to the locker room, Doc Jane met John's eyes. "I'm going to take good care of her—"

What's wrong? Why is she bleeding? he signed.

"I'm going to take care of her."

And then the door shut again.

When V came back, he looked every bit the warrior even though he was out of his leathers, and John hoped like hell the guy's competency on the field translated into the medical racket.

Those diamond eyes of his flashed and he clapped John on the shoulder before slipping into the exam room . . . which evidently was now functioning as an OR.

As the door closed, John felt like doing a little screaming of his own.

Instead, he kept with the walking, going up and down the corridor. Up and down. Up . . . and down. Eventually, the others dispersed, heading into a nearby classroom, but he couldn't stand to join them.

With each pass by the door that was closed to him, he went wider afield, until the trip took him all the way to exit into the parking area and then back to the locker room. His long legs ate up the distance, turning what was a good fifty yards into a matter of mere inches.

Or at least it seemed that way.

On what must have been his fifth trip down toward the lockers, John pivoted around and found himself in front of the office's glass door. The desk and the filing cabinets and the computer seemed relentlessly normal and he took a strange comfort from the inanimate objects.

But the deep breath was lost when he stepped forward once again.

In his peripheral vision, he saw the cracks in the concrete wall across the way, the fissures spidering out from a single impact source.

He remembered the night it had happened. That horrible night.

He and Tohr had been sitting together in the office, him doing schoolwork, the Brother trying to keep calm as he called home over and over again. Every time Wellsie didn't answer, every time he got voice mail, the tension was cranked up more—until Wrath had appeared with the Brotherhood behind him.

The news that Wellsie was gone was tragic . . . but then Tohr had learned the "how": Not because she was pregnant with their first child, but because a *lesser* had killed her in cold blood. Murdered her. Taken her out and the baby with her.

That was what had caused these marks.

John walked over and ran his fingertips across the fine lines in the concrete. The rage had been so great, Tohr had literally imploded into a supernova, the emotional overload dematerializing him to some other place.

John never had learned where he'd gone.

A sense of being observed had him lifting his head and looking over his shoulder. Tohr was on the far side of the glass door, standing in the office, staring out.

The two met each other's stare and it was male to male, not elder to younger.

John was a different age now. And like so many things in this situation, there was no going back.

"John?" Doc Jane's voice came from far down the hall and he wheeled around, then ran to her.

How is she? What happened? Is she—

"She's going to be okay. She's just coming out of the anesthesia. I'm going to keep her in bed for the next six hours or so. I understand she fed from you?" He flashed his wrist and the doc nodded. "Good. I'd appreciate it if you'd stay with her in case she needs to again?"

Like he would be anywhere else.

As John stepped inside the exam room, he moved on his tiptoes, not wanting to disturb anything; but she wasn't there.

"She's been moved into the other room," V said from over by the autoclave.

Before he went through to the far door, he stared at

the aftermath of whatever had been done to Xhex. There was an alarming pile of bloody gauze on the floor and more blood on the table she'd been on. The sheet and towels she'd been wrapped in were off to the side.

So much blood. All of it fresh.

John whistled loudly so that V would look over. *Can someone tell me what the fuck went on in here?*

"You can talk to her about it." As the Brother got out an orange biohazard bag and started to gather up the used gauze, V paused, but did not meet John's eyes. "She's going to be okay."

And that was when John knew for sure.

However bad he'd thought she'd been treated, she'd gotten it worse. Much worse.

Generally speaking, when there were injuries sustained in combat or on the field, the information was traded back and forth without a thought—femur broken, ribs crushed, stab wound. But a female came in, was examined without males present, and no one would speak a word of what had been operated on?

Just because *lessers* were impotent didn't mean they couldn't do other things with . . .

The cold breeze that shot through the OR brought V's head up again. "Word of advice, John. I'd keep your suppositions to yourself. Assuming you want to be the one who kills Lash, true? No sense Rehv or the Shadows, much as I respect them, doing what is your right."

My God, the Brother was cool, John thought.

Nodding once, he went over to Xhex's room, thinking those males weren't the only reason he was going to keep a lid on things. Xhex didn't need to know the lengths he was going to go to, either.

Xhex felt like someone had parked a Volkswagen bus in her uterus.

The pressure was so great, she actually lifted her head

and looked down her body to see if she was swollen to garage dimensions.

Nope. Flat as always.

She let her head fall back.

On some level, she couldn't believe where she was now: on the other side of the operation, lying in a bed with her arms and legs and head still attached . . . and the tear in her uterine wall repaired.

When she was in the grips of her iatrophobia, she couldn't see past what her brain had marked as deadly. To her, in that flipped-out state, she was not in a safe environment, surrounded by people she knew and could trust.

Now, having gone through the fire, the fact that she was unscathed and well gave her a weird buzz of endorphins.

There was a soft knock, and she knew who it was by the scent beneath the door.

Touching her hair, she wondered what the hell she looked like and decided it was better not to know. "Come in."

John Matthew's head ducked inside and his eyebrows lifted in a how're-you-feeling arch.

"I'm okay. I'm better. Groggy from the meds."

He slipped through and leaned back against the wall, shoving his hands in his pockets and crossing one shit-kicker over the other. His T-shirt was nothing but a white Hanes, which was probably a good call, given that it was stained with *lesser* blood.

He smelled like a male should. Soap and clean sweat.

And he looked like a male should. Tall and broad and deadly.

God, had she really lost it that badly in front of him?

"Your hair's shorter," she said for no particular reason.

He unplugged one of his hands and awkwardly brushed at the skull trim. With his head tilted down, the powerful muscles that ran from his shoulders up into his neck flexed under his golden skin.

Abruptly, she wondered if she would ever have sex again.

It was an alien thought, to be sure. Considering how she'd spent the last—

She frowned. "How many weeks have I been gone?"

He held up four fingers and then made a pinching motion.

"Almost four?" When he nodded, she took elaborate care straightening the fold on the sheet that ran across her chest. "Almost . . . four."

Well, the humans had had her for a matter of months before she'd been able to get away from them. Just under four weeks should be a cakewalk to get over.

Ah, but she wasn't sticking around, was she. There was no "getting over." There was just "getting done."

"Do you want to sit down?" she said, indicating a chair by the side of the bed. The thing was standard-issue institutional, which meant it looked about as comfortable as a stake up the ass, but she didn't want him to leave.

John's brows lifted again and he nodded as he came over. Arranging his huge body on the little seat, he tried first to cross his legs at the knees, then the ankles. He ended up jacked halfway around, his shitkickers under the bed and his arm over the back of the chair.

She fiddled with her goddamn sheet. "Can I ask you something?"

In her peripheral vision, she saw him nod, then shift around and take a pad and pen out of his back pocket.

Clearing her throat, she wondered exactly how to phrase her question.

In the end, she copped out and went with something impersonal. "Where was Lash last seen."

He nodded and curled over his paper, writing quickly.

As his words took form on the white page, she got to watch him . . . and realized she never wanted him to go. She wanted him here beside her forever.

Safe. She was truly safe with him around.

He straightened and flashed the pad. Then seemed to freeze.

For some reason, she couldn't focus on what he'd written and she strained—

John slowly lowered his arm.

"Wait, I haven't read it. Could you . . . What. What's wrong?" Damn it, now her eyes were refusing to see him clearly.

John leaned to the side and she heard a quiet *pfft* sound. Then a Kleenex was presented to her.

"Oh, for fuck's sake." She took what he offered and pressed it against both eyes. "I hate being a girl. I really fucking despise being a girl."

As she went on a rant about estrogen, and skirts, and pink nail polish, and frickin' stilettos, he fed her Kleenex after Kleenex, gathering up the red-stained ones she'd used.

"I never cry, you know that." She glared over at him. "Ever."

He nodded. And handed her another cocksucking tissue.

"Jesus Christ. First I get a case of the screams, now the dripping nonsense. I could kill Lash for this bull-shit alone."

A frigid blast shot through the room and she looked over at John—only to recoil. He'd gone from sympathetic to sociopath in a split second. To the point where she was almost positive he had no conscious clue that he'd bared his fangs.

Her voice dropped to a whisper and what she'd really wanted to ask came barreling out. "Why did you stay? In the OR, back then." She dropped her eyes from his, focusing on the red blotches that marked the tissue she'd just used. "You stayed and you . . . you just seemed to get it."

In the silence that followed, she realized she knew the context of his life so very well: who he lived with, what he did in the field, how he fought, where he spent his time. But she knew none of his specifics. His background was a black hole.

And for some unknown reason, she needed illumination on it.

Fuck that, she knew exactly why: In that incandescent horror she'd faced in the OR, the only thing that had tethered her to the earth had been him and it was strange, but she felt welded to him on some core level now. He had seen her at her absolute worst, at her weakest and most insane, and he hadn't looked away. He hadn't left and he hadn't judged and he hadn't been burned.

It was as if in the heat of her meltdown they had been melded together.

This was more than emotion. It was a matter of soul.

"What the hell happened to you, John. In your past."

His brows drew tight and his arms crossed over his chest as if now he was the one trying to figure out how to express himself. What was more, his emotional grid suddenly lit up with all kinds of dark things and she got the impression he was thinking of bolting.

"Look, I don't want to pressure you." Shit. Fuck. "And if you want to deny that you've had anything but complete hunky-dory in your life, I will totally accept it and move on. But I just . . . Most people would have at least flinched. Hell, even Doc Jane came in with a tread-carefully on her puss after I lost it. You, though? You just hung in there." She stared into his hard, closed face. "I looked into your eyes, John, and there was more than hypothetical understanding in them."

After a long pause, he flipped to a new page on the

pad and wrote quickly. When he flashed what he'd written, she could see his point, but she wanted to curse:

Tell me what they did in the OR. Tell me what was wrong with you first.

Ah, yes, classic tit for tat.

It only took Lash about an hour to get himself, the whore, and the Mercedes from the farmhouse back to the ranch in town. He was in raw survival mode, moving fast and decisively, making only one stop on the way.

And that was at a cabin out in the woods where he picked up some mission-critical shit.

When he pulled into the ranch's garage, he waited until the door was shut before getting out and dragging the prostitute from the backseat. As he carried her squirming body in through the kitchen, he threw up a good dose of what he'd imprisoned Xhex with.

The magical barrier was not for Plastic Fantastic, however.

The Omega knew where his *lessers* were on this side. Could sense them as echoes of his own existence. And along those lines, slayers could tweak to their fellow members.

So the only chance Lash had at keeping hidden was to in effect imprison himself. Mr. D hadn't known that Xhex was up in that bedroom—his say-what? confusion had been obvious every time he'd been told to leave food there.

Of course, the big question was whether the masking would keep the Omega at bay. And for how long.

Lash threw the whore into the bathroom with all the care and concern he'd show toward a cheap duffel bag full of dirty laundry. As she landed hard in the tub and moaned against the duct tape over her mouth, he went back out to the car.

Unpacking took about twenty minutes and he put

the shit in the basement on the concrete floor: seven sawed-off shotguns. A Hannaford plastic shopping bag full of cash. Three pounds of C4 plastic explosives. Two remote detonators. A hand grenade. Four auto loaders. Ammo. Ammo. Ammo.

As he came up the stairs and shut off the cellar light, he went to the back door, opened it, and put his hand out. The cool air of the night infiltrated the shield just fine, but his palm sensed the restriction. It was strong . . . but needed to be stronger.

Helllllllllllllo, 'hood rat.

Lash shut the door, dead-bolted it, and stalked to the bathroom.

He was all business as he took out his knife, sliced the bindings that held her wrists behind her back and—

She flailed around until he punched her in the head, knocking her out cold. Slice. Slice. Slice. He made three deep cuts in her wrists and in her neck and then sat back to watch the blood drain out of her in a sluggish ooze.

"Come on . . . bleed, bitch, *bleed*."

As he checked his watch, he thought maybe he should have kept her compos mentis, because that would have ensured a higher pulse rate and blood pressure. And shortened this do-nothing wait while she drained out.

Watching the process, he had no idea how dry she had to be, but the red pool beneath her was rising, her pink basque staining dark.

His foot was going a mile a minute as time droned on . . . and then he noticed that her skin was not just pale but gray and the blood wasn't really getting any higher on the walls of the tub. Calling it done, he cut open her basque, exposing a truly awful set of implants, and stabbed open her chest, the blade of his knife going right through her sternum.

The next cut he made was in his own flesh.

Holding his wrist over the gaping hole he'd made, he watched black drops free-fall into her motionless heart. Again, he wasn't sure how much he should be giving her, and tried to err on the side of overdoing it. Then it was a case of summoning energy into his palm, his will forcing air molecules to start spinning in a tornadic circle until they became a unit of kinetic power that he could control.

Lash looked down at the whore, her body all defiled, her makeup smudged on her cheeks, her ratty hair more fright wig than anything you'd expect to see on the street.

He needed this to work. Already, with nothing more than the barrier spell in place and this little fireball in his hand, he could feel his strength ebbing.

This had to fucking work.

He cast the blast into her chest cavity and her dead limbs flopped like fish tails against the sides of the tub. As the flash of light lit off and then dispersed, he waited . . . praying to—

The gasp she let out was god-awful. And also a godsend.

He was fascinated as her heart began to pump and his black blood was absorbed into the raw meat of her rib cage, the reanimation causing his cock to twitch in excitement. This was power, he thought. Fuck the shit money could buy.

He really was a god, just like his father.

Lash sat on his heels and watched the color return to her skin. As life came back to her, her hands curled against the edge of the tub and the withered muscles of her thighs twitched.

The next step was something he didn't fully understand but wasn't going to question. When she looked as if she was firmly back on the side of the living, he reached in with his bare hand and ripped that heart of hers right out of her chest.

More gasping. More choking. Blah, blah, blah.

He was fascinated with what he'd accomplished, especially as he put his palm over her sternum and commanded her flesh to reknit itself: What do you know, her very skin and bone followed his will and she was once more as she had been.

Except better. Because she was useful to him now.

He reached to the side and cranked on the shower, the spray hitting her body and face, her eyes blinking against the cold rain, her hands batting at it pitifully.

How long did he wait now? he wondered. How long until he could see if he was one step closer to what was really going to sustain him?

As a wave of exhaustion crept up his spine and fogged out his brain, he slumped against the cupboards that ran under the sink. Kicking the door shut, he balanced his forearms on his knees and played witness to the whore flailing around.

So weak.

So fucking weak.

It should have been his Xhex. He should have done this to her and not some random, skank-ass human.

Putting his hands to his face, he hung his head as his elation washed out of him. This was not how it was supposed to be. This was not what he'd planned.

On the run. Hunted. Scrambling in the world.

What the hell was he going to do without his father.

TWENTY-EIGHT

While John waited for Xhex to respond to his question, he focused on the words he'd written, tracing them with his pen, darkening them as he passed over them again.

He probably shouldn't be making demands given the shape she was in, but he needed something back from her. If he was going to expose his blanket chest of not-so-hot, he couldn't be the only one getting that kind of naked.

He also really wanted to know what was doing with her, and she was the only one who was going to tell him.

As the silence droned on, all he could think of was . . . shit, she was shutting the door on him. Again. On one level it so wasn't a surprise and therefore shouldn't have mattered. God knew he'd been on the receiving end of her rejections plenty of times.

The reality was that it felt like another death for him to face—

"I saw you. Yesterday."

Her voice yanked his head up. *What?* he mouthed.

"He kept me in that bedroom. I saw you. You came in and went to the bed. You left with a pillow. I was . . . beside you the whole time you were there."

John's hand lifted to his cheek and she smiled a little. "Yes, I touched your face."

Jesus Christ . . .

How, he mouthed.

"I'm not sure precisely how he does it. But that was the way he got me in the first place. We were all in that cave where Rehv was being kept in the colony. The *symphaths* had come in and Lash got me—it happened so damned fast. I was suddenly off my feet, being dragged out, but I couldn't fight and no one could hear me scream. It's like a force field. If you're inside, and you try to breach it, the shock is painful and quick—but it's more than aversion. There's a physicality to the barrier." She lifted her palm and pushed at the air. "A weave. The strange thing is, though, you can have other people in the same space. Like when you came in."

John was dimly aware that his hands hurt for some reason. Glancing down, he saw that he'd cranked them into fists and the pad was digging into his flesh. So was the Bic he'd been writing with.

Flipping to a new page he scribbled, *I wish I'd known you were there. I would have done something. I swear I didn't know.*

When she read what he wrote, she reached out and put her hand on his forearm. "I know. It's not your fault."

Sure felt like it on his end. To have been right with her and not had a clue that she was—

Oh. Shit.

He wrote fast, then flashed, *Did he come back. After we'd been there.*

When Xhex shook her head, his heart started beating again. "He drove by, but kept on going."

How did you escape, he signed without thinking.

While he scrambled for a fresh page, she said, "How did I get out?" As he nodded, she laughed. "You know, you're going to have to teach me sign language."

He blinked. Then mouthed, *Okay.*

"And don't worry. I'm a fast learner." She took a deep breath. "The barrier had been strong enough to keep me in since the moment that he took me. But then you came and left and . . ." She frowned. "Were you the one who did in that slayer downstairs?"

As his fangs punched out into his mouth, he mouthed, *Fuck, yeah.*

Her little smile had the edge of a dagger. "Nice job. I heard the whole thing. Anyway, it was after everything went quiet that I knew I had to get out or . . ."

Die, he thought. Because of what he'd done in that kitchen.

"So I was—"

He held his hand up to stop her, then wrote fast. When he showed her his words, she frowned and then shook her head.

"Oh, of course you wouldn't have done it if you'd known I was in there. But you didn't. And it sounded as if you couldn't help it. Trust me, I'm the last person you need to apologize to for slaughtering one of those bastards."

True, but he still got a case of the cold sweats thinking of how he'd inadvertently endangered her.

She took another long inhale. "So anyway, after you left, it became apparent the barrier was weakening, and when I was able to punch my fist through a window, I knew I had a shot." She lifted one of her hands and looked at the knuckles. "I ended up taking a runner through the doorway. I figured I was going to need the extra force working with me and I was right."

Xhex shifted around in the bed, wincing. "I think that's where I got the tear. On my inside. I got wrenched badly breaking out—it was like pulling my body through concrete that was about set. I hit the hallway wall hard as well."

There was the temptation to believe the bruises he'd seen on her skin were a result of her escape. But he knew Lash. He'd stared into the face of the guy's cruelty enough times to be absolutely sure that she'd been put through a lot at the hands of the enemy.

"That's why I needed to be operated on."

The statement was voiced in a clear and level way. Trouble was, she did not meet his eyes.

John flipped to a new page, wrote six letters in capitals and tacked on a question mark. When he turned the pad around, she barely glanced at the *REALLY?*

That gunmetal gray stare of hers swung away and locked on the far corner. "It could have been an injury I sustained fighting him. But I hadn't been bleeding internally before I got out, so . . . there you go."

John exhaled and thought of those scratched and stained walls he'd seen in that room. What he wrote next made him ache.

When she looked at what he'd put on the page, her face grew tight to the point of anonymity. It was as if he were staring at a stranger.

He glanced down at his words: *How bad did it get?*

He shouldn't have asked, he thought. He'd seen the condition she was in. Had heard her scream in the OR and been right in front of her as she had a nervous breakdown. What more did he need to know?

He was writing up an I'm-sorry when she spoke in a thin trail. "It was . . . okay. I mean . . ."

His eyes locked on her profile and he willed her to continue.

She cleared her throat. "I don't believe in fooling myself. Doesn't serve any purpose. I was pretty clear on the fact that if I didn't get out, I was going to die soon." She slowly shook her head back and forth on the white pillow. "I was getting really goddamned weak from lack of blood and the fighting. Thing is, I was okay with the dying part, actually. I still am. Death is nothing but a process, albeit typically a painful one. Once it's over and done with? You're fine because you don't exist and all the bullshit is over."

For some reason, the fact that she was so blasé made him anxious and he had to rearrange himself on the little chair to keep from pacing.

"Was it bad?" she murmured. "I'm a fighter by nature. So to some degree it was nothing special. Nothing I couldn't handle. I mean, I'm tight. I lost it in the clinic because I hate medical crap, not because of Lash."

That past of hers, he thought to himself.

"I will tell you this." Her eyes shot back to his and he actually jerked away at the burn in her stare. "What will make it bad? What will make the last three weeks totally unbearable? If I don't kill him. *That* will be insupportable to me."

The bonded male in him sat up and howled, to the point where he wondered if she knew he wouldn't be able to let her be the one to off the motherfucker: Males protected their females. It was the universal law if you had the cock and balls.

Plus the idea of her going anywhere near that guy made John mental. Lash had already taken her once. What if he pulled that cloaking shit again?

They weren't going to get a second chance to get her back. No way.

"So," she said. "I showed you mine. Your turn."

Right. Okay.

Now he was the one staring into that far corner. Jesus Christ. Where to start.

He flipped to a fresh page on his pad, put the Bic nib down, and . . .

Whole lot of nothing came to him. The problem was, there was too much to write, too much to tell her, and wasn't that depressing as shit.

A sharp knock brought both of their heads around.

"Goddamn it," she said under her breath. "Give us a minute!"

The fact that there was someone waiting for an audience on the other side of the door didn't exactly put him in a sharing kind of mood. That, coupled with the communication barrier and his innate cover-it-up tendencies, made his head hum.

"Whoever it is can hang outside all night and all day as far as I'm concerned." She smoothed the blanket over her stomach. "I want to hear what you have to say."

Funny, that was what unlocked him, and he wrote quickly.

It would be easier to show you.

Her brows went in tight together when she read that, and then she nodded. "Okay. When."

Tomorrow night. If you have clearance to go out.

"It's a date." She lifted her hand . . . and put it lightly on his forearm. "I want you to know—"

The knock that cut her off had them both cursing.

"We need a minute!" she snapped before refocusing on him. "I want you to know . . . that you can trust me."

John locked eyes with her and was instantly transported to a different plane of existence. Mighta been heaven again. Who the fuck knew or cared. All he knew was that there was only her and him together, the rest of the world drifting away into a fog.

Was it possible to fall in love with someone twice, he wondered dimly.

"What the hell are you doing in there?"

Rehv's voice on the other side of the door broke the moment, but didn't erase it.

Nothing ever could, John thought, as she pulled back and he got up to his feet.

"Come in, asshole," she snapped.

The instant the mohawked male stepped into the room, John felt the change in the air and he knew, as they looked at each other and stayed silent, that they were communicating as *symphaths* did.

To give them privacy, he headed for the door, and just as he was ducking out, Xhex said, "Will you be back?"

At first, he thought she was talking to Rehv but then

the male snagged his arm and stopped him. "My man? You coming back?"

John glanced over to the bed. He'd managed to forget his pad and pen on the little side table, so he just nodded.

"Soon?" Xhex said. "Because I don't feel tired and I want to learn sign language."

John nodded again and then knuckle-tapped with Rehvenge before heading out into the OR.

As he walked by the empty gurney, he was glad that V had finished cleaning up and wasn't around. Because for the life of him, John wouldn't have been able to hide the smile on his face.

In silence, Blay walked side by side with Qhuinn through the underground tunnel that led between the training center and the mansion's foyer.

The sounds of their two sets of shitkickers mingled, but that was it. Neither he nor Qhuinn said anything. And there was no touching.

Absolutely no touching.

A while ago, before his big admission to the guy, before things had broken down between them, Blay would simply have asked what was on Qhuinn's mind because clearly he was in a churn about something. Now, though, what would have once been just an afterthought seemed like an inappropriate intrusion.

As they came out through the hidden door under the mansion's grand staircase, Blay found himself dreading the rest of the night.

Sure, there wasn't much left to it, but two hours could seem like a lifetime under the right circumstances. Or the wrong ones, as the case was.

"Layla should be waiting for us," Qhuinn said as he went to the foot of the stairs.

Oh . . . great. Just the kind of diversion he was looking for.

Not. After having seen the way that Chosen stared at Qhuinn, he just didn't feel up to getting a boatload of that shy crushing again. Especially not tonight. The near miss with Xhex had left him curiously raw.

"You coming?" Qhuinn asked, his frown pulling in the piercing on his left eyebrow.

Blay flicked his stare down to the hoop that rounded the guy's full lower lip.

"Blay? You okay? Look, I think you need to feed, buddy. Lot been going down lately."

Buddy . . . Christ, he hated that word.

But fuck him, he needed to get a grip. "Yeah. Sure."

Qhuinn gave him an odd look. "My bedroom or yours?"

Blay laughed harshly and started up the stairs. "Does it really matter?"

"No."

"Exactly."

When they got to the second floor, they went past Wrath's study, the doors of which were shut, and headed down the hall of statues.

Qhuinn's room was the first they came to, but Blay pressed on, thinking that something could finally be on his turf, his terms.

Opening the door wide, he left the thing as it was and ignored the soft clicking sound when Qhuinn shut them in together.

In the bathroom, Blay went to the sink, turned on the faucet and bent over, splashing his face. He was drying himself off when he caught the scent of cinnamon and knew Layla had arrived.

Bracing his palms on the marble, he leaned into his arms and sagged. Out in his room, he heard their voices mingling, the lower and the higher trading places for airtime.

Throwing the towel down, he turned and went to

face the music: Qhuinn was on the bed, his back against the headboard, his boots crossed, his fingers linked over his thick chest as he smiled over at the Chosen. Layla was flushed as she stood next to him, her eyes on the carpet, her smaller, daintier hands twisting in front of her.

As Blay came in, the two of them looked over at him. Layla's expression didn't change. Qhuinn's did, though, closing up tight.

"Who goes first?" Blay asked, approaching them.

"You," Qhuinn muttered. "You go."

Blay wasn't about to hop on the bed, so he went over to the chaise and sat down on the foot of it. Layla drifted toward him and sank to her knees before him.

"Sire," she said, offering her wrist.

The TV flipped on and the channels started changing as Qhuinn clicked the whacker at the screen. He settled on Spike and a replay of UFC 63 Hughes vs. Penn.

"Sire?" Layla said.

"Forgive me." Blay leaned down, taking that slender forearm in his big palms, holding firmly but without too much pressure. "I thank you for your gift."

He struck as gently as he could and winced as she jumped ever so slightly. He would have retracted his fangs from her to apologize, but that would have required another puncture when he resumed drawing against her vein.

As he fed, his eyes flicked to the bed. Qhuinn was all about the MMA fight on the screen, his right hand lifted and curled into a fist.

"Fuckin' A," the guy muttered. "That's what I'm talkin' 'bout!"

Blay concentrated on what he was doing and finished up quickly. As he released, he looked into Layla's lovely face. "You have been so gracious, as always."

Her smile was radiant. "Sire . . . you are as ever my joy to serve."

He extended his palm and helped her up, approving of her innate grace. And God, the strength she gave him was nothing short of miraculous. He could feel it powering him up even now, his head fogging out in deference to his body's focus on what he'd just given it.

What Layla had given him.

Qhuinn was still way into the fight, his fangs bared, not for Layla, but for whoever was losing. Or winning. Or whatever.

Layla's expression faded into a resignation that Blay knew waaaaay too much about.

Blay frowned. "Qhuinn. Are you going to feed?"

Qhuinn's mismatched eyes held the screen until the ref called the match; then the blue and the green irises slid to Layla. On a sensuous surge, the guy shifted over on the bed, making room for her.

"Come here, Chosen."

The three words, backed up by that low-lidded stare, was a sucker punch to Blay—trouble was, Qhuinn wasn't throwing anything special Layla's way. That was just how he was.

Sex in every breath, every beat, every move.

Layla seemed to feel the same way, because her hands fluttered around her robing, first to the sashed tie, and then to the lapels.

For some reason, Blay realized for the first time that she was fully naked under those white folds.

Qhuinn extended his hand and Layla's palm trembled as she put it against what he offered her.

"You cold?" he asked, sitting up. Underneath his tight T-shirt, his abs popped into a tight six-pack.

As she shook her head, Blay stalked into his bathroom, shut the door and turned on the shower. After stripping, he got under the spray and tried to forget all about what was happening on his bed.

Which was successful only to the point of taking Layla out of the picture.

His brain got stuck on a fantasy of him and Qhuinn stretched out together, mouths on each other's necks, fangs breaking the surface of velvet skin, bodies . . .

It was pretty common for males to get hard after feeding. Especially if they were thinking of all kinds of naked things. And the soap didn't help.

And neither did the images of what would come after the two of them penetrated throats.

Blay planted one palm on the slick marble and the other on his rigid cock.

What he did was quick and about as satisfying as a piece of cold pizza: good, but not even close to a real meal.

The second trip through the park didn't improve the situation and he refused his body the chance for a third. Because honestly. How skeevy. Qhuinn and Layla were taking care of business on the other side of the door while he was all Johnny Pneumonic in the hot water? Ew.

Getting out, he dried himself off, put on his robe and realized he hadn't brought anything in to get dressed with. As he turned the knob on the door, he prayed that things were where he'd left them.

And they were, thank you, Scribe Virgin: Qhuinn had his mouth to Layla's other wrist and was taking what he needed as the Chosen knelt beside him.

Nothing overtly sexual.

The relief that nailed Blay in the chest made him realize how angry he'd become—not just about this but everything that had to do with Qhuinn.

It was really not healthy. For anyone.

And besides, when everything boiled down, was it wrong that Qhuinn felt the way he did? You couldn't help who you were attracted to . . . and who you weren't.

Over at the closet, Blay pulled out a button-down and some black combats. Just as he turned around to head for the bathroom, Qhuinn lifted his mouth from Layla's vein.

The male let out a satiated groan and extended his tongue toward the wounds he'd made with his fangs. As a flash of silver glinted, Blay's brows popped. The ball piercing was a new one and he wondered who'd done it.

Probably Vishous. The pair were spending a lot of time together and that was how they'd gotten the ink for John's tat—Qhuinn had lifted the bottle.

Qhuinn's tongue lapped at the Chosen's skin, that metal winking with each pass. "Thanks, Layla. You're good to us."

He gave her a quick smile and then shifted his legs off the bed, clearly on his way out. Layla, on the other hand, didn't move. Instead of following suit and taking her leave, her head went down and her eyes locked on her lap—

No, on her wrists, which were flashing from under the yawning cuffs of her robe. As she swayed, Blay frowned.

"Layla?" he said, going over to her. "Are you all right?"

Qhuinn came right around the bed. "Layla? What's doing?"

Now they were the ones kneeling before her.

Blay spoke clearly. "Did we take too much?"

Qhuinn went front and center with his own wrist, offering it to her. "Use me."

Shit, she'd fed John the night before. Maybe this had been too soon?

The Chosen's pale green eyes lifted to Qhuinn's face, and there was no spacy disorientation to her stare. Just a sad, ancient longing.

Qhuinn recoiled. "What did I do?"

"Nothing," she said in a voice that was too deep. "If you will pardon me, I shall take myself unto the sanctuary once again."

Layla went to get up, but Qhuinn captured her hand and tugged her down. "Layla, what's doing."

God, that voice of his. So smooth, so kind. And so was his hand as he reached up and hooked her chin, lifting her eyes to his.

"I cannot speak of it."

"Yeah, you can." Qhuinn nodded in Blay's direction. "He and I will keep your confidence."

The Chosen took a deep breath and her exhale was one of defeat, like she was out of gas, out of options, out of strength. "For truth? You shall remain silent?"

"Yup. Blay?"

"Yes, absolutely." He put his hand on his heart. "I swear. We'll do anything to help you. Anything."

She focused on Qhuinn, her stare locking on his. "Am I unpleasant to your eye, sire?" As he frowned, she prodded her cheekbones, her forehead. "Do I deviate from the ideal in a fashion which renders me—"

"God, no. What are you talking about? You're beautiful."

"Then . . . whyfore do I remain un-called-upon."

"I don't understand—we do call on you. Regularly. Myself and Blay and John. Rhage and V. You are the one we all ask for because you—"

"None of you use me for aught save blood."

Blay rose from his kneel and backed up until his legs hit the chaise and he found himself sitting down. As his ass bounced on the cushion, the expression on Qhuinn's face almost made him laugh. The guy was never caught off guard. Part of that was because he'd been exposed to so much over his relatively short life, both by choice and by curse. And part was his personality. He handled himself in all situations. Period.

Except this one, evidently. Qhuinn looked like he'd been smacked in the back of the head with a pool cue.

"I . . ." Qhuinn cleared his throat. "I . . . I . . ."

Ah, yes, another first. Stuttering.

Layla filled the silence. "I serve the males and Brothers within this place with pride. I give without receiving anything in return because it is my training and pleasure to do so. But I tell you this because you have asked and . . . I find I must. Every time I return to the sanctuary or to the Primale's home, I find myself increasingly empty. To the point that I think I may step aside. Verily . . ." She shook her head. "I cannot keep doing this even though it is all I ever saw my endeavors entailing. It's just . . . my heart cannot go on."

Qhuinn dropped his hands and rubbed his thighs. "Do you want . . . Would you want to keep going if you could?"

"Of course." Her voice was strong and sure. "I am proud to be of service."

Now Qhuinn was dragging a hand through his thick black hair. "What would it take . . . to fulfill you?"

It was like watching a train wreck roll out. Blay should have left but he couldn't move; he just had to witness the collision.

And naturally, Layla's brilliant blush made her even more beautiful. Then her full, lovely lips parted. Closed. Parted . . . closed again.

"It's okay," Qhuinn whispered. "You don't have to say it out loud. I know what you want."

Blay felt a cold sweat break out over his chest and his hands cranked down on the clothes he'd picked out for himself.

"Who," Qhuinn asked hoarsely. "Who do you want."

There was another long pause and then she said one word: "You."

Blay stood up. "I'll leave you two."

He was utterly blind as he made for the exit and he snagged his leather jacket on his way on instinct.

As he shut the door, he heard Qhuinn say, "We'll go very slowly. If we're going to do this, we're going to go very slowly."

Out in the hall, Blay put some fast distance between himself and his bedroom, and it wasn't until he came up to the double doors that led into the staff wing that he realized he was walking around in a robe. Slipping into the set of stairs that led to the movie theater on the third floor, he changed into his clothes in front of the dormant popcorn machine.

The simmering anger deep in his gut was a kind of cancer, eating him up. But it was so baseless. So useless.

Blay stood facing the shelves of DVDs, the titles on the jackets nothing but a visual pattern to his eyes.

What he ended up reaching for wasn't a movie, however.

It was a slip of paper from his coat pocket.

TWENTY-NINE

As the door to the recovery room shut, Xhex felt like she should say something. Out loud. To Rehvenge.

"So. Ah." She pushed at her hair. "How are you—"

He cut off her awkward rambling by striding over to her, that red cane of his jabbing into the tile, his loafers clapping heel-toe, heel-toe. His expression was fierce, his violet eyes burning.

It was enough to give her a complex.

Pulling her sheet up higher, she muttered, "What the hell is wrong with y—"

Rehv swooped down with his long arms and gathered her up against him, tucking her with vital care to his chest. Ducking his head to hers, his voice was deep and grave.

"I never thought I would see you again."

As he shuddered, she lifted her hands up to his torso. After holding herself back for a moment . . . she embraced him as fully as he did her.

"You smell the same," she said roughly, putting her nose right into the collar of his fine silk shirt. "Oh . . . God, you smell the same."

The expensive spiced cologne took her back to the days at ZeroSum when it was the four of them: him at the helm, iAm on the books, Trez on operations, her on security.

The scent was the hook that snagged her and pulled her through the keyhole of the abduction, tying her to her past, bridging the horrid span of the last three weeks.

She didn't want the tether, though. It was just going to make her departure harder. Better to be grounded in immediate events and immediate goals.

And then just float away.

Rehv pulled back. "I don't want to wear you out, so I'm not going to stay. But I needed . . . Yeah."

"Yeah."

Together, they held on to each other's arms and as always she felt that commonality between them, their shared half-blood sides latching on as *symphaths* did with one another.

"You need anything?" he asked. "Food?"

"Doc Jane said nothing solid for another couple hours."

"Okay. Listen, we'll talk about the future—"

"In the future." As she spoke, she projected into her mind an image of them in deep discussion. Which was produced solely to buy him off in the event he was reading her.

Unclear whether he bought it. "I live here now, by the way," he said.

"Where am I exactly?"

"Brotherhood's training center." He frowned. "I thought you'd been here before."

"Not this part. But yeah, I thought that's where they'd taken me. Ehlena was really good to me, by the way. In there." She nodded in the direction of the OR. "And before you ask, I'm going to be fine. Doc Jane said so."

"Good." He gave her hand a squeeze. "I'll go get John."

"Thanks."

At the door, Rehv paused and then shot narrowed amethyst eyes over his shoulder. "Listen up." The *asshole* went unsaid. "You matter. Not just to me, but to a lot of people. So you do what you have to and get your head right. But don't think I'm clueless about what you're planning for afterward."

She glared right back at him. "Fucking sin-eater."

"You know it." Rehv cocked an eyebrow. "And I know you too well. Don't be a fucker, Xhex. You've got all of us on your side and you can get through this."

As he ducked out, she found his faith in her resilience admirable. But she wasn't buying it.

In fact, just the thought of any future beyond Lash's funeral sent a wave of exhaustion blowing through her bloodstream. With a groan, she closed her eyes and prayed that for the love of all that was holy, Rehvenge would stay out of her biz . . .

Xhex woke up with a gasp. She had no idea how long she'd been out. Or where John—

Well, that one was answered: John was on the floor across from her bed, lying on his side, his head resting on the inside of the arm he'd curled up into a pillow. He looked tired even as he slept, his brows tight, his mouth in a weary grimace.

The comfort she took in seeing him was a stunner, but she didn't fight it. Not enough energy—and besides, no witnesses.

"John?"

The instant she said his name, he was up off the linoleum, in a fighting stance, with his warrior's body between her and the door to the hall. Pretty clear he was prepared to shred anything that threatened her.

Which was . . . really sweet.

And better than a bedside bouquet that would have left her sneezing.

"John . . . come here."

He waited a moment, cocking his head as if listening for sounds. Then he dropped his fists and walked over. The instant his eyes swung toward her, his brutal glare and his bared fangs faded into a gut-wrenching compassion.

He went right for his pad, wrote something, and flashed it.

"No, thanks. I'm not hungry yet." Which had always been true for her. After a feeding, she didn't eat for hours, sometimes a full day. "What I would love . . ."

Her eyes shifted to the bathroom in the corner.

Shower, he wrote, and showed her.

"Yeah. Jesus . . . I would love some hot water."

He was all about the nursey-nursey, going in to start the spray, setting out towels and soap and a toothbrush on the counter.

Feeling like a piker, she went to sit up . . . and it became clear someone had tied a house around her chest; it literally felt like she was lifting a two-story colonial up with her shoulders. What got her legs swinging off the side of the mattress was a lot of effort—and the conviction that if she couldn't at least get partially vertical on her own, he was going to call the doc and she was going to lose her shower.

John came in just as her bare soles hit the floor and he was Johnny-on-the-spot with the steadying arm as she stood up. When the sheets fell away from her, they both had a moment of . . . *Holy shit—naked*. But this was hardly a time for modesty.

"What should I do about the dressing?" she murmured, looking down at the white bandage that stretched across her pelvis.

When John glanced over at his pad, as if he were trying to decide whether he could reach it while still holding her up, she said, "No, I don't want Doc Jane. I'm just going to take it off."

She picked a corner free and as she weaved on her feet, she figured it probably would have been better to do this lying down—and under medical supervision. But fuck it.

"Oh . . ." she breathed as she slowly revealed the line of black stitches. "Damn . . . V's female is good with a needle and thread, huh."

John took the bloodstained gauze pack and nothing-but-netted it into the trash can in the corner. And then he just waited, as if he was very aware she was thinking about getting back on the bed.

For some reason, the idea she'd been cut open made her light-headed.

"Let's do this," she said gruffly.

He let her set the pace, which turned out to be only slightly quicker than reverse.

"Can you turn the lights off in there?" she said as they shuffled along, her baby steps measuring at the most three inches. "I don't want to see what I look like in that mirror over the sink."

The instant he was in range, his arm snaked out and he clicked the switch on the wall.

"Thanks."

The feel of the humid air and the sound of the falling water eased her mind and her spine. Trouble was, the tension had helped keep her up and now she was sagging.

"John . . ." Was that her voice? So weak and thin. "John, will you get in with me. Please."

Talk about your long silences. But then in the light that streamed in from over at the bed, he nodded.

"While you undress out there," she said, "you can shut the door and I'll use the loo."

With that, she gripped the bar that was bolted into the wall and maneuvered herself over. There was another pause, and then John stepped back and the light source was dimmed.

After she took care of business, she dragged herself up and cracked the door.

What she got was that pad in her face: *I would have left my boxers on but I don't wear them under my leathers.*

"That's okay. I'm hardly the shy kind."

Although that proved to be not entirely accurate as the two of them got into the stall shower together. You'd think after all she'd been through that a little skin, in a darkened room, with a male she trusted and had already been with, wouldn't have been a big deal. It was, though.

Especially as his body brushed against the back of her as he shut the glass door.

Concentrate on the water, she told herself, wondering if she'd lost her damn mind.

As she tilted her head up, she started to list to the side and his big hand slipped under her arm to hold her vertical.

"Thank you," she said roughly.

Awkward as the situation was, the hot water felt great as it bled into her hair down to her scalp, and the idea that she could clean herself off was suddenly more of a priority than everything John Matthew wasn't wearing.

"I forgot the soap, damn it."

John pulled another lean and lunge, his hips pushing into hers. And although she tensed up, bracing herself for something sexual . . . he wasn't aroused.

Which was a relief. After the stuff Lash had done to her—

As the soap was pressed into her palm, she locked down all thoughts of what had happened in that bedroom and just wet the bar under the spray. Wash herself. Dry off. Back to bed. That's all she had to think about.

The strong, distinct smell of Dial wafted up and she had to blink fast.

It was exactly what she would have chosen herself.

Amazing, John thought as he stood behind Xhex.

If you looked down at your cock and balls and told them that if they behaved badly you would slice them up and bury them in the backyard, they actually listened to you.

He was going to have to remember this.

The shower stall was a generous size for a male, but it was close quarters with the two of them and he had to keep his ass pressed against the cool tile to make one hundred percent sure that Mr. Bright Idea and his twin sidekicks, Dumber and Dumberer, stayed away from her.

After all, the pep talk had done wonders, but he wasn't going to push it.

Besides, he remained shocked that Xhex was so weak he needed to hold her upright—even after feeding. Then again, you didn't just shake off four weeks of hell after a two-hour nap. Which was how long she'd been asleep, according to his watch.

As she hit the shampoo, she arched her back, her wet hair brushing against his chest before she turned around to rinse the suds. He switched his grip as necessary, holding first her right upper arm, then her left, then again her right.

Trouble hit when she bent over to wash her legs.

"Shit—" Her balance shifted so fast, his grip popped off her slick, soapy biceps and she fell right against his body.

He had a brief, vivid impression of slippery, wet, and warm and then he slammed himself back against the wall and scrambled for a less full-contact way of keeping her upright.

"I wish there was a seat here," she said. "I can't seem to keep my damn balance."

There was a pause . . . and then he took the soap from her. Moving slowly, he traded places with her, easing her into the corner he'd parked his ass in, and putting her palms on his shoulders.

As he knelt down, he turned the Dial bar in his hands, working up a good froth while the water pounded on the back of his head and rivered down his spine. The tile was hard under his kneecaps and one set of his toes pressed into the drain as if the thing had teeth and was taking a nibble, but he didn't care.

He was about to touch her. And that was all that mattered.

Wrapping his hand around her ankle, he gave her a gentle tug, and after a moment, she eased her weight to the opposite side and gave him her foot. He put the bar of soap down next to the door and smoothed over her sole and up onto her heel, massaging, cleaning . . .

Worshiping without expecting anything in return.

He went slowly, especially as he headed up onto her leg, pausing every now and again to make sure he didn't push on any of the bruises. Her calf muscle was rock-hard, and the bones that went up into her knee seemed strong as a male's, but she was dainty in her own way. At least compared to him.

As he went even higher, up onto her thigh, he gravitated to the outside. The last thing he wanted her to worry about was him coming on to her, and when he got to her hip, he stopped and picked up the soap again.

After rinsing the bottom of her foot off, he tapped her other ankle, and felt a spear of relief as she obligingly gave him a chance to repeat what he'd done.

Slow massages, slow hands, slow progress . . . and only on the outside up toward the top.

When he was finished, he stood, his knees cracking as he lifted to his full height and maneuvered her under the spray. Holding on to her arm again, he gave her the soap so she could wash whatever else there was to be done.

"John?" she said.

As it was dark, he whistled a *What?*

"You are such a male of worth, you know that. You really are."

She reached up and cupped his face.

It happened so fast, he couldn't believe it. Later, he would play and replay everything over and over again, stretching out the moment endlessly, reliving it and taking a strange kind of nourishment from the memory, again and again.

When it actually went down, though, it was just an instant. An impulse on her part. A chaste gift given in gratitude for a chaste gift received.

Xhex flexed up on her tiptoes and pressed her mouth against his.

Oh, so soft. Her lips were incredibly soft. And gentle. And very warm.

The contact was far too fleeting, but then again, he was ready to go for hours and hours and call that almost long enough.

"Come lie with me," she said, opening the door to the shower and stepping out. "I don't like you on the floor. You deserve much better than that."

Dimly, he shut off the water and followed her, accepting the towel she handed him. They dried off together, her wrapping her whole torso up, him covering his hips.

Outside, he got up on the hospital bed first and it felt like the most natural thing in the world for him to open his arms wide. If he'd thought about it, he wouldn't have made the gesture, but he wasn't thinking.

Which was okay.

Because she came to him as the spraying water in the shower had, drenching him in a warmth that leached through his skin and into his marrow.

But of course, Xhex went even farther through him than that. She always had.

Seemed like he'd lost his soul to her the very first time he'd laid eyes on her.

As he clicked off the light and she settled even closer to him, it felt like she was burrowing right into his cold heart and setting up shop, her banked fire thawing his soul out until he took the first honest-to-God deep breath in months.

John closed his eyes, not expecting to sleep.

He did, though. And very, very well.

THIRTY

In the staff room of Sampsone's mansion, Darius concluded his meeting with the daughter's maid.

"Thank you," he said as he rose to his feet and nodded at the female. "I appreciate your candor."

The doggen *bowed low. "Please find her. And bring her home, sire."*

"We shall endeavor to do just that." He glanced at Tohrment. "Would you be so kind as to show in the steward?"

Tohrment opened the door for the tiny female and the pair left together.

In their absence, Darius stalked around the bare floor, his leather boots making a circle about the ledger desk in the center of the room. The maid knew naught of relevance. She had been utterly open and unassuming—and added absolutely nothing to the puzzle.

Tohrment came back with the steward, and resumed his stance right beside the door, staying quiet. Which was good. Generally speaking during interrogation of the civil variety, you didn't need more than one inquisitor. The boy had another utility, however. His shrewd eyes missed nothing, so perhaps there was something he would pick up on that Darius missed during the discourses.

"Thank you for speaking with us," Darius said to the steward.

The doggen *bowed low. "It shall be my pleasure to be of service to you, sire."*

"Indeed," Darius murmured as he sat down on the hard stool he had used when speaking with the maid. Doggen *by nature tended to value protocol and therefore they would prefer*

those of higher station to be seated in this situation while they stood. "Whatever are you called, steward."

Another low bow. "I am Fritzgelder Perlmutter."

"And how long have you been with the family."

"I was born unto them seventy-seven years ago." The steward linked his hands behind his back and straightened his shoulders. "I have serviced the family with pride since my fifth anniversary of birth."

"Long history. So you know the daughter well."

"Yes. She is a female of worth. A joy to her birthed parents and her bloodline."

Darius watched the steward's face carefully. "And you were not aware of anything . . . that would lead one to expect such a disappearance."

The servant's left eyebrow twitched once.

And there was a long silence.

Darius lowered his voice to a whisper. "If it eases your conscience, you have my word as a Brother that neither myself nor my colleague shall reveal what you say to anyone. Even the king himself."

Fritzgelder opened his mouth and breathed through it.

Darius remained in silence: Pushing the poor male would only slow the process of revelation down. Indeed, he was either going to talk or not, and encouraging him would but delay his decision.

The steward reached into the interior pocket of his uniform and withdrew a bright white handkerchief that was pressed into a precise square. Blotting at his upper lip, he fumbled to put the thing away.

"Nothing shall breach these walls," Darius whispered. "Not a thing."

The steward had to clear his throat twice before his thready voice materialized. "Verily . . . she was above reproach. That I am certain of. There was no . . . consort with a male about which her parents were unaware."

"But . . ." Darius murmured.

At that moment the door swung wide and the butler who had let them into the mansion appeared. He seemed totally unsurprised by the meeting and utterly disapproving of it. No doubt one of his underlings had tipped him off.

"You run such a fine lot of staff," Darius said to the male. "My colleague and I are very impressed."

The low bow did nothing to ease the male's expression of distrust. "I am complimented, sire."

"We were just leaving. Is your master about?"

The butler straightened and his relief was obvious. "He has retired and that is why I came to see you. He has bidden you well adieu, but must needs look after his beloved shellan."

Darius got to his feet. "Your steward here was about to show us the grounds on our way out. As it is raining, I am certain you should prefer one of your staff to guide us o'er the wet grass. We shall return here after the sunset. Thank you for your accommodation of our requests."

There was no other response save for the one the male gave: "But of course."

Fritzgelder bowed to his superior and then extended his arm toward a door in the far corner. "This way."

Outside, the air carried little of spring's promise of warmth. Indeed, it was winter-cold as they trudged through the mist.

Fritzgelder knew exactly where to take them, the steward walking with purpose around the back of the mansion to the part of the gardens that were overlooked by the female's bedroom.

Did not this work out well, Darius thought.

The steward stopped right under Sampsone's daughter's window, but he didn't face the stout stone walls of the house. He looked outward . . . across the flower beds and the hedge maze . . . to the estate next door. And then he deliberately turned to face Darius and Tohrment.

"Lift thine eyes unto the trees," he said while pointing at the house as if describing something pertinent—because undoubtedly they were being watched from the leaded windows of the manse. "Regard well the clearing."

Indeed, there was a break in the crowd of barren tree limbs—which was how they'd seen the far-off mansion from the second floor.

"That vista was not created by our household, sire," the doggen said softly. "And I noticed it about a week before . . . she was found gone. I was upstairs cleaning the rooms. The family of the household had retired underground as it was lighted day. I heard the sounds of cracking wood and rendered my eyes unto the windows, whereupon I saw the branches being taken down."

Darius narrowed his stare. "Very deliberate, the cutting, isn't it."

"Very deliberate. And I thought nothing as it is naught but humans who reside therein. But now . . ."

"Now you wonder if there was a purpose other than landscaping. Tell me, to whom did you mention this."

"The butler. But he beseeched me to remain mum. He is a fine male, of good service to the family. He wants nothing more than to have her found . . ."

"But he wishes to avoid any conception that she might have fallen into human hands."

After all, they were just a tail away from being considered upright rats by the glymera.

"Thank you for this," Darius said. "You have done well your duty."

"Just find her. Please. I care not the source of the abduction—just bring her home."

Darius focused on what he could see of the manse next door. "We shall do that. In one manner . . . or another."

For their sakes, he prayed that the humans in that estate had not dared to take one of theirs. The other race was to be avoided, by the king's orders, but if they had the temerity to aggress upon a vampire? And a noble female at that?

Darius would slaughter each one of them in their beds and leave the bodies to rot into a stench.

THIRTY-ONE

Gregg Winn woke up with Holly curled against him, her lush fake breasts a pair of twin pillows pressing into his side.

A quick glance at the clock and he saw that it was seven a.m. Might as well get packed and head for Atlanta.

"Holly." He nudged her with his hand. "Wake up."

She let out something close to a purr and stretched, her body arching into his and turning his morning hard-on into a raw need that he was inclined to do something about. Memories of how she'd ended up in his bed curbed that impulse quickly, though.

Proving that he was a gentleman in some ways.

"Holly. Come on. Wakey-wakey." He pushed her hair back and smoothed it down her shoulder. "If we get a move on, we'll be in Atlanta by late afternoon."

Which, considering he'd cost them a day chasing after this Rathboone thing, was going to come in handy.

"Okay. I'm up. I'm up."

Actually, he was the only one of the two who got vertical. Holly just nestled into the warm space he'd left and went right back to sleep.

He took a shower and then filled up his suitcase as loudly as he could but she was dead to the world. Not so much asleep as in a coma.

He was just about to go a round with Stan, who was even worse at the whole rousing thing, when a knock sounded on the door.

Could the stoner fool already be awake?

Gregg started talking to his cameraman as he opened the door. "Listen, let's pack up the van—"

It was the tight-ass butler. Looking as if someone had dumped red wine all over his couch.

Gregg lifted his palm. "We're leaving, okay. We're taking off. Just give us—"

"The owner has decided to allow you to film here. For your special."

Gregg blinked like an idiot. "Excuse me?"

The butler's tone grew even more disgusted. If that was possible. "The owner spoke to me this morning. He said you are permitted to host your show herein."

One day too late, Gregg thought with a curse to himself. "Sorry. My team and I are—"

"Thrilled," Holly finished for him.

As he glanced over his shoulder, his narrator was pulling her robe into place and getting off the bed.

"That's great news," she said pointedly while smiling at the butler.

Who seemed to be yo-yoing between disapproval and enchantment at the sight of her all fuzzy and warm and au naturel.

"Very well then," the butler said, after he cleared his throat. "Do let me know if you need anything."

With a bow, he disappeared down the hall.

Gregg shut the door. "I thought you wanted out of here."

"Well . . . I was safe with you, right?" She sidled up to him, stroking his chest. "I'll just stay with you."

The satisfaction in her voice made him suspicious. "Did you play me. About that whole sex thing with . . . whoever it was?"

She shook her head without hesitation. "No . . . but I truly think it was all a dream."

"What about the fact that you said you'd actually had sex."

Her plucked brows furrowed as if she were trying to see through frosted glass. "It's just too hazy to have been real. Last night, I was totally confused, but in daylight . . . it all seems silly."

"You were pretty sure when you came in here."

She shook her head slowly. "Nothing except a really vivid, incredible dream . . . it didn't actually happen."

He searched her face and found nothing but certainty.

Abruptly, she put her hand up to her temple. "Do you have any aspirin?"

"Headache?"

"Yeah. It just came on."

He went over and took his dopp kit out of his suitcase. "Listen, I'm willing to give it a shot here, but if we decide to stay, there's no pulling out. We need to fill our time slot, so we can't just bolt for Atlanta in a day or two."

Frankly, they were already in last-minute land.

"I understand," she said as she sat on the bed. "I absolutely get it."

Gregg brought her the aspirin, then went into the bathroom and snagged her a glass of water. "Listen, why don't you go back to bed. It's early yet and Stan's no doubt still passed out."

"What are you going to do." She yawned as she handed him back the Bayer and the empty glass.

He nodded to his laptop. "I'll take this downstairs to the living room and start going through the footage we captured last night. It should have all uploaded from the remote cameras."

"Stay here?" she asked as she shifted her manicured toes under the sheets.

"You sure?"

Her smile as she put her head down on the pillow revealed her perfect caps . . . and the sweet side of her personality. "Yes. I'll sleep better, plus you smell nice after your shower."

Man, she had some kind of way about her: With her looking up from his bed like that, it would have taken an army to drag him out of the room.

"Okay. Go to sleep, Lolli."

She smiled at the pet name he'd given her after he'd first started sleeping with her. "I will. And thank you for staying with me."

As she closed her eyes, he went over to the wing chair by the window and fired up his laptop.

The feeds from the tiny cameras they'd hidden out in the hall and downstairs in the living room and outside in the big oak next to the porch had indeed uploaded.

Given what had happened, he wished like hell they'd put a remote in Holly's room, but that was the thing. As ghosts didn't actually exist, why would they have bothered? The shots had been taken just for selling the atmosphere of the place . . . and for doctoring up later when it came time to "call forth the spirits of the house."

As he started to look through the images that had been captured, he realized he'd been doing this for how long? Two years? And he had yet to actually see anything or hear anything that couldn't be explained.

Which was fine. He wasn't trying to prove the existence of spirits. He was out to sell entertainment.

The only thing he'd learned in the past twenty-four months was that it was a good job lying had never been a problem for him. Matter of fact, his total comfort with falsity was why he was a perfect television producer: It was all about the goal for him and the particulars, whether they were locations, talent, agents, home owners or whatever was on film or tape, were nothing but soup cans in a cupboard to be positioned at his will. To get the job done, he'd lied about contracts and dates and times and images and sounds. He'd fudged and misled and threatened with fallacies.

He'd manufactured and cued up and—

Gregg frowned and leaned into the screen.

Moving the cursor to the *rewind* button on the Windows Media Player, he replayed the segment that had been recorded in the hallway.

What he saw was a dark shape moving along the corridor outside their bedrooms and . . . disappearing into Holly's. The time on the lower right-hand corner: 12:11 a.m.

Which was just about forty-five minutes before she came to him.

Gregg replayed the segment, watching that huge shadow walk down the center of the dimly lit hallway, blocking the illumination that came in through the window at the far end.

In his mind, he heard Holly's voice: *Because I had sex with him.*

Anger and anxiety swirling in his head, he let the recording play on, the minutes ticking by in that right-hand corner. And then there it was, someone leaving Holly's room, stepping out, blocking the light, about thirty minutes later.

The figure headed off the opposite way it came almost as if it knew where the camera had been mounted and didn't want to show its face.

Just as Gregg was getting ready to call the local police . . . the damn thing disappeared into thin air.

What. The. Fuck.

THIRTY-TWO

John Matthew came awake, sensed Xhex beside him, and panicked.

Dream . . . was this a dream?

He sat up slowly, and when he felt her arm slip down his chest to his belly, he caught it before it hit his hips. God, what he held with care was warm and weighted and . . .

"John?" she said into a pillow.

Without thinking, he curled around her and smoothed her short hair. The instant he did, she seemed to fall right back to sleep.

A quick look at his watch told him it was four in the afternoon. They'd slept for hours, and if the growl in his stomach was anything to go by, she must be starving as well.

When he was sure she was out like a light again, he slipped free of her hold, and moved around quietly, writing her a quick note before drawing on his leathers and T-shirt.

In his bare feet, he padded out into the hall. Everything was quiet because there was no training here anymore, and that was a damn shame. There should have been shouts of sparring from the gym and the drone of lectures in the classroom and the slam of lockers being shut in the showers.

Instead, silence.

But he and Xhex weren't alone, as it turned out.

When he got to the office's glass door, he froze with his hand on the pull.

Tohr was asleep at the desk . . . well, on it. His head was down on his forearm and his shoulders were slumped.

John was so used to feeling anger toward the guy, it was a shock to have nothing of the sort light him up. Instead . . . he felt a crushing sadness.

He'd woken up next to Xhex this morning.

But Tohr was never, ever getting that again. He was never going to roll over and smooth Wellsie's hair. He was never going to go to the kitchen to bring her something to eat. He was never going to hug her or kiss her.

And he'd lost a baby along the way.

John opened the door and expected the Brother to snap up, but Tohr didn't. The male was out cold. Made sense, though. He'd been busy getting back into shape, eating and working out twenty-four/seven, and the effort was showing. His pants no longer hung off him and his shirts weren't sagging. But clearly the process was exhausting.

Where was Lassiter? John wondered as he went by the desk and into the closet. The angel usually stuck pretty close to the Brother.

Ducking into the hidden door in the supply shelves, he walked through the tunnel toward the house. As he went, the fluorescent lights in the ceiling stretched out far, far ahead of him, giving the impression of a predestined path—which considering how things were going was a comfort. When he came to a shallow set of stairs, he mounted them, entered a code, and went up another flight. Emerging into the foyer, he heard the TV in the billiard room and figured that was where the angel was.

No one else in the house would be watching Oprah. Not without a gun to his head.

The kitchen was empty, the *doggen* no doubt catching some food in their own quarters before they had to get First Meal made and set for the household. Which was just as well. He really didn't want help.

Moving fast, he snagged a basket from the pantry and filled the bitch up to the gunwales. Bagels. Thermos full of coffee. Jug of OJ. Cut fruit. Danish. Danish. Danish. Mug. Mug. Glass.

He was going for high calories and praying she liked sweets.

On that note, he made a turkey sandwich, just in case.

And for a different reason he slapped together a ham and cheese.

Striding out through the dining room, he headed back for the door beneath the grand staircase—

"Lot of food for two," Lassiter said, his usual smart-ass routine dialed down.

John wheeled around. The angel was in the doorway to the billiard room, lounging against the ornate archway. He had one boot crossed over the other and his arms linked across his chest. His golden piercings glinted, giving the impression there were eyes all over him, eyes that missed nothing.

Lassiter smiled a little. "So you're seeing things from a different angle now, are you."

As recently as the night before John would have thrown back a *fuck off*, but now he was inclined to nod. Especially as he thought of the cracks in the hallway concrete that had been caused by the pain Tohr had been through.

"Good," Lassiter said, "and about damned time. Oh, and I'm not with him at the moment because everyone needs to be alone. Plus I got to have my O fix."

The angel turned away, his blond-and-black hair swinging. "And you can shut it. Oprah's awesome."

John shook his head and found himself smiling. Lassiter might be a metrosexual pain in the ass, but he'd brought Tohr back to the Brotherhood and that was worth something.

Through the tunnel. Out the back of the closet. Into the office where Tohr was still asleep.

As John stepped up to the desk, the Brother woke up on a full-body spasm, his head whipping off the desk. Half of his face was mashed in, as if someone had hit him with a round of spray starch and ironed his shit badly.

"John . . ." he said roughly. "Hey. You need anything?"

John reached into the basket and took out the ham and cheese. Placing it on the desk, he slid it toward the male.

Tohr blinked as if he'd never seen two slices of rye pulling a cinch on some meat before.

John nodded down at it. *Eat*, he mouthed.

Tohr reached out and placed his hand on the sandwich. "Thanks."

John nodded, his fingertips lingering on the surface of the desk. His good-bye was a quick knock of his knuckles. There was too much to be said in the little time he had, his big concern being that Xhex not wake up alone.

When he hit the door, Tohr said, "I'm really glad you got her back. I'm so damned glad."

As the words drifted over to him, John's eyes latched onto those cracks out in the corridor. That would have been him, he realized. If Wrath and the Brothers had rolled up to his door with bad news about his female, instead of the good kind, he'd have reacted the exact same way Tohr had.

Tore up from the floor up. Followed by a big outtie.

Over his shoulder, John looked at the pale face of the male who had been his savior, his mentor . . . the closest thing to a father he'd ever known. Tohr had gained weight but his face was still hollow and maybe that would never change, no matter how many meals he ate.

As their stares locked, John had the sense that the

pair of them had been through so much more than just the sum of years they'd known each other.

John put the basket down at his feet. *I'm taking Xhex out tonight.*

"Yeah?"

I'm going to show her where I grew up.

Tohr swallowed hard. "You want the keys to my house?"

John recoiled. He'd meant just to include the guy in what was doing with him, kind of a toe-in-the-pool thing to mending shit between them.

I didn't expect to take her there—

"Go. It would be good for you to check it out. The *doggen* get over there just once a month, maybe twice." Tohr shifted and pulled open one of the desk drawers. As he took out a key fob, he cleared his throat. "Here."

John caught the keys and made a fist around them, shame constricting his chest. He'd been busy shitting on the guy lately and, even still, the Brother manned up and offered what had to be a killer for him?

"I'm glad you and Xhex have found each other. It makes cosmic sense, it truly does."

John shoved the keys in his pocket to free up his hand. *We're not together.*

The smile that briefly showed on the guy's face seemed ancient. "Yeah, you are. You two are *meant* to be together."

Jesus, John thought, guess his bonding scent was obvious. Still, there was no reason to go into all the why-nots that were surrounding the pair of them.

"So, you going to Our Lady?" When John nodded, Tohr reached down to the floor and picked up a Hefty bag. "Take this with you. It's drug money confiscated from that brownstone. Blay brought it back. Figure they could use it."

As Tohr got to his feet, he left the loot on the desk and picked up the sandwich, peeling back the Saran Wrap, and taking a bite.

"Good work with the mayo," he murmured. "Not too much. Not too little. Thanks."

Tohr headed for the closet.

John whistled softly and the Brother stopped, but didn't turn around. "It's okay, John. You don't have to say anything. Just be safe out there tonight, 'kay?"

With that Tohr ducked out of the office, leaving John alone in the wake of a kindness and dignity he could only hope to live up to someday.

As the closet door closed, he thought . . . he wanted to be like Tohr.

Heading out into the corridor, it was funny to have that running through his brain again, and its return kind of righted the world: Ever since he'd first met the guy, whether it was the Brother's size, or his intelligence, or the way he treated his female, or how he fought, or even the deep sound of his voice . . . John had wanted to be like Tohr.

This was good.

This was . . . right.

As he walked down to the recovery room, he wasn't exactly looking forward to tonight. After all, the past was oftentimes better left buried . . . especially his, because it stank.

But the thing was, he had a better chance at keeping Xhex from tearing off after Lash this way. She was going to need another night, maybe two, before she was at her full strength. And she should feed again at least one more time.

This way, he would know where she was and keep her by his side for the evening.

No matter what Tohr believed, John wasn't fooling himself. Sooner or later, she was going to bolt and he wasn't going to be able to stop her.

On the Far Side, Payne strolled around the Sanctuary, her bare feet tickled by the springy green grass, her nose filled with the scents of honeysuckle and hyacinth.

She hadn't slept for even an hour since her mother had reanimated her, and though at first that had seemed odd, she didn't give it much thought anymore. It just was.

More than likely her body had had enough repose to last a lifetime.

As she went by the Primale Temple, she didn't go inside. Same with the entrance to her mother's courtyard—it was too early for Wrath to arrive and her sparring with him was the only reason she ever went therein.

When she came to the sequestering temple, however, she did breach the door, although she couldn't have said what drew her to turn the knob and step o'er the threshold.

The bowls of water the Chosen had long used to stare into and thereby bear witness to the events that transpired on the Other Side were lined up in perfect order on the many desks, the rolls of parchment and quill pens likewise laid out, ready for use.

A glint of light caught her eye and she walked over to its source. The water in one of the crystal basins was moving in ever-slowing circles, as if the thing had been used just now.

She looked around. "Hello?"

There was no answer, just the sweet smell of lemon, which suggested No'One had been by recently with her cleaning cloth. Which was a bit of a waste of time, really. There was no dust, no grime, no dirt to be dealt with here, but then No'One was a part of the great Chosen tradition, wasn't she.

Nothing to do but make-work that served no great purpose.

As Payne turned to leave and passed by all the vacant chairs, the sense of her mother's failure was as prevalent as the silence that abounded.

She didn't like the female, for truth. But there was a sad reality to all the plans that had been made that had come to naught: Design a breeding program to weed out defects so that the race was strong. Face the enemy on the field on earth and win. Have her many children serve her with love, obedience, and joy.

Where was the Scribe Virgin now? Alone. Unworshiped. Unliked.

And the coming generations were even less likely to follow her ways, given the manner in which so many parents had strayed from tradition.

Leaving the empty room, Payne stepped out into the pervasive milky light and—

Down by the reflecting pool, a brilliant yellow shape shifted and danced like a tulip in a breeze.

Payne strode toward the figure and as she got closer, she decided Layla had evidently lost her mind.

The Chosen was singing a song that had no words, her body moving to a rhythm that had no fiddle, her hair swinging around like a flag.

It was the first and only time the female had not worn a chignon in the fashion of all Chosen—at least that Payne had seen.

"My sister!" Layla said, coming to a halt. "Forgive me."

Her brilliant smile was brighter than the yellow of her robing and her scent was louder than it had ever been, the fragrance of cinnamon ringing in the air as sure as her lovely voice had.

Payne shrugged. "There's nothing to forgive. Verily, your song is pleasing to the ear."

Layla's arms resumed their elegant swinging. "'Tis a lovely day, is it not?"

"Indeed." From out of nowhere, Payne felt a bolt of fear. "Your mood is much improved."

"'Tis, 'tis." The Chosen pirouetted around, pointing

her foot in a lovely arch before springing up into the air. "Verily, 'tis a lovely day."

"Whatever has pleased you so?" Although Payne knew the answer. Transformations of disposition, after all, were rarely spontaneous—most required a trigger.

Layla slowed her dance, her arms and hair drifting downward and coming to a rest. As her elegant fingers lifted to her mouth, she seemed at a loss for words.

She has been of proper service, Payne thought. No longer was her experience as an *ehros* just theory.

"I . . ." The blush on those cheeks was vibrant.

"Say no more, just know I am happy for you," Payne murmured, and that was largely true. But there was a part of her which felt curiously dejected.

Was it now just her and No'One who were of no use? Seemed so.

"He kissed me," Layla said, looking toward the reflecting pool. "He . . . laid his mouth upon mine."

With grace, the Chosen sat upon the lip of marble and trailed her hand through the still water. After a moment, Payne joined her because sometimes it was better to feel something, anything. Even if it was an ache.

"You enjoyed it, yes?"

Layla stared at her own reflection, her blond hair trailing over her shoulder until the blunt ends hit the silvery surface of the pool. "He was . . . a fire within me. A great burning rush that . . . consumed me."

"So you are virgin no longer."

"He stopped us both after the kissing. He said he wanted me to be sure." The sensuous smile that touched the female's face was a clear echo of the passion. "I was certain, and still am. So is he. Indeed, his warrior's body was ready for me. Hungry for me. To be desired in such a way was a gift beyond measure. I had thought . . . fulfillment in my education was what I was in search of, but now I know there is so much more waiting for me on the Other Side."

"With him?" Payne murmured. "Or through the pursuit of your duty?"

This caused a deep frown.

Payne nodded. "I ascertain that it is more of him than your position you seek."

There was a long pause. "Such passion betwixt us is surely indicative of a certain destiny, is it not?"

"On that I have no opinion." Her experience with fate had led her to one shining, bloody moment of activity . . . followed by a pervasive inaction. Neither of which enabled her to comment on the kind of passion to which Layla was referring.

Or reveling in.

"Do you condemn me?" Layla whispered.

Payne lifted her eyes to the Chosen and thought of that empty seeing room with all the vacant desks and the bowls left unwarmed by well-trained hands. Layla's joy now, rooted as it was in goings-on outside of the Chosen life, seemed another inevitable defection. And that was not a bad thing.

She reached out and touched the other female's shoulder. "Not at all. Verily, I'm pleased for you."

Layla's shy pleasure turned her from beautiful to something close to breathtaking. "I am so pleased to share this with you. I am full to bursting and there is no one . . . really . . . with whom to speak."

"You may always talk to me." Layla, after all, had never judged her or her masculine proclivities and she was very inclined to grant the female the same gracious acceptance. "Will you be going back soon?"

Layla nodded. "He said I could return unto him on his . . . How did he put it? Next night off. And so I shall."

"Well, you must keep me informed. Indeed . . . I shall be interested to hear of how you fare."

"Thank you, sister." Layla covered Payne's hand, a sheen of tears forming in the Chosen's eyes. "I have been so long unused and this . . . this is what I have wanted. I feel . . . *alive*."

"Good for you, my sister. That is . . . very good."

With a final smile of reassurance, Payne got to her feet and took her leave of the female. As she walked back to the quarters, she found herself rubbing that ache that had formed in the center of her chest.

Wrath couldn't get here fast enough, as far as she was concerned.

THIRTY-THREE

Xhex woke up to John Matthew's scent.

That and fresh coffee.

As her lids lifted, her eyes found him in the dim recovery room. He was back in the chair he'd started out in, his torso twisted around as he poured coffee out of a dark green thermos into a mug. He'd put his leathers and his T-shirt on again, but his feet were bare.

When he turned toward her, he froze, his brows shooting up. And even though the java had been on the way to his mouth, he immediately put it out for her to take.

Man, didn't that just sum him up in a nutshell.

"No, please," she said. "It's yours."

He paused as if considering whether or not to argue the point. But then he put the porcelain rim to his lips and sipped.

Feeling a little more steady, Xhex threw off the covers and slid her legs out from under. As she stood up, her towel fell from her and she heard John take a hissing breath.

"Oh, sorry," she muttered, bending down and snagging the terry cloth.

She didn't blame him for not wanting a gander at the scar that was still healing across her lower belly. Not exactly what you needed to see right before you ate your breakfast.

Wrapping herself up, she padded into the loo, used the facilities, and washed her face. Her body was rebounding well, her collection of bruises disappearing, her legs feeling stronger under her weight. And thanks to the rest and her feeding from him, her aches were no longer outright painful, but more just a series of vague discomforts.

When she came out from the bathroom, she said, "You think I can borrow some clothes from someone?"

John nodded, but motioned to the bed. Clearly he wanted her to eat first and she was on board with that plan.

"Thanks," she said, tightening the towel around her breasts. "What you got in there?"

As she sat down, he offered her a variety of things, and she took the turkey sandwich because the need for protein was a craving she couldn't turn down. From his chair, John watched her eat the thing, just drinking his coffee, and the second she was finished, he brought out a Danish that proved too tempting.

The combination of cherry and sweet glaze made her jones for some coffee. And what do you know, John was right there with a mug, as if he were reading her mind.

She polished off a second Danish and a bagel. And a glass of OJ. And two cups of coffee.

And it was funny. The silence of him had a bizarre effect on her. Normally, she was the quiet one in situations, preferring to keep her own council and not share her thoughts on anything. But with John's mute presence, she felt curiously compelled to talk.

"I'm stuffed," she said, lying back against the pillows. As he cocked a brow and lifted the last Danish, she shook her head. "God . . . no. I couldn't manage another thing."

And it was only then that he began to eat.

"You waited for me?" she said, frowning. When he ducked her gaze and shrugged, she cursed softly. "You didn't have to."

Another shrug.

As she watched him, she murmured, "You have beautiful table manners."

His blush was the color of Valentine's Day and she had to tell her heart to calm the fuck down as it started to beat fast.

Then again, maybe she was having palpitations because she'd just thrown close to two thousand calories into her empty gut.

Or not. When John started to lick the frosting from his fingertips, she caught sight of his tongue and for a moment, she felt a stirring in her body—

Memories of Lash crushed the fragile bloom between her legs, the images taking her back to that bedroom, back to him on top of her, forcing her legs apart with his hard hands—

"Oh, fuck . . ." Lunging off the bed, she scrambled to the toilet and just barely made it in time.

It all came up. The two Danishes. The coffee. That turkey sandwich. Complete evac of everything she'd eaten.

As she heaved, she didn't feel the vomiting. She felt Lash's awful mitts on her skin . . . his body inside of hers, pounding away—

Annnnd there was the orange juice.

Oh, God . . . how had she gone through that with the bastard time and time again? The fists and the struggle and the biting . . . then the brutal sex. Over and over and over . . . and then the aftermath. Washing him off of her. Out of her.

Fuck—

Another wave of heaving cut off her thoughts and though she hated throwing up, the shutdown on her brain was a relief. It was almost as if her body was trying to physically exorcise the trauma, just blow it out so that she could start over.

A reboot through booting, so to speak.

When the worst of the vomiting finished off, she sank onto her heels and rested her clammy forehead on her arm. As her breath sawed up and down her throat, her gag reflex quivered like it was considering getting organized again.

Nothing else in there, she told the damn thing. Not unless it wanted to try spring-loading her lungs.

Shit, she hated this part. Right after you'd been through hell, your mind and your environment were full of land mines and you never knew what could set off an explosion. Sure, over time, it faded, but the initial salvo back into "regular life" was a bitch and a half.

She lifted her head and hit the flusher.

As a cool washcloth brushed against her hand, she jumped, but it was just John, nothing for her to be frightened of.

And man, he had the only thing she really wanted at that moment: that clean, damp, cold washcloth was a godsend.

Burying her face in it, she shuddered in relief. "I'm sorry about that food. It was really good going down."

Time for Doc Jane.

As Xhex sat sprawled naked on the floor in front of the toilet, John kept one eye on her and the other on the phone as he texted.

The second he hit *send*, he tossed the cell up onto the counter and pulled a fresh towel down from the stack next to the sink.

He wanted to give Xhex some modesty, but he was also having a hard time looking at how her spine threatened to break through the skin of her back. Wrapping her up, he let his hands linger on her shoulders.

He wanted to pull her into his chest, but he didn't know if she'd be into getting that clo—

Xhex eased back flush against him and arranged the towel, crossing the two halves over her front. "Let me guess. You hit up the good doctor."

Moving himself around, he set his palms on the floor to support his torso and put his knees up so she was cradled on all sides by him. Not bad, he thought. The loo wasn't right in her face, but if she needed it, all she had to do was sit up straight.

"I'm not sick," she said, her voice hoarse. "From the operation or anything. Just ate too fast."

Maybe, he thought. But then, there was no harm in Doc Jane's checking her over. Besides, they needed clearance before they went out tonight, assuming that was even possible now.

"Xhex? John?"

John whistled at the sound of the doctor's voice, and a moment later Vishous's female put her head into the bathroom.

"A party? And I didn't get invited," she said, coming in.

"Well, technically, I think you were," Xhex muttered. "I'm okay."

Jane knelt down and though her smile was warm, her eyes were sharp as they went over Xhex's face. "What's going on here?"

"I got sick after I ate."

"Mind if I take your temperature?"

"I'd prefer not to have anything near the back of my throat right now, if you don't mind."

Jane took a white instrument out of her bag. "I can do it by your ear."

John was shocked when Xhex's hand found his and squeezed hard as if she needed some support. To let her know he was there for whatever she needed, he squeezed back, and the instant he did, her shoulders eased up and she relaxed again.

"Knock yourself out, Doc."

Xhex tilted her head and what do you know, it ended up right on his shoulder. So he really couldn't help but put his cheek on the downy soft curls and breathe in deep.

As far as he was concerned, the good doctor worked much too quickly. Just in, a beep, and she was pulling back—which meant Xhex put her head up again.

"No fever. Would you mind if I looked at your incision?"

Xhex pulled a reveal, parting the towel and exposing her belly and the stripe that ran across her lower abdomen.

"Looks good. What did you eat?"

"Too much."

"Fair enough. Any pain I should know about?"

Xhex shook her head. "I feel better. I really do. What I need is some clothes and shoes . . . and another shot at First Meal."

"I've got scrubs you can put on and then up at the house we'll take care of feeding you again."

"Good. Thanks." Xhex started to get to her feet and he helped her up, keeping the towel in place when it slipped. "Because we're going out."

"Not to fight, you aren't."

John nodded his head and signed at the doctor, *We're just going to stretch our legs. Swear.*

Doc Jane's eyes narrowed. "I can only render a medical opinion. Which is that I think you"—she glanced at Xhex—"should eat something and hang around here for the rest of tonight. But you're an adult, so you can make your own choices. Know this, though. You leave without Qhuinn and Wrath is going to have some serious issues with the pair of you."

That's fine, John signed. He wasn't psyched about the babysitter routine, but he wasn't taking chances with Xhex.

He was under no illusions about the female he loved. She could decide to bolt at any moment and if shit came down to that, he was going to appreciate the backup.

THIRTY-FOUR

Lash came awake in the same position he'd passed out in: sitting on the floor in the ranch's bathroom, arms linked on top of his knees, head down.

When he opened his eyes, he got a look-see at his hard-on.

He'd been dreaming of Xhex, the images so clear, the sensations so vivid it was a wonder he didn't come in his slacks. They'd been back in that room together, fighting, biting, and then he'd taken her, forcing her down on the bed, making her accept him even though she hated it.

He was so totally in love with her.

The sound of a wet gurgle brought his head up. Plastic Fantastic was coming around, her fingers twitching, her lids flickering like blinds that were broken.

As his eyes focused on her matted hair and her blood-stained basque, he felt a stinging pain at his temples, a hangover that sure as shit wasn't tied to a good time. The bitch disgusted him, lying all flopped around in her own filth.

She'd clearly been sick to her stomach, and thank God he'd slept through that commotion.

Pushing his hair out of his eyes, he felt his fangs elongate and knew it was time to put her to good use, but damn . . . she was about as appealing as spoiled meat.

More water. That's what this nightmare needed. More water and—

As he leaned up to crank the shower on again, her eyes drifted over to him.

Her scream pealed out of her bloody mouth and echoed around the tile until his ears rang like church bells.

Goddamn fangs scaring the shit out of her. As his hair fell into his eyes again, he shoved it back and debated ripping her neck open just to kill the noise. But there was no way he was biting into her before she had a bath—

She wasn't looking at his mouth. Her wide, crazy-ass eyes were locked on his forehead.

When his hair bugged him again, he swept it back— and something came off in his hand.

In slow motion, he looked down.

Nope, not his blond hair.

His skin.

Lash turned around to the mirror and heard himself shout. His reflection was incomprehensible, the patch of flesh that had let loose revealing a black oozing under-coat over his white skull. With his fingernail, he tested the edge of what was still attached and found that it was all slack; every square inch over his face was nothing but a sheet draped over the bone.

"No!" he screamed, trying to pat the shit back in place—

His hands . . . oh, God, not them, too. Flaps of skin were hanging off the backs of them, and as he yanked up the sleeves of his button-down, he wished he'd been more gentle, because his dermis came along with the fine silk.

What was happening to him?

Behind him, in the mirror, he saw the whore flash by at a dead run, looking like Sissy Spacek's Carrie only without the prom dress.

With a surge of strength, he went after her, his body moving with none of the power and grace he was used to. As he pounded after his prey, he could feel the fric-tion of his clothes against himself and could only imagine the tearing that was happening over every inch of him.

He caught the prostitute just as she got to the rear

door and started fighting with the locks. Slamming into her from behind, he grabbed her hair, yanked her head back, and bit hard, drawing her black blood into him.

He polished her off, drained her until his sucking pulls got him a whole lot of nothing in his mouth, and when he was done, he just let her go so that she crumpled down right on the carpet.

In a drunken shamble, he went back to the bathroom and turned on the lights that ran along both sides of the mirror.

With each piece of clothing he removed, he revealed more of the horror that was already showing on his face: His bones and muscles glistened with a black, oily sheen under the bulbs' illumination.

He was a cadaver. An upright, walking, breathing cadaver, the eyes of which rolled around in their sockets without lid or lash, the mouth of which showed nothing but fangs and teeth.

The last of his skin was that which anchored his beautiful blond hair to his head, but even that was sliding off the back, like a wig that had lost its glue.

He took off the final piece and, with his skeletal hands, stroked that which he'd taken such pride in. Of course, he fucked the shit up that way, the black ooze congealing on the locks, staining them, matting them . . . so that they were no better than what was still attached to that whore's head out by the door.

He let his scalp fall to the floor and stared at himself. Through the cage of his ribs, he watched his own heart beat and wondered in numb horror what else was going to rot off him . . . and what he was going to be left with when this transformation was finished.

"Oh, God . . ." he said, his voice no longer sounding right, a displaced echo fleshing out the words in a way that was chillingly familiar.

* * *

Blay stood with his closet door open, his hanging clothes all on display. Absurdly, he wanted to call his mother for advice. Which was what he'd always done before when it came to getting dressed up.

But that wasn't a conversation he was in a hurry to have. She'd assume it was a female and get all excited about the fact that he was going on a date and he'd be forced to lie to her . . . or come out of the closet.

His parents had never been judgmental . . . But he was their only son and no female meant not only no grand-babies, but a hit from the aristocracy. Unsurprisingly, the *glymera* was okay with homosexuality provided you were mated to a female and you never, ever spoke about it or did anything overtly to confirm the way you were born. Appearances. All about appearances. And if you did come out? You got shut out.

And so did your family.

On some level, he couldn't believe he was about to go meet up with a male. At a restaurant. And then head off to an after-hours bar with the guy.

His date was going to look amazing. Always did.

So Blay took out a Zegna suit that was gray with the palest pink pinstripe. A fine cotton button-down from Burberry was next, the shirt's body a faint blush, with its French cuffs and collar a bright white. Shoes . . . shoes . . . shoes . . .

Bam, bam, bam on the door. "Yo, Blay."

Shit. He'd already laid the suit out on the bed and he was newly showered, in his bathrobe, with gel in his hair.

Gel: Dead frickin' giveaway.

Going to the door, he cracked the sucker only an inch or two. Out in the hall, Qhuinn was ready for fighting, his chest holster of daggers hanging from his hand, his leathers on, his New Rocks buckled up.

Funny, though, the warrior routine didn't make much of an impression. Blay was too busy remembering what the guy had looked like stretched out on the bed the night before, his eyes on Layla's mouth.

Bad call to have had that feeding done in his own room, Blay thought. Because now he was stuck wondering how far things had gone on his mattress between those two.

Knowing Qhuinn, though, that would be all the way. You're welcome.

"John texted me," the guy said. "He and Xhex are going on a Caldie crawl and for once the motherfucker is—"

Qhuinn's mismatched eyes went up and down and then he leaned to the side and looked over Blay's shoulder. "What's doing?"

Blay brought the lapels of his robe a little closer. "Nothing."

"Your cologne is different—what did you do to your hair?"

"Nothing. What were you saying about John?"

There was a pause. "Yeah . . . okay. Well, he's heading out and we're going with him. We gotta lay low, though. They're going to want their privacy. But we can—"

"I'm off tonight."

That pierced brow dropped low. "So."

"So . . . I'm off."

"That's never mattered before."

"It does now."

Qhuinn shifted to the side again and glanced around Blay's head. "You putting on that suit just to impress the home team?"

"No."

There was a long silence and then one word: "Who."

Blay let the door go wide and stepped back into his room. If they were going to get into a thing, no sense doing it out in the corridor for people to see or hear.

"Does that really matter," he said, on a surge of anger.

The door shut. Hard. "Yeah. It does."

As a fuck-you to Qhuinn, Blay undid the sash of the robe and let it fall from his naked body. And he put the slacks on . . . commando.

"Just a friend."

"Male or female."

"Like I said, does it matter."

Another long pause, during which Blay slipped his shirt on and buttoned it up.

"My cousin," Qhuinn growled. "You're going out with Saxton."

"Maybe." He went over to the bureau and opened his jewelry box. Inside, cuff links of all kinds gleamed. He chose a set that had rubies in it.

"Is this payback for Layla last night?"

Blay froze with his hand on his cuff. "Jesus Christ."

"It is, right. That's what—"

Blay turned around. "Did it ever occur to you that it has nothing to do with you? That a guy asked me out and I want to go? That this is normal? Or are you so self-involved that you filter everything and everybody through your narcissism."

Qhuinn recoiled ever so slightly. "Saxton is a slut."

"Well, I guess you would know what makes one."

"He's a slut, a very classy, very elegant slut."

"Maybe all I want is some sex." Blay cocked a brow. "It's been a while for me, and those females I did in bars just to keep up with you weren't all that good to begin with. I think it's about time I got some, and in the right way."

The bastard had the gall to pale. He honestly did. And goddamn it if he didn't falter back and lean against the door.

"Where are you going?" he asked roughly.

"He's taking me to Sal's. And then we're going to that cigar bar." Blay did his other cuff up and went over to the dresser for his silk socks. "Afterward . . . who knows."

A wave of dark spice wafted across the bedroom, and stunned him into silence. Of all the ways he'd thought this conversation would go . . . his triggering Qhuinn's bonding scent was so not it.

Blay pivoted back around.

After a long, tense moment, he walked toward his best friend, drawn by the fragrance. And as he came closer, Qhuinn's hot eyes tracked him with each step, the link between them, that had been buried on both sides, abruptly exploding into the room.

When they were nose-to-nose, he stopped, his rising chest meeting Qhuinn's. "Say the word," he whispered harshly. "Say the word and I won't go."

Qhuinn's hard hands clapped onto both sides of Blay's throat, the pressure forcing him to tilt his head back and open his mouth so he could breathe. Strong thumbs dug into the joints on either side of his jaw.

Electric moment.

Incendiary potential.

They were going to end up on the bed, Blay thought as he locked his palms on Qhuinn's thick wrists.

"Say the word, Qhuinn. Do it and I'll spend the night with you. We'll go out with Xhex and John and when they're through, we'll come back here. *Say it.*"

The blue-and-green eyes Blay had spent a lifetime looking into locked onto his mouth and Qhuinn's pecs pumped up and down as if he were running.

"Better yet," Blay drawled, "why don't you just kiss me—"

Blay was whipped around and shoved hard against the dresser, the chest of drawers slamming against the wall with a thunder. As cologne bottles rattled and a brush hit the floor, Qhuinn forced his lips down hard on Blay's, his fingers biting into Blay's throat.

It didn't matter, though. Hard and desperate was all he wanted from the guy. And Qhuinn was clearly on board, his tongue shooting out, taking . . . owning.

With fumbling hands, Blay yanked his shirt out from the slacks and went for his own fly. He'd waited so long for this—

But it was over before it started.

Qhuinn spun away as Blay's pants hit the floor, and the guy positively lunged for the door. With his hand on the knob, he rammed his forehead into the panels once. Twice.

And then in a dead voice, he said, "Go. Enjoy yourself. Just be safe, please, and try not to fall in love with him. He'll break your heart."

Between one blink and the next, Qhuinn left the room, the door closing without a sound.

In the aftermath of the departure, Blay stood where he'd been left, his slacks around his ankles, his fading hard-on an utter embarrassment even though he was all alone. As the world grew wavy and his chest constricted into a fist, he blinked fast and tried to keep the tears off his cheeks.

Like an old male, he bent down slowly and pulled up the waistband of the pants, his hands fumbling with the zipper and fastenings. Without tucking his shirt in, he went over and sat on the bed.

When his phone rang over on the nightstand, he turned and looked toward the screen. On some level, he expected it to be Qhuinn, but that was the last person he wanted to talk to and he let whoever it was go to voice mail.

For some reason, he thought of the hour he'd spent in his bathroom fussing over his shave and clipping his nails and arranging his hair with the goddamn gel. Then the time in front of the closet. It all seemed wasted now.

He felt stained. Utterly stained.

And he wasn't going out with Saxton or anybody tonight. Not with the mood he was in. No reason to subject some innocent guy to the toxicity.

God . . .

Damn.

When he felt like he could talk, he stretched over to the side table and picked up his phone. Flipping the thing open, he saw that it was Saxton who'd called.

Maybe to cancel? And wouldn't that be a relief. Getting shut down twice in one night was hardly good news, but it would save him from having to beg off from the male.

Firing up voice mail, Blay propped his forehead on his palm and stared down at his bare feet.

"Good evening, Blaylock. I imagine that you are, at this very moment, standing in front of your closet trying to decide what to wear." Saxton's smooth, deep voice was a curious balm, so soothing and low. "Well, indeed, I am before mine own clothes . . . I believe I shall be going with a suit and vest coat in a gamine houndstooth. I think pinstripes would be a good accompaniment on your part." There was a pause and a laugh. "Not that I would tell you what to wear, of course. But do call if you're on the fence. About your wardrobe, of course." Another pause and then a serious tone. "I'm looking forward to seeing you. Bye."

Blay took the phone away from his ear and hovered his thumb over the *delete* option. On impulse he saved the message.

After a long, steady inhale, he forced himself to his feet. Even though his hands were shaking, he tucked in his fine shirt and went back to the now messy dresser.

He picked up the cologne bottles, righting them once again, and retrieved the brush from the floor. Then he opened up the sock drawer . . . and took out what he needed.

To finish getting dressed.

THIRTY-FIVE

Darius was due to meet his young protégé after the sun was well set, but before he headed over to the human mansion they'd spied upon through the trees, he materialized in the woods afore the Brotherhood's cave.

With the Brothers scattered thither and yon, communication could be delayed and a system had been set up for the exchange of notations and announcements. All came here once a night to see what had been left for the others or to leave missives of their own.

After ensuring that there were no eyes upon him, he ducked into the dark enclave, went through the secret rock wall, and made his way through the series of gates toward the sanctum sanctorum. The "communication system" was nothing but an alcove set in the rock wall, into which correspondence could be placed, and because of its simplicity, it was far down the way.

He didn't make it far enough to see if his brothers had anything to say to him, however.

Coming up to the final gate, he saw upon the stone floor that which at first glance appeared to be a pile of clothing folded up next to a rough sack.

As he unsheathed his black dagger, a dark head rose from the heap.

"Tohr?" Darius lowered his weapon.

"Aye." The boy turned over on his ragged bed. "Good evening, sire."

"Whatever are you doing herein?"

"I have slept."

"'Tis obvious, indeed." Darius went over and knelt down. "But why-for did you not return unto your home?"

307

After all he had been disowned, but Hharm rarely went unto his mated abode. Surely the young one could have stayed with his mahmen?

The boy pushed himself up to his feet and steadied himself on the wall. "Whatever time is it? Have I missed—"

Darius gripped Tohr's arm. "Did you eat?"

"Am I late?"

Darius didn't bother asking any more questions. The answers to what he wanted to know were in the manner in which the boy refused to lift his eyes: Indeed, he had been asked not to take shelter in his father's house.

"Tohrment, how many nights have you passed herein?" On that cold floor.

"I can find another place to tarry. I shall not retire here again."

Praise the Scribe Virgin, that would be true. "Wait here, please."

Darius ducked through the gate and checked for correspondence. As he found communications for Murhder and Ahgony, he thought about leaving one for Hharm. On the lines of, How could you possibly turn out your blooded son such that he is forced to spend the day with naught but stone for a bed and his clothes for a cover?

You arsehole.

Darius returned to Tohrment and found that the boy had packed his things up in his satchel and had his weapons strapped on.

Darius bit back a curse. "We shall go first to the female's mansion. I have something I must needs discuss with . . . that steward. Bring your things, son."

Tohrment followed, more alert than most would be after however many days without food or proper rest.

They materialized in front of Sampsone's manse and Darius nodded to the right, indicating that they should proceed around to the back. As they came to the rear of the house, he took them to the door they had exited from the evening before and rang the banging bell.

The butler opened the way and bowed low. "Sires, what-ever may we do to serve you in your quest?"

Darius stepped inside. "I should like to speak anew to the second-floor steward."

"But of course." Another low bow. "Perhaps you would be good enough to follow me to the front parlor?"

"We'll wait here." Darius took a seat at the staff's well-worn table.

The *doggen* paled. "Sire . . . this is—"

"Where I should like to speak with the steward Fritzgelder. I see no benefit to adding to the burden of your master and mistress by their encountering us unannounced in their house. We are not guests—we are here to be of service in their tragedy."

The butler bowed so deeply it was a wonder that he didn't fall on his brow. "Verily, you are right. I shall get Fritzgelder this very moment. Is there anything we can do to ease you?"

"Yes. We would greatly appreciate some victuals and ale."

"Oh, sire, but of course!" The *doggen* bowed his way out of the room. "I should have so offered, forgive me."

When they were alone, Tohrment said, "You don't need to do that."

"Do what?" Darius drawled, running his fingertips over the table's pitted surface.

"Get food for me."

Darius glanced over his shoulder. "My dear boy, it was a request calculated to put the butler at ease. Our presence in this room is a source of great discomfort for him as is the request to question anew his staff. The request for food shall be a relief for him. Now please sit, and when the victuals and libations arrive, you must consume them. I have had my fill prior."

There was the scraping sound of a chair being dragged back and then a creak as Tohrment's weight settled on the seat.

The steward arrived momentarily.

Which was awkward, as Darius didn't really have anything to ask him. Where was the food—

"Sires," the butler said with pride as he opened the door with a flourish.

Staff filed in with all manner of trays and tankards and provisions, and as the feast was laid out, Darius cocked a brow at Tohrment and then pointedly stared down at the various foodstuffs.

Tohrment, ever the polite male, helped himself.

Darius nodded at the butler. "This is a repast worthy of such a house. Verily your master should be most proud."

After the butler and the others left, the steward waited patiently and so did Darius until Tohrment had taken all he could. And then Darius got to his feet.

"Verily, may I inquire of you a favor, Steward Fritzgelder?"

"But of course, sire."

"Will you be so kind as to store my colleague's bag for us during the eve? We shall return after we have made our surveillance."

"Oh, yes, sires." Fritzgelder bowed low. "I shall take the best of care of his things."

"Thank you. Come, Tohrment, we are off."

As they went outside, he could feel the ire of the boy and was not at all surprised when his arm was caught.

"I can take care of myself."

Darius stared over his shoulder. "Of that there is no doubt. However, I do not need a partner who is weakened by an empty gut and—"

"But—"

"—if you think this family of great means would begrudge a meal to aid in the search of their daughter, you are vastly mistaken."

Tohrment dropped his hand. "I shall find lodging. Food."

"Yes, you will." Darius nodded to the ring of trees around the neighboring estate. "Now may we proceed?"

When Tohrment nodded, the pair of them dematerialized into the forest and then stalked their way onto the property of the other mansion.

With each forward stride toward their destination, Darius felt upon him a sense of crushing dread which increased until he found it hard to breathe: Time was working against them.

Every night that passed and they didn't find her was another step closer to her death.

And they had so very little to go on.

THIRTY-SIX

The Caldwell Greyhound terminal was on the far side of downtown, on the edge of the industrial park that stretched south of the city. The old flat-roofed building was ringed by a corral of chain-link fence, as if the buses were flight risks, and its porte cochere had a sag in the middle.

As John took form in the lee of a parked bus, he waited for Xhex and Qhuinn. Xhex was the first to arrive, and man, she was looking much better; the second attempt at eating had stayed down just fine and her color was really good. She was still in the scrub bottoms Doc Jane had given her, but on top she had on one of his black hoodies, and one of his windbreakers.

He loved the outfit. Loved that she was in his threads. Loved that they were too big on her.

Loved that she looked like a girl.

Not that he didn't totally get off on her leathers and her muscle shirts and her I'll-crack-your-balls-if-you-step-out-of-line routine. That was a complete turn-on, too. It was just . . . the way she looked now seemed private, for some reason. Probably because he was damned sure she didn't let herself get seen like this very often.

"Why are we here?" she asked, looking around. Her voice wasn't disappointed or annoyed, thank God. She was just curious.

Qhuinn took form about ten yards away and crossed his arms over his chest like he didn't trust himself not to hit something. The guy was in a vicious mood. Absolutely vile. He hadn't had two civil words to say in the foyer as John had told him the order of places they were going, and the cause hadn't been clear.

Well . . . at least not until Blay had walked by the group looking like a million bucks in a gray pin-striped suit. The guy had paused only to say goodbye to John and Xhex; he hadn't spared even a glance for Qhuinn as he'd gone out the vestibule and into the night.

He'd had fresh cologne on.

Clearly he was going on a date. But with who?

On a hiss and roar, a bus trundled out of the lot, the diesel fumes making John's nose threaten a sneeze.

Come on, he mouthed to Xhex, switching his backpack to his other shoulder and drawing her forward.

The two of them walked across the damp pavement toward the glowing fluorescent light of the terminal. Even though it was chilly, John kept his leather jacket open in case he needed to get to his daggers or his gun, and Xhex was packing as well.

Lessers could be anywhere and humans could be idiots.

He held the door open for her and was relieved to see that aside from the ticket taker who was behind bullet-proof Plexiglas, there was only an old man sleeping upright on one of the plastic benches and a woman with a suitcase.

Xhex's voice was low. "This place . . . you're saddened by it."

Shit, he supposed he was. But not from what he'd experienced here . . . more what his mother must have felt, being alone and in pain while she struggled through labor.

Whistling in a loud burst, he held up his palm as the three humans looked over. Dialing down their consciousness, he put them each in a light trance and then walked over to the metal door that had a sign screwed into it: WOMEN.

Planting his hand on the cold panel, he pushed his

way in a little and listened. No sounds. Place was empty.

Xhex walked past him, her eyes going around the cinder-block walls and the stainless-steel sinks and the three stalls. The place smelled like Clorox and damp, sweaty stone and the mirrors weren't made of glass, but of polished sheets of metal. Everything was bolted down, from the drooling soap dispensers to the No Smoking sign to the rubbish bin.

Xhex stopped in front of the handicapped stall, her eyes sharp. As she nudged open the flapping door, she recoiled and seemed confused.

"Here . . ." She pointed down to the floor in the corner. "Here was where you were . . . where you landed."

When she glanced back at him, he shrugged. He didn't know which stall precisely, but it made sense that if you were having a baby, you'd want to be in the one with the most space.

Xhex stared at him as if she were seeing through him and he briefly shifted around and checked to see if someone had joined them. Nope. Just her and him, together in the women's bathroom.

What, he mouthed as she let the stall door shut.

"Who found you?" When he made like he was mopping the floor, she murmured, "A janitor."

As he nodded, he felt ashamed of this place, of his history.

"Don't be." She came over to him. "Believe me, I'm not one to judge. My circumstances aren't any better. Hell, they're arguably worse."

Being a half-breed *symphath*, he could only imagine. After all the two breeds didn't mix willingly for the most part.

"Where did you go from here?"

He led her out of the bathroom and glanced around. Qhuinn was standing in the far corner, glaring at the doors of the terminal like he was hoping something that smelled like baby powder would walk in. When the guy looked over, John nodded; then he untranced and scrubbed the minds of the humans, and the three of them dematerialized.

When they took form again, it was in the backyard of Our Lady's orphanage, next to the slide and the sandbox. A bitter March wind swept over the grounds of the church's sanctuary for the unwanted, the links of the swings creaking and the bare branches of the trees offering no protection. Up ahead, the rows of four-paned windows that marked the dormitory were dark . . . and so were all the ones in the cafeteria and the chapel.

"Humans?" Xhex breathed as Qhuinn wandered over and sat his ass on one of the swings. "You were raised by humans? God . . . damn."

John walked toward the building, thinking maybe this wasn't such a hot idea. She seemed horrified—

"You and I have more in common than I thought."

He stopped dead and she must have read his expression . . . or his emotions: "I was raised around people I wasn't like, too. Although considering what my other half is, that could have been a blessing."

Stepping in beside him, she stared up at his face. "You were braver than you thought." She nodded toward the orphanage. "When you were in here, you were braver than you thought."

He didn't agree, but he wasn't about to argue her faith in him. After a moment, he held out his hand toward her, and when she took it, they walked together to the back entrance. A quick disappear and they were on the inside.

Oh, shit, they used the same floor cleaner. Acid lemon.

And the layout of the place hadn't changed, either. Which meant the headmaster's office was still down the hall, in the front of the building.

Leading the way, he went over to that old wooden door, slipped off the backpack and hung it on the brass doorknob.

"What's in there anyway?"

He held up his hand and rubbed his fingers against his thumb.

"Money. From the raid on . . ."

He nodded.

"Good place for it."

John turned around and stared down the hall to where the dormitory was. As memories bubbled up, his feet started in that direction before he had a conscious thought to go over to where he'd once laid his head. It was so strange being here again, remembering the loneliness and the fear and the nagging sense that he was totally different—especially when he was with other boys his own age.

That had always made it worse. Being around that which he should have been essentially identical to had alienated him the most.

Xhex followed John through the hallway, staying a little behind him.

He was walking silently, toe-heel in his shitkickers, and she took his example to heart, doing the same so that they were nothing but ghosts in the quiet corridor. As they went, she noted that although the physical plant of the building was old, everything was spotless, from the high-polish linoleum, to the much-painted beige walls, to the windows with the chicken wire embedded in the glass. There was no dust, no cobwebs, no chips or cracks in the plaster.

It gave her hope that the nuns and the administrators looked after the kids with similar attention to detail.

As she and John came up to a pair of doors, she could feel the dreams of the boys on the far side, the tremors of emotion that bubbled up through their REM sleep tickling her *symphath* receptors.

John ducked his head in, and as he stared in at those who were where he had been, she found herself frowning again.

His emotional grid had . . . a shadow to it. A parallel but separate construct that she had picked up on before, but now found screamingly obvious.

She'd never sensed anything like it in anybody else and she couldn't explain it . . . and didn't think John was consciously aware of what he was doing. For some reason, though, this trip into his past was exposing the fault line in his psyche.

As well as other stuff. He'd been just like her, lost and apart, cared for by others out of obligation, not blooded love.

On some level, she thought that she should tell him to stop this whole thing, because she could sense how much it was taking out of him—and how much farther they had yet to go. But she was captivated by what he was showing her.

And not just because as a *symphath* she fed off the emotions of others.

No, she wanted to know more about this male.

While he studied the sleeping boys and got pulled into his past, she focused on his strong profile as it was lit by the security light over the door.

When she lifted her palm up and laid it on his shoulder, he jumped a little.

She wanted to say something smart and kind, put togther some combination of words to reach him where he'd reached her with this. But the thing was, there was more courage in these revelations of his than she had ever shown anyone, and in a world that was full of taking and cruelty, he was fucking breaking her heart with what he was giving her.

He'd been so lonely here and the echoes of the grieving were killing him. And yet he was going to soldier on because he'd told her he would do so.

John's beautiful blue eyes met her stare, and as he tilted his head in inquiry, she realized words were bullshit in moments like this.

Stepping into his hard body, she wrapped one of her arms around the small of his back. With her free hand, she stretched up and captured his nape, pulling him down to her.

John hesitated and then came willingly, linking his arms around her waist and burying his face in her neck.

Xhex held him, lending him her strength, offering him shelter that she was more than capable of providing. As they stood one against another, she looked over his shoulders into the room beyond, at the small dark heads on their pillows.

In the silence, she felt the past and the present shift and mix, but that was a mirage. There was no way to comfort the lost boy he'd been back then.

But she had the grown male.

She had him right in her arms, and for a brief moment of whimsy, she imagined that she was never, ever going to let him go.

THIRTY-SEVEN

As he sat in his guest room at the Rathboone mansion, Gregg Winn should have felt better than he did. Thanks to some evocative camera shots of that soulful portrait down in the living room, coupled with some stills of the grounds taken in the gloaming, the brass back in L.A. was thrilled with the presell footage and was set to start running it. The butler had also come along nicely, signing the legal documents that gave permission for all kinds of access.

Stan the cameraman could perform a proctology exam on the damn house for all the places he could stick his lens.

But Gregg didn't have the taste of victory in his mouth. Nope, he had a case of the this-isn't-rights riding his gut and a tension headache that ran from the base of his skull all the way into his frontal lobe.

The problem was the hidden camera they'd put out in the hall the night before.

There was no rational explanation for what it had captured.

Ironic that a "ghost hunter," when confronted with a figure who disappeared into thin air, needed Advil and Tums. You'd think he'd be overjoyed that for once he didn't have to get his camera guy to fudge the footage.

As for Stan? He just shrugged it all off. Oh, he thought it was a ghost for sure—but that didn't faze him in the slightest.

Then again, he could have been tied to a set of railroad tracks on some *Perils of Pauline* thing and just thought, Perfect, time for a quick nap before he got greased.

There were advantages to being a pothead.

As the clock struck ten down below, Gregg got up from the laptop and went to the window. Man, he'd feel better about this whole thing if he hadn't seen that long-haired figure roaming the grounds the night before.

To hell with that: Better that he hadn't seen the fucker outside in the hall pulling a hallucination's trick of now-you-see-it, now-you-don't.

From behind him on the bed, Holly said, "Are you hoping to see the Easter bunny out there?"

He glanced over at her and thought she looked great propped up against the pillows, her nose in a book. When she'd taken the thing out, he'd been surprised to see it was the Doris Kearns Goodwin about the Fitzgeralds and the Kennedys. He'd have figured she was more a Tori Spelling–bio kind of girl.

"Yeah, I'm all about the cotton tail," he murmured. "And I think I'm going to go down and see if I can get the bastard's basket."

"Don't bring back any marshmallow Peeps. Colored eggs, chocolate bunnies, that fake fuzzy grass—all good. The Peeps freak me out."

"I'll have Stan come sit with you, 'kay?"

Holly's eyes lifted from Camelot's backstory. "I don't need a nanny. Especially not one who's liable to light up a joint in the bathroom."

"I don't want to leave you alone."

"I'm not alone." She nodded to the camera in the far corner of the room. "Just turn that on."

Gregg leaned back against the window jamb. The way her hair caught the light was really nice. Of course, the color was undoubtedly an expert dye job . . . but it was the perfect shade of blond against her skin.

"You aren't scared, are you," he said, wondering

exactly when it was that they'd traded places on that account.

"You mean about last night?" She smiled. "Nope. I think that 'shadow' is Stan playing a trick on both of us as payback for jerking him around between rooms. You know how he hates moving luggage. Besides, it got me back in your bed, didn't it. Not that you've done anything much about this."

He snagged his windbreaker and went over to her. Taking her chin in hand, he looked into her eyes. "You still want me like that?"

"Always have." Holly's voice dropped. "I'm cursed."

"Cursed?"

"Come on, Gregg." When he just looked at her, she threw up her hands. "You're a bad bet. You're married to your job and you'd sell your soul to get ahead. You reduce everything and everyone around you to a lowest common denominator and that allows you to use them. And when they aren't useful? You don't remember their name."

Jesus . . . she was smarter than he'd thought. "So why do you want to have anything to do with me?"

"Sometimes . . . I don't really know." Her eyes returned to the book, but they didn't go back and forth over the lines. They just locked onto the page. "I guess it's because I was really naive when I met you, and you gave me a shot when no one else would, and you taught me about a lot of things. And that initial crush is hanging on."

"You make it sound like a bad thing."

"It can be. I've been hoping to grow out of it . . . and then you do stuff like look after me and I get sucked in all over again."

He stared at her, measuring her perfect features and her smooth skin and her amazing body.

Feeling tangled and strange, and like he owed her an

apology, he went over to the camera on the tripod and turned it on to record. "You got your cell phone with you?"

She reached into her robe's pocket and took out a BlackBerry. "Right here."

"Call me if anything strange happens, 'kay?"

Holly frowned. "Are you all right?"

"Why do you ask?"

She shrugged. "Just never seen you quite this . . ."

"Anxious? Yeah, I guess there's something about this house."

"I was going to say . . . connected, actually. It's like you're truly looking at me for the first time."

"I've always looked at you."

"Not like this."

Gregg went over to the door and paused. "Can I ask you something weird? Do you . . . color your hair?"

Holly put her hand up to the blond waves. "No. I never have."

"It's really that blond?"

"You should know."

As she cocked her eyebrow, he flushed. "Well, women can get dye jobs down . . . you know."

"Well, I don't."

Gregg frowned and wondered who the hell was running his brain: he seemed to have all these odd thoughts playing over his airwaves, like maybe his station had been hijacked. Giving her a little wave, he ducked into the hall, and looked left then right while listening hard. No footsteps. No creaking. No one with a sheet pulled over his head, Casper-ing around.

Yanking his windbreaker on, he stalked over to the stairs and hated the echo of his own footsteps. The sound made him feel pursued.

He glanced behind himself. Nothing but empty corridor.

Down on the first floor, he looked at the lights that had been left on. One in the library. One in the front hall. One in the parlor.

Ducking around the corner, he paused to check out that Rathboone portrait. For some reason, he didn't think the painting was so fucking romantic and salable anymore.

Some reason, his ass. He wished he'd never called Holly over to look at the thing. Maybe it wouldn't have marked her subconscious such that she fantasized about the guy coming to her and having sex with her. Man . . . that expression on her face when she'd been talking about her dream. Not the fear part, but the sex, the resonant sex. Had she ever looked like that after he'd been with her?

Had he ever stopped to see if he'd satisfied her like that?

Satisfied her at all?

Opening the front door, he stepped out like he was on a mission, when in reality, he had nowhere to go. Well, except for away from that computer and those images . . . and that quiet room with a woman who might just have more substance than he'd always thought.

Kind of like a ghost being real.

God . . . the air was clean out here.

He walked out away from the house, and when he was about a hundred yards down the rolling grass, he paused and looked back. On the second floor, he saw the light on in his room and pictured Holly nestled against the pillows, that book in her long, thin hands.

He kept going, heading for the tree line and the brook.

Did ghosts have souls? he wondered. Or were they souls?

Did television execs have souls?

Now, that was an existential question and a half.

He took a leisurely loop around the property, stopping to tug at the Spanish moss and feel the bark on the oaks and smell the earth and the mist.

He was on his way back to the house when the light on the third floor came on . . . and a tall, dark shadow passed by one of the windows.

Gregg started to walk fast. Then broke out into a run.

He was flying as he leaped onto the front porch and hit the door, throwing it open and pounding up the stairs. He didn't give a shit about that whole don't-go-to-the-third-floor warning. And if he woke people, fine.

As he came to the second floor, he realized he didn't have a clue which door could take him to the attic. Walking fast down the hall, he figured the numbers on the jambs were dead giveaways that he was ripping past guest rooms.

Then he got to Storage. Housekeeping.

Thank you, Jesus: EXIT.

He broke through, hit the back staircase and took the steps up two at a time. When he got to the top, he found a locked door with a light glowing under the bottom.

He knocked loudly. And got a whole lot of nothing.

"Who's there?" he called out, yanking on the knob. "Hello?"

"Sir! Whatever are you doing?"

Gregg wheeled around and looked down the stairs at the butler—who was, even though it was after hours, still dressed in his tux.

Maybe he didn't sleep in a bed, but hung himself up in a closet so he didn't wrinkle overnight.

"Who's in there?" Gregg demanded, jabbing his thumb over his shoulder.

"I'm sorry, sir, but the third floor is private."

"Why?"

"That is none of your concern. Now, if you don't mind, I'm going to ask you to return to your room."

Gregg opened his mouth to keep arguing, but then slammed his gap shut. There was a better way to deal with this.

"Yeah. Okay. Fine."

He made a show of thumping down the stairs and brushing past the butler.

Then he went to his room like a good little guesty-poo and slipped inside.

"How was your walk?" Holly asked, yawning.

"Anything happen when I was gone?" Like, oh, say, a dead guy coming in here to bang you?

"Nope. Well, other than someone racing down the hall. Who was that?"

"No idea," Gregg muttered, going over and shutting off the camera. "Not a clue . . ."

THIRTY-EIGHT

John took form next to a streetlight that probably didn't have a lot of job satisfaction. The illumination pooling beneath its giraffe neck bathed the front of an apartment building that would have looked a hell of a lot better in total darkness: The bricks and mortar were not red and white, but brown and browner, and the cracks in various windows were fixed with zigzagged duct tape and cheap blankets. Even the shallow steps going up to the lobby were a pockmarked mess like they'd been hit with a jackhammer.

The place was just as it had been when he'd spent his last night inside except for one thing: the yellow Condemned notice that had been nailed to the front door.

File that under Well, *duh*.

As Xhex came out of the shadows and joined him, he did his best to project nothing but a calm dissociation . . . and knew he was failing. This grand tour of the shitscape of his earlier life was harder to go through than he'd thought, but it was like an amusement park ride. Once you got on and the cart got rolling, there was no reaching for the off/stop button.

Who knew that his existence should have come with a warning for pregnant ladies and epileptics.

Yeah, there was no stopping this; she'd totally tweak to him not finishing it. She seemed to know everything he was feeling—and that would include the sense of failure that would rip through him if he pulled out early.

"You ended up here?" she whispered.

Nodding, he led her past the front of the building

and around the corner to the alley. As he came up to the emergency exit, he wondered if the latch would still be broken—

The punch bar let go with just a little force and they stepped in.

The carpet in the hallway was more like the raw dirt floor in some kind of cabin, all packed down and sealed with stains that had leached into the fibers and dried up hard. Empty booze bottles and twisted Twinkie wrappers and stunted cigarette butts littered the corridor, and the breeze in the air smelled like a bum's armpit.

Man . . . even a tanker of Febreze couldn't make a dent in this nose-mare.

Just as Qhuinn came in through the emergency exit, John hung a louie into the stairwell and started an ascent that made him want to scream. As they went up, rats squeaked and scampered out of the way and the eau de tenement got thicker and more pungent, like it was fermenting in the higher altitudes.

When they got to the second floor, he led the way down the hall and stopped in front of a starburst pattern on the wall. Jesus Christ . . . that wine stain was still there—although why the hell was he surprised? Like Merry Maids was going to show up here and bleach it out?

Going one more door down, he pushed into what had once been his studio apartment and walked . . . inside . . .

God, everything was just as he'd left it.

No one had lived here since he had, which he supposed made sense. People had been gradually leaving back when he'd been a tenant—well, the ones who could afford to get better places had taken off. What had stayed had been the druggies. And what had taken up the vacancies had been the homeless who'd seeped in like cockroaches through the broken windows and busted ground-level doors. The culmination in the demographic shift had been that Condemned notice, the building having officially been declared dead, the cancer of declining fortune claiming everything but the shell.

As he looked at the *Flex* magazine he'd left on the twin bed by the window, reality warped on him, dragging him back even as his shitkickers were firmly planted in the here and now.

Sure enough, when he reached over and cracked the warm fridge . . . cans of vanilla Ensure.

Yeah, 'cause even hungry, penniless scavengers wouldn't take that shit.

Xhex walked around and then paused at the window he'd stared out of for so many nights. "You wanted to be other than you were."

He nodded.

"How old were you when you were found?" As he flashed two fingers twice, her eyes widened. "Twenty-two? And you had no idea you were . . ."

John shook his head and went over to pick up the *Flex*. Flipping through the pages, he realized he had become what he had always wished he would be: a big, badass motherfucker. Who'da thought. He'd been a real scrawny pretrans, at the mercy of so much—

Tossing the magazine back down, he cut off that thought pattern hard and fast. He was willing to show her almost everything. But not that. Never . . . that part.

They were not going back to the first building he'd lived in alone and she was not going to find out why he'd left there for this addy.

"Who brought you into our world?"

Tohrment, he mouthed.

"How old were you when you left the orphanage?" He flashed a one and a six. "Sixteen? And you came here? Right from Our Lady?"

John nodded and went over to the cupboards above

the sink. Opening one up, he saw the only thing he'd expected to find left behind. His name. And the date.

He stepped aside so Xhex could see what he'd written. He remembered doing it, so quick, so fast. Tohr had been waiting down at the curb and he'd scooted up to get his bike. He'd scribbled the markings as a testament to . . . he didn't know what.

"You didn't have anyone," she murmured, looking inside. "I was like that. My mother died in childbirth and I was raised by a perfectly nice family . . . who I knew I had nothing in common with. I left them early and never went back, because I didn't belong where I was—and something was screaming in me that it was better for them that I took off. I didn't have a clue I was part *symphath* and there was nothing out in the world for me . . . but I had to go. Fortunately, I met Rehvenge and he showed me what I was."

She glanced over her shoulder. "The near misses in life . . . man, they're a killer, aren't they. If Tohr hadn't found you . . ."

He would have gone into his transition and died in the middle of it because he didn't have the blood he needed to survive.

For some reason, he didn't want to think about that. Or the fact that he and Xhex had a lonely stretch of lost in common.

Come on, he mouthed. *Let's go to the next stop.*

Out among the corn fields, Lash drove along the dirt lane toward the farmhouse. He had his psychic cover in place so that the Omega and his new boy toy couldn't get a bead on him and he was also rocking a baseball cap, a raincoat with the collar turned up, and a pair of gloves.

He felt like the Invisible Man.

Fuck that, he wished he were invisible. He hated looking at himself, and after a good couple of hours of waiting to see what else was going to fall off on his descent into the living dead, he wasn't sure whether he was relieved that he appeared to have plateaued.

He was only half-melted at this point: his muscles were still hanging on to his bones.

About a quarter of a mile away from his destination, he parked the Mercedes in a stand of pines and got out. As his powers were all being used to keep himself masked, there was nothing left over for him to dematerialize with.

So it was a long frickin' walk to the goddamn shit-hole and he resented like hell having to work that hard just to move his body.

But when he came up to the clapboard house, he got hit with a surge of energy. There were three POS cars in the driveway—all of which he recognized. The Willy Loman rides were owned by the Lessening Society.

And what do you know, the place was hopping. There were a good twenty guys inside and there was a whole lot of partying going on: Through the windows, he could see the kegs and the liquor bottles, and all around, motherfuckers were lighting up bongs and snorting God only knew what.

Where was the little bastard.

Ah . . . perfect timing. A fourth car pulled up and it was not like the other three. The street racer's flashy-ass paint job was probably just as expensive as the souped-up sewing machine under the hood, and the under-carriage's neon glow made it look like it was coming in for a landing. The kid got out from behind the wheel and gee whiz, he was all spanked, too: He'd gotten himself some brand-new jeans and a sweet-ass Affliction leather jacket, and he'd taken up lighting his cigarettes with something gold.

Well, wasn't this going to be the test.

If the kid went in and just partied, Lash had been wrong about the fucker's smarts . . . and the Omega had gotten himself nothing other than a good lay. But if Lash was right, and the SOB had more to him than that, the party was going to get interesting.

Lash drew his lapels closer to the raw meat that was now his neck and tried to ignore how jel he was. He'd been in the sweet spot where that kid was. Reveled in the I'm-so-specials and assumed that glow would last forever. But whatever. If the Omega was willing to kick his own flesh and blood to the curb, this previously human piece of shit wasn't going to last long.

When one of the lushes inside stared out the window in Lash's direction, he supposed he was taking a chance getting this close to the hub, but he didn't give a crap. He had nothing to lose, and wasn't really looking forward to spending the rest of his days as nothing more than animated beef jerky.

Ugly and weak and leaky was not hot.

As the cold wind made his teeth rattle, he thought of Xhex and warmed himself with the memories. On some level, he couldn't believe that his time with her had been mere days ago. Felt more like ages since he'd had her under him. For fuck's sake, finding that first lesion on his wrist had been the beginning of the end . . . he just hadn't known it at the time.

Just a scratch.

Yeah, right.

Lifting his hand to push at his hair, he hit the bill of the baseball cap and was reminded that he had nothing to fuss with anymore. All he had left up there was a bone dome.

If he'd had more energy, he would have started ranting and raving at the unfairness and the cruelty of his decaying destiny. Life wasn't supposed to be like this. He wasn't supposed to be looking in from the outside. He had always been the focus, the driver, the special one.

For some stupid reason, he thought of John Matthew. When the motherfucker had come into the training program for soldiers, he'd been a particularly small pretrans with nothing but a Brotherhood name and a star scar on his chest. He'd been the perfect target to ostracize and Lash had gotten off on riding the kid hard.

Man, back then, he'd had no idea what it was like to be the odd man out. How it made you feel like worthless crap. How you looked at the other people who had it going on and would trade anything to be in with them.

Good thing he hadn't had a clue how it was. Or he might have thought twice about fucking with the cocksucker.

And here and now, leaning against the shaggy, cold bark of an oak tree and watching through the windows of the farmhouse as some other golden boy lived his life, he felt his plans shifting.

If it was the last thing he did, he was going to take that little shit down.

It was even more important than Xhex.

That the guy had dared to mark Lash for death wasn't the driver. It was the need to send a message to his father. He was, after all, a rotting apple that didn't fall far from the tree, and payback was a bitch.

THIRTY-NINE

"That's Bella's old house," Xhex said after she took form in a meadow beside John Matthew.

As he nodded, she looked around at the pastoral spread. Bella's white farmhouse with its wraparound porch and its red chimneys was picture-perfect in the moonlight, and it seemed a shame that the place was left empty with nothing but exterior security lights on.

The fact that its outbuilding had a Ford F-150 parked in its gravel drive and windows that were glowing seemed to make the sense of desertion even more acute.

"Bella was the one who first found you?"

John made an equivocal motion with his hand and pointed over to another little house on the lane. As he started to sign and then stopped himself, his frustration over the communication barrier was obvious.

"Someone in that house . . . you knew them and they put you in touch with Bella?"

He nodded as he reached into his jacket and brought out what appeared to be a handmade bracelet. Taking it from him, she saw that symbols in the Old Language had been carved into the hide.

"Tehrror." When he touched his chest, she said, "Your name? But how did you know?"

He touched his head, then shrugged.

"It came to you." She focused on the smaller house. There was a pool in the back and she sensed that his memories were sharpest there, because every time his eyes passed over that terrace, his emotional grid fired up, a switchboard with a lot of circuits flaring.

He'd come here at first to protect someone. Bella had not been the reason.

Mary, she thought. Rhage's *shellan*, Mary. But how had they met?

Odd . . . that was a blank wall. He was shutting her off from that part.

"Bella got in touch with the Brotherhood and Tohrment came for you."

When he nodded again, she gave him back the bracelet, and while he fingered the symbols, she marveled at the relativity of time. Since they'd left the mansion, only an hour had passed, but she felt as though they'd spent a year together.

God, he'd given her more than she'd ever expected . . . and now she knew precisely why he'd been so helpful as she'd flipped out in the OR.

He'd endured a hell of a lot, having not so much lived through his early life as been dragged through it.

The question was, How had he gotten lost to the human world in the first place? Where were his parents? The king had been his *whard* when he'd been a pretrans—that was what his papers had said when she'd first met him in ZeroSum. She'd assumed his mother had died, and the visit to the bus station didn't disprove that . . . but there were holes in the story. Some of which she got the impression were deliberate, others of which he didn't seem to be able to fill.

With a frown, she sensed his father was still very much with him, and yet he didn't appear to have ever known the guy.

"You're taking me to one last place?" she murmured.

He seemed to take a final look about and then he poofed off and she followed him, thanks to all the blood of his that was in her system.

When they resumed form in front of a stunning modern house, his sadness overwhelmed him to such a degree that his emotional superstructure actually started to cave in on itself. With force of will, however, he managed to stop the disintegration in time, before it couldn't be righted.

Once your grid collapsed, you were cooked. Lost to your inner demons.

Which made her think of Murhder. On the day that he had learned her truth, she could remember exactly how his emotional construct had appeared to her: The steel girders that were the basis of mental health had been nothing but a crumbled mess.

She had been the only one who hadn't been surprised when he went insane and took off.

With a nod to her, John walked up to the formal front door, put in a key and opened the way in. As a draft ushered out to meet them, she could smell the dust and the damp, indicating that this was another structure that was empty. But there was nothing rotten inside, unlike John's former apartment building.

As he turned on the light in the foyer, she nearly gasped. On the wall, to the left of the door, was a scroll proclaiming in the Old Language that this was the home of the Brother Tohrment and his mated *shellan*, Wellesandra.

Which explained why it pained John so much to be here. Wellesandra's *hellren* wasn't the only one who had saved the pretrans from the projects.

The female had mattered to John. A helluva lot.

John walked down the hall and flicked on more lights as he went, his emotions a combination of bittersweet affection and roaring pain. When they came to a spectacular kitchen, Xhex went over to the table in the alcove.

He had sat here, she thought, putting her hands on the back of one of the chairs . . . on his first night in this house, he had sat here.

"Mexican food," she murmured. "You were so afraid of offending them. But then . . . Wellesandra . . ."

Like a bloodhound following a fresh trail, Xhex tracked what she sensed of his memories. "Wellesandra served you ginger rice. And . . . pudding. You felt full for the first time and your stomach didn't hurt and you . . . you were so gateful you didn't know how to handle it."

When she looked across the way at John, his face was pale and his eyes a bit too shiny and she knew he was back in his little body, sitting at the table, all curled into himself . . . becoming overwhelmed at the first kindness anyone had shown him in a very long time.

A footstep out in the hall brought her head up and she realized Qhuinn was still with them, the guy loitering about, his bad mood a tangible shadow around him.

Well, he didn't have to tag along any longer. This was the end of the road, the final chapter in John's story that pretty much caught her up-to-date. And unfortunately, it meant by all which was right and proper, they should go back to the mansion . . . where no doubt John would make her eat some more and try to get her to feed again.

She didn't want to return there, though, not yet. In her mind, she'd decided to take one night off, so these were her last few hours before she got on the vengeance trail . . . and lost this soft connection between her and John, this profound understanding they now had of each other.

Because she wasn't going to fool herself: The sad reality was the powerful tie that linked them was nonetheless so fragile, she didn't doubt it was going to snap once the present came back into better focus than the past.

"Qhuinn, will you excuse us, please."

The guy's mismatched eyes shot over to John, and a series of hand motions got traded between them.

"Fuckin' A," Qhuinn spat before turning on his heel and marching out the front door.

After the slam finished echoing through the house, she stared at John. "Where did you sleep?"

When he swept his hand to a corridor, she went with him past many rooms that had modern fixtures and antique art. The combination made the place feel like an art museum you could live in and she explored a little, ducking her head into the open doors of parlors and bedrooms.

John's crib was all the way at the other end of the house, and as she walked in to it, she could only imagine the culture shock. Squalor to splendor, all in the change of a zip code: Unlike the crappy studio apartment, this was a navy blue haven with sleek furniture, a marble bathroom, and a carpet that was as thick and full as a marine's brush cut.

Plus it had a sliding glass door that led out onto a private terrace.

John went over and opened the closet, and she looked over his strong, heavy arm to the small clothes that hung on wooden hangers.

As he stared at the shirts and fleeces and pants, his shoulders were tight and one of his hands was curled into a fist. He was sorry about something he'd done or the way he'd acted and it didn't have anything to do with her . . .

Tohr. It was about Tohr.

He was regretting the way things had been lately between them.

"Talk to him," she said softly. "Tell him what's doing. You'll both feel better."

John nodded and she could sense his resolve sharpening.

God, she wasn't quite sure how it happened—well, the mechanics were pretty damn simple, but what was surprising was the fact that once again, she found herself going over and hugging him, her arms wrapping around his waist from behind. Laying her cheek between his shoulder blades, she was glad when she felt his hands covering hers.

He communicated in so many different ways, didn't he. And sometimes touch was better than words for saying what you meant.

In the silence, she drew him back to the bed and they both sat down.

As she just stared at him, he mouthed, *What?*

"You sure you want me to go there?" When he nodded, she looked him right in the eye. "I know you left something out. I can sense it. There's a gap between the orphanage and that apartment building."

Not one facial muscle moved or even twitched on him and he didn't blink, either. But the tells of a male who was good at covering up his reactions were irrelevant. She knew what she knew about him.

"It's okay, I'm not going to ask. And I'm not going to press."

His faint blush was something she would remember long after she was gone . . . and the thought of leaving him was what brought her fingertips to his lips. As he jerked in surprise, she focused on his mouth.

"I want to give you something of me," she said in a low, deep voice. "It's not about making the score even, though. It's just because I want to."

After all, it would have been great if she could have taken him to her places and walked him through her life, but his knowing more about her past was just going to make her suicide mission harder for him: however she felt about John, she was going after her captor and she wasn't about to fool herself on the odds of her surviving that showdown.

Lash had tricks.

Bad tricks that he did bad things with.

Memories of the bastard came back to her, horrible

ones that made her thighs tremble, ugly ones that nonetheless served to push her into something that she might not really be ready for. But she couldn't go to her grave with Lash having been her last.

Not when she had the one male she'd ever love in front of her.

"I want to be with you," she said hoarsely.

John's shocked blue eyes traced her face like he was looking for signs that he might be reading her wrong. And then a hot, hard lust broke through all his emotions, shattering them and leaving nothing behind but a full-blooded male's urge to mate.

To his credit, he did his best to beat back the instinct and hold on to some semblance of rationality. But all that meant was that she was the one who ended the battle between sense and sensibility—by putting her mouth against his.

Oh . . . God, his lips were soft.

In spite of the thundering she sensed in his blood, he kept himself in check. Even when she slid her tongue inside of him. And that restraint made it easier for her as her mind flickered back and forth between what she was doing now . . .

And what had been done to her mere days ago.

To help focus her, she sought out his chest and ran her palms down the pads of muscle over his heart. Easing him back onto the mattress, she breathed in his scent and smelled the bonding he felt for her. The dark spices were unique to him, and about as far as you could get from the sickening stench of a *lesser*.

Which helped her separate this experience from her most recent ones.

The kiss started out as an exploration, but it didn't stay that way. John moved closer, rolling his massive body against hers, his heavy leg riding up until the weight of it pushed down on her own. At the same time, his arms wrapped around her, bringing her in tight to him.

He was moving slowly, as was she.

And she was fine until his hand slipped onto her breast.

The contact scrambled her, yanking her out of this room and this bed, taking her away from John and the moment with him and landing her back in hell.

Fighting her mind's defection, she tried to stay connected to the present, to John. But as his thumb brushed over her nipple, she had to force her body to stay still. Lash had liked to hold her down and draw out the inevitable by scratching and pawing at her, because as much as he'd enjoyed his orgasms, he'd been even more into the foreplay of fucking with her head.

Psycho-smart move on his part. She'd have infinitely preferred to just get it over with—

John pushed his erection into her hip.

Snap.

Her self-control rubberbanded on her, reaching its limit and splitting in half: With a surge, her body bolted away from the contact of its own volition, breaking the communion with him, blowing up the moment.

As Xhex sprang off the bed, she could feel John's horror, but she was too busy reeling from her own fear to be able to explain. Pacing around, desperately trying to hold on to reality, she breathed in deeply, not from passion but derivative panic.

Well, wasn't this a bitch.

Fucking Lash . . . she was so going to murder him for this. Not for what she was going through, but for the position she'd put John in.

"I'm sorry," she groaned. "I shouldn't have started it. I'm really sorry."

When she was able, she stopped in front of the dresser and looked into the mirror that hung on the wall. John had gotten up while she paced and gone to stand before the sliding glass door, his arms crossed over his chest, his jaw clenched hard as he stared out into the night.

"John . . . it's not you. I swear."

As he shook his head, he didn't look at her.

Scrubbing her face, the silence and strain between them amplified her urge to run. She just couldn't deal with any of this, with what she was feeling and what she'd done to John and all that shit with Lash.

Her eyes went to the door and her muscles tensed for her exit. Which was straight from her playbook. For all of her life, she had always relied on her ability to ghost out of things, leaving behind no explanations, no trace, nothing but thin air.

Served her well as an assassin.

"John . . ."

His head swiveled around and his stare burned with regret as she met it in the leaded glass.

As he waited for her to speak, she was supposed to tell him it was best that she go. She was supposed to toss over another limp-ass apology and then dematerialize out of the room . . . out of his life.

But all she could manage was his name.

He pivoted to face her and mouthed, *I'm sorry. Go. It's okay. Go.*

She couldn't move, though. And then her mouth parted. As she realized what was in the back of her throat, she couldn't believe she was going to put it into words. The revelation went against everything she knew about herself.

For God's sake, was she really going to do this? "John . . . I . . . I was . . ."

Shifting the focus of her eyes, she measured her reflection. Her hollowed cheekbones and pasty pallor were the result of so much more than lack of sleep and feeding.

With a sudden flash of anger, she blurted, "Lash wasn't impotent, all right? He wasn't . . . impotent—"

The temperature in the room plummeted so fast and so far, her breath came out in clouds.

And what she saw in the mirror made her swing around and take a step back from John: His blue eyes glowed with an unholy light and his upper lip curled up to reveal fangs that were so sharp and so long they looked like daggers.

Objects all around the room began to vibrate: the lamps on the bed stands, the clothes on their hangers, the mirror on the wall. The collective rattling crescendoed to a dull roar and she had to steady herself on the bureau or run the risk of being knocked on her ass.

The air was alive. Supercharged. Electric.

Dangerous.

And John was the center of the raging energy, his hands cranking into fists so tight his forearms trembled, his thighs grabbing onto his bones as he sank down into fighting stance.

John's mouth stretched wide as his head shot forward on his spine . . . and he let out a war cry—

Sound exploded all around her, so loud she had to cover her ears, so powerful she felt the blast against her face.

For a moment, she thought he'd found his voice— except it wasn't vocal cords making that bellowing noise.

The glass in the sliders blew out behind him, the sheets shattering into thousands of shards that blasted free of the house, the fragments bouncing on the slate and catching the light like raindrops . . .

Or like tears.

FORTY

Blay had no idea what Saxton had just handed him.

Well, yeah, it was a cigar, and yes, it was expensive, but the name hadn't stuck in his head.

"I think you're going to like it," the male said, shifting back in a leather armchair and lighting up his own stogie. "They're smooth. Dark, but smooth."

Blay flicked up a flame off his Montblanc lighter and leaned forward for the inhale. As he took the smoke in, he could feel Saxton focusing on him.

Again.

He still couldn't get used to the attention, so he let his eyes wander around the place: vaulted dark green ceiling, glossy black walls, oxblood-color leather chairs and booths. Lot of human men with ashtrays at their elbows.

In short: no distractions that could come close to Saxton's eyes or voice or cologne or—

"So tell me," the male said, exhaling a perfect blue cloud that momentarily eclipsed his features, "did you put on the pinstripe before or after I called?"

"Before."

"I knew you had style."

"Did you?"

"Yes." Saxton stared across the short mahogany table that separated them. "Or I wouldn't have asked you to dinner."

The meal they'd had at Sal's had been . . . lovely, actually. They'd eaten in the kitchen at a private table and iAm had made them a special menu of antipasto and pasta, with café con leche and tiramisu for dessert. The wine had been white for the first course, and red for the second.

The topics of conversation had been neutral, but interesting—and ultimately not the point. The thread of will-they-or-won't-they was the real driver of every word and glance and shift of body.

So . . . this was a date, Blay thought. A subtextual negotiation slipcovered in talk of books read and music enjoyed.

No wonder Qhuinn just went for straight sex. The guy wouldn't have had the patience for this kind of subtlety. Plus he didn't like to read, and the music he pumped into his ears was metalcore that only the deranged or the deaf could stand.

A waiter dressed in black came up. "Can I get you guys something to drink?"

Saxton rolled his cigar between his forefinger and thumb. "Two ports. Croft Vintage 1945, please."

"Excellent choice."

Saxton's eyes returned to Blay's. "I know."

Blay looked to the window they were seated in front of and wondered if he was ever going to stop blushing around the guy. "It's raining."

"Is it."

God, that voice. Saxton's words were as smooth and delicious as the cigar.

Blay switched his legs around, crossing them at the knee.

As he searched his brain for something to kill the silence, it looked as if no-shit-Sherlock comments about the weather were as close to inspired as he was going to get. The thing was, the end of the date was starting to loom, and whereas he'd learned that he and Saxton both mourned the loss of Dominick Dunne and were fans of Miles Davis, he didn't know what he was going to do when it came to parting ways.

Would it be a case of *Call and we'll do this again*? Or

the infinitely more complicated, messy, and pleasurable, *Yes, as a matter of fact, I will come over and look at your etchings.*

To which his conscience compelled him to add: *Even though I've never done this with a guy before, and in spite of the fact that anyone but Qhuinn is going to be a poor man's substitute for the real thing.*

"When was the last time you were out on a date, Blaylock?"

"I . . ." Blay took a long draw on the cigar. "It's been a long time."

"Whatever have you been doing with yourself? All work, no play?"

"Something like that." Okay, unrequited love wasn't exactly in either of those categories, although the no-play was certainly covered.

Saxton smiled a little. "I was glad you called me. And a bit surprised."

"Why?"

"My cousin has a certain . . . territorial response to you."

Blay turned his cigar around and stared at the glowing tip. "I think you vastly overread his interest."

"And I think you're politely telling me to mind my own business, aren't you."

"There's no business to mind there." Blay smiled up at the waiter as the guy put two port glasses down on the round table and backed away. "Trust me."

"You know, Qhuinn's an interesting character." Saxton reached out with an elegant hand and picked up his port. "He's one of my favorite cousins, actually. His nonconformity is admirable and he's survived things that would crush a lesser male. Don't know that being in love with him would be easy, however."

Blay didn't go near that one. "So do you come here often?"

Saxton laughed, his pale eyes glinting. "Not for discussion, huh." He looked around with a frown. "Actually, I haven't been out much lately. Too much work."

"You said you're a solicitor in the Old Law. Must be interesting."

"I specialize in trusts and estates so the fact that business is booming is something to mourn. The Fade has become too full of the innocent as of last summer—"

At the booth next door, a bunch of big guts with gold watches and silk suits laughed like the blowhard drunks they were—to the point that the loudest of them slammed back in his seat and knocked into Saxton.

Which didn't go over well, proving that Saxton was a gentleman, but not a pussy: "I beg your pardon, but would you mind toning it down?"

The sloppy human cranked around, his belly fat bulging over his belt until it looked like he was going to pull a *Meaning of Life* and thin-mint it all over the place. "Yeah. I mind." His watery eyes narrowed. "Your types don't belong here anyway."

And he wasn't talking about the fact that they were vampires.

As Blay took a drink of his port, the high-priced liquor tasted like vinegar . . . although the bitter sting in his mouth wasn't because the stuff had gone bad.

A moment later, the guy banged back so hard, Saxton nearly spilled his drink. "Damn it to hell," the male muttered going for his napkin.

The fidiot human leaned into their space again, and you had to wonder if that belt wasn't going to snap free and take someone's eye out. "We interrupting you two pretty boys sucking on those hard things?"

Saxton smiled tightly. "You are definitely interrupting."

"Oh, sorrrrry." The man made an abrupt show of lifting his pinkie up from his stogie. "Didn't mean to offend you."

"Let's go," Blay said as he leaned in and snuffed out his cigar.

"I can get us another table."

"You running along, boys?" Mr. Mouth drawled. "You going to a party where there's all kindsa cigars? Maybe we'll follow you just to make sure you get there okay."

Blay kept his eyes locked on Saxton. "It's getting late anyway."

"Which means it's only the middle of our day."

Blay stood up and reached into his pocket, but Saxton put his hand out and stopped him from getting his wallet. "No, allow me."

Another round of commentary from the Super Bowl—and-stripper set soured the air even further and left Blay grinding his molars. Fortunately, it didn't take long for Saxton to pay the waiter and then they were making their way to the door.

Outside, the night's chilly air was a balm to the senses and Blay took a deep breath.

"That place isn't always like that," Saxton murmured. "Otherwise, I would never have taken you there."

"It's all right." As Blay started walking, he felt Saxton fall in beside him.

When they got to the head of an alley, they paused to let a car hang a louie on Commerce.

"So how are you feeling about all this?"

Blay faced the other male and decided life was too short to pretend he didn't know precisely what the "this" was. "To be honest, I feel strange."

"And not about those charmers back there."

"I lied. I've never been on a date before." This got him a cocked brow and he had to laugh. "Yup, I'm a real player."

Saxton's suave air slipped and behind his eyes, true warmth glowed. "Well, I'm glad I was your first."

Blay met the guy's stare. "How did you know I was gay?"

"I didn't. I merely hoped."

Blay laughed again. "Well, there you go." After a pause, he put out his palm. "Thank you for tonight."

As Saxton slipped his hand in, a frisson of pure heat flared between them. "You do realize that dates don't normally end this way. Assuming both parties are interested."

Blay found that he was unable to let go of the male's palm. "Oh . . . really?"

Saxton nodded. "A kiss is more customary."

Blay focused on the male's lips and abruptly wondered what they tasted like.

"Come here," Saxton murmured, pulling on their connection, drawing him into the shelter of the alley.

Blay followed into the darkness, swept up under an erotic spell he had no interest in breaking. When they were in the lee of the buildings, he felt the male's chest come up against his own and then their hips fused.

So he knew precisely how much Saxton was aroused.

And Saxton knew he was the same.

"Tell me something," Saxton whispered. "Have you ever kissed a male before?"

Blay didn't want to think of Qhuinn right now and he shook his head to clear the image. When that didn't work, and the guy's blue and green eyes lingered, he did the one thing guaranteed to get him to stop thinking of his *pyrocant*.

He closed the distance between Saxton's mouth and his own.

Qhuinn knew he should have gone right home. After he got summarily dismissed from Tohr's house, no doubt so that John and Xhex could do a little horizontal conversating, he should have gone back to the mansion and cozied up to some Herradura and minded his own goddamned business.

But nooooo. He'd taken form across the street from the only cigar bar in Caldwell and watched—in the rain like a loser—as Blay and Saxton took up res at a table right in the front window. He'd gotten a whole lot of bird's-eye as his cousin had looked at his best friend with an elegant lust, and then some knuckleheads gave them a hard time and they left their cigars barely smoked and their ports mostly unfinished.

Not wanting to get caught in the shadow game, Qhuinn had dematerialized into the alley beside the place . . . which quickly turned into a wrong place/wrong time kind of gig.

Saxton's voice drifted over on the chilly breeze. "You do realize that dates don't normally end this way. Assuming both parties are interested."

"Oh . . . really?"

"A kiss is more customary."

Qhuinn felt his fists tighten, and for a split second, he actually thought of stepping out from behind the Dumpster he was standing behind. But to do what? Ride on up into their space and be all red-light, break-it-up-boys?

Well, yeah. Exactly.

"Come here," Saxton murmured.

Shit, the bastard sounded like a sex-phone operator, all husky and mad sexed up. And . . . oh, man, Blay was going with it, following the guy into the darkness.

There were times when a vampire's incredible sense of hearing was a real ball-gnasher. And of course . . . it didn't help if you put your head around the corner of the trash heap you were next to so you could have a clear visual shot.

As the two of them came up against each other, Qhuinn's mouth dropped open. But not because he was

349

shocked and not because he wanted in on the action.

He simply couldn't breathe. It was as if his ribs had frozen along with his heart.

No . . . no, goddamn it, *no* . . .

"Tell me something," Saxton whispered. "Have you ever kissed a male before?"

Yes, he has, Qhuinn wanted to scream—

Blay shook his head. He actually shook his head.

Qhuinn squeezed his eyes shut and forced himself to calm down enough to dematerialize. As he took form in front of the Brotherhood's mansion, he was shaking like a motherfucker . . . and briefly considered bending over and fertilizing the bushes with the dinner he'd eaten before leaving with Xhex and John.

A couple of inhales later, he decided it was more appealing to go with plan A and get good and shitfaced. With that in mind, he walked into the vestibule, got let in by Fritz, and headed for the kitchen.

Hell, maybe he'd take it a little further than just a buzz. God knew Saxton wasn't going to want to stop at a kiss or two in a cold, damp alley, and Blay had looked like he was prepared to finally get what he'd needed all along.

So there was plenty of time to hammer the hooch until he blacked the fuck out.

Jesus . . . Christ, Qhuinn thought as he rubbed his chest and heard his cousin's voice over and over again: *Tell me something. Have you ever kissed a male before?*

The image of Blay shaking his head was like a scar on Qhuinn's brain, and didn't that just carry him right out the far side of the kitchen to the storage room where the cases of alcohol were kept.

Such a cliché. Getting sauced because you didn't want to deal.

But he might as well do one thing in his life according to tradition.

Heading back through the kitchen, he realized there was at least one saving grace. When the pair of them did the deed, it had to be back at Saxton's house, because no casual visitors were allowed in the king's home, ever.

As he came out into the foyer, he stopped dead.

Blay was just ducking in through the vestibule.

"Back so soon," Qhuinn said gruffly. "Don't tell me my cousin is that fast."

Blay didn't even pause. Just kept on going up the stairs. "Your cousin is a gentleman."

Qhuinn fell in behind his best friend, getting right on the guy's heels. "You think? In my experience, he just looks like one."

That got Blay to turn around. "You always liked him before. He was your favorite. I can remember you talking about him like he was a god."

"I grew out of that."

"Well, I like him. A lot."

Qhuinn wanted to growl, but killed the impulse by cracking open the Herradura he'd snagged off the shelf and taking a swallow. "Good for you. I'm just *thrilled* for you both."

"Really. Then why aren't you even using a glass."

Qhuinn marched around his buddy and didn't stop as Blay said, "Where're John and Xhex?"

"Out. In the world. On their own."

"I thought you were supposed to stay with them?"

"I was momentarily dismissed." Qhuinn paused at the top of the stairs and tapped the tear that had been tattooed under his eye. "She's an assassin, for God's sake. She can take care of him just fine. Besides, they were hanging at Tohr's old place."

When he got to his room, Qhuinn kicked the door shut and stripped his clothes off. After swigging from the bottle, he closed his eyes and sent out a summons.

Layla would be good company right about now.

Right up his alley.

After all, she had been trained for sex, and all she wanted to do was use him as an erotic gymnasium. He didn't have to worry about hurting her or her getting attached to him. She was a professional, so to speak.

Or she would be when he was done with her.

As for Blay? He had no idea why the guy had come back instead of heading off into Saxton's bed, but one thing was clear. The pair of them were attracted to each other and Saxton wasn't the kind to wait when it came to somebody he wanted.

Qhuinn and his cousin were related, after all.

And that wasn't going to save the sonofabitch in the slightest if he broke Blay's heart.

FORTY-ONE

The party at the farmhouse went on and on and more people kept coming, their cars parking on the lawn, their bodies jamming into the downstairs rooms. Most who showed were ones that Lash had seen at the Xtreme Park, but not all of them. And they kept bringing more booze. Six-packs. Bottles. Kegs.

God only knew what kinds of illegal were in their pockets.

What the fuck, he started to think. Maybe he'd been wrong and the Omega had been snowed by his perversions—

As a rolling breeze developed out of the north, Lash went perfectly still, keeping his camo in place and locking his mind down.

Shadow . . . He projected a shadow in him and through him and around him.

The Omega's arrival was preceded by an eclipse of the moon and the idiots inside didn't have a clue what was doing . . . but that little shit did. The kid stepped out of the front door, the light from inside spilling out around him.

Lash's blooded father came into form on the scruffy lawn, his white robes swirling around his body, his arrival driving the ambient air temperature down even further. As soon as he'd taken form, the Shit walked up to him and the two embraced.

There was the temptation to go off on the pair of them, to tell his father he was nothing but a fickle cocksucker and warn that little rat bitch his days and nights were numbered—

The Omega's hooded face turned in Lash's direction.

Lash stayed perfectly motionless and projected in his mind an utterly blank slate such that he was invisible inside and out. Shadow . . . shadow . . . shadow . . .

The pause lasted a lifetime, because without a doubt if the Omega sensed Lash was around, it was game-over.

After a moment, the Omega refocused on his golden boy, and just as he did, some fuck-twit tripped out the front door, his flailing arms and loose legs going haywire as he tried to keep upright. Once on the grass, the guy got close to a cabbage patch but didn't quite make it, before landing on his knees and hurling all over the foundation of the house. As people inside laughed at him and the sounds of the party rolled out into the night, the Omega swept up to the doorway.

The party just kept raging as he went into the house, no doubt because the shwasted bastards were too far gone to realize that under that white drape, evil had just come into their mix.

They weren't clueless for long, though.

A massive light bomb went off, the blast of illumination sweeping through the house and streaming out of the windows to the tree line. As the roaring illumination dimmed to a soft glow, there were no upright survivors: All those lushes had dropped to the floor on a oner, the good times over and then some.

Holy shit. If this was headed where it seemed to be going . . .

Lash sidled up to the house, being careful to leave no footprint literally or figuratively, and as he got closer, he heard an odd scraping sound.

Coming to one of the living room's windows, he looked inside.

The Shit was dragging bodies around, lining them

up side by side on the floor so that their heads were all facing north and there was a foot or so between them. Jesus . . . there were so many of the stiffs that the good-little-dead-soldier routine stretched all the way out into the hall and into the dining room.

The Omega hung back as if he liked the view of his boy toy muscling the men around.

How. Precious.

It took almost a half hour to get everyone in the row, the guys from the second floor getting dragged down the stairs so that their heads bounced on each step and left a bright red trail of blood.

Made sense. Easier to pull a deadweight by the feet.

When everybody was together, the Shit got to work with a knife and it became an assembly line of inductions. Starting in the dining room, he sliced throats and wrists and ankles and chests and the Omega followed behind, bleeding black into the open ribs then hitting them with electricity before performing cardio-ectomies.

No jars for this batch. When the hearts were extracted, they were pitched into a corner.

Slaughterhouse much?

By the time it was done, there was a pond of blood in the center of the living room where the floorboards had sagged, and another at the base of the stairs in the hall. Lash couldn't get a look-see all the way to the dining room, but he was damn sure there was one there as well.

The moans of the inducted started up soon after, and the crop of misery that had been reaped was going to get louder and messier as the transition was bridged and the last of their humanity was vomited out of them.

In the midst of the chorus of agony and confusion, The Omega twirled around, stepping over the writhing masses, dancing to and fro, his white robes trailing through the congealing crap on the floor and remaining unstained.

In the corner, the Shit lit up a joint and toked away

like he was taking a breather after a good job done well.

Lash stepped back from the window and then retreated toward the trees, all the while keeping his eyes on that house.

Damn it, he should have done something like this. But he hadn't had the contacts in the human world to pull it off. Unlike the Shit.

Man, this was going to change everything for the vampires. Those fuckers were going to actually face a legion of the enemy again.

Back at the Mercedes, Lash started the engine and eased out of farmlandia the long way so he didn't go anywhere near that house. Behind the wheel, with the cold air hitting his face thanks to the shot-out window glass, he was grim. Fuck females and all that bullshit, for real. His sole goal in life was to knock out the Shit. Take the Omega's little prize. Destroy the Lessening Society.

Well . . . females were mostly out of it. He felt absolutely drained because he needed to feed—whatever was happening to his outer layer, his inside was still craving blood and he had to solve this problem before he could face his daddy-o.

Or he was going to get popped.

As he drove toward downtown, he took out his phone and marveled at what he was about to do. But then, a common enemy had a way of making strange alliances.

Back at the Brotherhood compound, Blay got undressed in his bathroom and stepped under the shower. As he took the soap and frothed up some suds, he thought about the kiss in that alley.

About that male.

About . . . that kiss.

Moving his palms over his pecs, he tilted his head back and let the warm water run down his hair and his back to his ass. His body felt like it wanted to arch harder and he let it do its thing, stretching, luxuriating in the warm rush. He took his time shampooing his hair and running that slippery, soapy hand of his around.

While he thought of that kiss some more.

God, it was as if the memory of their lips together was a magnet that dragged him back to home again and again; the pull too strong to fight, the connection too enticing for him to want to avoid it.

Sweeping his palms down his torso, he wondered when he was going to see Saxton again.

When they were going to be alone again.

Moving lower with his hand, he—

"Sire?"

Blay spun around, his heel squeaking on the marble. Covering his hard, heavy cock with both hands, he ducked around the glass door. "Layla?"

The Chosen smiled at him shyly and ran her eyes down his body. "I was called forth? To serve?"

"I didn't call." Maybe she was confused? Unless—

"Qhuinn summoned me forth. I assumed it was to this room?"

Blay briefly shut his eyes as his erection faded. And then he gave himself a boot in his Key West and canned the hot water. Reaching around, he snapped a towel free and wrapped it around his hips.

"No, Chosen," he said quietly. "Not here. His room."

"Oh! Forgive me, sire." She began to back out of the room, her cheeks flaming.

"It's all right—watch out!" Blay lunged forward and caught her just as she bumped into the tub and lost her balance. "You okay?"

"Verily, I should look where I goeth." She glanced up into his eyes, her hands coming to rest on his bare arms. "Thank you."

Staring down at her perfectly beautiful face, it was

obvious why Qhuinn was interested. She was ethereal for sure, but there was more to it—especially as her lids lowered and her green eyes flashed.

Innocent, but erotic. That was it. She was that captivating combination of purity and raw sex which to normal males was undeniable—and Qhuinn was not even close to normal. He'd bang anything.

Wonder if the Chosen knew that? Or whether it would matter to her if she did?

With a frown, Blay set her back from him. "Layla . . ."

"Yes, sire?"

Well, hell . . . what was he going to say to her? It was damn clear she hadn't been called back to feed Qhuinn, because they'd just done that the night before—

Christ, maybe that was the point. They'd already had sex once and she was returning for more.

"Sire?"

"Nothing. You'd better go. I'm sure he's waiting."

"Indeed." Layla's fragrance surged, the cinnamon spice flaring in Blay's nose. "And for that I am so grateful."

As she turned and left, Blay watched her hips sway and felt like screaming. He did not want to think of Qhuinn having sex next door—for fuck's sake, the mansion had been the one place uncontaminated by all the extracurricular grind.

Now, though, all he could see was Layla walking into Qhuinn's room and letting that white robe fall down from her shoulders, her breasts and her belly and her thighs revealed to his mismatched stare. She'd be in his bed and under his body in the blink of an eye.

And Qhuinn would do her right. That was the thing, at least when it came to sex: He was generous with his time and his talents. He'd be all over her with everything he had, his hands and his mouth—

Right. No need to go there.

Toweling off, it occured to him that maybe Layla was the perfect partner for the guy. With her training, she would not only please him on every level, she would never expect monogamy from him or resent him for his other exploits or push him for emotional connections he didn't feel. She would probably even join in the fun, because it was obvious by the way she walked that she was comfortable with her body.

She *was* perfect for him. Better than Blay, for sure.

Besides, Qhuinn had made it clear he was going to end up with a female . . . a traditional female with traditional values who was preferably from the aristocracy, assuming he could find one who would take him even with the defect of those mismatched peepers.

Layla totally fit that bill—nothing more old-school or highbred than a Chosen and it was clear she wanted him.

Feeling like he was cursed, Blay went into his closet and changed into nylon shorts and an Under Armour shirt. No way was he going to sit here and cozy up with a good book while whatever was going down next door went down—

Yeah. Didn't need those pictures either, even in the hypothetical.

Stepping out into the hall of statues, he rushed down past the marble figures, envying them their calm poses and their serene faces. Sure as shit the everything's-cool routine made being inanimate seem like a good deal. Whereas it meant they felt no joy, they didn't have to go through this burning pain, either.

When he got down to the foyer, he shot around the banister's curling end and ducked through the hidden doorway. In the tunnel to the training center, he struck up a jog as a warm-up and as he emerged through the back of the office closet, he didn't slow down. The weight room was the only place he could stand to be right now. Good hour or so on the StairMaster and he might not feel like peeling his own skin off with a rusty spoon.

Coming out into the corridor, he pulled up short as he saw a lone figure propped against the concrete wall.

"Xhex? What are you doing here?" Well, other than clearly staring a hole in the floor.

The female glanced over and her dark gray eyes seemed like hollow pits. "Hey."

Blay frowned as he walked up to her. "Where's John?"

"He's in there." She nodded at the door to the weight room.

Which would explain the dull pounding he heard. Somebody was clearly running the shit out of one of the treadmills.

"What happened?" Blay said, putting her expression and what John's Nikes were doing together—and coming up with a whole lot of oh-shit.

Xhex let her head fall against the wall that was holding her body up. "It was all I could do to get him back here."

"Why?"

Her eyes flicked over. "Let's just say he wants after Lash."

"Well, that's understandable."

"Yeah."

As the word drifted out of her mouth, he had a sense he didn't know the half of it, but it was clear that was as far as she was going to go with the commentary.

Abruptly, her storm cloud–colored stare sharpened on his face. "So you're the reason Qhuinn was in such a bad mood tonight."

Blay recoiled, and then shook his head. "It's got nothing to do with me. Qhuinn is usually in a bad mood."

"People going in the wrong direction will get like that. Round pegs just don't fit in square holes."

Blay cleared his throat, thinking *symphaths*, even ones who were arguably not against you, were not the kind of thing you wanted to be around when you were raw and exposed. Like, say, when the male you wanted was doing right by a Chosen who had a face like an angel and a body built for sin.

God only knew what Xhex was picking up on from where his head was at.

"Well . . . I'm going for a workout." Like his rig wasn't a dead giveaway.

"Good. Maybe you can talk to him."

"I will." Blay hesitated, thinking Xhex looked a little too much like he felt. "Listen, not for nothing, but you're clearly spent. Maybe you could go up to a guest room and sleep?"

She shook her head. "I'm not leaving him. And I'm out here waiting only because I was making him crazy. The sight of me . . . isn't good for his mental health at the moment. I'm hoping that's no longer true after he breaks this second treadmill."

"Second?"

"I'm pretty damn sure the flapping and the smell of smoke about fifteen minutes ago meant he ran one of them into the ground."

"Damn."

"Yup."

Bracing himself, Blay ducked into the weight room— "Jesus . . . Christ. *John.*"

His voice didn't carry at all. Then again, the roar of the treadmill and John's slamming strides would have drowned out a car backfiring.

The guy's massive body was in a full-out bolt on the machine, his T-shirt and torso dripping with sweat, droplets flicking off his cranked fists and creating twin tracts of damp on either side on the floor. Both his white socks had red blushes streaking up from his heels as if he'd worn patches of skin off, and the black nylon shorts he had on his hips slapped like a wet towel.

"John?" Blay shouted, as he measured the burned-out machine next to the one the guy was on. "John!"

When yelling didn't bring that head around, Blay stalked over and waved his hands right in the guy's visual field. And then wished he hadn't. The eyes that locked on his were blazing with a hatred so vicious, Blay took a step back.

As John refocused on the air in front of his face, it was pretty damn clear that the fucker was going to keep this up until he was a yard shorter from having run his legs into stubs.

"John, how 'bout you step off!" Blay hollered. "Before you fall off?"

No response. Just the screaming whirl of the treadmill and the carpet-bombing sound of those feet.

"John! Come on, now! You're killing yourself!"

Fuck this.

Blay walked around behind the piece of equipment and yanked the cord out of the wall. The abrupt slowdown caused John to trip and fall forward, but he caught himself on the console's arms. Or maybe just collapsed onto them.

His heaving breaths tore in and out of his lax mouth as his head lolled on his arm.

Blay pulled a weight bench over and parked it so he could look into the guy's face. "John . . . what the hell's going on?"

John let go of the console and fell back on his ass, his legs giving out from under him. After a series of sawing breaths, he drew his hand through his wet hair.

"Talk to me, John. I'll keep it just between us. I swear it on the life of my mother."

It was quite a while before John lifted his head, and

when he did, his eyes were shiny. And not from sweat or exertion.

"Talk to me and it goes nowhere," Blay whispered. "What happened? Tell me."

When the guy eventually signed, it was messy, but Blay read the words just fine.

He hurt her, Blay. He . . . hurt her.

"Well, yeah, I know. I heard about the shape she was in when she—"

John squeezed his eyes shut and shook his head.

In the tense silence that followed, the skin on the back of Blay's neck tightened. Oh . . . *shit.*

There had been more to it. Hadn't there.

"How bad," Blay growled.

Bad as it gets, John mouthed.

"Motherfucker. Bastard ass *motherfucker*. Cocksucking rat-bitch bastard mother*fucker*!"

Blay wasn't big into the swearing thing, but sometimes that was all you had to offer the ears of others: Xhex wasn't his female, but you didn't hurt the fairer sex as far as he was concerned. For any reason . . . and never, *ever* like that.

God, her pained expression hadn't been just worry for John. It had been about memories. Awful, hideous memories . . .

"John . . . I'm so sorry."

Fresh drops fell from the guy's chin onto the treadmill's black band, and John wiped his eyes a couple of times before he looked over. In his face, anguish warred with the kind of fury that made your balls get tight.

Which made perfect sense. With his history, this was a crusher on so many levels.

I've got to kill him, John signed. *I can't live with myself if I don't take him out.*

As Blay nodded, the whys of the vengeance were obvious. Bonded male with a bad history?

Lash's death warrant had just had PAID stamped on it.

Blay curled up a fist and offered his knuckles. "Anything you need, anything you want, I'm with you. And I won't say a word."

John waited a moment and then met fist with fist. *I knew I could count on you*, he mouthed.

"Always," Blay vowed. "Always."

FORTY-TWO

Eliahu Rathboone's house went fully silent again about an hour after Gregg's aborted trip to the third floor, but he waited long after that butler had gone back downstairs before he gave the ascension another shot.

He and Holly passed the time not by fucking, which was their old MO, but by talking. And the thing was, he realized the more they said, the less he knew about her. He didn't have a clue that her hobby was something as apple pie–ish as knitting. Or that her larger ambition was to segue into real television news—which wasn't a shocker on the face of things: Lot of bobble-headed females in the reality world had loftier ambitions than introducing amateur high-steppers or commenting on how cockroaches were eaten. And he even knew that she'd given local news a shot in the Pittsburgh market before getting fired from that entry-level position.

What he hadn't had a clue about was the real reason why she'd left that first job of hers. The married general manager had expected her to perform for a different, more private kind of camera, and when she'd told him no, he'd pink-slipped her after setting her up to fail on air.

Gregg had seen the tape of the reporting job where she'd butchered her words. After all, he did his homework, and though her audition for him had gone great, he always checked references.

Guess that was what had started him off with his assumptions about her: pretty face, great rack, nothing much else to offer.

But that wasn't the worst of his misconceptions. He'd never known she had a brother. Who was handicapped. Who she was supporting.

She'd shown him a picture of the two of them together.

And when Gregg had asked out loud how it was possible he hadn't known about the boy? She'd had the honesty to tell him the way it was: *Because you'd laid out the lines and that was over the line.*

Naturally, he'd had the normal male reaction to defend himself, but the fact was, she was right. He had drawn the boundaries pretty fucking clearly. Which meant no jealousy, no explanations, nothing permanent and nothing personal.

Not exactly the environment you wanted to make yourself vulnerable in.

That realization was what had had him pulling her up against his chest and putting his chin on her head and stroking her back. Right before she'd gone to dreamland, she'd mumbled something in a soft voice. Something like, it was the best night she'd ever had with him.

And this in spite of the monstrous orgasms he'd given her.

Well, given her when it suited him. There had been a lot of dates that he'd canceled at the last minute and phone messages that went unreturned and brush-offs both verbal and physical.

Man . . . what a shit he'd been.

When Gregg fianlly got up to go, he tucked Holly in, turned the motion-activated camera on, and slipped out into the hallway. Silence all around.

Padding down the corridor, he went back to the Exit sign and ducked into that rear stairwell. Up the steps, around the landing, another flight, and then he was at the door.

No banging this time around. He took out a thin

screwdriver that was normally used on the camera equipment and got to work jimmying the lock. It was easier than he'd thought, actually. Just one poke and shift and the thing sprang loose.

The door did not squeak, which surprised him.

What was on the other side, however . . . shocked the ever loving hell out of him.

The third floor was a cavernous space with old-fashioned, rough-hewn floorboards and a ceiling that sloped at a steep angle on either side. Down at the far end, there was a table with an oil lamp on it and the glow turned the smooth walls into a golden yellow . . . as well as illuminated the black boots of whoever was sitting in a chair just outside the pool of light.

Big boots.

And suddenly, there was no question who the SOB was and what he'd done.

"I have you on tape," Gregg said to the figure.

The soft laugh that came back at him made Gregg's adrenal gland go into overdrive: Low and cold, it was the kind of sound killers made when they were about to get to work with a knife.

"Do you." That accent. What the fuck was it? Not French . . . not Hungarian . . .

Whatever. The idea Holly had been taken advantage of made him taller and stronger than he really was. "I know what you did. The night before last."

"I'd tell you to take a chair, but as you can see, I only have one."

"I'm not fucking around." Gregg took a step forward. "I know what happened with her. She didn't want you."

"She wanted the sex."

Motherfucking asshole. "She was asleep."

"Was she." The boot tip swung up and down. "Appearances, like psyches, can be deceiving."

"Who the hell do you think you are?"

367

"I own this fine house. That is who I am. I'm the one who gave you permission to play with all your cameras."

"Well, you can kiss that shit good-bye now. I'm not advertising this place."

"Oh, I think you will. It's in your nature."

"You don't know dick about me."

"I think it's the other way around. You don't know . . . dick, as you call it . . . about yourself. She said your name, by the way. When she came."

This made Gregg furious, to the point that he took another step forward.

"I would be careful there," the voice said. "You don't want to get hurt. And I'm considered to be insane."

"I'm calling the police."

"You have no cause. Consenting adults and all that."

"She was asleep!"

That boot shifted around and planted on the ground. "Watch your tone, boy."

Before there was time to get fired up about the insult, the man leaned forward in the chair . . . and Gregg lost his voice.

What came into the light made no sense. On a shit-load of levels.

It was the portrait. From downstairs in the parlor. Only living and breathing. The only difference was that the hair was not pulled back; it was down over shoulders that were two times the size of Gregg's and the stuff was black and red.

Oh, God . . . those eyes were the color of the sunrise, gleaming and peach-colored.

Utterly hypnotic.

And yes, partially mad.

"I suggest," came a drawl in that odd accent, "that you back out of this attic and go down to that lovely lady of yours—"

"Are you a descendant of Rathboone's?"

The man smiled. Right, okay . . . there was something *very* wrong with his front teeth. "He and I have things in common, it's true."

"Jesus . . ."

"Time for you to run along and finish your little project." No more with the smiling, which was a relief of sorts. "And a word of advice in lieu of the ass-kicking I'm tempted to give you. You might take care of your woman better than you have been lately. She has honest feelings for you, which is not her fault, and which you clearly have been undeserving of—or you wouldn't smell like guilt at this moment. You're lucky to have the one you want by your side, so stop being a blind fool about it."

Gregg didn't get shocked all that often. But for the life of him, he didn't have any idea what to say.

How did this stranger know so much?

And Christ, Gregg hated that Holly had been with someone else . . . but she had said his name?

"Wave good-bye." Rathboone lifted his own hand and mimed a child's gesture. "I promise to leave your woman alone, provided you quit ignoring her. Now go on, bye-bye."

Out of a reflex that was not his own, Gregg brought up his arm and did a little flapping before his feet turned his ass around and started walking toward the door.

God, his temples hurt. God . . . damn . . . why was . . . where . . .

His mind ground to a halt, as if its gears had been glued up.

Down to the second floor. Down to his room.

As he took off his clothes and got into bed in his boxers, he put his aching head on the pillow next to Holly's, drew her up against him, and tried to remember . . .

He was supposed to do something. What was—

369

The third floor. He had to go up to the third floor. He had to find out what was up there—

Fresh pain lanced through his brain, killing not only the impulse to go anywhere, but any interest in what was above them in the attic.

Closing his eyes, he had the strangest vision of a foreign stranger with a familiar face . . . but then he passed the fuck out and nothing else mattered.

FORTY-THREE

The infiltration into the mansion next door posed no problem at all.

After regarding the activity of the manse, and finding nothing to suggest movement within the walls, Darius declared that he and Tohrment would go in . . . and in they went. Dematerializing from the ring of woods that separated the two estates, they re-formed beside the kitchen wing—whereupon they simply walked right in through a stout wooden-framed door.

Indeed, the biggest obstacle to breaching the exterior was overcoming the crushing feeling of dread.

With every step and every breath, Darius had to force himself to go forward, his instincts screaming that he was in the wrong place. And yet he refused to turn back. He was out of other practical roads on which to traverse, and though Sampsone's daughter might well not be here, with no other leads, he had to do something or go mad.

"This house feels haunted," Tohrment muttered as they both looked around the servants' common room.

Darius nodded. "But recollect that any ghosts rest solely in your mind, and are not among whoever tallies under this roof. Come, we must locate any subterranean quarters. If the humans have taken her, they must needs keep her underground."

As they made their way silently past the massive kitchen hearth and the curing meats that hung from hooks, it was so very clearly a human house. All was quiet up above and all around; in contrast to a vampire manse, where this would be an active time of preparation for Last Meal.

Alas, that this household was made up of the other race was no confirmation the female was not held herein—and could perhaps recommend that conclusion. Although vampires knew for certain of the existence of mankind, there was naught but myths of vampires abounding on the human cultural periphery— because that was how those with fangs survived with greater ease. Still, from time to time there were inevitable and bona fide contacts between those who chose to remain hidden and those with prying eyes, and these infrequent brushes with one another explained humans' scary stories and fantastical whimsies of anything from "bean-sidhe" to "witches" to "ghosts" to "bloodsuckers." Indeed, the human mind appeared to suffer from a crippling need to fabricate in the absence of concrete proof. Which made sense, given that race's self-referential understanding of the world and their place in it: Anything that didn't fit was forced into the superstructure, even if that meant creating "paranormal" elements.

And what a coup for a wealthy household to capture physical evidence of such ephemeral superstitions.

Especially lovely, defenseless evidence.

There was no telling what had been observed by this household over time. What oddities had been witnessed in their neighbors. What racial differences had been unexpectedly exposed and noted by virtue of the two estates being brothers in landscape.

Darius cursed under his breath and thought that this was why vampires should not live so close among humans. Separation was best. Congregation and separation.

He and Tohrment covered the first floor of the mansion by dematerializing from room to room, shifting as the shadows thrown in the moonlight did, passing around the carved furnishings and tapestries without sound or substance.

The biggest concern, and why they did not traverse the stone floors on foot? Sleeping dogs. Many of the manses had them for guards, and that was a complication they could well do without. Hopefully, if there were some within the household, they were curled at the feet of the master's bed.

And would the same be true for any personal guard.

However, they had fortune on their side. No dogs. No guard. At least, not that they saw, heard, or scented—and they were able to locate the passage that led underground.

Both of them produced candles and lit the wicks, the flames flickering over the hurried, careless workmanship of the rough-hewn steps, and the uneven walls—all of which seemed to indicate that the family never made this sojourn below, only the servants.

More proof this was not a vampire household. Underground quarters were among the most lavish in such homes.

Down on the lower level, the stone beneath their feet yielded to packed earth and the air grew heavy with cold dampness. As they progressed farther under the great mansion, they found storage rooms filled with caskets of wine and mead and bins of salted meats and baskets of potatoes and onions.

At the far end, Darius expected to find a second set of stairs that they could take back up out of the earth. Instead, they just came to a termination of the subterranean hall. No door. Just a wall.

He looked around to see if there were tracks on the ground or fissures in the stones indicating a hidden panel or section. There were none.

In order to be certain, he and Tohrment ran their hands over the walling surface and over the floor.

"There were many windows on the upper stories," Tohrment murmured. "But perhaps if they kept her above, they could have drawn the drapes. Or mayhap there are windowless interior rooms?"

As the pair of them faced the dead end they'd hit, that sense of dread, of being in an incorrect place, swelled in Darius's chest until breath was short and sweat formed under his arms and down his spine. He had a feeling Tohrment was suffering from a similar bout of anxious trepidation, for the male shifted his weight back and forth, back and forth.

Darius shook his head. "Verily, she appears to be else-where—"

"Very true, vampire."

Darius and Tohrment wheeled around while unsheathing their daggers.

Looking at what had taken them by surprise, Darius thought . . . *Well, that explains the dread.*

The white-robed figure blocking the way out was not human and was not vampire.

It was a symphath.

FORTY-FOUR

As Xhex waited outside of the weight room, she regarded her emotions with dispassionate interest. It was, she supposed, like staring at a stranger's face and taking note of the imperfections and the coloring and the features for no other reason than that they had presented themselves for observation.

Her urge for revenge had been eclipsed by an honest concern for John.

Surprise, surprise.

Then again, she'd never imagined seeing that kind of fury up close and personal, especially from the likes of him. It was as if he had an inner beast that had roared free from some interior cage.

Man, the bonded male was not something you fucked around with.

And she wasn't kidding herself. *That* was the reason he'd reacted the way he had—and was also the cause of those dark spices she'd scented around him since she'd gotten out of Lash's prison: Sometime during the weeks of her brutal holiday, John's attraction and respect for her had jelled into the irrevocable.

Shit. What a mess.

As the sound of the treadmill got cut off abruptly, she was willing to bet Blaylock had pulled the cord out of the wall, and good for him if he had. She'd tried to get John to stop pulling a death-by-Nike, but when reasoning with him had gotten her absolutely nowhere, she'd taken up sentry duty out here.

No way she could watch him run himself into the

ground. Listening to the punishment was bad enough.

Down the hall, the glass door to the office swung open and the Brother Tohrment appeared. Given the glow that emanated from behind him, Lassiter had come into the training center as well, but the fallen angel hung back.

"How is John?" As the Brother he walked over, his concern was in his hard face and his tired eyes, and also in his grid, which was lit up in the regret sectors.

Made sense on a lot of levels.

Xhex glanced at the weight room door. "Appears to have rethought a career change to marathoner. Either that or he just killed another treadmill."

Tohr's towering height forced her to tilt her head up, and it was a surprise to see what was behind his blue eyes: There was knowledge in his stare, deep knowledge that made her own emotional circuits fire with suspicion. In her experience, strangers who looked at you like that were dangerous.

"How are you?" he asked softly.

It was strange; she hadn't had a lot of contact with the Brother, but whenever their paths had crossed, he'd always been particularly . . . well, kind. Which was why she always avoided him. She dealt much better with toughness than she did with anything tender.

Frankly he made her jumpy.

As she stayed quiet, his face tightened as if she'd disappointed him but he didn't blame her for the shortfall. "Okay," he said. "I won't pry."

Jesus, she was a bitch. "No, it's all right. You just really don't want me to answer that right now."

"Fair enough." His eyes narrowed on the weight room door and she got the distinct impression he was trapped outside of it as much as she was, shut down by the male who was suffering on the other side. "So you called up to the kitchen to get me?"

She took out the key John had used to let them into the guy's former house. "Just wanted to give this back to you and tell you there was a problem."

The Brother's emotional grid went black and vacant, everything lights-out. "What kind of problem?"

"One of your sliding glass doors is broken. It's going to need a couple of sheets of plywood to cover it up. We were able to reengage the security alarm so the motion detectors inside are on, but you've got a hell of a draft. I'll be happy to fix it today."

Assuming John either finished off the rest of the exercise machines, ran out of running shoes, or fell over in a dead heap.

"Which . . ." Tohr cleared his throat. "Which door?"

"The one in John Matthew's room."

The Brother frowned. "Was it broken when you got there?"

"No . . . it just spontaneously busted."

"Glass doesn't do that without a good reason."

And hadn't she given John Matthew one. "True enough."

Tohr stared at her and she looked right back at him and the silence grew thick as mud. The thing was, though, as nice a guy and as good a soldier as the Brother was, she had nothing to share with him.

"Who do I talk to about getting some plywood," she prompted.

"Don't worry about it. And thanks for letting me know."

As the Brother turned and walked back into the office, she felt like hell—which she supposed was yet another connection she had with John Matthew. Except instead of setting a land/speed record, she just wanted to take a knife and cut her inner forearms to release the pressure.

God, she was such a crybaby emo sometimes, she truly

was. But those cilices of hers not only kept her *symphath* side in check, they helped her dim down the things she didn't want to feel.

Which was aboooooooout ninety-nine percent of emotion, thank you very much.

Ten minutes later, Blaylock ducked his head out of the door. His eyes were locked on the floor and his emotions were in an upheaval, which made sense. No one liked to see a buddy self-destruct, and having to conversate with the person who'd sent the poor bastard into a free fall wasn't exactly a happy-happy.

"Listen, John's gone into the locker room to take a shower. I got him to quit the *Running Man* impression, but he's . . . He needs a little more time, I think."

"Okay. I'll keep waiting for him here in the hall."

Blaylock nodded and then there was this awkward pause. "I'm going to go work out now."

After the door eased shut, she picked her jacket and her weapons up and wandered down toward the locker room. The office was empty, which meant Tohr had gone along his merry way, no doubt to set up some Tim the Tool Man Taylor time with a *doggen*.

And the resonant quiet told her there was no one in any of the classrooms, gym, or clinic.

Sliding down the wall, she let her ass bottom out on the floor and hung her arms off her knees. Letting her head fall back, she closed her eyes.

God, she was exhausted . . .

"John's still in there?"

Xhex snapped awake, her gun pointed right up at Blaylock's chest. As the guy leaped back, she immediately flipped on the safety and lowered the muzzle.

"Sorry, old habits die hard."

"Ah, yeah." The guy motioned his white towel toward the locker room. "Is John still in there? It's been over an hour."

She flipped her wrist up and looked at the watch she'd snagged. "Christ."

Xhex got to her feet and cracked the door. The sound of the shower running wasn't much of a relief. "Is there any other way out?"

"Just through the weight room—which opens only into this hall."

"Okay, I'm going to go talk to him," she said, praying it was the right thing to do.

"Good. I'll finish my workout. Call me if you need me."

She pushed through the door, and inside, the place was standard-issue, all banks of beige metal lockers separated by wooden benches. Following the sound of falling water to the right, she passed by a bay of urinals, stalls, and sinks that seemed lonely without a bunch of sweaty, naked, towel-snapping males putting them to use.

She found John in an open area with dozens of showerheads and tile on every square inch of the floors, walls, and ceiling. He was in his T-shirt and running shorts and was sitting against the wall, his arms hanging off his knees, his head down, the water rushing over his huge shoulders and torso.

Her first thought was that she had been outside in exactly the same position.

Her second was that she was surprised he could stand being so still. His emotional grid was not the only thing lit up; that shadow behind it was likewise afire with anguish. It was as if the two parts of him were both in a kind of mourning no doubt because he'd suffered or been witness to too many cruel losses in this life . . . and perhaps another. And where all that put him emotionally terrified her. The dense black void created in him was so powerful, it warped the superstructure of his psyche . . . taking him where she had been in that fucking OR.

Taking him to the pinpoint of madness.

Stepping over the tiled lip in the floor, her skin goose bumped at the chill in the air that came from his feelings . . . and the reality that she'd done it again. This was Murhder, only worse.

Jesus Christ, she was a fucking black widow when it came to males of worth.

"John?"

He didn't look up, although she wasn't sure whether he was even aware she was in front of him. He was back in the past, sucked in and held in the vise of memory . . .

Frowning, she found her eyes following the path of the water that rivered its way out from under him and traveled across the tilted tile plane . . . to the drain.

The drain.

Something with that drain. Something to do with . . . Lash?

Within the embrace of the solitude and against the backdrop of the quiet sound of the water's spray, she unleashed her bad side for a good purpose: In a great rush, her *symphath* instincts dove into John, penetrating through his physical territory and going deep into his mind and his recollections.

As he lifted his head and looked up at her in shock, everything went red and two-dimensional, the tile becoming a blush pink, John's dark, damp hair changing to the color of blood, the water twinkling like rose champagne.

The images she got were drawn with a quill of terror and shame: a dark stairway in an apartment building not unlike the one he'd taken her to; him a small pretrans being forced by a fetid human male . . .

Oh. God.

No.

Xhex's knees gave out and she wobbled—then just

let herself go to the ground, landing on the slick tile so hard her bones rattled and her teeth clapped together.

No . . . not John, she thought. Not when he was defenseless and innocent and so very alone. Not when he was lost in the human world, scrounging to survive.

Not him. Not like that.

With her *symphath* side out and her eyes undoubtedly glowing red, they sat there staring at each other. He knew she'd read him and he hated her knowledge with such a fury she wisely kept any sorrow or commiseration to herself. He didn't appear to resent that she'd invaded him, though. It was more like he wished like fuck he didn't have that to share with anybody.

"What does Lash have to do with it," she said roughly. "Because he's all over your mind."

John's eyes shifted to the drain in the center and she got the impression he was seeing blood pooling around the stainless-steel cap. Lash's.

Xhex narrowed her eyes, the backstory becoming pretty damned guessable: Lash had found out about John's secret. Somehow. And she didn't need her *symphath* side to tell her what the fucker would have done with information like that.

A baseball announcer would seek less of an audience.

As John's stare came back to her, she felt a shattering communion with him. No barriers, no worries about being vulnerable. Even though they were both fully clothed, each was naked before the other.

She knew damn well she was never going to find this with any other male. Or any other person. He knew without words all she had been through and everything that those kind of experiences spawned when they were triggered. And she knew the same for him.

And maybe that shadow on his emotional grid was a kind of bifurcation of his psyche caused by the trauma he'd been through. Maybe his mind and his soul had gotten together and agreed to cut the past out and put it toward the back of his mental and emotional attic. Maybe that was why these two parts of him were so vividly animated.

Made sense. And so did the vengeance he was feeling. After all, Lash had been intimately involved in both sets of wrongs, his and hers.

Information like John's in the wrong hands? Almost as bad as the horror that had actually happened because you relived that shit every time someone else learned of the story. Which was why she never talked about her time up in the colony with her father, or that shit in the human medical clinic . . . or . . . yeah . . .

John raised his forefinger and tapped beside his eye.

"Mine are red?" she murmured. When he nodded, she rubbed her face. "Sorry. I'm probably going to need to get another pair of cilices."

As he shut the water off, she dropped her hands. "Who else knows. About you."

John frowned. Then mouthed, *Blay, Qhuinn. Zsadist. Havers. A therapist.* When he shook his head, she took that to mean it was the end of the list.

"I'm not going to say anything to anyone."

Her eyes went over his huge body from those shoulders to his powerful biceps and his tremendous thighs— and she found herself wishing he'd been this size back in that grungy stairwell. At least he wasn't as he'd been when he'd been hurt anymore—although that was true only on the outside. Inside, he was all the ages he'd ever lived through, the infant who'd been abandoned, the child who'd been unwanted, the pretrans who'd been out in the world on his own . . . and now the grown male.

Who was an ass-kicker in the field and a loyal friend and, going by what he'd done to that *lesser* in the brownstone and what he undoubtedly wanted to do to Lash, a very nasty enemy.

And didn't this add up to a problem: As far as she was concerned, the son of the Omega was *hers* to murder.

Not that they needed to cover that right now.

As the dampness from the tile sneaked into the seat of her scrubs, and water dripped off of John, she was surprised by what she wanted to do.

On a lot of levels, it didn't make sense and it certainly wasn't a hot idea. But logic wasn't a big player in this moment between them.

Xhex shifted forward and put her palms on the slick shower floor. Moving slowly, going hand, knee, hand, knee, she went toward him.

She knew when he caught her scent.

Because under the sopping wet running shorts his cock twitched and hardened.

When she was face-to-face with him, she locked her eyes on his mouth. "Our minds are already together. I want the flesh to follow."

With that, she leaned in and tilted her head. Just before she kissed him, she paused, but not because she was worried he was going to turn away—she knew by the dark bonding spice he was throwing out that John was not interested in pulling back.

"No, you've got it all wrong, John." Reading his emotions, she shook her head. "You're not half the male you could be because of what was done to you. You're twice what anyone else is because you survived."

You know, life put you in places you never expected.

Under no circumstances, not even in the worst nightmares his subconscious had burped up, had John ever thought he would be able to handle Xhex knowing about how he'd been hurt when he was young.

The thing was, no matter how big or strong his body

got, he'd never shed the reality of how weak he'd once been. And the threat of those he respected finding out brought that weakness back not just once, but perpetually.

Yet here they were with his skeleton not just out of the closet, but draped in strobe lights.

And as for his two-hour shower? He was still dying inside that she'd been hurt like that. . . It was too painful to think about, too horrible not to dwell on. Then add in his need as a bonded male to protect her and keep her safe? And the fact that he knew exactly how awful it was to be victimized in that way?

If he'd only found her sooner . . . if he'd just worked harder . . .

Yeah, but she'd freed herself. Hadn't she. He hadn't been the one to spring her—for fuck's sake, he'd stood in the goddamn room she'd been raped in *with her* and not even known she was *there*.

It was almost too much to live with, all the layers and the intersections making his head hum to the point where he felt like his brain had turned into a helicopter that was on the verge of levitating up, up, and away, never to return again.

The only thing keeping him grounded was the prospect of killing Lash.

As long as he knew the fucker was out there breathing in the world, John had a focus that kept the roof on his house.

Killing Lash was his link to sanity and purpose, the galvanizing in his steel.

One more intrinsic weakness, though, like not avenging his female, and he was game-over.

"John," she said, clearly in an effort to pull him out of his tailspin.

Focusing on her, he stared into her red, glowing eyes and was reminded that she was a *symphath*. Which meant she could burrow into him and trigger all of his inner trapdoors, springing his demons just to watch them dance. Except she hadn't done that, had she—she'd gotten into him, yes, but only to understand where he was at. And upon seeing into his dark parts, she wasn't yukking it up and pointing fingers at him, or recoiling in disgust.

Instead, she'd prowled over to him like a she-cat, looking like she wanted to kiss him.

His eyes dropped down to her lips.

What do you know, he could stand some of that kind of connection. Words weren't enough to assuage the self-loathing he felt, but her hands on his skin, her mouth on his, her body up against his own . . . that, not talking, was what he needed.

"That's right," she said, her eyes burning, and not just from the *symphath* in her. "You and I need this."

John reached up and put his cold, wet hands on her face. Then he looked around. Now might be the time, but here was not the place.

He was not making love to her on the hard tile.

Come with me, he mouthed, standing up and pulling her to his side.

His hard-on tented the front of his running shorts as they left the locker room, the urge to mate a roar in his blood that was nonetheless held in check by the need to do right by her and give her something gentle in place of the violence she'd suffered.

Instead of heading for the tunnel back to the main house, he took them to the right. There was no way he was going up to his room with her under his arm and him sporting an erection the size of an I-beam. Besides, he was soaking wet.

Way too much to explain to the perma–peanut gallery the mansion offered.

Next to the locker room, but not connected to it, was a stretching facility with massage tables and a whirlpool bath in the corner. Place also had a shitload of blue mats

385

that hadn't been used since they'd been laid down—the Brothers barely had time to spar, much less play ballerina with their precious hamstrings and glutes.

John buttressed the door closed with a plastic chair and turned to face Xhex. She was walking around, her lithe body and smooth strides better than an entire strip show, as far as he was concerned.

Reaching to the side, he killed the lights.

The red-and-white Exit sign over the door created a pool of dim light that his body split in half, his shadow a tall, dark divide that stretched all the way across the blue flooring to Xhex's feet.

"God, I want you," she said.

She wasn't going to have to say that twice. Kicking off his Nikes, he pulled his shirt over his head and let it fall to the mats in a flap. Then he linked his thumbs in the waistband of his running shorts and drew them down his thighs, his cock popping free and standing straight out of him. The fact that it pointed to her like a divining rod was no big surprise—everything from his brain to his blood to his beating heart was focused on the female who stood no more than ten feet away.

But he wasn't going to just jump on her and pound away. Nope. Not even if it gave him balls the color of a Smurf—

His thoughts stopped being logical as her hands went to the bottom hem of her sweatshirt and, in an elegant shift, she pulled it up her torso and over her head. Underneath, she had on nothing except for her beautiful, smooth skin and her tight, high breasts.

As her scent roared across the way and he began to pant, those nimble fingers of hers went to the tie on the scrubs and loosened it, the thin green cotton falling in a rush to her ankles.

Oh . . . sweet God, she was gloriously bared to him, and the impressive lines of her body were astonishing:

Although they'd had sex two times, both had been fast and hot, so he'd never had the chance to look at her properly—

John blinked hard.

For a moment, all he could see were the bruises that had been on her when he'd found her, especially the ones on the insides of her thighs. To know now that she hadn't gotten them from just hand-to-hand fighting . . .

"Don't go there, John," she said hoarsely. "I'm not and you shouldn't. Just . . . don't go there. He's already taken too much from both of us."

His throat tightened around a roar of vengeance, which he managed to stifle only because he knew she was right. With sheer force of will, he decided that that door behind him, the one he'd jammed shut with the chair, was going to keep out not just passersby of the living variety, but the ghosts of wrongs as well.

There would be time on the other side of this private commune for evening the score.

You are so beautiful, he mouthed.

But of course she couldn't see his lips.

Guess he was going to have to show her.

John took a step forward and another and another. And it wasn't just him going toward her. She met him in the middle, halfway between her point A and his point B, her form encased in the shadow thrown by his body and yet nevertheless the only thing he saw.

As they came together, his chest was pumping and so was his heart. *I love you*, he mouthed in the dark slice he'd cut out of the light.

They each reached for the other at the same moment: He went for her face. She put her hands on his ribs. Their mouths finished the journey in the still, electrified air, their lips latching on, soft to soft, warm to warm. Drawing her against his bare chest, John wrapped his thick arms around her shoulders and held her tight as he deepened the kiss—and she was right there with him, sliding her palms around his sides and slipping them down to the small of his back.

His cock folded up between them, the friction of his stomach and hers sending shafts of heat licking up and down his spine. But he wasn't in a hurry. With lazy pushes, his hips moved in and back, stroking his arousal against her as he shifted his hands onto her arms and then to her waist.

Thrusting deep with his tongue, he dragged one hand up to the short hair at the base of her neck and let the other fall to the back of her thigh. Her leg came up on his gentle pull, the sleek muscles flexing—

With a lithe surge, she jumped the gun, leaping onto him and wrapping the remaining leg that had borne her weight around his hips. As his cock hit something hot and wet, he groaned and took them down to the floor, holding her to him as he sank them to the mats and stretched her out underneath him.

John broke the seal of their kiss and pulled back enough so he could run his tongue up the side of her throat. Latching on, he sucked on the cords of her neck and followed them downward until his fangs, which throbbed to the beat of his erection, traced over the thrust of her collarbone. As he went south, her fingers were deep in his hair and holding him down to her skin, moving him toward her breasts.

Pulling back, he towered over her and traced with his eyes the way her body was set off by the glowing light of the Exit sign. Her nipples were tight and her ribs were pumping hard and her six-pack flexed as she rolled her hips. Between her thighs, her smooth sex had him opening his mouth in a soundless hiss—

Without warning, she reached up and put her hand on his cock.

The contact had him rearing back to the point where

he had to throw his arms out and catch himself on his palms.

"Goddamn, you're beautiful," she said on a growl.

Her voice snapped him into action and he shifted forward, popping his cock free of her palm and positioning himself so he was kneeling between her thighs. Dropping his head, he covered one of her nipples with his mouth and flicked at it with his tongue.

The moan that rippled out of her nearly had him coming all over her sex and he had to freeze his body to regain control. When the tingling tide retreated enough, he resumed sucking at her . . . and let his palms drift slowly down her ribs and her waist and her hips.

Typical of her, she was the one who put him to her sex.

Xhex covered one of his hands with her own and got him right where they both wanted him to be.

Hot. Silky. Slick.

The orgasm at the head of his erection broke free the instant his fingers slipped through and came flush against the entry he was dying to breach: There was absolutely no holding the release back and she laughed in a throaty way as he jetted his marking on her legs.

"You like the way I feel," she murmured.

He looked into her eyes and instead of nodding, brought the hand that she had drawn down onto herself up to his mouth. As he extended his tongue and slid what was covered with her between his lips, she did some shuddering of her own, her body jacking up off the mats, her breasts surging, her thighs falling further open.

From beneath lowered lids, he kept his stare locked on hers as he planted his palms on either side of her hips and bent down to her sex.

Might have been smoother to do that butterfly-kisses

bullshit. Might have shown more finesse to tease her with his tongue and his fingertips.

Fuck that.

With a raw, whipping need, he latched onto her core with his mouth, sucking her into him, taking her deep, swallowing her up. His orgasm had left some of him on her and he tasted that along with her honey—and the bonded male in him relished the combination.

Which was lucky for him. By the time he was through with this session, his dark spice was going to be all over her, inside and out.

As he lapped and flicked and penetrated, he dimly felt one of her legs get thrown over his shoulder and then she was working herself against his chin and lips and mouth, adding to the magic, driving him to drive her harder.

When she orgasmed, she said his name. Twice.

And didn't it make him glad that even though he had no voice, his ears worked just fine.

FORTY-FIVE

Jesus Christ, John knew what he was doing.

That was the one thought which shot through Xhex's mind after she came down from the soaring release he'd given her with his mouth. And then she promptly got swept up again. His bonding scent was a roar in her nose, and his lips were blisteringly delicious on her core, and his erection was a teasing hot length on her legs—

As he extended his tongue and went in deep, she flew apart again. The wet heat he brought to her, the shifting strokes that were soft when they were his lips and rasping when it was his chin, the circling of his nose against the top of her sex, it all blew off the top of her brain—a loss she was so willing to enjoy.

In the midst of the fire, there was nothing but John . . . no past, no future, nothing but their bodies. Time had no meaning and location had no matter and other people held no interest.

She wished they could be like this forever.

"Come in me," she groaned, as she pulled at his shoulders.

John lifted his head and moved up her body, his arousal nudging against her inner thighs, getting closer.

She kissed him hard, grinding her mouth against his as she shoved her hand down between them and guided him where she needed him—

His massive body torqued at the contact as she bit out, "Oh, *God . . .*"

The blunt head of him parted her and he slid in nice and slow, filling her, stretching her. She arched so he could go all the way in and shifted her palms down his smooth back to the dip at the end of his spine . . . and even lower so that she could sink her nails into his ass.

His muscles bunched and released under her hands as he started to pump, and her head rocked back and forth against the mat as he pushed in and pulled out, pushed in and pulled out. He was heavy as a car on top of her, and his body had a lot of hard edges—and what do you know, she was so okay with all of that: She had enough curves to accommodate where he needed space, and she was so close to coming again that her lungs were burning for air anyway.

Linking her ankles behind the backs of his thighs, she moved with him until their bodies smacked and their breath exploded, and then John pushed his torso up and drove his fists into the mat on either side of her ribs, bracing the weight of his chest on the carved muscles of his arms—so he could pound harder.

His face was an erotic mask of the features she had seen so often, his lips drawn back off his long, white fangs, his brows down tight, his eyes blazing, his jaw clenched so hard that his cheeks had hollows in them. With every thrust, his pecs and his abdominals popped, the sweat on his skin gleaming in the dim light. The sight of him was the chaser to what he felt like deep in her, the sucker punch that came on the heels of the body shot, knocking her out completely.

"Take my vein," she growled at him. "Take it—*now*."

As she ricocheted off into another orgasm, he came to her throat in a lunge, his bite slicing into her neck as his own release jerked into her.

Once he started to come, he couldn't stop and she didn't want him to. He kept moving and drinking and shuddering into her, the rolling multiples that racked him saturating her sex as he fed and took her hard.

But it was what she wanted.

When he finally stilled, he didn't so much stop as collapse on her. Running her hands up his shoulders, she held him as he drew lazy laps over his puncture marks.

Sometimes you had to sandblast in order to clean something properly. Delicate little circles with a sponge or a cloth just couldn't get the dirt and grime out well enough. And what they'd just done was a sandblast and a half—and, given the way he was still hard, she knew that there was more to come.

Literally.

John lifted his head and looked down at her. His eyes were worried and he was careful as he brushed at her hair.

She smiled. "Nah, I'm fine. I'm more than fine."

A sly grin bloomed on his handsome face as he mouthed, *Ain't that the truth.*

"Hold up there, big man. You think you can make me blush like I'm some girl? Pulling that sweet talk?" As he nodded, she rolled her eyes. "I'll have you know I'm not the kind of female who goes all dizzy, popping a stiletto off the floor just because some guy kisses her deep."

John was all male as he cocked a brow. And damn it if she didn't feel a tingle in her cheeks.

"Listen, John Matthew." She took his chin in her hand. "You're not turning me into one of those females who goes gaga over her lover. Not happening. I'm not hardwired for that."

Her voice was stern and she meant every word—except the instant he rolled his hips and that huge arousal pushed into her, she purred.

Purred.

The sound was utterly foreign and she'd have sucked it back down her throat if she could have. Instead, she just let out another of those decidedly non-tough-guy moans.

John bowed his head to her breast and started suckling on her as he somehow managed to keep thrusting in slow, even penetrations.

Swept away, her hands found his hair again, spearing through the thick softness. "Oh, John . . ."

And then he stopped dead, lifted his lips from her nipple, and smiled so wide it was a wonder he didn't bust off his front teeth.

His expression was one of total and complete *gotcha*.

"You are a bastard," she said on a laugh.

He nodded. And pressed into her with his full length again.

It was perfect that he was giving her shit and showing her a little of who was boss. Just perfect. Somehow, it made her respect him even more—but then, she'd always loved strength in all its forms. Even the teasing kind.

"I'm not surrendering, you know."

He pursed his lips and shook his head, all *oh, no, of course not*.

And then he started to pull out of her. As she growled low in her throat, she sank her nails into his ass. "Where do you think you're going?"

John laughed silently, stretched her thighs wide, and went down the length of her until he was back where he'd started on her . . . with his mouth all over her sex.

His name echoed loud in the room, bouncing around the tiled walls as he gave her more of exactly what she wanted and needed.

Studiously ignoring the sounds of sex was a skill Blay was getting waaaaaay too much practice at.

As he came out of the weight room, he heard the echo of John's name through the closed door of the rehab suite. Given the pitch and the tenor, it was clear a whole lot of conversating wasn't the cause.

Not unless Xhex was a closet meteorologist and John was giving her the weather report of her life.

And good for them. Considering how hard-core things had been with John and those treadmills, it was a blessing.

Blay took a second to debate returning to the mansion, and decided that given how long Qhuinn could go, it was too early to head for his room. Ducking into locker-landia, he took a quick shower and changed into a pair of scrubs from the Vishous collection. Out in the corridor once again, he hustled along, pushing through into the office and shutting the door tight.

Quick hearing test and everything was quiet as far as he knew, which was just what he was after. Unfortunately, a check of his watch showed he'd blown through only about an hour and a half total. To think he'd always assumed an efficient shower was a wonderful thing.

Considering his alternatives, he decided to sit behind the desk. After all, studiously not listening to Xhex and John was an issue of decorum. Tuning out Qhuinn and Layla? Self-preservation.

Much better to rock the former than the latter.

Parking it in the swivel chair, he stared at the phone.

Saxton had been one hell of a kisser.

One . . . hell . . . of a kisser.

Blay's eyes briefly closed as heat wafted through him, like someone had started up a banked fire in his stomach.

He reached out to the receiver . . . and couldn't commit, his hand hovering, but not picking up.

And then he remembered Layla sauntering out of his bathroom, heading for Qhuinn.

Snatching the receiver from its cradle, he dialed Saxton's number and wondered what the hell he was doing as the line rang.

". . . Hello . . ."

Blay frowned and straightened in the office chair. "What's wrong?" Long pause. "Saxton?"

There was a cough and a wheeze. "Yes, 'tis I . . ."

"Saxton, what the hell is going on?"

There was a terrible silence. "You know, I loved kissing you." The strangled voice became wistful. "And I loved"—another cough—"being with you. I could look into your face for ages."

"Where are you?"

"At home."

Blay looked at his watch again. "Where is that."

"Are you seeking to play hero?"

"Do I need to?"

This time the coughing didn't stop after just one hitch. "I'm afraid . . . I . . . must go."

There was a click and the call went dead.

With his instincts screaming, Blay bolted through the closet into the underground tunnel, and dematerialized past the steps that led up to the mansion.

He took form again in front of another door hundreds of yards down.

At the Pit's entry, he put his face in the camera's eye and hit the intercom. "V? I need you."

As he waited, he prayed to the Scribe Virgin that Vishous was—

The stout panel whipped open and V was on the other side, his hair wet, a black towel around his waist. Jay-Z's *Empire State of Mind* was thumping in the background and the scent of fine Turkish tobacco drifted out.

"Whassup?"

"I need you to get me an address."

Those icy silver eyes narrowed, the tattoo on his left temple flexing. "What kind of addy you looking for."

"Off a civilian's cell phone number." Blay recited the digits he'd just dialed.

V rolled his eyes and stepped back. "Child's play."

And it was. Couple of keystrokes at the Brother's Four Toys and V looked up from his computers. "Twenty-one oh five Sienna Court— Where the fuck are you going?"

Blay spoke over his shoulder as he strode past the leather couches and the wide-screen television. "Out your front door."

V dematerialized and blocked the exit. "Sun's coming up in twenty-five minutes, true?"

"Then don't keep me here a second longer." Blay slid his eyes to the Brother's. "Let me go."

The whole lot of nonnegotiable he was feeling must have shown in his face because V cursed low. "Make it quick or you aren't coming back."

As the Brother opened the door, Blay thin-aired it right out . . . and took form on Sienna Court, a tree-lined street with Victorians of various colorful extractions. He flashed down to 2105, a perfectly conditioned clapboard number painted in dark green with gray-and-black trim. The front gingerbread porch and the side door were lit with lanterns, but inside everything was dark.

Which made sense. Going by the way the glass panes double-reflected, there were internal shutters down in place.

No getting in through them.

Without a lot of options for infiltration, given that those window shields undoubtedly had steel in them, he went up to the front door and rang the bell.

The weak sunlight coming from the east heated his back even though the rays were barely strong enough to throw shadows. Damn it, where was the camera? Assuming V got the house right—and come on, he was always right—there would be a closed-circuit monitoring system . . .

Ah, yes, in the eyes of the lion door knocker.

Leaning forward, he met the brass face and pounded with his fists.

"Let me in, Saxton." As his shoulders and spine heated even further, he reached behind himself and fluffed out the top of the scrubs he'd put on.

The clicking shift of the lock and turn of the knob had him brushing quickly through his damp hair.

The door opened only a crack and the house beyond was shrouded in dense shadows. "What are you doing"— cough—"here."

Blay went cold as he smelled blood.

Slamming his shoulder into the heavy panels, he pushed inside. "What the hell—"

Saxton's voice receded. "Go home, Blaylock. As much as I adore you, I'm not in a position to receive at the moment."

Yeah, big whatever on that. With a quick shift, Blay shut them in together to keep the sun out.

"What happened." Even though he knew. On án instinctual level, he knew. "Who beat you?"

"I was about to take a shower. Perhaps you'll join me?" As Blay swallowed hard, Saxton laughed a little. "All right. I'll take one and you have a coffee. Because it seems as though you are my guest for the day."

There was the sound of the lock turning on the door, and then the male shuffled away—which suggested he might have a limp.

Although it wasn't possible to see Saxton in the dense black, the sounds of him walking headed over to the right. Blay hesitated. No sense in checking his watch again. He knew that the chance to get back had likely passed.

He was indeed staying the day.

The other male opened the way into a cellar, revealing a set of dimly lit steps that descended below. In the soft glow of illumination, Saxton's beautiful blond hair was matted with a rusty stain.

Blay marched forward and snatched hold of the guy's arm. "Who did this to you?"

Saxton refused to glance over, but his deep shudder said plenty about what his voice had already revealed:

he was tired and in pain. "Let us say . . . that I shan't be going for more cigars anytime soon."

That alley by the bar . . . shit, Blay had taken off first, but he'd assumed Saxton had done the same. "What happened after I left?"

"It doesn't matter."

"The fuck it doesn't."

"If you'd be so kind, permit me"—more of that damned cough—"to go back to bed. Especially if you're going to get testy. I'm not feeling particularly well."

With that, he looked over his shoulder.

Blay's breath shot out of his lungs.

"Oh . . . my God," he whispered.

FORTY-SIX

The sun was just about to pierce the veil of forest when Darius and Tohrment took form in front of a small, thatch-roofed cottage miles and miles and miles away from the site of the abduction and the mansion beside it . . . and the reptilian thing who had greeted them in that dank underground hallway.

"Are you sure about this?" Tohrment asked, switching his satchel to his opposite shoulder.

At the present, Darius felt sure about nothing. For truth, he was surprised that he and the boy had managed to get free of that symphath's house without a fight. In point of fact, however, they had been escorted out as though they had been invited guests.

Then again, sin-eaters always kept their own best advantage in sight, and verily, Darius and Tohrment were of far greater use to the head of that household alive as opposed to dead.

"Are you sure?" Tohrment prompted again. "You hesitate to go therein."

"Alas, my tarrying has naught to do with you." Darius walked forward, picking up the beaten path that led to the front door, said groundway having been created by the repeated passing of his own boots. "I shall not have you sleeping on the cold stone floor of the Tomb. My home is rough, but has a roof and walls sufficient to shelter not one, but two."

For a brief moment, he entertained a fantasy that he lived as he had once done, in a castle full of rooms and doggen and lovely appointments, in a luxurious place where he could open his doors to friends and family and have those whom he loved safe and secure and tended to.

Perhaps he would find a way to have that again.

Although given that he had no family and no friends, it was hardly something to pursue with alacrity.

Popping the cast-iron latch free, he put his torso to the oak door—which, considering its size and heft, was more of a movable wall. After he and Tohr went inside, he lit the oil lamp that hung by the entrance and closed them in, laying a broad beam thick as a tree trunk across the panel.

So modest. Only one chair before the hearth and a single pallet across the way. And there was not much more to be had down below the earth, just some precious supplies and a hidden tunnel that terminated well into the bounds of the forest.

"Shall we have a repast?" Darius said as he began to disarm.

"Yes, sire."

The boy removed his own weapons and went to the hearth, settling down onto his haunches and lighting the peat that was always set when there wasn't a fire burning. As the scent of the smoking moss wafted over, Darius pulled up the trapdoor in the dirt floor and went underground to his food and ale and his parchments. He returned with cheeses and breads and smoked venison.

The fire cast a glow over Tohr's face as he warmed his hands and asked, "What dost thou make of it all?"

Darius joined the boy and shared what little he had to offer with the only guest he had ever had in his home. "I have always believed destiny makes for strange bedfellows. But the concept that our interests could be aligned with one of those . . . things . . . is an anathema. Then again, he seemed equally disposed toward shock and dismay. For truth, those sin-eaters favor us in no greater regard than we favor them. We are but rats at their feet."

Tohrment partook of the ale flask. "I should never wish to mix my blood with theirs—they disgust my senses. All of them."

"And he feels similarly. The fact that his blooded son took the female and held her even for a day within his walls made

401

him ill. He is as incented as we to find both parties returned unto their families."

"But why use us?"

Darius' smiled coldly. "To punish the son. 'Tis the perfect corrective action—to have the female's kind rip his 'love' from him and leave him with the burden of that absence as well as the knowledge that inferiors had bested him. And if we bring her home safe? Her family will move and take her away, and never, ever allow ill to befall her again. She will live long on the earth and that sin-eater's spawn shall have to know that for every day he draws breath. This is in their nature—and precisely the kind of soul shattering that the father could not attempt without you or me. That is why we were told where to go and what we would find."

Tohrment shook his head like he didn't understand the way the other race thought. "She will be ruined in the eyes of her bloodline. Indeed, the glymera *will shun them all—"*

"No, they won't." Darius held up his palm to halt the boy's talk. "Because they shall never know. No one shall. This secret shall be betwixt me and thee. Verily, the sin-eater has no cause to come forward for his own kind would shun him and his— and thus the female shall be protected from the fallout."

"How will we accomplish such a deceit with Sampsone, though?"

Darius brought the ale flask to his lips and swallowed. "Upon the fall of night tomorrow, we shall head north, as the sin-eater suggested. We shall find what is ours and bring her home to her blooded family and tell them that it was a human."

"What if the female talks?"

Darius had considered that. "I suspect that as a daughter of the glymera *she is well aware of how much she stands to lose. Silence shall protect not only her but her family."*

Although the foregoing logic assumed she was in her right mind when they got to her. And that might well not be the case, may the Virgin Scribe ease the female's tortured soul.

"This could be an ambush," Tohrment murmured.

402

"Perhaps, but I do not believe so. Further, however, I am not afraid of any conflict." Darius lifted his stare to his protégé's. "The worst thing that can happen is that I die in the pursuit of an innocent—and that is the very best way to go. And if 'tis a trap, I will guarantee you I shall take out a legion on my way unto the Fade."

Tohrment's face positively shone with respect and reverence and Darius felt saddened at the pledge of faith. If the boy had had a real father, instead of a brutish lush, he wouldn't have felt as such toward a relative stranger.

Wouldn't be in this modest shelter, either.

Darius didn't have the heart to point this out to his guest, however. "More cheese?"

"Yes, thank you."

As they finished their repast, Darius's eyes went to his black daggers, which were hanging from the harnesses he wore o'er his chest. He had a strange conviction that it wouldn't be long before Tohrment got a set—the boy was smart, and resourceful, and his instincts were good.

Of course, Darius hadn't seen him fight yet. But that would come. In this war, that would always come.

Tohrment's brow furrowed in the firelight. "How old did they say she was?"

Darius wiped his mouth on a cloth and felt the nape of his neck get tight. "I don't know."

The pair of them fell silent and Darius guessed that what was suddenly in his mind was spinning in Tohrment's as well.

The last thing the situation needed was a further, dire complication.

Alas, ambush or not, they were going up north to the coastal area the symphath had directed them to. Once there, they would head a mile out of the small village and find upon the cliffs the retreat the sin-eater had described . . . and they would discover whether they had been sent forth into a lie.

Or used to further a purpose that aligned both them and that whip-thin reptile.

Darius was truly not worried, however. Sin-eaters were untrustworthy, but they were compulsively self-serving . . . and vindictive even against their own young.

It was a case of nature over character: The latter made them a bad bet; the former made them utterly predictable.

He and Tohrment were going to find what they were in search of up norih by the sea. He just knew it.

The question was, in what condition the poor female would be . . .

FORTY-SEVEN

When John and Xhex finally reemerged from their little slice of privacy, the first stop was the shower in the locker room. And as food was mission-critical after all the exercise, they took turns with Xhex going first.

As John waited his turn out in the hall, it was funny—he should have been exhausted. Instead, he was energized, alive, coursing with power. He hadn't felt this strong . . . ever.

Xhex came out of the locker room. "You're up."

Man, she looked hot as hell, her short hair curling as it air-dried, her body clad in scrubs, her lips red. Flashes of what they'd done together got him jazzed and he ended up backing his way through the door just so he could keep his eyes on her.

And what do you know, when she smiled up at him, his heart snapped in half: The warmth and gentleness in her transformed her into something north of lovely.

She was his female. Evermore.

As the door eased shut between them, he felt a marauding panic when the latch clicked in place, like she wasn't just blocked from view, but gone entirely. Which was nuts. Crushing the paranoia, he showered quickly and pulled on scrubs, studiously ignoring how fast he went.

She was still there when he came out and though he meant to take her hand and head for the mansion, he ended up hugging her, hard.

The thing was, all mortals were going to lose the ones they loved. It was the way life worked. But for most of the time, that reality was so far off in the mind that it had no more weight than a mere hypothetical. There were reminders, however, and the almosts, the near-misses, the oh-God-please-nos, snapped your chain and got you to stop and feel what was in your heart. Like when a bad headache was just a migraine; or when a car accident totaled the station wagon, but the baby seats and the air bags saved all the lives inside; or when someone who had been taken came back to the fold . . . the aftermath shook you up and made you want to hold on to your person to steady yourself.

God, he'd never thought about it properly before, but from the first heartbeat struck within a vital body, a bell got tolled and the clock started to run. A bargain you weren't even aware of having made was put into play, with destiny holding all the cards. As minutes and hours and days and months and years passed, history was written as you ran out of time until your last heartbeat marked the end of the ride and the time to tally wins and losses.

Strange how mortality made moments like this with her infinite.

And as he held Xhex against him, feeling her warmth amplify his own, he was rejuvenated down to his marrow, his scale rebalanced, his sum total squarely in life-was-all-worth-it territory.

His growling stomach was what parted them.

"Come on," she said, "we need to feed your beast."

He nodded, clasped her hand, and started walking.

"You have to teach me sign language," Xhex said as they went into the office and opened the supply closet door. "Like, now."

He nodded again as they filed into the tight space and Xhex shut them in together. Hmm . . . another shot at privacy. Closed door . . . loose clothes . . .

The rat bastard in him measured the maneuvering room they had, his cock twitching behind the scrubs. If she put her legs around his hips, they could fit just fine—

Xhex stepped in close, her hand going to the erection behind the thin cotton across his hips. Rising onto her tiptoes, she brushed her lips against his neck, one fang scratching over his jugular.

"We keep this up, we're never going to find a bed." Her voice dropped even lower as she rubbed him. "God, you're big . . . Have I told you how deep you go in me? Very deep. Niiiice and very deep."

John fell back against a stack of yellow legal pads, knocking them off the shelf. As he scrambled to catch them before they hit the floor, she stopped him by pushing him upright again.

"Stay where you are," she said, going down on her knees. "I like the view too much."

As she picked up what had gone flying, her eyes locked on his arousal—which naturally made a bid for freedom, pushing out against what kept it hidden from her stare, her mouth, her sex.

John's hands cranked onto the lip of one of the shelves as he watched her watch him, his breath sawing in his lungs.

"I think I got all the pads," she said after a while. "Better put them back."

She leaned into his legs as she slowly rose up, her face caressing his knees, his thighs—

Xhex went right over his cock, her lips brushing the underside of the damn thing. As his head went loose and flopped onto the shelving, she continued the ascent so that her breasts were the next thing that hit him on that electric spot.

She ended the torture by sliding the legals back in place . . . while grinding her hips against his.

In his ear, she whispered, "Let's eat fast."

Fucking. Too. Right.

She backed off of him with a nip on his lobe, but he stayed riiiiiiight where he was. Because if the scrubs added even a hint of friction to this sex-quation, he was going to come all over himself.

Which was ordinarily not a bad thing, at least not with her around, but on reconsideration, this was not really a private place. At any moment, one of the Brothers or the *shellans* could pop in and get an eyeful nobody was going to be comfortable with.

After a curse and some serious repositioning below the waist, John punched a code in and opened the way to the tunnel.

"So what is the hand position for 'A'?" she said as they stepped through and started walking.

By the time they got to "D," they were out through the hidden door under the mansion's grand staircase. "I" took them into the kitchen to the refrigerator. "M" got them to a pair of sandwiches—because their hands were busy with the roasted turkey and the mayo and the lettuce and bread, there wasn't much forward progress through the alphabet. They didn't do any better during the eating part of things, just "N" and "O" and "P," but he could tell she was practicing in her mind, her eyes focused on the middle distance between them as she obviously mentally reviewed what he was teaching her.

She learned fast and that was not a surprise. Cleanup led to "Q" through "V," and they were coming out of the kitchen as he showed her "X" and "Y" and "Z"—

"Good, I was going to go find you." Z pulled up short in the archway of the dining room. "Wrath's called a meeting now. Xhex, you're going to want to be there."

The Brother wheeled around, jogged across the mosaic apple tree on the foyer's floor and headed up the grand staircase.

"Your king usually do this in the middle of the day?" Xhex asked.

John shook his head and both mouthed and signed, *Something's up.*

The pair of them followed quickly, taking the steps two at a time.

Up on the second floor, the whole Brotherhood was crammed into Wrath's study and the king was seated on his father's throne behind the desk. George was curled into a sit by his master's side and Wrath was stroking the golden retriever's boxy head with one hand while flipping a dagger-shaped letter opener in the air with the other.

John stayed back, and not just because it was SRO, given the number of large male bodies in the room. He wanted to be near the door.

Xhex's mood had completely shifted.

Sure as if she'd changed her emotional clothes, she'd gone from a flannel nightgown to chain mail: She was twitchy as she stood beside him, her weight shifting back and forth from one foot to the other.

He was feeling much the same.

John looked around. Across the way, Rhage unsheathed a grape Tootsie Pop and V lit up a hand-rolled while he got Phury on speakerphone. Rehv, Tohr, and Z were pacing and Butch was on his sofa, pulling a Hugh Hefner in his silk pajamas. Qhuinn, meanwhile, was propped up near the pale blue drapes, and clearly fresh from some grind: His lips were red and his hair had had a lot of fingers through it and his shirt was partially tucked in— hanging loose in front.

Which made you wonder if he was sporting a hard-on.

Where was Blay? John wondered. And who the hell had Qhuinn just balled?

"So V got one fuck of a voice mail in the general mailbox." As Wrath spoke out, his wraparounds scanned the crowd, even though he was totally blind behind them. "Instead of doing a lot of bullshit explaining, I'm going to have him play it for you."

Vishous left the hand-rolled between his lips as he pulled trig on the phone and danced across the numbers on the console putting in mailbox numbers and passwords.

And then John heard that voice. That snarky-ass, cocksucking voice.

"Bet you never expected to hear from me again." Lash's tone was one of grim satisfaction. "Surprise, motherfuckers, and guess what? I'm about to do you a favor. You might want to know that there was a mass induction into the Lessening Society tonight. Farmhouse out RR 149. Happened around four a.m., so if you get off your asses and head there as soon as night falls, you might find them still throwing up all over the place. FYI, wear your waders—it's a mess. Oh, and tell Xhex I can still taste her—"

V canned the speakerphone.

As John's lips peeled off his fangs, and he let out a soundless snarl, the painting on the wall behind him trembled.

When George whimpered, Wrath soothed the dog and pointed the letter opener across the way. "You'll get your chance at him, John. I swear it on my father's grave. I need your head in this game now, though, dig?"

Easier said than done. Reeling in the urge to kill was like restraining a pit bull with one hand behind his back.

Next to him, Xhex frowned and crossed her arms over her chest.

"We cool?" Wrath demanded.

When John finally whistled an assent, Vishous exhaled a cloud of Turkish tobacco and cleared his throat. "He didn't leave an exact address for this so-called massacre. And I tried to trace the number he called from and got nothing."

"The question I'm wondering," Wrath said, "is what the fuck's doing. He's head of the Lessening Society—so if his tone was all I've-got-the-biggest-balls-of-them-all? Hey, cool, I get that shit. But that wasn't my read."

"He's tattling." Vishous stabbed out his hand-rolled in an ashtray. "That's what it sounded like to me—although I'm not willing to bet my big balls on it."

Now that John had his inner pit recaged and was able to think properly, he was inclined to agree with the Brother. Lash was a self-serving shit, and about as trustworthy as a rattlesnake, but the thing was, when you couldn't rely on morality, you could absolutely bank on narcissism: It made the bastard utterly predictable.

John was sure of this—to the point where he felt like he'd been through it all before.

"Is it possible he's been dethroned," Wrath murmured. "Daddy-o maybe decide that the son was not so amusing after all? Or did the evil's shiny, pretty new toy break—is there some shit in Lash's bizarre biology that's just coming out now? I want us to go in assuming it's an ambush . . ."

There was broad consensus in the room for the plan, as well as some cheap shots involving Lash's ass and various kinds of large-bore instruments of impact: size-fourteen boots being the most likely to come to pass, but hardly the most creative.

For example, John seriously doubted Rhage could in fact park his GTO in the guy's sun-don't-shine. Or would want to.

Man . . . what a turn of events. And yet it wasn't really surprising—if what they were guessing had actually happened. The Omega was known to go through *Fore-lessers* like shit through a goose, and blood wasn't necessarily thicker than evil, so to speak. And if Lash had been kicked to the curb, his calling the Brotherhood out to pull a middle finger on his father was brilliant maneuvering—especially as *lessers* were weakest right after their inductions, and therefore incapable of fighting back.

The Brothers could clean house.

Jesus Christ, John thought. Destiny could make for strange bedfellows.

Xhex was on a low boil as she stood next to John in a study that, but for the desk and throne, could have been mistaken for a French female's parlor.

The sound of Lash's voice coming from that phone made her feel like her stomach had been scrubbed down with ammonia, the burning, churning routine doing a nasty on that poor, well-intended turkey sandwich she'd just had.

And Wrath's assumption that John was going to defend her honor didn't calm things down in there.

"So we infiltrate," the Blind King was saying. "At nightfall, all of you go out 149 and—"

"I'll go now," she said loud and clear. "Give me a pair of guns and a knife and I'll go check it out right now."

Okaaaaaay. Short of pulling the pin on a hand grenade and chucking it into the center of the room, she couldn't have commanded more attention.

As John's emotional grid went dark with oh-no-you-don't, she started the countdown before the explosion hit.

Three . . . two . . . one . . .

"That's a kind offer," the king said as he slid into full cajole-the-female mode. "But I think it's best—"

"You can't stop me." She dropped her arms to her sides—and then reminded herself that she wasn't about to physically attack the guy. Really. She wasn't.

The king's smile was about as warm as dry ice. "I'm sovereign here. Which means if I tell you to hang tight, you're going to goddamn well do that."

"And I'm a *symphath*. Not one of your subjects. More

to the point, you're smart enough not to send your best assets"—she motioned around the room at the Brothers—"into a possible ambush set up by your enemy. I'm disposable—unlike them. Think about it. You going to lose one of them just because you didn't want me to get a little sun today?"

Wrath laughed hard. "Rehv? You want to weigh in on this as king of her kind?"

From across the room, her old boss and dear friend, the fucker, stared at her with amethyst eyes that knew way too much.

You're going to get yourself killed, he thought at her.

Do not hold me back, she returned at him. *I'll never forgive you.*

You keep acting like this and forgiveness is the last thing I'm worried about. Your funeral pyre's more like it.

I didn't stop you from going up to that colony when you needed to. Hell, you tied my hands so I couldn't. You saying I don't deserve my revenge? Fuck you.

Rehvenge's jaw clenched so hard she was surprised that when he finally opened his mouth, he didn't spit out his teeth in pieces. "She can go do what she wants. You can't save someone if they don't want the fucking lifeboat."

The male's anger sucked most of the air out of the room, but she was so focused she didn't need her lungs to work properly anyway.

Obsession was as good as oxygen. And anything that had to do with Lash was fuel to her fire.

"I need weapons," she said to the group. "And leathers. A phone for communication."

Wrath growled low and deep. Like he was going to try and lock her down in spite of Rehv's pass.

Walking forward, she planted her palms on the king's desk and leaned in. "Lose me or run the risk of losing them. What's your answer there, Your Highness."

Wrath rose to his feet, and for a moment she got a clear sense that although he was on the throne, he was still lethal as hell. "Watch. Your. Tone. In my fucking house."

Xhex inhaled deeply and calmed herself down. "I apologize. But you've got to see my point."

As the silence expanded, she could feel John looming—and knew that even if she could break through the king's roadblock, she was still going to have a hell of a time getting around the male by the door. But her departure was not open for discussion from anyone.

Wrath cursed low and long. "Fine. Go. I won't be responsible if you get yourself killed."

"Your Highness, you never were responsible. No one but me is—and no crown on your head or anybody else's is going to change that."

Wrath looked in V's direction and all but snarled, "I want this female covered with weapons."

"No problem. I'll hook her up right."

As she went to follow Vishous out, she stopped in front of John and wished she had a different hand to play—especially as he took her biceps in a hard grip. But the fact was, an opportunity was out there and she had until sundown to take advantage of it: If there were any clues to where Lash was, she'd better use them to get to him if she wanted a clear shot at the bastard. Come nightfall? John and the Brotherhood were going to get unleashed on the situation—and they weren't going to hesitate to kill their target.

Yes, Lash had to pay for what he'd done to her, but she needed to be the one to collect on that debt: She was batting a thousand when it came to burying those who had wronged her, the living, breathing "bitch" in that jolly little saying about payback.

Quietly, so no one else heard, she said, "I'm not someone you need to protect, and you know *exactly* why

I have to do this. You love me like you think you do, you're going to let go of my arm. Before I rip it out of your hold."

As he paled, she prayed she wasn't going to have to get forceful.

But she didn't. He released his grip on her.

Heading out the door of the study, she marched past V and barked over her shoulder, "Time's wasting, Vishous. I need some steel."

FORTY-EIGHT

As Xhex took off with V, John's first thought was to go downstairs, put himself in front of the door that opened into the great outdoors, and physically block her from leaving.

Second thought was to go with her—although that would just turn him into the vampire equivalent of a Roman candle.

Jesus Christ, every time he thought he'd reached a new low with her, the rug got pulled out from under him and he landed at an even harder, hellish place: She'd just volunteered to go into a total unknown that she herself admitted was too dangerous for the Brothers. And she was doing it without backup and without any way of him reaching her if she got hit.

As Wrath and Rehv walked up to him, the study came back into focus and he realized everyone else had left—except for Qhuinn, who was hovering in the corner, frowning at his cell phone.

Rehvenge exhaled hard, clearly in the same fuck-me boat John was in. "Listen, I—"

John signed fast: *What the fuck are you doing, letting her go out like that?*

Rehv drew a hand over his brush-cut mohawk. "I'm going to take care of her—"

You can't go out during the day. How the hell are you going—

Rehv growled deep and low. "Watch your attitude, kid."

Right. Okay. Such the wrong thing to say on the

wrong day: John got right in the guy's grille, bared his hardware, and thought loud and clear: *That's my female going out there. Alone. So you can* fuck *my attitude.*

Rehv cursed and nailed John with hard eyes. "Be careful with that 'your female' stuff—I'm just telling you. Her end game doesn't involve anyone but herself, feel me?"

John's first instinct was to punch the bastard, just pop him in the headlights.

Rehv laughed hard. "You want to throw down? Fine with me." He put his red cane aside and dumped his sable trench coat on the back of an ornate chair. "But it's not going to change a damn thing. You think anyone can read her better than I can? I've known her for longer than you've been alive."

No, you haven't, John thought, for some strange reason.

Wrath stepped between them. "Okay, okay, okay . . . go to your corners, boys. This is a nice Aubusson carpet you're standing on. You get blood on it and I'll have Fritz so far up my ass I'll be coughing on his hankie."

"Look, John, I'm not trying to bust your balls," Rehv muttered. "I just know what it's like to love her. It's not her fault that she's the way she is, but it makes for hell on other people, trust me."

John dropped his fists. Shit, as much as he wanted to argue, the purple-eyed son of a bitch was probably right.

Strike the "probably." He *was* right—John had learned that the hard way. Too many times.

Fucking A, he mouthed.

"That pretty much covers it."

John left the study and went down to the foyer with some vain hope that he could talk her out of leaving. As he paced over the mosaic floor, cutting paths over the depiction of the apple tree, he thought of that embrace they'd shared outside of the locker room. How the hell had they gone from being that close to . . . this?

Had that moment even happened? Or had his stupid-ass nancy side just pulled it out of thin air because he was a sap?

Ten minutes later, Xhex and V came out from the secret door beneath the grand staircase.

As she strode toward across the foyer, she was as John had first met her: black leathers, black boots, black muscle shirt. There was a leather jacket hanging from her hand and enough weapons strapped to her body to outfit a SWAT team.

She paused when she came up to him, and as their eyes met, at least she didn't bother feeding him a line of bullshit like, *It's going to be all right.* On the other hand, she wasn't going to stay. Nothing he could say was going to derail this—the resolve was in her eyes.

As things stood now, he found it very hard to believe she had ever wrapped her arms around him.

As soon as V opened the vestibule's door, she turned away and slipped through without a word spoken or a look back.

Vishous locked up again as John stared at the heavy panels and wondered exactly how long it would take to claw his way through them with his bare fucking hands.

The rasp of a lighter was followed by a slow exhale. "I gave her the best of everything. Forties. Matched. Three clips for each gun. Two knives. New cell phone. And she knows how to use the shit."

V's heavy hand clapped him on the shoulder and squeezed and then the Brother took off, his boots making a heavy rhythm across the mosaic floor. A second later, the hidden door Xhex had emerged from clamped shut as the guy went down into the tunnel to go back to the Pit.

Helplessness really didn't suit him, John thought, his mind starting to hum in the same way it had when Xhex had found him on the floor of the locker room shower.

"You want to watch TV?"

John frowned at the quiet voice and glanced to the right. Tohr was in the billiard room, sitting on the couch that faced the wide-screen over the ornate fireplace. His shitkickers were up on the coffee table and he had his arm running along the back of the sofa, the remote facing the Sony.

He didn't look over. Didn't say anything else. Just kept flipping through the channels.

Choices, choices, choices, John thought.

He could rush out after her and torch his ass. Stay in front of this door like a dog. Peel his own skin off with a knife. Drink himself into a stupor.

From the billiard room, he heard a muted roar and then the screams of a crowd of people.

Drawn to the sound, he went in and stood before the pool table. Over the back of Tohr's head, he saw Godzilla trampling the shit out of a model of downtown Tokyo.

Kind of inspiring, really.

John went over to the wet bar and poured himself a Jack, then sat down next to Tohr and put his feet up on the table as well.

As he focused on the television screen and tasted the whiskey in the back of his throat and felt the warmth of the fire that had been lit across the way, he felt the blender in his brain slow down a little. And then a little more. And further still.

Today was going to be brutal, but at least he wasn't contemplating death by sun ray anymore.

Sometime later, he realized it was Tohr who he was sitting beside, the two of them stretched out as they'd done back home when Wellsie had still been alive.

God, he'd been so pissed off at the guy lately that he'd forgotten how easy it was just to hang with the Brother: On some level, it felt like they had done this for ages, the pair of them before a fire, drink in one hand, exhaustion and stress in the other.

As Mothra flew in for some wing-to-claw action with the big guy, John thought of his old bedroom.

Turning to Tohr, he signed, *Listen, when I was at the house tonight—*

"She told me." Tohr took a drink from his squat glass. "About the door."

I'm sorry.

"Not to worry. Shit like that can be fixed."

True that, John thought, turning back to the television. Unlike so much else.

From way against the far wall, Lassiter let out a sigh that suggested someone had cut off his leg and there wasn't a medic in sight. "I should never have given you the remote. This is just some guy in a monster suit, batting around at a piñata. Come *on*, I'm missing *Maury*."

"What a shame."

"Paternity tests, Tohr. You're button-blocking paternity tests. This sucks."

"Only to you."

While Tohr held steady on 'zilla-vision, John let his head fall back against the leather cushions.

As he thought about Xhex out there alone, he felt as if he'd been poisoned. The stress was literally a toxin in his bloodstream, making him light-headed and nauseated and twitchy.

He thought back to all that "Kumbaya" shit he'd been spouting before he'd found her. How he was owning his feelings, how even if she didn't love him, he could still love her and do what was right and let her live her life and blah, blah, blah.

Yeah, he was so choking on that self-actualization Kool-Aid right now.

He was *not* okay with her out there by herself. Without him. But she clearly wasn't going to listen to him or anyone else.

And how much you want to bet she was scrambling

to get to Lash before nightfall—when John could finally be in the field. On some level, it shouldn't matter which of them took out the piece of shit—but that was rationality talking. The inner core of him couldn't bear another weakness—like, oh, say, sitting idly by while his female tried to kill the son of evil and likely got mortally wounded.

His female . . .

Ah, but wait, he told himself. Just because he had her name tattooed on his back didn't mean he owned her—it was just a lot of black letters in his skin. Fact was, it was more like she owned him. Different. Very different.

Meant she could walk away quite easily.

Just had, as a matter of fact.

Fuck. Rehv seemed to have summoned up the sitch better than anyone could: Her end game didn't include anyone else but herself.

Couple hours of good sex wasn't going to change that.

Nor was the fact that, like it or not, she had taken his heart out there into the daylight with her.

Qhuinn went to his bedroom and headed straight for the bath on legs that were surprisingly steady. He'd been pretty drunk before the emergency meeting had been called, but the idea of John's female out in broad daylight, walking into a shitstorm all by herself, had a way of slapping down the waves of heeeeeey-noooow.

Then again, he was kind of dealing with a twofer along those lines.

Blay was also off in the world all by his little lonesome.

Well, he wasn't alone; he was unprotected.

That text that had come through from an unknown number had settled the mystery of where he was and then some: *I am staying the day with Saxton. I'll be home after dark.*

So like Blay. Everyone else in the world would have shortened that message to: *Stayn t day w Sax b hm afta drk*

Guy's texts were always grammatically correct, though. Like the idea of busting out of the King's English made him scratch.

Blay was funny like that. All proper and shit: He changed for meals, trading leathers and T-shirts for French-cuffed button-downs and pressed slacks. He showered at least twice a day, more if he sparred. Fritz found his room a complete frustration because there was never any mess to clean up.

He had table manners like a count, wrote thank-you letters that could make you tear up, and he never, ever swore in the presence of females.

God . . . Saxton was perfect for him.

Qhuinn sagged in his own skin at that realization, imagining all the proper English that Blay was calling out at this very moment as the other guy had him.

Merriam-Webster had never been used so well, no doubt.

Feeling like he'd been punched in the head, Qhuinn ran the cold water in the sink and splashed his face with the shit until his cheeks tingled and the tip of his nose started to go numb. As he toweled off, he thought back to that tat shop, to the bump and grind he'd had with the receptionist there.

The curtain that had separated the two of them from the rest of the place had been thin enough so that with his mismatched, but highly functional eyes, he'd been able to see everything that was going on on the far side. Everyone, too. So that when that chick had been on her knees in front of him and he'd turned his head, he'd looked out . . . and seen Blay.

The wet mouth he'd been drilling into abruptly morphed from some stranger's to his best friend's and that shift had cranked up the sex from servicing a generic need to something incendiary.

Something important.

Something raw and erotic and lose-your-soul right.

Which was why Qhuinn had pulled her up and spun her around and taken her from behind. Except as he'd pounded into his fantasy, he'd realized that Blay was watching him . . . and that had changed everything. He'd abruptly had to remind himself who he was fucking—which was why he'd pulled the girl's head up to his and forced himself to stare into her eyes.

He hadn't orgasmed.

As she'd come hard, he'd faked it—the truth was his erection had started to fade the instant he'd looked into her face. The only saving grace had been that she clearly hadn't known the difference, having been wet enough for the two of them—and besides, he'd fronted like a pro, laying it on thick like he was all satisfied and shit afterward.

But it had been a total lie.

How many people had he fucked like that in his lifetime, all wham-bam-forget-I-ever-met-ya? Hundreds. Hundreds and hundreds—and this was even though he'd been on the sex ride for only a year and a half. Thing was, though, those late nights at ZeroSum, picking up three and four chicks at a clip, could get you into those big numbers fast.

Of course, a lot of those sessions had been with Blay, he and his buddy balling the women together. The pair of them hadn't actually been with each other during those bathroom orgies at the club—but there had been a lot of watching. And wondering. And maybe a private hand job from time to time when the remembering got too vivid.

At least on Qhuinn's part.

That had all ended, though, when Blay had put the

kibosh on it by realizing that he was gay and that he was in love with someone.

Qhuinn didn't approve of his choice. Not at all. Guy like Blaylock deserved somebody much, much better.

And it appeared he was heading down a road that would get him just that. Saxton was a male of worth. All the way around.

The fucker.

Looking up at the mirror over the sink, Qhuinn couldn't see a thing because it was totally dark in both the bathroom and the bedroom. And wasn't it just as well that he couldn't see his reflection.

Because he was living a lie, and in quiet moments like this he knew it with such conviction he got sick to his stomach.

His plans for the rest of his days . . . oh, his glorious plans.

Such perfectly "normal" future plans.

Involving a female of worth, not a long-term relationship with a male.

The thing was, males like him, males with something wrong with them . . . like, oh, say, one iris that was blue and another that was green . . . were despised in the aristocracy as evidence of a genetic failure. They were embarrassments to be hidden away, shameful secrets to be buried: He'd spent years watching his sister and his brother get elevated on pedestals while everyone who crossed his path performed evil-eye rituals to protect themselves.

His own father had hated him.

So it didn't take a therapist with a diploma on the wall to see that he just wanted to be "normal." And settling down with a female of worth, assuming he could find one who could stand to be mated to somebody with a genetic glitch in the system, was mission-critical to that happy little tag.

He knew if he got tangled up with Blay that wasn't going to happen.

Knew also that all it would take was one fuck and he was never going to leave the guy.

It wasn't that the Brothers didn't accept homosexuals. Hell, they were cool with it—Vishous had been with males and no one blinked an eye, or judged him, or cared. He was just their brother, V. And Qhuinn had crossed the line every now and again just for shits and giggles and they all knew about that and didn't give a crap.

The *glymera* cared, though.

And it galled him that he still gave a crap about those motherfuckers. With his family gone, and the nucleus of the race's aristocracy scattered around the East Coast, it wasn't as if he had any contact with that stick-up-the-ass crowd anymore. But he was a dog too well trained to be able to forget they existed.

He simply couldn't come out.

Ironic. His outside was all about the hard-core. Inside? He was straight-up pussy.

Abruptly, he wanted to punch the mirror, even though all it was showing was a whole lot of shadow.

"Sire?"

In the darkness, he squeezed his eyes shut.

Shit, he'd forgotten Layla was still in his bed.

FORTY-NINE

Xhex wasn't precisely sure which farmhouse she was looking for, so she materialized in a wooded area off Route 149 and used her nose to tell her what direction to head in: The wind was coming out of the north, and when she caught the slightest whiff of baby powder, she tracked the scent, vaporizing herself at hundred-yard intervals through the scruffy, mowed-down cornfields that had been lambasted by winter's winds and snow.

The spring air tingled in her nose and the sunlight on her face warmed wherever the breeze didn't brush over her skin. All around, skeletal trees had halos of bright green, their tentative buds drawn out of hiding by the promise of warmer hours.

Lovely day.

For a killing spree.

When the stench of *lessers* was all she could smell, she unsheathed one of the knives Vishous had given her and knew that she was so close she could—

Xhex took form at the next row of maples and stopped dead.

"Oh . . . fuck."

The white farmhouse was nothing to write home to Mom about, just a wilted structure next to a cornfield, surrounded by a ring of pines and bushes. Good thing it had a lawn, though.

Otherwise the five police cars that were jammed up close to the front entrance wouldn't have had enough room to get their doors open.

Masking herself as *symphaths* did, she ghosted her way up to a window and looked inside.

Perfect timing: She got to see one of Caldwell's finest throw up into a bucket.

Although it wasn't as if he didn't have good reason to. The house looked like it had been bathed in human blood. Actually, scratch the "looked." It *had* been covered in the shit, to the point where she tasted copper on the back of her tongue even though she was out in the fresh air.

It was like Michael Myers's kiddie pool in there.

The human cops were walking around the living room and dining room, picking their way with care not only because it was a crime scene, but obviously because they didn't want the stuff splashing up on their pants.

No bodies, though. Not one single body.

At least, not that was visible.

There were nascent *lessers* in the house, however. Sixteen of them. But she couldn't see them and neither could the cops, even though from what she sensed, the men were walking right over them.

Lash's cloaking again?

What the fuck was he up to? Calling the Brothers, announcing this shit . . . and then getting the cops to come? Or had someone else done the dialing to 911?

She needed answers to so much . . .

Mixed in with all the blood was some inky residue and one of the officers was frowning over a patch of it, looking like he'd found something icky. Yup . . . that amount of oily mess wasn't sufficient to explain the strong sweet scent she'd followed—so she had to assume that the inductions had been successful and what was hidden was no longer human.

She glanced around the forest behind and before her. Where was the Omega's golden boy in all of this?

Moving around to the front of the house, she saw a

postman who was clearly struggling with some PTSD as he gave a statement to a uniform.

U.S. Postal Service to the rescue.

No doubt he'd been the one to drop a dime . . .

Staying camo'd, she just observed the scene, watching the cops fight their gag reflexes to do their jobs, and waiting for Lash to make himself known—or for any other *lesser* to make an appearance. When the television crews showed up about a minute and a half later, she played witness to an almost beautiful blond woman doing a poor man's Barbara Walters on the lawn. The second the taping was finished, she started pestering the cops for information until she annoyed them enough that they let her get a gander of what was doing inside.

Didn't that just slap the serious journalist right out of her.

As she went full chick and passed out into the arms of one of the uniforms, Xhex rolled her eyes and headed around back again.

Shit. She might as well get comfy. She'd come jonesing for a fight, but as so often happened in war, she was in a waiting game until the enemy showed.

"Surprise."

She wheeled around so fast, she nearly lost her balance: The only thing that saved her from falling over was the counterbalance of her dagger hand, which was raised up high, over her shoulder, ready for use.

"I wish we'd showered together."

As Blay choked on the coffee he'd made them both, Saxton sipped at his cup just fine. To the point where it was pretty obvious the guy both engineered and enjoyed the reaction he'd gotten.

"I really like surprising you," the male said.

Bingo. And naturally, those damn fool redhead genes made hiding a blush impossible.

428

Easier to put a sedan in your pocket. It was *that* obvious.

"And you know, the environment is important. Water conservation and all that. Go green . . . or naked as it were."

Saxton was lounging against the satin pillows of his bed in a silk robe, whereas Blay was stretched out all along the base of the mattress, weighing down the extra duvet that had been folded so precisely. Candlelight turned the scene into something out of a fantasy, the glow blurring all kinds of lines and boundaries.

And what do you know, Saxton was beautiful amid all the dark chocolate bedding, his pale hair so thickly waved, it seemed sculpted even though it was unmoussed, unsprayed. With his half-mast eyes and his smooth chest partially exposed, he was ready, willing . . . and, given the scent he was throwing off, able to be what Blay needed.

At least on the inside. His exterior wasn't quite up to the job: His face remained swollen, his lips puffy not from an erotic pout, but some asswipe's punch, and he moved carefully, as if there were still a lot of black-and-blues on him.

Which was not cool. His injuries should have been healed up by now, some twelve hours following the attack. He was an aristocrat, after all, and had a good bloodline.

"Oh, Blaylock, whatever are you doing here." Saxton shook his head. "I still don't know why you came."

"How could I not have."

"You like being a hero, don't you."

"It's not heroic just to sit with someone."

"Don't underestimate that one," Saxton said gruffly.

Which made Blay wonder. The guy had been his usual cool, slightly sarcastic self all morning and afternoon—but he had been attacked. Brutally.

"Are you okay?" Blay said softly. "Really okay."

Saxton stared into his coffee. "I find it difficult to fathom humanity sometimes, I truly do. Not just in that race, but our own."

"I'm sorry. About last night."

"Well, it got you in my bed, didn't it." Saxton smiled as much as he could, given that half of his mouth was distorted. "Not exactly the route I had planned to take to get you here . . . but it is lovely looking at you in the candlelight. You have the body of a soldier, but the face of an earnest scholar. The combination is . . . intoxicating."

Blay finished what was in his cup on a oner and nearly choked. Or maybe that was less what he was drinking and more what he was hearing. "Do you need a refill on the coffee?"

"Not right now, thank you. It was perfectly made, by the way, and that was also an excellent, if obvious, deflection."

Saxton put his cup and saucer on his ormolu bed stand and resettled himself with a groan. To keep himself from staring at the guy, Blay put his cup on the blanket chest below and let his eyes wander around. Upstairs was all Victorian Empire, with heavy mahogany furniture and Oriental rugs and gorgeous, lush colors—which he'd learned during his excursions to the kitchen. The understated and proper and reserved got left at the cellar door, however. Down here it was all straight-up boudoir, everything French, with curving marble-topped tables and dressers and formal needlepoint rugs. Lot of satin and . . . black-and-white pencil drawings of gorgeous males reclining very much in the same way Saxton was.

Only without the robe.

"Do you like my etchings," Saxton drawled.

Blay had to crack up. "What a line."

"I use it sometimes. I'm not going to lie."

Abruptly, Blay had an image of the male naked and making love on this very bed, his flesh twisting and turning with another's.

Surreptitiously checking his watch, he realized he had another seven hours here and he wasn't sure whether he wanted them to pass at a crawl or in a blink.

Saxton closed his lids and didn't so much sigh as shudder.

"When was the last time you fed?" Blay asked.

Those heavy lids lifted and bright gray flashed. "Are you volunteering?"

"I meant from a female."

Saxton grimaced as he rearranged himself on the pillows. "A while. But I'm fine."

"Your face looks like a chessboard."

"You say the *sweetest* things."

"I'm serious, Saxton. You won't show me what's going on under that robe, but if your face is any indication, you're hurting in other places."

All he got back was an *mmm*.

"Now who's deflecting."

There was a long pause. "Saxton, I'm going to get you someone to feed from."

"You keep females in your back pocket?"

"Mind if I use your phone again?"

"Suit yourself."

Blay got up and went into the bathroom, preferring a little privacy because he had no clue how this was going to go.

"You could use the one right here," Saxton called out as he shut the door.

Blay came back out ten minutes later.

"I didn't know eHarmony worked that quickly," Saxton murmured, his eyes remaining shut.

"I have connections."

"Yes, you do."

"We're going to be picked up here at nightfall."

That raised the blinds on those eyes. "By whom? And where are we off to?"

"We're going to take care of you."

Saxton drew in a breath and exhaled on a wheeze. "Coming to the rescue again, Blaylock?"

"Call it a compulsion." On that note, he went over to a chaise longue and lay on it. Pulling a luscious fur throw over his legs, he blew out the candle next to himself and got comfortable.

"Blaylock?"

God, that voice. So low and quiet in the dim light. "Yes."

"You're turning me into a poor host." There was a slight hitch of breath. "That chaise is no place for you to sleep."

"I'll be fine."

There was a silence. "You won't be cheating on him if you join me in bed. I'm in no condition to take advantage of your virtue, and even if I were, I respect you enough not to put you in an awkward position. Besides, I could use the body heat—I can't seem to get warm enough."

Blay wished like hell he had a cigarette. "I wouldn't be cheating on him even if . . . something happened between you and me. There's nothing there. Friends, just friends."

Which was the reason this situation with Saxton was so damned weird. Blay was used to being in front of that closed door, the one that kept him out and away from what he wanted. Saxton, however, offered an archway, something he could walk through easily . . . and the room on the other side was gorgeous.

Blay held out for about a minute and a half. Then, feeling as if he were moving in slow motion, he shifted the white fur to the side and stood up.

As he crossed the room, Saxton made space for him, lifting up the sheets and duvet. Blay hesitated.

"I don't bite," Saxton whispered darkly. "Unless you ask."

Blay slipped in between all that satin . . . and got an immediate idea why silk bathrobes were the way to go. Smooth, so smooth.

Something more *naked* than naked.

Saxton turned on his side to face Blay, but then moaned . . . in pain. "Damn it."

As the male eased over onto his back again, Blay found himself following and putting his arm over Saxton's head. When the male leaned upward, Blay made a pillow of his biceps and Saxton took full advantage, nestling in.

The candles extinguished one by one except for the votive in the bathroom.

Saxton shivered and Blay moved closer, only to frown.

"God, you are cold." Drawing the male into his arms, he held Saxton and willed his body heat into the guy.

They lay together for the longest time . . . and Blay found himself stroking that thick, blond, perfect hair. It felt good . . . soft, springy at the ends.

Smelled like spices.

"That feels divine," Saxton murmured.

Blay closed his eyes and breathed deep. "I agree."

FIFTY

"What the hell are you two doing here?" Xhex hissed as she lowered her dagger.

Trez's expression gave her a big-ass helping of *well, duh.* "Rehv called us."

Characteristically, iAm stayed quiet at his brother's side; he just nodded and crossed his arms over his chest, doing an excellent impression of an oak tree that was going nowhere. And as the twin Shadows stared down at her, they were shielding themselves, revealing their bodies and voices only to her.

For a moment, she regretted their discretion. Hard to knee the busybodies in the balls when they were in their ghosting form.

"No hugs?" Trez murmured while he searched her face. "Been a lifetime since we saw you."

Answering him back on a frequency the humans and any *lessers* wouldn't be able to hear, she muttered, "I'm not a hugger."

Except then she cursed and wrapped her arms around the two steakheads anyway. The Shadows were notoriously private with their emotions and harder to infiltrate than humans or even vampires, but she could feel their pain over what she had been through.

As she went to pull back, Trez tightened his hold and shuddered. "I'm . . . Jesus Christ, Xhex . . . we didn't think we were ever going to see you again—"

She shook her head. "Stop. Please. There's never a good time for that and here is certainly not the place. I love you both, okay, and I'm tight. So let's drop it."

Well, sort of tight. As long as she didn't think about John stuck back at that mansion, no doubt going insane. Thanks to her.

Ah, how history repeated itself.

"I'll stop before we get morbid." Trez smiled, his fangs showing bright white against his ebony face. "We're just glad you're all right."

"Stipulated. Or I wouldn't be here."

"Not sure about that," he said under his breath as he and his brother looked through the window. "Wow. Someone had fun in there."

A stiff breeze whiffled through, bringing a fresh blast of baby powder from a new direction, and all three of their heads turned.

Out on the dirt lane in front of the house, a car rolled by that had no business anywhere near cornfields. The thing was all *Fast & Furious*, a Honda Civic that had been to the automotive plastic surgeon's and gotten a *Playboy* makeover: With a whale tail and an air dam that left about a three-inch ground clearance as well as a paint job that was gray and pink and a retina-burning yellow, it was like a Midwestern girl who'd fallen into porn.

And what do you know . . . the *lesser* behind the wheel had an expression that didn't match the juice he was driving. Unless someone had just pissed in his gas tank.

"I will bet my forties that's the new *Fore-lesser*," Xhex said. "No way Lash would allow a second in command that kind of ride. I spent four weeks with that fucker and everything was all about him."

"Switch at the top." Trez nodded. "Happens a lot with them."

"You've got to follow that car," she said. "Quick, get on him—"

"Can't leave you. Orders from the boss."

"Are you fucking kidding me?" Xhex looked from

the Civic to the crime scene, then back to the departing whale tail. "Go! We need to track him—"

"Nope. Unless you want to . . . and then we'll hit it with you, right, iAm."

As the other Shadow nodded once, Xhex felt like punching the aluminum siding she'd been leaning against. "This is fucking ridiculous."

"Hardly. You're waiting for Lash to show up here and I know you're not going to want to just talk to him. So no way we're leaving you—and don't bother hitting me with the you're-not-the-boss-of-me shit. I have selective deafness."

iAm actually spoke up. "He really does."

Xhex locked eyes on the license plate of that ridiculous Honda, thinking, Oh, for fuck's sake . . . Then again, if the two Shadows weren't here, she would have stayed put; just taken the numbers down and stayed right where she was. She could always trace them later.

"Make yourself useful," she snapped. "And give me your cell phone."

"You calling in a pizza? I'm hungry." Trez flipped her his BlackBerry. "I like a lot of meat on mine. My brother prefers the cheese."

Xhex called Rehv out of contacts and hit him up because it was the fastest way to get to the Brothers. When voice mail kicked in, she left the specs and the tag on that car and asked for Vishous to track them.

Then she hung up and fired the phone back to Trez.

"No Domino's then?" he muttered. "They deliver, you know."

Swallowing a curse, she frowned and remembered that V had given her a phone. Shit . . . she was not as sharp as she should be in this situation—

"And another department is heard from . . ." iAm said.

Her eyes shot to the road as an unmarked came to a

stop in front of the house. The homicide detective who got out was someone she knew. José de la Cruz.

At least the humans had sent in a good man. Then again, maybe that kind of competence wasn't great news. The less involvement of that other race in a situation like this, the better, and de la Cruz had the instincts and follow-through of a bloodhound.

Man . . . it was going to be a looooooong frickin' day. A very, very long frickin' day.

As she watched the humans mill about and spin their wheels, and felt the collective weight of her bodyguards pressing down on her head, her right hand began to move, her fingers forming the curves and straightaways John had taught her.

A . . .

B . . .

C . . .

Lash woke up to the sound of moaning. And not the good kind.

Lying facedown on a bare mattress in that cheesy-ass ranch was another buzz kill. Third strike was the fact that when he finally got up, his body left a black stain behind.

Kind of like a shadow thrown on the ground, a reflection of what actually was.

Jesus f'n Christ. He was like that Nazi guy at the end of *Raiders of the Lost Ark*, the one whose face melted off . . . the one the DVD extras had said was special effected by hitting Jell-O with a hot fan.

Not exactly the sort of movie role he wanted to rock in RL.

As he walked out toward the kitchen, he felt like he was dragging a refrigerator behind him, and what do you know, Plastic Fantastic wasn't doing much better as she lay on the floor by the back door. She'd been drained enough to incapacitate her, but not enough to zap her back to the Omega.

Bummer for her. To be forever on the brink of death, with all that pain and suffocation, and yet aware that the vast peace on the other side of all that was never coming? It was enough to make you want to kill yourself.

Cue laugh track.

Then again . . . she didn't have a clue that she was going nowhere. That she would be forever in "as-is" condition. Probably best to keep that info on the down-low—it would be his good deed for the day.

As she marshaled a pathetic groan for him to help, he stepped over her and went to check on the food sitch. To conserve cash, he'd sucked back McCrap for dinner on his way here. Shit had been one step up from dog food, and that had been warm and fresh from the fryer.

Age did not improve the half he hadn't been able to stomach at the end of the night, but he ate what was left over anyway. Cold. Standing up over the crumpled bag on the countertop.

"Want some?" he said to the woman. "Yes? No?"

All she could do was plead with her bloodshot eyes and her gaping, oozing mouth. Or . . . maybe it wasn't pleading. She looked kind of horrified—which suggested that whatever condition she was in, his appearance was startling and ugly enough to draw her out of her agony for a moment.

"Whatever, bitch. The sight of you ain't doing wonders for my appetite, either."

Turning away, he stared out the window to the sunny day and felt a whole lot of fuck-this-shit-for-real.

Man, he hadn't wanted to leave that farmhouse, but he'd been a narcolepsy candidate, he'd been so exhausted—and no way he was risking a nap with that many of his enemy around. It was a case of retreat to fight again as opposed to pull a dreamland and bite the muzzle of a gun. Or worse.

But at least the sun was still on its rise in the cloudless sky, which was good news for him—it gave him the time he needed. The Brotherhood wasn't showing up in one form or another until it was dark enough, and what kind of host would he be if he wasn't there waiting.

The Omega's fucking kiss-ass bitch may have started the party, but Lash was going to damn well finish it.

He needed more ammo, though, and not for his heat.

Grabbing his raincoat and putting on his hat, he tugged on his gloves and stepped back over the prostitute. As he was unlocking the dead bolt on the door, her shrunken hand skittered over to his shoe, her bloody fingers scratching at the leather.

He looked down at her. She no longer had speech, but her red-rimmed, bulging eyes said it all: *Help me. I'm dying. I can't kill myself . . . do it for me.*

Apparently she'd gotten over her revulsion of him. Or maybe the fact that he'd covered up helped.

Ordinarily, he would have just left her as she was, but he couldn't shake the memory of peeling his own face off. He was operating under the assumption that he wasn't going to end up a perpetually rotting nightmare, but what if that was his destiny? What if he continued to melt away until he could no longer support his skeleton and he ended up in the condition she was . . . nothing but suffering for eternity?

Lash withdrew a knife from the small of his back, and when he came at her with it, she didn't shrink back. Instead, she rolled herself over, offering the fresh meat of her chest.

One stab was all it took and her immediate misery was over: On a bright flash of light, she puffed into thin air, leaving nothing but a scorched circle on the matted rug.

Lash turned to leave—

He didn't make it through the door. His body ricocheted back and he slammed into the far wall, lights flashing in front of his eyes as a rush of power blasted through him.

It took a moment to figure out what the fuck was doing . . . and then it became clear: What he had given the prostitute had come home to him.

So that was how it worked, he thought as he breathed deep and felt less like death on roller skates.

Whatever was stabbed with steel returned to sender, so to speak.

Well, it went back provided that the Brotherhood's secret weapon didn't get there first. Butch O'Neal was the Omega's Achilles' heel, capable of circumventing that reunion by absorbing the evil essence that animated a slayer into himself.

Having just gotten the rush, Lash now knew what a threat O'Neal was. If you didn't get your LEGOs back, eventually you couldn't build much of anything—or worse, your toy box was empty . . . and then what. You disappeared?

Yeah, avoiding that Butch bastard was important. Good tip.

Heading into the garage, Lash left the ranch in the Mercedes and went not out to the sticks, but downtown to the 'scrapers.

As it was just a little past eleven thirty in the morning, there were suits and ties out everywhere, the fleet of wingtips stopping at intersections, waiting for the go-ahead, and then striding across the streets right in front of the grilles of cars. They were all so fucking self-righteous, these humans with their chins up and eyes straight ahead like nothing existed except whatever meeting, lunch, or waste-of-time errand they were speeding to.

He wanted to stomp on the accelerator and turn them into sloppy bowling pins, but he had enough to worry about and better things to do with his time. His destination? Trade Street and the hub of the bars and nightclubs. Which, unlike the business district, would be dead at this time of day.

As he cut down toward the river, it was clear that the two different parts of town functioned as a yin and yang when it came to crowds as well as appearances. In the sunlight, the tall financial buildings with their glass windows and steel frames sparkled and flashed. In the land of dark alleys and neon signs, however, shit looked like an old whore well used: dirty, seedy, and sad.

When it came to people? Former was packed with the productive and the purposeful. Latter was lucky if it could pull together more than a couple of bums at this hour.

Which was precisely what he was banking on.

Heading for Caldwell's twin bridges, he passed by a vacant lot that had a chain-link fence around it and had to slow a little. Christ . . . that was where ZeroSum had been before it was reduced to a pile of rubble. And the real estate sign that was in front had a Sale Pending sticker slapped on it.

Wasn't that how things worked. Nasty, like nature, abhorred a vacuum—so if the new club going up on the site met a similar MacGyver end as Rehv's had, another would take its place just as fast.

Kind of like the sitch with his father. In no time at all, Lash had been replaced by something right up his own alley, so to speak.

Made you feel fucking dispensable. It really did.

Down under the bridges, it didn't take long to find what he was looking for, but wished he didn't need. His trolling beneath the overpasses quickly brought out the raggedy humans who slept in cardboard boxes

441

or burned-out cars, and he thought of how similar to stray dogs they were: drawn by the hope of sustenance, suspicious from experience, riddled with disease.

The mange parallel worked, too.

He wasn't picky and neither were they. Soon enough he had a female in his passenger seat, oohing and ahhing not over the AMG's leather, but the plastic Baggie of coke he gave her. While she pinkied some up and went Hoover on it, he drove her over to a dark cave formed by the massive concrete foundation of the incoming bridge.

One snort was all she got.

He was on her in a flash, and whether it was his need or her physical weakness, he was able to completely subdue her while he drank.

Her blood tasted like dirty dishwater.

When he was finished, he got out of the car, went around, and yanked her out by the collar. Her color had been pale to begin with; now it was the gray of the concrete.

She would be dead soon if she wasn't already.

He paused and looked down at her face, measuring the thick lines in the skin and the busted capillaries that had given her an unhealthy blush. She had been a newborn once. She had been fresh to the world years ago.

Time and experience had certainly battered her, and now she was going to die like an animal, alone and on the dirt.

After he dropped her, he reached forward to shut her eyelids—

Jesus . . . *Christ.*

Lifting his hand up, he looked through his palm out to the river.

No longer rotting flesh, but dark shadow . . . in the

442

form of what he used to write with and punch with and drive with.

Dragging the cuff of the raincoat up, he saw that his wrist was still corporeal.

A surge of strength powered through him, the loss of skin no longer something to mourn, but a source of rejoicing.

As is the father . . . so be the son.

He wasn't going to end up like that whore he'd just stabbed back to himself. He was heading for the Omega's territory, not rotting . . . but transforming.

Lash began to laugh, great belly rolls of satisfaction percolating from his chest and boiling up his throat and leaping out of his mouth. He fell to his knees next to the dead woman and let the relief—

With a sudden surge, he jacked to the side and threw up the spoiled blood he'd taken in. When there was a pause, he wiped his chin with his hand and looked at the glossy red as it covered the shadowy outline of what had once been flesh.

No time to admire his nascent new form.

Violent vomiting racked him so hard he was blinded by the stars exploding in his vision.

FIFTY-ONE

Sitting in her private quarters, Payne stared out over the Far Side's landscape. The rolling green grass and the tulips and honeysuckle reached only so far before they were cut off by a ring of trees that encircled the lawn. Above it all, the arching milky sky stretched from fluffy treetops to fluffy treetops, the lid on the wardrobe trunk.

From personal experience, she knew that if you walked to the edge of the forest and penetrated its shadows, you ended up emerging . . . right where you entered.

There was no way out, except through the Scribe Virgin's permission. She alone held the key to the invisible lock and she wasn't going to let Payne go—not even to the Primale's house on the Other Side, as the others were allowed to do.

Which proved that female knew well what she had birthed. She was very aware that once Payne got loose, she was never coming back. Payne had said as much—in a yell that made her own eardrums hum.

In retrospect, her outburst had been a victory for honesty, but not the best strategy. Better to have kept that to herself, and perhaps been allowed to traverse to the Other Side—and stayed there then. After all, it wasn't as if her mother could force her back to the land of the living statues.

Well, at least theoretically.

On that note, she thought of Layla, who had just returned from having seen her male. The sister had been glowing with a kind of happiness and satisfaction that Payne had never felt.

Rather justified the urge to leave here, didn't it: Even if what awaited her on the Other Side was nothing like she remembered from her small slice of freedom, she would have choices to make on her own.

Verily, it was a strange curse to have been born and yet not have a life to live. Short of killing her mother, she was stuck herein, and however much she hated the female, she wasn't going to take that trail. She wasn't sure she'd win in such a conflict, for one thing. For another . . . she had already disposed of her sire. Matricide was not an experience that held any new or particular fascination for her.

Oh, the past, the painful, wretched past. How awful to be stuck here with an infinite, bland future whilst burdened with a history that was too awful to dwell on. Suspended animation had been a kind gift when measured up against this torture—at least in the frozen state, her mind hadn't been able to wander and tangle with things she wished hadn't transpired, and things she would never get to do—

"Would you care for some victuals?"

Payne looked over her shoulder. No'One was in the archway of the room, bended into a bow with a tray in her hands.

"Oh, yes, please." Payne shook off her moribund musings. "And won't you join me?"

"I thank you kindly, but I shall serve you and depart." The maid put the provisions down on the window seat beside Payne. "When you and the king set to your physical conflicts, I shall return to collect—"

"May I ask you something?"

No'One bowed again. "But of course. How may I be of service?"

"Why have you never gone on to the Other Side? Like the others?"

There was a long silence . . . and then the female

gimped over to the pallet on which Payne slept. With shaking hands, No'One straightened the bedding into a precise order.

"I have no particular interest in that world," she said from under her robing. "I am safe here. Over there . . . I would not be safe."

"The Primale is a Brother of stout arm and fine dagger skill. No harm would e'er befall you under his care."

The sound that drifted out from the hood was noncommittal. "Circumstances have a way of spinning into chaos and strife there. Simple decisions have ramifications that can be shattering. Here, everything is in order."

Spoken as a survivor of the raid that had taken place in this sanctuary some seventy-five years ago, Payne thought. Back on that horrible eve, males from the Other Side had infiltrated the barrier and brought with them the violence that often existed in their world.

Many had died or been hurt—the Primale at the time included.

Payne looked back out at the static, lovely horizon— and at once understood the female's thinking, and yet wasn't swayed by it. "The order herein is precisely what galls me. I would seek to avoid this kind of falsity."

"Can you not leave when you wish?"

"No."

"That is not right."

Payne's eyes shot over to the female—who was now at work refolding Payne's modified robes. "I never expected you to say something counter to the Scribe Virgin."

"I love our dearest mother of the race—please do not misunderstand. But to be imprisoned, even in luxury, is not right. I choose to stay herein and ever will—you should be free to go, however."

"I find myself envying you."

No'One seemed to recoil under her robes. "You must never do that."

"'Tis true."

In the silence that followed, Payne recalled her conversation with Layla by the reflecting pool. Same exchange, different twist: Then, Layla had been the one to envy Payne's lack of desire when it came to sex and males. Here, it was No'One's contentment with inertia that was of value.

And 'round and 'round we go, Payne thought.

Turning her head back to the "view," she regarded the grass with a jaundiced eye. Each blade was perfectly formed, and precisely the right height such that the expanse was less a lawn than a carpet. And the result was not gotten by mowing, of course. Just as the tulips stood in their beds with everlasting blooms upon their slender stalks and the crocuses were perpetually unfurling and the roses were always fat-headed with petals, so too were there no bugs or weeds or disease.

Or growth.

Ironic that it appeared to be all cultivated and yet was attended to by no one. After all, who needed a gardener when you had a god capable of engineering everything to its best state—and keeping it there.

In a way, that made No'One a miracle, didn't it. That she had been allowed to survive her birth herein and permitted to breathe the nonair, even though she was not perfect.

"I don't want this," Payne said. "I truly do not."

When there was no comment, she looked over her shoulder . . . and frowned. The female had left as she had come in, without noise or fuss, leaving the surroundings bettered by her careful touch.

As a scream welled inside of her, Payne knew she had to be freed. Or go mad.

*   *   *

Back in Caldwell's farm country, Xhex finally got a shot to have inside the house when the police left at five in the afternoon. As they walked out, that bunch of blue unis looked ready not so much for a night off, but a week's vacation—then again wading through congealing blood for hours'll do that to a guy. They locked everything up, put a seal over the front and back doors, and made sure there was a ring of yellow crime scene tape around the yard. Then they got in their cars and drove away.

"Let's get in there," she said to the Shadows.

Dematerializing, she took form smack in the middle of the living room and Trez and iAm were right with her. Without needing to talk, they fanned out, traipsing through the mess, searching for things the humans wouldn't have known to look for.

Twenty minutes of ooey-gooey on the first floor and nothing but dust on the second left them with a whole lot of nada.

Damn it to hell, she could sense the bodies and the emotional grids that were marked with suffering, but they were like reflections in water—and she just couldn't get to the forms that were throwing the wavy images.

"You hear from Rehv yet?" she said, lifting one boot and measuring how far up the sole the blood came. Onto the leather. Great.

Trez shook his head. "Nope. But I can call again."

"Don't bother. He must be crashed." Shit, she was hoping that he'd gotten her message and started hunting down that license plate already.

Standing in the front hall, she looked around the dining room, and then focused on the pitted table that had clearly been used as a cutting board.

The Omega's little buddy with the Vin Diesel ride was going to have to come back for the new recruits. They weren't useful hidden like this, because, assuming the lockdown worked as hers had with Lash, they couldn't get out of the parallel plane they'd been relegated to until they were released.

Unless the spell could be called off from afar?

"We've got to stay longer," she said. "And see who else shows."

She and the Shadows took up res in the kitchen, pacing around and leaving fresh, bloody footprints on the cracked linoleum—ones that were no doubt going to fuck with the level, earnest heads of all those cops.

NHP.

Not. Her. Problem.

She checked the clock on the wall. Measured the empty kegs and the liquor bottles and the beer cans. Glanced over the tail ends of joints and the talc-y residue of coke lines.

Rechecked the clock.

Out in the back, the sun seemed to have stopped its descent, as if the golden disk was scared of getting skewered by the tree branches.

Stalled in her pursuit, she had nothing else to think about other than John. He must be climbing the damn walls right now, all up in a headspace that was hardly what you wanted somebody to meet the enemy with: He was going to be pissed off at her, distracted, revved up in the wrong way.

Wasn't like she could call and talk to him. He couldn't answer her.

And what she had to say wasn't the kind of thing you wanted to text.

"What's the matter?" Trez asked, as she began to fidget.

"Nothing. Just ready to fight with no target."

"Bullshit."

"Annnnd we can stop the chatter right here, thank you very much."

Ten minutes later, she was staring up at the clock on the wall again. Oh, for hell's sake, she couldn't stand this.

"I'm going back to the Brotherhood's for a half hour," she blurted. "Stay here, will you. Call my cell if anyone shows."

As she gave them her number, the peanut gallery did themselves a favor and didn't ask any whys—then again Shadows were like *symphaths* in that they tended to know where people were at.

"Roger that," Trez said. "We'll hitchu the second anything happens."

Dematerializing, she took form in front of the Brotherhood mansion and crossed the pea gravel to the basilica-size steps. After she went into the vestibule, she put her face to the security camera.

Fritz opened the way after a moment and bowed low. "Welcome home, madam."

The H-word sent a jolt through her. "Ah . . . thanks." She looked around at the empty rooms off the foyer. "I'm just going to go upstairs."

"I've prepared your previous room."

"Thanks." But she wasn't heading there.

Drawn by the sense of John's blood, she jogged up the grand staircase and went down to his crib.

Knocking, she waited, and when there was no answer, she cracked the door into the darkness and heard the hush of a running shower. Across the way, a lateral strip of light showed at carpet level, indicating he'd shut the way into the bathroom.

Crossing the Oriental, she shed her leather jacket and left it on the back of a chair. At the bath, she knocked again. Without hesitation. Loudly.

The door opened by itself, swinging free and revealing humid air and the dim glow of the inset lights above the Jacuzzi.

John was facing her behind the glass enclosure, the water rushing down his chest and his six-pack and his thighs. His cock sprang up into a massive erection the moment her eyes met his, but he didn't move and he didn't look glad to see her.

In fact, his upper lip curled in a snarl, and that wasn't the worst of it. His emotional grid was completely closed off to her. He was blocking her and she wasn't even sure he was aware of doing it: She couldn't get a bead on anything that she had always sensed so clearly before.

Xhex lifted up her right hand and spelled out awkwardly: *I came back.*

His brow twitched. Then he signed much more smoothly and quickly: *With intel for Wrath and the Brothers, right. Feel like a hero? Congratulations.*

He shut off the water, stepped out, and leaned for a towel. He didn't cover himself, but dried off, and it was hard not to notice that with each move and arch, his erection bobbed.

She never thought she'd curse her peripheral vision.

"I haven't talked with anyone," she said.

This left him pausing with the towel stretched across his back, one arm angled up, the other down. Naturally, the pose popped his pecs and pulled the muscles that ran over his hip bones out in stark relief.

He snapped the towel free and draped it over his shoulders. Leaving it to hang, he signed, *Why did you come here?*

"I wanted to see you." The ache in her voice made her wish she'd used ASL.

Why.

"I was worried—"

You want to see how I'm hanging together? You want to know what it was like to spend the past seven hours wondering if you were dead or—

"John—"

He ripped the towel free and snapped the end in midair to shut her up. *You want to know how I handled the idea that you were dead, fighting alone, or worse, back where you'd been? Your* symphath *side need a little diversion for kicks and giggles?*

"God, no—"

You sure about that? You're not wearing your cilices. Maybe you're feeding that hunger, coming back here—

Xhex wheeled around for the door, her emotions too much for her to handle, the guilt and the sadness choking her.

John caught her arm and they ended up against the wall, his body holding hers in place while he signed up close to their faces.

Hell no, you do not get to run. After what you put me through, you do not get to run the fuck out of here just because you can't deal with shit you created. I couldn't run from today. I had to stay caged here and you can damn well return the favor. Her eyes wanted to focus elsewhere, but then she couldn't track what he was saying with his hands. *You want to know how I am? Fucking resolved, that's how I am. You and I are turning a corner tonight. You say you have a right to go after Lash? I do, too.*

That locker room, in the shower, she thought. The betrayal that she didn't know the details of, but that she sensed had everything to do with what had happened to John when he'd been young, and alone, and defenseless.

Here's the deal and it's nonnegotiable. We work together to find him and get him and kill him. We work as a team, which means where one of us is, the other goes. And at the end, whoever takes him to ground gets the honors. That's where we stand.

Xhex exhaled with relief, instantly knowing it was the right answer. She hadn't liked how it felt being at that farmhouse without him. It had seemed wrong.

"Deal," she said.

His face didn't register surprise or satisfaction—which

told her whatever he'd planned if she said no must have been a doozy.

Except then she learned why he was so calm.

After it's over, we go our separate ways. We're done.

The blood drained out of her head and abruptly, her hands and feet went numb. Which was such bullshit. What he was proposing was the best arrangement and the best outcome: two fighters working together and once their goal was accomplished, there was no reason to retain any tie between them.

Matter of fact, this was precisely what she'd seen of the future when she'd first come out of that nightmare with Lash. Get him good and dead. Then end this fiasco of life.

Trouble was . . . her plans that had been so clear were foggy now, the path that she had set with her head the instant she got free obscured by things that had nothing to do with what was in her skull and everything to do with the male who was naked against her.

"Okay," she said hoarsely. "All right."

Now that caused a reaction in him. His body relaxed against hers and he planted his hands on the wall on either side of her head. As their eyes met, her body roared with a blast of heat.

Man, desperation was gasoline to a match for her when it came to John Matthew—and given the way he subtly rolled his hips against her, he felt the same way.

Xhex reached up and clamped a hold on the side of his neck. She wasn't gentle and neither was he as she pulled him down to her mouth, their lips crushing together, their tongues not so much meeting as dueling. When she suddenly heard a tearing sound, she realized he'd grabbed both sides of her muscle shirt and ripped it in half down the front—

Her breasts came up against his bare chest, her nipples rubbing against his skin, her core weeping for him. To hell with desperation; the need to have him inside went farther than that, until her emptiness without him was an agony.

Her leathers were on the floor a split second later.

Then with a quick hop, she jumped up and locked her thighs around his waist. Reaching down, she positioned him against her sex and squeezed her heels into his ass, making the penetration so very real. As his arousal sank deep, she took all of him, the sliding push enough to make her orgasm wildly.

Riding her release, her fangs shot out into her mouth, and John broke the kiss to tilt his head and flash his vein.

The puncture was sweet. The strength that came from him meteoric.

With hard draws, she drank as his body hammered into her, pitching her off that cliff again, sending her into a crazy descent that somehow had no hard landing— and he followed her, making that glorious leap without a parachute, his orgasms shuddering into her.

There was only the briefest of pauses . . . and then John started pumping again—

No, he was carrying her to the bed in the darkened room, the motion of his striding thighs pushing him inside of her and pulling him free and pushing him back.

She remembered every single sensation, storing each one deep in her mind, making the moment infinite and ageless by virtue of the power of memory. And as he settled on top of her, she did what he had done for her: offering her vein to him, she ensured that they were the most powerful team they could be.

Partners.

Just not the permanent kind.

FIFTY-TWO

As John's body got it on with Xhex's, his mind briefly retreated to that moment in the bathroom when he'd waited for her to agree to their arrangement.

Sure, he'd sounded all lay-down-the-law, but the truth was he'd had no leverage: She was either going to go with it or not, and if she didn't, he had nothing to hold over her. Bottom line? There was absolutely no threat of withdrawal, no proactive anything, no if-this-then-that he could bring to the situation.

And that was what had dawned on him while he'd sat on the sofa in the billiard room, pretending to watch TV with Tohr. All day long, he'd heard Rehvenge's voice in his head, over and over again.

Her end game doesn't include anyone but herself.

John was not a fool, and he was not prepared to let his bonding for her paralyze him anymore. They had a job to do and they had a better shot at getting it done if they worked together. After all, this wasn't any ordinary *lesser* they were going after.

Besides, the story of the two of them was written in the language of collision; they were ever crashing into each other and ricocheting away—only to find themselves pulled back into another impact. She was his *pyrocant* and there was nothing he could do to change that. But he could sure as shit cut the bungee cord that was torturing him.

Man, he wished that tattoo of his weren't permanent. Then again, at least it was on his back and he didn't have to look at the goddamn thing.

But whatever. They were going to get Lash and then go their separate ways. And between now and then? Well . . .

John let his thoughts drift away as he reconnected with the surging sex and the roaring taste in his mouth as he fed. Dimly, he once again caught the bonding scent rising from his own skin, but he shut that reality out. He wasn't going to allow his head to get scrambled just because of that dark spice. Not for a minute longer.

Bonded males were crippled without their females, true enough—and a huge part of him would always be hers. But he was going to keep living, goddamn it. He was a survivor.

As he moved inside Xhex's tight hold, his cock was a solid shaft of power and another release soon slammed through him and into her. Breaking the seal on her vein, he lapped the punctures with his tongue and then latched onto one of her breasts. With a shift of his leg, he split her thighs farther apart and rolled onto his back so she was on top.

Xhex took it from there, bracing her hands on his shoulders, swinging her hips on the base of her spine, her tight stomach curling and releasing as she rode him. With a silent curse, he grabbed onto her thighs and squeezed, her muscles shifting under his hold, and he didn't stop there. He drew his hands farther up, to the juncture where her legs met her torso, that electric crease drawing him to where they were joined.

His thumb slipped into the carnal heart of her and found the top of her sex, rubbing it in circles—

In the dim light from the bathroom, he watched her arch back, her fangs cranking down on her lower lip in an effort to keep herself from crying out. He wanted to tell her to let her roar free, but he didn't have time to pity her discretion—he came hard, his lids squeezing shut as he shuddered beneath her.

Catching his breath, he felt her pause to breathe deep . . . and then she was changing position.

When he opened his eyes, he nearly orgasmed again. She'd shifted back so that she was leaning on his legs, balancing her weight on his shins. With her feet up by his sides, he got one hell of a show . . . and that was before she started moving. The sight of him emerging shiny and thick from her folds, his shaft revealed right to the ridge of his cock head, pitched him off into another release.

She didn't stop.

He didn't want her to.

John needed more of watching their sexes up close, more of seeing the tips of her breasts and the thrust of her chin and the smooth strength of her body as she had him deep and hard. He wanted to stay captured in her . . . forever.

But that was his problem with her, and one that was ending here and now.

They climaxed together, with his hands locking onto her slender ankles and her mouth opening to let his name out of her throat.

Afterward, there was nothing but a lot of heavy breathing and air that seemed cold.

With a lithe shift, she disengaged them by swinging a leg over his head and landing on the floor beside the bed without a sound.

As she looked over her shoulder, her spine twisted in an elegant curve. "Can I use your shower?"

When he nodded, she walked with confident, long strides into his bathroom—and in spite of all the sex they'd just had, he felt a driving need to take her from behind.

A moment later, the rushing water sounded . . . and then her voice echoed. "The human police have found the scene."

That got John out of bed and hungry for more intel. As he came into the bath, she turned around under the showerhead and arched back to rinse the shampoo he used out of her hair.

"The place was crawling with cops, but the new initiates were hidden in the same way I had been—all those humans saw was enough blood to paint a house red. No sign of Lash, but there was a drive-by of a street racer with something that smelled like fake strawberries behind the wheel. I called Rehv with the license plate number to pass on to Vishous and I'll make the report to Wrath right now."

When she looked over at him, he signed, *We go back the second night falls*.

"Yup. We do."

Qhuinn woke up alone, having sent Layla back to the Far Side after they had done a little more business. He'd meant to tell her to go right away, but a goodbye embrace had led to other things . . .

She was still a virgin, though.

Not untouched, any longer, but defo still a virgin . . . Seemed like there were two people in the world he couldn't have sex with. The trend continued and he was going to end up celibate.

As he sat up, his head pounded, proof positive that Herradura was an opponent of worth.

Rubbing his face, he thought back to kissing the Chosen. He'd taught her how to do it properly, how to suck and stroke, how to open the way for someone's tongue, how to penetrate a mouth when she wanted to. Female learned fast.

And yet it hadn't been hard to keep things from getting out of hand.

What had killed the urge to seal the deal was the way she stared at him. When he'd started down the Lewis-and-Clark highway with this sex-ploration shit, he'd assumed she was just looking for the practical course after all her textbook training. But on her side, there had quickly been more to it than that. Her eyes had started to get stars in them, like he was the key to the door that kept her locked in herself, like he alone held the power to spring her dead bolt and set her free.

Like he was her future.

Rather ironic because, on paper, she was his ideal female. Might well have solved his mating problem permanently.

Except his heart wasn't in it.

So yeah, no way he was taking on the responsibility for her hopes and dreams. And not a chance he was going all the way with her. She was already being seduced by a fantasy of him—if he actually made love to her, it was only going to get worse: When you didn't know any better, that kind of physical rush could easily be mistaken for something deeper and more meaningful.

Hell, that sort of delusion could happen between two people who had experience.

Like that chick at the tat place, for instance, slipping him her number. He'd had no interest in calling her before, during, or after. He couldn't even remember her name—and the intel vacuum didn't bother him in the slightest. Any woman willing to fuck a guy she didn't know in a public place with three other males around was not someone he needed to have a relationship with.

Harsh? Yes. Double standard? Not a chance. He had no respect for himself either, so it wasn't like he judged his own low, filthy standards with any less distaste.

And besides, Layla had no clue what he'd been doing with humans since his transition . . . all the sex in bathrooms and alleys and dark corners of clubs, that dirty math adding up to his being able to know exactly what to do with her body.

With any body. Male or female.

Shit. Didn't that make him think about how Blay had spent the day.

Qhuinn fumbled with his phone and flicked the thing open. Calling up the text that Blay had sent from that unknown number, he read and reread and reread it again.

Had to have come from Saxton's phone.

Probably typed out on the guy's bed.

Qhuinn tossed his BlackBerry onto his table and stood up. In the bathroom, he kept the lights out because he was sooo not interested in what he looked like in the jeans and shirt he'd slept in.

Hot mess. No doubt.

As he was washing his face, a subtle whirring sound emanated from all around, the shutters rising from the windows. With water dripping off his chin and a can of Barbasol in his mitt, he glanced out into the new night. In the moonlight, the buds on the silver-trunked birches by the window had come out even farther, indicating the day had been a warm one.

He totally ignored any parallel to Blay's being awakened to his own sexuality.

By Qhuinn's own cousin.

Disgusted with himself, he skipped the razor action and stalked out of his room. Gunning for the kitchen, he went as fast as he dared, given that the barometric pressure in his skull was making him worried about the health and longevity of his optic nerves.

Down in Fritz's fiefdom, he made a pot of coffee as *doggen* scurried around making First Meal. Good thing they were already so preoccupied. Sometimes, when you felt like shit inside and out, you wanted to work your own Krups.

Pride mattered in moments like this.

Mind you, first trip through the park, he forgot to add the grounds, so all he got was a nice, steaming pot of clear water.

Once more with feeling.

He was coming out of the dining room with a camping thermos full of dark brown miracle juice and a bottle of aspirin when the door to the vestibule was opened by Fritz.

The pair who stepped past the good *doggen* ensured that there was a shitload of Bayer in Qhuinn's immediate future: Blay and Saxton entered the house arm in arm.

For a split second, he nearly growled as possessiveness made him want to drive his Hummer between the two and park it there—until he realized their huggy-huggy was evidently for medicinal purposes. Saxton didn't seem too steady on his feet, and his face had clearly been used as a punching bag.

Now Qhuinn growled low for a different reason. "Who fucking did that to you."

Couldn't be the guy's own family. Saxton's folks were cool with what and who he was.

"Tell me," he demanded. And once that question was answered, the pair could follow it up with how in the fuck Blay thought he could bring an outsider not only into the Brotherhood's seat, but the home of the First Family.

Oh, but number three: *How was it?* was actually going to stay right where it was. Namely choking his throat.

Saxton smiled. Sort of. His upper lip wasn't working all that well. "Nothing but some human trash. Let us not get emotional, shall we?"

"Fuck that. And what the hell are you doing here with him?" Qhuinn stared at Blay and tried not to measure the guy's face for stubble burn. "He can't be in this house. You can't bring him—"

From up above, Wrath's voice cut him off, the king's deep baritone filling the foyer. "Blay wasn't kidding about you, was he. You got some kind of cracked there, didn't you, son."

Saxton wheezed as he bowed. "Forgive me, Your Majesty, for not providing a more agreeable presentation. You are most kind to welcome me herein."

"You did me right when it mattered. I return the favor. Always. That being said, you compromise my happy home in any way, I'll slice off your balls and feed them to you."

I love Wrath, Qhuinn thought.

Saxton bowed again. "Understood."

Wrath didn't look down the stairs, his wraparounds remaining straight ahead so that it seemed as if he were staring up at the frescoes on the lofty ceiling. And yet even with his blindness, he missed nothing. "Qhuinn's got coffee, from what I can scent, so that'll help, and Fritz has fired up a bedroom for you. You want something to eat before you feed?"

Feed? *Feed?*

Qhuinn didn't appreciate being out of the loop, even when it came to little shit like what was being served for dinner. Saxton, the mansion, Blay, and someone's vein? Yeah, not knowing what was doing with the likes of all that made the tips of his fangs tingle.

Saxton bowed once again. "Indeed, you are a very kind host."

"Fritz, get the male some chow. The Chosen should be arriving very soon."

A Chosen's vein?

Christ, what exactly had Saxton done for the king? Whose ass had he saved?

"And our physician will see you." Wrath held his palm up. "Nope. I smell the pain you're feeling—it's a combo of kerosene and raw peppers in my sinuses. Now get moving. Take care of yourself and we'll talk later."

As Wrath and George did a wheel-around up on the balcony, Qhuinn fell into the wake of Fritz's hospitality, walking behind the butler as the guy led a slow ascension of the grand staircase. At the top, the elderly *doggen* paused in favor of Saxton's limp, whipping out his handkerchief to polish the carved brass curlicues.

With nothing to do but wait as well, Qhuinn popped open the aspirin and took a handful, noting that through the open doors of the king's study, John and Xhex were talking to V and Wrath, the four of them standing over a map that was stretched flat on the desk.

"This is a spectacular manse," Saxton said while he stopped to regain his breath. Leaning on Blay's strength, he fit under the guy's arm . . . fucking perfectly.

The miserable bastard.

"My master, Darius, built it." Fritz's ancient watery eyes drifted around before focusing on the apple tree that was depicted in mosaic tile down below. "He had always wanted the Brotherhood herein . . . had constructed the facility for their every purpose. He would be so pleased."

"Let us continue then," Saxton said. "I am eager to see more."

Down the hall of statues. Past Tohr's room. Past Qhuinn's and John Matthew's. Past Blay's . . . and right next door.

Why not farther down, Qhuinn thought. Like in the basement.

"I shall bring you a tray of various and sundry." Fritz went inside and double-checked that everything was in order. "Dial star-one if you should need anything before I return or at any other time."

With a bow, the butler took off, leaving a whole lot of awkward behind. Which didn't smooth out in the slightest as Blay took Saxton over to the bed and helped the male get horizontal.

SOB was in a gorgeous gray suit. With a waistcoat. Which made Qhuinn in his clothes-as-sleeping-bag feel like he was dressed in some of Hefty's best.

Standing a little taller, so at least he clearly beat Sax

on the vertical front, he said, "It was those guys at the cigar bar. Those fucking assholes. Wasn't it."

As Blay stiffened, Saxton laughed a little. "So our mutual friend Blaylock here told you about our date? I wondered what he was doing on my phone in my bathroom."

Uh-huh, whatever. Deduction not daytime minutes had led him to that conclusion. Hell, he'd only gotten that one text from the guy. One measely, short text that didn't offer so much as a hi-how're-ya—

Holy. Shit. Was he actually bitching about phone etiquette? Was he really chicking out like that?

Um . . . short of wearing panties under his jeans, he guessed that would be a big yuppity-yup-yup.

Getting back in the game, he snapped, "Was it them?"

When Blay said nothing, Saxton sighed. "Yes, I'm afraid they felt the need to express themselves—well, the head ape in the group did." The male's lids lowered and he glanced over at Blay. "And I'm a lover not a fighter, you see."

Blay hurried to fill the silence after that little bomb. "Selena will be here shortly. You'll like her."

Thank God it wasn't Layla, Qhuinn thought for absolutely no good reason . . .

The silence that followed had the consistency of tar and the smell of guilty conscience.

"Can I talk to you," Qhuinn said to Blay abruptly. "Out in the hall."

Not a request.

As Fritz arrived with the tray, Qhuinn stepped from the room and waited in the corridor, facing off at one of the muscular statues. Which made him think about what Blay looked like naked.

Cracking the thermos lid, he took a swig from his coffee, burned his throat, and drank more anyway.

After Fritz left, Blay emerged and shut the door. "What is it?"

"I can't believe you brought him here."

Blay recoiled with a frown. "You've seen his face. How could I not? He's hurt and not healing well and he needs to feed. And Phury would never allow one of his Chosen to just show up in the world somewhere. This is the only safe way to do it."

"Why didn't you just find him someone else? It doesn't have to be a Chosen."

"Excuse me?" That frown got even deeper. "He's your *cousin*, Qhuinn."

"I'm well aware of the relation." And of how petty he sounded. "I just don't get why you pulled all these strings for the guy."

Bullshit. He knew exactly why.

Blay turned away. "I'm going back in now—"

"Is he your lover."

That stopped the male dead . . . just froze him like he was one of the Greek statues, his hand halting on its reach for the doorknob.

Blay glanced over his shoulder, his face hard. "That is none of your business."

Not a blush in sight, and Qhuinn exhaled slowly in relief. "He isn't, is he. You haven't been with him."

"Leave me alone, Qhuinn. Just . . . leave me alone."

As the door shut behind the guy, Qhuinn cursed under his breath and wondered if he would ever be able to do that.

Not anytime soon, a voice said in his head. Maybe not ever.

FIFTY-THREE

Lash woke up with his face in the dirt and someone going through his pockets. As he tried to turn over, something hard cupped the back of his skull and held him in place.

A palm. A human palm.

"Get the car keys!" somebody hissed from the left.

There were two of them. A pair of humans, both of whom smelled like crack smoke and old sweat.

Just as the rummaging hand went to the other side of him, Lash caught the man's wrist and, with a twist and a jump, traded places with the looting bastard.

As the guy went fish-mouth in shock, Lash bared his fangs and swept down from above, catching the ruddy skin of a cheek and ripping it free of the bone. A quick spit and he ripped the cocksucker's throat wide-open.

Yelling. Serious yelling from the guy who'd given the order about the keys—

Which was quickly extinguished as Lash withdrew his knife and pitched it at the running back of Mr. Grand Theft Auto, catching the fucker right between the shoulder blades. As the son of a bitch yard-saled into the dirt, Lash curled up a fist and punched the temple of the man who'd mounted him.

With the threat now neutralized, Lash went wobbly again, his body falling to the side as he briefly considered another round of throwing up. Not a great condition to be in—especially as the human he'd nailed on the fly began to grunt and claw at the ground like he was determined to get away.

Lash forced himself to his feet and shuffled over. Standing above the crackhead, he braced a foot on the guy's ass and yanked his knife out of that back. Then he kicked his target over and lifted his arm—

He was about to do the plunge-into-the-chest thing when he realized the bastard was built strong, his frame packed with muscle. Given his wild eyes, he was clearly into the pipe, but he was young enough so that the ravages of the addiction had yet to eat away at his body mass.

Well, wasn't this the SOB's lucky night. Thanks to a whim and a good body, he'd just gone from corpse to lab rat.

Instead of stabbing him in the heart, Lash slashed the human's wrists and nicked his jugular. As red blood flowed into the earth, and the man started in with the moans, Lash looked to the car and felt like the thing was a hundred miles away.

He needed energy. He needed . . .

Bingo.

While those veins drained, Lash dragged himself to the Mercedes, popped the trunk, and lifted the carpet section up. The panel that covered where the spare would normally go pulled out easily.

Hello, wakey-wakey.

The kilo of cocaine was supposed to have been cut down and repackaged for street sale days ago, but then the world had exploded and it had been left right where Mr. D had stashed it.

Wiping his knife off on his pants, Lash punctured a corner of the cellophaned block and dipped in the tip of the blade. He snorted the shit right off the stainless steel, loading up first his right then his left nonexistent nostril.

For good measure, he did another round.

Annnnnd . . . one more.

467

As he rocked some keep-it-in-there sniffing, the rush that thundered through him saved his ass, perking him up so that he could keep going even after his vomiting and passing-out routine. Why he'd had those problems was a mystery . . . Maybe that 'hood rat's blood had been tainted, or maybe it wasn't only Lash's body but his internal chemistry that was changing. Either way, he was going to need that powder in the back until things stabilized.

Shit worked, too. He felt *great*.

After rehiding his stash, he returned to the crackhead. The cold didn't help the draining process, and waiting around here while the fucker bled out wasn't the brightest idea, no matter how well hidden they were under the bridge. Riding his considerable buzz, he strode over to the dead guy he'd done a Hannibal Lecter on; he ripped open the man's filthy jacket and tore the undershirt beneath into bandage-size strips.

Fuck his father.

Fuck that little Shit.

He was going to make his own army. Starting with that bulldog addict.

It didn't take long to wrap up the seeping wounds on the human, and then Lash picked him up and threw him in the trunk with all the regard a cabdriver would pay to cheap luggage.

Driving out from under the bridge, his eyes were bouncing around. But shit . . . every car he saw, from the ones on the surface roads to the traffic that whizzed by on the highway, every single one of them was a Caldwell PD unmarked.

He was sure of it. They were police. Humans with badges looking into his car. The police, the CPD, the police, the CPD . . .

As he headed for the ranch, he hit every single red light in Caldwell, and as he was forced to brake it, he stared straight ahead, praying that all the police behind and in front of him didn't sense he had a dying man and a fuckload of drugs in the car.

It would take too much effort to deal with being pulled over. Besides, talk about buzz kill. He was finally feeling like himself, every single heartbeat drumming through his veins, the steel-shod hooves of all that cocaine trampling through his brain, creating a cacophony of creative inspiration—

Wait. What had he been thinking of?

Aw, hell, what did it matter. Half-formed ideas winged around his mind, plans forming and disintegrating, every single one of them brilliant.

Benloise, he had to get to Benloise and reestablish the connection. Make more *lessers* of his own. Find the little Shit and stab him back to the Omega.

Fuck his father like the guy fucked him.

Fuck Xhex again.

Go back to the farmhouse and fight with the Brothers.

Money, money, money—he needed money.

As he passed by one of Caldwell's parks, his foot eased off the accelerator. At first, he wasn't sure whether he was actually seeing what he thought he was . . . or whether his coked head was warping reality.

But no . . .

What was going down in the shadows by the fountain presented the opportunity he'd planned on manufacturing for himself. Or infiltrating if need be.

Pulling the Mercedes into one of the metered parking spaces, he turned off the car and got his knife out. As he went around the hood of the AMG, he was vaguely aware he wasn't thinking straight, but as he rode the cocaine rush, that felt just fine.

John Matthew took form in a stand of pines and bushes along with Xhex and Qhuinn, and Butch, V and Rhage.

Up ahead, the ratty farmhouse with the yellow crime scene tape around it looked like something out of *Law & Order*.

Although if that were true, without Smell-o-Vision, you wouldn't get an accurate pic even with great camera work. Despite the acres of fresh air around, the scent of blood was strong enough to make you clear your throat.

To properly cover Lash's intel dump, the Brotherhood had split in half, with the others staking out the address which had been tied to the license plate on that souped-up Civic. Trez and iAm had just taken off to handle their own biz for the night, but they were ready to come back at the drop of a text. And according to the Shadows, there was nothing too special to report since Xhex had left them except for the fact that Detective de la Cruz had returned, spent an hour, and left again.

John searched the scene before him, focusing on the shadows more than what the risen moon illuminated. Then he closed his eyes and let his instincts bleed out from him, giving that indefinable, invisible sensor in the center of his chest free rein.

In moments like this, he didn't know why he did what he did; the urge just came upon him, the conviction that he had done this before—to good effect—so strong it was undeniable.

Yeah . . . he could feel something was off . . . There were ghosts in there. And the certainty reminded him of what he'd felt when he'd been in that dreaded bedroom where Xhex had been so close and so far away. He had sensed her too, but been blocked from making the connection.

"The bodies are in there," Xhex said. "We just can't see or get to them. But I'm telling you . . . they're in inside."

"Well, let's not fuck around out here then," V said, dematerializing.

Rhage followed, poofing it right into the farmhouse while Butch took a more labor-intensive approach, hotfooting it across the scruffy lawn, with gun drawn and down at his thigh. He looked in the windows until V let him in the back.

"You going in?" Xhex asked.

John signed carefully so she could read his hands. *You've already reported what's doing inside. I'm more interested in who's going to show up at the front door.*

"Agreed."

One by one the Brothers came back.

V spoke softly. "Assuming that Lash isn't just showing off his induction efforts, and assuming Xhex is right—"

"No assumption there," she bit out. "I am."

"—then whoever turned the poor bastards has to come back."

"Thank you, Sherlock."

V glared in her direction. "You want to dial back the attitude, sweetheart?"

John straightened, thinking that however much he loved the Brother, he was so not appreciating that tone.

Xhex evidently agreed. "Call me sweetheart one more time and it'll be the last word you ever speak—"

"Don't threaten me, swee—"

Butch stepped behind V and clapped his palm over the guy's piehole while John put his hand on Xhex's arm, urging her to calm down as he glared in Vishous's direction. He'd never understood the enmity between the pair of them, even though it had been there since he could remember—

He frowned. In the aftermath of the flare-up, Butch was looking at the ground. Xhex was focused on a tree over V's shoulder. V was growling and staring at his fingernails.

Something is off with all this, John thought.

Oh . . . Jesus . . .

V had no reason to dislike Xhex—in fact, she was precisely the kind of female he'd typically respect. Unless, of course, she happened to have been with Butch . . .

V was known to be possessive about his best friend with everyone but the guy's *shellan*.

John stopped his extrapolations right there; he so didn't need to know any more. Butch was one hundred percent about his Marissa, so if anything had happened with Xhex . . . it was a lifetime ago. Probably before John had even met her—or maybe when he'd been just a pretrans.

Past was the past was the past.

Besides, he shouldn't—

Any further thoughts on the sitch were mercifully derailed as a car drove by the farmhouse. Instantly, all their attention was crosshaired on a ride that was done up like an outfit some twelve-year-old girl might have wanted to find in her closet. In, like, 1985.

Gray and acid yellow and hot pink. Really? You really think that's hot? Man . . . assuming that was a slayer behind the wheel, John just had another reason to kill the Flock of Seagulls motherfucker.

"That's the souped-up Civic," Xhex whispered. "That's it."

All at once there was a subtle shift in the scenery, like a screen had been pulled into place from above. Fortunately, visual acuity suffered only until what shielded them was settled; then everything was clear again.

"I've fired up the *mhis*," V said. "And what a fucking asshole. That ride is too flashy to be in this part of town."

"Ride?" Rhage snorted. "Please. That thing is a sewing machine with an air dam taped to it. My GTO could dust the fucker in fourth gear from a dead stop."

When there was an odd sound from behind, John looked back. So did the three Brothers.

"What." Xhex bristled and crossed her arms over her chest. "I can laugh, you know. And that's . . . pretty damn funny."

Rhage beamed. "I knew I liked you."

The sewing machine went past the house and then came back . . . only to turn around and do a third drive-by.

"I'm getting really bored with this." Rhage shifted his weight back and forth, his eyes flashing neon blue—which meant his beast had a case of the snores and was getting twitchy as well. Never a good thing. "Why don't I just hood-ornament it and drag the fucker face-first out the windshield."

"Better to chill and lay the trap," Xhex murmured just as John thought the very same thing.

The guy behind the wheel might have been color-blind when it came to car paint, but he wasn't a total moron. He drove on and about five minutes later, just as Rhage was practically pulling a split personality he was so itchy, the slayer who'd been doing the drive-bys came striding out across the rear cornfield.

"That kid's a ferret," Rhage muttered. "A little, shifty ferret."

True enough, but the ferret had a pair of reinforcements with him, of a size that wouldn't have fit in his ride. Clearly, they'd met up elsewhere and dumped another car.

And they were smart about their approach. They took their time and looked all around the lawn and house and forest. But thanks to V, when they saw the stand of trees their enemy was among, their eyes wouldn't register anything but landscape: Vishous's *mhis* was an optical illusion that effectively fogged out the shitstorm the enemy was walking into.

As the trio went to the back of the house, their boots made a crunching sound over the cold, stiff grass. A moment later, there was a shattering sound . . . glass breaking.

To no one in particular, John signed, *I'm going to close in.*

"Wait—"

V's voice didn't slow John in the slightest and neither did the cursing he left behind as he dematerialized right to the side of the house.

Which meant he was the first to see the bodies as they became visible.

The instant the ferret climbed through a window in the kitchen, the house shivered and . . .

Hello, *Texas Chainsaw Massacre.*

Stretching from the living room to the hall to the dining room, there were some twenty guys lined up with their heads facing the rear of the house and their feet toward the front. Dolls. Grotesque naked dolls with black vomit on their faces and slowly pinwheeling arms and legs.

John felt Xhex and the others take form right behind him at the window just as the ferret strode into view.

"Fuckin A!" the kid hollered as he looked around. *"Yes!"*

His triumphant, skittering laughter bordered on hysteria—which might have been disturbing, except for the fact that he was surrounded by blood and guts and gore. As it was? The keening cackle was a bit of a snooze—a horrible cliché.

But then, so was the bastard's car. Vin Diesel much?

"You are my army," he shouted at the bloodied guys on the floor. "We are gonna rule Caldwell! Getcha asses up, it's time to go to work! Together we are . . ."

"I can't wait to kill this little shit," Rhage muttered. "If only to shut him up."

Too. Right.

The fucker was on a serious Mussolini kick, all blah-

blah-taking over-blah, which was all well and good for the ego but ultimately didn't mean shit. The response from the sorry sons of bitches on the ground was the critical thing . . .

Huh. Maybe the Omega had chosen well: The dolls appeared to be drinking the Kool-Aid. The assembled drained, butchered, reanimated, and now soulless former humans stirred, lifting their torsos up off the floorboards, struggling to their feet at the ferret's command.

Too bad for them it was going to be a wasted effort.

"On three," Vishous whispered.

Xhex was the one who counted it down. "One . . . two . . . *three*—"

FIFTY-FOUR

As soon as night fell o'er the landscape and granted its dark grace upon the good earth, Darius dematerialized from his modest abode and took form on the shore by the ocean with Tohrment. The "cottage" the symphath *had described was in fact a stone manse of some size and distinction. There were candles lit inside, but as Darius and his protégé tarried amid an outcropping of foliage, there were no overt signs of life: No figures walked past the windows. No dogs barked a warning. No scents from the kitchen wing wafted on the cool, calm breeze.*

There was, however, a horse turned out in the field and a carriage by the barn.

As well as a crushing sense of foreboding.

"A symphath is therein," Darius murmured as his eyes probed not just the visible, but the shadowed.

There was no way to know whether there was more than one sin-eater within the walls, as it took only a single of them to create the barricade of fear. And no way to ken whether it was the symphath *they sought.*

At least, not as long as they stayed on the periphery.

Darius closed his eyes and let his senses penetrate what they were able of the scene afore him, his instincts beyond that of sight and hearing focusing to ascertain danger.

Verily, there were times when he trusted what he knew to be true more than what he beheld.

Yes, he could feel something inside. There was frantic movement within the stone walls.

The symphath *knew they were here.*

Darius nodded at Tohrment and the two of them took a chance and tried to dematerialize into the living room.

Metal embedded in the masonry itself prevented them penetrating the stout walls and they were forced to re-form at the house's cold flank. Undeterred, Darius lifted his leather-covered elbow and smashed the leaded glass of a window; then he gripped the dividers and pulled out the frame. Tossing it aside, he gusted in with Tohrment, becoming corporeal in the living room—

Just in time to catch a flash of red ducking through an internal door down toward the back of the house. In silent accord, he and Tohrment took off in pursuit, reaching the exit that had been taken as the pins of the lock were turning.

Copper mechanism. Which meant there was no moving it mentally.

"Stand aside," Tohrment said as he leveled the muzzle of his gun.

Darius briefly stepped clear as a shot rang out, and then he shoulder-rushed the door, forcing it wide.

The stairs down below were dark except for a jostling, everfading light.

They descended the stone steps with pounding boots and sprinted over the packed-dirt floor, running after the lantern . . . and the scent of vampire blood that was in the air.

Urgency thundered in Darius's veins, wrath warring with desperation. He wanted the female back . . . Dearest Virgin Scribe, how she must have suffered—

There was a slamming sound and then the underground tunnel went pitch-black.

Without losing his stride, Darius powered onward, putting his hand out against the walling to keep straight on his path. Tight on his heels, Tohrment was with him in pursuit, and the echoes of their clamoring boots helped Darius determine the termination of the passageway. He pulled up short just in time, using his hands to locate the latch on the door.

Which the symphath *hadn't taken the time to lock behind himself.*

Ripping open the heavy wooden panels, Darius got a deep

lungful of fresh air and caught sight of the jangling lantern up ahead, across the grasses.

Dematerializing and re-forming up close, he caught the symphath *male and the vampire female next to the barn, blocking their escape such that the abductor was forced to halt.

With shaking hands, the sin-eater held a knife to his captive's throat.

"I shall kill her!" he screamed. "I shall kill her!"

Up against him, the female didn't struggle, didn't try to pull away, didn't beg to be saved or set free. She just stared ahead, her haunted eyes listless in her bleak face. Indeed, there was no paler skin to behold than that of the dead by moonlight. And verily, the daughter of Sampsone might have possessed a beating heart betwixt her ribs, but her soul had passed away.

"Let her go," Darius commanded. "Let her go and we shall let you live."

"Never! She is mine!"

The symphath's eyes glowed red, his evil lineage shining in the night, and yet his youth and his panic evidently rendered him incapable of using his race's most powerful weapon: Although Darius braced himself for a mental onslaught, an invasion of his cranium did not ensue from the sin-eater.

"Let her go," Darius repeated, "and we shall not kill you."

"I have mated with her! Do you hear me! Mated with her!"

As Tohrment leveled his gun right at the male, Darius was impressed by how calm he was. First time in the field, captive situation, symphath . . . and the boy was right in the midst without being consumed by the drama.

With deliberate composure, Darius continued trying to reason with their opponent, noting with vicious anger the way the female's nightgown was stained. "If you release her—"

"There is nothing you can give me worth more than her!"

Tohrment's low voice broke through the tension. "If you let her go, I won't shoot you in the head."

It was a good enough threat, Darius supposed. But of course, Tohrment wasn't going to fire the weapon—too much risk to the female in the event his aim was off by even a fraction.

The symphath *began walking back toward the barn, dragging the vampire with him.* "I shall slice her open—"

"If she's so precious to you," *Darius said,* "how could you bear the loss?"

"Better she die with me than—"

Boom!

As the gun went off, Darius shouted and jumped forward, even though he couldn't possibly catch Tohrment's bullet with his hands.

"What have you done!" *he hollered as the* symphath *and the female landed in a heap.*

Racing over the grass and then falling to his knees, Darius prayed that she had not been hit. With his heart in his throat, he reached out to roll the male off of her . . .

As the young symphath *flopped over onto his back, he stared in blind fixation at the heavens, a perfectly round, black hole in the center of his forehead.*

"Dearest Virgin Scribe . . ." *Darius breathed.* "What a shot."

Tohrment knelt down. "I wouldn't have pulled the trigger if I hadn't been sure."

They both leaned toward the female. She too was staring at the galaxy above, her pale eyes locked and unblinking.

Had her throat been cut after all?

Darius rifled through her frothy, once-white nightdress. There was blood on it, some of which had dried, some of which was fresh.

The tear that spilled forth from her eye twinkled silver in the moonlight.

"You are saved," *Darius said.* "You are safe. Be not afraid. Be not of sorrow."

As her pale stare shifted over to meet his own, her despair was as cold as a winter wind and just as isolating.

"We shall take you back from whence you came," Darius vowed. "Your family shall—"

Her voice was nothing more than a croak out of her throat. "You should have shot me instead of him."

FIFTY-FIVE

As the countdown hit "one," Xhex took form in the farmhouse's living room, thinking that the concerns of an ambush were right—except the slayers were the fuckers getting jumped. Facing off at the nearest lesser and falling into hand-to-hand with the guy, she knew she had to work fast.

You had the element of surprise only once in any given fight, and she and her crew were outnumbered four to one—in a sitch where no guns could be used. Bullets were accurate only if you had clean shots on static targets and there was none of that going down. Arms and legs and bodies were flying all around as the Brothers and John and Qhuinn did exactly what she was doing—picking a random inductee and going Bruce Lee on their ass.

Xhex had her dagger out in her left hand while she threw a right hook at the slayer in front of her. The cracking blow knocked the guy senseless, and as he slumped against the wall, she drew her arm back and aimed the tip of her blade right for the chest of—

With a slap, Butch caught her wrist. "Let me finish it."

Positioning himself between them, he locked eyes on the slayer and put his mouth down close. On a slow, steady inhale, he began to draw the essence out of that body, a nasty cloud—like smog transferring from the *lesser* to Butch.

"Jesus . . . Christ . . ." she whispered as the slayer who once had had form disintegrated into ash at the Brother's feet.

As Butch wobbled and reached out for the wall like he was having trouble standing, she took his arm. "Are you okay—"

A shrill whistle from John brought her head around just in time—another *lesser* was rushing at her, prepared to use the switchblade in its hand. Thanks to John, she ducked down and lunged forward, grabbing a thick wrist and taking control of the weapon while she stabbed upward, catching the slayer under the ribs.

Bright lights, big bang.

And on to the next.

She was all in the zone with the fighting, fast on her feet, quick with her hands. And even though she was going a mile a minute and she'd poofed off that one slayer, she was going to respect Butch's role in this show-down. She didn't understand precisely what that ashes-to-ashes routine was all about, but she was willing to bet that it was a special end for the enemy.

In that vein, she took to slicing the backs of knees and the fronts of thighs. Incapacitation was something she had excelled at as an assassin, because a lot of times she'd had a message to share before she struck mortally. And sure enough, as she left moaning bodies in her wake, Butch swept up behind her, inhaling and turning to fine powder that which they had come to kill.

As she carved and slashed her way through the inductees, she found herself keeping a second eye on John and . . . holy hell. He was one slick fighter.

Who seemed to specialize in snapping necks. He was lethal for closing in behind the enemy, grabbing on and then with brute strength—

The blow came from out of nowhere, catching her on the shoulder and sending her spinning into the wall, her knife popping from her hold as all kinds of Looney Tunes stars bloomed in her vision.

The slayer who had hockey-checked her lunged forward

and nabbed her dagger from the bloody living room floor, palming the weapon and coming at her with it.

At the last minute, she bobbed left so that he stabbed the wall she'd hit, trapping the blade in the Sheetrock. As he went to try to get the thing free, she whirled around and nailed him in the gut with her backup blade, springing a hole in his lower intestines.

Meeting his shocked stare, she said, "What, like you didn't think I'd have a second knife? Fucking idiot."

She punched him in the head with the butt of her backup, and as he crumpled at the knees, she unsheathed her primary from the plaster and faced off at the fray. As grunts and smacks resounded around the house, she shifted through the fighting to find what was being unattended to—

One of the slayers was flying through the front door, on a bolt for the great outdoors.

She dematerialized out of the house and right into his path. As he went Three Stooges and pinwheeled to a stop, she smiled. "No, you may not be excused."

The *lesser* took off again and headed back for the fight—which was stupid because there was no one who would help him in there. Well, not to survive, that was.

Her body was lithe and strong as she burst after him and the two of them came around in a fat circle. Just as he got to the door, she leaped into the air and took him down in a flying tackle, catching him around the neck and shoulder and wrenching him around, using the combination of her strength and her trajectory to crank the guy into a living, breathing question mark.

They landed hard, but even as the air punched out of her lungs, she was smiling.

God, she loved a good fight.

John saw Xhex flash out the front door, but he couldn't go after her because he had a pair of initiates so far up his ass he was coughing on their eyebrows. But he was going to take care of the crowding PDQ.

Funny how when your female beat feet into the night on her own you got an extra burst of energy—

Not that she was his female.

Funny how reminding yourself of something like that made you mean as a snake.

Reaching out to the slayer in front of him, John snapped the bastard's neck clean off the top of his spine. As he bowling-balled the head, he thought it was a goddamned pity there wasn't time to do the same to the kid's arms and legs—so he could beat the other one senseless with the stumps.

Unfortunately, number two had just grabbed John around the chest and was trying to bear-hug him into hypoxia.

John palmed those wrists and locked the fucker in place, then pivoted around, jumped up, and pulled a straight horizontal in midair. They slammed onto the ground with John on top and the slayer putting the L-E-S-S-E-R in *mattress*. Rearing upward, John smashed the back of his head right into his opponent's face, turning that nose into a geyser.

Quick flip and John raised his fist high in the air.

His second strike caused a round of twitching, which suggested the guy's frontal lobe was having serious electrical transmission problems and the bastard was now in seizure-land.

Wasn't going to be any trouble as he waited for Butch to come at him.

John lunged for the doorway that Xhex had dematerialized out of, his shitkickers skidding on the blood that was now running both rusty red and glossy black.

Just as he came to the open doorway, he caught himself on the jambs.

It was the most spectacular tackle he'd ever seen. The

lesser she was chasing was gunning back for the house, having obviously rethought his escape strategy, and he was hauling balls, his bare feet screaming over the frosty grass. Xhex, however, was closing fast, triangulating an interception that was possible only because she was stronger and more focused than the former human.

John didn't have time to intervene even though he wanted to: Xhex jammed into the air, springing up and stretching out for the *lesser*. She clipped him right around the waist and winged him around, pasting him on the ground and slicing the backs of both his thighs so deep he screamed like a girl.

She dismounted and was ready to go again—

"John! Behind you!"

As she shouted at him, he swung around and got faced by a slayer, the guy bull-rushing him right out the door. John landed on his ass, skidding back on the crappy concrete walkway.

Which proved why you needed to wear good leathers. Dermabrasion much?

Pissed off that he'd been parked on the front lawn with Xhex playing witness, he grabbed the hair of the slayer and yanked the thing into an arch that would leave the guy's spine humming like a motherfucker.

With a soundless growl, John pulled a reveal on his fangs and bit the fucker in the neck. Ripping all kinds of gross former human anatomy free, he spat the shit out and then dragged the gurgling thing back into the party by the hair. As he passed Xhex, he nodded at her.

"You're welcome," she said with a small bow. "And nice move with that bite action."

Looking over his shoulder at her, the respect she paid him hit him harder than any of the slayers had or could: His heart swelled and he felt as if he filled out his skin better all around.

Fucking sap that he was—

The unmistakable pop of a gun going off behind him froze him where he stood.

The loud ring was so close his eardrums felt pain rather than hearing anything specific, and for a split second afterward, he wondered who'd done the shooting and who, if anyone, had been shot.

The latter was answered when his left leg went loose under his weight and he went down like an oak.

FIFTY-SIX

Xhex's knife flew from her hand a split second after she saw the *lesser* come around the corner and level a gun muzzle right at John's back.

Her dagger traveled hilt over tip through the air, crossing the distance in the blink of an eye, winging past John's ear so close she prayed to a God she didn't believe in that he wouldn't suddenly decide to turn his head for any reason.

Just as the slayer pulled the trigger, her blade caught him in the meat of his shoulder, the impact shifting his torso, the pain making him drop his arm.

Which meant John took the slug in the leg instead of the heart.

As her male went down, she leaped over him with a war cry.

Fuck Butch O'Neal. This kill was hers.

The *lesser* was scrambling as he tried to disengage her weapon from his torso—at least until he heard her yell. Then he looked toward her and shrank back in horror— which suggested her eyes were glowing red and her fangs were fully extended and flashing.

She landed in front of him, and as he cringed and put his hands up to shield his face and neck, she didn't move: Her backup dagger stayed by her side and her third-stringer remained holstered on her thigh.

Other plans for this boy.

Using her *symphath* side, she burrowed into the slayer's brain and popped the tops on his memories so that all at once, he felt the impact of every horrible thing he'd ever done and every terrible act that had been perpetrated against him.

Lot of shit. Looooot of shit. He'd apparently had a thing for underage girls.

Well, wasn't this going to be satisfying on so many levels.

As he went down to the floor, he screamed and clutched his temples—like he had a chance in hell of stopping the deluge—and she let him suffer and wallow in his sins, his emotional grid lighting up in all the sectors that indicated fear and loathing and regret and hatred.

When he started to bang his skull against the dirty wallpaper, leaving a black stain where his ear was, she planted one and only one thought in his mind.

Planted it like an ivy streamer . . . a poison ivy streamer that would take hold and infiltrate and own his mental real estate.

"You know what you have to do," she said in a deep, warping voice. "You know the way out."

The slayer dropped his arms and revealed his wild eyes. Under the weight of what she'd released, and as a slave to the dictate she gave him, he grabbed the hilt of her dagger and ripped it out of his flesh.

Turning the point back toward himself, he doublegripped the weapon, his shoulders tensing as he prepared to send the blade on a rocking descent.

Xhex halted him, freezing him so she could kneel down right beside him. Going face-to-face, she looked into his eyes and hissed. "You don't go after what's mine. Now be a good boy and gut yourself."

A splatter of black blood hit her leather pants as the guy nailed himself right in the stomach and dragged the blade crosswise, making a nice messy hole of things.

And then on her mental command, even as his eyes

were rolling back in his head, he withdrew the weapon and handed it to her hilt first.

"You're welcome," she muttered. Then she stabbed him in the heart and in a flash, he was gone.

As she pivoted around, the sole of her boot squeaked on the wet floor.

John was looking up at her with eyes that were not dissimilar to the slayer's, his stare peeled so wide he was showing no lid at all on the top or the bottom.

Xhex wiped her first blade on her leathers. "How bad are you?"

As John gave her a thumbs-up, A-OK, she realized the house was quiet and looked around. Everyone was still standing: Qhuinn was just straightening from a decapitation, and wheeling around to see if John was okay. And Rhage was coming in at a run from the kitchen with Vishous on his heels.

"Who's hit—" Rhage skidded to a halt and stared at the hole in John's leathers. "Man, three inches up and to the left and you'da been a soprano, buddy."

V went over and helped John to his feet. "Yeah, but at least he could have taken up knitting with you. You could've taught him how to crochet socks. Brings a tear to the eye."

"If I recall, I'm not the one with the wool fixation—"

As a wheezing boiled up from the living room, Vishous cursed and rushed to Butch's side as the guy all but fell into the hallway.

Oh . . . man. Maybe she needed to revise the "everyone standing" thing. The former cop looked like he had food poisoning, malaria, and H1N1 all at the same time.

She focused on Qhuinn and Rhage. "We need a car. He and John need transport back to the mansion—"

"I'll take care of my boy," Vishous said gruffly as he became a crutch for Butch and escorted him back over to the living room couch.

"And I'll go get the Hummer," Qhuinn said.

Just as he turned away, John slammed a fist into the wall to get everyone's attention and signed, *I'm fine to fight—*

"You need to get seen by the doctor," she said.

John's hands started to fly so fast she couldn't track the words, but it was pretty damn clear that he was not on board with getting benched just because of the slug of lead in his leg.

Their argument was interrupted by a brilliant glow that had her leaning to the side and glancing over her shoulder. What she saw explained so much and not just what had happened in the fight they'd all been in: on the ratty sofa, V had Butch in his arms and their heads were together, the pair of them so close there was no gap whatsoever between them. And in the midst of their embrace, Vishous's whole body was glowing, with Butch seeming to draw strength and healing from him.

V's obvious care and sympathy for the guy made her dislike him less—especially as he turned his face and looked over at her. For once, his icy mask slipped and the despair showing in his eyes proved he wasn't a total asshole. On the contrary, he seemed to feel the pain of his Brother's sacrifice for the race. Truly, it ate him alive.

Oh, and . . . Butch was apparently his. Which explained why V had it in for her. He was jel that she'd had a piece of what he'd wanted, and as rational as he was, he couldn't stop resenting her for it.

Only once, though, she thought at him. *And never again.*

After a moment, V nodded, as if he appreciated the reassurance, and she returned the respect. Then she refocused on the males in front of her. Rhage had hopped on the hell-no-you're-not-fighting train, picking up the slack she'd left.

"I'm going back with you, John," she cut in. "We're going back together."

As John met her eyes, his emotional grid was lit up like the Vegas Strip.

She shook her head at him. "I'm going to keep to our deal. And you're going to take care of yourself."

With that, she resheathed her knives, crossed her arms over her chest, and leaned back against the wall, all going-nowhere-fast.

She'd saved his life.

Without a doubt, Xhex had given John his future back before he'd even known he was going to lose it: The only reason he was still alive was because she'd clipped that slayer in the shoulder with her knife.

So, yeah, he was grateful for all that, but he really wasn't interested in her playing nursemaid.

Besides, it wasn't as if candy striper was the highest and best use for her talents.

John glanced past her to the scorched mark on the floor—which was all that was left of the slayer who'd shot him. Goddamn . . . to think she'd done the worst of the damage without even touching the fucker? That was one fancy-dancy weapon she had in her mind. Shit, the horror on that bastard's face . . . Then he'd slit his own abdomen open. What the hell had he been seeing?

Now John knew why *symphaths* were feared and segregated.

And man, between that little show and the Heisman move she'd pulled out on the front lawn, he realized she was precisely what he'd always known her to be: a fighter to the core.

She could more than handle herself in the field—she was an out-and-out asset in the war. Which was why they both needed to keep going tonight and not waste time back at the house getting a Band-Aid put on his boo-boo.

Shoving himself up off the floor, he put weight on

the injured leg and the thing howled like a bitch. But he ignored the yelling—as well as the conversation that sprang up all around him.

Cheap talk from the peanut gallery: free. Opinions about his leg: not worth the powder to blow up.

Selective deafness? Priceless.

What he was interested in was how many they'd killed tonight. And whether they'd gotten the ferret. Looking into the living room, he—

Rhage stepped in front of him. "Hey, hi! How are you?" Hollywood stuck his hand out. "I'd like to introduce myself. I'm the piece of meat that's going to force you headfirst into your buddy Qhuinn's Hummer as soon as it gets here. Just figured I'd introduce myself before I rope your ass and throw you over my shoulder like a bag of sand."

John glared at the guy. *Not going anywhere.*

Rhage smiled, his incredible beauty looking like something heaven sent. But that was just the external shit. Internally, he was straight from hell—in this situation. "Sorry, wrong answer."

I'm fine—

That piece-of-shit, motherfucker, cocksucking son of a bitch actually ducked forward, grabbed John on the wound, and squeezed the bullet's new home.

John screamed without making a sound and went down in a free fall, landing on the blood-soaked floor with a splash. Bringing up his leg, he tried to cradle his thigh, as if showing some belated TLC would convince the thing to calm down.

As it was, he felt like he had jagged glass jammed into his muscle.

"Was that really necessary?" Xhex demanded overhead.

Rhage's voice was no longer teasing. "You want to reason with him? Good luck. And if you think any slayer would do differently, you've got your head wedged. There's an obvious circular hole in the front of his leathers and he walks with a limp. Any half-wit asswipe's going to know what his weakness is. Plus he smells like fresh blood."

The rat bastard probably had a point, but Christ on a crutch . . .

It was entirely possible that John passed out from the pain, because next thing he knew, the self-proclaimed "piece of meat" was picking him up to carry him out of the house.

Yeah, whatever. That was a no-go. John shoved himself free of the guy's hold and tried to land without cursing or throwing up. With his mouth making up all kinds of *fuck*-oriented words, he limped past Butch, who was looking much better, and V, who'd lit up a hand-rolled.

He knew right where Xhex was: behind him, with her hand at his back like she knew he was wobbly and might go down at any minute.

Not a chance, though. Sheer grit got him to the Hummer and in the backseat on his own. Of course, by the time Qhuinn hit the gas, he had a cold sweat all over him and couldn't feel his hands or his feet.

"We did a body count," he heard Xhex say.

When he looked over, she was staring across the seat at him. Man . . . she was fucking beautiful in the distilled light from the dash up front. Her lean face had a smudge of black *lesser* blood on it, but her cheeks had high color and her eyes had a special sparkle to them. She'd gotten off on tonight, he thought. She'd enjoyed it.

Fuck him. She really was the perfect female.

And how many did we take out? he signed, trying to distract his inner nancy.

"Twelve of the sixteen new recruits as well as both of the slayers who came across the field with the ferret.

Unfortunately, that new *Fore-lesser* was nowhere to be found—so we have to assume the little bastard bolted as soon as we infiltrated and took a handful of inductees with him. Oh, and Butch inhaled all of those downed except two."

At least one of which you dealt with.

"Actually both were mine." Her eyes held his. "Did that bother you? Seeing me . . . go to work like that?"

Her tone suggested she assumed it did and that she didn't blame him for feeling yucked-out. Except she was wrong.

Beating back the pain he was in, John shook his head and signed with floppy hands. *It's an incredible power you have. If I looked shocked . . . it's because I'd never seen one of your kind in action before.*

Her face tightened ever so slightly and she glanced out the window.

Tapping her on her arm, he signed, *That was a compliment.*

"Yeah, sorry . . . just the 'your kind' always throws me. I'm half-and-half, therefore I'm neither. I have no kind." She batted away her words with her hand. "Whatever. While you were passed out, V hacked into the Caldwell PD database with his phone. The police didn't find any IDs at the scene either, so we have nothing to go on except for that addy from the Civic's license plate. I'll bet that . . ."

As she continued talking, he let her words wash over him.

He knew all about that "no kind" thing.

Just one more way they were compatible.

Closing his eyes, he sent up a prayer to anyone who was listening, asking please, for God's sake, stop sending him signals that they were right for each other. He'd read that book, seen the movie, bought the sound track, the DVD, the T-shirt, the mug, the bobble-head, and the insider's guide. He knew every reason they could have been lock and key.

But just as he was aware of all that aligned them, he was even clearer on how they were damned to be ever apart.

"Are you all right?"

Xhex's voice was soft and closer, and when he cracked his lids, she was practically in his lap. His eyes traced her face and her coiled, leather-bound body.

Pain and a sense that time was running out for them made him toss out his filter and say what was truly on his mind.

I want to be in you when we get back to the mansion, he signed. *As soon as I get a bandage on this fucking leg of mine, I want in you.*

The flare of her scent in his nostrils told him she was so on board with that plan.

So at least one thing, aside from his cock, was looking up.

FIFTY-SEVEN

Up on the second floor of Eliahu Rathboone's plantation house, Gregg Winn had to open the door to his and Holly's room with two fingers and a prayer that he didn't dump hot coffee down his leg. He'd filled the pair of mugs in his hands with brew he'd made himself at the "guest" pot on the sideboard in the dining room.

So God only knew what it tasted like.

"You need help?" Holly said as she looked up from the laptop.

"Nope." He kicked the door shut and headed for the bed. "I got it."

"You are so thoughtful."

"Wait till you try it . . . I had to jerry-rig yours," he said, giving the pale one to her. "They didn't have whole milk, which was what you had yesterday at breakfast. So I went to the kitchen and took half-and-half and some skim, mixed them together, and tried to get the color right." He nodded to the computer's screen. "What do you think of those scans?"

Holly stared down into the mug as she held it over the Dell's keyboard. She was stretched out on the bed, propped up against the headboard, analyzing the data he'd become obsessed with . . . looking sexy and smart.

And as if she didn't trust what he'd given her.

"Listen," he said, "just try the coffee—if it sucks, I'll wake up that proper butler."

"Oh, it's not that." She ducked her blond head and he heard her sip. The "ahhh" that followed was more than he could have hoped for. "Perfect."

Going around the edge of the bed, he settled in beside her on top of the duvet. As he took a drink from his own mug, he decided if his career in TV went tits-up, he might have a future at a Starbucks counter. "So . . . come on, tell me what you think of the footage."

He nodded at the screen and what it was showing: The night before, there had been a shot of something walking through the living room and going out the front door. Now, it could have been a guest up for a midnight snack, like Gregg had just been—except for the fact that it dematerialized right through the wooden panels. The thing just disappeared.

Kind of like the shadow outside her bedroom from the first night. Not that he liked thinking of it. Or that dream of hers.

"You haven't retouched this?" Holly said.

"Nope."

"God . . ."

"I know, right? And the network just e-mailed me while I was downstairs. They're so on fire, apparently the Internet's gone nuts over the promos already—all we have to do is pray that thing shows up a week from now when we go live. You sure your coffee's okay?"

"Oh, yes, it's . . . amazing." Holly glanced up over the rim of her mug. "You know, I've never seen you like this before."

Gregg leaned back against the pillows and couldn't help but agree. Hard to know what had changed; there had been a shift inside of him, however.

Holly took another sip. "You seem really different."

Unsure what he should say, he kept it about the work. "Well, I never actually thought ghosts existed."

"You didn't?"

"Nah. You know as well as I do all the fixes I've pulled. But here in this house . . . I'm telling you, something is here and I'm dying to get onto the third floor.

I had this crazy dream about going up there . . ." As a sudden headache cut off his thoughts, he rubbed his temple and decided he had eyestrain from having been on a computer for the past seventy-two hours straight. "There's something up in that attic, I'm telling you."

"The butler said it was off-limits."

"Yeah." And he didn't want to buck the guy too much. They had so much good TV to roll out, it wasn't like they needed more—and no sense pushing it. Last thing he wanted was to run into trouble with the management this close to airdate.

And it was very clear Mr. Spit and Polish didn't like them.

"Here, let me show you again . . . this is what really amazes me." Gregg reached forward and restarted the file so he could watch that figure disappear through the solid door again. "That's pretty damn incredible, right? I mean . . . did you ever think you'd see something like that?"

"No. I didn't."

Something about the sound of her voice brought his head toward her. Holly was staring at him, not the screen, while cradling her mug right to her heart.

"What?" he said, checking to see if he'd spilled on his shirt.

"Actually . . . it's about the coffee."

"Bad aftertaste?"

"No, not at all . . ." She laughed a little and drank some more. "I just never would have guessed you'd remember what kind of coffee I like, much less go to the trouble of making it for me. And you've never asked me what I thought about work before."

Jesus . . . she was right.

She shrugged. "And I guess I'm not surprised that you never believed in what you were doing. I'm just glad you do now."

Unable to keep the eye contact going, Gregg looked out over their two pairs of socked feet, to the windows on the far side of the room. The moon was barely visible through the lace of the curtains, nothing but a soft glow on the dark horizon.

Holly cleared her throat. "I'm sorry if I made you feel awkward."

"Oh . . . yeah . . . no." He reached over and took her free hand, giving it a squeeze. "Listen . . . there's something I want you to know."

He felt her stiffen—which made two of them. He was suddenly bracing himself as well.

Gregg cleared his throat in the thick silence. "I color my hair."

There was a tense pause—at least on his part. And then Holly broke into bubbling laughter, the sweet, happy kind that came with relief.

Leaning into him, she ran her nails through his falsely dark waves. "You do?"

"I'm gray at the temples. Really gray. I started doing something about it a year before I met you—have to stay young in Hollywood."

"Where do you get it done? Because you're never rooty."

With a curse, he shifted off the bed and went to his suitcase, rummaging around to the bottom of the thing. Flashing the box in question, he muttered, "Just for Men hair color. I do it myself. I don't want to be caught in a salon."

Holly smiled at him so widely, she got crinkles around her eyes. And what do you know, he liked the way they looked. Gave her pretty face some character.

He glanced down at the box. Staring at the model on the front, all kinds of truths came to him, the kind that he simply couldn't fight or even argue with. "You know what, I hate Ed Hardy T-shirts. Damn things'll burn your retinas. And distressed jeans give me the scratch . . . and those square-toed loafers I wear bother my feet. I'm tired of being suspicious of everyone and working for money just so I can spend it ahead of everybody else on something that will be out of style next year." He tossed the hair color back into his suitcase and liked the fact that it could sit out in the fresh air, so to speak. "Those files? On that computer? First ones Stan and I haven't doctored up. I've been a fake for a long time working in a fake industry doing fake shit. The only thing that was real was the cash, and you know what? I don't know if that's going to do it for me anymore."

As he got back up on the bed, Holly finished her coffee, put the computer and the mug aside, and draped herself across his chest.

Best damn blanket he'd ever had.

"So what do you want to do next?" she asked.

"I don't know. Not this. Well, I'm kind of getting off on the ghost-hunter stuff, actually. The producer crap? Meh." Looking down at the top of her head, he had to smile. "You're the only one who knows about my old-man hair."

And he had the weird feeling that the secret was safe with her.

"It doesn't matter to me." She stroked his pec. "And it shouldn't to you."

"How come I never knew you were so smart?"

Her laugh resonated through his own chest. "Maybe because you were being stupid."

Gregg threw his head back and howled. "Yeah, maybe." He kissed her temple. "Maybe . . . definitely. I'm through with that, though."

God . . . he was still unsure exactly what had changed. Well, everything . . . but the precise why was unknown. He felt like someone had set him right, but he couldn't remember who or where or when.

His eyes went to the computer and he thought of that shadowy ghost. For some reason, he had an image of a cavernous, empty room on the third floor of this house— and a huge man sitting in a chair with a pool of light hitting only his knees and lower legs.

And then the man leaned forward . . . into the light—

The pain in Gregg's head made him think someone had *Basic Instinct*ed his temples, spearing him with a pair of ice picks.

"Are you okay?" Holly asked, sitting up. "Your head again?"

He nodded even though the motion made his vision swim and his stomach feel like he'd chugged spoiled milk. "Yeah. Probably I need new glasses. Bifocals, even . . . damn."

Holly stroked his hair, and as he stared into her eyes, the agony faded and he felt a strange feeling in his chest. Happiness? he wondered.

Yup. Had to be. Because in all of his adult life he'd been through the full gamut of emotions . . . and he'd never once felt like this. Whole. Complete. At peace.

"Holly, you are so much more than I thought you were," he whispered, brushing her cheek.

As those lovely eyes of hers grew watery, she said, "And you've turned out to be everything I wished you'd be."

"Well, hasn't this been the show of a lifetime, then?" He kissed her slowly. "And I have the perfect ending."

"You do?"

Gregg nodded and put his mouth to her ear. In a soft whisper, he said, "I love you."

First time those words had come out of him . . . when he'd actually meant them.

As she croaked out an "I love you, too," he kissed her and kissed her some more . . . and felt like he owed the moment to a ghost.

Turned out his Cupid was a big shadow with a bad attitude. That didn't exist in the "real" world.

Then again . . . stranger things had brought people together, hadn't they. And all that really mattered was that the right pair ended up doing the Hallmark at the end. The means that got them there? Not what ultimately counted.

Besides, now he might be able to stop with the hair color.

Yeah, life was good. Especially when you powered-down your ego . . . and had the right woman in your bed for the right reasons.

He wasn't letting Holly go this time.

And he was going to take care of her the right way, just as she deserved for . . . well, forever had a nice ring to it, didn't it.

FIFTY-EIGHT

Back at the Brotherhood's private clinic, Xhex stood at John's side while Doc Jane X-rayed his leg. Once the pictures were up, it didn't take the good doctor long to come to the conclusion that he had to be operated on—and even Xhex, in spite of her usual panic at being where she was, could see the problem on the X-ray. The bullet was just too close to the bone for comfort.

While Jane called for Ehlena and then went to change into scrubs, Xhex crossed her arms over her chest and started pacing.

She could not breathe. And that had been true even before she'd taken a gander at what was doing with John's leg.

When he whistled softly at her, she just shook her head and kept moving, making a circle around the room. Turned out the trip by all the stainless-steel cabinets with their glass-front doors and their caged medications wasn't a big help: Her heart thundered even more in her chest, going all Bon Jovi on her—the pounding so loud her eardrums were getting an aerobic workout.

God, she'd been struggling since the moment she'd come in here with him. And now he was being cut open and then sewed back together?

She was going to fucking lose it.

Although honestly . . . if she tried to be logical about it, that was nuts. One, it wasn't her body getting worked on. Two, leaving that slug of lead in him was clearly not a good idea. And three . . . helllllllo . . . he was being

503

treated by someone who'd already proven she knew her way around a scalpel.

Great rationalizations. All of which her adrenal gland middle-fingered and then carried right on.

Weren't phobias fun.

The second whistle was a demand and she stopped opposite John, lifting her eyes to his face. He was cool and relaxed. No hysterics, no freak-out, nothing but calm forbearance of what was coming.

I'm going to be fine, he signed. *Jane's done this a million times before.*

Jesus Christ, where the hell was all the air in this room, Xhex thought—

Like he knew he was losing her, he whistled again and held out his hand with a frown.

"John . . ." When no coherent words came, she shook her head and went back to the pacing. She hated this. She truly hated this.

As the door swung wide, Doc Jane came back in with Ehlena. The two were in the middle of a conversation about the procedure and John whistled at them. When he held up his forefinger to indicate he needed a minute, the females nodded and ducked out again.

"Shit," Xhex said, "don't stop them. I'll be all right."

As she headed for the door to call the doctor back in, a thunderous sound reverberated through the room. Thinking John had fallen off the gurney, she wheeled around—

No, he'd punched the stainless-steel table and left a dent in it.

Talk to me, he signed. *And they're not coming in until you do.*

She had the urge to argue and the vocabulary to do it—just not the voice, evidently. Try as she did, she couldn't manage to say a thing.

Which was when he opened his arms to her.

Cursing herself, she said, "I'm going to man up here. I'm going to so be twenty-one. You're not going to believe how tight in the head I'm going to be. Really. For real."

Come here, he mouthed.

"Oh . . . hell." Giving up, she went over and embraced him.

Into his neck, she said, "I don't do this medical thing well. In case you haven't noticed before. I'm sorry, John . . . damn it, I'm always letting you down, aren't I."

He caught her before she could pull away. Holding her in place with his eyes, he signed, *You saved my life tonight. I wouldn't be alive right now unless you'd thrown that blade. So you aren't always letting me down—and as for this? I'm not worried and you don't have to watch—go and wait up at the house. It's going to be over quickly. Don't torture yourself.*

"I'm not running scared." Moving quickly so she couldn't think too much and neither could he, she took his face in her hands and kissed him hard. "But maybe waiting outside is a good idea."

After all, she couldn't very well have Doc Jane stop in the middle to treat some pansy bystander with a case of the vapors. Or a concussion because the idiot had passed out cold on the floor.

Probably for the best, John mouthed.

Breaking away, she put one foot after the other to the door and let in Ehlena and Doc Jane. As the physician passed, Xhex grabbed the female's arm.

"Please . . ." God, what could she say.

Doc Jane nodded. "I got him. Don't worry."

Xhex took a shuddering breath and wondered how in the hell she was going to get through the wait out in the hall. Knowing the way her mind worked, she'd have John screaming silently in pain and Doc Jane removing his whole leg as the minutes dragged by—

"Xhex . . . mind if I suggest something?" Doc Jane said.

"Hit me. In fact . . . hit me. A good uppercut might help me pull it together."

Doc Jane shook her head. "Why don't you watch."

"*What?*"

"Stay here and watch what I do and how I do it and learn the whys. There are a lot of people who are terrified of medical situations—with very good reason. But phobias are phobias, whether it's an airplane or a dentist or a doctor—and exposure therapy works. Take the mystery out of it and the sense of not being in control? The fear can't get at you in the same way."

"Nice piece of logic. But what happens if I faint."

"You can sit down if you get dizzy and leave whenever you like. Ask questions and look over my shoulder if you're able."

When she glanced at John, his solemn nod sealed her fate. She was staying.

"Do I need scrubs?" she said in a voice that was utterly foreign.

Shit, it was so damn girly. Next thing you knew, she was going to start crying at TV ads and doing her nails. And getting a frickin' pocketbook.

"Yup, I'm going to want you in greens. Follow me."

When they came back five minutes later, Doc Jane took her over to the sink, handed her a sealed pack with a Betadine sponge inside, and showed her how to get properly cleaned.

"Good job." The doctor turned off the water by releasing a foot pedal down on the floor. "You won't need gloves because you're not going in."

"You got that right. Tell me, you have a crash cart around, just in case I go over?"

"Right in the corner and I know how to use those paddles." Doc Jane snapped on blue gloves and went

506

over to John. "You ready? And we'll be putting you under. Given where the bullet is, I'm going to have to go deep and there's no way in hell I'll be able to get you numb enough."

Gas me, Doc, John signed.

V's *shellan* put her hand on his shoulder and stared right into his eyes. "I'm going to fix you, don't worry."

Xhex frowned and found herself in awe of the female. To be that sure and certain, given what was at stake, was pretty amazing: If Doc Jane didn't do her job right, John could be way worse off than he was now. But if she pulled it off, he would be good as new.

This was power, Xhex thought. And the polar opposite of what she did in her profession—a knife in her hand was a very different instrument.

No healing there.

Doc Jane began a running commentary, her voice strong and calm. "In a human hospital, you'd have an anesthesiologist present, but you vampires tend to be very stable under heavy sedation—it flips you into a kind of dormancy. I don't understand it, but it makes my job easier."

As she spoke, Ehlena helped John take off both his shirt and the leathers Doc Jane had cut up; then the female spread blue cloths over his nakedness and started an IV.

Xhex tried to stop her eyes from bouncing around and largely failed. There was too much threat in the place, all those scalpels and needles and . . .

"Why?" Xhex asked, forcing herself to respond. "The difference between the species, I mean?"

"Not a clue. You have a six-chambered heart and we have a four. You have two livers, we have one. You don't get cancer or diabetes."

"I don't know much about cancer."

Doc Jane shook her head. "Would that we could beat

that thing in everyone who gets it. Bastard fucking disease it is, I'll tell you. What happens is a cellular mutation occurs whereby . . ."

The doctor kept talking, but now her hands were moving around on the stainless-steel tables that had been rolled over to John, organizing what she was going to use. When she nodded at Ehlena, the female went to John's head and covered his face with a clear plastic mask.

Doc Jane went to his IV with a syringe full of something milky. "You ready, John?" When he gave a thumbs-up, she depressed the plunger.

John glanced over to Xhex and winked. And then he was out like a light.

"First thing is disinfection," Doc Jane said, opening up a packet and taking out a dark brown sponge. "Why don't you stand opposite from me? This is Betadine, the same stuff we washed our hands with, just not in a soap form."

As the doctor scrubbed around the bullet wound in wide streaks, leaving John's skin tinged reddish brown, Xhex walked around his feet in a daze.

Actually, this was a better position. She was right next to an orange biohazard bin—so if she needed to throw up, she was good to go.

"The reason the bullet has to be removed is because it's going to cause trouble over time. If he were a less active guy, I might leave it in. But I think being extra-conservative in a soldier is best. Plus you guys heal so fast." Doc Jane discarded the sponge in Xhex's bin. "Based on my experience with you, any injury to the bone will regenerate by tomorrow night."

Xhex wondered if the doctor or the nurse was aware that the floor underneath all of their feet was moving in waves. Because it sure as shit felt like they were standing on the deck of a boat.

Quick check of the professionals and both seemed steady as rocks.

"I'm going to make an incision"—Doc Jane leaned over the leg with the knife—"here. What you're going to see directly under the skin is the fascia, which is the tough outer casing that's responsible for keeping our insides together. Your average human would have fat cells between the two, but John's in great shape. Beneath the fascia is the muscle."

Xhex bent at the waist, intending to take a rudimentary glance . . . except she stayed where she was.

As Doc Jane drew the blade again, the sinewy wrapper pulled back, exposing deep pink ropes of muscle . . . which had a hole through them. Staring at the internal damage, Xhex wanted to kill that slayer all over again. And Jesus, Rhage had been right. A couple of inches up and to the left and John would have been—

Yeah, let's not go there, she thought as she repositioned herself for an even better look.

"Suction," Doc Jane said.

There was a hissing sound and Ehlena put a small white hose down and cleared away John's red blood.

"Now, I'm actually going to use my finger to probe—sometimes the human touch is best . . ."

Xhex ended up watching the whole operation. Start to finish, from the first cut to the last stitch and all the retracting and lead removal in between.

". . . and that's it," Doc Jane said about forty-five minutes later.

As Ehlena bandaged John's leg and the doctor recalibrated whatever was getting pumped into his vein, Xhex picked the bullet off the tray and looked the thing over. So small. So damned small. But capable of creating havoc of the mortal kind.

"Good job, Doc," she said harshly as she slipped the thing into her pocket.

"Let me bring him around so you can look in his eyes and know that he's really all right."

"You read minds?"

The physician's eyes were ancient as they lifted. "Nope. Have just had a lot of experience with families and friends. You're going to need to see the eyes before you take a deep breath. And he's going to feel the same way when he looks up into your face."

John regained consciousness about eight minutes later. Xhex timed it, checking the wall clock.

As his lids rose, she was right next to his head and holding his hand. "Hey . . . you're back."

He was groggy, which was to be expected. But that bright blue stare was exactly as it had always been, and the way he squeezed her hand left nothing in doubt— he was back with a vengeance.

The breath Xhex hadn't been aware of holding slowly eased out of her lungs, a singing relief elevating her mood sure as if her heart had been put on a rocket to the moon. And Doc Jane had been right about staying. As soon as Xhex got involved listening and seeing and learning, the panic receded until it was just a quiet hum that she could control. And it was fascinating, the way the body was put together.

Okay? John mouthed.

"Yup, Doc Jane got the bullet out just fine—"

John shook his head. *You? Okay?*

God . . . damn, she thought. He was such a male of worth.

"Yeah," she said roughly. "Yeah, I am . . . and thanks for asking."

Staring down at him, she realized that she hadn't allowed herself to think too much about how she'd saved his life.

Man, she'd always known she was good with a blade. But she'd never thought that skill would matter as much as it had during that split second in that nasty-ass farm-house.

A blink of an eye later and . . . no John. For anyone, anymore.

Ever.

The mere thought of that made her panic come back full force, her palms getting sweaty, her heart not so much beating as flipping out in her chest. She knew they were going their separate ways after all this was over . . . but that didn't seem to matter in the slightest when she considered a world in which he didn't breathe or laugh or fight or do the sort of kindnesses he shared with all around him.

What, he mouthed.

She shook her head. "It's nothing."

Yeah, what a lie that was.

It was everything.

FIFTY-NINE

They used the carriage that had been left by the stables to transport the female back to her family's home. Tohrment took the reins up front and Darius stayed in the cabin with the female, wishing there was some comfort to give her and knowing there was little to offer. The trip was long and the thundering hooves up in front and the creaking of the seat and the clanging of tack were very loud and precluded much discussion.

Although Darius knew well that even if their mode of transport had been whisper quiet and still as water in a goblet, their precious cargo would have uttered nothing. She had refused drink and sustenance, and did naught but focus on the landscape as they sped through farmland and village and forest.

As they proceeded in a southerly direction, it occurred to him that the symphath must have chained her mind in some way following her initial capture, assuming this carriage was the manner in which the pair had gone up to that stone manse—otherwise she would have been at risk for dematerializing free from the rushing confines.

Tragically, such an egress was not a worry now because she was so weak—although he had to wonder. Given her expression of painful forbearance, he had the distinct impression that she felt imprisoned even though she had regained her freedom.

The temptation had been to send Tohrment ahead to tell her mother and father the good news that she'd been rescued, but Darius held back. A lot could happen during the trip and he needed Tohrment to drive the horses whilst he minded the female. Given the threats from humans and lessers and symphaths, both he and Tohr had their weapons out, and still, he wished

512

he had more backup. If only there was a way to get in touch with the other Brothers and call them forth . . .

It was just on the verge of dawn when the exhausted horse pulled them into the village that came afore the female's home.

As if recognizing where they were, she lifted her head and her lips moved, her eyes growing wide and tearful.

Leaning forward and holding out his palms, Darius said, "Be of ease . . . it shall be—"

As her eyes shifted to his, he saw the scream she held within her soul. It shall not be, she mouthed.

Then she dematerialized right out of the carriage.

Darius cursed and pounded on the side panel with his fist. As Tohrment brought the horse to a clattering halt, Darius leaped out—

She didn't make it far.

The flash of her white nightgown appeared in the field to the left and he followed her suit, flashing over to her as she started to run. Lacking any true vigor, her weaving gait was that of the desperate but injured and he let her go for as long as she could.

Later, he would reflect that it was then when he knew for sure, during that mad rush she put upon them both: She couldn't go home. It wasn't what she had been through . . . it was what she was carrying forth from her ordeal.

When the female tripped and fell to the ground, she did nothing to shield her belly.

And verily, she clawed at the ground to keep going but he simply couldn't bear to watch the struggle anymore.

"Arrest your exertions," he said, pulling her up from the cold grasses. "Arrest thee now . . ."

She fought him with all the strength of a fawn and then fell still in his arms. In the frozen moment between them, her breath came out hard from her mouth and her heart raced— he could see her flickering jugular in the moonlight, could feel the quiver in her veins.

Her voice was weak, but she meant truly what she uttered.

"Do not take me back there—not even to the start of the drive. Do not render me returned."

"You cannot mean what you say." With gentle hands, he pulled her hair back from her face and abruptly remembered seeing the blond strands in the brush in her room. So much had changed since she'd last sat before her vanity mirror and readied herself for a night with her blooded family. "You have been through too much to think clearly. You must needs rest and—"

"If you take me back there, I shall run again. Do not put it upon my father to see that."

"You must go home—"

"I have no home. Anymore and evermore."

"No one needs to know what has transpired. That it wasn't a vampire is of aid, as no one shall ever—"

"I am with the symphath's young." Her eyes grew cold and hard. "My needing came to pass the very night that he forced himself upon me and I have not bled as females do since. I am with its young."

Darius's exhale was loud in the silence, his warm breath bearing forth a cloud of mist in the cool air. Well, this did change everything. If she held the young to term and brought it unto this world, there was a possibility it could pass for a vampire, but half-breeds of that sort were unpredictable. You never could be sure of the balance of the genes, whether they would lean to one of their sides over the other.

But perhaps there was a way to implore her family . . .

The female grabbed the lapels of his sturdy overcoat. "Leave me for the sun. Leave me to the death I wish for. I would take mine own hand to my throat if I could but I am not that strong of arm and shoulder."

Darius looked back at Tohrment, who was waiting by the carriage. Calling the boy forward with his hand, Darius said to the female, "Let me talk with your father. Let me pave the way."

"He shall never forgive me."

514

"It was not your fault."

"Fault is not the quandary, the outcome is," she said bleakly.

As Tohrment dematerialized over and took form before them, Darius rose to his feet. "Take her back to the carriage and render you both into that stand of trees. I shall go to her father now."

Tohrment bent down, awkwardly arranged the female in his arms and stood. In the boy's strong but gentle hold, Sampsone's daughter reverted to the listless condition she had passed the trip home in, her eyes open but vacant; her head lolling to the side.

"Take good care of her," Darius said, tucking the female's loose nightgown closer 'round her. "I shall return anon."

"Worry not," Tohrment replied as he began striding away through the grass.

Darius watched them go for a moment and then cast himself upon the wind, re-forming on the grounds of her family's estate. He went directly up to the front door and put the massive lion's head knocker to use.

As the butler opened the portal wide, it was obvious that something terrible was afoot within the manse. His pallor was that of fog and his hands were shaking.

"Sire! Oh, blessed be, do come in."

Darius frowned as he stepped through the door. "Whatever is—"

The master of the house came forth from the males' parlor . . . and right behind him followed the symphath whose son had triggered the series of tragedies.

"Whatever are you doing here?" Darius demanded of the sin-eater.

"Is my son dead. Did you kill him."

Darius unsheathed one of the black daggers that were strapped, handles down, to his chest. "Yes."

The symphath nodded once and appeared not to care. Damn reptiles. Had they no feeling for their young?

"And the girl," the sin-eater demanded. "What of her?"

515

Darius quickly pinned the vision of a blooming apple tree to the front of his mind. Symphaths could read more than emotions and he had knowledge that he did not want to share.

Without answering the thing, he looked at Sampsone, who seemed to have aged a hundred thousand years. "She's alive. Your blooded daughter is . . . well and alive."

The symphath *drifted over to the door, its long robes trailing on the marble floor. "Then we are even. My son is dead and his progeny is ruined."*

As Sampsone put his face in his hands, Darius went after the sin-eater, grabbing its arm and yanking the thing to a halt just outside of the house. "You did not have to reveal yourself. This family has well suffered."

"Oh, but I must." The symphath smiled. "Losses must be borne equally. Surely the beating heart of a warrior must respect this truth."

"You bastard."

The sin-eater leaned in. "Would you prefer that I have her kill herself? That was another path I could have trodden o'er."

"She did nothing to deserve this. Neither did the others of her bloodline."

"Oh, indeed? Perhaps my son only took what she offer—"

Darius put both his hands upon the symphath *and spun him around, slamming him into one of the massive columns that held up the mansion's great weight. "I could kill you now."*

The sin-eater smiled again. "Could you? I think not. Your honor will not allow you to take an innocent and I have done nothing wrong."

With that, the sin-eater dematerialized out of Darius's hold and re-formed on the side lawn. "I wish that female a life-time of suffering. May she live long and bear her burden without grace. And now, I shall go anon and deal with my son's body."

The symphath *disappeared, gone as if he had never existed . . . and yet the ramifications of his actions were borne out as Darius looked through the open door: The male of the great*

516

house was weeping upon the shoulder of his servant, the two taking comfort from each other.

Darius breached the arch of the grand entrance, and the sound of his boots brought up the head of the family's patriarch.

Sampsone broke away from his loyal doggen *and he didn't bother to stop his tears or obscure his sorrow as he came forward.*

Before Darius could speak, the male said, "I shall pay you."

Darius frowned. "For what?"

"To . . . take her away and see that she is provided with a roof o'er her head." The master turned to the servant. "Go unto the coffers and—"

Darius stepped forth and took Sampsone's shoulder in a tight grip. "Whatever are you saying? She lives. Your daughter is alive and she should well render herself under this roof and within these walls. You are her father*."*

"Go and take her with you. I beg of you. Her mother . . . could not live through this. Permit me to provide—"

"You are a scourge," Darius spat. "A scourge and a disgrace to your bloodline."

"No," the male said. "She is. Now and evermore."

Darius was momentarily stunned into silence. Even knowing the debased values of the glymera*, and having been subjected to them, he was as yet shocked anew. "You and that* symphath *have much in common."*

"How dare thee—"

"Neither of you has the heart to mourn your offspring."

Darius headed for the door and didn't stop as the male called out, "The money! Permit me to give you the money!"

Darius did not trust himself to respond and dematerialized back unto the wooded glen he had left mere minutes ago. Taking form by the carriage, his heart was afire. As one who had been discarded, he knew well of the hardship of being rootless and unsupported in the world. And that was without the extra burden the female carried, literally, within her body.

Although the sun was threatening to break free of the earth's edge, he required a moment to compose himself and formulate what he could say—

The female's voice emerged from behind the carriage's window drapery. "He told you to keep me away, didn't he."

Indeed, Darius found that there was no manner of expression with which he could cast what had transpired in better light.

He laid his palm on the cool wood of the carriage door. "I shall care for you. I shall provide and protect."

"Why . . ." came the aching response.

"Verily . . . it is right and proper to do so."

"A hero you are. But what you seek to save cares not for the gift you offer."

"You will. In time . . . you will care."

When there was no reply, Darius hopped up onto the driving seat and took the reins. "We shall go unto mine home."

The jangle of the horse's tack and the clapping of shod hooves on packed dirt accompanied them out of the woods and on their way. He took them a different route, keeping them far from the mansion and that family whose social expectation was thicker than blood.

And as for the money? Darius was not a rich male, but he would have sooner cut off his own dagger hand than accept a pence from that weak-souled father of hers.

SIXTY

As John went to sit up on the gurney, Xhex helped him and he was amazed at how strong she was: The instant her hand went to the middle of his back, he felt as though his entire upper weight was totally supported.

Then again, as she'd often said, she wasn't just your normal female.

Doc Jane came over and started talking to him about what was doing under his bandage and what he needed to do to care for the incision . . . but he wasn't tracking.

He wanted to have sex. With Xhex. Right now.

It was pretty much all he knew or cared about—and the carnal need went waaay deeper than just a hard-on looking for a garage to park in. A brush with death had a way of making you want to live out loud, and sex with the person you wanted to be with was the best way of expressing that noise.

Xhex's eyes flared as she caught the scent he clearly was putting off.

"You're going to stay put for another ten minutes," Doc Jane said as she started to put instruments in the auto-clave. "And then you can crash down here in the clinic's bed."

Let's go, he signed to Xhex.

Swinging his legs off the table gave him a shot of whoa-nelly pain, but the owie shit didn't make him rethink his plan in the slightest. It did, however, get the attention of everyone else in the room. As Xhex steadied him with a curse, the good doctor started in with a whole lot of lie-down-big-guy—except John wasn't having any of that prone stuff.

Would you have a robe I could wear out of here? he signed, well aware that he had a massive erection and not a lot over his hips.

There was some arguing after that, but eventually, Doc Jane threw her hands up and allowed as how if he wanted to be an idiot, she couldn't stop him. When she gave the nod, Ehlena disappeared and returned with something that was fluffy and thick and big enough to cover him up . . . from collarbone to maybe midthigh. It was also pink.

Clearly, this was the sleepwear version of a dunce cap, payback for his refusing to stay in the clinic. And you'd think all the Barbie would pull a deflate on his arousal— but not a chance.

His cock was standing firm against the assault on his masculinity.

Kind of made him proud of the bastard.

Thank you, he signed, slipping the robe onto his shoulders. With some straining, he managed to get it to fold over his chest and cover up his southern exposure. Barely.

Doc Jane leaned back against the counter and crossed her arms over her chest. "Isn't there any way I can get you to stay longer? Or go back with crutches? Or . . . get you to *stay longer?*"

I'm good—thanks, though.

Doc Jane shook her head. "You Brothers are all a pain in the ass."

Abruptly, a stinging shaft went through him that had nothing to do with his leg. *I'm not a Brother. But I don't think I'm going to argue the second part with you.*

"Wise male. And you should be. A Brother, that is."

John hitched up his ass and gently lowered his weight off the table, all the while keeping an eye on the front of his Miss Priss of the Year robe. Fortunately, everything stayed suitable for mixed company and remained that way as Xhex ducked under his arm.

Man . . . she was the best crutch he could ask for, taking a hell of a lot of the load as they walked to the door. Together, théy went down to the office, ducked through the closet, and emerged into the tunnel.

He made it about, oh, ten yards before he stopped, moved her around so she was standing before him, and then . . .

Killed the lights. All of them.

On his mental command, the fluorescents on the ceiling went dark one by one, starting with the pair directly above their heads and then stretching out in both directions. As everything went pitch-black, he worked fast and so did she. They knew damn well that Doc Jane and Ehlena were going to be busy cleaning up in the OR for at least another half hour. And it was Last Meal up at the mansion, so no one was working out, about to work out, or taking a shower in the locker room from working out.

Limited window.

Darkness was key.

Despite the difference in their heights, which even with her being near six feet was still more than half a dozen inches, he found her mouth sure as if her lips were spotlit. As he kissed her deep and slipped her his tongue, she moaned low in her throat and held on to his shoulders.

In this glorious stretch of neither here nor there, in this one step off the path they had agreed on, he let his bonded male out, unleashing himself to ride the wave of that moment that had happened back at the farmhouse . . .

That moment when her dagger had left her hand and flown through the air . . . and given him nights still to be lived.

His palm slipped around to her breast, finding the tight nipple, rubbing it with his thumb while he ached to put his mouth where his fingers were. Good thing she'd left her jacket and her weapons back at the house in the foyer, so all there was between him and her skin was the muscle shirt she had on.

He wanted to rip another one down the front, but this was a quick quencher until they could make it up to the privacy of his bedroom: Instead of the grab and split, he slid both of his palms down and under, then shoved the shirt up until her breasts popped out. Shiiiiit . . . she didn't wear a bra even to fight, and for some reason that was a gigantic turn-on.

Not that he needed the help when it came to her.

As the sounds of their kissing echoed, he tweaked the tips that were ready for his lips and ground his arousal against her. And what do you know . . . she took the hint he wasn't even aware of making and dragged her hand down his stomach right to—

John jacked his head back, the slam of electricity bolting up his spine so great he couldn't hold the kiss together.

Faster than he could say, *Fuck me hard*, Xhex pushed him back against the tunnel wall and then he felt cool air as she parted the robe. Her lips moved across his chest, her fangs making a twin trail that tingled though every single nerve in his body—especially the ones at the top of his cock.

John let out a silent shout as her warm, wet mouth found that hot, hard place, sliding down over him, taking him fully, encompassing him in heat and suction. On the withdraw, she was slow and steady, until his head popped out of her lips with a soft smack—and then her tongue lapped around. As she worked him, his eyes were open, but the darkness surrounding them made it seem as if he'd squeezed his lids shut—and oh, man, blindness was just fine in this sitch: He had a clear image of what she had to look like on her knees before his spread legs, her muscle shirt up over her breasts, her nipples still peaked, her head going forward and back, forward and back.

Her breasts would sway with every move she made.

As his breath dragged into and out of his mouth, he had a feeling his weight was equally distributed between his injured and uninjured leg, but damned if he felt anything other than what she was doing to him. Hell, he could have been on fire, for all he knew or cared.

He *was* on fire, as a matter of fact—and the flames got hotter as Xhex folded his erection up against his lower belly and ran the flat of her tongue down him until she got to the heavy weights below his cock. One by one they were pulled into her mouth and then she went back to lollipopping his arousal.

She found a rhythm and he didn't last long. Stroke and suck, stroke and suck, stroke—

John's body arched and his palms smacked against the wall as he came.

After it was done, he dragged her to her feet and kissed her long and hard . . . with an inkling of returning the favor on her—

Xhex nicked his lower lip on purpose and lapped at the tiny slice she'd made. "Bed. Now."

Roger. That.

John relit the ceiling fixtures and they all but ran up to the mansion.

Funny, that bum leg didn't bother him in the slightest.

Blay stayed out of the room Saxton had been given during and after the feeding, but he wasn't allowed to leave the mansion to get some head space. Qhuinn's cousin was considered, under the Old Laws, a male guest of his within the house of the First Family, and as such, protocol demanded that he remain on the premises.

523

At least fighting with the others would have given him a sense of accomplishment and helped the time to pass faster.

After Phury had arrived with Selena, and introductions had been made, Blay had gone to his own room and rationalized the peace out by telling himself he had to straighten things up there. Unfortunately, the Maids R Us routine had taken all of two minutes and involved repositioning the book he'd been reading on the bedside table . . . and moving a pair of black silkies out of his colored-socks drawer to their brethren down below.

One of the curses of being neat was that there was never any major overhauling to be done on the tidy-up front.

He'd also had a haircut recently, too. Nails were clipped. No manscaping to do, thanks to the fact that vampires were hairless except for on their heads.

Ordinarily if he had time to kill, he called home to catch up with his parents, but given what was going through his mind, the number to the family safe house was not something he was dialing. Bottom line? He sucked at lying and wasn't about to loop his mom and dad: Hey, guys, you don't know this yet, but I'm gay . . . and I'm thinking about dating Qhuinn's cousin.

Oh, and he's here, by the way.

Feeding.

God, the idea that Saxton was taking someone's vein was hot as hell—even though it was Selena's.

And except for the fact that Phury was in there with the pair of them. For decorum rather than her protection of course.

So, yeah, no way he was going anywhere near that room. Last thing he wanted was to get aroused in front of an audience.

Blay glanced at his watch. Paced. Tried to watch TV. Picked up the book he'd repositioned for a while.

From time to time his phone went off with reports from the field, none of which helped his twitchy mood. The Brotherhood always sent out regular communiqués so everyone had up-to-the-moment intel, and things were not great: John had been injured, so he and Xhex and Qhuinn were down with Doc Jane in the clinic. The infiltration at the farmhouse had been successful, but only up to a point—the suspected *Fore-lesser* was still at large and they had gotten many, but not all, of the new recruits they'd found. Address tied to that street racer had yielded nothing but snores. Tensions were running high.

He checked his watch. Then the clock on the wall.

And felt like screaming.

Christ, it had been so long since Saxton and Selena had started. Why had no one come and gotten him when it was done?

What if something was wrong? Doc Jane had said the guy's injuries were not life-threatening and that feeding would put him well on the road to recovery—

Then again, if any Brother was likely to get along with Saxton, it was the Primale. Phury loved opera and art and good books. Maybe the two had gotten to talking afterward?

Eventually he couldn't stand his own company and went downstairs to the kitchen, where the *doggen* of the household were getting Last Meal ready. He tried to help, offering to put out plates or silver, or chop vegetables in the kitchen, or baste the turkeys that were roasting—but the staff got so flustered, he backed off.

Man, if there was one thing guaranteed to get a *doggen* all turned around, it was a bid to pitch in. By nature, they couldn't bear someone they served doing anything except getting waited on—*but* they also couldn't handle denying a request from said party.

Before spinning heads led to burned dinner and

possible mass suicide, he left the pantry and came out through the dining room—

The vestibule's door opened and shut and Qhuinn stalked across the foyer's mosaic floor.

There was red blood on the guy's face and hands and leathers. Fresh, glistening blood.

Of the human variety.

Blay's first instinct was to shout to his buddy, but he held back because he didn't want to draw a ton of attention to the fact that Qhuinn had very obviously been where John wasn't.

Noooot a lot of Homo sapiens down at the clinic in the training center.

And he'd supposedly been fighting initiates, who bled black.

Blay hit the stairs and caught up with the guy right in front of Wrath's study—the doors of which were mercifully closed. "What the hell happened to you?"

Qhuinn didn't stop, just powered onward to his room. Slipping inside, he made like he was going to close the door in Blay's face.

So not having any of that, Blay thought, as he shoved himself inside. "What's up with the blood?"

"I'm not in the mood," Qhuinn muttered as he started to undress.

He discarded his leather jacket on the bureau, disarmed himself at the desk, and kicked his boots off halfway to the bathroom. His T-shirt got tossed over his shoulder and ended up on a lamp.

"Why's there blood on your hands?" Blay repeated.

"None of your business."

"What did you do." Even though he had a feeling that he knew. "What the hell did you do?"

As Qhuinn leaned into the shower to start the water, the corded muscles along his spine flexed above the waistband of his leathers.

God, that red blood was on him in other places, too—which made Blay wonder just how far the beat-down had gone.

"How's your boy?"

Blay frowned. "My boy—oh, Saxton."

"Yeah. 'Oh. Saxton.'" Steam began to rise from the glass-encased shower, the mist boiling up and then falling between them. "How's he doing?"

"I guess he's been fed by now."

Qhuinn's mismatched eyes focused somewhere behind Blay's head. "Hope he feels better."

As they faced off at each other, Blay's chest hurt so badly he had to rub it. "Did you kill him."

"Him? Who?" Qhuinn put his hands on his hips, his pecs and his pierced nipples standing out in high relief, thanks to the lights over the sinks. "I don't know no 'him.'"

"Stop bullshitting. Saxton is going to want to know."

"Protective of him, are you." There was no hostility to the words. Just an uncharacteristic resignation. "Okay, fine, I didn't kill anyone. But I gave that homophobic asshole something to think about other than the throat cancer those cigars will be giving him. I won't have my family members being disrespected." Qhuinn turned away. "And—well, fuck, I don't like you upset, believe it or not. If Saxton had been left for dead and the sun came up? Or humans had found him? You'd have never gotten over it. Couldn't not settle that score."

God, wasn't that just like the son of a bitch. Doing the wrong thing for the perfect reason . . .

"I love you," Blay whispered so quietly that the sound of the rushing water drowned out the words.

"Listen, I need a shower," Qhuinn said. "I want to get the nasty off of me. And then I need to sleep."

"Okay. Yeah. You want me to bring you some food?"

"I'm good. Thanks."

As he started to leave, Blay glanced over his shoulder. Qhuinn was stripping his leathers off, his ass making a spectacular appearance.

With his head still cranked around, he made it out of the bathroom okay, but slammed into the desk, and had to catch the lamp from falling to the floor. Righting the thing, he peeled the shirt off the shade and, like a pathetic nancy, brought the soft cotton to his nose for an inhale.

Closing his eyes, he cradled what had been on Qhuinn's chest to his own and listened to the sound of the water falling in flips and flops as the other male washed himself.

He wasn't sure how long he stayed like that, dangling in the purgatory of so-close-yet-so-far-away. What got him on the move again was the fear of getting caught being a sap. Carefully replacing the T-shirt to its former drape, he forced himself to go to the door.

He was about halfway there when he saw it.

On the bed.

The white sash was tangled in the sheets, just one more rumpled stretch of cloth.

As his eyes went upward, he found two head indentations on a pair of pillows that were close together. Clearly, the Chosen Layla had forgotten the tie to her robe when she'd left. Which could happen only if she'd been naked while she was here.

Blay put his hand to his heart once more, a sense of constriction making him feel as if he were underwater . . . with the surface of the ocean far, far above him.

The shower was cut off in the bathroom and a towel flapped around.

Blay walked passed the well-used bed and ducked out the door.

He was unaware of having made a conscious decision, but his feet had direction; that was obvious. Going down the hall, they stopped two rooms over and then his hand lifted of its own volition and knocked quietly. When a muffled answer sounded out, he opened the door. On the other side, the room was dark and it smelled divine . . . and as he stood in the light from the hall, his shadow reached the foot of the bed.

"Perfect timing, they just left." Saxton's husky voice was a promise of things Blay wanted. "Have you come to see how I am?"

"Yes."

There was a long pause. "Then shut the door, and I'll show you."

Blay's hand tightened on the knob until his knuckles cracked.

And then he stepped inside and closed them both in. As he kicked off his shoes, he threw the lock.

For privacy.

SIXTY-ONE

On the Far Side, Payne sat on the edge of the reflecting pool and stared down at her own face in the still water.

She recognized well the black hair and the diamond eyes and the strong features.

Was all too aware of who had sired and birthed her.

Could recite the days of her history thus far.

And yet, she felt as though she had not a clue as to who she truly was. In many ways, more than she took comfort in adding up, she was naught but this echo on the surface of the pool, an image that lacked depth and substance . . . and would leave nothing of permanence in her wake when she departed.

As Layla came up from behind her, she met the female's eyes in the mirror of the water.

Later, she would consider that Layla's smile was what changed everything. Even though of course, 'twas more than that . . . but her sister's radiant expression was what ultimately cast her upon the winds of change, the subtle push that had her tumbling off the cliff.

That smile was real.

"Greetings, my sister," Layla said. "I have been searching for you."

"And alas you have found me." Payne forced herself to turn about and stare up at the Chosen. "Please. Sit and join me. I infer from your good cheer that your time with the male continues apace."

Layla lowered herself for but a moment, and then her kinetic joy had her up on her feet again. "Oh, yes, indeed. Indeed, yes. He is to call me anon this day and I shall go to him again. Oh, dearest sister, you cannot imagine . . . what it is like to be held within a circle of fire and yet emerge unscathed and o'erjoyed. 'Tis a miracle. A blessing."

Payne turned back to the water and watched as her own brows tightened. "May I ask you something intrusive."

"Of course, my sister." Layla came over and settled once more on the pool's white marble edge. "Anything."

"Are you thinking of mating him? Not just mating with him—but becoming his *shellan*?"

"Well, yes. Of course I am. But I am waiting to find the right time to broach it."

"What shall you do . . . if he says no?" When Layla's face froze, as if she had never considered such a thing, Payne felt as though she had crushed a rosebud in her palm. "Oh, damn me . . . I don't mean to upset you. I just—"

"No, no." Layla took a bracing breath. "I am well aware of the construction of your heart and you have not a cruel chamber within it. Which in truth is why I feel as though I may speak with such candor to you."

"Please forget I asked."

Now Layla stared into the pool. "I . . . we have yet to actually have relations."

Payne's brows popped. Verily, if just the precursor to the actual event was eliciting such elation, the act itself must be incredible.

At least for a female like the one before her.

Layla brought her arms around herself, no doubt because she was remembering the feel of another, stronger set. "I have wanted to, but he holds back. I hope . . . I believe it is because he wishes to mate me properly first, in ceremony."

Payne felt the awful weight of premonition. "Beware, sister. You are a gentle soul."

Layla got to her feet, her smile now saddened. "Yes, I am. But I would rather my heart be broken than unopened and I know that one must ask if one is to receive."

The female was so certain and steadfast that in the shadow of her courage, Payne felt small. Small and weak.

Just who was she? A reflection? Or a reality?

Abruptly, she stood up. "Will you permit me my leave?"

Layla seemed surprised and bowed low. "But of course. And please, I mean no offense by my ramblings—"

On impulse, Payne embraced the other Chosen. "You have given none. Worry not. And best of luck with your male. Verily, he would be blessed to have you."

Before anything more could be said, Payne walked off, moving quickly past the dorm and surmounting with ever gathering speed the hill that led up to the Primale Temple. Going beyond that sacred bedding place, which was never used anymore, she entered her mother's marble courtyard and strode down the colonnade.

The modestly sized door that marked the Scribe Virgin's private quarters was not what one would expect to herald such a devine space. But then when the whole world was yours, you had nothing to prove, did you.

Payne did not knock. Given what she was about to do, the inappropriateness of bursting in uninvited was going to be so far down her list of sins, it was barely going to count as one.

"Mother," she demanded as she stepped into the empty white room.

There was a long wait before she was answered and the voice that came to her was disembodied. "Yes, daughter."

"Let me out of here. Now."

Whatever consequence came upon her head from this

renewed confrontation was better than such a castrated existence.

"Throw me out," she reiterated to the blank walls and the nonair. "Let me go. I shall never return herein if that is your wish. But I shall not stay here anon."

In a flash of light, the Scribe Virgin appeared before her without the black robing she usually wore. Indeed, Payne was quite sure no one ever saw her mother as she truly was, energy without form.

Bright no longer, however. Dim now, barely more than a ripple of heat to the eye.

The difference was arresting and tempered Payne's rage. "Mother . . . let me go. Please."

The Scribe Virgin's response was long in coming. "I'm sorry. I cannot grant you your wish."

Payne bared her fangs. "Damn you, just do it. Let me out of here or—"

"There is no 'or,' my dearest child." The Scribe Virgin's thready voice drifted off and then returned. "You must remain here. Destiny demands it."

"Whose? Yours or mine?" Payne slashed her hand through the paralytic stillness. "Because I am not truly living here, and what kind of destiny is that."

"I am sorry."

And that was the end of the argument—at least as far as her mother was concerned. With a sparkle, the Scribe Virgin disappeared.

Payne hollered into the vast blankness, "Release me! Damn you! Release me!"

She half expected to be slain on the spot, but then the torture would be over, and where was the fun in that.

"Mother!"

When there was no reply, Payne wheeled around and wished to *Dhunhd* there was something to throw—but there was nothing to set her grip upon and the symbolism was a scream in her head: nothing for her, there was absolutely *nothing* for her here.

Approaching the door, she unleashed her anger, ripping the thing from the hinges and throwing it backward into the cold, empty room. The white panel bounced twice and then skidded freely across the unobstructed expanse, a pebble upon the surface of a still pond.

As she stalked out toward the fountain, she heard a series of clicks, and when she looked over her shoulder, she saw that the portal had fixed itself, magically resealing its empty jambs, forming exactly what had been there before with nary a scratch to show for what she'd done to it.

Fury rose within her such that it choked her throat and made her hands shake.

In the corner of her eye, she saw a black-robed figure coming down the colonnade, but it was not her mother. It was merely No'One with a basket of offerings for the Scribe Virgin, her limp shifting her gait from side to side.

The sight of the misfortunate, excluded Chosen fueled her rage even further—

"Payne?"

The sound of the deep voice whipped her head around: Wrath stood by the white tree of colorful songbirds, his massive form dominating the courtyard.

Payne sprang at him, turning him into a target she could fight. And the Blind King clearly sensed her violence and her vicious approach: In the blink of an eye, he fell into his fighting stance, becoming powerful, prepared, and ready.

She gave him everything she had and more, her fists and legs flying at him, her body becoming a whirl of punches and kicks, which he deflected with his forearms and dodged by ducking his torso and head.

Faster, tougher, deadlier, she kept at the king, forcing

him to return what she was putting to him or risk getting seriously injured. His first hard strike caught her in the shoulder, his fist crashing into her, throwing her off balance—but she recovered quickly and spun around, leading with her leg and foot.

The impact to his gut rocked him so hard he grunted—at least until she spun once more and struck him in the face with her knuckles. As blood exploded, and the dark lenses o'er his eyes skittered away, he cursed.

"What the fuck, Pay—"

The king didn't have a chance to finish her name. She plowed into him, catching him around the waist, driving his huge weight backward. There was no true contest, however. He was twice her size, and he took charge with ease, peeling her off of him and flipping her around to hold her, back to his front.

"What the fuck is your problem?" he snarled in her ear.

She slammed her head backward, nailing him in the face, and his grip loosened for a split second. Which was all she needed to break away. Flipping free of him by using his oak-strong body as a platform to fly from, she—

Vastly underestimated her momentum. Instead of landing with her weight perpendicular to the ground, she pitched forward—which meant she hurt one foot badly, her body tumbling wildly to the side.

The marble edge of the fountain kept her from hitting the ground, but the impact was worse than if she'd fallen flat.

The crack of her back was loud as a scream.

And so was the pain.

SIXTY-TWO

When Lash woke up at his hideaway ranch, the first thing he did was look at his arms.

Along with his hands and wrists, his forearms were now shadows as well, a kind of smog-like form that moved as he told it to, and either be nothing more than air or could bear weight at his command.

Sitting up, he shoved off the blanket he'd pulled over himself and stood. What do you know, his feet were pulling a disappear, too. Which was good, but . . . shit, how long was the transformer bit going to take? He had to assume that if his body still had physical form, with a heartbeat and needs like food and drink and sleep, he wasn't completely safe from bullets and knives.

Plus, frankly, given all the pieces that had fallen off him, bio-waste management was really fucking messy.

He'd turned the mattress he'd slept on into the biggest Depends on the planet.

A squeak from outside drew him over to the blinds and he parted a seam with his nonfingers. Through the crack, he watched humans going along their lame-ass days, driving by, biking along. Frickin' morons with their simple little lives. Get up. Go to work. Come home. Bitch about their day. Wake up and do the same thing again.

As a sedan went by, he implanted a thought in the driver's mind . . . and smiled as the Pontiac swerved out of its lane, bumped up over the curb, and gunned right at the two-story across the street. The fucking POS powered straight into a bank of windows, smashing through the glass and the wood framing, air bags exploding inside the car.

Better than a cup of coffee to start the day.

He turned away and went to the shitty bureau, firing up the laptop he'd found in the back of the Mercedes. The drug deal he'd interrupted on the way home had been worth the effort. He'd grifted a couple thousand dollars as well as some OxyCs, some X, and twelve crack rocks. More important, he'd thrown the two dealers and the one customer under a trance, gotten them back to the AMG, brought them here, and turned them.

They'd trashed the hall bath by throwing up all night long, but frankly he was about done with this house and was thinking of burning it down.

So . . . he had a team of four. And whereas none of them had been volunteers, once he'd drained them and brought them back to "life," he'd promised them all kinds of shit. And what do you know. Junkies who dealt to supply their own habits would believe just about anything you told them. You just had to sell them on a future—after you'd scared the colons out of them.

Which was a no B.F.D. for him. Naturally, they'd been shitting themselves when he'd unmasked his face, but the good thing was they'd hallucinated so many times on acid trips, it wasn't completely outside their experience to talk to a living corpse. Plus he was persuasive when he wanted to be.

Damn shame he couldn't brainwash them permanently. But that parlor trick with the Pontiac driver was as far as he could go with the influence: brief and unsustainable for longer than a couple of seconds.

Fucking free will.

After the computer booted up, he went to the *Caldwell Courier Journal* site . . .

Hello, front page. The "Farmhouse Massacre" was covered in a number of articles—the blood and the body parts and the strange oily residue garnering all kinds of Pulitzer-light description. Reporters also interviewed the police who'd been there, the postman who'd called 911 in the first place, twelve kinds of neighbors, and the mayor—who was evidently "calling upon the fine men and women of the CPD to solve this terrible crime against the Caldwell community."

Consensus was: ritual deaths. Perhaps tied to an unknown cult.

All of which was just background chatter obscuring what he was really looking for—

Bingo. In the last article, he found a short two-paragrapher reporting that the crime scene had been broken into the night before. The "fine men and women of the CPD" had grudgingly allowed as how one of their late-night patrol cars had done a drive-by and found that person or persons unknown had ransacked the scene. They were quick to point out that relevant evidence had already been removed and they were putting a black-and-white there full-time from now on.

So the Brotherhood had followed up on his little message.

Had Xhex gone there, too? he wondered. Maybe waited to see if he'd show up?

Shit, he'd missed a goddamn shot at her. And the Brothers.

But he had time. Hell, when his body went full-on shadow? He had an eternity.

Checking his watch, he got his hustle on, changing quickly into black slacks and a turtleneck and that hooded raincoat. Drawing on his leather gloves, he slid his black baseball cap on and gave a gander in the mirror.

Yeah. Right.

Rummaging around, he found a black T-shirt that he ripped to ribbons and wound around his face, leaving room for his lidless eyes and the cartilage that was left of his nose and the gaping maw that was now his mouth.

Better. Not great. But better.

First stop was the bathroom to check and see how his troops were getting along. They had all passed out in a heap on the floor, their arms and legs intertwining, their heads here and there . . . but the fuckers were alive.

Man, they were so bottom-of-the-barrel, dregs-of-humanity types, he thought. If they were lucky, collectively their IQ might creep into the triple digits.

They were going to be useful, however.

Lash locked the house up tight with a spell and stepped out into the garage. Popping the Mercedes' trunk, he lifted the carpeted panel, took out the bundle of coke, and loaded up both his non-nostrils before getting behind the wheel.

Gooooooooood *mornnning*! As a choir of chaos lit him up from the inside, he backed down the drive and headed out of the neighborhood, going the opposite way from the cops and ambulances that had arrived at the house across the street.

Which now had a drive-through as opposed to a living room.

Once he hit the highway, the trip downtown should have been ten minutes, but because of rush-hour traffic, it was more like twenty-five—although with the racing in his mind and his body, he felt like he was at a total standstill the entire time.

It was a little after nine o'clock when he pulled into an alley and parked next to a silver van. As he got out, he thanked God for the blow—he actually felt like he had some energy. Trouble was, if his Extreme Makeover didn't finish up fast, he was going to go through that stash in the trunk in a matter of days.

Which was why he'd called for this meeting now instead of waiting any longer.

And what do you know, Ricardo Benloise was on time and already in his office: The maroon AMG he was squired around in was docked on the far side of the GMC van.

Lash approached the back door of the art gallery, and waited by the video camera. Yeah, he'd have preferred to chill on this face-to-face for a couple of days, but his own needs notwithstanding, he had sellers curing in his bathroom and he needed product for them to hit the streets with.

Then he had to turn some soldiers.

After all, the little Shit hadn't wasted any time filling his ranks—although there was no way of telling how many were left after the Brotherhood's raid at the farm-house.

Never thought he'd be glad those motherfuckers were lethal at their jobs. Go. Fig.

Lash had to assume that the Omega's boy toy was going to quickly cook up another batch of inductees. And given that the kid had been a successful dealer, he was going to resume making paper as soon as he could. Both of which would give him the resources not only to fight the vampires, but come after Lash.

So it was a case of the clock ticking. Lash was damn confident that the Shit couldn't get a meeting with Benloise right now because he was small potatoes—but how much longer would that be true? Sales mattered. Smarts mattered. If Lash could get a foot in the door, someone else could.

Especially if they had the special talents of a *Fore-lesser*.

With a click, the door locks were sprung and one of Benloise's enforcers opened up. The guy frowned at Lash's Lady Gaga rig, but got back in the game quick. No doubt he'd seen a lot of crazy shit—and not just on the drug-trade side of things: artists were no doubt wacky nut jobs for the most part.

540

"Where's your ID," the guy said.

Lash flashed his fake driver's license. "About to be up your ass, motherfucker."

Clearly, the combination of the laminated card and Lash's familiar voice was enough because a moment later, he was allowed in.

Benloise's office was on the third floor in the front, and the trip up there was silent. The guy's private space was bowling-alley uncluttered, nothing but a long expanse of black varnished floorboards that culminated in a raised platform—which was the desk equivalent of a set of lifts for shoes. Benloise was parked on the dais, seated behind a teak table that was the size of a Lincoln Town Car.

Like a lot of guys who had to stand tall to hit five-six on a tape measure, everything the short man did was big.

As Lash came forward, the South American stared out over his steepled fingers and spoke in his smooth, cultured way. "I was so pleased to receive your call after you failed to make our last meeting. Wherever have you been, my friend."

"Family problems."

Benloise frowned. "Yes, blood can be trouble."

"You have no idea." Lash looked around at all of the absolutely nothing, locating the hidden cameras and doors—which were in the same positions they'd been in the last time. "First off, let me assure you that our business relationship remains my top priority."

"I am very pleased to know this. When you didn't arrive to buy the pieces you were contracted for, I wondered. As an art dealer, I depend on my regular customers to keep my artists busy. I also expect my regulars to fulfill their obligations."

"Understood. Which is the real reason I've come. I need an advance. I have an empty wall in my house that has to be filled with one of your paintings, but I won't be able to pay with cash today."

Benloise smiled, showing orderly little teeth. "I'm afraid I don't make those arrangements. You must pay for the art you leave with. And why ever is your face covered up?"

Lash ignored the question. "You're going to make an exception in my case."

"I don't make exceptions—"

Lash dematerialized across the space, taking form behind the guy and putting a knife to his throat. With a shout, the guard over by the door went for his heat, but there wasn't a lot to shoot at when your boss's jugular was on the verge of springing a leak.

Lash hissed in Benloise's ear, "I've had a really bad fucking week and I'm tired of playing by human rules. It is my full intention to continue our relationship, and you are going to make that possible not only because it benefits us both, but because I'm going to take it personally if you don't. Know this, you cannot hide from me and there is nowhere you can go that I can't find you. There is no door strong enough to keep me out, no man I can't overpower, no weapon you can use against me. My terms are this—one major piece to fill up my wall, and I will take it with me right now."

When he discovered who Benloise's overseas contacts were, he might just off the bastard—but that would be jumping the gun. The South American was the pipeline for product into Caldwell, and that was the only reason the son of a bitch had a good shot at having lunch later today.

As opposed to a date with an embalmer.

Benloise dragged in a breath. "Enzo, the new Joshua Tree pastels are due to arrive early this evening. When they do, you will pack up one of them and—"

"I want it now."

"You will have to wait. I cannot give you that which I don't possess. Kill me at this moment and you shall have none of it."

Fucker. Motherfucker.

Lash thought back to how much was left in the trunk of the Mercedes—and considered the fact that even now, the coke buzz was draining from him, leaving a whole lot of snooze in its wake. "When. Where."

"Same time and place as always."

"Fine. But I'll be taking a taste with me now." He dug the knife into that neck. "And don't tell me that you're totally dry. That's going to make me cranky . . . and twitchy. Twitchy is bad for you—FYI."

After a moment, the guy murmured, "Enzo, go get him a sample of the artist's new work, will you."

The meat across the way seemed to be having trouble processing everything, but then seeing someone disappear into thin air was no doubt a new one for him.

"Enzo. Go now."

Lash smiled underneath his mummy wraps. "Yeah, beat some feet there, Enzo. I'll take excellent care of your boss until you come back."

The bodyguard backed out and then there was the retreating sound of his boots clapping down the stairwell.

"And so you are the worthy successor to the Reverend," Benloise said with a strain.

Ah, Rehvenge's former nomenclature in the human world. "Yeah, I'm right up his alley."

"There was always something different about him."

"You think that shit was special?" Lash whispered. "Wait'll you get a load of me."

Back at the Brotherhood mansion, Qhuinn was sitting up in his bed, leaning against the headboard. He had the cable remote balanced on one thigh, yet another short-and-squat full of Herradura on the other side, and next to him, hanging tight?

Good ol' Captain Insomnia.

In front of him, the television glowed in the darkness, the morning news droning on. Turned out the police had found the homophobe Qhuinn had worked over in the alley next to the cigar bar and taken him to St. Francis Hospital. Guy was refusing to identify his attacker or comment on what had happened, but it wouldn't have mattered if he opened his piehole. There were hundreds of pierced, leather-wearing, tatted up sons of bitches in town and the CPD could kiss Qhuinn's ass.

But whatever, that motherfucker wasn't going to say shit to nobody—and Qhuinn was willing to bet his left nut he never gay-bashed again either.

Next came an update on what the humans were calling "the Farmhouse Massacre"—said report basically amounting to a whole lot of no new information, but plenty of hysteria-inducing hyperbole. Cults! Ritual sacrifices! Stay indoors after dark!

All of which was, of course, based on circumstantial evidence, because the blue-uni-and-badge brigade had nothing but aftermath to go on—no bodies. And although the identities of a rash of missing lowlifes were starting to percolate to the surface, the dead end was going to stick: Those few slayers who had escaped the Brotherhood's infiltration were now firmly entrenched in the Lessening Society, never to be seen or heard from again by their former friends and families.

So, yeah, basically, the humans were left with a ServiceMaster cleanup job out there and not much else: Fuck the CSI types; what they really needed was a carpet steamer, a shitload of mops, and a bathtub of Formula 409. If they thought they were ever going to "solve" the crime, those cops were just masturbating the soles of their shoes and the nibs on their pens.

What actually had happened was just a ghost they could sense, but never capture.

As if on cue, a promo for the all-new *Paranormal Investigators* prime-time special aired, the camera panning around some Southern mansion with trees that looked as if they needed a beard trimmer.

Qhuinn swung his feet off the edge of his bed and rubbed his face. Layla had wanted to come over again, but when she'd called out to him, he'd sent her back a thought that he was exhausted and needed to sleep.

It wasn't that he didn't want to be with her, it was just . . .

Goddamn it, she liked him, she wanted him, and he clearly was into her body. So why didn't he just call her over here, mate her, and put a check mark next to the biggest goal in life he had?

As he thought about the plan, an image of Blay's face came to mind and forced him to take a cold, hard look at the shaggy fabric of his life: The shit wasn't pretty and all the threads he'd started and could neither clip free nor stitch together suddenly became more than he could bear.

Getting up, he went out into the hall of statues and looked down to the right. To Blay's room.

With a curse, he walked over to the door he'd been in and out of as much as he had his own. When he knocked, the contact was a soft one, not his usual *bang-bang-bang*.

No answer. He tried again.

Turning the knob, he pushed inside barely an inch— and wished he hadn't had cause to be discreet. But maybe Saxton was in there with the guy.

"Blay? You up?" he whispered into the darkness.

No reply . . . and the lack of running water suggested the pair of them weren't taking a pneumatic shower together. Stepping in, Qhuinn flicked on the lights . . .

The bed was made up, neat as a pin, totally undisturbed. Fucking thing looked like an ad in a magazine, with all its pillows arranged and the extra duvet folded up like a cloth taco at the foot of the mattress.

Bathroom had dry towels, no condensation on the glass shower, and a Jacuzzi without a bubble bath ring.

His body went numb as he went back out into the hall and walked farther on.

At the door to the crib Saxton had been given, he stopped and stared at the panels. Excellent carpentry work, the pieces put together seamlessly. Paint job was perfect as well, with no brushstrokes marring the smooth surface. Nice brass knob, too, that was as shiny as a newly minted gold coin—

His acute hearing picked up on a soft sound and he frowned—until he realized what he was listening to. Only one thing made that kind of rhythmic . . .

Staggering back, he got goosed in the ass by the Greek statue directly behind him.

With stumbling feet, he blindly walked somewhere, anywhere. When he got to the king's study, he looked over his shoulder and checked the carpet over which he'd trodden.

No trail of his blood. Which, considering the way his chest was hurting, was a surprise.

Sure as shit felt like he'd been shot in the heart.

SIXTY-THREE

Xhex woke up screaming.

Fortunately, John had left the bathroom light on, so she had at least half a chance at convincing her brain where her body was: in fact, she was *not* back in that human clinic, being worked on like a lab rat. She was here in the Brotherhood mansion with John.

Who had leaped out of bed, and pointed a gun at the door to the hall like he was prepared to blow a hole right through the frickin' thing.

Slapping a hand over her mouth, she prayed she'd shut herself up in time, before she woke the entire house. The last thing she needed was a bunch of Brothers showing up at the doorstep with a whole lot of what's-doing.

In a silent shift, John swung the forty's muzzle around to the shuttered windows, and then he swept it over to the walk-in closet. As he finally lowered his weapon, he whistled an inquiry.

"I'm . . . okay," she answered, finding her voice. "Just a bad—"

The knock that cut her off was about as subtle as a curse in a quiet room. Or the scream she'd just let rip.

As she pulled the sheets up to her collarbones, John opened the door a crack and Z's voice drifted in. "Everything all right in here?"

Nope. Not even close.

Xhex rubbed her face and tried to replug into reality. Tough assignment. Her body felt weightless and disconnected, and man, that floaty thing was so not helping her on the get-grounded front.

It didn't take a genius to figure out why her subconscious had burped up that shit about her first trip through the abduction park. Staying in the OR while John had had his lead-ectomy had obviously been like a hot, spicy meal for her brain, with the nightmare being the cranial version of acid reflux.

Christ, she had a case of the fop sweats, her upper lip beading, her palms wringing damp.

In desperation, she focused on what she could see through the partially open door to the bathroom.

Turned out the toothbrushes on the marble counter saved her. The pair were standing up in the silver cup between the two sinks, looking like a couple of kibitzers who'd tilted their heads together to swap gossip. Both were John's, she was guessing, because guests were on the whole not welcome in this house.

One was blue. The other red. Both had the green bristles in the center that turned white over time to let you know when to get new ones.

Nice. Normal. Boring. Maybe if she'd had a little more of all that she wouldn't be looking for life's exit door. Or having nightmares that turned her voice box into a bullhorn.

John bade Z good-bye and came back over to her, leaving his gun on the bedside table and slipping under the covers. His warm body was solid and smooth against hers, and she went to him with an ease that she guessed was common among lovers.

But something she'd never had with anyone before.

As he pulled his head back so she could see his face, he mouthed, *What was it?*

"Dream. Very bad dream. From back when . . ." She took a deep breath. "When I was in that clinic."

He didn't press her for details. Instead, she just felt her hair getting stroked.

In the silence that followed, she didn't intend to talk

about the past—especially when the last thing she needed was more echoes of the nightmare. But somehow, words formed in her throat and she couldn't hold them back.

"I burned the facility down." Her heart thumped as she remembered, but at least the recall of what had happened wasn't as bad as being back there in a dream. "It's weird . . . I'm not sure the humans thought they were doing anything wrong—they treated me like a prized zoo animal, giving me everything I needed to survive while they poked and prodded at me and ran test after test . . . Well, most of the humans were good to me. There was a sadistic fuck in the group." She shook her head. "They kept me for about a month or two and tried to give me human blood to keep me going, but they could read the clinical indicators that I was getting weaker and weaker. I got free because one of them set me loose."

John rolled over on his back and put his hands into the shaft of light. *Shit, I'm so sorry. But I'm glad you dusted the place.*

In her mind, she pictured her return trip to where she'd been held—and the sooty aftermath. "Yeah, I had to burn the thing down. I'd been free for a while when I went back and did it—but I couldn't sleep for the nightmares. I lit the facility up after they'd left for the day. Although," she held a forefinger up, "there might have been one rather nasty death. But the son of a bitch deserved it. I'm an eye-for-an-eye kind of girl."

John's hands reappeared to sign, *That's pretty obvious—and not a bad thing at all.*

Provided it wasn't Lash, she thought to herself.

"Mind if I ask you something?" When he shrugged, she whispered, "The night you took me around town . . . had you been back to any of those places before?"

Not really. John shook his head. *I don't like to dwell on the past. I go forward.*

"How I envy you. Me, I can't seem to get free of history."

And it wasn't just about the clinic shit or Lash's little love-nest nightmare. For some reason, the fact that she'd never fit in—not with the family she'd grown up with, or the larger vampire society, or even the *symphath* one—resonated through her, defining her even when she wasn't consciously thinking about it. Her lock-and-key moments had been few and far between—and tragically seemed focused on when she'd gone out on jobs as an assassin.

Except then she thought of her time with John . . . and recalibrated the depressing arithmetic slightly. Being with him, their bodies together, that fit. But it was kind of a parallel to her murdering for hire—ultimately not a healthy thing for all involved. Hell, look at what had just happened: She woke up screaming and John was the one who weaponed up and faced off . . . while she played poor widdle scared female with the sheet clutched to her widdle scared heart.

That wasn't her. Just wasn't.

And God, that she'd fallen so easily into the role of being protected . . . that frightened her even more than dreams that made her scream. If life had taught her one thing, it was that your best bet was to take care of your own biz. The last thing in the world she wanted was to chick out and rely on anyone—even somebody as honorable and worthy and kind as John.

Although . . . man, the sex was good. Seemed base and a little crude to put it like that, but it was so very true.

When they'd come up here after their little tête à tête in the tunnel, they hadn't even bothered with the lights. No time, no time—clothes off, on the bed, going hard. She'd ended up passing out, and sometime later, John must have gotten up to use the loo and left the light on. Probably to make sure she didn't feel lost if she woke up.

Because that's the kind of male he was.

There was a click and whirl and the steel shutters began to lift for the night, the darkened sky revealed, her mental gyrations mercifully cut off.

She hated ruminating. Never solved anything and only made her feel worse.

"Hot water is calling us," she said, forcing her body upright. The delicious aches in her muscles and bones made her want to sleep for days in this big bed next to John. Maybe weeks. But that wasn't their destiny, was it.

She leaned over and looked down into his shadowy face. After tracing his handsome features with her eyes, she just had to bring up her hand and caress his cheek.

I love you, she mouthed in the shadows.

"Let's go," she said roughly.

The kiss she gave him was a sort of good-bye—after all, maybe tonight they finally got Lash, and that would mean an end to moments like this.

Abruptly, John gripped her upper arms, his brows tightening, but then, as if he read her mind and knew all too well the score, he released her.

As she got up and walked away from the bed, his eyes followed her . . . she could feel it.

In the bathroom, she started the water for them and went over to get some towels out of the cupboard.

She stopped as she saw her reflection in the mirror over the sink.

Her body was the same as it had always been, but she thought of the way it felt when she and John were together. She'd gotten so used to thinking of her corporeal form as little more than a weapon, something that was useful and necessary to accomplish things. Hell, she'd fed it and cared for it the same way she looked after her guns and her knives—because that was how she maintained its utility.

In their hours together, John had taught her differently, had shown her that there was profound pleasure to be had from her flesh. Which was something not even her relationship with Murhder had managed to do.

As if he'd been summoned by her thoughts, John came up behind her, his height and shoulder width dwarfing her reflection.

Meeting his eyes, she put her hand to her breast and rubbed her own nipple, remembering how it felt to have his touch there, his tongue, his mouth. The instant she made contact, his body responded, his bonding scent flooding the bathroom, his erection punching out of his hips.

Reaching behind herself, she pulled him against her, his arousal penetrating the wedge formed by her sex and her thighs. As his hips pushed in against her ass, his warm hands circled around her and stroked down her stomach. Bringing his head to her shoulder, his fangs flashed white as he delicately dragged them over her skin to the crook of her neck.

Arching back to him, she stretched way up and ran her hands through his thick dark hair. Although he'd cut it short, it was growing in, which was nice. She preferred it long because it felt so damn good going through her fingers, so silky, so smooth.

"Come inside me," she said hoarsely.

John swept his hand up and captured the breast she'd stroked for him; then he reached between their bodies, angled himself, and eased into her sex. At the same moment, he ran his fangs across her throat to her vein.

He didn't need to feed. She knew this. So she was strangely thrilled when he struck because it meant he was doing it just because he wanted to: He wanted her in him, too.

Beneath the overhead lighting, she watched as he took her from behind, his muscles flexing, his eyes burning, his erection pushing in and pulling out, pushing in and pulling out. She watched herself, too. Her breasts were tight at the tips, her nipples rosy, not just because that was the color of them, but because he'd been working on them so much over the day's hours. Her skin was aglow all over, her cheeks blazing, her lips puffy from the kissing, her eyes low-lidded and erotic.

John broke the seal he'd formed over her vein and his pink tongue came out, licking over the punctures, sealing them up. Turning her head, she captured his mouth with her own, relishing the slick slide of their tongues as their bodies followed the same rhythm down below.

It didn't take long for the sex to grow urgent and raw, no longer sensual, but powerful. As John's hips pistoned against her, their bodies slapped and their breath roared. Her orgasm tackled her so strongly that if he hadn't had a death grip on her hip bones, she would have lost her knees and fallen from him. And just as she came, John's own shudders rolled through her, the ripples emanating outward from his erection and sweeping through her body . . . and her soul.

And then it happened.

At the pinnacle of their release, her vision flipped into red and went flat—and as ectascy eventually faded, the unsummoned appearance of her bad side was a wake-up call she'd been subconsciously waiting for.

Gradually, she became aware of the growing humidity and warmth from the shower . . . and the twinkling sound of falling water . . . and the thousand points of contact between them . . . and how all things were in shades of blood.

John reached up to her face and touched next to her red eyes.

"Yeah, I need my cilices," she said.

He brought his hands forward in front of her and signed, *I have them.*

"You do?"

I saved them. He frowned. *But are you sure you have to—*

"Yes," she bristled. "I am."

The hard expression that tightened his face reminded her of the way he'd been when he'd sprung out of that bed as she'd screamed: Tough. Intractable. All-male. But there was nothing she could do to help him out of his current disapproval. She had to take care of herself, and whether or not he was down with what she did to keep herself in a "normal" bandwidth wasn't going to change her reality.

Man, they just weren't meant to be together, no matter how compatible they could be sometimes.

John withdrew from her core and stepped back, running his fingers down her spine as a kind of a thank-you . . . and given the dark knowledge in his eyes, probably a good-bye of his own. Turning away, he headed for the sh—

"Oh . . . my . . . God . . ."

Xhex's heart stopped as she looked at him in the mirror. Across his upper back, in a glorious spread of black ink . . . in a declaration that didn't whisper, but shouted . . . in a billboard-size font with flourishes . . .

Her name in the Old Language.

Xhex wheeled around as John froze. "When did you get that done?"

After a tense moment, his shoulder shrugged and she was captivated by the way the ink moved, stretching and then returning into place. Shaking his head, he reached in to test the warm spray, and then stepped through the glass door, put his back to the running water and grabbed the soap, frothing up the bar in his hands.

As he refused to look at her, he sent a clear message that her name in his skin was none of her business. Which was the same kind of line she'd drawn with her cilices, wasn't it.

Xhex went up to the glass door that separated them. Putting her hand up, she knocked hard.

When, she mouthed.

His eyes squeezed shut, as if he were remembering something that made his stomach hurt. And then with his lids down, he signed slowly . . . and broke her in half:

When I thought you weren't coming home.

John made quick work with the soap and the shampoo, very aware that Xhex was standing on the cold side of the glass, staring at him. He wanted to help her out with the surprise and all, but given where things stood between them, he was so not about to throw himself on the sword of all his feelings.

Or the tattoo needle, as it were.

When he'd asked her about the cilices, she'd been pretty clear about shutting him out—and that had rebooted his brain. Since he'd been injured the night before, they'd fallen back into their sex connection, and that had a way of blurring reality. But no more.

After he was finished with his wash-up, he stepped out of the shower and went past her, nabbing a towel from a brass bar and wrapping it around his hips. In the mirror, he met her eyes.

I'll go get your cilices, he signed.

"John . . ."

When she didn't say anything more, he frowned, thinking this was the pair of them in a nutshell: Standing three feet away from each other and being separated by miles.

He left and went into the bedroom, picking up a pair of jeans and pulling them on. His leather jacket had been brought in with him to the clinic the night before and he'd left it there. Somewhere.

In his bare feet, he walked past the marble statues, down the grand staircase, and around the corner to duck through the hidden door. Man . . . going back into the tunnel was a total crusher; all he could think about was Xhex and him together in the dark.

Like a complete nancy, he wished like hell they could return to those suspended moments when nothing existed except their roaring bodies. Down here, their hearts had been free to pound . . . and sing.

Fucking real life.

Sucked ass.

He was striding toward the training center's entrance when Z's voice stopped him.

"Yo, John."

John pivoted around, his bare feet squeaking on the tunnel floor. As he raised his hand in greeting, the Brother came striding down from the mansion's door and Z was dressed for fighting, his black leathers and muscle shirt something that they would all be wearing before they headed out once again to hunt Lash. With the Brother's skull trim, and the ceiling lights streaming down across that jagged scar on his face, it was no wonder people were scared shitless of him.

Especially with his stare narrowed like that and his jaw set grimly.

What's up, John signed as the Brother stopped in front of him.

When there was no immediate reply, John braced himself, thinking, Oh . . . fuck, now what.

What, he signed.

Zsadist exhaled a curse and started to pace around, his hands on his hips, his eyes locked on the floor. "I don't even know where to frickin' start."

John frowned and eased back against the tunnel wall, ready for more bad news. Although he sure as shit couldn't imagine what it was, life had a way of getting pretty damned creative, didn't it.

Eventually, Z halted and when he looked over, his stare was not golden yellow, as it usually was when they were home. It was pitch-black. Vicious black. And the male's face had gone the color of snow.

John straightened. *Jesus . . . what's wrong?*

"You remember all those walks you and I used to take in the woods. Just before your transition . . . after you lost it with Lash the first time." When John nodded, the Brother continued. "You ever ask yourself why Wrath put us together?"

John nodded slowly. *Yeah . . .*

"It wasn't a mistake." The Brother's eyes were cold and dark as the cellar in a haunted house, shadows making up not just the color of the irises but what lay behind that stare. "You and I have something in common. Do you understand what I'm saying. You and I . . . we have something in common."

At first John frowned again, not catching the drift—

Suddenly, he felt a cringing blast of cold shiver through his own body, one that reached his marrow. Z . . . ? Wait, had he heard it wrong? Was he taking this wrong?

Except then, clear as day, he remembered the two of them facing off at each other—right after the Brother had read what that psychologist had put in John's medical record.

You get to pick how you deal with it, because it's no one else's biz, Z had said. *You never want to say another fucking word on the subject, you're getting no lip from me.*

At that moment, John had been amazed by the Brother's unexpected understanding. As well as the fact that Z didn't seem to judge him or view him as weak.

Now he knew why.

God . . . *Z?*

The Brother held his palm up. "I'm not telling you

this to freak you out, and fuckin' A, I'd have preferred you never know—for reasons I'm sure you get. But I'm bringing it up because of your female's scream this morning."

John's brows pulled tight as the Brother took up pacing again.

"Look, John, I don't like people in my biz and I'm the last person who wants to talk about crap. But that scream . . ." Z faced off at John. "I've thrown too many of those out not to know what kind of hell you gotta be in to holler like that. Your girl . . . she's got some dark in her on a good day, but after Lash? I don't need no deets—but I can guess she's rattled and then some. Hell, sometimes after you're safe again—it's almost worse."

John scrubbed his face as his temples started to pound, and then he lifted his hands . . . only to find he had nothing to sign. The sadness that crushed him took his words away, leaving him with a strange, blank numbness in his head.

All he could do was nod.

Zsadist clapped him briefly on the shoulder and then resumed his back-and-forth. "Meeting and getting with Bella, that was my lifeboat. But it wasn't the only thing I needed. See, before we were mated proper, Bella left me—she took off and just left my ass for no damn good reason. I knew I had to do something to get my head on right if I was ever going to have a shot with her. So I talked to someone about . . . everything." Z cursed again and slashed his hand through the air. "And no, not some white coat at Havers's. Someone I trusted. Someone who was part of the family—who I knew wouldn't see me as dirty or weak or some shit."

Who, John mouthed.

"Mary." Z exhaled. "Rhage's Mary. We had the sessions down in the boiler room under the kitchen. Two chairs.

Right next to the furnace. It helped then and I still go back to her from time to time."

John could see the logic instantly. Mary had that kind, calm thing going on—which explained how she'd been able to tame not only the wildest Brother, but the son of a bitch's inner beast.

"That scream tonight . . . John, if you want to mate this female, you gotta help her with that. She needs to talk about her shit because if she doesn't, sure as fuck it's going to rot her from the inside out. And I spoke with Mary just now—without using any names. She's gotten her counseling degree and she said she's ready to work with someone. If you get a chance and the time is right with Xhex . . . tell her about this. Tell her to go talk to Mary." As Z rubbed his skull trim, the nipple rings he wore stood out in sharp relief under his black muscle shirt. "And if you want a testimonial, I can tell you on the life of my daughter that your female will be in good hands."

Thank you, John signed. *Yeah, I'll totally say something to her. Jesus . . . thank you.*

"No problem."

Abruptly, John locked eyes with Zsadist.

As the two held stares, it was hard not to feel part of a unique club that no one would ever volunteer to be associated with. Membership wasn't sought or desirable or something to crow about . . . but it was real and it was powerful: Survivors of similar wrecks could see the horrors of those jagged shoals in the eyes of others. It was like recognizing like. It was two people with the same tattoo on their insides, the divide of a trauma that separated them from the rest of the planet unexpectedly bringing a pair of weary souls closer together.

Or three, as was the case here.

Zsadist's voice was husky. "I killed the bitch who did it to me. Took her head with me when I left. You get that satisfaction?"

John shook his head slowly. *Wish I had.*

"Not going to lie. That helped me, too."

There was a tight, awkward silence, as if neither of them knew how to hit the *reset* button and get back to normal. Then Z nodded once and stuck out his fist.

John knocked those knuckles with his own, thinking, Shit, you never knew what was in someone's closet, did you.

Z's eyes glowed yellow once more as he turned away and walked back toward the door that would take him into the mansion and to his family, to his Brothers. In his back pocket, like he'd shoved it there and forgotten about it, was a pink baby's bib, the kind that had Velcro patches on the straps and a little skull and crossbones in black on the front.

Life goes on, John thought. No matter what the world did to you, you could survive.

And maybe if Xhex talked to Mary she wouldn't . . .

God, he couldn't even finish the thought because he feared defining her exit strategy.

Hustling on down into the training center, he headed for the clinic, where he found his jacket and his weapons and what Xhex needed.

As he picked up the shit, his mind was churning over things . . . things in the past, and in the present. Churning, churning, churning . . .

When he got back to the mansion, he beelined up the grand staircase and down the hall of statues. As soon as he walked into his room, he heard the shower running in the bath and had a brief, vivid image of Xhex gloriously naked and slick from the water and the soap suds— but he didn't go in and join her. He pulled the bed together and laid the cilices at the foot of it, then changed into his fighting gear and left.

He didn't go to First Meal.

He went down the hall to another bedroom. As he

knocked on the door, he had the sense that what he was about to do was a long time in coming.

When Tohr opened up, the Brother was half-dressed—and obviously surprised. "What's doing?"

Can I come in? John signed.

"Yeah, sure."

As John stepped inside, he felt an odd sense of premonition. But then when it came to Tohr, he'd always had them . . . that and a sense of deep connection.

He frowned while he looked at the male, thinking of the time they'd spent on that sofa downstairs, watching Godzilla movies while Xhex was out fighting in the daylight. It was funny; he was so comfortable around the guy that being with Tohr was like being alone without the solitude . . .

You've been following me, haven't you, John signed abruptly. *You're the one . . . the shadow I've sensed. At the tattoo parlor and the Xtreme Park.*

Tohr's eyes narrowed. "Yeah. That was me."

Why?

"Look, for real, it wasn't that I don't think you can handle yourself—"

No, it's not that. What I don't understand is . . . if you're well enough to be out in the field, why aren't you killing them? For . . . her. Why waste time with me?

Tohr breathed out a curse. "Ah, shit, John . . ." Long pause. And then, "You can't do anything more for the dead. They're gone. It's done. But the living . . . you can take care of the living. I know what kind of hell you've been in—and still are in—and I lost my Wellsie because I wasn't there when she needed me . . . I couldn't go through losing you for the same reason."

As the Brother's words faded, John felt like he'd been sucker punched—and yet he wasn't shocked. Because this was the kind of male Tohr was—steadfast and true. A male of worth.

The guy laughed harshly. "Don't get me wrong. Soon as you're out from under this Lash bullshit, and that bastard is good and dead, I'm going hard-core on those mother-fuckers. I will kill slayers in her memory for the rest of my natural life. But the thing is, I remember . . . see, I've been where you were when you were thinking your female was gone. No matter how levelheaded you believe your-self to be, you're insane in the membrane—and you were blessed to get her back, but life doesn't just return to rational that quick. Plus, let's face it—you'd do anything to save her, even put your chest in front of a bullet. Which I can understand, but would like you to avoid if at all possible."

As the Brother's words sank in, John signed automat-ically, *She's not my female.*

"Yeah, she is. And the two of you make so much sense. You have no idea what kind of sense you make together."

John shook his head. *Not sure who you're talking about there. No offense.*

"Doesn't have to be easy to be right."

In that case, we're meant for each other.

There was a long silence, during which John had the oddest sense that life was resetting itself, that the gears which had previously been slipping and missing had once more locked into place.

And here it was again, the Shitstorm Survivors' Club.

Christ, for all the crap that the people living in the mansion had been through, maybe V should design a tat they could each get on their asses. Because sure as shit, the bunch of them had won the lottery when it came to hard knocks.

Or, God, maybe this was just life. For everyone on the planet. Maybe the Survivors' Club wasn't something you "earned," but simply what you were born into when you came out of your mother's womb. Your heartbeat put you on the roster and then the rest of it was just a question of vocabulary: The nouns and verbs used to describe the events that rocked your foundation and sent you flailing were not always the same as other people's, but the random cruelties of disease and accident, and the malicious focus of evil men and nasty deeds, and the heartbreak of loss with all its stinging whips and rattling chains . . . at the core, it was all the same.

And there was no opt-out clause in the club's bylaws—unless you offed yourself.

The essential truth of life, he was coming to realize, wasn't romantic and took only two words to label: Shit. Happens.

But the thing was, you kept going. You kept your friends and your family and your mate as safe as you were able. And you kept fighting even after you were knocked down.

Goddamn it, you dragged your ass off the ground and *you kept fighting*.

I've been awful to you, John signed. *I'm sorry.*

Tohr shook his head. "Like I was any better? Don't apologize. As my best friend and your father always told me, don't look backward. Only forward."

So that's where it came from, John thought. The belief was in his blood.

I want you with me, by my side, John signed. *Tonight. Tomorrow night. For however long it takes to kill Lash. Do this with me. Find the bastard with me, with us.*

The sense that the pair of them would work together seemed so right. After all, for their individual reasons, they were united in this deadly game of chess: John needed to avenge Xhex for obvious reasons. And as for Tohr . . . well, the Omega had taken his son when that *lesser* had killed Wellsie. Now the Brother had a chance to return the motherfucking favor.

Come with me. Do this . . . with me.

Tohr had to clear his throat. "I thought you would never ask."

No knuckle-tap this time.

The two of them embraced, chest-to-chest. And when they pulled apart, John waited for Tohr to throw on a shirt, get his leather jacket, and grab his weapons.

Then they went downstairs side by side.

As if they had never been apart. As if it was as it always had been.

SIXTY-FOUR

The bedrooms at the back of the Brotherhood's mansion had the benefit not only of a view of the gardens, but a second-story terrace.

Which meant if you were antsy, you could step out and grab some fresh air before you faced the rest of the household.

The second the shutters lifted for the evening, Qhuinn opened the French doors by his bureau and walked into the brisk night. Bracing his palms on the balustrade, he leaned in, his shoulders accepting the weight of his chest easily. He was dressed for war in his leathers and shit-kickers, but he'd left his weapons inside.

Staring out over the battened-down flower beds and the spindly fruit trees that had yet to bloom, he felt the cool, smooth stone under his hands and the breeze in his still-damp hair and the tight pull of the muscles across the small of his back. The scent of freshly roasting lamb was floating up from the blowers on the roof over the kitchen and lights were glowing all over the house, the warm golden illumination pouring out onto the lawn and the patio on the lower level.

Pretty fucking ironic—to feel so hollow because Blay finally got fulfilled.

Nostalgia dropped its rose-tinted lens and through it he saw back to all those nights at Blay's, the two of them sitting on the floor at the end of the bed, playing PS2, drinking beer, watching vids. There had been serious and important shit to talk about then, things like what was doing in training classes and what game was coming

565

out over the human Christmas season and who was hotter, Angelina Jolie or anybody else in a skirt.

Angelina had always won. And Lash had always been an asshole. And Mortal Kombat had still ruled back then.

God, they hadn't even had Guitar Hero World Tour out in those days.

The thing was, he and Blay had always seen eye-to-eye, and in Qhuinn's world, where everyone hated his ass, having someone who understood him and accepted him as he was . . . It had been a shaft of tropical sunlight in the North fucking Pole.

Now, though . . . it was hard to comprehend how they'd started out so close. He and Blay were on two different paths . . . Having once had everything in common, now they had nothing except the enemy—and even there, Qhuinn had to stick with John, so it wasn't like he and Blay were partners.

Shit, the adult in him recognized that this was the way some things went. But the child in him mourned the loss more than—

There was a click and the breaking of a weather seal.

From out of a dark room that was not his own, Blay stepped onto the terrace. He was wearing a black silk dressing robe and was in bare feet, his hair wet from the shower.

There were bite marks on his neck.

He stopped as Qhuinn stood up from the balustrade.

"Oh . . . hey," Blay said, and immediately glanced back as if making sure the door he'd come through was shut.

Saxton was in there, Qhuinn thought. Sleeping on sheets they'd messed up royally.

"I was just going back inside," Qhuinn said, jabbing over his shoulder with his thumb. "It's too cold to be out here for long."

Blay crossed his arms over his chest and looked out over the view. "Yes. It's chilly."

After a moment, the guy stepped over toward the balustrade and the scent of his soap burrowed into Qhuinn's nose.

Neither of them moved.

Before he left, Qhuinn cleared his throat and threw himself off a bridge: "Was it okay. Did he treat you right?"

God, his voice was hoarse.

Blay took a deep breath. Then nodded. "Yeah. It was good. It was . . . right."

Qhuinn's eyes shifted away from his buddy—and just happened to measure the distance down to the stone patio below. Hmm . . . doing a swan dive onto all that slate might just get the images of those two out of his head.

Of course, it would also turn his brain into scrambled eggs, but really, was that such a bad thing?

Saxton and Blay . . . Blay and Saxton . . .

Shit, he'd been quiet awhile. "I'm glad. I want you to be . . . happy."

Blay didn't comment on that, but instead murmured, "He was grateful, by the way. For what you did. Thought it was a little overkill, but . . . he said you always were secretly chivalrous."

Oh, yeah. Totally. That shit was his middle name, riiiiiight.

Wonder what the guy would think if he knew Qhuinn wanted to drag him out of the house by all that gorgeous blond hair. Maybe stretch him flat on the pea gravel by the fountain and run him over with the Hummer a couple of times.

Actually, no, gravel wasn't the right surface. Better to drive the Hummer right into the foyer and do it there. You wanted something really hard beneath the body—like you would if you were pounding a cutlet on a cutting board.

He's your cousin, for godsakes, a small voice in him pointed out.

And . . . ? the larger half of him countered.

Before he totally freaked out and rocked a multiple personality disorder, he stepped back from the balustrade—and the whole homicidal thing. "Well, I'd better go. I'm heading out with John and Xhex."

"I'll be down in ten minutes. Just need to change."

As Qhuinn looked at his best friend's handsome face, he felt as if he'd never not known that red hair, those blue eyes, those lips, that jaw. And it was because of their long history that he searched for something to say, something that would get them back to where they had been.

All that came to him was . . . *I miss you. I miss you so fucking bad it hurts, but I don't know how to find you even though you're right in front of me.*

"Okay," Qhuinn said. "See you down at First Meal."

"Okay."

Qhuinn got his ass in gear and walked over to the door to his room. As he slid his grip around the cold brass handle, his voice rang out of his throat, loud and clear: "Blay."

"Yeah?"

"You take care of yourself."

Now Blay's voice was hoarse to the point of cracking. "Yeah. You, too."

Because of course, "take care of you" was what Qhuinn always said when he was letting someone go.

He went back inside and shut the door. Moving mechanically, he got the holsters for his daggers and his guns and picked up his leather jacket.

Funny, he could barely remember losing his virginity. He recalled the female, of course, but the experience hadn't made any kind of indelible impression. Neither had the orgasms he'd given and gotten since. Just a lot of fun, lot of sweaty gasping, lot of targets identified and realized.

Nothing but fucking that was easily forgotten.

Heading down to the foyer, though, he realized he was going to remember Blay's first for the rest of his life. The two of them had been drifting apart for some time, but now . . . the fragile cord that had been the last of their connection, that dwindling tie, had been cut.

Too bad the freedom seemed like a prison instead of a horizon.

As his boots hit the mosaic floor at the bottom of the stairs, John Mellencamp's old-school, Bic-lighter anthem echoed in his head—and though he'd always liked the song okay, he'd never truly understood what it meant.

Kind of wished that were still the case.

Life goes on . . . long after the thrill of living is gone . . .

In John's bathroom, Xhex stood under the hot water, her arms over her chest, her feet planted on either side of the drain, the water hitting her in the back of the head before blanketing her shoulders and flowing down her spine.

John's tattoo . . .

Goddamn . . .

He'd done it as a memorial to her—putting her name in his skin so she'd be with him always. After all, there was nothing more permanent than that—hell, that was why in the mating ceremony males got their backs carved up: Rings could get lost. Documents could be shredded or burned or misplaced. But it wasn't like you didn't take your epidermis with you everywhere you went.

Man, she'd never really cared two shits about those females in the dresses with their hair so long and pretty and the makeup all over their pusses and the gentle nature crap. If anything, those trappings of femininity had seemed like a declaration of weakness. But now, for a quiet moment, she found herself envying the silk and perfume set. What pride they must take in knowing that their males carried their commitment around on their bodies for every night they were alive.

John would be a wonderful *hellren*—

Jesus . . . when he did mate, what the hell was he going to do about that tattoo? Put his female's name under it?

Right, Xhex was not psyched at having top billing on his shoulders for the rest of his life. Really. Not at all. Because that would make her a selfish bitch, wouldn't it.

Oh, wait, that had pretty much been her theme song.

Forcing herself out of the shower, she toweled off and traded all the toasty warm, humid air in the bath for the cold smack of the stuff in the bedroom.

She stopped just past the doorjamb. Across the way, the duvet had been straightened with a casual hand, what had been messy now pulled up sort of into place.

Her cilices were at the base of the mattress. And unlike the covers, they had been arranged with care, the links smoothed out, the two lengths lined up together.

She walked over and ran a fingertip down the barbed metal. John had kept them for her—and instinct told her he would have held on to them even if she had never come back.

Helluva legacy to leave behind.

And if she was staying in the house for the night, she would have put them on. Instead, she drew her leathers on without them, pulled on her muscle shirt, and gathered up her weapons and her jacket.

Thanks to her having played lawn sculpture under the showerhead, she'd missed First Meal so she went directly to the meeting in Wrath's study. All of the

Brotherhood as well as John and his boys were jammed into the pale blue French study—and most everyone, including George, the Seeing Eye dog, was milling around.

Only person missing was Wrath. Which kind of put the brakes on things, didn't it.

Her eyes sought out and held on to John, but short of a nod in her general direction, he stared straight ahead, looking only at those people who wandered through his field of vision. At his side, Tohrment was standing tall and strong, and reading the pair's emotional grids, she got the sense they had reestablished a connection that meant a hell of a lot to both of them.

Which made her honestly happy. She hated the idea of John being alone after she left, and Tohrment was the father he'd never had.

With a nasty curse, Vishous stabbed out one of his hand rolls. "Damn it to hell, we've got to go even if he isn't here. We're wasting darkness."

Phury shrugged. "He gave a direct order for this meeting, though."

Xhex was inclined to take V's side, and given the way John shifted his weight back and forth on his shitkickers, she wasn't the only one.

"Look, you people can hang around," she barked. "But I'm leaving now."

As John and Tohr looked over at her, she had the oddest ripple go through her mind, as if it wasn't just the two males who'd been reunited in the quest to find Lash, but that she was likewise in the mix with them.

Then again, they all had scores to settle, didn't they. Whether it was the Lessening Society or Lash specifically, the three of them all carried the kind of grudges that made you want to kill.

Ever the voice of reason, Tohrment cut through the tension. "Okay, fine, I'll assume responsibility for the go order. Clearly his little 'exercise' sesh over on the Far Side is still rolling, and he wouldn't want us pissing away the night just for him."

Tohr split everyone up into teams, with John, Xhex, Z, himself, and the boys going to the address the street racer was registered to, and the rest of the Brotherhood apportioned between the farmhouse and the Xtreme skate park. In no time at all, the group was down the staircase, through the vestibule, and out the front door. One by one, they disappeared into the cold air . . .

When Xhex took form again, it was in front of an apartment building downtown in the old meatpacking district—although *building* was probably too kind a word for the place. The six-story brick structure had walleyed windows and a sagging roof that needed the construction equivalent of a chiropractor—or maybe a body cast. And she was pretty sure the line of pockmarks across the front had been created by the spray of a machine gun or maybe an autoloader whose shooter had had a case of the DTs.

Made you wonder how the humans at the DMV had accepted the address as a residence when that car got its license plate. Then again, maybe no one had checked to see whether what was listed was inhabitable.

"Charming," Qhuinn bit out. "If you want to breed rats and cockroaches."

Let's go around back, John signed.

There were two alleys that ran down both sides of the shithole, and they randomly picked the one on the left for absolutely no good reason. As they jogged along, they passed by your standard-issue city detritus—nothing new, nothing remarkable, just beer cans, candy wrappers and newspaper pages. The good news was that there were no windows on the flanks of the fugly building, but then it wasn't like there was anything to see other than the other slaughterhouses and packing facilities—plus maybe the stability of all that load-bearing brick was the reason the roof hadn't become the floor.

Xhex bounced on the balls of her feet as she ran with the males, the bunch of them falling into a quick rhythm that carried them down the alley efficiently and in relative quiet. The back of the structure was nothing but more red brick streaked with metro-grime. Only difference was that the reinforced-steel door opened out into a small parking lot instead of a surface road.

No *lessers*. No human pedestrians. Nothing but stray cats, filthy asphalt, and the distant wailing of sirens.

A sense of powerlessness overcame her. Goddamn it, she could show up here or across town at that ridiculous park or out in the sticks. But there was no making the enemy come to her. And they had so little to go on.

"For fuck's sake," Qhuinn muttered. "Where the hell's the party."

Yup, she wasn't the only one spoiling for a fight—

From out of nowhere, Xhex felt a tingling go through her, the resonant echo something that at first she didn't understand. She glanced at the rest of the team. Blay and Qhuinn were studiously not looking at each other. Tohr and John were pacing around. Zsadist had his phone out to report to the Brothers they were at the mark.

That pull . . .

And then she realized: She was sensing her blood in another.

Lash.

Lash was not far.

Blindly turning on her heel, she headed off . . . walking, then breaking into a run. She heard her name being shouted, but there was no stopping to explain.

Or stopping her.

SIXTY-FIVE

On the Far Side, as Payne lay in an unnatural position on hard marble, her namesake overwhelmed her—but only above her waist. She felt no agony in her legs or feet, only a disassociated tingling that made her think of fire sparks over damp kindling wood. Directly above her broken body, the Blind King was leaning o'er, his face tight—and the Scribe Virgin had also made an appearance, that black robe and dim light floating around in circles.

It was not a shock that her mother had come to magically fix her. Like that door which had gone from shambles to saved, her darling mother wanted to wipe away everything, neaten it all up, make everything perfect.

"I . . . refuse," Payne said again through gritted teeth. "I do not consent."

Wrath glanced over his shoulder at the Scribe Virgin, then looked back down. "Ah . . . listen, Payne, that's not logical. You can't feel your legs . . . your back's probably broken. Why won't you let Her help you?"

"I am not some inanimate . . . object She can manipulate at will . . . to please her whims and fancy—"

"Payne, be reasonable—"

"I am—"

"You're going to die—"

"Then my mother can watch me expire!" she hissed—and then promptly moaned. In the wake of her outburst, consciousness ebbed and flowed, her eyes blurring and then regaining focus, Wrath's shocked expression becoming that by which she measured whether she had fainted or not.

"Wait, she's . . ." The king braced his hand against the marble floor to steady his crouching position. "Your . . . *mother?*"

Payne cared not that he knew. She had never felt any pride associated with being the birthed daughter of the race's founder—had in fact sought at every turn to distance herself—but what did it matter now. If she refused "divine" intervention, she would go unto the Fade from here. What pain she did feel told her this.

Wrath twisted around to the Scribe Virgin. "This is the truth?"

No affirmative answer came back to him, but nor did a denial. And there was no chastisement that he had dared offend by his inquiry, either.

The king looked back at Payne. "Jesus . . . Christ."

Payne dragged in a breath. "Leave us, dear King. Go forth unto your world and lead your people. You need no help from this side or Her. You are a fine male and a brilliant warrior . . ."

"I'm not going to let you die," he spat.

"You have no choice, do you."

"The fuck I don't." Wrath shot to his feet and glared downward. "Let Her heal you! You're out of your goddamn mind! You can't die like this—"

"I most certainly . . . can." Payne shut her eyes, a wave of exhaustion rolling through her.

"Do something!" Clearly the king was now yelling at the Scribe Virgin.

Too bad she felt like such hell, Payne thought. Otherwise, she most certainly would have enjoyed this final declaration of independence. Verily, it had come upon the wings of her death, but she had done it. Stood up to her mother. She had gotten her freedom through her refusal.

The Scribe Virgin's voice was barely louder than breath. "She has denied my help. She is blocking me."

She certainly was. Her fury was directed at her mother to such an extent, it wasn't hard to believe that it functioned as a barrier to whatever magic the Scribe Virgin might seek to bear upon the "tragedy" that had occurred.

Which in fact felt more like a blessing.

"You're all-powerful!" The king's voice was a rough charge—the frantic nature of which was a tad confusing. But then, he was a male of worth who would no doubt place the blame upon himself. "Just fix her!"

There was a silence and then a weak reply: "I can no more reach her body . . . than I can her heart."

Verily, if the Scribe Virgin was finally getting a sense of what it was to be without power . . . Payne could die in peace.

"Payne! Payne, wake up!"

Her lids lifted. Wrath was inches from her face.

"If I can save you, will you let me?"

She couldn't understand why she was so important to him. "Leave me—"

"If I can do it, will you let me?"

"You can't."

"Answer the fucking question."

He was such a good male, and the fact that her demise would be upon his conscience e'ermore was a sorrow. "I'm sorry . . . about this. Wrath. I'm sorry. This is not your doing."

Wrath turned upon the Scribe Virgin. "Let me save her. *Let me save her!*"

Upon the demand, the Scribe Virgin's hood lifted of its own volition, and her once glowing form appeared nothing but a dingy shadow.

The visage and the voice she put forth was that of a beautiful female in tremendous agony: "I did not want this destiny."

"That and a pile of shit gets you nothing. *Will You let me save her.*"

The Scribe Virgin shifted her stare to the opaque heaven above her and the tear that fell from her eye landed on the marble flooring as a diamond, bouncing with a shimmer and a flash.

That lovely object would be the last thing Payne ever saw, she thought as her eyes became so heavy, she could no longer keep her lids open.

"For fuck's sake," Wrath bellowed. "Let me—"

The Scribe Virgin's answer came from a vast distance. "I can fight this no longer. Do what you will, Wrath, son of Wrath. Better she be away from me and alive, than dead upon my floor."

Everything went quiet.

A door was shut.

Then Wrath's voice: *I need you on the Other Side. Payne, wake up, I need you on the Other Side . . .*

Odd. It was as if he were speaking into her skull . . . but he was more likely leaning back down over her and talking aloud.

"Payne, wake up. I need you to get yourself over to my side."

In a haze, she started to shake her head—but that impulse wasn't borne out well. Better to hold still. Very still. "I don't . . . can't get there—"

A sudden, twirling vertigo sent her reeling, her feet swinging around and around her body, her mind the vortex about which she spun. The sense of being sucked downward was accompanied by a pressure in her veins, as if her blood were expanding, but was confined to tight quarters.

When she opened her eyes, she saw a lofty white glow above her.

So she hadn't moved, then. She was where she had been lying all along, beneath the milky sky of the Far Side—

Payne frowned. No, that wasn't the strange heaven o'er the sanctuary. That was a . . . ceiling?

Yes . . . she recognized what it was—and indeed, in her peripheral vision, she sensed walls . . . four pale blue walls. There were lights as well, although not ones that she remembered—not torches or lit candles, but things that glowed without flame.

A fireplace. A . . . massive desk and throne.

She hadn't moved her body here herself; she hadn't the strength. And Wrath could not have cast her corporeal form forth. There was but one explanation. She had been expelled by her mother.

There would be no going back; she had her wish. She was free, e'ermore.

An odd peace o'ercame her, one that was either the calming pall of death . . . or the realization that the fight was over. Indeed, live or die, that which had defined her for years had passed, a weight lifted that sent her flying anew in her as yet still flesh.

Wrath's face came into her field of vision, his long black hair slipping free of his shoulders and falling forward. And at that moment, a blond dog ducked under the heavy arm of the king, its kind face holding a welcoming inquiry, as if she were an unexpected but very appreciated guest.

"I'm going to get Doc Jane," Wrath said, stroking the flank of the dog.

"Who?"

"My private physician. Stay here."

"As if . . . I'm going anywhere?"

There was the jangle of a collar and then the king left, his hand on a harness that connected him with the beautiful dog, the animal's paws clipping on the floor when they reached the edge of the rug and hit hardwood.

He truly was blind. And here on this side, he needed someone else's eyes to function.

A door shut and then she thought of naught but the

pain. She was floating, rendered buoyant by the agony in her body—and yet, in spite of the incredible discomfiture, she was aloft on a strange peacefulness.

For no evident reason, she noted that the air had a lovely smell here. Lemon. Beeswax.

Just lovely.

Fates be, her time on this side had been long ago and, going by how strange things looked, in a different world. But she remembered how much she had liked it. Everything had been unpredictable and therefore captivating . . .

Sometime later, the door opened and she heard once more the jangle of the dog's collar and caught Wrath's powerful scent. And there was someone with them . . . who didn't register in a way that Payne could process. But there was definitely another entity in the room.

Payne forced open her eyes . . . and nearly recoiled.

It was not Wrath standing o'er her, but a female . . . or at least it appeared to be a female. The face had feminine lines—except the features and the hair were translucent and ghostly. And as their stares met, the female's expression shifted from concerned to shocked. Abruptly, she had to steady herself on Wrath's arm.

"Oh . . . my God . . ." The voice was rough.

"Is it that obvious, Doc?" the king said.

As the female struggled to respond, it was not the sort of reaction one hoped to engender in a physician. Verily, Payne had thought that she was well aware of how injured she was. However, it might well be that she was unclear as to the gravity of her condition.

"Verily, am I—"

"Vishous."

The name froze her heart.

For she had not heard it in well over two centuries.

"Wherefore speaketh thou of my dead?" she whispered.

The physician's ghostly face took tangible form, her forest green eyes revealing a deep confusion, her flesh carrying the pallor of someone fighting emotions. "Your dead?"

"My twin . . . is long passed unto the Fade."

The physician shook her head, her brows dropping low over that intelligent stare. "Vishous is alive. I'm mated to him. He's alive and well here."

"No . . . it cannot be." Payne wished she could reach up and grab the doctor's solid arm. "You lie—he is dead. He is long—"

"No. He is very much alive."

Payne couldn't understand the words. She had been told he was gone, lost to the Fade's tender mercies—

By her mother. Of course.

Verily, had the female cheated her out of knowing her own brother? How could one be so cruel?

Abruptly, Payne bared her fangs and growled low in her throat, the fire of anger displacing her agony. "I will kill Her for this. I swear I will treat Her as I did our blooded sire."

SIXTY-SIX

John took off after Xhex the instant she left the group and started running. He didn't like the independent thinking or her direction—she was heading into an alley where no one knew whether there was an exit or a brick wall at the end.

He caught up with her, taking her arm to get her attention. Which got him exactly nowhere. She didn't stop.

Where are you going? he tried to sign, but it was tough to do that to a person who was ignoring you while you were gunning full tilt . . .

He would have whistled but that was too easy to ignore, so he tried again to get her arm, but she shook him off, focused solely on a destination he could neither see nor sense. Finally, he just jumped in front of her and blocked her way; then forced her to see his hands.

Where the hell are you going?

"I can feel him . . . Lash. He's close."

John went for his dagger as he mouthed, *Where?*

She jogged around him and resumed her pursuit, and as he followed, Tohr fell in step with them. When the others started to come along, John shook his head and motioned for them to stay put. Additional support in the field was a smart thing, but too many weapons in this sitch were not a value-add: He was going to take Lash out, and the last thing he needed was more trigger-happy fingers pointed at his target.

Tohr understood, though. He knew viscerally why John had to avenge his female. And Qhuinn had to come along. But that was it, no more cups and saucers welcome at the tea party.

John stuck close to Xhex—who seemed to have chosen wisely when it came to alleys. Instead of a dead end, the uneven lane rolled around to the right and wheedled in between other vacant warehouses as it headed down to the river. He knew they were getting really close to the water when the smell of dead fish and algae wafted up into his nose and the air seemed to grow colder.

They found the black Mercedes AMG parked in front of a fire hydrant. The sedan stank of *lesser*, and as Xhex looked around as if searching for the next directive, John wasn't in the mood to wait.

He curled up a fist and punched out the front windshield.

The alarm went apeshit, and he glanced into the interior. There was some kind of oily residue on the steering wheel, and the cream leather was trashed with stains— he was damn sure the inky ones were *lesser* blood . . . and that rusty-colored shit was human. Jesus, the backseat looked as if it had been hit with a spastic cat, the scratches so deep in places, the stuffing underneath was showing.

John frowned, remembering back to training-center days. Lash had always been so particular about his stuff, from the clothes he wore to the way his locker was organized.

Maybe this wasn't his car?

"This is his," Xhex said, placing her palms on the hood. "I can smell him everywhere. Engine's still warm. I don't know where he is, though."

John snarled at the thought of the guy getting so close to his female that she knew him by nose. Fucking bastard son of a bitch—

Just as his anger was getting away from him, Tohr grabbed him by the back of the neck and gave him a shake. "Deep breath."

"He's got to be around here . . ." Xhex looked at the building in front of them and then glanced up and down the alley they were in.

When John felt a burning pain in his left hand, he brought up his arm. His grip on his dagger had tightened so hard, the handle was creaking in protest.

His eyes slipped to Tohr's.

"You're going to get him," the Brother whispered. "Don't you worry about that."

Lash half-expected Benloise's men to pop some shit as he faced off at the pair of thick necks. He was separated from them by about ten yards of cold air, and everyone had their twitch on.

As he looked them over, he hoped they did John Wayne it and try something. The two thugs would have made an excellent addition to his growing stable—they knew the trade and had obviously earned their stripes under Benloise: there were a lot of kilos in those metal suitcases they had in their hands, but the humans were coolheaded and calm.

Armed to the teeth, too.

Just like Lash. Goddamn, it was a real Lead Rave here with all the guns and ammo—and wasn't he going to feel a whole lot better after there was less of him to get shot at. Shadow was better than flesh, anytime.

"Here's the art," the guy on the left said as he hefted the cases. "Sir."

Ah, yes, the one who'd watched the shit roll out with Benloise. Explained why they were both being so polite.

"Let's see what you got," Lash murmured, keeping the muzzle of his forty trained on them. "And let's have your hands stay nice and visible."

The flash of goods was efficient and satisfactory, the pair working together with the shuffle and reveal.

Lash nodded. "Leave the product. Go."

The humans pulled a Simon Says and put down the drugs, backed away, and then briskly walked in the opposite direction, keeping their hands by their sides.

As soon as they turned a corner and their footfalls continued to echo away, Lash strode over to the briefcases and opened his shadowy palms. On command, the handles popped up and the two loads of coke levitated from the asphalt into his grip—

The shrill sound of a car alarm brought his head around, the mad beeping coming from the alley where he'd left his AMG.

Fucking human pieces of shit downtown—

Lash frowned as his instincts rippled outward and located that which had been taken from him.

She was here.

Xhex . . . his Xhex was here.

As what was left of his vampire side roared with possession, Lash found his body vibrating until his feet were removed of their burden and he moved over the asphalt with the wind, leaning into the momentum he created with his mind, not his legs. Faster. Faster—

He came around the corner and there she was, standing by his car, looking like pure sex in her leathers and her jacket. The instant he appeared, she turned toward him as if he had called out to her.

Even with no lights shining down on her, Xhex was resplendent, the ambient illumination of the city gathering to her body, like her inner charisma demanded it. Fucking wow. She was one hot bitch, especially in the fighting gear, and as the hollow space in front of his hips tingled, he reached down.

Something was hard. Behind his fly, something was there and ready for her.

With a shot of adrenaline that was better than any kind of coke, he entertained how much fun it would be to take her with an audience. His cock had returned in .

some form or another and that meant he was back in business—just in time.

As she met his eyes, he slowed his speed and focused on who was with her. The Brother Tohrment. Qhuinn, the mismatched genetic failure. And John Matthew.

The perfect peanut gallery for some *Clockwork Orange* shit.

How. Fucking. Fabulous.

Lash lowered himself down to the ground and set the briefcases on the asphalt. The idiot males she was with were all busy popping various kinds of heat—but not his Xhex. Nope, she was stronger than that.

"Hey, baby," he said. "Miss me?"

Someone let out a growl that reminded him of his rottweiler, but whatever, now that he had everyone's attention, he was going to take advantage of the stage time. Willing the raincoat's hood from his head, he reached up, his shadow hands undoing the black strips that covered his face to reveal his features.

"Jesus Christ . . ." Qhuinn muttered. "You look like a Rorschach test."

Lash didn't dignify that with a response, mostly because the only one he cared about was the female in the leather. Obviously, she hadn't expected his transformation, and the way she recoiled? Better than a hug and a kiss. To disgust her was just as good as turning her on—and much more fun when he got her back and booked their asses some time in a honeymoon suite.

Lash smiled and sent his new, improved voice out into the air. "I have such plans for you and me, bitch. 'Course, you're going to have to beg me for it—"

The goddamn fucking female disappeared.

Right into thin air.

One moment she was standing by his car; the next there was nothing but air where she had been. Bitch was still in the alley, though. He could sense her, just not see her—

The first gunshot that rang out came from behind him and caught him in the shoulder—or didn't, as was the case. The trench coat shredded on impact, blowing out a flap, but the nonflesh beneath couldn't have cared less—and all he felt was an odd echoing sting.

Niiiiiice. Otherwise that might have hurt.

He cranked his head around, frankly unimpressed by how obvious she was being and how bad her aim was.

Except Xhex hadn't been the one throwing the lead. Benloise's boys had shown up with reinforcements, and good thing they couldn't aim for shit. Last time he'd checked, his chest was still solid, so a couple of inches down and to the center and he might have had a sieve for a heart.

Rage at the goddamn nerve of those fucking drug slingers had Lash boiling up a ball of lights-out-asshole in his palm.

As he flashed back into an inset doorway, he cast the energy force down at the humans, the blast providing a helluva show as it bowling-balled the bastards, illuminating their bodies all manga-style as they were thrown to the sides in the wake of the rollout.

By this point, more Brothers had arrived and all kinds of people had started shooting, various guns getting a workout—which was no big deal until Lash took a slug in the hip, the pain scorching through his torso and making his heart ricochet around. As he cursed and fell to the side, his eyes shifted to the alley.

John Matthew was the only one who hadn't taken cover: Team Brother had ducked behind the Mercedes and Benloise's guys had dragged themselves behind the rusted-out shell of a Jeep.

But John Matthew had his shitkickers planted on the ground and his hands down at his sides.

Fucker made himself one hell of a target. It was almost a bore.

Lash summoned up another ball of energy in his palm and shouted, "You're killing yourself sure as if you put a gun to your head, you bitch-ass motherfucker."

John started walking forward, his fangs bared, a cold rush waving out ahead of him.

For a moment, Lash felt a prickle of tension filter through the nape of his neck. This couldn't be right. No one in their right mind would ride up on his grille like this.

It was suicide.

SIXTY-SEVEN

Plans, plans, plans . . .

Or, in other words, bullshit, bullshit, bullshit . . .

Xhex had had the perfect plan when she'd cloaked herself in the manner of *symphaths* and whispered out of sight. As an assassin, she had prided herself not only on her success rate, but the flair she brought to her work, and this payback was going to be good. Her "plan" had been to flank up on Lash unseen and slice his throat before going to work on him—while she looked in his eyes and smiled like the crazy bitch she was.

First wrinkle? What the *fuck* had happened to him since she'd seen him last? The reveal he'd pulled unwrapping his head had stunned the crap out of her. He had no flesh left on his face; there was nothing but black-slicked muscle fibers and jarring bones, his bright white teeth looking fluorescent in contrast. And his hands weren't right, either. They had form, not substance. In the shadowy night . . . they were nothing but a deeper shade of darkness.

Thank God she'd gotten away from him when she did—although maybe all that decaying was the reason she'd been able to break out of her prison: It seemed logical to assume his powers were weakening as well.

But whatever . . . her second problem in Plan Land? John. Who right now was standing in the center of the alley with everything but a sign saying SHOOT ME HERE on his chest.

It was pretty frickin' obvious that there would be no reasoning with him—even if she took form right next to his ear and screamed into his brain, she knew there was no derailing him. He was all animal as he faced off at his enemy, his fangs bared like a lion's, his body arching forward like he was going to pile-drive the guy.

Pretty good bet that he was going to die if he didn't take cover, but he didn't seem to care and the why was clear: His bonding scent was louder than any noise he could have made with his throat, the dark spice a roar that overcame every other smell, from the city's body odor to the river's sweat to the *lesser* stench that was wafting up from Lash's rotting body.

Standing in the gritty alley, John was the primordial male protecting his female—and everything she hadn't wanted in this situation for precisely this reason: Clearly, his personal safety meant nothing to him, his objective overriding all his common sense and specific training.

Bottom line? He wasn't going to be able to survive whatever energy ball Lash was palming up . . . and that reality shifted everything in her world.

New plan. No cloaking anymore for her. No disable, disarm, dismember. No extraction of pain for the agony she had been through, no Jack the Ripper routine.

As she took form and lunged at Lash, it was about saving John, not avenging herself. Because when it came down to it? Turned out John was the only thing that mattered to her.

She tackled Lash around the waist at the very moment he started to throw his ball of knock-down, and though she took him to the ground with her, he managed to course-correct his aim . . . and hit John square in the chest.

The impact blew her male off the pavement, sweeping him up and back, all but blowing him out of his boots.

"You fucking bastard!" she screamed into Lash's stripped face.

The son of a bitch's arms snapped around her, locking on with incredible strength. And as he flipped her around and pinned her to the pavement beneath him, his breath was hot and foul on her face.

"Gotcha," he sneered, grinding his hips into hers, his erection enough to make her sick.

"Fuck you!" With a quick jerk, she nailed him right in the . . . well, what passed for a nose . . . with a head butt that had him howling.

Unfortunately, she didn't get another clean shot as they struggled for control, rolling around, their legs intertwining, that horrible arousal of his pushing at her. He managed to snag one of her wrists, but at least she kept the other one out of his way.

Which meant when the time was right, she was able to reach between them, grab his balls, and twist them so hard, if it hadn't been for his pants, she'd have broken the fuckers off.

Lash wheezed out a curse and went rigid, proving that he might have been a demigod on the dark side, but he was pretty fucking mortal when it came to taking a hit in the jewels.

Now she was the one in control of the ground game, spinning him over onto his back and straddling him. "Got *you*," she snapped at him.

As she held him down, rage got the better of her— instead of stabbing him outright, she gripped him around the neck and squeezed the air out of his throat.

"You don't fuck with what's mine," she growled at him.

Lash's ugly-ass puss went vicious pissed and somehow his voice emanated up even with the lock she had on his larynx. "He's already been fucked good. Or didn't he tell you about that human who—"

Xhex cuffed the SOB so hard, she took a tooth with her on the follow-through. "Don't you dare go there—"

"I'll go anywhere the fuck I want, sweetheart."

With that, he ghosted on her, dissolving into nothing—but that didn't last. An instant later, she was taken from behind, grabbed, and pulled up hard against his body. In the still seconds that followed, she had a brief impression of the humans who were moaning on the asphalt, and then she was swung around and used as a shield as she and Lash faced the Brothers.

Her eyes didn't waste time checking her team's positions behind the Mercedes or measuring what weapons were pointed in her and Lash's direction.

John was the only thing that mattered.

And thank God, the Scribe Virgin . . . or whoever granted mercies . . . that he was sitting up and shaking off whatever strobe-light nightmare had ass-over-elbowed him.

At least he was alive.

She was probably not going to survive this, but John . . . he was going to live. Provided she got herself and Lash out of here.

"Take me," she hissed to the bastard. "Just take me and leave them."

There was a whisper of metal against metal and then a switchblade appeared in front of her face, the blade flashing right next to her eye—so close, she could make out the inscription of the manufacturer's name.

"You like to get real personal with your kills." Lash's voice was so not right, the distortion in it making his words ripple in her ear. "I know this because of what you did to that fool Grady. Gave him one hell of a last meal—wonder if he liked sausage in life as much as he did in death?"

The point of the weapon dipped out of her visual field . . . and then she felt the tip go into her cheekbone and drag slowly downward.

The breeze was cool. Her blood was warm.

Closing her eyes, all she could do was repeat, "Take me."

"Oh, I will. Don't you worry about that." Something wet drew up over the wound—his tongue lapping at what had welled up. Then he called out, "She tastes as good as I remember— Stop *right* there. Anyone takes another step forward, and I'll slice her where it counts."

The blade went to her throat and Lash started walking backward, dragging her with him. On instinct, she tried to get inside his head in the event her *symphath* side could influence him, but she was blocked sure as if she were in front of a stone wall. Not a surprise.

Abruptly, she wondered why he didn't cloak them both—

He was limping. He'd taken a bullet somewhere— and now that she was properly focused, she could smell his blood, and see it glistening on the pavement.

As Lash kept going, those sorry-ass humans came into sight again, and they looked like corpses, all pale and stiff to the point where she was amazed they could make any noises at all. Their car, she thought. Lash was going to try to take the two of them back to whatever ride those boys had come in. And although he was compromised on some levels, his grip on her was viciously strong, and that knife? Steady and ready.

Xhex stared down at John and knew she would remember the magnificent sight of his warrior's vengeance forever—

She frowned as she sensed his emotions. How . . . strange. That shadow she had always sensed in the lee of his grid wasn't a mere second-stringer anymore—it was as tangible and vivid as that which had always been the primary construct within his psyche.

In fact, as he stared up the alley, the two parts of him . . . became one.

After John had been hit with that bomb of energy, he was dazed and disoriented, but he forced his head to get back in the game and somehow managed to heave himself off the ground. He couldn't feel some portion of his body, and the other half that wasn't numb screamed in pain, but neither mattered. Deadly purpose animated him, replacing the beat of his heart as the driver of his physical form.

Locking his eyes on the scene before him, his hands twitched and his shoulders tightened. Lash was using Xhex as a living shield, all his best target points hidden behind her as he pulled her away.

That knife to her throat was right on her vein. Pressing against her . . .

In a quick twist, reality warped and distorted on him, his sight fuzzing out and becoming clear, only to lose its grip on the alley they were all in once more. Blinking hard, he cursed the tricks that Lash had at his disposal—

Except the problem wasn't what John had been hit with. It was something inside of him—a vision. A vision was boiling up from somewhere deep in his mind, wiping out what he was actually seeing . . .

A field by a barn. In the dark of night.

He shook his head and was relieved when the alley in Caldwell came back—

A field by a barn. In the dark of night . . . a female who mattered held in an evil lock, a knife to her throat.

And then he was abruptly back in the present, returning here to the warehouse district . . . where a female who mattered was held in an evil lock, a knife to her throat.

Oh, God . . . he felt like he had done this before.

Fuck that . . . he *had* done this before.

The epileptic fit came over him as it always did, scrambling his neurons, sending him flying in his own skin.

Usually he ended up on his ass, but the bonded male in him kept him upright, giving him a kind of power that came from the soul, not the body: His female was in the arms of a killer and every cell in John's body was going to rectify the situation in as violent and fast a manner as possible.

Or maybe even a little bloodier and quicker than that.

He moved his hand into his coat for his gun . . . but shit, what was there to shoot at? Lash wasn't taking any chances with his own vital organs and his grotesque head was so close to hers, there was no room for error.

John's fury screamed inside of him—

In his peripheral vision, he saw a gun muzzle come up.

Blink.

A field by a barn. In the dark of night. A female who mattered held in an evil lock, a knife to her throat. A gun brought to bear—

Blink.

Back here in Caldwell, the love of his life in the hands of his enemy.

Blink.

A gun going off—

The explosion right next to John's ear shocked him firmly back into reality, and he let out a wordless scream, lunging forward as if he could catch the bullet.

No! he screamed soundlessly. *Noooo—*

Except it was a perfect shot. The slug caught Lash in the temple—about two inches away from Xhex's own head.

In slow motion, John glanced over his shoulder. Tohrment's forty was held straight out from the guy's body, the weapon unwavering in the cold air.

For some reason, neither the shooter nor the accuracy was a surprise even though it had been a one-in-a-million Hail Mary.

Oh, God, they'd done this before, hadn't they. Just . . . like this.

Real time snapped back into place and John whipped his head around again. Across the way, Xhex was brilliant as Lash staggered. She ducked down into a crouch to give Tohr a bigger target and was almost totally out of the way as the second bullet got sent flying.

Impact number two popped Lash right off his precious little loafers, landing him flat on his back.

John threw off the vestiges of his vertigo and pounded down to his female, his shitkickers grabbing the ground and holding tight, his thighs shoving all his strength into his feet as he burst into action.

His only thought was of saving Xhex, and he went for the weapon he needed to do the deed with: the six-inch black dagger that was holstered to his chest. As he came up to them, he raised his arm over his head, prepared to fall upon his enemy and stab Lash back to—

The scent of Xhex's blood changed everything, derailing the slice.

Oh, Jesus . . . The fucking bastard had had two knives. One that had been at her throat. And another that had penetrated her in the gut.

Xhex rolled over on her back, grabbing her side with a grimace.

As Lash writhed and clasped his head and chest, Tohr arrived with Qhuinn and Blay and the other Brothers, all their guns pointed at their enemy, so John didn't have to worry about coverage as he assessed the damage.

John leaned down to Xhex.

"I'm okay," she gasped out. "I'm okay . . . I'm okay . . ."

The hell she was. She could barely breathe, and the hand that she had against the wound was covered with shiny, fresh blood.

John started to sign frantically. *Call for Doc Jane*—

"No!" she burst out, grabbing his arm with her bloody hand. "I only care about one thing right now."

As her eyes locked on Lash, John's heart slammed against his rib cage.

From overhead, Z said, "Butch and V are bringing the Escalade over from the Xtreme Park—mother*fucker* . . . we got company."

John glanced down the alley. Four *lessers* had stepped into view . . . evidence that the address on the Civic's registration had been right, even though the timing was now very wrong.

"We've got 'em," Z hissed as he and the group raced back to engage the new arrivals.

The sound of laughter refocused John. Lash was grinning widely, the unholy anatomy of his face pulled into a crazy-ass smile.

"John, boy . . . I fucked her, John . . . I fucked her hard and she liked it."

White rage tore through John, the bonded male in him screaming, the dagger in his hand rising up once again.

"She begged me, John . . ." The breath that was drawn in was ragged, but satisfied. "Next time you're with her . . . remember I fill—"

"I never wanted it!" Xhex spat. "Never!"

"Filthy female," Lash sneered. "That's what you were and what you'll stay. Filthy and mine—"

Everything slowed down for John, everything from how the three of them were clustered together to the way the wind whiffled through the alley to the fight that had broken out a hundred yards away by the Mercedes.

He thought of his own violation long ago in that stairwell. Pictured Xhex going through similar humiliation and degradation. Recalled what Z had said he'd been through. Remembered what Tohr had suffered.

And in the midst of the recollections, he felt the echo of something long, long ago, something of another abduction, another female hurt wrongly, another life ruined.

Lash's horrific face and his decrepit, melting form became the embodiment of all of it: a festering, rotting, tangible representation of all the evil in the world, all the pain caused with deliberation, all the cruelty and debasement and malicious joy.

All the deeds done in a moment that had repercussions which lasted a lifetime.

"I fucked her, John, boy—"

With a slashing arch, John's dagger arm plunged downward.

At the last second, he twisted his wrist so that the head of the hilt caught Lash right in the face. And the bonded male in him wanted to do what he'd done to that slayer back at the brownstone—nothing but complete evisceration.

Except then he'd be cheating this situation of the kind of divine justice so few people got. His wrong had never been righted—that human piece of shit who'd hurt him had gotten clean away. And Tohr's wrong could never be righted, because Wellsie was never coming back.

But Z had gotten his closure.

And goddamn it, so would his Xhex . . . even if that was the last thing in this world she did.

John had tears in his eyes as he took one of her bloodied hands from her wound . . . and opened it wide.

Turning his dagger around, he placed the hilt onto her palm. As her eyes flared, he closed her hold on his weapon and moved around to help prop her up and get her within range.

Lash's chest was going up and down, his skinless throat flexing while he drew his breath and blew it back out. As light dawned on him and he got a picture of what was coming, lidless eyes stretched in their sockets and his lipless mouth pulled off his teeth in a smile that was the stuff of horror movies.

He tried to say something, but he couldn't quite get it out.

Which was good. He'd already said too much, done too much, hurt too much.

Time had come for his reckoning.

In his arms, John felt Xhex gathering her strength and he watched as she took her other hand from her wound to aid in gripping his weapon. Her stare burned with hatred as she took over from there, a sudden surge of power in her body lifting her arms to form an arch above Lash's sternum.

The bastard knew what was coming, though, and blocked the blow by covering his chest.

Oh, hell, no. John shot out and grabbed both of the guy's biceps, forcing the asshole flat onto the ground, exposing the expanse she needed to hit, giving her the clearest and best shot.

As her eyes rose to John's, there was a telltale sheen of red across them, her tears making her irises glow: All the pain she'd borne in her heart was as exposed as Lash's ugliness, all the burden on her and in her made manifest in her stare.

When John nodded at her, his dagger in her hands swept down and hit Lash directly in the heart . . .

The evil's scream echoed in between the buildings, ricocheting back and forth, gathering in volume until it became the great Pop! that accompanied a vivid flash of light.

Which took Lash back to his unholy sire.

As the sound and illumination faded, all that was left was a faint scorched circle on the asphalt and the stench of burned sugar.

Xhex's shoulders went limp and the dagger blade squeaked across the pavement as she fell backward, her strength gone. John caught her before she hit the ground, and she stared up at him, her tears mixing with the blood on her face and running down her neck, past the vital beating pulse that was her life force.

John held her tight against him, her head fitting perfectly under his chin.

"He's dead," she sobbed. "Oh, God, John . . . he's dead . . ."

With his hands occupied, all he could do was nod so that she knew that he was agreeing with her.

End of an era, he thought, looking over at Blay and

Qhuinn, who were fighting side by side with Zsadist and Tohrment against the slayers who had shown up.

God, he had the oddest sense of continuity. He and Xhex might have briefly stepped out of the way of the war, taking this momentary respite at the side of the struggle trail. But the fight in the shadows of the alleys in Caldwell was going to continue without . . .

Her.

John closed his eyes and buried his face in Xhex's curling hair.

This was the end game she'd wanted, he thought. Get Lash . . . and get out of life.

She had exactly what she'd wanted.

"Thank you," he heard her say roughly. "Thank you . . ."

Against the tide of sadness that overtook him, he realized that those two words were better than *I love you.* They actually meant more to him than anything else she could have uttered.

He had given her what she wanted. When it had really mattered, he had done right by her.

And now he was going to hold her as her body grew colder and she drifted away from where he was going to stay.

The separation was going to last longer than the number of days he knew her.

Taking her slick palm, he flattened it once more. And then with his free hand, he signed against her skin in slow, precise positions:

L. O. V. E. U. 4. E. V. E. R.

SIXTY-EIGHT

Death was messy and painful and largely predictable . . . except when it didn't feel like behaving and decided to exercise its bizarre sense of humor.

An hour later, as Xhex opened her eyes a crack, she realized she was in fact not in the foggy folds of the Fade . . . but in the clinic at the Brotherhood's mansion.

A tube was being pulled out of her throat. And her side felt like someone had parked a rusty spear in it. And somewhere over on the left, gloves were being snapped off.

Doc Jane's voice was low. "She coded twice, John. I got the bleeder in her gut . . . but I don't know——"

"I think she's awake," Ehlena said. "Are you coming back to us, Xhex?"

Well, apparently she was. She felt like hell, and after having sliced open a variety of stomachs over the years, she couldn't believe she still had a heartbeat . . . but yeah, she was alive.

Hanging by a thread, but alive.

John's pasty white face entered her line of vision, and in contrast to the ill cast of his skin, his blue eyes were like fire.

She opened her mouth . . . but all that came out was the air in her lungs. She didn't have the strength to speak.

Sorry, she mouthed.

He frowned. Shaking his head, he took her hand and smoothed it . . .

She must have passed out, because when she woke

up, John was walking beside her. What the hell—oh, she was being moved into the other room . . . because they were bringing someone else in—someone strapped down to a gurney. A female, given the long, black braid that swung off the side.

The word *pain* came to mind.

"Pain is in here," Xhex murmured.

John's head whipped around. *What?* he mouthed.

"Whoever's there . . . is pain."

She passed out again . . . and came to feeding from John's wrist. And passed out again.

In her dreams, she saw parts of her life going all the way back to a time she didn't consciously remember. And as in-flight movies went, the drama was pretty depressing. There were too many crossroads to count where things should have been different, where fate had been more of a grind than a gift. Destiny was like the passage of time, however, immutable and unforgiving and uninterested in the personal opinion of those who breathed.

And yet . . . as her mind churned beneath the leaden weight and still surface of her unconscious body, she had the sense that everything had worked out as it was supposed to, that the path she had been set upon had taken her precisely where she was supposed to go:

Back to John.

Even though that made no sense whatsoever.

After all, she'd met him only a year or so ago. Which hardly justified the sprawl of history that seemed to unite them.

But then, maybe that did make sense. While you were unconscious on morphine and teetering on the brink of the Fade . . . things looked different. And time, like priorities, shifted.

On the other side of the door to Xhex's recovery room, Payne blinked hard and tried to ascertain where she had been moved to. There was naught to inform her, however. The chamber's walls were tiled in a pale green and gleaming fixtures and storage casings abounded. But she hadn't a clue what it all meant.

At least the transport had been slow, careful, and relatively comfortable. But then something had been put into her veins to calm her and ease her—and verily, she was grateful for whatever potion it was.

Indeed, the specter of her dead was more agitating than her discomfort or whether she had a future on this side. Had the good doctor truly spoken the name of her twin? Or had that been a figment of her scattered, muddled mind?

She knew not. But cared a great deal.

In the periphery of her vision, she saw many attending upon her arrival herein, including the doctor and the Blind King. There was also a blond female of comely visage . . . and a dark-haired warrior who people were calling by the name Tohrment.

Exhausted, Payne closed her eyes, the patter of voices carrying her off into a drifting sleep. She did not how long she was out . . . but what brought her back was the sudden awareness of a new arrival within the hushed space.

The personage was one whom she knew so very well, and the appearance was a greater source of shock than the reality that she was away from her mother.

As Payne opened her eyes, No'One approached her, her limp shifting her across the smooth flooring, the hood of her robe shielding her face from view. The Blind King loomed behind the female, arms crossed over his chest, his beautiful blond dog and his beautiful brunette queen on either side of him.

"Whatever . . . are you here?" Payne said hoarsely, aware she was making more sense on the inside of her head than her words would suggest.

The fallen Chosen seemed very nervous, although how that was exactly evident, Payne wasn't sure. It was something sensed but not seen, given that the Chosen's black robes were covering all of her.

"Taketh my hand," Payne said. "I should want to ease you."

No'One shook her head beneath her hood. "It is I who have come to ease you." As Payne frowned, the Chosen glanced back at Wrath. "The king has permitted me to tarry in his household for to serve as your maid."

Payne swallowed, but her dry mouth offered no relief to her parched throat. "No serve me. Be here . . . but serve yourself."

"Indeed . . . there is that as well." No'One's soft voice grew tight. "Verily, upon your departure from the Sanctuary, I approached the Scribe Virgin—and my request was granted. You inspired me to long o'erdue action. I have been cowardly . . . but no longer, thanks to you."

"I . . . am . . . glad . . ." Although what she could have done to justify such motivation escaped her. "And I am grateful you are here—"

With an explosive shove, the door in the far corner was thrown open, and a male dressed in black leather and smelling of sickly death burst into the room. Right on his heels was the private physician, and as he jerked to a halt, the ghostly female put her hand upon his shoulder as if to soothe him.

The male's diamond eyes locked on Payne, and though she hadn't seen him in forever, she *knew* who he was. Sure as if she was staring at her own reflection.

Tears sprang unbidden to her eyes for last she had known, he breathed no longer. "Vishous," she whispered desperately. "Oh, brother mine . . ."

He was at her side in a flash, taking form right next to her. His incredibly intelligent stare traced her features and she had the sense that their expressions were as identical as their coloring: her surprise and incomprehension were likewise upon his harsh, handsome features.

His eyes . . . oh, his diamond eyes. They were her own; she had seen them staring back at her in countless mirrors.

"Who are you?" he said roughly.

Abruptly, she felt something in her ever-numbing body—and the great heavy weight came not from physical injury, but inner calamity. That he didn't know who she was, that they had been kept separate by a lie, was a tragedy she could hardly bear.

Her voice became strong. "I am . . . your blood."

"Jesus Christ . . ." He lifted a hand that was encased in a black glove. "My sister . . . ?"

"I have to go," the doctor said urgently. "The break in her spine is beyond my expertise. I need to go get—"

"Find that goddamn surgeon," Vishous growled, his eyes still locked on Payne's. "Find him and bring him here . . . no matter what it takes."

"I won't come back without him. You have my word."

Vishous turned to the female and captured her mouth in a quick, hard kiss. "God . . . I love you."

The physician's ghostly face became solid as they stared at each other. "We're going to save her, trust me. I'll be back the second I can—Wrath's given his permission and Fritz is going to help me get Manny here."

"Fucking sunlight. It's coming all too soon."

"I'd want you here with her anyway. You and Ehlena need to watch her vitals, and Xhex is still in critical condition. I want you to take care of them."

When he nodded, the physician disappeared into thin air, and then a moment later, Payne felt a warm palm encompass hers. It was Vishous's ungloved hand against her own and the connection between them eased her in ways she couldn't name.

Verily, she had lost her mother . . . but if she lived through this, she still had family. On this side.

"Sister," he murmured, not as an inquiry, but a statement of fact.

"Brother mine," she groaned . . . before her consciousness slipped from her grasp and she drifted away.

But she would come back to him. One way or the other, she would not leave her twin ever again.

SIXTY-NINE

Xhex woke up alone in the room off the OR, and yet she sensed that John wasn't far.

The draw to find him gave her the strength to push herself up and swing her legs off the bed. As she waited for her heart to stop thumping from the effort, she noticed dimly that her hospital johnny had hearts on it. Little pink and blue hearts.

She couldn't even marshal up the energy to be offended. Her side was killing her and her skin was prickling all over. And she had to get to John.

Glancing over, she saw that the IV in her arm was plugged into a bag that hung off the bed's monitoring headboard. Crap. What she needed was one of those rolling poles they used to put 'em on. Could have used the help with the whole balance-while-upright thing.

When she finally put some weight on her feet, she was relieved to find she didn't face-plant right away. And, after a moment of orientation, she slipped the bag of fluids free and carried it with her, giving herself a pat on the back for being such a good little patient.

Thing was kind of like a handbag. Maybe she'd start a new trend.

She took the door that led directly out into the corridor, as opposed to going through the OR. After all, the episode with Doc Jane and John's procedure had helped her phobia, but she had quite enough to deal with at the moment and the last thing she needed was to walk into another operation—and God only knew what they were doing to that poor female who'd been rolled in after her.

Xhex stopped with one foot into the hallway.

John was all the way down by the office, standing outside the glass door and facing the wall across from it. His eyes were locked on the fissures that ran through the concrete and his emotional grid was dimmed to the point where it left her instincts squinting.

He was in mourning.

He didn't know for sure whether she had lived or died . . . yet he felt as if he had already lost her.

"Oh . . . John."

His head snapped toward her. *Shit*, he signed, hustling down to her. *What are you doing out of bed?*

Xhex started to walk in his direction, but he got to her first, rushing up as if he were going to scoop her into his arms.

She held him off, shaking her head. "No, I'm steady—"

At which point, her knees buckled and he was all that kept her from hitting the floor . . . which reminded her of being in that alley and Lash stabbing her.

John was what had saved her from falling back then, too.

With smooth strength, he carried her back into the recovery room, easing her down on the bed and rehanging her IV bag.

How're you feeling? he signed.

She stared up at him, seeing him for all he was, the fighter and the lover, the lost soul and the leader . . . the bonded male who was nonetheless prepared to let her go.

"Why'd you do it?" she said through an aching throat. "Back in that alley. Why did you let me kill him?"

John's vivid blue eyes locked on hers as he shrugged. *I wanted you to have that. It was more important for you to*

607

have the . . . closure, I guess it's called. There's a lot of shit in this world that never comes back around right and you deserved the satisfaction.

She laughed a little. "In a weird way . . . it's the most considerate thing anyone's ever done for me."

A faint blush hit his cheeks, and juxtaposed against his square jaw, it was pretty damned appealing. But then, what part of him wasn't?

"So, thank you," she murmured.

Well, you know . . . you're not exactly the kind of female a guy would get flowers for. Sort of limits my options.

Her smile faded. "I couldn't have done that without you. You realize that. You made it happen."

John shook his head. *The mechanics don't matter. The job got done in the right way, by the right person. That's all that counts.*

She thought back to him holding Lash down flat, pinning the fucker to the pavement to give her the best shot. Short of putting the bastard on a silver plate and shoving an apple in his mouth, John couldn't have served her captor up any better.

He had presented her enemy to her. He'd put her needs before his own.

And as she thought about all their ups and downs, that was the one constant, wasn't it. He always put her first.

Now Xhex was the one shaking her head. "I think you're wrong. The mechanics were everything . . . *are* everything."

John just shrugged again and glanced at the door he'd brought her in through. *Listen, do you want me to get Doc Jane or Ehlena? Do you need food? Help to the loo?*

Annnnnnnnnnnnd there it was again.

Xhex started laughing . . . and once she lit off, she couldn't seem to stop, even as her side began to holler and red tears sprang to her eyes. She knew John was looking down at her like she'd lost her mind and she couldn't blame him. She too heard the high note of hysteria coming out of her mouth . . . and what do you know, not long thereafter, she wasn't laughing; she was weeping.

Covering her face with her hands, she just sobbed until she couldn't breathe, the emotional explosion so great that there was no sucking it up or trying to keep it in. She just fell apart and for once didn't fight the unraveling.

When she finally eased into the station at Get-a-grip-ville, she was entirely unsurprised to find a box of Kleenex right in front of her . . . courtesy of John's hand.

She snapped a tissue free. And then promptly went back for seconds and thirds: After that show, cleanup was going to take a lot more than one.

Hell, on that theory, maybe she should just use the sheets on the bed.

"John . . ." She sniffled as she mopped her eyes, and that, coupled with all the little hearts she was wearing, pretty much sealed the deal on her nancy status. "I have to say something to you. It's been a long time in coming . . . so long. Too long."

He grew so still he didn't even blink.

"God, this is hard." More with the frickin' sniffles. "You wouldn't think three little words would be so hard to say."

John's exhale was loud—like someone had punched him in the solar plexus. Funny, she felt the same way. But sometimes, in spite of the waves of nausea and a crushing sense of suffocation, you had to speak what was in your heart.

"John . . ." She cleared her throat. "I . . ."

What, he mouthed. *Just tell me. Please . . . just say it.*

She straightened her shoulders. "John Matthew . . . I'm *such* an ass-hat."

As he blinked and looked like his mouth was about to unhinge, she sighed. "Guess that's four words, huh."

Well, yes . . . that was four words.

God, for a second there . . . John forced his head to get back to reality—because only in a fantasy would she ever I-love-you him.

You're not an asshole, he signed. *Hat, I mean.*

She sniffled some more and the sound was just too fucking adorable. Shit, the *sight* of her was too adorable. Lying back against the thin pillows, with crumpled tissues all around her, and her face flushed, she seemed so fragile and lovely, almost soft. And he wanted to take her into his arms, but he knew she liked her space.

Always had.

"I so am one." She snatched out another tissue, but instead of using it, she folded the thing into precise squares, halving it and then quartering it, then working some triangles until it was nothing but a tight wedge between her fingers.

"Can I ask you something?"

Anything.

"Can you forgive me?"

John recoiled. *For what?*

"For being a hardheaded, narcissistic, single-minded, emotionally repressed nightmare? And don't tell me that I'm not." She sniffed again. "I'm a *symphath*. I'm good at reading people. Can you ever forgive me?"

There's nothing to forgive.

"You're so wrong."

Then color me used to it. Have you seen the fools I live with?

She laughed and he loved the sound. "Why have you hung in with me through everything—wait, maybe I know the answer to that one. You can't choose who you bond with, can you."

Her sad voice trailed off.

As Xhex's eyes stayed locked on that Kleenex in her hand, she started to unfold what she had done to it, opening up the shapes she'd made from its corners and flat stretches.

He brought up his hands, getting ready to sign—

"I love you." Her gunmetal gray stare lifted to his. "I love you and I'm sorry and thank you." She laughed in a short, harsh burst. "Check me out, being all ladylike."

John's heart thumped so loudly in his ribs, he nearly glanced out in the hallway to see whether a marching band was going by.

Xhex's head eased back onto the pillows. "You've always done the right thing by me. I've just been too wrapped up in my own drama to be able to accept what's been in front of me the whole time. That or too much of a wimp to do anything about it."

John was having a hard time believing what he was hearing. When you wanted something or someone as badly as he did her, you were liable to translate things wrong—even if they were in your native tongue.

What about your end game? he signed.

She took a deep breath. "I think I'd like to change my plans."

How? Oh, God, he thought, please say—

"I'd like you and me to be my end game." She cleared her throat. "It's easier to check out. Just do yourself and be done with the whole living-breathing thing. But I'm a fighter, John. Always have been. And if you'll have me . . . I'd like to fight with you." She extended her hand to him, palm up. "So what do you say. How'd you like to sign on for a *symphath*?"

Fucking. Bingo.

John grabbed that hand of hers and brought it to his lips, kissing the thing hard. Then he put it over his heart, and as she kept it there, he signed, *I thought you'd never ask, you meathead.*

Xhex laughed again and then he was smiling so hard his cheeks felt like they were full of buckshot.

Gingerly, he gathered her to his chest and held her with care.

"God, John . . . I don't want to fuck this up, and I have a bad track record with so much."

He pulled back and stroked her silky, curling hair from her face. She looked so damned anxious—which was not how he wanted her to be feeling at a moment like this.

We're going to work it out. Now and in the future.

"I hope so. Shit, I've never told you this, but I had a lover once . . . It wasn't like you and me, but it was a relationship beyond just physical stuff. He was a Brother—he was a good male. I didn't tell him about what I was, which was so not fair. I just didn't think anything would come of it . . . and I was totally wrong." She shook her head. "He tried to save me, he tried so damned hard. He ended up going into that colony to get me, and when he found out the truth, he just . . . lost it. Dropped out of the Brotherhood. Disappeared. I don't even know if he's still alive. That's the main reason I've fought this . . . thing . . . between you and me. I lost Murhder, and it nearly killed me—and I didn't feel for him half of what I do for you."

This was good, John thought. Not that she'd had to go through all that—Christ, no way. But now their past made even more sense—and it made him trust better where they were now.

I'm so sorry, but I'm glad you told me. And I'm not whoever that was. We're going to take it night by night and not look back. We look forward, you and I. We look forward.

She laughed in a quiet burst. "I think that's it for revelations, by the way. You know everything I do about myself."

Right . . . how to put this, he wondered.

John lifted his hands and slowly signed, *Listen, I don't know whether you'd be up for this, but there's a female in this house, Rhage's shellan? She's a therapist and I know that some of the Brothers have used her to sort things out. I could introduce you to her? And maybe you could talk with her? She's very cool and very discreet . . . and maybe it will help you with the past as well as the future.*

Xhex took a deep breath. "You know . . . I've been living with buried shit for so long—and look where it's gotten me. I'm a meathead, but I'm not a moron. Yeah . . . I'd like to meet with her."

John leaned in and pressed his lips to hers; then he stretched out beside her. His body was exhausted, but his heart was alive with a joy so pure it was like the sunlight he didn't get to see anymore: He was a mute-ass motherfucker with a nasty past and a night job that involved fighting evil and slaughtering the undead. And in spite of all that . . . he'd gotten the girl.

He'd gotten *his* girl, his true love, his *pyrocant*.

Of course, he wasn't fooling himself. Life with Xhex wasn't going to be normal on so many levels—good thing he was down with the wild side.

"John?"

He whistled an ascending note.

"I want to get mated to you. Properly mated. Like in front of the king and everyone. I want this to be official."

Well . . . didn't that just make his heart stop.

As he sat up and looked at her, she smiled. "Jesus, the expression on your face. What? You didn't think I'd want to be your *shellan*?"

Not in a million years.

She recoiled a little in surprise. "And you were okay with that?"

It was hard to explain. But what was between them went further than a mating ceremony or a back carving or a witnessed exchange of commitment. He couldn't put his finger on the why of it . . . but she was his missing puzzle piece, the twelfth in his dozen, the first and the last pages of his book. And at some level that was all he needed.

All I want is you. However that comes.

She nodded. "Well, I want the whole deal."

He kissed her again, softly, because he didn't want to hurt her. Then he pulled back and mouthed, *I love you. And I'd love to be your* hellren.

She blushed. She actually blushed. And didn't that make him feel like he was the size of a mountain.

"Good, then it's settled." She put her hand to his face. "We're going to be mated now."

Now? As in . . . now? Xhex . . . you're having trouble standing.

She looked him straight in the eye, and when she spoke, her voice ached—God . . . how it ached. "Then you would hold me up, wouldn't you."

He traced over her features with his fingertips. And as he did, for some strange reason, he felt the arms of infinity wrapping around them both, holding them close . . . linking them forever.

Yes, he mouthed. *I would hold you up. I will ever hold you up and hold you dear, lover mine.*

As he fused their mouths, he thought that was his vow to her. Mating ceremony or not . . . that was his vow to his female.

SEVENTY

*Tragedy struck during a brutal winter storm, and verily, it
was not at all like the long labor of the female on her birthing
bed. The ruination took naught but the blink of an eye . . .
and yet the ramifications changed the course of lives.*

"No!"

*The sound of Tohrment's shout snapped Darius's head up
from the steaming, slippery newborn in his bare hands. At
first, there was no telling what had occurred to cause such
alarm. Indeed, there had been much blood during the birthing,
but the female had survived the delivery of her offspring unto
this world. In fact, Darius was just cutting the cord and going
to wrap the young for presentation—*

"No! Oh, no!" *Tohrment's face was ashen as he reached
out.* "Oh, dearest Virgin Scribe! No!"

"Whyever are you—"

*At first, Darius could make no sense of what he saw. It
appeared . . . that the hilt of Tohrment's dagger protruded from
the sheets covering the female's still-rounded belly.*

*And her pale, now bloodied hands were slowly slipping
down from the weapon to land at her sides.*

"She took it!" *Tohrment gasped.* "From my belt—I . . . It
was so fast . . . I bent down to cover her and . . . she unsheathed
the—"

*Darius's eyes shot to the female's. Her stare was locked on
the fire in the hearth, a single tear easing down her cheek as
the life light began to drift out of her.*

*Darius knocked over the tub of water by the bed in his
scramble to get to her . . . to take out the dagger . . . to save
her . . . to . . .*

615

The wound she had imparted to herself was a mortal one, in light of all she had been through during the birthing . . . and yet Darius could not help himself from fighting to save her.

"Leave not your daughter!" he said, leaning down with the squirming young. "You have brought forth a healthy babe! Lift thine eyes, lift thine eyes!"

As the sound of water dripping from the upended bowl seemed loud as a gunshot, no answer came forth from the female.

Darius felt his mouth moving and had the sense that he was talking—but for some reason, all he could hear was the soft rain of that spilled water while he begged for the female to stay with them . . . for her daughter's sake, for the hope of the future, for the ties that he and Tohrment were prepared to forge with her so that she was never alone as she sought to raise what she had birthed.

As he felt something upon his britches, he frowned and glanced down.

'Twas not water that fell to the floor. 'Twas blood. Hers.

"Oh, dearest Virgin Scribe . . ." he whispered.

Verily, the female had chosen her course and sealed her fate.

Her last breath was naught but a shudder and then her head listed to the side, her eyes seemingly still locked upon the flames licking at the logs . . . when in fact, she saw nothing and would be sightless e'ermore.

The wail of the newborn and that forsaken dripping were the only sounds in Darius's thatched cottage that he could hear. And indeed, it was the young's plaintive mewling that threw him into action, for there was naught to accomplish about the spilled blood or the life lost. Grabbing the swaddling blanket that had been made for the little one, he carefully wrapped up the wee innocent and held her to his heart.

Oh, the cruel fate that had brought about this miracle. And now what?

Tohrment looked up from the bloodied birthing bed and the now cooling body, his eyes burning with horror. "I but turned away for a moment . . . may the Scribe Virgin forgive me . . . but for a moment did I—"

Darius shook his head. When he went to speak, he had no voice, so he placed his palm upon the boy's shoulder and squeezed to offer comfort. As Tohrment sagged in his own skin, the wailing grew louder.

The mother was gone. The daughter remained.

Darius bent down with the new life in his arms, and retracted Tohrment's dagger from the belly of the female. He put it aside, and then he closed the lids on those eyes and drew up fresh sheeting o'er the face.

"She will not go unto the Fade," Tohrment moaned as he put his head in his hands. "She has doomed herself . . ."

"She was doomed by the actions of others." And the greatest sin among them was the cowardice of her father. "She was doomed long afore . . . oh, merciless fate, she was doomed long afore . . . Surely the Scribe Virgin shall look upon her in her death with a favor she was not granted in her life."

Oh . . . damned . . . cursed, damned fate . . .

Even as he railed against so much in his head, Darius took the tiny young closer to the fire, because he was worried about the chill in the air. As the two of them came within the circle of warmth, she opened her mouth and routed about . . . and for lack of a better alternative, he offered his pinkie for her to suckle on.

With the tragedy still loud as a scream, Darius took in the tiny features and watched as the little one reached out toward the light.

The eyes were not red. And upon that hand there were five digits, not six. And the jointing of the fingers was normal. Briefly opening the swaddling cloth, he checked the feet and the belly and the little head . . . and found that the abnormal length of feature and limb characteristic of sin-eaters was not represented.

Darius's chest roared with pain for the female who had carried this life within her body. She had become a part of both him and Tohrment—and even though she rarely spoke and never smiled, he knew that she had cared for them as well.

The three of them had been a kind of family.

And now she had left this wee one behind.

Darius retucked the blanket and realized that the swaddling cloth was the only way the female had acknowledged her impending birth. Indeed, she herself had made this coverlet that her new daughter was wrapped in. It was the only interest she had taken in the pregnancy . . . likely because she had known this would be the outcome.

All along, she had known what she was going to do.

The young's wide eyes stared up at him, her brows arching in concentration, and with a sense of grave burden, he recognized how vulnerable this bundle was—left on her own to the cold, she would die in a matter of hours.

He had to do the right thing by her. That was all that mattered.

He had to take care of her and do right by her. She had started with so much against her and now she was an orphan.

Dearest Virgin Scribe . . . he would do the right thing by her if it was his last action on earth.

There was a shuffling sound, and as Darius looked over his shoulder, he saw that Tohrment had wrapped the female's body in the sheeting and gathered her into his arms.

"I shall take care of her," the boy said. Except . . . his voice was not that of a boy. It was of a fully grown male. "I . . . shall care for her."

For some odd reason, the way he held her head was the only thing Darius could see: That big, strong hand of Tohrment's was cradling the departed as surely as if she lived, holding her as if comforting her to his chest.

Darius cleared his throat and worried whether his shoulders were strong enough to bear this weight. However would he complete his next breath . . . the next beat of his heart . . . the next step that must needed to happen?

For truth, he had failed. He had gotten the female free but ultimately, he had failed her . . .

Except then he dug deep and turned to face his protégé. "The apple tree . . ."

Tohrment nodded. "Yes. That is what I thought. Beneath the apple tree. I shall take her there now and to hell with this storm."

It was not a surprise that the boy would battle the elements to bury the female. He no doubt needed the exertion to ease his agony. "She shall enjoy the blooms in the spring and the sound of the birds that light upon the boughs."

"What of the babe?"

"We shall care for her, too." Darius stared down into that small face. "By giving her to ones who shall look after her as she deserves."

Indeed, they could not keep her here. They were out all night fighting, and the war did not stop for personal loss . . . The war did not stop for anything or anybody. Besides, she needed things two males, however well intended, could not provide.

She required a mother's succor.

"Is it night yet?" Darius asked roughly as Tohrment turned for the door.

"Yes," the male said as he unlatched the lock. "And I fear it will be ever so."

The door swung open, blown asunder by the wind, and Darius curled himself around the babe. When the gust was shut off, he looked down at the tiny new life.

Tracing her features with his fingertips, he worried over what the years ahead had in store for her. Would they be kinder than the circumstances of her birth?

He prayed that they would. He prayed that she found a male of worth to protect her and that she bore young and lived as a normal within their world.

And he would do whatever he could to ensure that.

Including . . . giving her away.

SEVENTY-ONE

As night fell the following evening over the Brotherhood's mansion, Tohrment, son of Hharm, strapped on his weapons and got his jacket from his closet.

He was not going out to fight, and yet he felt as if he were facing a kind of enemy. And he was going alone. He'd told Lassiter to chill and get a mani-pedi or some shit, because there were some things you just needed to do by yourself.

The fallen angel had simply nodded and wished him good luck. Like he knew precisely what ring of fire Tohr was about to walk through.

God, the sense that nothing surprised the guy was almost as annoying as everything else about him.

The thing was, though, John had come in about a half hour ago and shared his joyous news. Personally. The kid had been grinning so wide, there was a good chance his face was going to freeze in that position, and that was a pretty goddamn fantastic thing.

Shit, life was so strange sometimes. And all too often this meant that bad things mowed good folks down. Not in this case, though. Thank God, not this time.

And it was hard to think of two people who deserved it more.

Leaving his room, Tohr strode down the hall of statues. The happy announcement about John and his Xhex getting mated had spread throughout the household, bringing a much-needed shot in the arm to everybody. Especially Fritz and the *doggen*, who loved to put on a big party.

And man, from the sounds down below, they were in the throes of preparations. Either that or West Coast Choppers was doing a Harley over in the foyer.

Nah. Turned out the buzzing wasn't some pimp job on a cycle, but a fleet of floor buffers going to town.

Pausing, Tohr braced his hands on the balustrade and looked down at the mosaic depiction of the apple tree in full bloom. As he watched the *doggen* with their whirling machines go over the branches and the trunk, he decided life was right and fair on occasion. It truly was.

And that was the only reason he could summon the strength to do what he had to.

After descending the grand staircase at a jog, he waved at the *doggen* while dodging in and out of their paths and ducking out through the vestibule. In the courtyard, he took a deep breath and braced himself. He had a good two hours before the ceremony, which was a bene. He wasn't sure how long this was going to take.

Closing his eyes, he sent his atoms scattering and took form . . . on the terrace of his mated home, the place where he and his beloved had lived out a good fifty years.

As he lifted his lids, he didn't look at the house. Instead, he tilted his head back and searched the night sky above the roofline. The stars were out, their shimmering brightness undimmed by the moon which had yet to reach any appreciable height.

Where were his dead? he wondered. Which among the tiny lights were the souls of those whom he'd lost?

Where were his *shellan* and their young? Where was Darius? Where were all the others who had pared off from the trudging path his boots still strode so that they could take residence in the velvet ever-afterlife of the Fade?

Did they watch what happened down here? Did they see what transpired, both the good and bad?

Did they miss those they'd left behind?

Did they know they were missed?

Tohr slowly brought his head to level and steeled himself.

Yup, he was right . . . hurt like a motherfucker just to look at the place.

And the metaphor was too frickin' obvious: What he was staring at was a huge hole in his house, the glass slider to John's old room blown clean out of its frame, a whole lot of nothing left where there was meant to be something.

As a breeze blew by, the drapes that hung on either side of the casing wafted gently.

So very obvious: House was him. Hole was what remained after he'd lost . . . Wellsie.

Still difficult to think her name. Much less say it.

Over to the side, there were half a dozen sheets of plywood along with a box of nails and a hammer. Fritz had brought them over as soon as Tohr had learned about the accident, but the *doggen* had been under strict orders not to fix the problem himself.

Tohr fixed his own house. Always.

As he walked forward, the soles of his shitkickers crushed the glass shards into flagstone, the crackling sound following him as he got to the door's threshold. Taking a key fob out of his pocket, he pointed it into the house and pressed the disarm button on the remote. There was a distant *beep-beep*, which meant the security system had registered the signal and was now off.

He was free to go in: Motion detectors were deactivated and he could open any exterior door or window in the place.

Free to go in.

Yup.

Instead of taking that first step, he went over to the plywood, picked up one of the four-by-eight sheets, and muscled it over to the busted slider. Leaning the thing against the house, he returned for the nails and the hammer.

It took him about a half hour to cover the hole, and when he stepped back to inspect the effort, he thought it looked like shit. The rest of the place was pristine in spite of the fact that it hadn't been lived in since . . . Wellsie's murder: Everything was battened down, and his former staff were good enough to look after the landscaping and to check the indoors once a month—even though they'd moved on to serve another family out of town.

Funny, he'd tried to pay them for what they still did here now that he was back in the land of the living, but they'd refused the money. Just returned it with a kindly note.

Guess everyone mourned in their own way.

Tohr put the hammer and remaining nails on top of the one sheet of board he hadn't used and then he forced himself to walk around the outside of the house. As he went along, from time to time he peered into the windows. The drapes had all been pulled, but nonetheless, his vision penetrated through the folds of cloth to readily view all the ghosts that lived within the walls.

In the back, he saw himself sitting at the kitchen table, with Wellsie cooking at the stove, the two of them arguing over the fact that he'd left his weapons out the night before. Again.

God, she'd turned him on when she handed him his own ass.

And when he came around to the living room, he remembered taking her into his arms and making her dance with him as he hummed a waltz in her ear. Badly.

She'd always been so fluid against him, her body built for him and his for her.

And at the front door . . . he recalled walking in with flowers. Every anniversary.

Her favorite had been white roses.

As he got to the driveway and faced the garage, he focused on the one on the left, the one closest to the house.

The one Wellsie had backed that Range Rover out of for the last time.

After the shooting, the Brotherhood had taken the SUV and disposed of it, and Tohr didn't even want to know what had become of the thing. Never had asked. Never would.

The scent of both her perfume and her blood was too much for him to handle even in the hypothetical.

He shook his head as he stared at the closed door. You never knew the last time you were seeing someone. You didn't know when the last argument happened, or the last time you had sex, or the last time you looked into their eyes and thanked God they were in your life.

After they were gone? That was all you thought about.

Day and night.

Heading around the side of the garage, he found the door he was looking for and had to force it open with his shoulder.

Shit . . . it still smelled the same: the dry breath of concrete and the sweet oil from the 'Vette and the lingering gas from the mower and the Weedwacker. He flicked a switch. Christ, the place was like a museum of an era long, long ago; he recognized the objects from that kind of life, could extrapolate their uses . . . but damned if they had a place in his existence now.

Focus.

He went over toward the house and found the stairwell to the second floor. The attic over the garage was fully finished and heated and filled with an eclectic combination of trunks from the 1800s and wooden boxes from the twentieth century and plastic Rubbermaid containers from the twenty-first.

He didn't actually look at what he'd come to get, but he got what it had always been stored in and humped the old LV wardrobe down the stairs.

No dematerializing with it, though, damn it.

He was going to need a ride. Why hadn't he thought of that?

Glancing over his shoulder, he saw the 1964 Sting Ray he'd rehabbed himself. He'd spent hours on the engine and the body, even during the day sometimes— which had made Wellsie mental.

Come on, honey, like the roof is going to blow off?

Tohr, I'm telling you, you're pushing it.

Mmm, how 'bout I push something else, too . . .

He squeezed his eyes shut and wiped the memory away.

Going over to the car, he wondered if the key was was still in the . . . Bingo.

He opened the driver's-side door and squeezed in behind the wheel. The top was down as always, because he couldn't really fit in the thing with the roof in place. Punching his left boot into the clutch, he turned the key and—

The roar fired off like the damn thing had been waiting for way too long and was pissed off at having been ignored, thank you very much.

Half a tank of gas. Oil level was fine. Engine was turning over in perfect sync.

Ten minutes later, he reengaged the security alarm and backed out of the garage with the LV wardrobe trunk roped onto the ass of the convertible. Securing the thing had been easy; he'd put a blanket over the paint job, braced the weight on top of the boot, and tied it down every which way to Sunday.

He was going to have to go slowly, though. Which was okay.

The night was cold and the tips of his ears went numb before he'd gone so much as a mile. But the heater was kicking out a bonfire's worth of BTUs and the steering wheel was good and solid against his palms.

As he headed back for the Brotherhood's mansion, he had the sense that he had lived through a mortal test. And yet he felt no triumph at the besting.

He was resolved, though. And as Darius had said, prepared to look forward.

At least when it came to killing his enemy.

Yeah, he was looking forward to that all right. Starting tonight, it was all he had to live for and he was nothing if not prepared to meet his obligations.

SEVENTY-TWO

They took the young to her new home on the backs of warhorses.

The family who was adopting her lived villages and villages away, and Darius and Tohrment traveled through the night following the birth fully weaponed, aware of all the ways they could be stopped en route. When they got to the cottage they sought, it was not unlike Darius's own, with a thatched roof and walls made of stone. Surrounding trees offered protection from the weather, and the barn out back had goats and sheep and milking cows milling about in paddocks.

The household even had a doggen, *as Darius had learned the previous evening when he had come to reach out to this modest but prosperous family. Of course, he had not been introduced to the female of the manse at that time. She had not been receiving and he and her male had spoken of the private matter on the front stoop.*

As he and Tohrment pulled up on their reins, the horses clattered to a halt and refused to stay still. Indeed, the massive stallions were bred for fighting, not patience, and after Darius dismounted, his protégé managed to subdue both animals only by sheer strength of shoulder.

Every mile they had covered on the way to this end, Darius had second-guessed the choice, but now that they had arrived, he knew this was where the infant needed to be.

He approached the door with his precious cargo, and it was the master of the house who opened the stout portal. The male's eyes were shining in the moonlight, but it was not joy that made them so. Indeed, an all too familiar loss had struck this household of virtue—which was how Darius had found them.

Vampires kept in contact o'er hill and dale in the same

*manner as humans did: by sharing stories and commiser-
ating.*

*Darius bowed to the gentlemale in spite of his own higher
station. "Greetings on this cold night."*

*"Greetings, sire." The male bowed very low, and as he rose,
his kind stare went to the tiny bundle. "'Tis getting warmer
anon, however."*

*"Indeed." Darius unfolded the top of the swaddling blanket
and looked once more upon the tiny face. Those eyes, those
arresting iron gray eyes, stared back at him. "Do you care to
. . . inspect her first?"*

*His voice broke, for he wanted no judgment upon the young,
now or ever—and indeed he had done his best to ensure that.
Verily, he had not shared the circumstances of her conception
with the male. How could he? Who would then take her? And
as she lacked the conspicuous traits of her other half, no one
would ever know.*

*"I shall need no inspection." The gentlemale shook his head.
"She is a blessing to fill my shellan's empty arms. You have
said she is healthy; that is all that we care about."*

*Darius exhaled a breath he wasn't aware he'd been holding
and continued to stare down upon the babe.*

*"Are you sure you wish to give her up?" the gentlemale said
softly.*

*Darius glanced back at Tohrment. The male's eyes burned
as he looked over from upon his mincing stallion, his warrior's
body clad in black leather hides, his weapons strapped upon
his chest and saddle, his appearance a harbinger of war and
death and blood spilled.*

*Darius was aware he presented a similar picture as he
turned back to the gentlemale and cleared his throat. "Would
you permit me one license?"*

"Yes, sire. Please take any you shall require."

"I . . . I should wish to impart her nomenclature."

*The gentlemale bowed low once again. "That would be a
most kind and welcome gesture."*

Darius looked over the shoulder of the civilian to the cottage door that had been closed against the chill. Inside, somewhere, there was a female in mourning, one who had lost her young upon the birthing bed.

For truth, he knew something of that dark void's vast shadow as he prepared to give what was in his arms to another. He would ever be missing a part of his heart when he rode off from this wooded glen and this broken family who would now be made whole—but the young deserved the love that awaited her herein.

Darius's voice rang out, pronouncing, "She shall be called Xhexania."

The gentlemale bowed anew. "'Blessed one.' Yes, that suits her beautifully."

There was a long pause during which Darius resumed his regard of that angelic face. He knew not when he would see her again. This family was her own now; she needed not two warriors o'erseeing her—and better that they not intrude. Two fighters visiting this quiet locale regularly? Questions might well be raised as to why and perhaps endanger the secret that had to surround her conception and birth.

To protect her, he must disappear from her life to ensure she was raised as a normal.

"Sire?" the gentlemale asked meekly. "Are you sure you wish to do this?"

"I'm sorry. But of course . . . I am very sure." Darius felt his chest burn as he leaned forward and placed the young in the arms of a stranger.

Her father.

"Thank you . . ." The male's voice cracked as he accepted the small weight. "Thank you for the light you have presented us in our darkness. Verily, though, is there naught we may do for you?"

"Be . . . be good to her."

"We shall." The male went to turn away and paused. "You are never coming back, are you."

As he shook his head, Darius could not take his eyes off the swaddling cloth the young's mother had made. "She is yours sure as if your bloodline had borne her. We shall leave her here in your fine care and trust you shall treat her well."

The gentlemale came forward and took Darius's upper arm. With a squeeze, he offered commiseration and reassurance. "You have put your faith in us wisely. And know that you are always welcome here to see her."

Darius inclined his head. "Thank you. May the blessed Virgin Scribe look with favor upon you and yours."

"And the same for you."

With that, the gentlemale walked through his door and entered his mated home. On a final lifted palm by way of goodbye, he shut himself in with the wee one.

As the stallions snorted and stamped their hooves, Darius walked around and glanced through wavy leaded glass, hoping to see—

O'er by a fire, upon a bed of clean linens, a female lay with her face turned toward the flaming warmth. She was pale as that which covered her, and her empty eyes reminded him of the tragic female who had passed unto the Fade before his own hearth.

The gentlemale's shellan did not sit up or look over as her hellren entered the bedchamber, and for a moment, Darius worried that he had made a mistake.

But the young must have let out a sound, because the female's head suddenly snapped around.

As she beheld the bundle that was presented to her, her mouth fell open, confusion and then awe filtering through her lovely features. Abruptly, she cast the coverlet from her arms and reached for the babe. Her hands were shaking so badly, her hellren had to place the young against her heart . . . but she held her newborn daughter in place all by herself.

'Twas the wind which made Darius's eyes water. Verily, 'twas but the wind.

As he brushed over his face with his palm, he told himself

that all was well and how it should be . . . even if he felt a mourning within his breast.

Behind him, his charger let out a roar and reared up against the hold on his reins, his massive hooves pounding against the earth. At the sound, the female in the bedchamber looked up with alarm and cradled her precious gift closely, as if she needed to protect the babe.

Darius wheeled away and blindly jogged over to his steed. With a leap, he was up on the back of the great beast, taking control of the animal, harnessing the power and rage that had been bred into its every muscle and bone.

"We shall go unto Devon," Darius said, needing a purpose more than he needed breath or heartbeat. "There are reports of lessers."

"Aye." Tohrment looked back at the house. "But are you . . . of a proper spirit to fight now?"

"The war waits for no male to be of sound mind." Indeed, at times 'twas better to be in lunacy.

Tohrment nodded. "Onward to Devon, then."

Darius gave his stallion all the head it wanted and the warhorse burst forth from its enforced halt, galloping off into the woods, tearing o'er the ground. The wind in Darius's face cast his tears away, but did naught to cure the ache in his chest.

He wondered as he rode off back to the war whether he would see the babe again—but he knew the answer. There was no way their paths would cross. How could they? In what manner of life's twists and turns could they find themselves united once more?

Verily, it defied destiny, did it not.

Oh, the wee one. Ill begotten. Ne'er to be forgotten.

E'er to have a piece of his heart.

SEVENTY-THREE

Later Xhex would reflect that good things, like bad, came in threes.

She'd just never had that particular experience before . . . not with the three thing, but with the "good" part.

Thanks to John Matthew's blood and Doc Jane's handiwork, she was up and around the night after the rollout with Lash, and she knew she was back to her normal self because she'd put her cilices on again. And trimmed her hair. And been to her house on the Hudson River to get clothes and weapons.

And spent about . . . four hours making love with John.

She'd also met with Wrath and it looked like she had a new job: The great Blind King had invited her to come fight with the Brotherhood. In the wake of her initial shock, he'd maintained that her skills were much needed and welcome in the war—and gee, yeah, kill some *lessers*?

Great. Idea. She was so on board with that.

And speaking of on board, she'd moved into John's room properly. In his closet, her leathers and her muscle shirts were hanging next to his, and their shitkickers were lined up together, and all her knives and her guns and her little toys were now locked up in his fireproof cabinet.

Their ammo was even stacked together.

Too frickin' romantic.

So, yup, business as usual.

Except . . . well, except for the fact that she'd been reduced to sitting on this big bed, rubbing her sweaty palms on her leathers for, like, the last half hour. John was having a workout down in the training center before their ceremony and she was glad he was busy elsewhere.

She didn't want him to see her nervous like this.

Because it turned out, in addition to a phobia about medical crap, there was another little glitch in her hard-wiring: The idea of standing up in front of a ton of people and being the focus of attention during their mating made her want to vomit. Guess it shouldn't have been a total surprise, though. After all, in her job as an assassin, the whole point was to remain unseen. And she'd long been an introvert by both circumstance and character.

Pushing herself back to the pillows, she leaned against the headboard, crossed her feet at the ankles, and grabbed the remote. The little black Sony number discharged its duties with admirable flair, the thing firing up the flat-screen and switching the channels until they flicked by quick as the beat of her heart.

It wasn't just the fact that there were going to be so many witnesses to her and John's ceremony. It was because getting hitched made her think of the way things should have been if she'd had a normal life. On nights like this, most females were getting dressed in gowns made just for the occasion and being strewn with family jewels. They were looking forward to being presented to their intended by their proud fathers, and their mothers were supposed to be sniffling now as well as when the vows were exchanged.

Xhex, on the other hand, was walking down the aisle by herself. Wearing leathers and a muscle shirt, because that was all she'd ever owned for clothes.

As the TV stations flipped before her eyes, the distance between herself and "normal" seemed as great a divide as that of history itself: There would be no recasting of the past, no editing the peaks and valleys of her story.

Everything from her mixed blood, to the kindly mated couple who had raised a nightmare, to everything that had happened to her since she'd left that cottage . . . all of it was written in the cold stone of the past.

Never to be changed.

At least she knew that the wonderful male and female who had tried to raise her as their own had finally had a babe of their bloodline, a son who had grown up strong and mated well and given them a next generation.

All that had made the leaving of them so much easier.

But everything else in her life, save for John, had not had a happy resolution. God, maybe that was the cause of her nerves as well. This mating stuff with John was such a revelation, almost too good to be true—

She frowned and jacked upright. Then rubbed her eyes.

She couldn't be seeing what was on the screen correctly.

It wasn't possible . . . was it?

Scrambling for the right button on the remote, she turned up the volume. ". . . Rathboone's ghost haunting the halls of his Civil War mansion. What secrets await our *Paranormal Investigators* team as they seek to uncover . . ."

The narrator's voice faded from hearing as the camera drew closer and closer upon a portrait of a male with dark hair and eyes that were haunted.

Murhder.

She'd know that face anywhere.

Leaping up, she rushed at the TV—but like that was going to help?

The camera panned back to show a beautiful parlor and then shots of the grounds of a white plantation house. They were talking about some kind of live special . . . during which they were going to try to flush out the ghost of a Civil War abolitionist who so many maintained still roamed the halls and the grounds of where he'd once lived.

Tuning in to the commentary again, she desperately tried to catch where the mansion was located. Maybe she could . . .

Just outside Charleston, South Carolina. That's where it was.

Stepping back, she hit the bed with her calves and sat down. Her first thought was to flash there and see for herself whether it was her former lover or a real live ghost or just some talented television producers making a lot of noise.

But logic overrode the impulse. The last time she'd set her eyes on Murhder, he'd made it clear he wanted nothing to do with her. Besides, just because there was an old oil painting that resembled the male didn't mean he was taking up res in that old manse playing Casper.

Although that was a helluva portriat. And terrorizing humans actually did sound right up his alley.

Shit . . . she wished him well. She totally did. And if she wasn't convinced she'd be as unwelcome as the secret she should have told him about after they'd gotten involved, she would have made the trip.

The fact was, however, sometimes the best thing that you could do for someone was stay away from them. And she'd given him her address on the Hudson. He knew where to find her.

God, she hoped he was okay, though.

The knock on the door brought her head around. "Hello?" she said.

"Is that a come-in?" a deep male voice answered.

She got to her feet and frowned, thinking that sure as hell didn't sound like a *doggen*. "Yeah. It's unlocked."

The door swung wide to reveal . . . a trunk—as in a wardrobe trunk. A Louis Vuitton wardrobe trunk from back in the day. And she assumed the guy holding it was a Brother—given the shitkickers and leathers showing down below.

Unless Fritz had eschewed the vanilla lifestyle for something out of V's playbook. And put on a hundred pounds.

The LV lowered enough so that she got a clear shot at Tohrment's face. The Brother's expression was serious, but then, he wasn't a Lite-Brite kind of guy. Never had been . . . and given where his life had ended up, never would be ever.

He cleared his throat and then inclined his head toward what was up against his chest. "I've brought you something. For your mating."

"Um . . . well, John and I haven't registered anywhere." She motioned for him to come in. "Not like Crate and Barrel carries handguns. But thanks."

The Brother stepped through the jamb and put the trunk down. The thing was five feet tall and about three feet wide and seemed to be the kind to split wide down the middle.

In the quiet that followed, Tohrment's eyes traced over her face and yet again she had this odd sense that the guy knew too much about her.

He cleared his throat. "It is customary upon the mating of a female for her family to proffer vestments for the ceremony."

Xhex frowned again. Then slowly shook her head from side to side. "I have no family. Not really."

God, that grave, knowledgeable stare of his was freaking her out . . . and in a rush, her *symphath* side reached out to thread through his grid, assessing, measuring.

Right. This made no sense. The resonant grief and pride and sadness and joy he was feeling . . . were reasonable only if he knew her. And as far as she was aware, they were strangers.

To find the answer, she tried to penetrate his mind and memories . . . but he was blocking her from getting into his brain. Instead of a read on his thoughts . . . all she got was a scene from *Godzilla vs. Mothra.*

"Who are you to me?" she whispered.

The Brother nodded at the trunk. "I have brought you . . . something to wear."

"Well, yeah, but the why is what I'm more interested in." Sure, that sounded ungrateful, but manners had never been her strong suit. "Why would you bother?"

"The particular reasons are not relevant, but they are well sufficient." Read: He wasn't going to go into it. "Will you let me show you?"

Normally, this would be a no-go for her on so many levels, but this was not a normal day or a normal mood she was in. And she had the oddest sense . . . that he was protecting her with all his mental blocking. Protecting her from some series of facts that he feared would cut her to the core.

"Yeah. Okay." She crossed her arms over her chest, feeling uncomfortable. "Open it."

The Brother's knees cracked as he knelt in front of the trunk and took a brass key out of his back pocket. There was a click and then he released the latches on the top and the bottom and moved around behind the thing.

But he didn't split it wide. Instead, his fingers trailed across the trunk reverently—as his emotional grid nearly collapsed from the pain he was feeling.

Concerned for his mental health and the suffering he was going through, she raised a hand to stop him. "Wait. Are you sure you want to—"

He cracked the trunk open, pulling the front halves wide—

Acres of red satin . . . acres of deep bloodred satin spilled out of the LV's confines, falling onto the carpet.

It was a proper mating gown. The kind of thing that was passed down from female to female. The sort of dress that took your breath away even if you weren't a girlie-girl.

Xhex's eyes snapped up to the Brother. He wasn't looking at what he'd brought for her. His stare was locked on the wall across the room, his expression one of forbearance as if what he was doing was killing him.

"Why are you bringing me this?" she whispered, recognizing it for what it had to be. She knew little about the Brother, but she was well aware his *shellan* had been shot by the enemy. And this had to be Wellesandra's mating gown. "It's agony for you."

"Because a female should have a proper dress to walk down . . . the . . . ." He had to clear his throat once more. "This dress was last worn by John's sister on her mating day to the king."

Xhex narrowed her eyes. "So this is from John?"

"Yes," he said hoarsely.

"You're lying—I mean no disrespect, but you're not telling me the truth." She glanced down at all that red satin. "It's incredibly beautiful. But I just don't understand why you would show up here now, tonight, and offer to let me wear it—because your emotions are very personal at this moment in time and you can't even look at the thing."

"As I said, my reasons are private. But it would be . . . a well-intended gesture if you would be mated in it."

"Why is this so important to you."

A female voice interrupted them. "Because he was there at the very beginning."

Xhex wheeled around. In the doorway, standing between the jambs, was a black hooded figure and her first thought was that it was the Scribe Virgin . . . except there was no light glowing beneath the robes.

Her second thought was that the grid of this female . . . was a blueprint of Xhex's own.

To the point where it was identical.

The figure limped forward and Xhex found herself stumbling back and tripping on something. As she went down, she tried to catch her balance on the bed and missed, landing on her ass on the floor.

Their grids were absolutely identical, not in terms of emotions, but the construction itself. Identical . . . as a mother's and daughter's would be.

The female brought her hands up to her hood and slowly lifted that which covered her face.

"Jesus . . . *Christ*."

The exclamation came from Tohrment, and the snap of his voice shifted the female's iron gray eyes to him. She bowed in slow reverence. "Tohrment . . . son of Hharm. One of my saviors."

Xhex was vaguely aware of the Brother bracing himself on the trunk, as if his knees had voted to take a holiday on him. But what she was truly concerned with were the features that had been revealed. They were so like her own, more rounded, true . . . more delicate, yes . . . but the bone structure was the same.

"Mother . . ." Xhex breathed.

As the female's eyes swung back, she did the same search-and-memorize routine on Xhex's face. "Verily . . . you are beautiful."

Xhex touched her own cheek. "How . . ."

Tohrment's voice was full of shock as he demanded, "Yes . . . *how?*"

The female came forward a little farther with that limp—and Xhex instantly wanted to know who or what had harmed her: Although there was no sense to any of this—she'd been told her true mother had died in child-birth, for godsakes—she wanted no injury to ever befall this sad, lovely creature in the robes.

"The night of your birth, daughter mine, I . . . I did die. But when I sought entry unto the Fade, I was not permitted to pass. The Scribe Virgin, however, in all

Her mercies, did allow me sequestering on the Far Side and therein I have e'er stayed, serving the Chosen as penance for my . . . death. I am still in service to a Chosen, and have come here to be on this side to care for her. But . . . in truth, I have arrived unto this plane to finally look upon you in person. I have long watched and prayed for you from the Sanctuary . . . and now that I see you, I find . . . I am well aware that there is much you would need to consider and have explained and be angered over . . . But if you should be of an open heart to me, I should like to forge . . . an affection. I can understand if it is too little, too late . . . ."

Xhex blinked. As lame as it made her, it was all she could do . . . apart from absorb the female's incredible sorrow.

Eventually, in an attempt to understand something, anything, she tried to pierce the mind of the robed figure before her, but didn't get far at all. Any specific thoughts or memories, like Tohrment's, were blocked from her perception. She had emotional context, but no detail.

She knew, however, that the female told the truth.

And though there had been many times she had felt deserted by the one who had birthed her, she wasn't stupid. The circumstances of her conception, given who her sire had been, could not possibly have been joyous.

Horrific was more like it.

Xhex had always felt that she must have been a curse on the mother who had borne her, and so now, meeting the female face-to-face? She felt no acrimony toward the still, tense figure before her.

Xhex got to her feet, and as she stood, she sensed Tohrment's rank despair and disbelief, and knew some of that for herself. But she would not turn away from this opportunity . . . this gift that destiny had given her on the night of her mating.

She walked slowly across the rug. As she came up to

her mother, she noticed the other female was much smaller than she, and thinner of stature, and more timid of nature.

"Whatever is your name?" Xhex asked roughly.

"I am . . . No'One," came the reply. "I am No'One—"

A shrill whistle whipped everybody's heads around to the door. John was standing just inside the room, his sister the queen by his side, a small red bag with MARCUS REINHARDT JEWELERS, EST. 1893 written on it in his hand.

John clearly hadn't gone for a workout. He'd gone with Beth into the human world . . . to pick out a mating ring.

Xhex looked around at the assembled and saw the tableau they all made: Tohrment by the LV trunk, John and Beth in the doorway, No'One by the bed.

She would remember this moment all the days of her life. And though there were more questions in her mind than answers, she found the strength in her own soul to voice a reply to John's mute question about who her mystery guest was.

And actually, it was because of him she was able to answer at all: Always look forward. There was much in the past that was best left in the annals of history. Here in this room, with these people, she needed to look forward.

Clearing her throat, she said loudly and clearly, "John . . . this is my mother. And she shall stand for me at our mating."

John seemed utterly nonplussed—but he got over it quickly. Like a perfect gentlemale, he approached No'One and bowed at the waist. After he signed, Xhex translated hoarsely.

"He said he is grateful for your presence on this night and that you are e'er welcome within our home."

No'One put her hands over her face, clearly overcome with emotion. "Thank . . . you. Thank you."

Xhex wasn't a hugger, but she was damned good at holding people up, and she clasped her mother's terribly thin arm so the poor thing didn't go down onto the carpet.

"It's okay," she told John, who was obviously freaking about having upset the female. "Wait—don't look over there, you can't see my gown."

John froze with his eyes halfway across the room. *Gown*, he mouthed.

Yeah, hard to know what the biggest shocker was: her mother showing up for the first time in three hundred years. Or the fact that, yes, it appeared she was jacking her ass into a mating gown.

You never knew where life was going to take you, did you.

And sometimes, the surprises were not bad, not bad at all.

One . . . John.

Two . . . a gown.

Three . . . her mother.

Tonight was a good night, a very good night, indeed.

"Here, we'll go down the hall," she said, heading over and shutting the dress in. "I've got to get dressed . . . don't want to be late for my very own mating."

As she hustled the wardrobe out of the room, turning down help from the males, she asked No'One and Beth to come with her. After all, when it came to her mother and John's sister, they all needed to start getting acquainted . . . and what better way than to get her well and properly dressed for her future *hellren*.

For her male of worth.

For the love of her life.

Tonight was actually the very best thing that had ever happened to her.

SEVENTY-FOUR

John Matthew was forced to stand aside and watch his *shellan* heft a trunk the size of a Chevy off down the hall with his sister . . . and her mother?

He was thrilled about the latter two females; not so much about the former deadweight. But he knew better than to play he-man with the muscles. If Xhex needed his help, she'd ask for it.

And what do you know, she was strong enough to do it all by herself.

Right, for reals . . . that was hot—he wasn't going to lie.

"Have you got your duds?" Tohrment asked gruffly.

As John glanced over at the guy, it was clear the Brother had just been rocked to his core. He was absolutely reeling in his shitkickers. Except, given the hard line of his brow and his jaw, he was not going to go into it.

Ah . . . I don't know what I'm wearing, John signed. *A tuxedo?*

"No, I'll go get you what you need. Hold on."

Bam—the door was shut.

John looked around his room, and when he saw the closet, that clown smile he seemed to wear all the time came back. Walking over, he put the little red bag he'd gotten at the jewelers on the bureau and paused to admire the display of their coupledom.

Oh, man . . . she'd moved in. She'd really moved in. Her clothes and his were hanging together.

Reaching out, he touched her leathers and her muscle

shirts and her holsters . . . and felt his flush of pride and happiness dim a little. She was going to fight in the war. Side by side with him and the Brothers. The Old Laws might have expressly forbidden it, but the Blind King had already proven he wasn't a slave to the ancient ways—and Xhex had already proven she could more than handle herself in the field.

John headed for the bed and sat down. He wasn't sure how he felt about her out in the night with the slayers.

Okay. Fuck that. He knew *exactly* how he felt about it.

Wasn't going to tell her not to go out there, though. She was who she was and he was mating with a fighter.

Just as she was.

His eyes shifted to the bedside table. Leaning over, he popped open the top drawer and took out his father's diary. Smoothing his hand down the supple leather, he felt history slide out of the intellectual and into the actual. Long, long ago another's hands had held this book and written on its pages . . . and then through a series of accidents and luck the journal had come down through the nights and days to John.

For some reason, on this evening, his tie to his father Darius seemed strong enough to best the foggy ether of time and pull the two of them together, uniting them until . . . God, it seemed as if they were almost one person.

Because he knew his father would have been thrilled with this. Knew surely as if the guy were seated next to him on this bed.

Darius would have wanted him and Xhex to end up together. Why? Who knew . . . but that was a truth as real as the vows he would soon be taking.

John reached forward for the drawer again, and this time, he took out the small old box. Lifting the lid, he stared down at the heavy gold signet ring. The damn thing was huge and sized to fit a warrior's hand, its surface glowing through the fine network of scratches that covered the crest and the sides.

It fit the forefinger on his right hand perfectly.

And he abruptly decided he wasn't taking it off again even when fighting.

"He would have so approved of this."

John's eyes flashed up. Tohr had come back and brought a bunch of black silk with him—as well as Lassiter. Standing behind the guy, the fallen angel's light spilled in all directions, as if a sunrise had happened out in the hall.

You know, for some reason I think you're right, John signed.

"I know I'm right." The Brother came forward and sat down on the bed. "He knew her."

Who?

"He knew Xhex. He was there when she was born, when her mother . . ." There was a long pause, as if Tohr had had his brain scrambled and the sloshing hadn't quite quieted down yet. "When her mother died, he took Xhex to a family who could care for her. He loved that young—and so did I. That was why he called her Xhexania. He watched her from afar—"

The epileptic attack came on so suddenly, John didn't have time to try to fight the seizure—one moment he was sitting upright listening to Tohr; the next he was down on the floor doing the not-this-again jitterbug.

When his synapses finally stopped snap-crackle-popping, and his flopping limbs fell still, his breath heaved in and out of his mouth. To his relief, Tohr was right over him, crouching down.

"How you doing?" the guy asked tightly.

John shoved against the floor and sat upright. Rubbing his face, he was glad to find his eyesight still worked. Never thought he'd be glad to get a clear picture of Lassiter's mug.

Struggling for control of his hands, he managed to sign, *Feel like I've been in a blender.*

The fallen angel nodded gravely. "And you look it, too."

Tohr shot the guy a glare, then refocused on John. "Don't mind him, he's blind."

"No, I'm not."

"In another minute and a half, you're going to be." Tohr hitched a hold on John's biceps and dragged him back onto the bed. "You want a drink?"

"Or maybe a new brain?" Lassiter offered.

Tohr leaned in. "As a public service, I'll make him mute, too, 'kay?"

You are such a giver.

There was a long pause and then John signed, *My father knew her?*

"Yes."

You did, too, didn't you.

"Yes."

In the silence that followed, John decided that some things were best just left at their definition. And this was one of them, given the Brother's tight expression.

"I'm glad you're wearing his ring," Tohr said abruptly as he got to his feet. "Especially on a night like tonight."

John looked at the hunk of gold on his finger. It felt so right. As if he'd been wearing it for years.

Me, too, he signed.

"Now, if you'll excuse me, I'm going to get dressed myself."

As John glanced up, he was taken back to a moment all that time ago when he'd answered the door to his shitty studio and leveled a gun up, up, way up, into the guy's face.

And now Tohr had brought him his ceremonial mating robes.

The Brother smiled a little. "I wish your father was here to see this."

John frowned and rolled that signet ring around on his finger, thinking about how much he owed the male. Then on a quick surge, he burst to his feet . . . and embraced the Brother hard. Tohr seemed momentarily surprised but then strong arms reciprocated.

When John pulled back, he stared straight into those eyes. *He is here,* he signed. *My father is right here with me.*

An hour later, John was standing on the mosaic floor in the foyer, shifting his weight back and forth between his two feet. He was dressed in the traditional mating ceremony garb of a noble male of worth, the black silk pants falling to the floor, the loose top secured with a jeweled belt that had been presented to him for use by the king.

The decision had been made to conduct the ceremony at the base of the grand staircase, in the archway that was formed by the dining room. The double doors of where everyone ate had been shut to form a wall, and on the other side of them, the *doggen* had set out a feast.

Everything was arranged, the Brotherhood standing in a line next to him, the *shellans* and other members of the household assembled in a loose half-circle across the way. Among those playing witness, Qhuinn was on one end; Blay and Saxton were on the other. iAm and Trez were in the middle, having been invited as special guests.

As John looked all around the space, he took note of the malachite columns and the marble walls and the chandeliers. There had been so many times since he had come here to stay when people had told him how much his father would have enjoyed people filling up all the rooms and living their lives under the sturdy roof.

John focused on the apple tree depicted on the floor. It was so lovely, a sign of spring, eternally flowering . . . the kind of thing that uplifted you every time you saw it.

He'd loved the tree since he'd moved in—

A collective gasp snapped his head up.

Oh . . . sweet . . . Mary . . . Mother . . . of . . .

His brain conked out at that point. Just went blank. He was pretty sure his heart was still ticking, given that he remained upright, but other than that?

Well, he'd just died and gone to heaven.

Standing up at the top of the grand staircase, with her hand poised on the golden balustrade, Xhex had appeared in a breathtaking glory that rendered him senseless and astonished.

The red gown she was wearing suited her perfectly, the black lace at the top playing to her black hair and her dark gray eyes, the miles of satin skirting falling about her slender body in resplendent waves.

As she met his eyes, she fussed with the waist, then smoothed the front.

Come to me, he signed. *Come down to me, my female.*

In the far corner, a tenor began to sing, Zsadist's crystal-clear voice sailing up toward the warrior paintings on the ceiling far, far above them all. At first John didn't know what the song was . . . although if he'd been asked what his name was, he would have said Santa Claus, or Luther Vandross, or Teddy Roosevelt.

Maybe even Joan Collins.

But then the sounds coalesced and he caught the tune. U2's "All I Want Is You."

The one John had asked the male to sing.

Xhex's first step brought out the sniffles from the females. And Lassiter, evidently. Either that or the angel had dust in his eye.

With every descending footfall Xhex took, John's chest swelled further until he felt as if not only his body was buoyant, but he was lifting the great weight of the stone mansion up with him.

At the base of the stairs, she paused again and Beth rushed forward to arrange the long skirting.

And then Xhex was standing with him in front of Wrath, the Blind King.

I love you, John mouthed.

The smile she gave him started small, just a lift on one side, but it spread—oh, God . . . it spread until she was beaming so wide her fangs were showing and her eyes were lit up like stars.

I love you, too, she mouthed back.

The king's voice echoed to the high ceiling. "Hear ye, all assembled before me. We are gathered herein to witness the mating of this male and this female . . ."

The ceremony commenced and proceeded, with him and Xhex responding when they were supposed to. The absence of the Scribe Virgin was glossed over, with the king pronouncing that it was a good mating, and then when all the vows were made, it was time to get serious.

As Wrath gave the cue, John leaned in and pressed his lips to Xhex's; then he stepped back and took off the jeweled belt and the robe. He was smiling like a moth-erfucker as he gave them over to Tohr and Fritz brought forward the table with the bowl of salt and the silver pitcher of water on it.

Wrath unsheathed his black dagger and said in a loud voice, "What is the name of your *shellan*?"

To all and sundry, John signed, *She is called Xhexania.*

With Tohr's guiding hand, the king carved the first letter, right over the tattoo John had gotten. And then the other Brothers followed suit, marking across the ink in his skin, the blades of the Brotherhood cutting him along not just the four Old Language symbols, but the scrollwork the tat artist had drawn. With every slice, he bore down onto the depiction of the apple tree, taking the pain with pride, refusing to let even a silent hiss escape his lips—and after each letter or swirl, he looked up to Xhex. She was standing at the fore-front of the females and the other males, her arms locked over the bodice of the dress, her eyes grave, but approving.

When the salt hit his fresh wounds, he gritted his teeth so hard, his jaw cracked under the strain, the sound cutting through the dripping of the water. But he didn't gasp or mouth a curse even as the agony lanced through him and made his vision fuzz out.

As he straightened his torso on his hips, the war cry of the Brotherhood and the soldiers of the house echoed all around and Tohr blotted the raw design with a stretch of white linen. After the Brother was finished, he put the cloth into a black lacquered box and gave it to John.

Rising up off his knees, John approached Xhex with the swagger of a male in his full prime—who'd just been through the gauntlet and rocked it just fine, thank you very much. In front of her, he knelt back down, dropped his head, and held the black box up for her to take or refuse at her will. Tradition said if she accepted it, she accepted him.

She didn't even wait a heartbeat.

The weight was relieved from his hold and he looked up. Those beautiful red tears of hers were in her eyes as she cradled the box with his pledge to her against her heart.

As the assembled cheered and clapped, John burst to his feet and swept her and that big, gorgeous red dress right up into his arms. He kissed her hard and then, in front of the king and his sister and his best friends and the Brotherhood, he carried his female straight up those stairs she'd come down.

Yeah, there was a feast in their honor about to break out. But the bonded male in him needed to do a little marking—then they'd come down for food.

He was halfway to the top when Hollywood's voice sounded out. "Oh, man, I want mine done over with some of that curlicue crap."

"Don't even think about it, Rhage," was Mary's response.

"Can we eat now?" Lassiter asked. "Or is anyone else turning themselves into sushi?"

The party started to get rolling, voices and laughter and the beat of Jay-Z's "Young Forever" filling the space. At the head of the stairs, John paused and looked down. The sight below, coupled with the female in his arms, made him feel as though he'd climbed a great mountain and had finally, inexplicably, unbelievably gotten to the top.

Her husky voice sealed the deal on his hard-on: "You just going to stand around, or did you bring me up here for a good reason?"

John kissed her, slipping his tongue between her lips, penetrating her. He kept at it as he walked her down to his—

Their room.

Inside, he set her down on the bed and she stared up at him, looking as if she were more than ready for what he was going to give her.

Except she seemed surprised when he just turned away.

But he had to present her with the gift he'd bought.

When he came back to the bed, he had the red bag from Reinhardt's with him.

I was raised human, and when they do their matings, the male gives the female a token of affection. Abruptly, he got nervous. *I hope you like it. I tried to do you right.*

Xhex sat up and her hands shook a little as she took out the long, thin box. "What did you do, John Matthew—"

Her gasp as she cracked the lid was too frickin' fabulous.

John reached out and took the thick chain off the velvet nest. The square diamond set in the middle of the platinum links was six carats—whatever that meant. All he cared about was that the damn stone was big enough and bright enough and sparkly enough to be seen from goddamn Canada.

Just in case any males saw her and maybe had a head cold or something, he wanted it to be known that she was taken. And if John's bonding scent didn't reach their noses, the flash of that rock sure as shit would bounce off their retinas.

I didn't get you a ring because I know you're going to be fighting and won't want your hands encumbered. And if you like it, I'd love it if you'd wear it all the time—

Xhex grabbed his face and kissed him so long and so deep he couldn't breathe. And didn't care. "I'll never take it off. Ever."

John fused their mouths and mounted her, pushing her and that gown back against the pillows, his hands riding up her breasts, then scooping under her hips. As he arched into her body, he started fishing around the acres of satin . . .

Took him about a second and a half to get frustrated.

And turned out that the dress looked even better off.

John made slow love to his female, luxuriating in her body, caressing it with his hands and his mouth. When he finally joined them together, the fit was so perfect, the moment so right, he just fell still. Life had brought him here to this time with her, with them together . . .

This was the history he would be living from now on.

"So, John . . ." she said in a husky voice.

He whistled in an ascending note.

"I was thinking about getting a little ink of my own." As he cocked his head to the side, she ran her hands up his shoulders gingerly. "How about we head over to that tattoo place . . . maybe get your name in my back?"

The orgasm that rocked out of his body and into hers

652

evidently served as a well enough reply in the absence of his being able to voice one.

Xhex laughed in a throaty way and moved her hips against his. "I'll take that as a yes . . ."

Yes, John thought as he started to pump inside of her. Yes, oh, fuck, yes . . .

After all, what was good for the gander was even hotter for the goose. And fair was fair.

God, he loved life. Loved life and everyone in this house and all the people of worth in all the corners of the world. Fate was not easy . . . but it got things right.

Eventually, everything that came to pass was exactly how it was meant to be.